Also by Ann Aguirre

Fix-It Witches
Witch Please
Boss Witch
Extra Witchy

The Only Purple House in Town

ANN AGUIRRE

sourcebooks
casablanca

Published by Sourcebooks Casablanca, an imprint of Sourcebooks
P.O. Box 4410, Naperville, Illinois 60567-4410
(630) 961-3900
sourcebooks.com

Cataloging-in-Publication Data is on file with the Library of Congress.

Printed and bound in the United States of America.
VP 10 9 8 7 6 5 4 3 2 1

For my son, Alek

CHAPTER ONE

WHOEVER SAID IT WAS ALWAYS darkest before the dawn clearly had never lived like Iris Collins.

Sometimes she felt like a cave creature that never saw sunlight; it was dark at sunrise, sunset, and all the hours in between. She stared at her account balance on her phone with anxiety chewing away at her insides, a behavior she mirrored by gnawing on her cuticle until it bled. Her roommates would be home soon, and she didn't look forward to that conversation. They'd covered her for the last two months, but she doubted they would be willing to triple down.

I can't even leave until I pay them back, and I can't find a new place either.

She had no clue how to earn her back rent or come up with what she needed for this month. Her sisters had money, but Rose would lecture if she bailed Iris out; Lily would refuse to help while talking about how Iris should live within her means; and Olive didn't have reliable internet since she was currently doctoring without borders. Her three sisters were a how-to guide for success, while Iris was the cautionary tale. Her mother had made life hell the last time she lent financial assistance, so that was out of the question.

Should I sell my car?

In the movies, vampires were essentially immortal and had been accruing wealth for centuries. Unfortunately for Iris, she came from a different line entirely. Her type didn't feed on blood but human emotions, and Iris had come up shy in that department as well. Unlike the rest of her family, she had no special abilities that sprang from her vampiric nature. At least, nothing had ever *manifested*. Olive could feed on her patients' pain and improve their lives as she did so. Lily feasted on grief, and Rose thrived on anger, whereas Iris was basically *human*. Or so her mother had said more than once; her tone made it clear that wasn't a compliment. But then, even among the paranormal community, psychic vampires weren't well liked. They were known as "takers" for obvious reasons. Five years ago—when the witches made their big announcement—others had followed suit.

Now, Iris didn't have to hide who she was, and there were dating apps devoted to various types of supernatural folk. Iris had been on Shifted for a while, but she kept meeting lone wolf types who just wanted to hit and quit. In this case, they happened to be able to turn into actual wolves. Then she tried Bindr, but witches could be touchy about lineage, apparently. The skeptics and conspiracy theorists amused her the most. There were forums devoted to debunking magic, calling it "the greatest hoax since the moon landing," and sometimes Iris did a deep dive through the most ridiculous suggestions to distract herself from the reality of how screwed she was.

In fact, she was doing that now. She scrolled on her phone, snickering. "Sure, lizard people have replaced all our nation's leaders—that's real. And there are mole people living underneath Capitol Hill."

Enough of that.

From there, she clicked through to a site offering various magical charms. *I could really use one for prosperity, but they're so expensive. And what if it doesn't work?* Shaking her head, she resisted the urge to max out her card with an impulse purchase. But damn, it was tough. She *really* wanted to find out if the magical lipstick was permanently kiss-proof. In the news, Congress was trying to pass a new law requiring all paranormal individuals to self-identify and register in some kind of national database. *Yeah, that won't end well.* And some douchebag senator in Iowa wanted even sterner sanctions, special housing projects, and tracking devices. Someone else had proposed a *tax* on supernaturals. *How does that even make sense? And good luck enforcing it.* She shook her head and went back to window-shopping. So many cool magic items she'd love to get her hands on...

For Iris, life hadn't changed that much. The paranormal communities were still close-knit, and most didn't reveal themselves readily, even if a few people had identified themselves for clout and were giving interviews about what it was like growing up "other" among humans. Some were pursuing a fortune or building social media empires, capitalizing on the interest focused their way.

I can't even do that. Too bad—it would help the shop.

Sighing, she trudged to her room, currently crammed with supplies for her jewelry-making business, but nobody was buying the finished products. She'd invested in the idea, but she hadn't earned more than twenty bucks on her pieces. She supposed she could register as a driver, but she was scared of letting strangers get in her car. Iris lowered her head. It was ridiculous that she was afraid of…so many things. Pacing back to the dining room, she feverishly tried to think of a solution.

Do I have anything *left to sell besides my car?*

"You owe me six hundred bucks," Frederic said.

Iris let out a cry, juggled her phone, and then dropped it. Screen down, because of course. That was how her luck ran. When she picked it up, there was a tiny nick on the corner, exactly what she didn't need today. *I didn't even hear him come in.*

Stifling a squeak, she spun to face Frederic.

She'd been dodging the others—Regina, Frederic, and Candace—for the last week, even though she had nowhere to go. The diner staff was sick of her ordering a cup of coffee and staying for hours, while the dollar cinema didn't seem to care if she stayed all day. But now, it was too late.

Frederic tapped her shoulder briskly. "Did you hear me? Where's my money?"

He owned the house and had rented three of the four bedrooms. It was a decent place, decorated in bachelor style, and everyone was nice enough. But like everywhere else Iris had lived, she didn't quite fit. Frederic hadn't even wanted to rent to her in the first place since she didn't have a day job, but Iris had gone to high school with Regina, and she vouched for Iris. Now Regina was mad because Iris was making her look bad, and Candace was tired of the tension.

Everyone quietly wanted Iris gone, but she had to *pay* them first. She raised her gaze from the polished-oak dining table, trying to figure out what to say. *Sorry, I'm broke* was only three words, but she couldn't make herself say them, mainly because she'd said them so often, and she'd burned through any good will the others felt for her.

But before Regina and Candace arrived to exacerbate the situation, the doorbell rang. "I'll get it," she said swiftly.

Iris raced past Frederic to the front door where a postman in a blue uniform asked her to sign for a certified letter. *That's never good news. I hope it's not another bill that I let slide until it went to collections.* The way her luck ran, it probably was, and the return address stamp on the envelope only reinforced that impression. Digby, Davis, and Moore sounded like a law firm.

I hope I'm not being sued.

She didn't want to read it, but the alternative was facing Frederic, so she closed the door with a quiet snick, blocking the early-autumn breeze. Through the window, she watched the leaves skitter on the sidewalk, caught by that same wind. She tore open the packet and found a wealth of legal documents.

IN THE ESTATE OF GERTRUDE VAN DOREN, DECEASED...

Poor Aunt Gertie. I wish I'd gone to her funeral.

Iris skimmed the pages with growing disbelief. Her great-aunt Gertrude had left the bulk of her estate to Iris: a small amount of cash, her collection of ceramic angels, and a house in St. Claire,

Illinois, including all contents within. Iris had no clue why Great-Aunt Gertie had done this, but the bequest burned like a spark of hope. Her great-aunt—her paternal grandfather's sister—had been reckoned rather odd, something of a misanthrope just because she never married.

Maybe she thought I'm the weirdest, the most like her. Or the one who needs the most help? Either way, true enough.

Iris hadn't seen Great-Aunt Gertie since the summer after graduation, when her parents had dragged her to St. Claire for a courtesy visit. Iris had sent yearly Christmas cards, however, mostly because she enjoyed the ritual of writing them out and mailing them, and occasionally, her great-aunt sent snail mail in return. *Maybe that haphazard correspondence meant something to her?* Whatever the reason, this inheritance couldn't come at a better time.

Quickly she read the letter telling her how to proceed, and when she folded up the packet of papers, she had a response for Frederic at least, who was standing behind her with his arms folded. "Well?" he prompted.

Iris handed him the will. "It'll take a little while, but I'll pay you soon. You can start looking for someone to take over my room."

"You're moving out?" Though he tried to sound neutral, she read relief in the flicker of his eyes, in the faint upward tilt of his mouth.

Over the years, she'd gotten good at gauging people's moods, actively looking for the disappointment and impatience her mother tried to mask, usually without success. Her face silently said, *Why aren't you more like your sisters? Why are you so exhausting? Why can't you get yourself together?*

"Not right away, but yeah."

You're running away again, her mother's voice whispered.

Some people would see it that way, but Iris viewed it as a fresh start. While she didn't have a plan per se—when did she ever?—she'd figure it out when she saw the house. At the least, it was a place she could live rent free. Her expenses would be lower, and she wouldn't have witnesses when she failed. People in St. Claire didn't really know her either, so maybe she could shake off her reputation as well.

"I can be patient," Frederic said with a magnanimous air.

Now that he's seen proof that I have money incoming.

When Iris had gotten word about Great-Aunt Gertie's passing, she'd scraped up enough to send flowers, living on ramen that week. *If I'd known she meant to leave me everything, I would've sold something for gas money to show my face at her service.* That was a crappy feeling, one that she couldn't shake even as Regina and Candace got home.

She heard Frederic in the kitchen, explaining the situation in a low voice. Then Regina headed into the living room, where Iris was curled up on the couch. "I'm so glad you figured out your next move," she said in an overly cheerful tone.

Regina wasn't really a friend, more of an acquaintance who'd vouched for Iris. She tried not to take the comment the wrong way. "Yeah, it's a minor miracle."

Candace came to the doorway, folding her arms. "You realize you're praising her for having a dead relative."

When you put it that way...

"Sorry, I didn't mean to be hurtful," Regina said.

"When are you going to see about your inheritance?" Frederic asked.

Though he'd said he could be patient, he wanted his money. Iris headed for her room to pack a weekend bag. According to the navigation app on her phone, it was six hours in the car from here to St. Claire. *If I go now, I could be there by midnight.* She knew where Great-Aunt Gertrude used to keep the spare key too.

It was impulsive and absurd, the kind of behavior that made Iris an odd duck in a family of swans. Thankfully, none of her relatives knew about this yet, and her roommates didn't care enough to stop her. Her mind made up, Iris crammed socks and underwear into her backpack, along with a few clean shirts, plus one pair of pants and something to sleep in. She dropped toiletries into her purse and snagged her keys.

"I'll see you later," she said. "I don't know how long it will take to square things away, but I'll be back to pay my back rent and to collect my stuff."

"Drive safely," Regina said, seeming relieved that she wouldn't wind up pissing off everyone in the house.

Frederic waved and Candace watched from the doorway as Iris drove into the night, away from the house where she was a square peg in a round hole.

Eli Reese wasn't the kid everyone made fun of anymore.

He owned a condo in Cleveland and a vacation cottage in Myrtle Beach, by virtue of two successful apps steadily feeding his bank account—one to gamify household management, including to-do lists and budgeting, and another social platform that focused on sharing recipes. The second had taken off in a modest way; users were collaborating on dishes, doing recipe challenges, and sending food pics to each other, and he'd just patched in an update supporting video clips. The revenue was decent on both, and he was already getting offers. A German tech company wanted Task Wizard, which let users create an avatar and level up based on the amount of real-world work accomplished, while a Chinese communications conglomerate had made an offer for What's Cooking?

If he sold one, it would give him enough capital to fund his next project. He just hadn't decided what that should be yet. Eli never imagined he'd be in a position where he didn't need to work, but there was no urgency fueling his productivity anymore. It was strange being free to do what he wanted with his life; the problem being—he didn't know what that was.

His favorite thing was flying; it was magical stepping out onto the balcony of his condo, leaving his clothes and cares behind. Transforming into a hawk and soaring over the city and then far beyond—over the whorls of trees and the scurries of small mammals in the underbrush, hidden colors in a spectrum his human eyes couldn't glimpse. Red-tailed hawks were common enough that he didn't attract unwanted attention from ornithologists, although he was larger than usual in his shifted form. Those nightly flights were the closest Eli came to pure freedom, but multiple people would disapprove of him withdrawing from personhood in favor of joining bird-dom.

Mostly Liz and Gamma, to be honest.

Music played in the truck, soft classical that didn't distract him from his thoughts. Currently, his most pressing concern was his grandmother. He'd come to St. Claire to help her relocate, as she was selling her house in the Midwest and moving to New Mexico. Gamma had looked at Florida and Arizona as well, but she'd bought a condo in a retirement community in a suburb outside Albuquerque and was looking forward to all the activities and built-in social life.

Eli had offered to assist with cleaning her basement, attic, and garage, getting the stuff she didn't want hauled away, and prepping the house to be put on the market, which involved painting and staging to make buyers picture themselves living there, undistracted by the current owner's clutter. He could've contracted the work out—hired someone to do this. But Gamma hated strangers touching her belongings, and unlike the other grandkids, he didn't have a day job or a limit to his vacation time. Plus, some of them agreed with Gamma's ex-wife or had been conditioned to do so, so there was a certain distance between them. And Eli appreciated the chance to spend time with Gamma and help her out.

She wasn't the kind of grandparent who said stuff like *You'll regret not visiting me when I'm gone*, but since Gamma had held Eli's hand as they buried his dad and then helped raise him, he understood that it was important to see people while he still could. Words like *orphan* were really Oliver Twist, but his mom had died when he was six, and his dad had passed away when he was thirteen.

Friends took turns inviting him for the holidays, which was awkward as hell. Usually, he said he had plans, and sometimes he did hang out with people, but even then, he felt...extraneous. In every space he occupied, while he might be welcome, he wasn't necessary. Nobody needed him. If he made his excuses and stayed home, wallowing in solitude, no one followed up. He didn't have the sort of friends who barged in with pizza and beer, determined to keep him company.

Hell, Eli didn't even know if he wanted that anyway. He did know something was missing, though.

He focused on reaching his destination, turning down the narrow street. Gamma's house sat on the right side of a cul-de-sac, a three-bedroom Cape Cod house with white siding where he'd spent his teen years. In this neighborhood, the houses were mostly homogenous, built around the same time with similar designs— Cape Cod, bungalow, and ranch. He pulled into the driveway, seeing the minute signs of neglect that had crept up.

The hedges had to be trimmed, and the yard was a bit tall and weedy, while the gutters needed to be cleaned, and he might need to get on the roof to have a closer look at that soggy patch. Those were issues prospective buyers would notice right away. As ever, the porch was welcoming with a profusion of potted plants and blooming flowers. Two Adirondack chairs painted forest green framed the front door with the single step leading inside. Gamma opened the screen door and popped her head out.

"Come in! I made your favorite."

Eli smiled, wiping his feet on the mat. He took his shoes off on the uncarpeted tile just inside and padded across the improbably pink carpet, through the living room and into the kitchen. He breathed in deep, savoring the smell of barbecued chicken. There was also macaroni and cheese and garden salad with a bottle of ranch dressing on standby.

She put the platter of drumsticks on the table and hugged him, smelling faintly of Poison perfume. For as long as Eli could remember, she'd been using that brand. He'd been so proud of saving up to buy her some the year after he moved in.

"You didn't have to go to any trouble," he said, as his stomach growled.

Gamma waved dismissively. "It's the least I can do. Besides, it was nothing. I used the air fryer for the drumsticks and finished them in the broiler with barbecue sauce. The macaroni and cheese is blue box, and the salad came from a bag."

He grinned. "When you put it that way..."

"Let's eat. After dinner, we can talk more about the projects you've volunteered for."

"Why do I feel like you should've made me steak instead of chicken legs?"

She smirked right back. "It's not my fault your taste buds are cheap."

As Eli sat, he reflected that she was nothing like most other grandmothers. She didn't own a set of pearls, preferring feather earrings, leopard print, and spandex. Honestly, he was a bit concerned about the havoc she'd wreak on the local populace when she moved.

"I won't be a cliché, so I refuse to ask if you're seeing anyone," Gamma said.

"And I greatly appreciate your forbearance."

"But at the same time, I *worry*. You were uprooted from your friends, and you never settled in here properly."

"Oh no. You played the *worry* card. Seriously, I'm fine. I have friends. And you'll be the first to know if I find someone special."

"I'd better be!"

He pretended to be stern. "But I expect the same courtesy. You're a catch, and you're better at socializing. I'll probably get a wedding invitation by Christmas."

"That fast?" Gamma pretended to wipe sweat from her brow. "I can see I have my work cut out for me, but I suspect I'm up to the challenge."

By the time they finished, it was getting dark. He helped her rinse the plates, put the food away, and load the dishwasher. "Thanks for dinner," he said.

"You don't need to thank me." Gamma donned a determined look. "It's too late to start today, but you should see what we're working with. I apologize in advance for the state of my hidden assets."

Assets? I'm sure she means junk.

Nevertheless, he followed her into the basement, which was piled ridiculously high with unmarked boxes. He stared. "What's in here anyway?"

"I have no idea," she said airily. "To be honest, some of this stuff was your father's, and I didn't have the heart to go through it. I still don't. The rest has been in here since I moved, and that was…" She paused, apparently trying to count back the years.

"1988?" he suggested, based on the amount of dust on the cartons.

"Could be."

"Is the attic like this?"

Gamma bit her lip. "Possibly, it's worse. I haven't been up there in forever. Those drop-down stairs are terrifying. I'm not turning into a cautionary tale for Life Alert. I'm not old. I *refuse* to be old."

"You're immortal," Eli said, wishing that were true.

He had a lump in his throat when he imagined going through his father's belongings, but it had been twelve years. *It's beyond time. Maybe I'll find something that makes me feel closer to him.* But the melancholy truth was, he'd lived longer without his dad. And that gap would only grow because that was how time worked. To reward himself for facing down these bad memories, he'd go for a long flight later.

"Watch your step, okay? I'll get you a flashlight."

"There's one on my phone."

She cocked her head. "Have you ever watched a horror movie? You'll drop your phone after being startled by a cat. Or maybe a raccoon. Anyway, I'll be right back."

When she returned, he said, "Tell me you're kidding. There are raccoons?"

Gamma put the sturdy flashlight in his hands, patted them, and made no promises. "Be careful. I'll send help if you're not back in an hour."

CHAPTER TWO

IRIS PULLED INTO THE DRIVEWAY beside the ramshackle Victorian house she was set to inherit, if the correspondence from Digby, Davis, and Moore could be believed.

It was past one in the morning, and her body ached from the long drive. She'd paused once to fuel up, stretch her legs, and use the restroom. It was impossible not to think about her sisters in this situation. Any of them would have energy to burn, siphoning from humans they encountered along the way. That aptitude had given them an unfair advantage in pursuing higher education too.

Shrugging, she grabbed her backpack, locked the doors of her crappy Sentra, and headed toward the rickety front porch. Even in the faint glow of the streetlights, she could see the ravages of time, peeling paint and weedy front lawn. The plants were all dead, dry leaves spilling listlessly over the stone lip of the pot. She levered the one on the left up and found a rusty key.

Yes. Still here.

Thankfully, nobody had meddled with the property or Iris would be sleeping in the car. There was no money for a motel, barely enough for her gas tank. With a little coaxing, she got the door open and stepped inside. The first breath smelled of... loneliness—liniment that carried faint eddies of camphor and menthol—dusty books and stale air.

She flipped the light switch, but there was no power. *Looks like I'll be charging my phone in the car. Better than nothing.* Using the light on her phone, she crept through the dark house to the kitchen and tested the tap. *At least the water is still on.* She could take a quick cold shower in the morning and arrive at the law office looking presentable.

Bless Great-Aunt Gertie, she had a whole cupboard full of emergency candles, along with books of matches from the oddest of places. Iris examined them one at a time: Minden's Wax Doll Workshop, The Murder Room, Noise Factory (a club in Germany), and a host of other places that made Iris believe that Gertie had led a fascinating life.

She lit one candle and decided she didn't feel up to exploring further in the dark. The house was large and creepy at this hour with narrow hallways and staircases. Rooms had generally been smaller when this house was built, and apart from adding electricity and indoor plumbing, few renovations had been made over the years. Iris found four knitted throws scattered around the living room and snuggled under them on the overstuffed sofa. Between those and the hoodie she had on, it was cozy enough, even without heat.

Possibly she ought to be nervous, alone in this big old house. But sleep claimed her immediately, and she rested better than she had in a long while, deep and dreamless. Iris awoke feeling surprisingly alert. She didn't have an appointment, but hopefully the attorneys could work her in if she called first thing. Her cell phone had battery life to complete the call, at least.

A professional voice answered on the second ring. "Digby, Davis, and Moore, how may I help you?"

"I received a letter about my great-aunt's estate. Gertrude Van Doren. I was hoping to speak with the person in charge." Iris loathed talking on the phone, and she hoped she didn't sound as nervous as she felt.

"Just a moment, please."

Calming yet bland music piped into her ear, and two minutes later, the woman returned to the line. "Can you come in at two? We have a cancellation. Otherwise, Mr. Davis won't have time until next week."

"Two is perfect. I'll see you then."

"Excellent. I'll let Mr. Davis know."

Quickly, Iris checked the time. She had over four hours until the meeting. *Best to get the cold shower over with.* In daytime, the house was even more dated, with pink and gray walls that had probably been painted in the nineties. Everything was dated cottage chic, echoing trends that died long before Great-Aunt Gertie. The bathroom was even older looking, harking back to the seventies. Or maybe the fifties? Iris wasn't a professional decorator, but the lime-green tile and Pepto-pink tub, sink, and toilet truly were astonishing.

On the bright side, she was delighted to coax some warm water out of the shower. Apparently the heater ran on gas, not electricity. She could even use the stove if she lit the burner with a match. *Wonder if there's anything left to eat.*

She dried her hair with a towel, combed out the tangles, and then put on clean clothes: jeans, wrinkled button-up blouse, concealed by a chunky cardigan. *That's probably good enough.* It wasn't like she'd had lots of reasons to meet with lawyers, just the times she'd ended up as a defendant, and those damn sure weren't happy memories.

The house had five bedrooms, though several were quite small, and the closet space was terrible. Luckily, most of Iris's stuff was in her mom's basement while Mom waited for her to get her life together enough to send for it.

That…might never happen.

In the kitchen, in the light of day, it was simultaneously better and worse than she'd imagined. Everything was white with black accents and fairly clean, but the cupboards were ancient particleboard, and the counters were scarred-up butcher block. The room was tidy, and judging by the empty fridge, the attorneys must've sent someone to clean out the perishables. What a relief not to be dealing with rotten groceries on top of everything else.

In the cabinets, she found instant coffee and a kettle she could use to boil water. The cleaners had left all the staples that hadn't expired—a bag of flour, sugar, some rice, powdered milk, sweetener, a few cans of soup, various spices, and a bottle of cooking oil. It was like a vacation rental in some ways, though all of Great-Aunt Gertie's belongings were still here.

I'll have to go through everything. Her auntie must've known that when she made her will—that Iris would be the one sorting her things, deciding what to keep and what to donate. *I hope I don't disappoint her.* Was that even possible? To let a ghost down?

Hopefully, her great-aunt wasn't here, watching Iris assess the pantry contents.

She added spoons of instant coffee, dry milk, and sugar to her mug and poured in the hot water. While it cooled, she walked through the house. In the middle of what must've been the parlor a hundred years ago stood a proud display case stuffed full of ceramic angels. Iris remembered Great-Aunt Gertie telling stories about them as if they were real people who lived with her, something that had enchanted her at age seven.

Now she couldn't decide if it was sweet or sad—that these figurines had taken the place of family. Hell, maybe it was for the best, because the ceramic angels wouldn't tell her that she was a failure because she earned less than her sisters, she was single at twenty-seven, she had no psychic aptitude, and her ideas always fell apart.

Gertie probably hadn't planned on dying alone, either. That made Iris feel closer to her, and she searched her memory, but she couldn't recall what Gertie's ability had been. On Iris's dad's side, they tended to feast on the positive emotions—anticipation, joy, excitement, and the like. She imagined that Gertie had nourished herself over her long life through joyous friendships, never taking enough to make anyone feel deprived.

Suddenly, her phone rang, making her jump. Mom's picture flashed on the screen, like she'd summoned the woman with those thoughts. *I need to put down a salt circle. Or maybe hang some garlic. If only Mom couldn't enter without an invitation...* Sadly, none of those remedies were effective at warding off her mother. Iris had heard that those old wives' tales didn't work on their blood-drinking counterparts, either, not that she'd met any of them. They were more reclusive than the fae.

"Hey, what's up?" she said, trying to sound more cheerful than she felt.

New beginning. Don't let her get in your head.

"What time will you be here?" Mom demanded.

"Pardon me?"

"The party, don't tell me you forgot. We're celebrating your sister's promotion! It's a huge deal, Iris. Do you know how rare it is for someone Rose's age to make partner?" Sheer incredulity oozed down the phone line.

I hate my family.

No, I...love them. I'm supposed to, right?

But I hate them.

Rose was thirty-two, five years older than Iris. She was married to a judge who might run for state senate. Privately, Iris loathed her brother-in-law, Greg Connery. He was smug and pretentious, prone to name-dropping and boasting about his connections. If that wasn't bad enough, he also *watched* Iris in ways that made her deeply uncomfortable, his gaze lingering on her ass, on her cleavage, while he lectured about her life choices. The one time she'd mentioned it to Rose, her sister practically hissed like a cat and threatened to tell Mom what a jealous liar Iris was.

So Rose either had no clue that her husband was a creep or refused to admit it. She fed all on the glorious negativity associated with law and politics in addition to adoring the upper-crust sound of Rose Collins-Connery, such elegant alliteration, and—

Fuck. I totally forgot about the party.

Honestly, that was typical. Iris tended to shove things she didn't want to deal with out of her brain, and that worked fine until someone showed up to yell about how she'd let them down.

Like now.

At this point, she was pretty good at coming up with off-the-cuff lies to cover her own ass. This time, she decided to pretend this was an *intentional* decision, not a mental glitch. "Nobody will miss me," she said lightly. "Something came up, so I'm not even in Ohio right now. Congratulate Rose for me, though."

"Iris, please, just—"

"By the way, do you happen to recall how Great-Aunt Gertie's powers worked?" If she had any.

"Why are you asking that all of a sudden?"

"Because I'm curious, obviously."

A long-suffering sigh slid out of her mother like a tire deflating. "Iris, tell me the truth. Are you in trouble again?"

"Everything's fine."

"Are you boycotting this event because Lily is dating your ex? It's not fair to punish Rose because you're mad at Lily."

Iris ignored that. "I have an appointment soon, so I need to go. Talk to you soon!" For once, Iris got the last word.

She disconnected while Mom was gearing up the interrogation, and that silence after she tapped the red phone icon felt like a *huge* victory.

———

Eli Reese wasn't an internet stalker.

Which, come to think of it, sounded like something an internet stalker would say.

I should stop this.

It had been fifteen years since he first saw Iris Collins; he had been ten, and she was twelve. He had been a tiny kid, diminutive compared to the rest of his class. He couldn't say he had a particular bully, one person devoted to making his life a living hell. But a few jerks took turns giving him shitty nicknames or knocking him over, and some of them took his stuff when he had something they wanted that he wasn't big enough to protect. Those who didn't participate looked away, in case they pissed someone off by standing up for him.

This was before his ability to shift kicked in, or he'd have had another means of escape. It would've been nice if he could've flown away from all the pain. Then came Iris, the rainbow after a violent storm. Honestly, it was embarrassing how clear and sharp his memory was, even after all this time. Roddy Frierson had shoved Eli down and was rummaging in his bag for Pokémon cards when an older girl strode up. She was in sixth grade, the highest level at Ridgecrest Elementary, and she had sunny brown hair in two braids, gray eyes brightened by outrage. She'd kicked Roddy right in the ass, tipping him over so he hit the floor next to Eli.

She took the bag away and handed it back. "Are you okay?" she'd asked.

Mutely, Eli had nodded, accepting her hand when she helped him up. Her hands were sticky from an open bag of gummy worms, and she offered him one. He ate it without hesitation, though he secretly thought gummy worms were freaking creepy. Bears were the way to go because they didn't look like actual bears.

She'd folded her arms and glared at Roddy. "I'm bigger, and I picked on you anyway. You probably feel bad, huh? That's how you're making *him* feel, so stop it. If I hear about anybody bothering…" She paused, glancing at Eli. "What's your name?"

"Eli Reese," he said in a small voice.

"Eli again, I'm telling *everyone*. I'll tell your teacher, the principal, and your parents. I'll call your grandmother. Do you want that?"

Roddy burst into tears. "Don't tell Nonna!"

Since they'd gathered an interested audience, the girl glared at everyone. "You're all on my list! Anyone could've helped him, but none of you did. So cut it out, you cowards!"

The girl stomped off like an avenging angel, swinging her arms wildly. A bracelet slipped off her wrist, and he hurried to pick it up. Eli hadn't known her name then, but he found out by asking around quietly. Iris Collins. Unbelievably, people left him alone after that. Well, they still used the mean nicknames, but he could live with that.

He carried the bracelet around for weeks. He should've given it back, but he couldn't work up the nerve to interrupt when she was with her friends. Each time he tried, it felt like his insides were on fire, and he wound up running away. The next year, Iris went to middle school, and he saw her in passing when he got there later. But they never talked.

Because I didn't have the courage to speak to her.

Then his parents died, and he moved to St. Claire to live with

Gamma. At the new school, he kept to himself and read a lot of books, played computer games, and made friends online while telling himself the real world would be better. That summer, he finally inherited his dad's ability to shift and unlocked a whole different world, one that didn't care how tall he was or how many friends he had.

Gamma had shown him the online communities where he could connect with people like himself, but he'd never had the inclination to socialize. Pack shifters probably felt otherwise. At school, nobody paid much attention to him, and by the time he got a growth spurt late in his senior year, it irritated him to suddenly qualify as attractive. Classmates saw him with new eyes, and they wanted to date him, but he had no use for those who had treated him like he was invisible before. He left for college without looking back.

But over the years, he never lost track of Iris.

Eli had developed this habit of checking out her social media. Once a month, no more. He'd skim posts and look at pictures, trying to imagine what her life must be like. It wasn't as if he was nursing a deathless love or something. He was just...curious about her. Because she'd changed his life in one moment, by caring, just a little, about someone nobody else at that school gave a damn about.

Yesterday, he'd inspected the attic; thankfully there hadn't been any raccoons. And today, he had errands to run. Instead, he was staring at his phone. Today was the day he usually skimmed Iris's socials. Last month, she'd been excited about the launch of her online jewelry business. He was already planning to order Gamma some earrings; she'd love the blue enamel flower ones.

Really, Eli had no idea if this was normal behavior, checking up on someone he'd gone to school with. It wasn't like they'd been friends, although he wished they had. Making friends required talking to people, however, and Eli was bad at that. He was better with code and numbers, better where the data could be analyzed meticulously and relied upon to provide consistent results.

He was good at flying too. Soaring beyond the reach of human hands. There was no conversation above the treetops, just the occasional shrill call of distant birds. He saw so much, though, and it didn't matter that he was a silent observer.

The thought came again. *I should stop.*

Even though his interest wasn't harming anyone, it probably wasn't healthy. Instead of following what had become a sort of comfort ritual—because it made him happy knowing she was out there, alive and well—he showered and went downstairs without looking at any of her accounts. Gamma had breakfast waiting, an odd assortment of toast, sausage links, sliced fruit, and hot tea. His grandmother had gone to the UK once, and she hadn't quite gotten a handle on English breakfast, but she tried.

"Looks good," he said. "I'm heading to the hardware store later to get a few things to help with the..." What to call it? Packing up Gamma's life and tidying it up so other people would want to live beneath this roof?

"Move?" she suggested.

"Yeah. That. Do you need anything while I'm out?"

"I'd love some cinnamon rolls. There's a little bakery downtown. It's one of the things I'll miss when I move to New Mexico."

"Anything else?" he asked.

Gamma thought for a moment. Even in the morning, she was fabulous—with fake eyelashes, purple-red lipstick, and slippers with feathers on the front. "The changing seasons, I suppose. But not the snow."

"Not your grandson, either, it seems." He pretended to sulk, knowing it amused her.

"You're not a *thing*. Of course I'll miss you. Once I'm settled, visit me, or I'll look up 'how to guilt my grandson' on the inter-web. Not my forte, but I learn fast."

"I'd rather you didn't acquire that skill. Cinnamon rolls then. I'll get those and the stuff I need to wrap up here. When are you leaving?"

"Two weeks," she said. "Are you sure it's not too much, asking you to finish this?"

Eli smiled and got up to hug her. "Not at all. It's the least I can do, what with you raising me as a single grandma and all."

He had vague recollections that there had been big upheaval in Gamma's life. She'd had a wife who couldn't accept it when Gamma transitioned, so they divorced. And Gamma changed... basically everything, around the time that Eli's parents died. She'd had so much on her plate, wrestling with her own identity, but she never hesitated to take Eli, and she'd loved him so much and taught him how important it was to accept everyone as they were.

He was...incredibly grateful to her. Gamma was the most precious person to him, and he sort of hated that she was going to New Mexico because they'd never lived this far apart before. Even when he'd relocated for college, he'd had the security of knowing they were only a short plane ride or a reasonable drive away.

But damned if he would clip Gamma's wings. She deserved to spread them and fly and find a partner if she wanted. He knew she was lonely and that she'd make someone tremendously happy if they were lucky enough to be loved by her.

Like I was. Like I am. Damn, am I tearing up?

He blinked away the emotions and focused on his breakfast. Hopefully, he wouldn't lose it over breaking the ritual of checking Iris's socials. Habit. *Habit* sounded less compulsive.

A few hours later, as he stepped out of the hardware store, it seemed like the universe was screwing with him. He dropped the two bags he was carrying. Thank God he hadn't bought the cinnamon rolls yet.

There she was, in the flesh. *Iris Collins.* He'd recognize her freaking anywhere.

Something else a stalker would say.

And she was headed into a law office across the street.

Maybe this was a sign. *I ought to thank her. That's why our paths crossed, why it feels like there's unfinished business. I never told her how much that meant to me back in the day.*

I need to acknowledge my appreciation and move on. Eli touched the charm bracelet in his pocket that he carried like a talisman. *Right?*

Right.

CHAPTER THREE

THE LAW OFFICE WAS DECORATED in brown and beige, and the chair was vinyl.

Whenever Iris moved, it let out an embarrassing squeak. The receptionist had already given her several disapproving looks; she was a middle-aged white woman with carefully permed brunette hair and an ornate manicure, and she honestly was wearing the hell out of that pink pantsuit, even if she vibed like she should be selling cosmetics.

"Mr. Davis will see you now."

Taking a breath to steady herself, Iris went down the hall and went into the first office, clearly marked with a nameplate that read *Carl Davis, attorney at law*. He greeted her with a squishy, damp handshake and a smile that worried her vaguely, as if he was about to ask her to sign something she didn't understand. He was an avuncular man, balding and clad in a gray suit that bagged in the wrong places.

"Come, sit down. Would you like coffee?" When Iris shook her head, he offered with a hopeful expression, "Tea?"

"No, I'm fine. Thank you."

"First, let me say that I'm sorry for your loss. Your aunt was quite a woman."

It didn't seem worth correcting him on the "great" part, so she merely nodded. "Did you know her well?"

"Unfortunately not. We met near the end of her life, and I helped get her affairs in order. She seemed to know..." He paused delicately.

"That her time was coming to an end?"

"Precisely. Most of the details are resolved now, as we've completed inventory and valuation and paid off all outstanding creditors. What remains to you will be disbursed..."

Iris listened as Mr. Davis explained everything in simple terms, letting her know that it would probably take a couple more months to get her money. He went on, "There's also a 1988 Chevy Impala, but it needs repairs. In the will, Ms. Van Doren specified that it's yours to do with as you please."

Hopefully, her great-aunt wouldn't be hurt by this decision. "I already have a car, and I can't afford to fix hers. Can we sell it?"

The attorney nodded briskly. "We may be able to find a collector. If not, there will be someone who needs it for parts. In that scenario, it won't bring in much cash, but—"

"That's fine." Somehow she refrained from saying, "Anything helps," because she didn't want Mr. Davis knowing that she was broke and desperate.

Adjusting his glasses, he checked his files. "I also have questions about a few more items in the house, particularly the ceramic angel collection."

"I'll keep it," she said at once.

That was sheer instinct. It had been important to Gertie, and Iris couldn't bring herself to liquidate it. Not now, anyway. She was still getting used to the idea of inheriting anything. How could she be heartless right from the jump?

"Understood. Then there are just some documents to sign…"

All told, the meeting took less than an hour, and the attorney provided all the documentation she needed to turn the power on in her name. None of this solved her immediate cash flow problem, but hopefully, Frederic would be chill. While she understood that he needed the money too, she couldn't sell enough plasma to pay him off any sooner. She had been doing that to pay down her credit card, but the donations didn't cover rent, her phone bill, food, or her share of the utilities.

She wrapped things up and said, "Contact me if you need anything to make the process go smoother."

"I'll be in touch as needed. Take care." Mr. Davis didn't walk her out.

Soon she found herself on the sidewalk again with people going about their day, running errands in the cute and bustling downtown district in St. Claire. Iris cast a longing look at a bakery across the square, but she talked herself out of spending the money. Learning to bake would be more sensible. She thought a man across the street was looking at her, but then he turned and hurried in the opposite direction, so maybe not.

———

Weeks later, Iris stood in the driveway of what was now *her* house.

So freaking wild.

Her car was packed to the brim. She had no furniture, just clothes and bedding, various personal effects, and some kitchen items. Great-Aunt Gertie had accumulated a lifetime of stuff, and dealing with it was Iris's problem. She had mixed feelings about that responsibility because she wasn't good at detail management, but it had to be done, whether she liked it or not. At least she'd gotten an inventory list from Mr. Davis, so she knew exactly what the house held in store.

By selling Gertie's car, Iris had gotten enough cash to pay off her roommates in Ohio, freeing her to hit the road. Two weeks ago, she'd been forced to turn off her cell phone; first order of business, get a prepaid SIM with some data and minutes on the cheap. She'd probably donate more plasma to install Wi-Fi. She couldn't live without that, and her prospective roommates would expect to use it too.

The long drive had given her lots of time to think about the future, at least. Iris had a vague idea about renovating the place and turning it into a bed-and-breakfast, but she was wary of her own enthusiasm. *Just look at the boxes of jewelry-making supplies in my trunk.* With a sigh, Iris stretched, popped her back, and started unloading.

As she stacked boxes near the porch, a woman cut across an immaculate yard that was somehow still emerald green even though summer was over. Idly Iris wondered if they paid to have the dead grass painted. The woman was tall and statuesque with carefully curled hair, and she beamed a smile that alarmed Iris for some reason.

"Hey there! So good to get some fresh blood in the neighborhood!"

"Right," said Iris, hoping she wasn't about to meet her first real-life sanguine vamp.

"I'm Susan Calhoun. You must be moving into Crazy Gertie's place. So glad she's finally out of the way. Now you can spruce up the place! That porch is positively a death trap. I told her so many times that the mailman would fall through someday and then she'd get sued." Susan clicked her tongue against her teeth. "But did she listen? Of *course* not!"

Before Iris could get a word in edgewise, Susan took a breath and kept going. "Anyway! I just wanted to welcome you to the neighborhood. I would've brought a casserole, but these days people are *so* picky. 'I don't eat meat, don't eat dairy,' and don't get me *started* on people who think they're allergic to gluten."

Yelling at her new neighbor probably wasn't the way to go, so Iris mumbled something noncommittal. She was actually kind of impressed at how wrong and awful Susan had managed to be in the space of two minutes. "Uh, thanks. I need to get my things inside, so…"

Susan didn't take the hint, peering at Iris with judgmental eyes. "Hmm. At least you *look* normal. I was scared to death that a real weirdo would move in next door. You know, one of those types," she added.

"I don't follow," she said.

The other woman shot her an incredulous look. "You must've read the news! Humanity is under siege. Witches have been intermingling with us secretly for *years*. They're a major threat to our way of life. And I've read that—"

"Sorry to cut this short. If I don't get these boxes inside soon, I'm afraid they might get rained on."

"Right! We'll talk more later. I do appreciate someone who

knows the value of hard work. I'm expecting good things from you, oh, what was your name? You didn't tell me."

You didn't let me.

"Iris Collins. Gertrude Van Doren was my great-aunt," she said deliberately.

Susan let out a nervous cough. "Right. Well, I'm sure you knew she was a few hot dogs shy of a picnic, so it's not like I spoiled the ending of a good movie. TTYL!"

"Who says TTYL?" Iris mumbled, hoisting a box and hauling it into the house.

She wished she'd put Susan in her place, but at this juncture, she couldn't cope with additional problems. Once she got settled in, she'd make it clear to that awful woman just where Iris stood on all that bigoted BS. It took her an hour to drag everything inside, and she left it cluttering up the foyer, too tired to put anything away after the long drive.

Like the last time she'd visited, it was late, but at least she had the utilities sorted out. The power, water, and gas were in her name, thanks to some guidance from Mr. Davis.

Iris couldn't bring herself to sleep on any of the mattresses because who knew how long it had been since they were cleaned. Maybe never. And while she wasn't ordinarily that picky about housekeeping, there was something unnerving about being in a house by herself that had belonged to someone who'd passed away.

Yeah, I can't let myself think along those lines. My imagination will kick in.

Before the world changed and the witches stepped out of the shadows, sometimes she'd even imagined she caught glimpses of

the elusive fae while walking in the woods. Since her family was…
unusual, she'd believed in ghosts, unicorns, and mermaids too. To
Iris, it always seemed strange that her sisters didn't wonder at *all*
about the other paranormal communities that might be quietly
coexisting nearby, hidden in plain sight just like her family. But
no, instead of being curious, her sisters used to wind her up with
far-fetched stories, which usually ended with Iris in tears and Mom
scolding her for being difficult and dramatic.

Good times.

Her phone pinged, and Rose popped up in the notifications.
Until now, nobody had messaged her since she'd skipped Rose's
party, and if she was honest, she'd welcomed the silence. Things
hadn't been the same since Iris brought home her boyfriend of two
months …and her sister Lily had snapped him up.

She hadn't been in *love* with Dylan, but in her view, both he and
Lily were wrong. He shouldn't have flirted with her sister, and Lily
damn sure shouldn't have gone along with it, even if those two were
a better fit. Now everything was awkward, and Iris couldn't help
feeling resentful toward everyone currently enabling that relationship.

It felt like she didn't even have a family anymore, frankly. She
wished she could opt out, like people did with newsletters they
didn't want anymore. But there was no button to press that would
get her out of those blood ties. Iris sucked in a calming breath,
wishing that she was enough for someone. Anyone. Without
changing who she was or—

She could practically hear her mother's admonition—*Get your
head out of the clouds. Dreams won't get you anywhere. It's all
about hard work. Look at how well Rose is doing.*

Mom usually didn't add the last, unspoken sentence: *Why can't you be more like your sister?* But Iris didn't have to hear the words to know Mom was thinking them. Pretty much everyone believed that Iris was wasting her life.

It was yet another layer of disappointment that Iris was so... average, unable to share in the family legacy or even know what it was like to...feed. Which was a gross way to put it, but her family seemed to look on most humans as a snack pack rather than individuals with their own hopes and dreams. Olive was the only exception, as she genuinely cared about others. Iris *should* be able to relate better to humans, but her sisters were *experts* in mental and emotional manipulation; they had...well, *minions* seemed like the right word to Iris, even if Lily and Rose called them "friends."

Anger and envy burned within her in a bitter, blazing knot.

Most people could hold on to friendships at least, but people always drifted away from her, as if she had nothing they needed long-term. Her family, on the other hand, cultivated sycophants addicted to the faint euphoria that came from draining their emotions, a blissful numbness that approached inner peace. Her mother's "best friend," Misty, had been running errands for Delphine Collins for over thirty years, whereas Iris's bestie from high school had ghosted after graduation. Since Iris had gone to four different colleges before dropping out, she hadn't made lasting impressions there either. As she rolled up in a blanket and curled up on the couch, she thought, *Nobody would care if I disappeared.* That was a lot grimmer than she usually felt. Maybe exhaustion was making her emotional. Things would look better in the morning, right?

The next day, things were still messy.

She hauled all her stuff upstairs and then got started sorting Great-Aunt Gertie's earthly effects. Her family would have simply paid someone to do this, but that felt deeply wrong, even if she could've afforded it. To her surprise, she wept as she sorted. When she found a bundle of letters, she couldn't resist opening them.

In a romantic movie, these would be a collection of love letters from some tragic affair, perhaps a soldier who'd perished in some long-ago war, the reason Auntie had never married. But no, these were chatty notes from various friends, illuminating what life had been like for her great-aunt over the years. Those she elected to save because discarding responses to Gertie's words and emotions while living in this house seemed like an act of violence.

Iris saved all the photos because they too felt like stories with a life of their own. Most of the clothes went, though she salvaged some vintage sweaters. Random bric-a-brac got discarded, along with musty decorative objects and muddy watercolors. Little by little, over the course of three days, she packed most of what should be donated and called a charity service to collect it.

Then she popped out for the cheapest prepaid SIM she could find. She'd probably keep the data turned off and stick to free hotspots, as this purchase had to last her for the foreseeable future. Between credit cards, student loans, and paying to deep-clean the house, there was no room in her budget for extras. Hell, she'd probably be eating oatmeal for weeks.

Iris cringed at paying online for hired cleaning professionals. "It'll be worth it," she told herself and put the transaction on her card. *I'll never pay this off.* But the site promised that they'd scrub the place, top to bottom, and they'd also deep-clean all the mattresses and rugs. The next day, the team showed up in pristine uniforms, ready to scour.

Iris spent the afternoon weeding while the crew blitzed the house with cleaning agents. When she came in hours later, the place smelled much better. It couldn't make up for years of neglect, of course, but stripping away the junk helped. So did making the woodwork gleam. Now, the house itself felt...lighter, somehow, as if she'd lessened its architectural burden; even the air seemed easier to breathe.

"You paid online," the team leader said. "So we're finished unless you'd like to schedule regular appointments?"

"I can't afford that," she admitted. "Sorry if—"

"No, it's fine. We often do one-shot visits when houses are changing hands. Good luck!" With that, the crew headed out, getting into the van with the anthropomorphized vacuum cleaner stenciled on the side.

After that, Iris sent a few requests for quotes to various home reno sites and shuddered when they called her back. "Yes, this is Iris Collins."

"What's your renovation budget?" a deep-voiced contractor asked.

"Eh, I was hoping to find out how much it would cost," she hedged.

"To turn your old Victorian into a B and B? I'd have to do a walkthrough, but you're looking at a minimum of 50K."

"Okay, thanks."

"Did you want to set a time for me to come out and take a look at your property?"

How much would *that* cost?

"I'm talking to a few companies," she said swiftly. "I'll be in touch."

Her credit wouldn't qualify for a loan, and she didn't want to get in more debt over an idea that even *she* wasn't convinced would pan out. To say she'd lost confidence was a misnomer. That would mean she'd had some in the first place.

And she still had to get the Wi-Fi turned on. She'd be charged for the installation visit, probably for equipment, and then the monthly fee—that was why she'd turned off her cell phone service. Not to mention electric, gas, and there was water and sewage as well, though she hadn't seen the bills yet. Iris hoped she hadn't bitten off more than she could chew.

Of course you have, her mother's voice said. *That's your specialty.*

She shook her head fiercely. It occurred to her then that the house had income potential. Not as a B and B, but there were five bedrooms she could rent—one behind the kitchen, two on the second floor, two on the third. And she wouldn't need to cater to roommates, hovering around with plates of scones or whatever. They'd fix their own food, and she'd collect the money. That base amount should be enough for her to live on while she continued with her jewelry business.

I can fix up the attic for myself. At least it's finished, and I like the space. It's big enough for me to set aside part of it as a studio. I'll probably need to buy an air con, though. There was even enough old furniture stored up there that she could arrange it in a way that made sense for her private living space.

Her mind made up, she opened her laptop and wrote the ad before she could change her mind.

SEEKING ROOMMATE(S) FOR SPACIOUS VICTORIAN HOME IN QUIET NEIGHBORHOOD. PRIVATE ROOM, SHARED BATH. COMMUNAL USE OF KITCHEN, LIVING AREAS, AND LAUNDRY FACILITIES. NONSMOKERS, LIGHT DRINKING OK, NO DRUG USE AND NO PETS. IF INTERESTED, PLEASE GET IN TOUCH.

With an emphatic nod, she hit Send.

Eli had blown his chance to speak with Iris again.

When he'd spotted her, he froze, just like when they were in school. Instead of going over to say hi, he'd bolted like a coward. He told himself it was no big deal; he'd run into Iris again before she left town. St. Claire wasn't a huge city by any means…only that hadn't happened. He never saw her again, and he'd tucked away the vague disappointment.

Not meant to be, that's all.

For the past two weeks, he'd focused on spending time with Gamma. They watched movies, chatted, ate meals together, and worked on the house. Eli did the heavy lifting while Gamma shared her many opinions regarding his work. Thankfully, she *never* asked about his social life or when he was planning to get married, and she respected his need to slip away to fly when the prospect of saying goodbye to her overwhelmed him.

And today, he drove her to the airport, reassuring her that he—and her house—would be fine.

"I'll take pictures," he promised, as they hugged in front of the security line. "So you can see how nice it looks when I list it."

She hesitated. "You're sure you don't mind handling the sale for me?"

"It's my pleasure, least I can do—"

"I didn't raise you so you'd be grateful," she cut in. "I love you to bits, little man."

He grinned. That was what she'd called him his whole life, and it used to be more applicable than it currently was. Back then, it rubbed him raw since he was *so* freaking small, but now, he found it cute, a cornerstone of their history. She'd never meant it as an insult either, unlike the kids at school.

"Love you more," he said, kissing the top of her head. "Now go catch a plane. New Mexico needs some of your energy."

"I'll text you when I land!" she called, falling in with the other travelers.

It was a little ironic for an avian shifter to get on a plane, but she couldn't take her belongings if she flew all the way to Albuquerque in bird form. On that mildly amusing thought, Eli wheeled and headed to the parking garage. He lined up and paid to exit, driving on automatic. Good thing he knew the way back to Gamma's—what used to be Gamma's house—in his sleep because when he came to himself again, he was turning left off the interstate, reflexively taking the main road that led into town.

He'd been up early, and he could use a coffee before he went back to painting. The house was almost empty; they'd kept only enough furniture for staging, removing all the clutter. Eli had read up on what he needed to do to get the best price for the house, and he took such matters seriously. His earnestness had gotten him in trouble more than once.

Do you see everything as a major deal? Lighten up; it's not that deep.

It was, though. To him.

Eli snagged a choice parking spot in front of Java House and headed in for an iced coffee. He got his usual—almond milk latte with a shot of vanilla. Perfect. Then he stopped, gaze locked on the person he most wanted to see and never thought he would again.

Before he could even call it a decision, his feet carried him over to her. Iris Collins.

She looked up with a brilliant smile. "You're here about the ad, right? You're a bit early, but that's fine. I like your enthusiasm."

Uh, what?

She carried on talking, not seeming to read his befuddlement. "Have a seat. I'll be honest, I'm so new at this that I don't know what I'm doing. But I have a few questions."

Eli sat...because Iris was asking him to. He'd hardly spoken to her in his life, just...observed her from a distance. And having all her attention focused on him shorted out his brain. Her smile was bright, and her voice came across soft and smooth, like he could listen to her for days, even if he had no clue what she was talking about.

"Go ahead," he said.

"Which room are you interested in? Since you're the first person I'm talking to, you have your choice." She ran down a list for him, summarizing amenities and related costs.

Honestly, the rates she was quoting for a monthly rental sounded low. Instead of clearing up the misunderstanding, he heard himself say, "That's a bargain."

She beamed. "The house isn't fancy, and it needs some work, but it's really clean, I promise. I guess I should ask, do you have any pets?"

He shook his head. "No, but I—"

"That's great. I like animals, but I'd rather not bring in any right now."

Her smile stole his breath, so wide and lovely, even down to the way one of her front teeth overlapped the other. *Why is that so cute?* He'd been about to crack a joke—*I can turn into a bird.* Probably just as well he hadn't been able to finish. Most people didn't believe in his abilities, and he didn't care enough to prove them wrong.

After pausing to make a note, Iris went on, "Do you smoke?"

"No, definitely not."

She brightened. "Excellent! The smoking is a deal breaker. We're off to a great start."

He blinked. *What's even happening here? What are you doing? Tell her—*

"What's your name?"

Shit. She doesn't recognize me. That shouldn't hurt; it had been ages, and she clearly hadn't thought about him in all that time. It wasn't like she'd been looking at *his* socials, making sure he was okay.

"Eli Reese." He watched her face, but there wasn't even a flicker of recognition.

Dammit.

She made a note on her tablet. "And what do you do?"

"Well, I was getting coffee. Before that, I was updating a house that'll be sold soon." Once the words were out, he realized that was probably not what she was asking. It had been a "source of income" question, and he'd kind of lied. Not on purpose, but she had his head in a spin.

"A house flipper! That's so cool."

"I do some freelance work online too," he said, desperately trying to get back on top of the situation. "Coding—"

"Like websites? That's awesome. You're handy and techy! The total package."

Wow. Nobody had ever said that about him, and he went silent, feeling heat sting his cheeks. "Uh. Yeah. I pick stuff up quickly when I need to learn, so..."

What am I even doing?

Just tell her who you are. Thank her. And get out of here. This is getting weird.

"You seem like you'd have your stuff together. Why do you need to rent a room at my place?" Iris asked.

"It just kind of...happened," he heard himself say. "The house I'm staying at, it'll be sold soon."

That was all true, but he had other places to go. The condo. The vacation cottage. Yet he paused, staring at her, gauging her expression.

Her face softened, eyes getting a little brighter. "Yeah, I know how it is. Sometimes things don't work out or your plans don't come together."

She asked a few more questions about his habits—clean or sloppy, drugs or alcohol, loud parties, overnight guests—and at the end of the quick interview, she said, "I'd be happy to have you as a roommate if you're interested."

She must need financial help if she's doing this. One thing Eli had was money. He was great at coming up with app ideas, and when he got tired of managing them, he'd sell them for a tidy profit. Inspiration would strike again soon. He still hadn't decided whether to sell Task Wizard or What's Cooking?

"I'll take the main bedroom," he said. "Five hundred a month is fair. How much is the damage deposit?"

She blinked as if she'd never even thought of that. This woman was too soft to live in the real world. It made him want to protect her from those who'd take advantage.

"Is that...?" Seeming to think better of whatever she was about to ask, she stopped and changed directions. "Could you manage $250?"

"No problem," he said. "If you give me your email, I can pay you online."

"That's perfect." She asked for his number and texted him her email. Eli saved her information in his contacts right away.

"Anything else?" he asked.

She shook her head. "I'll have the rental agreement ready to sign next time we meet. You can move in whenever you like—just give me a heads-up first. The rooms are furnished but not fancy. I hope you like living with me." Then she bit her lip, eyes wide. "I meant rooming, I didn't mean—"

"It's fine. I know."

With a casual wave, he got the coffee he'd come in for and headed out to his truck as an elderly man sat down at the table. Eli leaned his head on the steering wheel. *What the hell have I done?* Then he straightened. It wasn't like he had any pressing reason to rush off. Maybe things happened for a reason; this could be his chance to finally get to know her.

Eli got out his phone, stared at her number for a moment, then quietly changed Iris's contact info to "Dream Come True."

CHAPTER FOUR

"HENRY DALE MACABEE," THE OLDER man said, offering his hand with a pugnacious tilt of his unshaven chin.

"Iris Collins. Have a seat."

He wore a short-sleeved, button-up plaid shirt, carefully tucked into worn jeans. The man shook her hand firmly and took a seat, hot coffee in hand. Iris was a little surprised he'd bought any, but it seemed to be plain and black. No frills for this senior citizen.

"I'm on a fixed income," he said without waiting for her to begin. "And I won't tolerate a lot of nonsense. No smoking indoors. No loud parties."

She was torn between the desire to laugh and the urge to set him straight. The former would likely offend him, so she tried for the latter, tactfully. "I'm the homeowner, so *I'm* setting the conditions. But smoking and loud parties are deal breakers for me as well, so you'll have to host your ragers somewhere else."

The old man's eyes snapped up, and for a moment, he glared at her, eyes narrowed, then eventually, a reluctant smile tugged at the edge of his thin mouth. "You're sassy. I don't...entirely mind a bit of pertness."

"That's good." From there, she described the four available rooms and showed him pictures on her phone. Then she added, "The house is really clean, but it's old and—"

"Well, I'm old too," he cut in, "so you can put a pin in whatever you were about to say. There aren't many options for my budget, so if you're willing, let's do this."

She hesitated. Maybe renting to an old grouch wasn't the best idea, but she couldn't bring herself to say no. "Which room did you want?"

"I'll take the one off the kitchen. It's away from everyone else."

Yeah, she'd read him right. He was a curmudgeon who didn't *want* to live with other people. Iris quoted him the total: one month up front, half a month for a damage deposit. She was grateful to Eli Reese for bringing that up, as she hadn't even thought of it. She hoped nobody would wreck the place, but inviting five strangers to live with her? Anything could happen. It was tough not to be nervous about that, but she planned to run criminal checks on everyone using an online service that promised a complete national report for a reasonable price.

It'll be fine. Probably.

"I don't have my checkbook with me, but I can pay right away."

"I'll be here for a couple more hours, talking to people. If—"

"I'll go right now," the old man interrupted. "I don't intend to let someone else snatch the room I want out from under me. Don't give the kitchen room to anyone else, understand? I'll be back soon."

He was gone before Iris could say another word. She blinked and tried to decide if Henry Dale Macabee's eagerness was a good thing. He seemed a little desperate, and that made her feel bad for him, but maybe she shouldn't do this first come, first served. It might be better to take applications and—

The next candidate arrived, a buff guy in his thirties who kept winking for no reason. "Clint McMahon. I had no idea you'd be so cute. I would've worn better underwear."

"Uh, what?"

"Just kidding! I don't sleep with people I'm rooming with. Too bad for you! I know, it's very sad. So let's see, I manage Big Fitness. That's a gym, if you didn't know. And honestly, you could be really hot if you just put in the time. I hate seeing people not living up to their potential, you know?"

"I really would rather—"

"Don't worry about it, doll. Once I move in, I'll help you manage your lifestyle. You'll get fitness and nutrition tips, free of charge." Clint winked again. "If you play your cards right, I might even make you one of my special breakfast shakes."

"Thank you. I'll be in touch," Iris said, fighting to keep a straight face.

Clint seemed both surprised and disappointed that there were no further questions. He flexed as he pushed back from the table, winking at four other people before he made it out the door. Iris imagined how much she'd enjoy taking a shower later.

Two more potential candidates arrived. With these folks, Iris did a better job of controlling the encounters, and she promised to call them once she made a decision.

Unlike Clint, they seemed normal enough, and maybe that was the issue. With Eli, it seemed like he was in a jam due to poor planning, and Henry Dale had said he was on a fixed income. Iris realized she was leaning toward people who...*needed* to rent a room at her place, who didn't easily have other options.

Maybe she had her shoes on the wrong feet—something she'd done literally as a kid—but to her, that seemed like a safe way to choose her new roommates. People who had no other fallbacks ought to be more considerate, easier to live with. Since Iris had been in that situation, she knew how it felt to be dependent on someone else's goodwill. She'd never take advantage of that desperation, but she understood it for sure.

As she was about to leave, Henry Dale rushed in with a check in hand. Once she had it, she input her number into the old man's flip phone and wrote down the address. "You can move in whenever you like," she said. "Just let me know beforehand. I'll have the rental agreement ready to sign then as well. And if you don't like the furniture in your room, I'll remove it."

He shook his head. "I'm sure it's fine. I just need a place to lay my head at night." He hesitated. "Listen, from the photos you showed me, it's an old place. Could use some looking after. I like to keep busy. Would you have a problem with me...puttering?"

Iris blinked. "You mean, like, working on the house?"

"Exactly. Just from looking at the photos, I *know* I can improve that kitchen."

"I'd love the help. Anything you feel like fixing, I'll knock it off your rent." She hoped Henry Dale would be honest about the value of his work, however, because she had no clue about that sort of thing.

"That's a generous offer," he said, visibly brightening. "And

I'm happy to take you up on it. I'll know better what I ought to be doing once I check the house in person. I'm…looking forward to this, Miz Collins."

"Iris."

"Miz Collins," he repeated with a firm nod.

Looks like I'm Miz Collins.

As she stood, Eli's payment popped up in her phone notifications. In the end, she'd conducted ten interviews and only promised rooms to Eli and Henry Dale. *I'll post another ad. This is enough money to get by for the first month.* She could cover necessities, though she needed to be careful with groceries. As ever, eating out wasn't an option.

"When will you move in?" she asked, deciding not to bicker over what he called her.

"Monday all right? I need the weekend to pack up and organize my things."

"It's fine. I'll see you then."

She stood and stretched, stiff from two hours on a coffee shop chair. Henry Dale left without looking back, and she stifled a laugh. She'd never been close to her own grandparents—like Mom, they compared Iris to her sisters and found her wanting—so this might be a nice change of pace. Dad's parents were long gone; she'd never met them. And Dad? Well, he rarely glanced up from his professorial pursuits to intervene in the way his wife saw fit to run their home.

After buying a sandwich to go, Iris headed out to her Sentra, parked a block away because she hadn't wanted to occupy a primo parking spot for that long. Her meter had two minutes left—perfect timing—and she drove home slowly, satisfied with how the day had gone. Iris rarely felt this way, as if she'd done an adequate job. Her phone rang, and she let it go to voice mail. It wasn't safe to answer the phone while she drove, at least not without a headset, and she didn't bother with such things. Whatever anyone wanted could wait until she got home. Besides, she wasn't talking to Lily currently, Rose would nag about how she was being petty for not getting over Lily and Dylan, and she'd rather dodge calls from Mom, who insisted she get over her resentment for the sake of family unity. *Funny how it's* always *me being asked to swallow my emotions and be the bigger person.* Once she pulled into the driveway, she checked and found a missed call from Olive.

Dammit. The one sister I'm not *avoiding.*

Olive rarely got a signal, and it must be important if she was trying to get in touch. Or maybe the others had dragged her into this low-key feud. That wasn't the right word, though. More like Iris was just...done. Lily had wanted Dylan more than she'd wanted a relationship with her own sister. And Rose had a perfect life, so why didn't she just live it instead of meddling?

Taking a deep breath, she rang Olive back. No surprise—it went to voice mail. "Sorry, I was driving," she said after the tone. "Hope you're well. Love and miss you."

Now Olive could tell everyone else, *She's not dodging me. She called back right away. You're imagining things.* Because Olive tried to play peacemaker and she wanted everyone to get along— without dragging her into their problems. That was probably part of why she was living in an African tukul, not chasing success in the same way as Rose and Lily. Of her three sisters, Iris liked Olive best despite the ten-year age gap. She also approved of the way Olive deployed her special abilities, using them for good instead of her own gain.

At least Iris finally had her own place, far enough away from her family to discourage drop-in visits. They'd rarely come to see Great-Aunt Gertie, after all.

Things might finally be looking up.

───────────

This is ridiculous.

Eli had paid hundreds of dollars to avoid clearing up a misunderstanding. His chagrin didn't stem from spending the money; he could afford it. But now he was connected to Iris through deception, and as he finished the final coat of paint in Gamma's dining room, he let out a breath, irritated with himself. It would've been simple to square everything away, but no.

And now look, you made it worse.

Yet part of him also simmered with excitement. Becoming Iris's roommate would allow him to get to know her without her suspecting that he'd known her for most of his life. Regrettably, the opposite wasn't true, but she might like him if they spent time together. And then, once they became friends, he could mention the fact that they'd gone to elementary school together. Casually, though, like he'd just remembered. In time, he could work up to thanking her for what she did back then.

And then...

Well, he didn't have all the answers. She might not even handle it well if she discovered his hawk shifter lineage. Already there were whispers about groups being formed among humans, dedicated to ferreting out those who were different. His people hadn't come out like the witches had, but they'd stopped worrying about being discovered. There was no central body since shifters were rare, and hawks were solitary by nature, so everyone was playing it by ear, doing what seemed best individually.

For Eli, that meant keeping his cards close to his chest, as he'd learned all too well just how cruel humans could be. And that was when they had no concrete reason for hurting him, apart from him being small. There was no telling what they'd do if they learned his actual secret. While the world might've changed some, he still feared that human nature remained essentially the same.

Rather than fret about issues he couldn't change, he went out the attic window, reveling in his wings catching the wind. He glided in a slow circle and eventually located Iris's place from two miles away. It wasn't difficult; she lived in the only purple house in town, and he flew that way on instinct until he circled above the fanciful Queen Anne roof that had sparrows nesting in the broken bits. Though repairs were needed, the place had a certain ramshackle charm, and he could envision Iris here. He flew on until the colors of sunset bled out into the darkness of night.

Sometimes he imagined living as a hawk, just packing in the human side. The call grew a little stronger year after year. Some shifters were more comfortable with their wild side, and that was true for Eli as well. But he still had a few ties to the world. So far, they always drew him back.

Eli spent the weekend feverishly working on Gamma's house, getting the yard in shape—as much as possible with general autumn messiness. This was a tough time of year to sell a house, as the leaves dropped constantly, and he'd bulked up his raking muscles. At least the hedges were uniform, and he cleaned the gutters and then scrubbed the porch, ending with a power wash. Before the sun went down Sunday evening, he took a ton of photos for the listing agent. He emailed them to Gamma as well, who had been texting him about her welcome party. She'd chosen a fifty-five-plus community, where she'd bought a condo and was already getting involved in all the activities on offer.

Gamma: I'm having a great time. I signed up for salsa lessons.

Eli: That sounds fun.

Gamma: Should I learn how to write HTML or how to speak Spanish?

Eli: Can it be both?

Gamma: I only have so much time and energy!

Eli: Then Spanish. I might decide to find my relatives on Mom's side at some point and you can come with me to Mexico.

Gamma: !! That would be amazing. I've been telling you to look for years. Gotta run, little man. I've been invited to a wine tasting.

He was glad she seemed to be doing well. There were no problems with her house; thanks to his efforts today, the outside looked fantastic too. He had faith that the place would sell like a dream, and it would be easier without him getting in the way. The real estate agent could show the house at any time without worrying about Eli eating toast in his boxers. And since he was hoping for a quick sale, it might be better if he was living locally, available to sign the closing papers when a solid offer came in. Eli knew he was rationalizing, but those were all excellent—and valid—reasons to stick around.

On Monday morning, Eli packed his suitcase and polished away the last traces of his own presence. After taking one last look at the house where he'd spent his teen years, he drove over to the real estate agent's office and left the keys with her, signing all the papers necessary for her to set up showings. Keshonda Jennings was a professional, driven Black woman who set records moving properties around town, and he had a good feeling about what she could do for Gamma's place.

Keshonda shook his hand with a polite smile. "I had a chance to review the photos you sent. You've staged the place well, but we should get a professional in there to upgrade the listing. Are you on board?"

"For photos or staging?"

"Both. I can invoice you for the work."

He didn't even hesitate. This was an investment, one that would benefit Gamma. "Let's do it. The house is nice, but if you can take it to the next level—"

"I can and will. I just need your approval," Keshonda cut in.

"Where do I sign?" he joked.

As it turned out, there were documents for that as well, so he scrawled his signature until Keshonda said they were done. "That should do it. Thanks so much for trusting me with your grandmother's home."

"You come highly recommended."

She walked him out, past the receptionist tapping away on her keyboard. "I'll keep you posted throughout the process."

Eli nodded and jogged to his car. Everything he'd brought from home was in the trunk, a suitcase and a backpack. *Can't believe I'm doing this.* After texting Iris as requested, he input her address into his phone's navigation app. He'd done the flyby, but the streets didn't look quite the same in his truck. Better not to get lost and show up late. He drove carefully, minding the turns. Since it was past noon by now, it shouldn't be too early, but he was still nervous as hell.

In the daylight, the flaws he'd glimpsed as a hawk were even more obvious. The house desperately needed to be sanded and painted, and half the gingerbread trim was rotten or had fallen off entirely. The porch didn't look stable, and one of the upstairs windows had a massive crack.

This was the sort of house that kids on the block told stories about; they claimed the old woman who lived in it was a witch, and they'd cook up tales about the ghosts who haunted the place. But ghosts and witches didn't frighten a hawk shifter. With a mental shrug, he navigated past Iris's Sentra in the narrow drive, parking in front of her. If everyone who rented from her had a car, parking would become an issue. If they didn't, that would be a separate problem because life in St. Claire could be challenging without transportation.

He opened the tailgate and hauled his stuff out. A woman came outside next door and stood on her front porch with folded arms, watching like a creeper. Ignoring the woman's strange interest, Eli dragged his suitcase to the steps, avoiding the soft spots.

Gathering himself, he rang the bell.

A few minutes later, Iris flung the door open. She had her hair up in a messy bun, and she was still in pajamas, adorable pink ones with sleeping kittens on them with little *zzz*s coming from their tiny mouths. *Okay, it should be illegal for anyone to be this cute.*

"Oh wow, you're here already. I just saw your text two minutes ago. The papers are around here somewhere, and...I had keys made! Where are they? I was in the shed and..." Her voice faded as she moved away from the door without inviting him in.

Am I supposed to wait?

She rushed back. "Sorry, I'm bad at this. Come in! This is your home now too. You don't need to be polite. You've paid for in-and-out privileges."

She probably didn't mean for that to sound suggestive. It totally did. Somehow, he pretended he didn't notice it either. "Thank you," he mumbled, hauling his bag up the single step into the foyer.

Inside, it was cool and dim. Overall, the house gave a nice impression, though it didn't fit Iris's personality in the slightest. Everything was a bit faded, colors chosen in a time when dusty mauve and country blue ruled the world. But the furniture looked comfortable enough, and there wasn't too much of it crammed into the living area. She had a good eye for flow, it seemed.

"None of this is mine," she said, seeming to misread his silence. "I did the best I could with Great-Aunt Gertie's stuff, but—"

"It's nice." He meant that. The place already had a homier feel than either of his professionally decorated residences, a lived-in air that only came through wear and tear.

"I'm glad. Here's your key." Iris handed him a key chain with two charms on it—one was a tiny functional measuring tape and the other a small USB drive. Apparently responding to his look, whatever that was, she hurried on, "I thought those were cute, and based on what you said at the interview, I thought..."

Oh. It's because she thinks I flip houses and build websites.

"That's sweet of you. I'm sure I'll get a lot of use out of these."

"Really?"

"Sure." Hell, he'd measure his own dick to keep her smiling with such delight. Not a thought he'd ever expected to have, but Iris had a way of doing that to him.

"That's good. I'll show you to your room." Gesturing toward the stairs, she picked up his backpack, the sort of person who always helped without being asked. With a pang in his chest, he recalled the little girl with twin plaits and a fearless demeanor.

Some things never change.

CHAPTER FIVE

IRIS TRIED TO VIEW THE bedroom through Eli's eyes.

It wasn't huge by modern standards, and the closet was an afterthought. She'd painted this room sage green and covered the freshly cleaned mattress with old sheets and a handmade quilt. At least the house was spotless, thanks to the professional crew who had scrubbed everything from top to bottom.

"What do you think?" she asked, trying not to sound as nervous as she felt.

If he threw a fit and left, she'd have to give back his money. It wasn't like he'd signed the rental agreement yet. She hadn't known how long to set the terms for, so she'd chosen three months with two weeks' notice required before moving out. Iris had adapted a free agreement she found online, mostly because she couldn't afford to pay Mr. Davis to write one specific to her situation. Carefully, she set the printed page on the old dresser, which was currently more shabby than chic.

"It's fine," he said eventually.

"Fine" was what people said when they'd expected something else, different or better or both. Iris bit her lip and pretended she didn't realize that. "I'm glad you like it. I'll put the paperwork here. You can sign and return it later. I'll leave you to get settled in." She set his backpack on the floor by the door. "Oh, and if you're hungry, I made oatmeal."

She caught herself before she explained that she didn't particularly like it, but it was good for her. And *cheap*. Cheap was the important bit until her jewelry business took off.

"I already ate breakfast, but thanks."

"If you need anything, let me know."

That was so awkward. She'd had roommates before, obviously, but she'd never been the responsible party. Hopefully, it wouldn't be another disaster; she needed a break from relentless failure. Hell, if this fell through, there *was* no plan B.

"I will. Um. Iris?"

"Yeah?"

She paused in the hall, casting a curious glance back at her new roomie. Who really was distractingly attractive. During the interview she'd thought so as well, but having him in the house only reinforced her initial opinion. Hopefully, she wouldn't embarrass herself by being even more awkward than normal around him.

Eli hesitated and then shook his head. "Never mind."

With a mental shrug, she went back downstairs to finish washing her breakfast dishes and to put her leftover oatmeal away. As she opened the fridge, she realized she was barefoot, still in kitty pajamas and with unbrushed hair. *OMG.* Iris buried her face in her hands. This wasn't the impression she'd wanted to make... Too late now. She supposed it was better to dispel all illusions since they'd be living together while Eli worked on houses. Or built websites? She wasn't clear on what exactly he'd be doing, but as long as he paid the rent on time, it was none of her business.

She wanted to get upstairs to organize her studio—which wasn't a word she normally used—but this was a fresh start. If she took some nice photos, updated her online store, and did some advertising, maybe she'd start getting orders. Every little bit would help. But she was expecting Henry Dale Macabee today as well, and she'd thought he might show up at the crack of dawn. But it was just past noon, and she still hadn't heard from him. She had his check, and he had seemed desperate, so he'd turn up sooner or later.

Once she put her clean bowl in the drainer, Iris went upstairs, up, up, up—all the way to the attic. Fortunately, she'd only needed to haul a mattress up here on her own. The rest of the furniture had been hibernating here for decades, and she'd had this space cleaned as well, so at least she wasn't breathing in a quarter century of dust. Once, she'd read that dust was mostly made of dead skin cells, and—

Yeah. Stop thinking about that.

She'd built herself a bed from old pallets she'd found tucked away up here, and she'd set up a seating area with two armchairs and a side table. Across the room, a dated dining table served as a workstation. Her clothes were still in boxes, bags, and suitcases, shoved up against the wall to clear a footpath. The sloped ceilings might bother some people, but for Iris, this space felt cozy. In summer she might feel otherwise, but since it was fall trundling toward winter, she had some time before sweltering heat became an issue.

She'd showered the night before, so she dressed in a ratty sweater and yoga pants and followed through on her plan to set up her workspace properly—bins full of beads, pendants and cabochons, pins and earring hooks, various wires and strands and tools. There was a certain peace in putting everything in its place, but it was impossible to focus when she was listening for the bell. When Henry Dale arrived, she'd have to sprint down three flights of stairs.

Finally, she took her sketchbook and sat in the front room, listening for the old man's arrival. An hour later, he turned up in a rideshare with even less fanfare than she'd imagined, carrying only a small suitcase and a duffel bag. Iris couldn't decide if it was impressive or sad to have lived so long and to own so little.

"Hey," she said, stepping back so Henry Dale could come in.

She snagged his paperwork from the dining room table and led the way to the kitchen. The old man inspected everything with critical eyes; hopefully, he was imagining all the fun projects he could take on, not judging the house defective. She already felt protective of the place, even if she lacked the resources to restore its former glory.

The bedroom off the kitchen was on the small side: a single bed with an antique brass headboard, a small trunk, a night table with a vintage lamp, and a wardrobe. If Henry Dale needed more furniture, he could check the attic or supply it himself. Again, she'd tapped into old sheets and quilts that had been hidden away in various trunks, though she'd had the linens professionally cleaned also.

"Is it okay?"

He stood for a moment in silence, then he set his duffel on the bed. "I like it. No clutter. No nonsense."

"Here's your rental agreement. I haven't deposited your check yet, but I will now that you're officially rooming with me."

His mouth pressed together, but she couldn't tell if he was annoyed at the reminder or repressing a smile. Henry Dale had a weathered face that reminded her of an old map, as if it had been used well, folded often, and the lines represented roads he'd traveled and stories he could share. Then his shoulders rounded, as if he was repressing a sigh of relief.

Over having somewhere to stay? Relatable.

"Thank you," he said quietly.

Iris figured she shouldn't make a big deal out of his gratitude. "Welcome. I forgot to mention, certain items will be communal— like cooking oil, spices, sugar, tea, and coffee. I'll figure out how much we use in a month and tell you how much to contribute to keep the kitchen stocked. Label your food to avoid confusion and let me know if you need anything."

Henry Dale nodded, and she got the impression he was done with the conversation. Since he was older, it would be challenging not to slip into the misguided dynamic that he had authority over her, simply by virtue of greater age. *I'm in charge. This is my house.* If she repeated that often enough, she might even believe it.

There were three rooms left to rent, but she'd worry about that next month.

Part of her felt like she ought to be making food or offering to entertain these strangers since they felt like guests. But really, she just needed to leave them alone. Iris ate a sandwich and a yogurt for lunch and was about to head back to her room when Henry Dale came into the kitchen.

"I noticed the shed out back. Do you mind if I take a look? There might be tools I could use, and I'll need somewhere to work."

"Work?" He'd mentioned that he wanted household projects to keep busy, but she never imagined he would get started on day one.

"Yes, ma'am. I can take down these cabinet doors, wash and sand them and paint them. It should only cost for the paint, and you said you'd knock the labor off my rent."

Crap. What does he charge per hour? I wonder if he's planning to work full-time and bill me for the work while living here.

Quickly she said, "I did say that. But I can't afford to pay you outright, and I can't afford projects that will cost a ton up front. So it's probably best if we set an hourly limit."

"I understand. You need the cash or you wouldn't be renting rooms in the first place," Henry Dale said brusquely. "I can't get handyman work at my age. People are worried I'll break a hip. So I'll charge you minimum wage for the work and no more than twenty hours a month."

Iris did the math. That would mean he was only paying around a hundred dollars a month in cash, but if he slowly improved the condition of the house, it would be a good investment, even if she had to tighten her belt.

"That works for me."

———————

Eli was eavesdropping.

He hadn't intended to, but he came down the stairs and heard

Iris discussing plans for home repair with their other roommate, an older man he hadn't met. Somehow, it helped knowing he wouldn't be rattling around this big house alone with Iris. With her, he felt like he was ten years old again and awkward as hell. Because it would be weird to do otherwise, he came into the kitchen.

The older man glanced over but didn't smile. *Time to make a good impression.*

"I'm Eli," he said, offering his hand. "Nice to meet you."

"Henry Dale Macabee. Likewise. Do you know anything about jigsaws?" The handshake was firm but not to the point that Henry Dale appeared to be compensating for something. Just a polite handshake, no more, no less.

"They're best used for curves," he answered.

Henry Dale nodded as if Eli had passed a test. "If I decide to take on that gingerbread, I'll need a hand. I'm not so nimble these days."

If he hadn't noticed the rotten trim outside himself, that declaration might not have made sense. "Just let me know."

Why am I here? Offering to help an old man update Iris's house?

"Will do. I'm off to the shed." With that baffling assertion, the older man let himself out the back door and left Eli staring at Iris.

"He's okay," she offered. "A bit abrupt in his manners and rough around the edges. I don't think he likes people very much."

Eli surprised himself by saying, "Sometimes I don't either."

Iris laughed. "We all have those days, I suspect."

For him, it was more than that. After his shape-shifting ability kicked in, he'd wondered if his solitary hawkish nature was bleeding through, leaving him predisposed to silence, to those rare and lofty heights where he was alone on the perfect wind stream, carried ever higher and farther from humanity. For some reason— with Gamma moving on—this felt like his last chance, and he didn't even know why.

Last chance for what?

His brain wouldn't cooperate. Just being in the kitchen with her made him anxious. His heart fluttered as he produced the rental agreement. "I signed both copies. I brought one for your records."

"Ah, right! Thank you. I'll...file this."

It was adorable because it was so obvious she had no clue what she was doing. Eli could relate. When he'd bought the cottage as a vacation house in Myrtle Beach, it blew him away to realize he was responsible for everything from roof to floor tiles. *No landlord to call. Just me.*

He opened his mouth to reassure her, then realized he wasn't supposed to know about homeowner issues and wound up saying, "Do we have laundry facilities on site?"

"Oh! I should have told you already. And Henry Dale too. But your clothes are probably clean for now. Who moves with a sack of dirty laundry?" She gave a laugh that sounded nervous to Eli, and his heightened senses—even in this form—picked up a certain quiver in her tone.

Something about Iris struck him as...different from other people. Not the energy of another shifter, no tingle of witchy magic, but she didn't smell human either. Eli couldn't pin down exactly what made Iris unique, and his curiosity brightened to unbearable intensity.

Eli needed to know her better. To know her and learn her secrets. Maybe then he could let her go.

"Then where…?" he prompted, referring to the laundry room.

Her cheeks flooded with color, and he bit back more comforting words. Now that he'd spent a little time with her as an adult, she no longer seemed as strong or fearless as she had when they were children. Did life siphon away her spirit? If that was true, it seemed like a crime.

"Down here."

Multiple doors led out of the kitchen. One opened to a mudroom with steps heading down. The basement was perfect for filming a horror movie, complete with skeletal stairs, stained cement floor, and exposed pipes and wiring. In the corner, he spotted the washer and dryer—old, bulky, and dinged up from years of use. Judging by the dials, these machines had to be twenty or thirty years old.

"Do they still work?"

Iris bit her lip and shrugged. "I presume so, but to be honest, I haven't done laundry yet. I let it pile up because I'm dreading the long haul from attic to cellar and back again."

"I can carry it for you," he offered.

She stared at him. "Uh, why?"

He shrugged. "Because you don't want to."

"And I'm sure you're *dying* to lug someone else's clothes."

"It's good cardio."

She laughed, evidently not realizing he was serious. "You're funny. Anyway, feel free to use the machines anytime. If they still work."

Eli peered at the brands. "Does Westinghouse still make washers and dryers?"

"I have no clue. I've never bought a major appliance. And the ones that came with the house will need to be nurtured."

He liked that word, liked it a lot. And he liked that she didn't immediately plan to gut the place. Sure, some of that prudence probably stemmed from being strapped for cash, but he pictured Iris as someone who cared about the mark she left on the world. She was the type to repurpose instead of discard whenever possible.

"Is the stove gas or electric?" Eli asked the question, not really caring about the answer, but it served to keep her with him a bit longer.

"It's gas. I was so glad when I first arrived. The power had been cut off, and I thought I'd be taking cold showers until I got it turned on. But apparently the hot water heater is gas too. The tank is on the small side, so we'll need to stagger our showers. I should probably consider a bathroom and laundry schedule—"

"It's probably okay for now," he cut in, seeing that she was getting stressed over all the little details.

Letting out a breath, she nodded with a grateful smile as they went back upstairs to the kitchen. "This is all new to me. I'm not great at…being in charge. But I'll worry about it when the rest of the rooms are rented."

"You're doing fine."

She blinked, gazing at him in wonder. "Am I?"

"Sure. My room is comfortable, everything is clean. And the bathroom is quite a unique experience. I've never seen a pink toilet before."

For some reason, Iris burst out laughing. "Purple house. Pink toilet. What was Great-Aunt Gertie thinking?"

Eli smiled. Not because he understood the joke, but her amusement was infectious. "It was a different time?"

"I guess so. By the way..."

He listened as she filled him in about a communal fund for cooking oil, coffee, and the like, then instructed him to label his food. Frankly, he wasn't worried about someone eating his protein bars or quaffing his canned beverages, but he nodded all the same.

"Anyway, that's about it. I hope you like living here and that we'll get along."

"Me too," he said.

It was difficult to imagine anyone *not* getting along with Iris, actually. She radiated a cartoon princess vibe. If she sang out in the yard, mice and squirrels and bluebirds would perch on her shoulder. Suddenly, they were just...staring at each other. Not speaking. Just staring. He was barely breathing, and she—

"I can definitely work out there," Henry Dale said, stepping into the kitchen. "It wants tidying up, but that's work I can do as well. And somebody left a really nice tool set. It's a wonder nobody's carted them off. Shed wasn't even locked."

"That's St. Claire for you," Iris said.

"Did you grow up here?" the older man asked.

Eli knew the answer, even as Iris shook her head. "No, my great-aunt lived in town. I inherited her house after she passed."

"I went to school here," Eli volunteered.

Then he realized that might mislead Iris even more if she thought he was local. *How am I supposed to tell her we went to grade school together when she thinks I'm from here?*

"From middle school on," he added, hoping to clarify, but he'd already lost them.

Henry Dale was checking the hinges on all the kitchen cabinets, and Iris was asking the old man if it was possible to remove scuffs and stains from the flooring. A skilled tech witch might be able to do it; they didn't just magically repair machines. They could also restore organic materials to pristine condition. But the old man wouldn't have anything to do if Eli suggested to Iris that she could call Fix-It Witches and get a complete kitchen face-lift for a reasonable price. He gazed at Iris for a moment longer, but she continued the conversation with Henry Dale.

Usually he preferred to slip away unnoticed, but this time, it stung.

CHAPTER SIX

A FEW DAYS LATER, SUSAN Calhoun came over again.

This time, she carried the promised/threatened casserole, which smelled like broccoli and cheddar cheese. Susan didn't wait to be invited in, breezing by Iris with a determined expression. She seemed to be taking inventory of the house, her eyes narrowed as they darted around the front room.

"Here," she said, shoving the glass dish into Iris's hands. "Enjoy! I'm a great cook, if I do say so myself. You can get me a cup of coffee while you pop that in the fridge, then we'll have a nice chat. It's *so* great to have someone close to my own age in the neighborhood!"

Since Iris estimated Susan to be on the other side of forty, she winced inwardly. She stared at the casserole she didn't want and wished she had the ability to teleport away. "Coffee. Right."

She met Eli in the kitchen, who shot a troubled look past her toward the front room. "We have a visitor?"

"Yeah, one of the neighbors. I'll get rid of her. She's…" Words actually failed her.

"Not great?" he offered.

"That's putting it mildly."

"You will be remembered for your service," he said solemnly.

After putting away the casserole, Iris intentionally made a bad cup of instant coffee and carried it out to her unwelcome guest. "Enjoy."

Susan didn't so much as sip the coffee, proving it had been an excuse to stick around. And Iris would have to interact with her again in returning the damn Pyrex dish. After dealing with Mom, Lily, and Rose, Iris was wise to the ways of manipulative people, but she wasn't so great at getting rid of them.

"I'm a little disappointed," Susan said.

"About what?"

"Your lack of progress in fixing up the place. You've been here for a while, haven't you? Now, I don't like to meddle, but I'm positive I mentioned that hazard of a porch when we first met! If you don't fix up this eyesore, I'll have to contact the city. You *do* realize there are certain safety standards?"

Iris finally lost her patience. She got up, strode to the kitchen, retrieved the casserole, and pushed it into Susan's hands. "Look, I'm not made of money. I'll do what I can, as I can, but I have no intention of being blackmailed. You should go."

That wasn't even half of what she wanted to say, and somehow she managed to swallow the rest of the tirade as she herded Susan onto the porch of doom. Good Lord, could the woman be more dramatic?

Iris tried to shake off the annoyance and bury herself in her work—to no avail. She wanted to vent to Eli or Henry Dale, but her two roommates kept to themselves, and she didn't feel free to dump her frustrations on them. Eli was so nice that he'd probably listen, even if he'd rather be doing literally anything else. As for Henry Dale...

The old man spent most of his time in the shed with machine noises periodically whirring as he worked on the cabinet doors. For some reason, he'd enlisted Eli's help, which she felt a bit bad about, as she hadn't promised to discount *his* rent in exchange for physical labor, and truthfully, she couldn't afford to either.

She waited for him to bring it up on his own, but he never said a word. Eli was shy and awkward, and he could barely make eye contact. That was surprising, as handsome men usually oozed self-confidence and made nuisances of themselves without any encouragement at all. Not that she should think of her roommates that way.

Whatever his motivation for helping out, Eli had packed all the contents of the cupboards into cardboard boxes and had washed, then sanded the wooden part of the cupboards. Now he was carefully repainting them, presumably according to Henry Dale's instructions, so everything would match. They'd also put down some kind of ammonia solution to brighten up the white squares on the vinyl flooring. The black tiles didn't show wear as much, and the end result was frankly impressive.

"It looks great in here," she said later that day after she calmed down from Susan's less-than-delightful drop-by.

Henry Dale nodded. "House has good bones, just needs a little elbow grease."

And paint.

"Could you hand me that pack of screws?" Eli asked.

Iris did that, and for a moment, she simply admired the pull and bunch of his muscles as he lifted the cabinet door into place while Henry Dale installed it. Then she shook her head, irritated with herself for noticing. She left them working in the kitchen with the cabinet doors glossy, finished, and looking good as new.

Upstairs, the attic was quiet and cozy. Autumn meant the heat felt just right up here, and she headed for her worktable and sketched for a bit, creating and discarding five different designs before settling on the sixth. Happily, she tapped the page and got to work making the necklace. In the online listing, she'd call this one Golden Sunrise, not that anyone would buy it. At least her expenses were covered for the month, even if she wouldn't be living in luxury.

The work kept both her hands and mind busy, so time flew. It was full dark when she finished. She didn't have the equipment she needed to take proper photos, such as special lights, but she could make do. Once she rented another room, the budget would loosen a bit, and she might be able to get some lights and props to make the photos look more professional. Using a desk lamp and a scarf, she took the best photos she could and then polished them in a photo-editing app. As the last step, she created the listing and wrote a poetic description for the necklace.

Is there any point to this? I need to promote the online shop, and—

"Iris?" A soft tap at the door pulled her from depressing thoughts.

"Yeah?"

Eli spoke from the stairs without intruding on her space. "The kitchen is done, and we made some food. Are you hungry?"

In her last share-house situation, everyone just ate at different times. She realized she was starving. "I am, actually. I'll be down in a minute."

Henry Dale was forking down pasta when she went into the kitchen. He didn't look up from his plate, and she smiled a bit as she served herself. This was simple tomato spaghetti, but it was nice having somebody care if she'd eaten or not. Eli served some and passed it to her before doing the same for himself. As she sat, she surveyed the kitchen. Already it was 100 percent better; between the cabinets, the floors, and the counters, it had a clean, retro charm.

"We sanded the counters," Henry Dale said. "Applied some elbow grease. Butcher block is forgiving, so it just needed some TLC."

"And wood polish," Eli added.

The counters did look nice. She'd had no idea the kitchen could be brought back so effectively without major expenditures. Even the appliances gleamed after being scrubbed by the professional cleaning crew, scouring away years of neglect.

"Thank you, seriously. I can't believe how good everything looks. And for dinner too. Who made this? It's delicious."

Eli smiled slightly while twirling pasta around his fork. "I did. Glad you like it."

"It's all right," Henry Dale said gruffly. "Not difficult to boil a noodle, is it?"

But she noticed the old man ate every last bite. Great-Aunt Gertie hadn't installed a dishwasher, so Iris washed everything by hand. That seemed fair since the men had cooked. Eli stuck around to dry the dishes and put them away. Oddly, the silence felt…companionable. There was no pressure for her to fill the quiet with pointless words.

"What do you think he'll work on next?" she asked eventually, as Eli put the second plate in the squeaky-clean cupboard.

Henry Dale had gone to his room to read, leaving them alone in the kitchen. Eli paused, staring thoughtfully at the old-fashioned pattern on the china. Iris quite liked these plates; they had scalloped edges and lavender flowers painted daintily on the border with one small blossom in the center. Actually, these plates *might* be valuable antiques, but she had no intention of selling them.

Then Eli said, "I think it'll be the porch. He's worried about the soft boards. Somebody could get hurt if they fall through."

Iris winced. "I might have gotten into it with our next-door neighbor over the porch earlier today. She threatened to report me to the city."

"I heard some of that while I was hiding out in the kitchen," Eli admitted. "I might have steered Henry Dale toward the porch as a result. Hope you don't mind."

"Not at all."

Still, she sighed, trying to imagine how much it would cost to replace the lumber. The kitchen work hadn't cost much, just paint and a few miscellaneous supplies. But porch repair… Yet Eli was right. If someone stepped wrong and got hurt, Iris might get sued. *Maybe I should sell the ceramic angel collection?* That felt borderline immoral, as Great-Aunt Gertie had considered those things her family.

"You look worried," Eli said.

"I'm sure you've guessed that I'm not exactly well off despite owning a house. So I was just wondering how to pay for everything."

"You mean the porch? Henry Dale has contacts in construction. I think he's planning to get scrap wood from a builder he knows. If that doesn't pan out, there's always something being torn down."

She stared, unable to believe this was real life. These two were so obviously going above and beyond that she didn't even know what to say. "Wow. I'm speechless. *Thank you* isn't enough, so dinner is on me next time."

How did I get so lucky? Henry Dale is a retired contractor, and Eli is a handyman who flips houses. Oh, and codes. I wonder...

Silently she shook her head. *I can't ask him for even* more *help.*

"I'd like that," he said quietly. "But you look like you want to say something else?"

Apparently, her mouth didn't obey her brain. "Thing is, you said you do web stuff, right? I have an online store for my jewelry-making business, but I don't get many hits. Is that something you could help with?" She couldn't read his reaction to the request, so she hurried on. "Like with Henry, I can discount your rent next month, accounting for the time you spend helping me. And if you don't want to or don't have time, it's totally okay—"

"Iris."

"Yeah?"

"Breathe."

"Okay. I hate asking for favors. Let's pretend I never said that."

Eli smiled and took a step toward her. She noticed that he smelled clean, like soap, evergreen, sage, and cinnamon. Idly, she wondered what cologne he was wearing.

"Nah, I have no reason to do that. I'd be happy to look at your online shop and make some recommendations. Send me the link. It's no trouble."

"Oh wow. *Thank* you!" Before she chickened out, she texted him the link and tried to pretend she wasn't imposing in a major way.

Hopefully Eli wasn't someone who'd choose to inconvenience himself for a stranger. He must have time and was truly willing, right? Deep breath. Everything would be fine. Thankfully he didn't look at the site with her standing right there.

"It's my pleasure."

"You're so nice. I don't want to take advantage."

"You're not. I never do anything I don't want to. So while we're on the subject, the other bedrooms need to be painted, I think. The main bedroom was done recently, but the others?" He made a face that she interpreted as "yikes."

Yeah, the other bedrooms were dingy, small, dismal, and smudged. Henry Dale didn't care, but other potential renters would. Of the folks she'd interviewed, three had declined after looking at the pictures because the available spaces were so basic and unappealing. Erasing the ravages of time on the house wouldn't be easy...or cheap.

"I should do that before I try to rent them," she said, stifling a sigh.

———————

"I can help. If you want." Eli made the offer immediately.

Spending more time with Iris would be a dream come true, and this provided the perfect excuse. He could see them now, spending hours painting together. They'd talk more, obviously, and then—

Well, he didn't have it all figured out. And maybe he didn't have to.

"I can't ask you to do that," she answered at once. "You're not on the job here."

Right, she thinks I rehab houses professionally.

He couldn't get himself to correct the misapprehension because that might make her disinclined to accept his help. But he'd painted every room in Gamma's house before turning the place over to the real estate agent, so that basically made him a pro now, right?

"I like staying busy, and if I do nothing but code, I'll develop back problems."

"That's true. I can't stay hunched over my worktable for too long either—for the same reasons."

When she smiled at him, directly at him, it felt like a punch in the heart, as if he'd been waiting for her to notice him all these years. Which was patently ridiculous. *I wonder how she'd feel if she knew who I really am. That I'm one of those special types.* Humans were as divided on that issue as any other; some thought the revelation of the paranormal was cool as hell, while others were lobbying for legislation to isolate and control their numbers. And, of course, there was the fringe element who believed this revelation heralded the apocalypse. Eli wanted to believe his personal truth wouldn't even faze Iris, but it was too soon to test that theory.

For now, painting.

"We'll go to the hardware store tomorrow. They're running a

sale on interior stain-resistant paints. The bedrooms are small, so I think one can per should work."

"Thankfully Great-Aunt Gertie stayed with Antique White and we're not trying to cover up navy blue or puce," Iris said.

Eli laughed. "God, yes. We'd need three cans of paint plus primer."

He felt a little proud of that knowledge, as he'd studied painting the way he did everything, reading all the hints and how-tos and watching endless tutorials. Now he might even be qualified to make his own guides. Iris seemed to make a decision, even nodding to herself with her eyes slightly narrowed.

"Okay. Clearly it's a sign from the universe if the paint is even on sale."

Why is it so cute that she believes in signs from the universe?

Frankly, it didn't surprise him, given the things he'd seen her post on social media over the years, but he still found it adorable. Soon, his vague interest might ripen into an embarrassing crush. But that was a problem for later.

"Tomorrow at ten? We can get to work as soon as we get home."

When Iris smiled, stars might as well be twinkling in her gray eyes. He lost his breath a bit. "Seriously, you're the answer to my prayers."

"Hardly," he mumbled, conscious that his face felt hot. "Have you thought about what color you want to use?"

"Should I stick with one?"

"Well, it'll be faster. Because otherwise, we'll need to clean the brushes, rollers, and trays. If you pick one shade for all three rooms, we can cover the floor in plastic, tape off the edges, and sweep through."

"You think we could do more than one room tomorrow?"

"Depends how long we work, how many coats are needed, and how fast we are. But by myself, I can do a room in four hours. So I suspect we can do two rooms tomorrow."

"Wow, you really know your stuff. I'm not that experienced, so I probably won't be fast." She bit her lip. "I hope I don't get in your way."

"That won't happen. Tomorrow at ten, okay?" He needed to get her confirmation, then dodge out before she could change her mind.

She nodded, seeming cautiously enthusiastic about the plan. "See you then."

Eli took that as his cue to finish drying the dishes and make himself scarce. He retreated to his room, which was sparsely furnished with a full-size bed, a night table, and a dresser, while the walls were painted a surprisingly restful sage green. There were no paintings or pictures. Iris had said he could hang some, but she'd prefer if he used putty or sticky tape hooks to avoid putting holes in the walls. His other residences didn't display much of his taste either, but here, for some reason, he wanted to leave his mark. Maybe he'd print out pictures of him and Gamma or something else to personalize the space.

I have plans with Iris tomorrow.

He tried not to feel absurdly gleeful over that, but it was impossible. The little kid he'd been did a victory dance over finally having her attention. He threw himself on the bed, cozy with floral sheets, a fuzzy blanket, and what seemed like a handmade quilt. Iris had done a fantastic job of appointing the rooms with her aunt's belongings without overwhelming the spaces with that certain old lady aspect. There were also homemade cushions, sewn in a variety of vintage fabrics. It felt...homey here in a way that nowhere else ever had, at least not since he'd left Gamma's house.

He set his laptop on his legs and opened the chat app in the browser so he could see her store on a bigger screen. First off, her banner needed improvement, and so did the shop icon. He wasn't amazing at design, but he didn't need to be. He had a subscription to a service that let him do high-quality drag-and-drop graphics that would serve her purposes.

Eli created three different branding sets using the colors she clearly preferred. The shop could also benefit from collages and carousels to draw the eye. Iris must not be paying for plus features, as she wasn't using any of the advanced site design options. Or maybe she didn't know how?

I can teach her.

With that enticing thought, he handled some issues related to his two apps and noted that the Chinese conglomerate had set a deadline. He had to respond in seventy-two hours or the offer would be withdrawn. Since he'd be busy helping Iris, it made sense to divest at this point. *I'll sell What's Cooking and keep Task Wizard.* By halving his workload, he could focus more on the house and Iris's shop.

He enjoyed knowing that he could be useful and that she'd appreciate his time. It clearly hadn't made an impression on her, but he carried a sense of debt for the way she'd stood up for him back in the day. Paying her back made him happy, even if she never knew the details. Once the house was in good shape, he might move on without even telling her truth, if that seemed like the best option.

What she doesn't know won't hurt her, right?

He was acutely aware that he might come off as a stalker or a creep if he explained things wrong, as he often did. Frequently, words were his enemy, and the *last* thing he wanted was to upset or frighten her. *Hell, I'd be alarmed if someone told me they'd been reading my socials for that long.*

And then I moved in with her...

Yeah, there probably wasn't a way for him to explain that wouldn't end with her calling the police. *Just...help her for now. Return the favor. And move on.*

Quickly, he checked the time in Shanghai. It was morning there already, so he typed out his response.

I'm pleased to say I'm considering your offer. Send all related paperwork to my attorney, Liz Fielding; I'm copying her on this email. Once she's reviewed the contract and given me the green light, we can proceed. I can't guarantee she will be able to fully assess the offer in less than 72 hours, but I hope we can come to a tentative agreement nonetheless.

Eli thought they'd just wanted to get an answer from him, one way or another, so hopefully, asking for a formal contract would satisfy them without the deal breaking down. More to the point, it was best to have an expert review the fine print and make sure there wasn't anything that could land him in hot water later.

Within fifteen minutes, he had affirmation from the rep who was handling the matter for WeiZhen International. Liu Han-Shou promised they'd send the contract before close of business. Eli sent a brief email acknowledging that. Then he stretched, rolling his neck. *Time to kick back.*

He was reading a web comic on his laptop when Liz messaged an hour later.

> Working this late? Wait, what time is it where you are?

He checked the time.

> Eli: Almost ten. I don't keep normal hours anyway.
>
> Liz: No kidding. I'll let you know when I get the contract.
>
> Eli: Just ping me if you find anything sus hidden in the legal-speak.
>
> Liz: You play too much Among Us.
>
> Eli: Or maybe you don't play enough.
>
> Liz: Are you really arguing with your own lawyer?
>
> Eli: ...I'm going to bed.
>
> Liz: Before you do, I'm forwarding a proposal. And don't say no immediately! I know you prefer lone wolf dev life, but this opportunity could be life-changing. For both of us.

That was enough to pique his interest, so he opened his laptop and skimmed through the documents.

Dear Ms. Fielding,

As Mr. Reese's legal representative, we hope you'll facil-
itate a meeting between us. We're looking to enter the
social media market, and to that end, we've researched
the best possible candidates to head up this project. We
love what we see in What's Cooking and feel that Mr.
Reese could provide exactly what we're looking for. I
have attached a project overview and look forward to
discussing the matter further.

Sincerely,
Kelsey Grant
Executive Assistant

Eli clicked through the attachments, and when he saw the proposed budget, his eyes widened. This wasn't just an app; they wanted a whole new social media platform with cross-compatibility and the potential to change how people spent their time online. It was an ambitious undertaking but also a risky one, as there was no guarantee a new platform would take off.

Liz was right, though. He loathed the idea of working for someone else, but it felt wasteful to trash this opportunity without even hearing them out. Before he could change his mind, he texted her.

Eli: Fine. I'll talk to them.
Liz: Awesome. I'm raising my billable rate when you start making Gates money.

CHAPTER SEVEN

IRIS WOKE AT 9:23 A.M. without needing an alarm.

She was sleeping well these days, comfortable in a way she'd rarely been anywhere else. Both Eli and Henry Dale were good housemates so far; they never left dishes in the sink, and they didn't scatter their belongings in the common area. If everyone else was as conscientious, this would be a successful endeavor.

Without a schedule, she'd taken to showering at night since Henry Dale used the bathroom practically at dawn and Eli went in a bit later. Iris didn't mind either way. Really, she needed another bathroom with a shower, but in a house this old, she was lucky to have even a half bath on the first floor and the full bath on the second.

She put on comfy clothes that would serve for the trip to the hardware store and for painting afterward, then she headed to the kitchen for more oatmeal. This bowl she topped with frozen berries, making the flavor a little different at least. She didn't mind eating the same food every day, especially if it meant not telling her family that she was having trouble making ends meet. Iris would rather eat oatmeal three times a day than get in touch with her family. But of course, as if she'd manifested the call, her phone rang anyway before she finished eating.

Her dad sounded perpetually vague, untethered to reality. Instead, he lived in the past, forever buried in texts from ancient Rome. "I haven't heard from you in a while, flower. Your mother said you're sulking over that boy Lily is dating. Is there something I should know?"

She stifled a sigh. "I was dating him first, Dad."

"Oh! Well, that's not right. Is that why you boycotted Rose's party? I do understand where you're coming from, but...as your mother says, aren't you punishing Rose for something Lily did?"

She wondered if anyone would ever take her side unconditionally. "I'm not even living in Ohio anymore, Dad. I inherited Great-Aunt Gertie's house in St. Claire."

There was a significant pause. "Hmm. Did your mother tell me that?"

"How would I know?" she asked with gentle exasperation.

"Then if I understand correctly, your mother and sisters are making mountains out of molehills again."

"In my opinion, yes."

"I'll see if I can smooth things over then. Do you need anything? Is Gertie's place in livable condition?"

The offer was so tempting because her dad would send her money if she asked, but he'd go through her mother since she controlled the purse strings. Dad didn't earn a whole lot writing scholarly articles about ancient Rome and Greece, and he'd lost his professor post due to a lamentable tendency to forget that he was supposed to be teaching and giving lectures.

"I'm fine," she lied.

"Love you, flower. Sorry you always end up in the center of all the drama."

"Love you too, Dad."

After she disconnected, she reflected that it would've been nice, had her father been the type to shield her. But when he "stepped in," the situation never improved, and Iris got accused of trying to pit her parents against each other. Dad wasn't forceful enough to make a difference, and his wishy-washy approach often made things worse. Her mood was a bit glum as she ate the rest of her oatmeal.

As she washed her bowl, Eli came into the kitchen. "Hungry?" she asked.

He shook his head. "I ate earlier."

"What did you have?" Iris was always looking for economical meal suggestions.

Eli tilted his head like that was an odd question. But he answered, "Scrambled eggs and toast."

"Oh, eggs. Eggs are cheap. Note to self, buy eggs. Let's go?" Oddly, she didn't even need to clarify that she meant to the hardware store, not the supermarket.

Eli was a rare bird who could follow her thought processes, which were an awful lot like six squirrels unexpectedly loosed in a bouncy house.

This morning, his truck was parked behind her Sentra in the driveway, so it made sense for him to drive. She suspected he would also volunteer to retrieve the porch-fixing lumber for Henry Dale when the time came. At the rate they were going, she'd owe them both far more than a meal. Not that her homemade food was anything to brag about.

She didn't say much as he drove to Carruthers Hardware. The men who ran the store were a married couple, and she thought one of them said his dad had owned the place before. Keeping track of details wasn't her strong point, however. Iris greeted the dark-haired man who managed the place with a friendly wave.

"Back for more supplies?" Bruce called.

"You know it. Mitch doing okay?"

"He's great. I'll let him know you asked about him. He was all excited about the sale flyer he posted on social media yesterday. Any chance you saw it?"

"We did," Iris assured him. "That's why we're here!"

That was the benefit of shopping at a store like this one instead of a big box place: learning people's names and feeling like part of the community. She headed for the paint section since she knew where it was; she'd been here to buy the sage green a couple of weeks ago. For a minute, she stood looking at the color cards, trying to make up her mind. As Eli had said, it would be easier to use one color, but it had to be the right one, something pretty and peaceful.

"Any winners so far?" Eli asked.

She jumped a bit. He'd come up behind her so quietly that she didn't even sense a flicker of his presence. "Not yet. This is an important decision. I can't rush it."

Her family would mock her for saying something like that. She could hear it now—*It's just paint, Iris.* But it wasn't, really. It was about building a mood, telling a story with each room, and picking a single color reduced the amount of personality she could imbue. But this was a safer and easier choice; she could use textiles to add visual interest, whatever the walls looked like.

Eli nodded. "Any favorites then?"

"I'm stuck between Snow Day and Harbor Mist." The first was pale and should brighten the walls, while the second was a cool gray.

"If the rooms were bigger, I'd say Harbor Mist, but with the space—"

"Snow Day then. We'll look at this as offering a clean canvas. I'll supply the basics, and our future roomies can figure out the rest."

"Sounds reasonable. I like how you did the main bedroom."

"I painted it green when I was planning to move in there," she admitted. "But then I realized I could turn the attic into a studio and sleep up there."

"And earn more," Eli said.

She grinned. "There is that as well."

"Do you have painting supplies already? If not, I have some in my truck."

That made sense if he'd just finished flipping a house. Iris wondered idly how that worked; did the owners often let him stay there while fixing it up? But when it was ready to be sold, he probably had to relocate quickly, and it was probably tough to know exactly what date that would happen.

"I have what I used for the main bedroom, not enough for two people, though. So if you're willing to dedicate your own—"

"Of course, it's no problem. Then we just need the paint and some new plastic sheets for the floors." He hesitated. "I know you don't have much to spend on house reno, but I was thinking... We'll probably have paint left over. If we buy some self-adhesive wallpaper, we could do an accent wall in the front room then use the leftover paint in there."

Iris could imagine the wall he meant; it was widest one in the space, and it was currently an eyesore, painted in some dreadful sponge-daubing technique that was supposed to make it look like a Venetian palazzo but failed on all counts. Neither the colors nor the style worked with the rest of the house. She'd figured that living with it was the only option, but now Eli gave her hope for a reasonably priced fix.

"Were you thinking of doing the paper above the wainscoting?" Which her great-aunt had painted dusty blue for some reason.

"Exactly. I have some primer left in my truck. We can do Snow Day on the wainscoting and other walls."

Just then, she spotted a bin of deeply discounted wallpaper. "I think I see why you're suggesting this. I'll tell Bruce what color we need and take a look." She headed to the counter with the color card. "We need four gallons of Snow Day. There will be other odds and ends, so don't ring us up yet."

"I would *never*," Bruce said with a smile. "You might find something else you can't live without."

As Iris went over to the discount wallpaper bin, the bell on the door jangled, and an older woman she'd never seen breezed in. She had white hair gloriously tumbled in unruly curls, haphazardly tied with a floral scarf that didn't match the different flower pattern on her billowing dress. This woman was also wearing lime-green Crocs, ruffled ankle socks, and a gorgeous rainbow cardigan that immediately made Iris jealous because she didn't own one just like it. She whipped past Iris in a swirl of blackberry and jasmine. Iris breathed in the scent and wondered what perfume the woman was wearing.

"Mom! I didn't know you were stopping in today." Bruce was beaming as he came out from behind the counter and gave her a hug.

"I didn't know myself. But I was baking today, and I thought of you and Mitch. You both like my cheesecake squares, right? I packed a few for you." She dug into her bucket bag and produced a small container.

"Are you kidding? We'll inhale them. Thank you!" Bruce pulled the lid off to snag one, and even from this distance, she could smell the lemony sweetness. "Are you still staying at Ethel's place?"

"Worrying about me again?" Exasperated tone, delivered with a gentle pat on his arm.

Bruce sighed. "You haven't had a permanent address since you and Dad divorced. I'm the *last* person who would insist you stay in an unfulfilling marriage, especially after what we talked about. But—"

"You're still worried. Look, I promised Ethel I'd take care of Percy until she gets back from the Caribbean. After that, I'll find a place, okay?"

"Sounds reasonable. I love you. And I'm proud of you, even if the rest of the family doesn't understand."

"I knew you would," Bruce's mom said in a fond tone.

The older woman swirled out as swiftly as she'd come, and Iris realized she had been staring at the wallpaper without really seeing it as she unashamedly eavesdropped. *Why?* Because it seemed like Bruce's mom *might* need somewhere to stay. *Wonder how she would get along with Henry Dale.*

Of the bargains offered, only two patterns spoke to her. The white-and-black herringbone would be difficult to line up properly, which would make it more time-consuming, and it didn't match the feel of the house. She picked up two rolls of the gray-and-white damask. That would class up the room and go nicely with the paint. *I can probably get covers for some of the furniture too.* Iris took the wallpaper to the counter while waiting for Eli.

"I wasn't trying to listen in," she said to Bruce. "But in a week or two, I'll have more rooms to rent if you think your mom might be interested."

"That would be *great*. She's never lived alone, and she's a social butterfly, so I've been concerned about her. My dad and mom were together for forty years, and then… Well, it's best if I let her tell you. If she chooses to."

"I hear senior divorces are on the rise," Iris said.

"True." The hardware store owner seemed unwilling to proffer more details, and she didn't pry. "I'll take your name and email if that's okay?"

"You can have my cell number too if you want."

"Perfect."

She entered the info into the Notes app on his phone as Eli walked up with the plastic and a few extra trays. "All set?" he asked.

Smiling, she said, "Yeah. Maybe more than I expected."

Eli wasn't sure what Iris meant by that.

But she explained without him asking as they hauled their purchases out to his truck. He laughed as she went into great detail describing the woman's hand-knit rainbow sweater. It sounded like Iris had already made up her mind about renting a room, even if she didn't even know the lady's name.

Why wasn't it this easy to talk with anyone else? With Iris, conversations just happened; he didn't need to fish frantically for new topics.

It's so restful.

He stopped, shading his eyes to be sure of what he was seeing. Across the square, two women were scrubbing what looked like a nasty piece of graffiti from their shop. Someone had added "WILL BURN" to the Fix-It Witches logo in sloppy red spray paint. Iris followed his gaze and sighed.

"I guess even St. Claire has some badness," Iris said.

"You're okay with them? Witches, I mean." That was definitely a fact-finding question. Her attitude toward witches would tell him a lot about how she might react to him being a shifter.

"I try to treat everyone equally," she said. "But honestly, I've never met one...that I know of. But I think that's what has people riled up. The sense that it could be *anyone* and that humanity has been...infiltrated. Ugh. I don't even know why we're talking about this."

That response didn't offer as much insight into her thoughts as he'd hoped, but it would likely seem strange to persist. He wanted to say something about HAPI—Humans Against Paranormal Influence—and see how she reacted. Chapters had sprung up all over, and a former local politician had been yelling online about it for several years. Now others were joining Dan Rutherford, and Eli hated to see the movement gain traction.

"Let's go see if they need help," she said.

Before he could respond, she jaywalked across the street and was animatedly offering her services. At least, he assumed so, as he couldn't hear Iris from this distance. When he caught up to her, a woman with sun-streaked curls was saying, "I really appreciate the offer, but we're good. I'm only doing this because Clem is afraid it'll make things worse if we cast spells on Main Street, so to speak."

The brunette woman sighed. "Gavin is reviewing the security footage now. Soon we'll know who did this, okay? There's no reason to—"

"I'd *love* to see you fix the sign with a spell," Iris said, wide-eyed.

"We're not giving demonstrations," said the second witch, as the first one studied the sign with a measuring look.

"Danica, I'm so sorry this happened again." Now someone else joined the convo, a slim, dark-eyed person in a hoodie.

"Rowan! Good to see you again. Do you have something for us to fix?"

Rowan raised a small paper bag. "My old iPod. I started feeling nostalgic, and I want to check out what I was listening to in middle school if you can get it working."

"Of course we can." The friendly witch turned to them with a warm smile. "Thanks for offering to help. St. Claire is great, mostly, but no place is perfect."

The other three headed for the door to the shop while Iris

glanced at Eli with an apologetic expression. "Sorry, I didn't mean to delay us."

"It's fine. You were trying to do a good deed."

She laughed. "Yeah, that didn't pan out."

They often don't.

Iris went on, "But at least now I can say I've met some witches. They seemed nice, right? Well, Danica more than... What was the other one's name?"

"Clem," Eli said.

The two retraced their steps and got in the truck. While Eli brooded, Iris filled the silence with ideas, projects, things she wanted to try for the house if they wouldn't cost a fortune. He only had to nod, put in a quiet opinion here and there, and it was perfect. Maybe he wouldn't be this happy listening to someone else, but her voice *soothed* him, as if there were deeply woven magical notes. Honestly, the woman could convince him to do almost anything.

Possibly I ought to be worried about that.

He was deeply curious to see her with a hawk's eyes because in that form, he could discern more, and he wondered what those extra color spectra would reveal. In some worldviews, they'd say he could perceive her aura as a hawk, but for Eli it was much simpler. Different people radiated energy in unique ways, and he wished to know as much about Iris as he could.

How would she react? If I told her.

Taking a breath as he turned down the road leading to their house, he decided to risk it. Otherwise, there might be issues down the line. "I'm not sure how to bridge this topic, so I'll just be direct because I think you should know. I'm...not like other people."

Iris laughed. "Neither am I. That's how I ended up with a purple house, few friends, no job, and hardly any money."

Despite the nerves making his palms sweat, he laughed. "Okay, fair. But I mean more than that. You know how we were talking about witches before?"

"Yeah, what about them?"

"I sympathize...because I'm a shifter. Red-tailed hawk. So I might leave my window open sometimes if I'm out flying. I hope that's okay. I won't do it often when it gets cold," he added quickly.

Iris stared at him. "That is the *coolest* thing I've ever heard."

"It...is?" He drove past Susan Calhoun, raking leaves in her front yard. Their neighbor stared hard at the truck and scowled at her pile of leaves. The woman already seemed far too invested in what Iris did with her own home. Eli suspected that the word *busybody* didn't do the woman justice.

"Definitely. But I'm glad you gave me a heads-up because if I noticed your window wide open, I might've shut it, and then you'd be pants-less in the yard without keys."

Eli chuckled, appreciating that she understood without him needing to elaborate. "I've been in that situation before. Less than ideal."

She grinned at him. "You have a gift for understatement. So what's your favorite movie? I bet it's *Ladyhawke*. Is it *Ladyhawke*?"

"It is, actually."

Iris beamed at him. "You are such a good sport to play along like that. Anyway..."

Eli pulled into the driveway behind her car. He could have told her it wasn't a joke—that he'd loved the movie after Gamma streamed it for him. Not just because of the hawk, but it was a beautiful fairy tale of a movie, and, yeah, he was absolutely that person.

She took a deep breath, seeming somewhat nervous.

"You were about to say something?" he prompted.

"Yeah. Since we're disclosing...and you trusted me with your personal business, I should offer the same. I'm...not exactly from a typical family either. If I was properly awakened, I'd have informed you before you moved in."

"I don't understand," he said, turning to face her with curiosity bubbling inside him, more potent than a witch's potion.

"My family are vampires," she replied without looking at him. "Not the blood-drinking kind. Psychic. And before you say it, no, I'm not joking, and yes, I'm sure."

In all honesty, that was news to him. He'd kept to the fringes of the shifter community and didn't really try to connect despite Gamma's urging. So he hadn't met too many like him, let alone others. Like anyone else, he'd encountered folks he found exhausting, but he'd always assumed that was *perception*. Now he was hearing some of them might have literally been draining his energy? Wild.

Eli hesitated. "I have questions, but I'm not sure if it's okay to ask."

"I can guess what they are. Yes, we eat food, and yes, we age. But we require that extra component to thrive. In return, we have small...aptitudes. My oldest sister is a healer. Not only can she absorb someone's pain, she can also expedite healing and cure some illnesses that are supposed to be untreatable. Not *all* of them, obviously, or she'd already be in a government lab."

"Holy shit," Eli whispered.

"I *know*. In my opinion, Olive is the best of us, but I also think that's why she left the country. 'Miracles' would attract too much attention here. She might not be safe, especially with groups like HAPI gathering momentum and hosting rallies."

"That actually makes sense." He'd been pretty tense there for a minute without even realizing it, and hearing that they had this in common as well set his mind at ease.

Not that they were the same, exactly, but she didn't hate him after learning who he really was. Eli wouldn't have been able to handle it if she'd flipped out and admitted to belonging to one of those hate groups.

She went on, "Rose eats anger, and she's wildly charismatic. I suspect that's why she's never lost a case. Lily 'counsels' people and devours their grief. She's lauded for her ability to help people resolve emotional trauma."

"I'm stunned. I didn't even know any of that was possible. But what about you?"

"Like I said, I'm not...awakened. I don't have the power to absorb anyone's energy, and I have no cool extras."

"So you're human?" That didn't necessarily align with the unusual traces at the edges of her scent, so fascinating that he couldn't even pin them down.

"You don't think so?"

"I'm not sure." He saw no reason to confuse her when he wasn't even sure what he was sensing about her. Though he'd been fairly certain that she wasn't a run-of-the-mill human, he couldn't be sure of anything else. So he let the matter go, choosing to dodge the questions he saw swirling in her gray eyes.

"This was a good talk," Iris said. "We definitely know each other better now."

Eli made an agreeable sound as he hopped out of the truck. Iris followed suit and immediately started unloading pails of paint. Together, they hauled all the supplies upstairs and got ready to work.

To Eli's surprise, Henry Dale had already moved the furniture in each bedroom to the center of the space, so setting up went even faster. Henry Dale had also expertly taped all the windows and trim, reducing the time wasted before they got started. Sooner than Eli could have imagined, he and Iris were painting away in the first bedroom while tunes played on a Bluetooth speaker she'd suctioned to the windowpane. The thing was cute, like a little gray mushroom, and he approved of her upbeat playlist, which started with "I Will Survive," slid into "No Scrubs," took a sidestep to "The Best," and grooved into "Hey Ya."

"Nothing modern in the painting rotation?" he asked.

They were working on opposite walls so they didn't get in each other's way. He was doing the high parts and she the low ones, and then they planned to swap. If they did it quickly enough, it should work out beautifully.

"I could dig some up, but these are easy. Old favorites that I heard when I was little in old movies or in a fan video somebody made."

"I *love* watching dance videos," he said.

"You too? I swear, the best ones are filmed in parking lots with everybody in sweats and then just *bringing* it."

"Let's swap links. I'll send you some of my favorites." Again, he was struck again by how easy this was. Effortless, like lolling in a warm bath.

"That would be amazing," Iris said. "Okay, so if dance videos are a yes, what about dance *movies*?"

"Yes, please," he said promptly, earning another of her dazzling smiles. "I can't dance at all myself, so I live vicariously."

"Have you tried taking lessons?"

He shook his head. "No, I figured there was no point."

"But…nobody is born amazing at anything. Babies are terrible at almost everything," Iris pointed out.

He moved the ladder and kept painting as he considered her comment. "That's a good point. I guess I tend to live in my comfort zone."

"Hmm. I saw a flyer on the way out of the hardware store on their community bulletin board. We should totally take ballroom dancing lessons together."

Eli almost dropped his roller. "What?"

This had to be a dream. *She didn't really ask me to do that with her, did she?* Because it felt like a fantasy he wouldn't even have been able to dream up on his own.

"Sure. If we go together, we get a discount! And if we use the code from the flyer, it's even cheaper." When she named the price, it did sound like a deal, but that wasn't the point.

No, the point was he'd be dancing with *Iris*. For six weeks. Up close and personal.

Eli didn't even need to think about it. "Absolutely, sign us up."

CHAPTER EIGHT

IRIS DID THE MATH.

And she *hated* doing math, but this was simple enough. If they went in as a couple, it would cost about the same as a weekly latte to take the lessons. It wasn't like she had cash to burn, but it sounded *so* fun. She could put on low heels and one of her swirly romantic dresses that she never got to wear. Dancing with Eli would be frosting on the cake.

"I will. Later, though. Once we stop for the day."

With his help, the work was going much faster than it had in the main bedroom. Within a couple of hours, the first bedroom was covered completely and Iris cracked the window, though this type of paint was supposed to be low odor. Low didn't mean none.

As she took care of that, Eli transferred their supplies to the next room.

She was a bit hungry, but not enough to stop working. Since she knew herself, if she relaxed and filled her belly, she wouldn't want to get back to work. Inertia was seductive, and she'd end up watching something in her room, reading, or sketching, and the walls wouldn't get painted. If Eli was willing to help out, she should throw herself into the task as well, even if she ended up exhausted and sore.

I can't believe he can turn into a hawk.

That was just cool as hell. She'd never told anyone about her family either, but something about Eli made her want to trust him. It gave her hope that they could become real friends, not just housemates. It would be nice to have someone who stuck around too. Who didn't find Iris inadequate or exhausting or both.

Iris turned the music on again and lost herself in the peaceful repetition of rolling paint on the scuffed walls. It felt good, as if they were bringing the place back to life. Hours later, she stretched and slid her roller across the last untouched spot.

"Done," she said.

"For today."

She aimed a playful scowl at Eli. "You couldn't just let me have that?"

"We'll be done with the bedrooms tomorrow. It went pretty fast because the rooms are small."

"You think one more day to do the front room?" she asked, stretching to relieve some of the stiffness in her shoulders.

"If Henry Dale helps us with prep? Absolutely. In fact, you could start on the painting while I put up the paper, and then I'll switch to painting when I'm done."

"Sounds like a plan. I'll shower first, then you can. I owe you food, I believe. I'll get started on dinner while you wash up." Even to Iris, that sounded... Well, it sounded like they were more than roommates.

She repressed the impulse to stammer nervously, to explain that she didn't mean anything by taking charge of his shower arrangements. It seemed best not to lie, after all. Because maybe she did despite countless articles warning people *not* to get involved with their housemates. It might seem like the best of both worlds at first, but if things soured, the living situation might swiftly become untenable. And Iris needed the money.

So I can't date him. Even if he's kind of perfect.

Besides, she wasn't even sure what was going on emotionally. She might be confusing gratitude with attraction. And sleeping with someone wasn't the only way to say thank you. Giving herself a stern, silent warning, she headed into the Pepto-Lime bathroom. Oddly, the colors were starting to grow on her. The curtains had to go, and so did the wallpaper, but otherwise, as long as everything worked properly, she had no plans to gut this room.

She took a quick shower to scrub off the paint, wrapped up in a thick cozy robe, and left the door open to air the room out. Eli met her in the hall, and she was absurdly aware of being nearly naked despite how the robe covered every inch of her. Her cheeks heated as he stepped to one side, averting his gaze with color darkening his cheeks.

"Sorry," he mumbled, rushing past her.

Did I make him blush? Okay, that's adorable.

No. Stop. You're not doing this.

As Iris headed up to the attic to get dressed, she wondered how Great-Aunt Gertie had managed here alone. *All these stairs will take care of my cardio.* She put on random comfy clothes— soft, baggy cotton pants with pockets and a T-shirt that said

UNICORN RIDER. Warm, fuzzy socks on her feet completed the ensemble, and Iris went downstairs to see what she could make for dinner. She found a bit of cream cheese, a rind of parmesan, penne, and half a bag of frozen spinach.

"That solved itself," she said, putting on the salted water to cook the pasta.

Just then, her phone beeped, signaling an incoming video call. Her hands were wet, and she accidentally tapped the accept icon. Silently she swore as Mom, Lily, and Rose appeared on her screen. It looked as if they'd gathered at Rose's house; Iris would recognize that accent wall anywhere.

"Hey," she said, picking up her cell so they weren't staring up her nose.

"You're crying to Dad again?" Lily demanded. "When are you ever going to grow up? This is absolutely ridiculous."

"What are you even talking about?"

Oh right. She'd spoken to Dad not long ago and explained her side of the situation. Evidently that counted as whining. "Look, I'll tell you exactly what I told him. I don't think dating Dylan is a good look for you, but that had nothing to do with me missing Rose's party. I wasn't in town, that's all."

"I worked really hard for this," Rose said. "You didn't send a gift or a card or anything. I've tried so hard to get closer to you, but you act like you don't care about any of us at all."

Iris stifled a sigh, wishing things weren't so fraught with Rose, but Rose was much closer to Lily than Iris, whereas Olive was the only one who ever understood where Iris was coming from. "Okay, that's fair. I'm sorry I didn't at least send something. I am proud of you. But…did *you* send me anything when I opened my store?"

"Why would I?" Rose asked, swapping a puzzled look with Mom and Lily.

"Because it's important to me." Honestly, this shit shouldn't even need to be explained.

"It's not like you're earning a living that way," Lily said.

"So only milestones that mark financial gain are worth celebrating—noted. That means I don't need to send gifts on normal holidays, right?" She could have said more, so much more, but there was no point. They expected her to give and yield, and always had. Those metrics didn't seem likely to change.

And…she was done.

Meanwhile, Mom was talking over everyone, a skill she'd perfected. "Stop blabbering nonsense. You're mad at Lily over nothing—it's not like you'd have married Dylan—and I think we all remember when you were trash-talking Greg for no reason."

"We're all doing our best here," Rose added.

Are you? Really?

"Why is everything always my fault?" Iris asked.

"You know that's not true." Mom immediately went on the defensive and started listing all the problems Iris had caused over the years.

"Did we make you drop out of college?" Lily snarked.

"Probably," Rose muttered. "You know how she is, blames us every time something doesn't go her way."

"Here's the thing. I'm never going to give Lily my blessing with Dylan. If he becomes my brother-in-law, it's whatever, I guess. But

I'm done pretending things are fine when they're definitely not. Make of that what you will. Rose, I'll send you a special necklace for your promotion." *Not that I expect you to wear it.* "What are you planning to send me to congratulate me for inheriting a house? That's a financial gain that should be acknowledged, according to the Collins' creed."

Rose sighed. "I can see there's no talking to you."

"Okay," Iris said. Once this conversation would've crushed her. "I need to finish dinner. Bye!"

She got the last word and cut the call just in time to plop the penne in the frothing water. The meal came together quickly—penne in creamy spinach sauce with plenty of black pepper and a hint of nutmeg. She dished out three portions and topped each plate with grated parmesan cheese. Eli paused in the kitchen, smiling at the food she was plating.

Last week, we were strangers. Now we live together, eat together, he sees me fresh out of the shower...

"It's ready. I hope you like it."

"I'll go get Henry Dale. I think he's in the shed."

"Still?" She shook her head ruefully. "I suspect he'd live out there if I let him."

Eli laughed. "Don't give him ideas."

Though Henry Dale grumbled a bit, he still joined them for dinner. They ate mostly in silence, and the old man seemed to be in a decent mood until Iris asked, "I'm just curious. Have you ever been married?"

At that apparently forbidden question, his mouth tightened. "I never wanted to. Something wrong with that?"

Abruptly he set his fork down and left the table, retreating to his room. She bit her lip, glancing at Eli. "I get the feeling I shouldn't have asked."

"With Henry Dale, I think we need to wait until he volunteers the information. We haven't known each other that long."

"True," Iris said.

It was a measure of how upset Henry Dale must have been that he'd just left his plate on the table. As a silent apology, she washed it; Eli helped with the rest, of course. She could get used to this constant camaraderie, feeling like she wasn't alone anymore.

The whole house smelled lightly of paint, but not in a bad way. Between the professional cleaners and the work they'd already done on the place, the house no longer felt so desolate, redolent of dust and loneliness. If she took it slow and spaced out the paint costs, they might be able to do the whole house. Not *soon*. But eventually. The hallways needed some TLC too, and the attic... She'd *love* to brighten all that dark paneling. It wasn't the quality kind either; this had been done in the seventies, so it was the cheap stuff, and she wouldn't hesitate over painting or papering it.

"What are you thinking about?" Eli asked suddenly.

"House stuff."

"There's a lot to do." In measured motions, he put away the last plate, then turned to her with a smile that warmed her from the inside out. "By the way, I had a look at your shop. If you have time, I have some suggestions. Should I get my laptop?"

"Already? Wow! It's like all you do is help me."

"Luckily, it's stuff I'm already good at," he said.

Which made Iris pause because...did that mean he'd learn *new* skills if she needed him to? The implications puzzled her so much that she didn't even notice him going upstairs until he returned to the table with his laptop. He drew his chair over so she could see his screen as he clicked through several design options.

"You made these?"

"They're just samples. I can revise them if you—"

"No! The second one is absolutely gorgeous." He'd captured the chaotic energy full of summery colors that she'd been going for, but unlike her, he'd nailed it. "I love the font, love everything about it."

"That's my first recommendation."

She listened as he suggested how she could increase the visual appeal of the site, and he'd apparently made a sample account to show her how to add collages and carousels to showcase her work. He finished with some recommendations about what she could do using social media, which included contacting influencers and people who hosted related podcasts.

"This is exactly what I needed," Iris said, fighting the urge to hug him. "It's not that I *can't* do these things, but I get bogged down and I don't know what to do first, you know? Then it feels so overwhelming that I end up doing nothing at all."

Eli nodded. "I feel the same way in social settings. I can't figure out who to talk to or what to say. Nine times out of ten, I duck out and wind up watching a movie by myself."

"Really? You're so easy to talk to! I never would have guessed." She paused, wondering if there was any way she could help him in turn. "Oh! If you ever need someone to be your plus one—for moral support or whatever—I'm there."

"That would be incredible. Anyway, let me know how it goes. I hope sales pick up. And I'll spread the word about your shop as I can."

Iris beamed. "You're seriously my hero. The dance lessons are on me."

Eli fought the impulse to say he'd pay.

Iris didn't want someone to make her problems vanish or to buy everything for her. Though he didn't know her well, he already understood that much. She preferred support to outright interference, and she was probably trying to thank him by paying for the ballroom dance classes.

"Then I'm looking forward to it."

He scooped up his laptop and retreated before he said or did something that revealed how *much* he already liked her. Hell, it had been awkward enough when he found her in her robe, wet hair tumbled back from her glowing face. And urges that he didn't struggle with or even think about sprang vividly, awkwardly to life.

Fortunately, he had business to conclude, as Liz had finished reviewing the contract while he was painting bedrooms like it was a path to inner peace. The documents were ready for his e-signature—just in time, as What's Cooking gained users daily and the need for more staff to maintain the platform would become WeiZhen's problem. Eli read the documents himself, perusing the sections Liz had flagged, but everything fell within reasonable parameters. He e-signed with the understanding he'd be paid within fifteen business days.

After checking the time, he called Gamma. She liked video calls, and he was the one person she'd never refuse to chat with regardless of what she had going on. Tonight, it sounded like she was at a party when she answered. That alone put a smile on his face.

"Sorry, it's a bit loud here. Let me step outside." The music and laughter got fainter when she closed the door. "Better?"

"I can hear and see you. Everything okay?"

"Settling in fine! I'm at a neighbor's barbecue, so I can't talk long."

"There's nothing urgent. I haven't heard anything about your house yet. I'm just checking in."

"Ah, well, I'm fine. How're you, little man?"

"Surprisingly well. I actually like St. Claire."

"If you'd realized that sooner," she said, "we could've spent more time together."

"Hey, I was a teenager. I thought I had to leave home to prove myself."

"I know. Oh, they're calling me. I have to run. Love you!"

"Love you more," he said as Gamma disconnected.

Home reno. Ballroom dancing. The business deal. A woman he couldn't get off his mind and a taciturn elderly gent.

There was too much happening in his head and not enough space for it. To reach that blissful, quiet place, he locked his bedroom door, opened the window, and stripped. That fast, he was soaring up and out, circling the house once, twice, riding the crisp autumn wind with gentle flicks of his wings. Then he arrowed away. A long flight was exactly what he needed tonight.

Eli lost track of time, flinging himself into the night. The wind smelled of the coming winter, brisk to the point of bitterness. Fewer animals about, mostly pets that had snuck out of the house for a small adventure. He let them be, though other predators wouldn't.

When he returned to the purple house, Iris stood on the front porch, gazing out.

He'd wanted to see her with hawk's eyes, but nothing could have prepared him for the glorious silver corona that shone from her. In fact, he'd never seen anyone who gleamed so, platinum so bright that other hues flickered about the edges, somehow opalescent with hidden fire full of rainbows. Because she was so beautiful, he almost flew straight into the side of the house. Eli corrected at the last moment and glided through the window. He shifted back, cold now and exhausted enough to sleep.

She's absolutely not human. They don't look like that. None of them do. But he was too tired to contemplate why she gleamed so brightly when she supposedly wasn't anything special. Not a psychic vampire, like the rest of her family. Something about that didn't add up, but he lost the thread in exhaustion. After shutting the window, he tumbled into bed naked and didn't dream.

The next couple of days, he focused on finishing the work he'd started with Iris and trying not to stare too much at her. Consequently, he lost his ability to speak naturally in her presence and started acting more like his weird self. On the fourth day, they wrapped up in the front room. Between the paint and the gray-and-white paper on the accent wall, it was a new space.

"It's great, isn't it?" Iris didn't seem to have noticed his odd behavior, at least. "You did an amazing job with the wallpaper."

"The wainscoting was all you, though."

"I did my best. I wonder if Great-Aunt Gertie would like what we're doing with the place," she added in a musing tone.

"Definitely. She's probably beaming right now, wherever she is."

"Hopefully not *here*," Iris said with a small shiver.

Eli couldn't resist teasing her. "You never know..."

"That is *not* funny."

"Should we host a séance?" he asked, just as Henry Dale came to inspect their handiwork.

The old man ran a hand over the walls and offered an approving nod. "Looks good. I like gray and white." He turned a hard look on Eli. "But no mucking about with spirits, you hear me? No candles. No table rapping. No asking if anybody's here. Even if they *are* here, there's no point getting them stirred up, is there?"

Iris tilted her head, visibly surprised. "I didn't know you believed in such things."

Henry Dale cleared his throat. "*Believe* might be a strong word, but I've lived a long time and seen some odd things. Not everything can or *should* be explained, Miz Collins."

"I actually agree with that," Eli said.

Iris smiled. "Neither of you needs to worry. I'm not planning to bother Great-Aunt Gertie, even if she walks among us." With that, she grabbed her keys from the bowl on the table near the front door. "I'm off to pick up some cheap couch covers I found online. Only forty minutes away!"

Both he and Henry Dale hurried after her. Henry Dale objected first. "You can't just randomly go to some stranger's house! There's no telling what'll happen."

"I don't need a bodyguard," she said, but her steps slowed, as if she was considering the validity of their concern.

"Eh, actually I agree with Henry Dale," Eli put in. "There have been killers who used online ads to—"

"I *know* that. But with couch covers…?"

Henry Dale scowled, his white brows contracting. "Could be bait. Don't risk it."

She sighed, but Eli noticed that her eyes twinkled a bit, as if she might be enjoying how protective they both were. "Fine, put your shoes on. We're all going on a mini road trip."

Eli complied right away, while Henry Dale's frown didn't abate. "Why do I have to be the third wheel? This guy can protect you."

"No way," Iris said. "We need your stern energy, and I'm stopping for lunch after."

Though Henry Dale mumbled complaints all the way to the kitchen and back, Eli could tell that the old man was secretly glad to be included. Outside, he got in the back of Iris's Sentra, letting Henry Dale ride shotgun. Iris turned the radio on and found an oldies station, again likely for Henry Dale.

"Bunch of nonsense," the older man muttered.

"You love it," Iris said. "Anyway, I just wanted to say I'm sorry for being nosy the other day. I hope we're okay."

"Are you worried about my feelings?" Henry Dale asked in an incredulous tone.

"Well, yeah," Iris said, as if that should be obvious.

God, she's sweet.

Henry Dale cleared his throat. "Hmm. Well, I'm fine. And… if you must know, I never wanted a wife. Or a husband. I never wanted to be kissing *anybody*, though I had some wonderful friends back in the day. They've all since passed on. My family too. And I guess that's my one regret—that I'm the last.

"I miss my older brother the most." Henry Dale took a steadying breath, as if bracing for the next revelation. "After his wife died, I moved in with him. They never had children, and we lived together up until the last two years of his life. His house had to be sold to pay for memory care. I spent my life's savings looking after him, and then..."

There was nothing left, nobody who could be there for Henry Dale the way he'd been there for his brother. *That's how he ended up with nowhere to go.*

Eli reached forward and patted Henry Dale on the shoulder. "You're not alone anymore. You can make new friends."

"You *have*," Iris added.

She met Eli's gaze briefly in the rearview mirror, and her gray eyes practically glowed. For some reason, tears stung Eli's eyes and his throat tightened, not just because of Henry Dale. Because of this woman and this moment and that look.

"Well, isn't that something?" Henry Dale said in a surprisingly deep tone, like he might be getting choked up.

Eli felt the same way.

CHAPTER NINE

AS IRIS HAD GUESSED, THERE was no problem picking up the couch covers.

"I was redecorating and thought somebody might want these gray ones," the woman said as Iris forked over the cash.

Ten bucks was a steal, and Iris took full advantage. But at the same time, it was *nice* having both Eli and Henry Dale care enough to come with her. Well, she'd offered a free lunch, but still. She hadn't lived here long enough to have a favorite restaurant, so Eli might know where to go. *He said he went to school here, right?* That meant he was sort of local. Like Iris, he'd probably moved around a bit.

"You pick the place," she said to Eli.

"Are you in the mood for anything?" he asked Henry Dale.

The old man glanced over his shoulder. "Oh, lord. This isn't turning into those 'I dunno, what do you wanna do' type situations, is it?"

Iris laughed. "I can make an executive decision. I was trying to be polite."

Henry Dale didn't quite smile. "Have you been to Bev's?"

"Not yet. Can you give me directions?"

"Of course I can."

Iris noticed that Eli got quiet when Henry Dale started navigating. Not GPS style, but according to odd landmarks and funny little details she never would've noticed. Driving this way felt like she was getting a glimpse of how Henry Dale saw the world. Soon, they reached a weathered white building on the outskirts of St. Claire. It had a gravel parking lot, a wide porch, and a faded sign that just said BEV's alongside an image of a steaming cup of coffee.

Iris parked and hopped out of the car, already loving the retro vibe. Inside, the place was a classic diner from the old jukebox to the torn red vinyl and the Formica-and-chrome tables. There were even a few stools at the counter so people didn't feel self-conscious about eating alone. Iris eyed the display of cakes and pies, trying not to look overeager. Henry Dale apparently had a usual spot here, as he headed to the second booth toward the back, right-hand side, and slid into the far seat.

Since Henry Dale parked himself in the middle, that left Iris to share with Eli, so she scooted in first. A blue-haired teen trotted over to their table; her name badge read *Not Bev*. "The menu's right there." She pointed.

Oh, that was an ingenious solution. The pages had been laminated and mounted on the wall next to the booth. It was a short list, not a lot to think about. For lunch, it was burger, chicken sandwich, country fried steak, or green salad. Breakfast was a little more varied, and it was served all day, though she'd noticed the café closed at 3:00 p.m.

"I'll have a cheeseburger," Eli said.

"Fries or onion rings?"

"Can I say neither?"

The waitress nodded. "Sure, but it costs the same. You want a milkshake instead?"

That was an interesting substitution, but Eli went for it. "Strawberry, please."

"Chicken fried steak for me," Henry Dale said. "With all the trimmings and a tall glass of ice water."

Not Bev laughed, flipping her notepad around so they could see her elegant penmanship. "Already wrote it down, Mr. Macabee. I'll tell Grandma you stopped in." She turned to Iris. "Are you ready to order?"

"Biscuit and gravy plate, please."

"How do you want your eggs?"

"Scrambled."

"Anything to drink?"

"Iced coffee?"

Not Bev smiled. "We don't normally serve it, but since you're with Mr. Macabee, I'll make you some and charge the same as a hot coffee. My name is Brooke, by the way. The name tag is just a running joke between Grandma and me."

"The famous Bev?" Iris guessed.

"Yep. She's on vacation right now. I'll put your order in and get your drinks while you wait."

Once the waitress walked off, Iris turned to Henry Dale. "This is such a cute place. Have you been coming here long?"

He thought about it. "Thirty years at least. The food is good, and they make you feel at home."

When her food arrived, it looked positively scrumptious, a full-on comfort feast. Eli eyed her fluffy biscuits with a hint of envy, and she offered him a bite. It surprised her when he opened his mouth instead of taking the fork, but she mentally shrugged and fed him. He seemed to enjoy it *so* much that she almost fed him another forkful just to see that sparkle in his eyes.

"That's amazing," he said.

She grinned. "I know, right? Have you had this before?" she asked Henry Dale.

"Sure have. Never had anything here I thought was bad. It's all a good bet. Just depends on what you're craving."

As they were finishing their meals, Iris's phone rang, an unfamiliar number. *If this is Lily or Rose trying to trick me—no, I doubt they'd bother.* She answered on the second ring with a tentative "Hello?" Because honestly, when her phone rang these days, it just generally gave her a bad feeling.

"Is this Iris Collins?"

"It is. Who's this?"

"Oh, thank goodness!" The bright and cheerful voice definitely didn't belong to any of Iris's relatives. But it *was* a bit familiar.

Where have I heard this woman before?

"This is Sally Carruthers. My son, Bruce, gave me your information. He said you're looking for a roommate?"

Right, the hardware store. Iris put the face with the voice and name straightaway. Bubbly, white-haired woman with the rainbow sweater and a smile sweet enough to put cherubs to shame. "I am! We repainted the room recently, you can stop by to see if you think it would be a good fit."

Normally, Iris would insist on meeting elsewhere for the first time, but this wasn't a stranger exactly. She was talking to Bruce's *mom*. Not that people's moms couldn't be criminals, but still.

"I could be there later this afternoon if that's convenient," Sally said at once.

"We'll be home in about an hour." She figured it was best to give some leeway.

"Fantastic. I'll see you around three then. Bye for now!" Sally sang.

"Sounds like we have an interview," Eli said.

"I hope that's okay. You and Henry Dale need to agree as well. If you don't like Sally, I won't move forward."

"As long as she leaves me alone, I don't *need* to like her," Henry Dale said.

Just from the brief impression, Iris suspected Sally wouldn't be quiet or reserved, but maybe it would all work out. Quickly, she signaled for the bill and paid for it before Eli could grab it. Luckily, she'd read that inclination beforehand. She really couldn't accept anything else from him without feeling awful.

It didn't take long to drive home, and she even had time to get the couch and love seat neatly covered and tied off. The pre-owned couch covers smelled like detergent, and the woman had promised that they had been laundered before being packed away. Amazing what a difference hiding those random patterns made. Now the pops of color from the knit throws and the flowered pillows looked cozy and charming. The neutral walls and the elegant wallpaper improved matters as well, as did the white wainscoting.

"I love this room now," she said to Eli.

"It's so much better," he agreed.

Henry Dale offered no commentary; he just tried to retreat to the shed, but Iris grabbed his arm. "Oh no, you don't. We're talking to Sally together."

The old man mumbled something unintelligible and likely uncomplimentary, but he still took a seat on the sofa, wearing a resigned look. They didn't have long to wait, as soon Sally arrived in a flurry of exuberant knocks. Iris answered the door and waved her in, confirming her initial impression. Again today, Sally was dressed in a bright floral dress adorned in scarves, the same lime-green Crocs, and her hair was a silvery cloud.

Smiling, Iris performed the introductions. "I'm Iris. This is Eli. And Henry Dale. There's one room available on the second floor and two rooms on the third. They're not large, but—"

"Let's take a look, shall we?" Sally cut in. "First I need to see what's available to know if I can envision myself here. Everything else follows."

———————

Eli stayed with Henry Dale while Iris gave the older woman a quick tour.

Neither one of them showed any sign of breaking the silence. For his part, he was a bit nervous about bringing in someone else. A new person could upset the balance, and Eli didn't love change at the best of times. Change usually meant his life being turned upside down and ensuring that it got worse.

"What do you think?" he asked eventually.

The older man shrugged. "Hard to say from a look, though she seems chipper." After a pause. "I don't much care for unfounded optimism."

"What do you mean, *unfounded*?" Eli wanted to know.

There was a lengthy pause, as if Henry Dale was considering whether he ought to answer. "Look at her situation. It's no better than mine."

"How do you know so much about Sally Carruthers?" Eli asked.

"Small town, coffee klatch. I go for cheap coffee and crullers, get the gossip for free. When Sally left Howard, it was all anybody could talk about for months."

"Huh," Eli said. "I never knew you went to senior gatherings."

Henry Dale snorted. "You don't know everything about me, not by a long shot. Anyway, I feel a bit sorry for Howard. Sally is a handful. As I was saying before you cut me off, I might even argue her situation is worse than mine because she left her husband and her family, and for what?"

"That's for me to figure out," Sally said crisply.

Oh damn.

Heat washed Eli's face, as it seemed they'd been caught gossiping. Well, Henry Dale had been talking about her, and he hadn't shut it down. "Right."

Do I need to apologize?

Iris came in right after, and since she didn't know what'd happened, she moved the conversation along. Thankfully Sally allowed it. "So that's the house. The only thing I didn't show you is the basement with the washer and dryer."

"Those are all the same," Sally said, waving a hand as she

took a seat opposite Iris. "The rest of the house is charming. I love the bathroom, *so* much personality."

This lady reminded him a bit of Gamma, and that was a big plus in his book. Her energy shone with similar light. He listened as she and Iris discussed which room she'd prefer, the terms of the rental, and so on.

"You can have any of those rooms," Iris was saying. "But we do need to have a house meeting about it as well."

"Oh good, I was afraid I had to decide here and now. I do tend to be impulsive, but I wanted to give this a little thought."

"That's a good idea," Henry Dale said.

Judging by his frosty tone, the old man was hoping Sally would pass. Eli considered speaking up, but Iris was already on it. "Keep an open mind, okay?"

When Iris patted Henry Dale's shoulder, he sighed, but he didn't say anything else.

Sally stood. "I'll take a copy of the rental agreement to look over and let you know in a couple of days."

"Perfect. You have my email and my number if anything comes up. And tell Bruce we said hello."

That brought a proud smile to Sally's face. She'd apparently been on the verge of leaving, but she joined Iris on the sofa, bringing up the gallery on her phone to show off pictures of Bruce and his family without being asked. Eli circled behind the sofa to dutifully admire the chubby babies who grew into sturdy children with each swipe of Sally's screen. Honestly, her grandkids *were* super cute.

"I have other grandchildren too," Sally was saying. "But

Megan is older. She's my daughter's daughter, and Kim is a lot older than Bruce."

Henry Dale sighed. "Is there a reason for us to know any of this yet? We're not even sure if you're moving in."

The older woman scowled at him. "Do you need a *reason* to be friendly?"

This time, Eli intervened before Iris had to. "I enjoyed seeing those pictures. Thanks for sharing them."

Sally bestowed on him a radiant smile. "You're sweet. I already know I'll like *you*. Do you like cheesecake squares?"

Eli blinked. "Uh. Maybe?"

"Anyway, I was on my way out. I'll be in touch."

It felt like much longer than forty minutes had passed. Weirdly it was like being released from a time-warp spell when Sally sailed out the front door, as if the normal passage of moments had resumed. Henry Dale grumbled beneath his breath, and this time nobody stopped him when he stomped off to the shed.

"They're going to clash," Iris predicted.

"I suspect you're right. Does that mean we should tell her she can't move in?" Eli hated doing that to such a sweet woman, especially one who reminded him of Gamma.

Iris shook her head. "I mean, honestly, Henry Dale is cranky. I like him, but if we let him, he'll veto basically everyone, and…"

You need the money.

He didn't finish the thought, but he was aware of her financial status. That was why he was working on a bot to scrape references on social media for people interested in handmade jewelry. This wasn't the right moment to mention that, however.

"We can let him mull the idea over," he said. "Today he socialized quite a lot. I'm sure he'll be okay with it once he has time to ponder."

"Well, even if he's not, if you vote with me, we win," Iris pointed out.

And oh hell. While he felt bad for Henry Dale, he'd probably vote yes on whatever she suggested just to keep her gazing at him like that. Her smile was a starry night, the kind that offered perfect weather for flying.

"True enough. Uh. If you have time, we can work on your shop tonight."

Iris bit her lip, seeming uncertain. "*I* have time, but—"

"I'm between projects right now, so I can absolutely show you those upgrades."

"Then let's do it. I'm so excited, you have no idea. I did use the graphics you provided, but I could use some help with the other features."

His heart pattered wildly as she followed him into the main bedroom. When she perched on his bed, his face went ridiculously hot. *Please don't let her notice. I don't want to her to think I lured her into my room for some weird reason.* Eli had no intentions other than to pay her back, but shivers of reaction went through him when she perched next to him on the bed, eyes fixed on his screen.

"Should I log in so we can just work on the shop directly?" she asked.

"Go ahead. I'll delete all traces of your login afterward."

Iris laughed. "Like I'm worried about you stealing my eight

dollars. I haven't even earned enough to get my first payout from the site yet."

"You will," he said.

She shot him a melting look. "You're the only one who thinks so."

"Everyone else is wrong."

A quiet sound escaped her, sweet and soft, and it raced through his veins like wildfire. "Careful you don't encourage me too much. You'll never be rid of me."

I should be so lucky.

Frankly, Eli had no idea how he focused well enough to explain, but he tried to make it clear, step-by-step, as he used photos she retrieved from the cloud. The quality of her photography needed improvement, but he suspected she was just using her phone and filters, so it couldn't be helped. She'd probably spent a lot of money on supplies to make the jewelry but hadn't factored in extra costs for displaying her work.

"Can I say something constructive?"

"Of course!"

"It's not enough to create beautiful pieces. You also have to show them off in a way that makes the person looking at the page feel like they can't live without them."

Iris frowned at him. "If I knew how to do that, I'd already be doing it!"

"I'm going somewhere with this. A tech witch could probably help. They can absolutely make social media posts go viral. I read something about it—there was some talk during the local election.

Apparently one of the councilwomen is a witch, and her opponent was yelling about it."

"Oh wow. I wonder what they'd charge. I probably can't afford it."

"We can do it in other ways," he said. "But it's something to consider."

Her open mind meant a lot to him, as it suggested that she wasn't simply pretending to be okay with what he'd confided about himself. It took a special sort of person to open their mind to new possibilities, and maybe he was asking too much, but it also seemed to offer hope that she might understand his motives one day. Maybe.

It's more than I had before.

CHAPTER TEN

SALLY MOVED IN A WEEK later, bringing joy and chaos and myriad knitting projects in various stages of completion.

She didn't have a car either, but it seemed like she had a never-ending stream of friends and relatives willing to pick her up on their way somewhere. Iris envied how *connected* the older woman seemed to be. She had clubs and lessons and lunches. Hopefully, Iris would be that engaged and busy when she got to a certain age. Henry Dale wasn't thrilled with the noise and energy Sally brought with her, but he spent so much time in the shed or in his room that it shouldn't become an issue.

For the next few weeks, Iris worked on her shop, following Eli's tips and strategies, and she was definitely seeing an uptick in page views. She'd even gotten a couple of orders, and she was *so* excited to pack and send them. Tiny steps toward success, but they counted. She hummed as she worked, turning her dreams into reality.

If I worked with a witch, we could sell magical jewelry. That would be amazing.

But she didn't know any witches well enough to suggest it, and—

"Iris! Are you home?" That was Sally.

Eli would often text, even if they were both in the house, and Henry Dale didn't communicate much. It amused her to be summoned with such urgency, especially when the issue wasn't usually that critical. But she still put aside her tools and headed downstairs.

Sally met her in the hall and grabbed her hands. "Now you know I'm not one to meddle…"

"Right," she said, somehow keeping a straight face.

The opposite was true. Sally *lived* to meddle. It was her favorite hobby. Well, that and knitting, though she'd been taking samba lessons at the senior center lately.

"But my granddaughter Megan—you remember Megan?"

"You've spoken of her before, yes."

"I need to invite her over sometime so you can meet her. But that's not the point."

"What *is* the point?" Iris asked.

"I'm getting there! Megan told me that her friend Mira needs a place to live urgently. I guess she broke up with her girlfriend and for some reason had to be the one to move out. Well, she had a sublet lined up, but the original tenant decided not to travel after all, and now Mira has all her things in storage and nowhere to go!"

"Wow, that's awful." Iris could relate to the perfect storm of seeing all plans fall through. Immediately she felt for Mira. "We have two rooms left, so if she's interested, I'm happy to meet her."

"You're a lifesaver! Megan never asks for anything, so it means a lot that her Sallygram can come through when it counts."

Iris laughed. "Sallygram? That is the cutest nickname I've ever heard." With Sally's personality, it was like she was a cheerful singing message. Actually, that was completely on point when Iris considered it.

Sally grinned. "The grandkids would always answer the phone when they were at my house. They loved it even when they were little. And my friends would ask for Sally, so the babies started calling me that, but my daughter, Kim, said it was disrespectful. 'You can't call her that. She's your grandma, not your friend!' I didn't mind, but the books say I'm not supposed to argue about parenting. So then Megan said the cutest thing. 'If she's Sally and she's my grandma, then she's my Sallygram,' and—"

"That's how you became Sallygram. Love it." It wasn't that she didn't want to hear the rest, but she wanted to finish that necklace before the end of the day. "You can give my contact info to Megan to pass to Mira. Since I work from home, any time works."

"Two retirees, two self-employed," Sally noted. "I wonder if Mira has a day job… I'll ask Megan more about her. And thanks again. You're a gem."

"What kind?" Iris asked, unable to resist.

It was the sort of silly, speculative question that made her an oddball among her own family. This would earn her that look from any one of her sisters and her parents too. But Sally paused, considering the matter with great concentration.

"Citrine or carnelian," she said eventually.

"Why, in particular?"

"Citrine attracts good fortune," Sally told her. "And you're pure luck for me, Iris. For everyone in the house, really. We were all in a pickle, but things got better as soon as you said we could stay here. I can honestly say I've never been happier."

"Wow. I feel like I want to hug you," she said.

"Go for it. Hugs are free." Sally winked at her then. "Kisses require more thought, and you're too young for me."

Oh, hey, Sally is flirting. She grinned. "It's my loss. Maybe we'll be born closer together in our next lives."

Iris cuddled close, as Sally gave *great* hugs; she smelled like tropical fruit and summertime, and the older woman knew just how long to hold on without letting things become awkward. If Iris had gotten more hugs like that growing up, maybe her life wouldn't have been so chaotic. She smiled as she stepped back, wondering if she should tell Sally how lucky Bruce and Kim were.

"Are you curious about the carnelian?" Sally asked.

"I am, but I might melt if you compliment me anymore today."

Besides, Iris already knew that carnelian related to trust and abundance, so she had some idea of what Sally might say. While Henry Dale might dislike the woman's endlessly chipper attitude, to Iris, it felt like Sally carried the sunshine with her wherever she went, even on rainy days. The older woman gave her a final pat before hurrying to her next engagement, and Iris returned to her studio to finish her necklace.

A bit past dinnertime, she got a text from Eli:

Food is done.

That was…beyond nice. When he cooked, he always made enough for everyone, and if somebody didn't feel like eating, he'd put it in the fridge for later. It was odd; she felt more like she had a family now than she ever had while living at home. Her father was the dreamy sort, prone to leave messy life details to his overbearing wife. If he had the option, he'd stay in his study writing papers no historical journal wanted to publish. And Mom was still busy pretending he was a professor to keep up appearances.

She'd never thought about whether it was normal until she saw how other families lived. Her relationship with her folks had been chilly since she dropped out of college for the fourth time anyway, and things went from frosty to absolutely arctic when the rest of the Collins crew realized she had no plans to apologize for missing Rose's promotion party. They probably found it incomprehensible that she was still pissed about Lily dating Dylan. Iris didn't intend to let Lily off the hook.

Not this time.

Really, she *should* be hurt, right? That she'd been cut off. But instead, it felt like freedom. No more dodging calls. No more inventing excuses.

"You look conflicted," Eli said, as she stepped into the kitchen.

She admired his and Henry's work all over again. The white cabinets looked fantastic with the wooden counters, and the black-and-white tile floor hardly showed its age. This kitchen really was a welcoming space now, albeit like stepping back in time.

"Not as much as I expected."

He flashed her a curious look. "Do you want to talk about it?"

"There's not much to say. I don't get along with my family, and I was just thinking that I'm happier now that we just... don't talk."

Eli didn't say he was sorry or offer any of the usual platitudes. "I have cousins I rarely see, and I'm only close to Gamma, so I don't quite know how it feels. I miss her a lot, but I'm glad she's happy and having fun."

"Gamma? That's so precious." As they ate the vegetable soup, she repeated the story Sally had shared with her.

"Sallygram? Kids are so funny."

"I know, right?" She glanced at the hall that led to Henry Dale's room. "Is he okay?"

"He took a bowl of soup to his room. Said he wanted to finish his book and it's rude to read at the table."

"This is really good, by the way."

Eli often made good use of Great-Aunt Gertie's old slow cooker, choosing soups and stews that were low effort, high reward, and perfectly suited to a chilly autumn evening. Tonight, he'd made a vegetarian minestrone, chock full of carrots, onions, celery, white beans, spinach, green beans, zucchini, tomatoes, and plump little pasta shells. It reminded her of going to an Italian restaurant in college that offered unlimited soup, salad, and breadsticks, likely without realizing how much starving students could eat.

"Glad you like it."

I like you too, she almost said, but that would be too much. They were housemates, right? He'd never indicated he saw her as more, and she shouldn't read into his kindness. She'd gotten in trouble being impulsive and making assumptions before.

Don't ruin this. Things are going well. Just...be happy.

Everyday magic.

If someone asked Eli to describe his current life situation, he'd choose those two words. Because there were small wonders every day, new things he learned about Iris just from being around her. She had a sweet tooth, and she had a habit of putting whatever was handy in her hair to keep it out of her face. So far, he'd seen her use pens, pencils, chip clips, a chopstick, and once a wooden spoon. From what he could tell, she hated shoes and she only wore natural fabrics, none of which helped him figure out her true nature.

He hadn't been able to get those colors out of his head. Because he was so baffled and fascinated, he'd even asked on a shifter forum—about how a psychic vampire's aura looked. Most commenters hadn't even run across them, but those who had? Described something bleaker than the incandescent beauty Iris radiated.

Who are *you, Iris Collins?*

Absurd how happy he was, simply washing dishes with her. She liked the scrubbing better than the drying, and he enjoyed putting things in their proper place. If he believed in fate, he might imagine they matched.

In time, Henry Dale brought out his empty bowl and insisted on washing it himself. Eli loved the warm feeling in his chest when Iris shot him a conspiratorial look, assuming they'd be on the same page. And while he did share her amusement at Henry Dale's prickly tendencies, he also understood the man.

Henry Dale felt *alone.* He'd lost everyone who mattered, and he was maintaining emotional distance to protect himself. Eli had grown up solitary despite Gamma's best efforts. He...just wasn't good at connecting to people either. So Henry Dale's emotional retreat made complete sense, even if Iris just saw him as a grumpy old man. But Eli saw a man who was hurting and needed friends.

"Do you think you could give me a ride tomorrow?" Henry Dale asked.

Eli nodded. "Did they finish the teardown?"

"Yup. They said I can take whatever's fit to haul away. I'm sure we can pick up enough lumber to repair the porch."

"Name the time," he said.

Soon after, Sally came home, but she'd already eaten with her friends. She hung around the kitchen to drink a cup of tea, however, chatting with Iris while they tidied up. Eli kept quiet and mostly listened to their conversation.

During a natural break, he asked, "Are you settling in all right?"

"Definitely! It's homier than home. I even have an old man to bicker with, so what could be more familiar than that?" Sally flashed Eli a smile.

Iris chortled. "Howard wasn't that bad, was he?"

"I suppose not. But...I just wasn't happy. Back in the day, they said we should stay together for the children, but my kids are thirty-nine and forty-seven. I figured I'd done my bit. I married young, and I've been taking care of someone else for my *entire* life."

Is that how Gamma felt?

He'd tried not to be a burden, but maybe Gamma had been waiting to cut loose all this time too. Iris touched his hand lightly. The woman might not be a natural at running a business, but she seemed attuned to his every flicker of expression. Maybe he shouldn't like that as much as he did.

"I don't blame you," Iris said in a supportive tone.

She glanced at Eli as if for confirmation. Quickly he said, "There's nothing wrong with choosing to pursue your own happiness."

Sally sniffed. "From what I hear, Howard's doing the same. He went after Gladys as soon as our divorce was finalized!"

Eli had no idea who that was, but he supposed it must be someone from their circle, so he made a sympathetic noise. "Did he start…" What was the right word? "Dating her?"

The older woman shook her head. "Nope. She ended up with Leonard. Howard is single and ready to mingle, just like I am."

Before Eli could reply, a sharp rap sounded at the front door. Iris hopped up, and he heard multiple voices coming from the foyer. Unable to stifle his curiosity, he went to see who'd arrived on their doorstep. He didn't recognize any of the new arrivals, but they felt…cold in a way he'd rarely experienced, radiating a bone-deep chill that threatened to suck away all light and joy. Three women, all dressed in fashionable attire, immaculately coiffed and each wearing expensive shoes while carrying designer bags.

This has to be Iris's family.

It didn't seem like an improbable conclusion, given her tight expression and the way her shoulders rounded. He stepped to her side instinctively, as the older woman said, "Aren't you planning to invite us in, Iris?"

"Mom. Lily. Rose. The front room is through here," she said, her whole body radiating tension. "I'll make tea."

"That won't be necessary."

Eli *felt* the sharp slice of the older woman's gaze as it roved past him; he'd never felt more inadequate or insignificant in his life. *And this is the woman who raised Iris? It's a wonder she didn't freeze to death.*

"Fine. What's this about?" Iris asked.

He didn't follow them into the living room, but he couldn't make himself walk away, even if they required privacy. Their relationship wasn't such that he could offer moral support, but he had the unshakable impression that she needed it. Sally came to the foyer and glanced around the doorway to the front room.

"What's going on?" she whispered.

Silently he shook his head, and she motioned to the kitchen and mimed pouring a hot beverage. Though they'd said no, if Sally made drinks, he could bring them in. Maybe Iris would want him to stick around.

"This wasn't something we could discuss over the phone," another woman said in a careful tone, the kind people heard in hospitals before bad news was delivered.

Likely one of her sisters, Lily or Rose. It definitely wasn't her mother's voice with its diamond chill. *Yeah, I'm definitely eavesdropping. This doesn't involve me. I should—*

"Let's cut to the chase," a third woman added. "We've learned something completely startling, but it makes so much sense. In time, you might even be relieved. I know I am."

"Lily!" the older woman said sharply.

So the first speaker must be Rose.

"What?" Sulky tone. "I didn't say anything *wrong*, did I?"

"Iris is having her world upended. There's no reason to be cruel." Strange how the words didn't match her tone.

"What is it? Why are you here?" Iris asked.

Her mother paused, so much weight in that stillness that Eli's forearms prickled. "Iris...there's no easy way to say this."

Rose offered, "Should I...?"

Iris's mom took a deep breath. "No. I will. You got some mail at the house, a card asking you to donate blood, and it reminded me to pick up your medical records. I was planning to send them. I thought you'd need them here, in case something happened."

To Eli, that sounded like a good deed. Records were supposed to be easily accessible digitally, but some offices made it more complicated than it needed to be. But maybe he didn't understand why Iris's mother was doing that. Context could change everything.

"Okay..." Iris sounded confused.

"But I noticed something that raised a few questions—"

"Just tell her already," Lily said.

"Don't rush me! This isn't an easy thing to say." Another long pause.

Eli could only imagine how baffled and worried Iris must be. It took all his self-restraint not to interrupt and get in the middle of a complicated situation that had nothing to do with him.

Finally, Rose spoke up. "Mom wasn't there when you got your physical before college. And none of us had any reason to check on your blood type. But it was in the records they sent—"

"Just tell me," Iris said, sounding resolute.

"You're AB," her mother said in a neutral tone. "Iris, I'm type A. Your father is O. And..."

Oh shit. That's not possible. Even basic bio informed him of that much. Eli wondered if the woman was about to confess to cheating or something. Maybe Iris was about to learn she had a different biological father? He glanced at Sally, who was standing beside him in silence, her eyes as wide as his own must be.

"This is better than a telenovela," she breathed.

Rose continued the narrative. "I asked Mom if she cheated."

"Never!" The woman sounded genuinely indignant, then she went on, "But...it raised serious concerns, so I went to the hospital. I...*we* hoped they'd simply gotten your blood type wrong, but everything seemed to be correct on that end. In the end, we found an old toothbrush... You're apparently not related to any of us biologically, Iris."

"There must have been a mix-up at the hospital," Rose said. "I'm considering filing suit. This has just about broken Mom's heart."

Iris didn't speak for several long excruciating moments. Then she whispered, "Did you come all this way to tell me I'm not family?"

He could *hear* the hurt in her voice, ached for her with every fiber of his being.

"That's your decision," her mother said quietly. "You've always found fault with us, and lately you've been giving us the silent treatment. So I suppose you can consider yourself free of obligation if that's how you—"

"Enough of this nonsense," Sally said, loud enough for the women in the front room to hear her.

Eli took a step, only to find Sally standing behind him on the verge of dropping her tray. He steadied her, and then she steam-rolled right past him into the front room. He hadn't known if he should step in, but Sally had no such qualms. Eli followed her just in case she needed backup.

"I'd like you to leave," Sally added. "You've just given Iris some shocking news. You should be comforting her, not telling her she can cut ties if she wants. That's not how family behaves."

Iris's mother snapped to her feet. "Who do you think—?"

"Her housemate. Do I need to get a broom to make a clean sweep? Or should I get salt, holy water, or garlic?"

"That's offensive," Lily snapped. "Iris, I can't believe you told her."

Sally blinked. "Told me what? That's just what you do to get rid of bad energy. Please leave if that's how you plan to handle this situation."

"This is none of your business," Iris's mom said.

Sally didn't back down. "It is, though. You're doing this in my home, and if I feel uncomfortable, I have the right to ask visitors to leave. It's in the rental agreement."

Lily stood with a frosty look at Sally. "I can see there will be no having civil discourse, Iris. Your quality of friends is precisely what I'd expect."

Rose seemed to feel incredibly awkward about it all. "Maybe we should...take some time? We can talk again when tempers cool."

"Indeed," said Iris's mother. "Reach out when you're ready."

CHAPTER ELEVEN

DAZED, IRIS STARED AT THE cup in her hand.

It was part of the china set she particularly liked—with the purple flowers and scalloped edges. She had no memory of picking it up. Sally sat beside her, gently rubbing her back while Eli hovered.

"I'm so sorry," Sally said softly.

She glanced between them with a growing sense of bewilderment. "My mom and sisters were really here, right?"

"Is there anything I can do?" Eli asked, sounding anxious.

Shaking her head, Iris whispered, "How does something like this even happen?"

There was no map for navigating this revelation. With shaking hands, she took a sip of the tea and gathered herself as best she could. This was the kind of reveal she'd enjoy in a Korean drama, but living it?

Not much fun.

Sally said, "I've heard of rare cases where infants have been switched at birth. Usually, staff made a mistake and mixed up the tags or something. I remember one case where it happened because both babies had jaundice and there was only one incubator."

"I don't know if that applies here." Oddly, hearing Sally discuss the possibilities in such a matter-of-fact manner? It helped.

"The most important thing for you to keep in mind? This isn't your fault. You didn't do anything wrong."

Iris drew in a shaky breath, trying not to cry. "I swear, Lily was glad. Now she doesn't have to feel guilty about Dylan, I guess. Because I'm not really her sister. It was harder to read Rose and Mom. Or should I call her Delphine now?"

"Lily is a piece of work," Sally muttered, shaking her head. "Bruce and Mitch adopted both their kids, and they're every bit as precious to me as Megan."

Iris tried to smile because Sally was right; blood ties shouldn't matter. The people who raised and loved you ought to be your family. But she didn't feel confident that Mom really wanted her to reach out later. Maybe everyone would be happier if Iris used this as an opportunity to cut ties for good, and that was a heartbreaking possibility.

Her voice came out unsteady. "It's odd; I never felt like I fit in, and now I have literal confirmation. It wasn't just a feeling. I *was* a cuckoo in the nest."

"I don't understand your mother. She was so cold!"

Iris couldn't muster a smile. "Delphine might be relieved. I was always the weird one, the child she couldn't explain."

"You don't need to be *explained*," Sally said in an indignant tone.

It was incredible that this was why they'd been calling lately. Not to argue about Rose's party or to demand that she forgive Lily or even to smooth things over in their usual dismissive way—by calling her dramatic. But…to tell her that she wasn't biologically related. Lily hadn't bothered to hide her opinion either—*You're not one of us. You never have been. And now we have documentation to prove it.*

Everything about this was messy, a scandal the rest of the family would hate other people knowing about. Iris wondered how Dad and Olive felt and what she was supposed to do now. *Do I change my last name? But I don't know what my actual last name is. How does this even* work? Presumably, if something went wrong at the hospital, there should be records regarding her biological family, but she wasn't sure she wanted to meet them.

What if they're even worse? What if they prefer the child they raised? And it turns out nobody *wants me?* She clenched her fist on the teacup to the point that it was faintly surprising that the delicate handle didn't snap off in her grasp. Sally seemed to feel the same way since she removed the fragile porcelain gently from Iris's hand.

"Breathe," Eli said softly.

He had been so quiet during the whole thing that she'd practically forgotten he was there. Yet when she glanced in his direction, she saw only gentle concern. Not pity, which would've wrecked her.

"Is it awful that I would rather just…not think about it?" Iris buried her face in her hands; avoidance was her favorite strategy for dealing with crap life chucked at her.

Sally shook her head. "Of course not. This came out of the blue. It would be strange if you were ready to sail off in search of your 'real' family. And I have strong opinions about that anyway. Your mother should have broken the news delicately and then fought tooth and nail to assure you that you're her daughter, no matter what."

"It doesn't work that way," Iris said. "Never has. I can't remember a single moment when she was happy with me. Or…proud of me."

"Then you're better off without her." Sally gave her a hug, and it almost balanced out the badness.

Almost.

"I…need some time." She got to her feet and headed upstairs without looking directly at either one of them.

If anything, Iris wished they hadn't witnessed that scene. Lily might even send messages about Iris collecting the rest of her things. Since Iris had decided not to give her sister a pass over Dylan, she turned everything into a personal grudge. That was entirely in character, so maybe Iris would surprise everyone and strike first.

Eli would probably let me borrow his truck. No, I bet he'll insist on driving me since it's quite a trek. Luckily, she had her own basement now, and she could house the boxes just fine. Maybe she'd even sort through them and sell some stuff, donating the rest, just as she'd done with Great-Aunt Gertie's belongings.

For a while, Iris tried to work, but her heart wasn't in it, and finally, in the privacy of her attic retreat, she let herself cry, fat and futile tears that did nothing to change her situation. Iris wept until she was spent and fell asleep in her clothes. She woke the next morning gummy-eyed but more resolved.

She also had three texts from Olive.

Olive: I don't care what the hospital said. You're my baby sister. If Lily gives you a hard time, tell me. I'll talk to her. I'm fed up with her lately anyway.

Olive: And if you need somewhere else to be, you can come

to me. I don't have much, but you're welcome, and you could
do some good while you're here.

Olive: Love you, sis. Just wanted to say that too.

Iris wiped her eyes because they were threatening to spill over again, but not in a bad way this time. Quickly, she tapped out a response.

Iris: I'm honestly not even surprised. I appreciate the offer,
but I'm at Great-Aunt Gertie's place now. I wonder if she'd be
horrified to realize she left her house to someone who's not
a blood relative.

Olive: Knowing Great-Auntie, she'd be delighted.

Iris: What time is it there anyway?

Olive: Don't worry about it. Hang in there, okay? I'm...virtually
here for you.

Iris: I have some great housemates now. I'll be okay.

Maybe that was pure optimism, but Iris felt better after the chat with Olive. *She always was my favorite.* There was still a faint ache in her chest, but not enough to keep her from going about her business. Iris washed up, had some food, and finished two more pieces before the end of the day. Then she took careful photos, filtered them, and used Eli's trick to make the new items pop. In checking her stat page, she saw that more visitors were cruising by. Actually, that could be Sally too; she was always telling people to check out Iris's work.

As Iris wrapped up, a text arrived from an unknown number.

Unknown: Hi, this is Mira Yoon. I got your number from Megan. I *think* you're rooming with her grandmother?

Iris: That's me. I'm not sure what you heard, but I have two rooms left. I own a big old Victorian house.

Mira: I'd love to swing by. I'm really in a bind.

Iris: I have time tonight.

Mira: I'll be there after I get off work. I have an afternoon meeting and they sometimes run long, so I'll text you when I'm leaving the office. Is that okay?

Iris: Yep! We'll be here. You can meet everyone.

Mira: Everyone? How many housemates do you have, exactly?

Iris: Right now? 3. You'd be the fourth.

Mira: ...OK. See you later.

Yeah, Mira definitely seemed dubious about living with this many people, and Iris would understand if she passed. The bathroom situation might become an issue, though since Mira had a day job, if a schedule had to be made, she'd get priority. *Damn, I never really thought about the logistics. I'm...bad at logistics.* Then she shrugged philosophically.

That was for future-Iris to worry about.

———————

Eli drove Henry Dale to the middle of nowhere.

Forty-seven minutes from St. Claire, away from all civilization—into the heart of corn country. This time of year, the fields were earthen dark, full of dried of husks, depressing and broken up by so many tiny towns with improbable names that

Eli lost track. Most didn't have stoplights or a post office. He saw hints that some of them had once been bigger with closed buildings and weathered houses telling the story. Periodically, he spotted wooden signs, hand-painted, for berries, honey, hay, or dirt.

In time, they reached a farm set well back from the road on a winding drive. There were a couple of silos, cows grazing in fenced fields nearby. Two barns on the property as well, and one of them was apparently being demolished. This wasn't what he'd expected when the older man mentioned a teardown, but he helped sort through the lumber alongside Henry Dale, then they loaded the truck with enough wood to repair the porch. There would probably be lumber left for other projects too. If he knew the other man a fraction as well as he suspected, Henry Dale would likely store the rest in the shed and find other things to fix.

"It's good of you to do this," Eli said as they got back in the truck.

"Hogwash," said Henry Dale.

"Excuse me?" He glanced over as he made a three-point turn on the gravel drive and headed back toward town.

"Kindness has nothing to do with it. I'm using old contacts to get a discount on my rent and to stave off boredom."

Eli let it go because Henry Dale seemed allergic to the idea that he'd get caught being nice to somebody. "Never mind, then." Taking the hint, he changed the subject. "I hear we might be getting another housemate."

The other man sighed. "Like the place isn't already busy enough. I understand it's not my place to object—Iris owns the house, not me—but don't you think we have enough people? Sally is loud enough for four folks."

Eli thought about that. "I've lived alone for years," he said slowly. "So I don't really mind. I like having dinner with everyone, and I enjoy the company. It's…" He paused. What was the right word, exactly? "Comforting."

Henry Dale made a scoffing noise, but he didn't offer further argument. The ride home passed quietly with Eli trying to decide how long he planned to stay. Three months might be long enough to wrap up the sale of Gamma's house. Keshonda had sent him an update, detailing how many calls she'd gotten and how many showings she'd set up. So far, no offers, but the market was a bit sluggish. Once the house sold, he'd play it by ear. He couldn't—in good conscience—move on until he was sure Iris had everything under control and could make ends meet.

Since he had the main bedroom, he was currently contributing most to her financial stability, and he couldn't just *walk away*. But maybe he could say he was traveling to check out properties or something while continuing to pay rent? It probably wasn't the best idea to stay for ages, as that would create deeper connections under false pretenses.

Damn, why is this so complicated? This was just him paying it forward, no hidden motives. But it probably wouldn't scan that way to anyone else.

"Back it in," Henry Dale said suddenly, interrupting his thoughts.

Without realizing it, Eli had driven all the way home.

He complied without asking why. It seemed pretty clear that Henry Dale intended to use the truck bed as the staging point for the porch repair. At least the weather was right for it, not so cold that working outside was difficult, not so hot that they'd sweat themselves sick. Together, they fetched necessary supplies from the shed, including a miter saw, a sawhorse, and various other tools. As the older man arranged things to his satisfaction, Eli got started tearing out the bad boards. Fortunately, this wasn't a complete overhaul; it was only two bad steps and a small section in the middle that needed to be replaced.

"How long do you think this will take?" Eli asked.

Henry Dale shrugged. "Hard telling. But I *think* we can do it before the end of the day. Just the construction, mind. We'll still need to sand everything, apply waterproofing, and then paint or stain, depending on what Iris prefers."

Frankly, the whole house needed to be painted, but that would be a *massive* undertaking. Iris probably couldn't even afford the cost of all the supplies that would be required, let alone manpower. Gamma had white siding on her house, so Eli had no experience with exterior work. He assumed it would require a fair amount of specialized equipment as well.

As Eli carefully pried up the rotten boards, Henry Dale checked the rest of the porch and found two more trouble areas. Fortunately, they had plenty of lumber for repairs. The older man got busy taking measurements while Eli worked on removal. They didn't speak much while they went about their tasks with Henry Dale cutting the pieces to fit, then sanding and waterproofing the back side of the replacement boards.

A black truck drove by and leaned on the horn; then a man in a ballcap shouted, "You forgot the rainbow flag on your gay purple house, losers!"

"What a turd wrapped in human skin," said Henry Dale.

Eli couldn't agree more. The world was better these days, but people like that still existed, unfortunately. It was also why groups like HAPI could grow their numbers at an alarming rate.

Later in the day, Iris came out with mugs of hot coffee. "It looks like rain," she said, peering at the clouds with a worried look.

"We can wrap up before it breaks." Henry Dale took the mug with his usual stoic air, but Eli could tell the old man was happy.

"Don't get sick," she said firmly.

"Thanks." Eli met her halfway, stepping around the gaps in the porch. "And be careful out here. It's kind of an obstacle course."

"This is amazing. I can't believe how much you've already gotten done. Can you imagine how pretty it will be when I have a chance to redo the flowers out front?"

Before he could respond, the next-door neighbor, Susan, marched across the yard like she was going to war. Granted, she normally looked like someone had pissed in her cereal, and today, she appeared no more cheerful, her face pulled into an expression of discontent. Though it wasn't freezing by any means, she was wearing a huge puffy coat, and her orange hair had been permed within an inch of its life. That might be new, both the perm and the color. He couldn't recall if she'd looked this way before.

"How much longer do you plan on keeping up this racket?" the woman demanded, addressing Henry Dale.

The older man shrugged. "Until the weather breaks, we lose daylight, or the work is done. Hard telling what will come first."

"The good lord knows I have tried to be polite. Welcoming

even! But you refuse to extend me the same courtesy." Susan stepped closer to glare at Iris.

What's wrong with this woman anyway?

"I don't understand the problem," Iris said. "You threatened me about contacting the city, and now that we're fixing the porch—like you wanted—you're mad about that too?"

"It's just good manners to advise close neighbors when you're starting a renovation project. Yes, I advised you to fix the porch, and you kicked me out of your house without even tasting the casserole I made. You obviously have no intention of being a good neighbor! As evinced by the way you do whatever the hell you want regardless of how it impacts the rest of the neighborhood."

An older woman across the street happened to be getting her mail. Eli didn't know her name, but he sighed as she came to the end of her driveway. If she ganged up on Iris too, he honestly didn't know how he'd keep himself in check. If he slipped away and shifted silently, they'd never know it was him dive-bombing Susan as an angry hawk. In that case, they couldn't charge him for assault either.

The older woman frowned. "That's enough, Susan! You drove Gertie to an early grave with your nagging. Don't start with her little niece now too."

Hearing the other neighbor lend some support allowed Eli to keep quiet.

I'm just her housemate. I don't have the right to step in.

CHAPTER TWELVE

CRAP.

At least all the neighbors don't hate me. Having said her piece, the woman across the street went back inside, leaving Iris to stare at Susan Calhoun, whose new hairstyle didn't suit her even slightly.

"I can tell you weren't raised right," Susan said.

Oh, Delphine would love that. Maybe I could introduce them to each other.

Yet Iris tried to stay civil since escalation would only make things worse. She'd already lost her temper with this woman once. No benefit in doubling down. "Look, I'm sorry we got off on the wrong foot. We won't be working on the porch late into the night or anything, so it shouldn't disturb your sleep."

The woman scowled. Lines on her face made it clear this was her usual expression. Then she let out an exaggerated sigh. "I should have known that anyone who's related to Crazy Gertie couldn't be normal."

Iris narrowed her eyes. "Excuse me?"

Susan had gotten a free pass the first day they met, but Iris had no intention of letting anyone trash-talk her auntie.

Susan didn't take the warning in Iris's sudden shift in posture. "We've discussed this before. It's nothing new. Gertrude Van Doren had a bunch of screws loose, bats in her belfry. Do I need to go on?"

"Don't talk about her that way! Actually, don't talk about *anyone* that way. That's incredibly hateful. And hurtful." Iris's palm itched to deliver a slap, but that would just get her hauled in by the police. Again.

"Fantastic. You're one of those. No wonder."

Iris spoke through clenched teeth. "What's that supposed to mean?"

"You're trying to police my thoughts and actions. This is a free country. I can say what I want! I wonder how you ended up so sensitive yet so rude at the same time. You don't even know basic manners and you're lecturing *me*?"

"Seems to me you're the rude one," Henry Dale said quietly. "Miz Collins apologized when you came looking for a scrap. And now you're disrespecting her deceased auntie. Does that seem like good manners to you, ma'am? Truly?"

Susan clamped her mouth shut, seeming at a loss for words. She aimed another hateful look at the house that didn't live up to her standards. In contrast, Susan's place was immaculate with no peeling paint; she'd chosen pale-yellow siding, and fake navy shutters framed the windows. Her hedges were geometric, and though it was autumn, everything about her property still somehow maintained a clean silhouette.

Finally, she said in a grudging tone, "I suppose I could have overreacted about not being apprised of your schedule for the repair work."

"We'll be out here for two or three days," Eli said. "But we'll try to keep it down."

Iris bit back a sharp retort. Henry Dale had reined Susan in, and Eli seemed to be taking a conciliatory approach, so she shouldn't fan the flames. "I intend for the house to be beautiful again, but it will take time."

And money. So much money.

"The first thing you should do is get the place painted. Purple is a ridiculous color. If only we had a homeowners' association to—"

"What color is preferable?" Iris asked tightly. She *loved* this purple house. Though she had no intention of painting it a "normal" color, she was curious what Susan would say.

Susan smiled, evidently imagining that she was being consulted. "White is a good choice. Or gray. A very pale blue might work. I believe the Victorians were fond of dark tones like olive or umber, but I'm not sure how it would look or how it would blend with the rest of the neighborhood. Whatever you decide, do be mindful of the rest of us. Your choices impact our property values."

"I'll remember that," she muttered. *But I don't promise to care.* Essentially, she was done with this conversation too. "If you'll excuse me, I have work to do."

She went inside without another word, still fuming. They hadn't even made that much noise. A few cuts on the saw? It hardly seemed worth all that drama, and how fucking unbeliev-able that Susan Calhoun imagined she had the right to advise Iris what to do with her own home. *What a...harridan.* Iris had been reading a historical romance the night before, and the word leapt into her mind from the pages of the book.

Wrath carried her all the way up to the attic, and she checked her online store for the first time today. *Ten orders. I have ten orders.* While she wouldn't get rich from this, she was moving in the right direction. Excited, she packaged up the chosen pieces along with thank-you cards and a code for 10 percent off their next orders. The packages were small; she'd bought a number of gift boxes and padded shipping envelopes in setting up, which was part of why she hadn't been able to pay rent at her old place.

Don't think about past failures. Fresh start, remember?

She got online and created labels for each envelope—small and light translated to economical shipping, and she scheduled the pickup for tomorrow. Diving into design work—her favorite part—Iris lost track of time. It was hours later when a knock at her door drew her out of the wondrous world she lived in, most of the time. Sometimes she felt like she was trying to design things she'd seen in her dreams, and the reality never quite lived up to her imagination. Marvelous artifacts, jewels made of fruit and flowers—ah, it was so disappointing to find that her creations didn't match what was in her mind.

Standing, she stretched, rolling her neck and shoulders. "What's up?" she called.

"You have a guest," Eli answered.

Oh right. I was supposed to meet Mira.

"I'll be right down! Can you offer tea or coffee?"

"On it."

Quickly Iris brushed her hair and made sure she didn't have any strange ink smears on her face, as sometimes happened when she was sketching. Then she hurried downstairs to meet their prospective housemate. When she got to the front room, Sally was chatting to Mira like they were old friends, showing off one of her knitting projects—a rainbow scarf to match the rainbow cardigan that Iris envied.

"It's *gorgeous,*" Mira said.

She stood as Iris offered her hand. "Mira Yoon. Well, *technically*, it's Mi-rae, but I go with Mira when I'm in the US. Which is most of the time."

Iris took a seat. The other woman had short hair with a side part and an undercut. She wore a tailored black trouser suit with tasteful accessories, no makeup apart from a hint of lip color. "To recap, your sublet fell through, is that right?"

Mira nodded. "I'm in a bit of a bind."

"Would you like to see the room first?" she asked.

"I think so. If I can't see myself in the space, then there's no point in chatting because I won't be staying, even if we get along well."

"Makes sense. You'd be on the third floor. This way."

Mira didn't say much on the way up, but Iris could tell she was making careful note. She probably noticed that all of the hallways needed to be painted, but that couldn't be helped. At least she and Eli had done the bedrooms. Otherwise, nobody would be tempted by such cramped, dingy offerings. Without fanfare, she opened the door and let Mira have a look. What would deter most people was the wardrobe in place of a proper closet. Technically speaking, this room couldn't be listed as a bedroom because of that.

"It's small," Mira said eventually.

"Yeah, that's why it's priced low. This is the bigger of the two rooms, to be honest."

Immediately, Mira went across the hall with apparent curiosity and peeked in. "Wow, you weren't kidding. This is...more of a nook, isn't it?"

"Yeah. I wasn't even sure if I should rent it at all."

For storage solutions in the tiny room, she'd mounted a short bar on the wall for hanging clothes and set up shelving with cinder blocks and scrap wood she'd found in the shed. She'd painted some crates, and in addition, she'd created a daybed out of palettes and topped it with a new foam mattress. In her own boxes, she'd unearthed a string of fairy lights, and she'd affixed those above the bed. At least the walls were bright, right? Maybe somebody with imagination could do more with the space, as Iris had thought it best to leave the room like a blank canvas.

"This is quite clever," Mira said.

"Thanks. I did the best I could."

When Eli brought out the coffee Mira had requested, he learned that she was upstairs with Iris.

"I like her," Sally said. "The woman asked all kinds of smart questions about my latest project." She raised her knitting bag to illustrate the point.

"Your crafts are beautiful. You should ask Iris about selling a few pieces on her site."

Sally stared at him. "Do you think people would buy them?"

"Absolutely! Handmade knit items are huge."

"I was planning to make everyone something for Christmas... I never even thought about *selling* my work." Sally looked thoughtful.

"I don't care so much about the income. I'm well enough off as it is. But ..."

"What?"

"Would it make people happy to buy something I made?"

Eli smiled. "Absolutely. Not everybody has a relative who knits, and there's something warm and comforting about wrapping up in a scarf that was handcrafted."

"That settles it," Sally said firmly. "I'll talk to Iris later."

Eli heard the voices in the stairway long before he caught a glimpse of Mira and Iris. Sally probably couldn't make out the words, and she was working on her scarf again. "If that's possible, then I think we can move forward," Mira was saying.

"It's no trouble. I can clear the room for you."

"That would be great. I have stuff in storage now, but I'd rather use my bedroom furniture and my own bed." She glanced around the house. "It looks like there would be room for some of my other decorative items as well, if you're willing."

"We can look at everything as a group," Iris said. "But if there are no objections, I'm fine with it. The house should represent everyone, even the common spaces."

"I doubt Henry Dale will care," Eli said.

He wasn't trying to be mean, but the older man just wasn't a "pick out curtains" type of person. Sally agreed with an emphatic nod, her fingers moving in hypnotic patterns.

"That's absolutely right. He'd have strong feelings about the type of kitchen tile we plan to use. Not the pattern."

Mira glanced between them, seeming confused. "Are we replacing the kitchen tile?"

Sally flashed her a gentle look. "Just an example, dear."

While Eli sat and picked up his own coffee, Iris went over the house rules, explaining about the condiment fund and general other points of clarity. Mira nodded along, seeming to approve of what she heard. Iris went on, "As for chores, I haven't come up with a schedule or anything yet. Generally, we pick up after ourselves and wash our own dishes. The washer and dryer is in the basement. I'll probably pay to have the house deep cleaned once a year, and I just had that done recently."

"I noticed how clean everything is," Mira said.

"It's an old house, so there's wear and tear—"

"I could help with that," Mira cut in. "Fact is, I'm a bit short of cash right now because I had to pay for a storage unit. All of my stuff won't fit here, so I need to keep paying for it, which means I was hoping you might be open to a barter arrangement for the deposit."

Eli read Iris's surprise, but she didn't look annoyed. "I'm listening."

Mira took a breath. "Damn. It feels strange being able to say this openly, but...I'm a witch. A tech witch, to be exact. And I can do all kinds of cool updates to the house, if you're willing to accept my services in lieu of cold hard cash."

Sally dropped her knitting needles, eyes wide. "Do you know Ethel? What about Gladys? No, they're old, you probably don't. What about Danica and Clementine? They own Fix-It Witches here in town."

Mira glanced at Sally, seeming startled. "Actually, I do know them. Well, *of* them, anyway. We belong to some of the same online forums, and we've chatted about various projects over the years. I was hoping—eh, we're getting off topic here."

"Are you serious?" Iris asked.

Eli had his own misgivings because if Iris accepted this at face value, Mira might end up living here for free or at least paying only a nominal amount. And it wasn't that he disagreed on principle—the house did need work. And he himself had thought that a tech witch might be the better option instead of doing deep and messy work in the house walls. Hell, from what he'd heard, tech witches could even transform pipes and wiring without needing to touch the plaster. But Iris also needed money to live on; if she kept taking in people and agreeing to barter, she might end up—

No, it's her decision. Not yours.

Mira nodded. "Absolutely. For instance, I could make the woodwork look like new. That would be one spell. I could renew the paint in the hallways upstairs. I could restore the gingerbread or revitalize the peeling exterior. Each task would be an additional spell."

"Doing everything all at once would require too much energy?" Iris guessed.

"Exactly." Mira paused, as if weighing her next words. "You're taking this better than I expected. Some people laugh and say I've read too many magic academy stories. Others get nervous and stop talking to me."

"We're trying not to make it weird," Eli said.

Iris added, "It must be harrowing to come out with it like this."

Mira nodded. "A little. There still some risk involved in self-identification, but I wanted you to know before I moved in."

She must be referring to the proposed legislation that would require a database monitoring all paranormal citizens and the rise of HAPI. Eli had his own fears connected to those issues. He would follow Iris's lead, however. At this point, only she knew about his double nature.

Sally bounced a little in her chair. "I've bothered Ethel and Gladys about this ever since I found out, but they won't tell me anything. Can I ask you a few questions?"

"Sure," Mira said warily.

Eli smothered a smile. He also noticed that Henry Dale was lurking in the hallway outside the kitchen beside the china cabinet full of ceramic angels. The old man was interested but refusing to admit he was. Henry Dale's irascible nature made him endearing rather than annoying. Eli had no idea why he felt that way, but he wanted to look after the old fellow, almost as much as he did Iris.

Sally got started right away. "I don't understand what a tech witch does, exactly. Danica and Clem seem to fix broken machines mostly. But you're talking about refreshing paint? How does that work?"

"'Tech' makes it sound like it needs to be a gizmo with moving parts for me to impact it. But actually, my magic works on pretty much any nonliving thing. Wood is a bit of a gray area because it was alive, but now it isn't. So it's inert if organic. But if you want *repair* work done on it, that's the tech side. If you want a witch to take an old cypress board and turn it into a living tree, that's on the vivimancer side."

Eli blinked. "Is that even possible?"

"It depends on how much...life is left to the board. And

that relates to a lot of esoteric factors that would take me ages to explain."

Henry Dale stomped out into the open. "What's this nonsense? You're all acting like this is real. Don't be taken in by such baloney."

CHAPTER THIRTEEN

"HENRY DALE!" IRIS SCOLDED. "YOU didn't want to hold a séance because you're willing to believe ghosts are real, but you draw the line at witches?"

Before Iris could say more, Mira stood. "I take it this is my other potential roommate?" She stepped toward him and offered a handshake. Looking bemused, Henry Dale accepted, and Mira went on, "Have you ever met a witch?"

"Of course not! They're fictional," the old man snapped.

"See, that's where your analysis breaks down. That would be like you claiming that because you've never met an Italian person, that they too are fictional. I'm a witch. You've met me. And hopefully, you'll see that it's merely one facet of my existence."

At that point, Iris stepped in because she could see that Henry Dale was about to escalate the argument. "So you were saying that you can actually use your magic to update the house?"

"Precisely. I'm willing to do one spell per month for a discount on the rent. Though bear in mind, for larger tasks, I need to break them down into more manageable stages."

That explanation made sense to Iris. Energy was finite, so

Mira wouldn't be able to snap her fingers and restore the whole house exterior. At least, not without more witches to increase the size of her magic pool. Otherwise, she'd be too exhausted to function at her day job. Sally was practically vibrating with excitement over the idea while Iris found Eli more difficult to read. He wasn't openly antagonistic like Henry Dale, but it seemed like he might be reserving judgment.

"Would it be possible to get a tiny demonstration? Not that I don't believe you, but..." She couldn't think of a way to finish that sentence.

"But you'd still like to see for yourself?" Mira's gentle suggestion took the pressure off, and Iris nodded gratefully.

"Me too!" Sally put in.

Henry Dale made a skeptical sound, but she noticed that he didn't make himself scarce either. Instead, he perched on the edge of the sofa next to Eli, as if he had no intention of missing whatever the next step might be. Mira glanced around the house as if seeking something in need of repairs, and Iris promptly pulled out her phone.

"It has a tiny crack, right here." She pointed at the lower right corner of the screen, showing the minor fault to everyone before she handed it over.

"Oh, this will be easy. It's a small problem and quite superficial." The tech witch took the phone and ran her fingers over the front, closing her eyes as she did so. "Everything is fine inside, so..."

A soft glow rose from Mira's fingertips as she smoothed them over Iris's screen, and then she handed the phone back. No nick. No fissure. It looked as it had when Iris had purchased it. *Holy crap.*

"I'm convinced," Sally declared. "You're incredible, Mira! Are you all right, though, dear? Do you need some cookies or orange juice?"

Mira laughed. "I didn't donate blood. Yes, I'm fine. That was a tiny working, so it scarcely impacted my magic at all."

"I've never been to Fix-It Witches," Sally said. "Now I have regrets. I bet their customers love seeing the magic happen."

"Literally," Iris added.

Henry Dale let out a long breath, not a sigh, exactly. And when he spoke, his voice was deeper than usual, laced with regret. "I owe you an apology, young lady. I've made it my policy not to put my faith in fanciful poppycock, but facts are facts, and I'm truly sorry."

"Forgiven and forgotten," Mira said promptly.

"I can waive the deposit," Iris said, refocusing their attention on the original issue. "But I need to decide what to ask in return... unless fixing my phone screen—"

"Oh, definitely not," Mira cut in. "A spell like that would cost less than having it physically fixed at a repair shop. Hmm. I could restore the paint in the hallway on the second floor?"

Iris nodded at once. "Sounds good to me. For each project, I'll discount your rent by 25 percent. Does that seem fair?"

Mira went on, "Definitely! Next month, I'll do the paint on the third floor for a discount on rent. With that, the whole house interior will be bright and fresh. And we can discuss the rest of the updates as we go."

"I like that idea." She paused, trying to decide what else to cover. "It's a three-month rental agreement and…I told you everything else. So are you interested in moving in?"

"Absolutely," Mira said. "But is everyone else okay with it?"

"I'm good," Sally said at once.

Eli nodded.

And Henry Dale didn't object, so Iris took it for agreement.

As did Mira, evidently, because she said, "Then if you give me your banking details, I'll transfer the first month's rent and move in next weekend. Right now, I'm borrowing a friend's couch, but I don't want to outstay my welcome."

"Miz Yoon?" It seemed like Henry Dale had been waiting for a break in the convo, less interested in general logistics, more concerned with a personal request.

Iris glanced at the older man and realized she'd never seen such a tentative expression on his face. She didn't interrupt since this felt like a pivotal moment. Eli and Sally sat quietly as well, watching with interest. Since Henry Dale had apologized, this must be something else, an important something if the gravity of his expression was any guide.

"Yes?" Mira had already stood up, her business concluded for the time being.

"You can decline if it's a lot of trouble, but I was wondering… Does that magic of yours work on *old* technology?"

Mira smiled. "Like a phonograph?"

"Not quite that old." Henry Dale laced his hands together and spoke quickly without looking at anyone directly. "I have a Walkman, a gift from my best friend. He's since passed on, and the thing stopped working twenty years ago. Nobody could get it running, but I didn't have the heart to throw it away. Kept it for sentimental reasons, as it reminds me of good times and Jack. Do you think—?"

"Go get it." Mira sat down with an expectant smile.

Iris expected Henry Dale to say something more, but he complied with an alacrity that made her sad. Something this important—and he owned *so* few things—had been gathering dust without him being able to use it for twenty years, but affection kept him hauling the cassette player around. Soon, Henry Dale returned with the Walkman and a cautiously optimistic look. The expression sat strangely on his weathered features, but he gazed at Mira like she might be the sunrise he'd been waiting but not hoping for.

As she had before, the tech witch cradled the old device in her hands, and a soft brilliance flickered between her fingers. She worked on it longer too, until drops of sweat trickled down her temples. This time, Iris could feel the magic in a way she couldn't before; it drifted over her skin, a mist that hovered somewhere between fog and rain.

In time, Mira opened her eyes and handed it back. "It should work like new. The parts were quite corroded inside, but not beyond my ability to restore. I hope it brings you joy, Henry Dale."

The old man's eyes were actually damp. "I can't thank you enough. If there's ever anything I can do for you, Miz Yoon, tell me right away."

"It was my pleasure." Mira turned to leave, clearly needing a break.

"What kind of music do you listen to?" Eli asked Henry Dale, as Iris followed Mira.

"I only have five tapes left; got rid of the rest years ago. Still got…Jim Croce, Johnny Cash, Aretha Franklin, Rush, and Dolly Parton."

Iris overhead Henry Dale's reply as they reached the foyer, then she said to Mira, "I hope that didn't tire you out too much."

"More than I was planning for, but I could see it meant a lot to him, and he doesn't strike me as someone who easily asks for favors."

Iris smiled then. "You'll fit in perfectly here."

The next day, Eli worked with Henry Dale on sanding the porch.

After getting proof that tech witches could renovate a house with magic, he'd expected the older man to be glum, as that might make it seem as if all their hard work was a waste of time. But Henry Dale gave no sign of such thoughts; he was listening to his Walkman as they worked, lost in his own world.

Music often had that effect, possessing the power to transport a listener to a certain moment in time. For instance, whenever Eli heard "Bad Moon Rising," he remembered the little dance his father did when he was making pancakes, using the spatula as his microphone. He had even fewer memories like that of his mother, but he did recall his mom singing "Ojos Así" while making picadillo for the family.

They were both so young, not much older than I am now. Sobering thought. With effort, he put those thoughts aside. Eli was prone to brooding and "being morose," as Liz put it. *Should be hearing from her soon.*

Better to think about their varied cooking styles. Gamma preferred ABBA when she was making culinary masterpieces like Kraft blue box and barbecued chicken legs. As for Eli, he hummed while he cooked, usually whatever song was currently earworming him.

That's right. Live in the now. Finish the porch.

Since they couldn't sand and stain only the boards they'd replaced without it looking like patchwork, they'd opted to refinish the entire porch. Hopefully, they could wrap up sanding and waterproofing today, before the rain. Tomorrow, it would be staining, which should dry before the weather got even colder.

Wonder what Henry Dale will propose next.

By anyone's standards, Eli had done enough at this point. Hell, Iris didn't even recall the moment of kindness that had changed his life. Yet curiosity kept him here, almost like the universe was nudging people in Iris's direction, slowly helping her realize her dreams. But that made no sense, even less than the family who'd driven however many hours to tell her that she didn't share their blood. And recalling that conversation annoyed him all over again.

"You're looking mighty sour," Henry Dale observed. The orange-foam headphones were around his neck now, signaling his readiness to talk.

"I was just thinking about Iris's so-called family."

Henry Dale curled his lip. "Sally had a lot to say on that subject as well. But I just have the one comment to make."

"What's that?"

"We're all misfits. And that makes us Iris's new family. Do your best, son."

Son. That word put his father back at the forefront of his mind. In ten years, he'd be older than his dad was when he died. Wild, unwelcome thought. He pushed it back into the box marked *SHIT I DO NOT WANT TO THINK ABOUT*, smoothly sanding the wood as if his life depended on it.

"I will," he said quietly.

Later, after he showered to scrub away the fine wood dust, Keshonda called to say there was an offer on Gamma's house. The couple had their financing in order, so everything looked good up front, but it was best not to count the coinage until everyone signed the papers.

"I'm fine to pay closing, as it's their first home. They can schedule the inspection whenever. Thanks for your hard work," he said.

"That's my job. I'll relay the good word to the other agent," Keshonda answered.

To his surprise, Iris knocked on his door as he was getting dressed. Heightened senses told him it was her even through the wood; he recognized her movements, the sound of her breathing, and even the faintest hint of the lotion she used. Probably best not to mention any of that.

"What's up?" he asked, throwing the door open.

She froze, her cheeks flushing bright as a red carnation. Belatedly, Eli realized that he hadn't buttoned up his shirt, but it would be weirder to slam the door in her face now. He maintained a neutral expression, carefully examining the possibility that she liked what she saw as he toweled his hair.

"Um. Yeah. It's tonight. You should… I mean. Put on your shirt all the way and find some shoes. Are you still going?"

That made remarkably little sense, even for Iris.

He stared at her. "What?"

"We agreed to do those ballroom dancing lessons together! I paid for everything and signed us up online. The first class is tonight."

Ohhhh. Holy shit, this is happening.

"Sorry, I didn't realize. Give me fifteen minutes and we can go."

She pressed a hand to her head, pretending she'd been about to faint. "Oh thank God. I would've been upset to waste that money. It's not like I'm rolling in it, and I keep bartering with people." Quickly, she added, "Not that I regret those decisions, but—"

"Things are tighter than you expected currently." She didn't need to explain her situation to anyone, least of all him.

Her smile widened, showing a hint of dimples. "Yeah. I finally earned a payout from my shop, but it's not much."

"Yet," he said.

"Anyway, I need to get changed too. Wait for me downstairs, okay?"

"Right, yes."

Eli got ready quickly, dressing as he would for a date in dress shirt and slacks with shoes that he hoped were suitable for ballroom dancing. He tried looking it up on his phone, but the search told him all about dance sneakers, which he didn't own. So he went with dark tennis shoes, hoping for the best. He found Iris in the front room, and oh lord, she had on the prettiest dress, all floral and swirly. Chunky, strappy heels on her feet, her hair tumbling around her shoulders, mink-brown shot with gold, and her *eyes*, gray as a stormy sea. His heart went wild in his chest, just gazing at her. Maybe she'd imprinted on him when he was young or something because nobody else *ever* made him feel this way, and he had *no* idea what to do about it.

"Have fun," Sally called. "I'll make sure the old man eats something."

"Don't call me that. You're not much younger than me," Henry Dale snapped.

Leaving them to bicker, Eli grabbed his keys from the bowl near the front door and headed to his truck. He hurried to open the passenger door for Iris, not realizing it might seem strange until she shot him a weird look as she hopped in.

"Thanks?" Her tone made it clear she was confused, though.

Don't mess this up.

He took a deep breath and forced himself to relax, offering a smile that he hoped didn't look strained or nervous. Sometimes when he focused too hard on looking happy, it came out seeming more like a grimace of pain. Getting photos taken had been nonstop fun. He could still hear Gamma saying, "Eli, no! Stop making that face. You look like someone is pinching you."

"Sorry, my brain wires got crossed. We're both dressed like this, and—"

"Oh! Yeah, I can see how that would happen. It does feel sort of date-ish," she said easily, buckling her seat belt. "Do you know where the community center is?"

"Not off the top of my head. Can you navigate?"

"On it!" Iris said cheerfully.

CHAPTER FOURTEEN

IRIS HADN'T EVEN KNOWN THAT the community center had a ballroom.

Well, it probably doubled as a studio, offering ballet or other types of dance lessons for kids. Not that she'd spent any time here personally—she'd just scoped the place out online when she registered for lessons. In any event, the space was perfect with a wall lined with mirrors and a gleaming wood floor. The other couples assembled were all much older, in their sixties or seventies, but the notice hadn't said there were any age restrictions.

She grabbed Eli's hand before he could chicken out, as he took a step back when all heads swiveled in their direction. Though she was nervous too, she'd made up her mind to try new things in this fresh start, not to let anxiety get the best of her. So nobody was reneging on this deal.

Not me. Not him.

The instructor was a lithe woman in her forties who clapped her hands in excitement. "There's our last couple now. We were just introducing ourselves. I'm Norma Jean Martinson, and no, you can't call me Marilyn."

Everyone said their names again for Iris and Eli's benefit, and Iris gave up trying to recall all the names halfway through. Only four of them stuck—Leonard, Gladys, Howard, and Hazel. Leonard was a tall distinguished man with heavy brows, broad shoulders, and silver hair, while Gladys was a small round woman with white hair and dark skin. She had the smile of an angel too. Hazel was plump with a puffy perm, while Howard was thin and lanky, peering at the world through horn-rimmed glasses.

"Good to meet you," Iris said four or five times.

"It's a pleasure," Eli added.

"Likewise," Hazel said. "Are you new to St. Claire? I don't recognize you, and I know almost everyone."

"It's true," Howard agreed.

"Newish. I inherited property from my great-aunt—"

"Oh, you're the new owner of Violet Gables," Gladys cut in.

"Violet Gables?" she repeated.

"Oh, you don't know the story?" Hazel tried to fill her in, but Norma Jean clapped her hands again, this time more peremptorily.

"That's enough chitchat. We're here to dance, right? So let's get started."

Belatedly, Iris realized just how close she'd be to Eli for the next two hours. Somehow, she hadn't factored that in, but she offered her gamest smile as he extended his hand and pulled her into the correct position. This close, she could smell the soapy clean smell of his skin and hints of pine and juniper that teased her senses. His hand was firm and strong in hers, and the other curved carefully at her waist.

At first, it was awkward, and she couldn't keep the beat. She stumbled and stepped on his feet. He never complained. Never faltered. And then…everything shifted, as if the world vanished apart from his golden eyes. One night, while getting some fresh air, she'd seen him gracefully glide through his bedroom window, and she could see Eli's hawk aspect, even in his human form, quietly watching, waiting, though for what, she had no clue. His movements guided hers, step and spin, four paces, back, forward, the music laying the magical lines they followed. Iris could have danced for two more hours when the melody suddenly stopped. Honestly, it was like being freed from a spell that prevented her from detecting the passage of time.

She gazed up at him for a long moment in breathless silence, and she saw…his mouth. A smile meant just for her. It was as if he *lived* for her. No, that was absurd, one of her wild flights of imagination. But before she could make sense of her chaotic impressions, Hazel and Gladys were beside her.

Gladys said, inexplicably, in an oddly formal tone, "It has been a long, long time since we welcomed one of your kinfolk. Please let me know if there is anything I can do to keep the peace, Lady."

Uh, what?

The statement felt weighted. She didn't get a chance to pursue that, as Hazel bumbled into the conversation, fairly glowing with anticipation. "You might not know this, but I was friends with your great-aunt back in the day. Are you interested in hearing why we called her house Violet Gables?"

As it turned out, the story wasn't as riveting as Hazel imagined, having to do with Anne of Green Gables, some homemade apple wine, and Great-Auntie's impulsive decision to paint her house purple. And while Hazel recounted that long-ago evening, the rest of the class trickled out, including Gladys and Leonard. Iris listened to every last word, feeling glad that Great-Aunt Gertie once had friends like Hazel, at least.

The other woman sighed, evidently realizing that Norma Jean wanted to lock up. "Looks like I've done it again, talked too much and made a nuisance of myself."

"That's why we like you," Howard said in a bracing tone.

"You're just saying that." But Hazel seemed pleased with the comment, a touch of pink in her round cheeks.

"I'd love to hear any stories you might want to share about Great-Aunt Gertie," Iris added. "You're welcome to come by and chat."

She gave Hazel her phone number, and the older couple walked out with Iris and Eli, who didn't open the door for her this time. *Why does that bother me? I can't afford for things to get complicated between us.* No, this was clearly for the better. Boundaries shouldn't get blurred when they lived together. The parking lot was almost empty, just Eli's truck and Howard's car.

Before Iris got into the truck, Howard said, "I hear you're living with my ex-wife."

Oh, wow.

"*You're* Sally's ex?" she exclaimed.

"That's me. I just...well. Can you make sure she's all right? Things didn't work out for us, but she's not used to being on her own."

"There are four of us in the house," Eli pointed out. "Sally isn't alone."

"Right. The woman lands on her feet, I'll grant her that. I heard she's dating—"

"So are you," Hazel snapped. "If you keep this up, I'll never go out with you again."

"I think this is our cue," Eli whispered.

Iris couldn't get in the truck fast enough while the old couple argued in the community center parking lot. She could understand Howard being concerned for his ex, but it was a bit insensitive to leave his date standing while he asked about Sally. *Ugh. So awkward.* But she smiled faintly as a sudden thought occurred to her.

"I hate when people pester me about what's making me smile," Eli said softly.

"But you're curious?" She grinned. "It just dawned on me... We think everything will be clear by their age. We'll have it all figured out, right? But living with Sally and Henry Dale has clarified a few things."

"Like?"

For Iris, it felt like a critical insight because it took the pressure off. There was no deadline after all to get her shit sorted and get all her ducks in a row. "Some people don't like ducks," she said, forgetting that Eli couldn't read her mind. "Or rows for that matter. Why do the ducks have to be in a row? What if they prefer circles?"

"You lost me," Eli said.

"Okay, back to my original point. Older people don't know what they should be doing either. They've lived longer and seen more, and they've learned some things, sure. But it doesn't mean they automatically have all the answers or act exactly like they should."

"From cradle to grave, there's a learning curve," he agreed with a gentle smile.

Eli never pictured himself taking dance lessons, but since reuniting with Iris, he'd been stepping out of his comfort zone more and more.

"I had fun tonight," Iris said, almost as if she could read his thoughts.

"Me too. I'm looking forward to the next class."

"I wonder what Hazel can tell me about Great-Aunt Gertie. I'm living in her house, and I feel a tad guilty about it because I didn't know her well. And I wonder if it's okay for me to be there. Because…"

He glanced at her, taking his eyes from the road only briefly. His sharpened senses made night driving easier, but there was no reason to be careless. "Because of what you found out recently?"

He couldn't bring himself to say "you're not biologically related" when that wasn't her fault.

"Yeah," she whispered. "That."

"I think it's enough that you care," he said. "The rest of your family doesn't."

"Well, Olive is cut from different cloth, but—"

"She's not here. Have you spoken to your dad since you got the news?"

"Not yet. But historically, he takes the path of least resistance. Whatever allows him to peacefully read books about ancient Rome."

"Write him a note and put it in a biography of Julius Caesar. That way you know he'll see it."

Iris finally smiled, lightening the load in Eli's heart. "Thanks. You always know what to say. It's wild how good you are at getting me out of the bad place in my head."

Eli didn't know how to respond to that, so he changed the subject. "Was it me, or did the other lady…Gladys? Seem a bit…strange?"

"You noticed that too? It was so weird how she mentioned my kinfolk and called me 'lady.' Like, it didn't sound like, 'Hey, lady, move your car or else!' It felt more like a title?" She made a softly disparaging sound. "Eh, that probably doesn't—"

"No, I agree with you." He cut her off because she was likely about to start second-guessing herself. Her so-called family had really done a number on her self-esteem. Now Iris acted like she was wrong about *everything*.

"Hmm. I do wonder what that was about. Do you think Hazel would know anything? I—oh." Her phone beeped. "She just texted me! She wants to come over tomorrow."

"I think you might've made a new best friend," Eli noted.

It was sweet the way she collected people. On some level, maybe they sensed her innate goodness. She'd demonstrated it for him long ago, and the warmth he felt for her was only growing as he got to know her. Before, it had been gratitude and curiosity, and now—well, he refused to pin a name on these emotions.

"I could always use more friends," she replied cheerfully. "Seems like she's bringing fresh-baked corn muffins and homemade raspberry jam."

"Tea or coffee, then?" He didn't really care about the answer, but as Iris gave full consideration to the question, the unease he'd noticed disappeared.

Halfway to the house, the rain he'd seen coming earlier in the day broke, rolling thunder and snaps of lightning flashing far on the horizon. The rain fell in sheets, spattering the truck and pavement. He switched on the defrost to keep the windows from fogging up and set the wipers to the right speed. Iris didn't seem to notice any of that, and by the time they got home, she'd decided that coffee would be best. "Tea is for tiny cakes and finger sandwiches, right? I'll definitely make coffee for Hazel. I wonder if Sally will be home..."

"You should ask her," he said, parking the truck behind Iris's car.

Lights were ablaze in the house, golden rectangles of warmth that promised Sally and Henry Dale were there going about their business. That was an unexpectedly welcome realization, as his other properties were always dark—cool and inviolate spaces that offered silence and privacy. There were no baskets of knitting, no dog-eared paperbacks. Henry Dale had a collection of well-loved books, and he would read the same stories until the bindings fell apart. Already, Eli was planning to get him a collector's edition copy of *The Last Unicorn* for Christmas.

If I'm still here by then. Briefly, he imagined the house covered in lights; he and Henry Dale would spend two days decorating, just to make it beautiful for Iris. Violet Gables would be a stately grand dame wreathed in snow, icicles dangling from the newly repaired gingerbread trim. Inside, the place would smell of sugar cookies and peppermint bark; something told him Sally would make all kinds of treats. All of that was a few months off, and he couldn't stay here forever.

I can't, right?

No. Not without telling Iris everything.

Iris bounded out of the vehicle before he could stop her, and she gaped up at the sky in sudden realization as the rain pelted down. He rounded the truck and pulled off his jacket, lifting it above her head. She didn't argue; instead, they raced around the house together, as the front porch was still roped off from the work earlier. Both of them were drenched despite his best efforts by the time they came in through the mudroom behind the kitchen.

Eli kicked off his sneakers while Iris toed off her heels, tugging at her damp dress in little flutters. She was beautiful, even bedraggled like this, with water spangled on her skin like silvery sequins. He had a powerful urge to touch her, but he made himself step back instead of yielding to it, giving her a clear path into the house. But she didn't move. She stared up at him with an expression that tugged at his heartstrings, an inexorable pull.

"I made hot tea," Sally called.

Iris quickly shook her head, as if dismissing some strange thought, and her smile didn't look as it usually did when she brushed past. "You're a lifesaver!"

After hanging up his coat, Eli followed.

Sally smiled at him. "What would you like, my dear? The water is hot, and we've got apple cinnamon, lemon ginger, chamomile, and English breakfast."

"Chamomile." Lord knew he could use a calming drink right about then. "I'll be right back. I need to put on some dry clothes."

That wasn't a lie, but the real truth was he needed a solitary moment to get his head in order. *You're* not *allowed to fall for her. That would be ridiculous under the circumstances.* And yet she had so many endearing facets, so much that made it difficult not to—

He cut the thought with the sharpest of mental shears and continued onward up the stairs, ignoring the rise and fall of feminine voices as Iris and Sally chatted over tea. He pulled on warm socks, athletic pants, and a gray hoodie. Warm, comfortable clothing that should have felt like being enfolded in a hug, but the clothes didn't do the trick. Truth was, he'd wanted to kiss Iris in the mudroom.

He still wanted that.

Oh hell. I'm in so much trouble.

CHAPTER FIFTEEN

FOR ONCE IRIS WOKE FEELING energized and excited.

Business was picking up at the store—twelve orders today—and she was making friends. Even if Hazel was older, she still counted, not to mention Sally, Henry Dale, and Eli. Eh, best *not* to focus on Eli. He was altogether too sweet and hot for her own peace of mind.

The bathroom was free when she went down, so she took a quick shower and continued to the kitchen in her robe. She could hear Eli and Henry Dale working outside on the front porch, and Sally seemed to be gone already. Iris made toast for breakfast and took it upstairs along with her coffee. Today was overcast, just as yesterday had been, so it was cozy tucked beneath the eaves of the roof as she got to work sketching new designs.

She didn't break focus until she got a message from Olive, much later in the day.

Olive: Just checking in. You doing okay?

Iris: Probably tough to believe, but I am. What about you?

Olive: I'm not the one who's recovering from a bombshell.

Iris: That reads like deflection.

Olive: If you must know, I might have...fallen for someone here. But there are barriers.

Iris: Oh. I feel like I should say something pithy like, "All you need is love," or "Love finds a way," but those might just be old song titles. Whatever you decide, I'm rooting for you.

Olive: That helps, more than you know.

Iris: I'm glad I didn't lose you in the family lotto.

Olive: You'll never lose me.

After the text convo ended, Iris felt warm and fuzzy, but she also realized how stiff she was. *I have to get a better chair.* That was the *first* thing she'd spend money on once her store was earning more. Tomorrow, she'd make a few new necklaces since the old ones were almost sold out. *Now there's a problem I couldn't have imagined, even a month ago.*

Iris went downstairs in time to see Eli and Henry Dale hauling in boxes. *Wow. I should have expected this.* These cartons had been stored at Delphine and Roger's place since college. There was no correspondence, just a delivery from the freight company. She glared at the boxes and nudged one with her foot, fighting the urge to kick it.

This is my stuff anyway.

"Are you okay?" Eli asked.

"I don't know. Let's take these to the basement, I guess. I'll go through them later. I'll pay you handsomely in grilled cheese sandwiches?"

"I do enjoy a fine grilled cheese," Henry Dale said, picking up a box.

Eli followed suit. "As do I."

With Iris pitching in, it only took four trips to get all her stuff to the cellar. If she hadn't needed any of this stuff in five years, she should streamline, right? *I'll worry about that later.* As promised, she made grilled cheese for everyone and raised the guys a can of creamy tomato soup.

"Thank you, Miz Collins. That was tasty," Henry Dale said.

She laughed as the men made their way out. "Come back anytime."

Later that afternoon, Hazel dropped in. The older woman was clad in a blue tracksuit, and she was *wearing* a ginger cat, like, on her chest, as one would do with a baby. "This is Goliath," Hazel said, handing over a decorative gift box.

She glanced around with interest, and she smiled over the changes Iris had made. "Love what you've done with the place. Oh, and there's Gertie's angel collection, completely untouched. You're a saint! It would mean *so* much to her, knowing that you didn't just sell them off piece by piece to various collectors."

Iris didn't know what to say. Of course it *had* occurred to her, but so far, she hadn't bothered to look into it, so she was being praised for being apathetic and unmotivated. She couldn't bring herself to set the record straight, not when Hazel was beaming at her.

"You know the way to the kitchen? I'll make some coffee."

Iris measured out the ground beans and put them in the filter. This coffeemaker had to be twenty years old, but it still worked fine. Hazel took a seat at the table, admiring the work Henry Dale had done in the kitchen.

"My word, it looks just like it did twenty-five years ago. Gertie always wanted to get quartz counters in here, but then she learned how costly they were, and she decided the butcher block would do."

"I like the wood," Iris confessed. "It balances the black and white."

"That's what I said!" Hazel opened the box she'd brought and set out a container of corn muffins. Then she produced a jar of dark-red jam tied with a yellow-gingham ribbon. Goliath wriggled in the cat sling and tried to touch everything with curious ginger paws while Hazel gently nudged his pink beans away from the food with the air of one who was practically a professional cat wrangler.

"This looks amazing. Let me make a plate for Eli and Henry Dale, then I'll be right back to chat."

It had become common practice for Iris to bring them coffee and a snack. While she wasn't sure about Eli, Henry Dale absolutely would skip meals, and now that his beloved Walkman was fixed, he'd get lost in the work and the music. Frankly, it was cute as hell to pop out the front door and hear him humming "9 to 5" or some other Dolly hit.

To her surprise, when she returned, Hazel had four cups of coffee ready to go. "I thought they'd probably want a drink to go with those muffins."

"Thank you! I should feel guilty since you're a guest, but—"

"Oh, I was here a lot before Gertie passed." A cloud flickered across Hazel's determinedly cheerful face. "We were close, you could say. And you still keep the cups and things exactly where she did."

"Be right back! I promise this'll be the last interruption."

This time, Eli met her inside, taking the mugs with a smile so warm that it did things to her insides. *Whew. Okay. Take a break. Be cool.*

"Thanks. We've almost got the stain done. Hopefully the rain holds off for a few more hours."

"We can dream," she said airily.

Iris wheeled and practically ran back inside. She was far too aware of him. Maybe the dance lessons hadn't been so great after all. When she returned to the kitchen, she found Hazel gazing wistfully out the window. From here, she could see into the backyards of the people who lived on the next street. At this time of year, there were covered aboveground pools and grimy playsets, bicycles turned on their sides and basketballs gone wrinkly with exposure.

"Now then, did you honestly want to hear some stories about Gertie, or were you being polite?" Hazel asked.

"I do want to learn more. I remember that I loved visiting her, but I was pretty young, and I've forgotten a lot of details. I'd like to feel that I know her better since…"

"Since you're here, bringing Violet Gables to life again."

Iris smiled, relieved that Hazel got it. "That's exactly it."

"Well, I first met Gertie in summer of 1976. I was twenty and trying to convince my parents that I didn't want to get married. I wanted to go to college, not secretarial school either. But *they* said I could either get married or pay my own way, and they didn't see how I could manage."

Iris had seen her great-aunt's date of birth on various

documents, so she did the mental math. "That would have made her thirty-two, quite a bit older than you."

"Oh yes. But I admired her. She never married, and I was curious how she made ends meet. We went to the same church, so I tried to get to know her. It wasn't easy. Gertie had no patience for silly questions."

"So what happened?"

"I got married like my parents wanted. Raised a couple of kids, and now I have grandchildren. Unlike Gertie, I picked the conventional path. But we got together every week to work in the garden. We'd rotate, hers or mine. We made apple wine together here, right in the basement, and got drunker than skunks. My husband was *not* amused by that, let me tell you."

These little details might not mean much to anyone else, but Iris loved hearing them. "Did you ever find out why she didn't get married?"

Hazel pressed her lips together briefly. "All she ever said on the subject was that she loved somebody who didn't love her back."

"That's so sad."

Hazel nodded. "Found out later that she'd taken care of her father until he passed away, leaving her alone in this big house. But it's not all sad. As soon as she could, she went traveling. I think she was gone for a whole year."

"Oh my god, that explains the matchbook collection." Iris jumped up and retrieved them to show Hazel. "Just look."

With reverent hands, the older woman sorted through what was left of Gertrude Van Doren's memories. "This takes me back. She had a story for each one of these. I wish I could tell them like she did."

"It would mean a lot to me if you tried, next time we get together," Iris said.

"You mean that?" Hazel blinked a bit, as if she might be fighting off tears. Then she sighed. "I always felt like this place should be full of people. I'm *so* glad you're here."

Unaccountably, tears filled Iris's eyes too, and she reached across the table to take Hazel's hand in hers. "Me too. It feels like I've come home."

Yard sale. Rummage sale.

Whatever the right name for it, they were having one. Eli had been hauling stuff all day. Last week, Iris's crappy family had sent all her belongings, and she'd sorted them, determining what could be sold for fun and profit. Plus, Mira was moving in later, and with the ruckus being created by the amount of used goods currently arrayed on the front lawn, Susan from next door might have a stroke. As he understood it, anything that didn't sell would be donated.

Along with Iris's old stuff, they were also offering the last of Gertrude Van Doren's worldly goods apart from the ceramic angels. Iris had donated some things earlier, but she'd held back some items she wasn't sure about—in case they were needed for furnishings or because she couldn't decide if the stuff should stay or go. Evidently, she was sure now.

Henry Dale grumbled beneath his breath. "I don't see why I'm even doing this. Not getting anything out of it. Neither are you, for that matter."

"The time has come for me to speak the truth." Eli grinned,

drawing out the momentous pause. "It's because you're a nice person beneath your grouchy exterior."

Henry Dale gave him a filthy look, but Eli glimpsed the hint of a smile crinkling the older man's eyes as he turned away to arrange the goods in a more orderly fashion. From Iris, there were old shoes and clothes, some crafts and knickknacks. From Gertrude, they had a few amateur paintings, canning supplies, some larger furniture pieces, and other odds and ends. Eli had no clue if this was even worth the time, but he did know that rummage sales were popular around here.

With the sun shining down, people wandered in and out for most of the morning. Iris joined them and peered in the tin box they were using to collect the cash. "Wow. Somebody bought the bed set I was using in Mira's room?"

"Fifty dollars for a bed, mattress, and dresser is a steal," Eli pointed out.

"I suppose so. You did tell them I had the mattress cleaned recently?"

"We did," Henry Dale answered.

Today was perfect for an outdoor event, brighter than usual but not so warm that it was a hardship to be outside. Perfect sweater weather, in fact, the kind of day that should end curled up with somebody special with a romantic movie playing. *And here I go again.* He really couldn't keep a lid on these thoughts when Iris was around.

She hurried off to intercept a kid who was about to see if the vase he was holding was breakable. Spoiler, it was. He laughed as the mother apologized profusely and tried to pay for the damage while Iris waved away the offer. In the end, they compromised and she took five bucks to assuage the woman's conscience. Eli got a broom and dustpan to sweep the broken glass up from the gravel driveway.

"Oh, you're two steps ahead of me. Thanks! I'm planning to split the proceeds with you and Henry Dale, by the way. Just so you don't think I'm making you work for nothing."

"You're not making me work," Eli said gently.

Like most other days, Sally had gone over to a friend's house. Actually, she spent a *lot* of her time with Ethel, come to think of it. Eli didn't want to make assumptions, but he did wonder if romance was blooming in that direction. Not that it was his business.

At the end of the day, there were only four boxes left. The charity service took them, and that truck was just pulling away when Mira showed up. That must have set their cranky neighbor off because Susan slammed out of her house, storming across the sea of dead leaves with an expression that boded ill for residential peace.

"I have *tried* to be tolerant, Lord knows that I have. But this is the last straw! Constant noise. Constant traffic. If I could, I'd sell my house and move, that's how terribly you're behaving!"

Mira seemed to catch the last part of that tirade as she got out of the truck, and she glanced at Eli and then Iris. "Uh, hi?"

"I'm sorry for..." Here, Iris stumbled because she didn't even seem to know what she should be apologizing for.

Her shoulders rounded.

And he couldn't stand seeing her this way, hurt and beaten down, searching for excuses that she had no earthly reason to make. Today, Eli couldn't fight off the urge to step in, regardless of whether it was his place. "To my knowledge, there's no law against holding a yard sale. And that was the last of Gertrude Van Doren's things."

"I'll head inside," Mira said, wisely choosing not to engage.

Susan scowled, focusing her wrath on Eli. "You have no right to get involved. You're just the handyman."

"I'm her roommate. And don't cut me off, I had more to say. You've never *once* expressed condolences to Iris for losing a loved one, so if anyone is guilty of bad manners, it's you, woman."

Susan's eyes widened, and she sucked in a shocked breath. "How many of you *are* there, exactly? Are you freaks starting a commune?"

He ignored her, continuing with his verbal takedown. He might be quiet, but everybody had a tipping point. "If you can sell your house, please do. Then maybe we can make friends with whoever replaces you. So move along. You're not welcome here."

To his amazement, the others acted as if he'd spoken for them as well. Henry Dale and Iris left Susan spluttering in the yard, and eventually, she was forced to return home when nobody would acknowledge her. Eli stepped right into the back of Mira's U-Haul, handing boxes to Iris and Henry Dale. When Mira returned, she seemed a little shaken by the encounter, but she soon threw herself into unloading.

With four people pitching in, it didn't take long to empty the truck. Everything was piled in the foyer, of course, so there were more trips up-and-downstairs. Henry Dale eventually tapped out and wandered off to his room to rest. Eli kept going until the last carton reached Mira's room on the third floor. Iris stayed to the end as well.

"That was painless, apart from the woman ranting when I got here," Mira said, blowing out a breath. "Thanks for helping out."

"The other neighbors are fine," Iris said quickly. "I don't know why, but Susan has an axe to grind for some reason."

Mira nodded. "It happens. At my last place, the neighbor would constantly leave passive-aggressive notes on the door."

"What kind?" Eli asked, idly curious.

At the condo, he rarely saw anyone else. He had the impression most owners were absentee and only rented the units for income. In fact, he couldn't recall the last place where he'd even known his neighbor's name. Probably in college—in the dorms?

"Stuff like, 'Your mail is overflowing the box. Please collect the sale flyers or discard them; they're making the building look messy.'"

"Oh, *that* kind," Iris said with a shiver.

"We were planning to make dinner to welcome you unless you have other plans," Eli said to Mira.

The other woman smiled. "No plans yet. So thank you. That sounds good."

CHAPTER SIXTEEN

IRIS *DEFINITELY* WASN'T JEALOUS THAT Eli had offered to fix dinner for Mira.

That was just who he was. He often cooked for her and for Henry Dale, Sally too, when she was home at mealtimes. There was no reason to think he meant anything by it. Even if Mira was really cute and she seemed to have her life together as well. Well, apart from the minor hiccup of an unexpected breakup with her girlfriend, but that only proved that someone had liked her well enough to move in with her.

I've never even gotten to that point.

Iris stifled a sigh and tried to give herself a mental pep talk. Maybe it was the run-in with Susan before, but she'd lost the happy glow from earlier in the week. The amount she earned from the shop still wasn't enough to live on, and she wasn't getting as much as she'd hoped from the house either. Sure, she still thought it was a good decision to have Mira update certain things using her magic, but—

"Are you helping or what?" Eli beckoned from the kitchen doorway, soothing some of her spiky edges.

He included me in that offer from the start. Oh. That means...we. Us.

Much happier now for reasons she refused to contemplate, Iris took two steps, then paused. "You can start unpacking if you want. We'll call you when the food is ready."

Mira inhaled softly, a hint of unsteadiness in her voice. "This...means a lot to me. We're basically strangers, and you took me in on the most tenuous of connections. I'm trying not to show it, but...things are really tough right now."

Impulsively, Iris backtracked and opened her arms. "Hug? Totally fine if you'd rather not. Like you said, we don't know each other well yet."

"I'm not a hugger," Mira said. "Unless I've known someone for a long time. But I do appreciate the thought. I'll be upstairs."

Judging by how the woman rushed off, Iris guessed Mira would probably burst into tears as soon as the door closed behind her. Iris caught up with Eli in the kitchen, where he was chopping potatoes into fine cubes. Intrigued, she watched him mince up the onions and tomatoes in the same way.

"What're you making?" she asked.

"Picadillo. My mom's recipe, or at least that's what Gamma says. She wrote it down before Mom passed away."

She glanced over at him, locked on to the fact that he hadn't mentioned his family much at all before. Actually, she knew more about Sally and Henry Dale than she did about Eli. "You don't remember her making it for you?"

"I *do* recall eating it, and I have faint memories of her singing and cooking. She liked Shakira." He paused, staring down at the ingredients sizzling in the skillet. "I was six when she passed away."

"I'm sorry," Iris said.

Eli lifted a shoulder. "It's okay. I don't talk about her a lot. My dad died seven years later, and I moved to St. Claire to live with Gamma."

"Ah, so that's what you meant when you said were sort of from here." *Crap, I should be more sensitive when he's opening up.* "Sorry for your loss."

Eli didn't look at her, busy sautéing the garlic, potatoes, and onions in olive oil. He added the tomatoes next. "It was a long time ago. Can you defrost some peas and carrots?"

It seemed pretty clear that he was done talking about his sad past, so she took the hint. "Sure. How much?"

"About a cup. There's an open bag in the freezer... A minute or two in the microwave should do it." With a little flourish, Eli crumbled the ground beef into the hot pan, where it made a satisfying hiss. "Can you make some tomato broth?"

Iris hadn't even known they *had* this in the kitchen, but in the cupboard, she found four jars of stock powder—chicken, beef, vegetable, and tomato. While he browned the beef, she dutifully mixed a cup, and he added it to the pan. In that moment, she realized how *much* she enjoyed watching him cook. Part of why this house felt like home? It was Eli.

And that was a *terrifying* realization.

He shot her a concerned look, now that everything was coming together for the meal. "You okay? I noticed that you seemed down earlier."

Wow, he reads me that well?

Iris decided to tell him part of the truth. "Honestly? I was thinking that at least Mira had someone who loved her enough to move in with her. As a partner, I mean. I've never even gotten there." She sighed softly. "Hell, the last person I dated decided my sister Lily was the better option. Wait, should I still call her that?"

"That's up to you," Eli said, carefully tending to the food in the skillet, which was starting to look sort of like corned beef hash.

She'd never tasted picadillo, but it smelled amazing, and the aroma only became richer when he added peas, carrots, and various spices to it. "What is?"

"Whether you still consider them family. Apart from Gamma, I'm not close to anyone in my family. On my mother's side, I have relatives in Veracruz." Eli turned off the burner, moved the skillet to a cool burner, and then started setting out sour cream, hot sauce, and the like, along with a bag of tostadas. "But that's not the point. Don't waste a second on some asshole who picked her over you."

Why did it feel so good hearing that, especially from him? He'd seen Lily and Rose too, which meant he had some basis for comparison. She forced herself to stay on the far side of the table, not to hug him like she wanted to.

"I've warned you, right? About being so nice to me."

He smiled, and her heart turned over. "I guess I'm a slow learner."

The look built between them, becoming powerful enough that Iris almost, almost closed the distance. What she would've done, she had no idea. Just as well that he ended the moment by turning away. Eli knocked on Henry Dale's door while Iris called Mira down.

"We're having hash?" Henry Dale asked with a dubious look.

"Picadillo," Eli corrected. "We have tortillas if you'd rather eat it that way. I didn't make rice. I usually put it on tostadas."

"This looks delicious," Mira said.

Iris bit her lip as a worrisome thought occurred to her. "You *do* eat meat? Sorry, we should have asked."

"Yep, I'm an omnivore. I don't know if it's related to the type of magic vivimancers use, but they're more likely to be vegan," Mira said, taking her seat.

"Interesting," Eli said.

Henry Dale eyed the food, but he followed Eli's example and put a spoon of picadillo on the tostada, then topped it with a drizzle of cream and a swirl of hot sauce. He took his first bite and smiled. "This is darn tasty."

Iris was too busy enjoying her own tostada to say much, so she let the others carry the conversation. She wondered if Eli spoke Spanish. If his mom died when he was six, he might have lost the language and all ties to that side of his family. That struck her as sad.

Maybe I could help him get in touch…if he even wants that.

After dinner, Eli allowed himself to be shooed away from the sink by Henry Dale.

The old man had an unshakable work ethic, and as he put it, "If I ate your food without bestirring myself, then I wash up. Nonnegotiable."

Mira stood, rubbing her stomach with a satisfied smile. "I think I'm going to like it here. You fed me, and now I'm not doing the dishes."

"It's your first day," Eli said gently. "Get settled in."

Iris added, "We already talked about it, and you have first pick for the bathroom since you have to be at work."

"I always shower at five," said Henry Dale.

Mira blinked. "Eh, I don't need to be up *that* early. Seven will be fine."

"We can talk about the rest later. But if you run into annoyances, let's talk about them before they become resentments," Iris said.

Eli smiled. That was just like her, really.

"Are you sure you make jewelry?" Mira joked.

"Oh? Why?" Iris asked.

Mira said, "Because you seem like you'd be an awesome therapist."

Iris laughed. "Well, maybe I have the temperament for it, but I couldn't get through all the schooling."

Henry Dale glanced over his shoulder as he soaped up the plates. "That's nothing to be ashamed of. College isn't for everyone. I never went."

"I graduated with a degree in nonprofit management," Mira said. "And I have the debt to prove it."

As he put the last of the leftovers in the fridge, Eli realized everyone was looking at him. "Oh, my turn?"

"Unless you'd rather not." Iris always tried to put him at ease, never pushing him.

"I majored in app development." He didn't say anything

about debt, as he'd paid that off after he sold his senior project. Most of his classmates had gone to work for someone else, but he'd gotten lucky.

"So flipping houses is a side hustle?" Iris asked.

"Whoa, you flip houses *and* develop apps?" Mira looked so impressed that he didn't have the heart to tell them that Gamma's house was the first and only.

Unless you count this place. There wouldn't be any flipping, however, unless Iris tapped out because of Susan's nonsense. Theoretically, he supposed it was possible that she'd sell after he, Henry Dale, and Mira put the shine back in the old house. Now that Eli had some experience with renovations and updates, he might turn his attention to the Myrtle Beach cottage he owned. It was a sunshine-yellow haven two miles from the ocean, nothing special, but he'd gotten a great deal, and he might fix it up someday.

But the idea of doing that alone sent a spike of loneliness straight through his heart. He couldn't tell anyone about his condo or the Myrtle Beach cottage—at least not without revealing the fact that he'd moved in under false pretenses. The idea of losing all the connections he'd formed made him break out in a cold sweat, clutching the edge of the table with desperate hands.

"Usually just the app thing," Eli said, realizing they were all waiting for him to respond to Mira's compliment.

"If you make a profit on the house you're flipping, will you look for your next project?" Iris wanted to know.

Now was the time to tell her that he'd met her before. *Go ahead, make it casual. Something like, "Hey, funny story, I finally remembered where I know you from, Iris..."*

Instead, he only got out, "I don't think so."

"A pity," Henry Dale said. "I'd have been willing to look at properties with you, give you an expert opinion on which places have the best bones."

"That's such a weird saying," Mira noted.

Iris pretended to shiver. "I prefer my houses *without* bones."

"Let me do the dishes in peace, you smart alecks." Henry Dale waved the dish towel at them, and Eli slipped out while the women teased the older man.

I have to get away.

From his guilty thoughts, from fear that he'd end up hurting Iris, even with good intentions. Since it wasn't raining, he needed to fly. Barely keeping his shit together, he ran upstairs and locked his door, undressed, and opened his window. Out into the night, hawk form borne aloft on the crisp autumn breeze. He glimpsed a bonfire several streets over, mice skittering from house to house, and cats prowling after them. Night was *alive,* and he drank it in as he flew, silently observing St. Claire from his great height.

Oddly, while it felt incredible to stretch his wings, he didn't bask in the solitude as he once had. Before, he'd taken comfort in being alone and *above* it all. No tethers holding him to the earth, apart from Gamma, and she was living it up in Albuquerque. Though they talked fairly often, Liz didn't fully count since she straddled the line between colleague and friend. Yet *he* was the one who'd never let her close the distance. He shut people down when they showed too much interest, firming up his walls brick by brick.

Everyone except Iris. She was always the exception to his rules.

Without realizing it, he flew the whole perimeter of town

and back again until he found himself circling above the house. Thoughtful now, his wings pulsing with a gentle ache, he perched on the edge of the roof, gazing up at the indistinct stars. It wouldn't take an expert to identify why he preferred to be alone; it was safer. Easier.

Because people left. It didn't matter how much he wished otherwise. Endings were inevitable, and he survived by avoiding those moments. He'd become successful, but he was still *alone*. And then he *heard* her, moving about in her room beneath the eaves.

I'm not *alone. Not unless I choose to be.*

Comforted, he swooped off the roof and glided through his room, flowing into his human form with an ease born of familiarity. It was chilly, so he dressed quickly and closed the window. Once, he'd considered simply living as a hawk and letting Liz administer his worldly goods in a philanthropic fashion. Now, though? Eli wasn't ready to let go.

He heard footfalls, so the knock didn't startle him. He found Sally outside with a hot cup of tea. Chamomile, which was the kind he'd asked her to make the night after the first dance lesson. It touched him that she recalled his preferences, looking out for him as soon as she got home. "I brought tea and Bundt cake. Can I come in?"

"Absolutely." He stepped back to allow her access.

Sally paused, glancing around the space with a surprised expression. He followed her gaze to the black bag by the wall. "Your room is so tidy. Are you still living out of your suitcase?" she asked.

A pang of guilt stabbed him. "I'll put things away sooner or later."

The older woman eyed him, but she didn't verbalize her doubts. "Hmm."

"Did you need something?"

"It's more that I had a question. Iris told me that you ran into my ex at the community center recently. And I…"

"What?" he prompted, sipping at the delightfully warm and lemony drink.

Though Sally had her own reasons for popping in, it still felt incredible to come back to a hot beverage after a long flight. Plus, there was cake. Maybe this was even why hawks and falcons let humans tame them to some degree. *They don't get reward cake. I'm sure it's mice or raw meat.*

"Did Howard make things awkward?" she asked in a rush. "Or suggest that you should talk me out of this 'nonsense'?"

"Not even slightly."

"Oh, thank goodness. For a while, that was all I heard from the family. They even tried to get me checked for dementia!"

Eli nearly dropped his teacup. "Really? Just because—"

"Because I wanted to make big changes. Because I wanted to live my last years as I choose. I had a husband. Now I want a girlfriend! But not a life partner. I don't want to be responsible for anyone else. I want to be able to go home to my own bed. I want to travel and learn new things and—"

"Do it," Eli cut in, sensing that Sally was getting upset. "Do it all."

"Bless you. I'm so glad. I was afraid that Howard was up to his old tricks again, but it seems he's finally realized this isn't a phase."

He wondered if this info would make things better or worse, but he decided to loop Sally in anyway. "Full disclosure, he was on a date with someone named Hazel."

"That's good news," Sally said with a relieved smile. "She's a nice person, so maybe *she* can put up with his quirks."

"Maybe. Thanks for the cake." Eli lifted the spoon.

"My pleasure, dear. I hope you enjoyed the flight."

Sally breezed out, leaving Eli staring after her. He didn't think Iris would've told anyone, so how...?

How does Sally know? He followed her, unable to refrain from asking. "How did you find out?" Eli called.

Sally laughed and answered without breaking stride. "Eli, you silly goose. I've seen a bird flying into your room so many times when I was coming home from Ethel's. You don't own a bird. No pets allowed, remember? Ergo, *you* must be the bird. Most explanations are simple when you let go of your preconceptions."

CHAPTER SEVENTEEN

A COUPLE OF PEACEFUL WEEKS passed with Iris's store slowly getting more orders and Mira settling in.

Since Mira preferred having things formalized, everyone got together and agreed on a work schedule for basic cleaning in the common areas. If they stuck to it, there wouldn't be a problem, and so far, Henry Dale was the most finicky of residents. The man turned up his nose at a dust mote, let alone a dust bunny. Sally sighed a little over being assigned to the first rotation of kitchen chores, but she didn't complain. As for Eli, he seldom revealed his true thoughts.

Man of mystery, that's you. Iris gazed at him wistfully while trying not to reveal just how intrigued she'd become in the time they'd been living together. The dance lessons granted her his attention one night a week, and she'd started looking forward to those evenings, doing her hair carefully, picking out the cutest dress.

It's not a date, she'd told herself, more than once. *We're not dating.* But her reckless heart wouldn't listen. Anyway, there were two more days until the next lesson.

"Any other business?" Sally asked.

The house meeting was wrapping up; they got together on

Sunday nights to discuss matters relevant to those sharing space at Violet Gables. *Such a cute name.* Honestly, Iris wanted to get a plaque made—something adorable and vintage—to post next to the house number, but so far, she hadn't seen anything that looked exactly right.

"Actually, I do have something," Mira said tentatively.

"What's up?" Eli asked at once.

He was always a bit more forthcoming with Mira than with most people, and the other woman shot him a grateful smile. Iris restrained another flicker of…something. *It's fine. It's great. We all get along. That's flipping fantastic.*

"You have the floor," Iris added.

"You have one last room, right? I wasn't planning to say anything, but I guess things got worse this weekend."

At hearing this, Sally frowned in concern, her knitting needles at a rare pause. "Worse for who?"

"Tell us from the beginning," Henry Dale put in.

"Right. Let me back up. I used to be Rowan's big sister in a volunteer mentor program. They're nineteen now, and we're still friendly. Evidently, things have gotten scary at home. I mean, it wasn't *great* before. Evangelical household."

"Oh no," Iris breathed. She could easily imagine what "scary" entailed under those circumstances.

"Before what?" Eli asked.

Henry Dale was frowning, and Sally set down her knitting bag. Both of the older folks seemed focused on the story now, worried for someone they'd never met. *I have the best housemates.*

"The gist is Rowan's cousin screenshotted their locked socials and outed them to the rest of their family."

Iris drew in a sharp breath. "Are they safe?"

"Things were tense last time I talked to them. But they stopped answering my messages last night, and the texts have been left unread."

"Does Rowan usually take a while to respond?" Sally asked.

"I forget that my phone can even get texts," Henry Dale said. "And it takes me forever to send one."

Iris tried not to laugh. That was because Henry Dale had a "classic" flip phone and he used his thumbs on the numeric pad. Anyone who wanted a quick answer should call him or ask face-to-face. She'd learned not to message the old man if she needed a fast turnaround.

Mira shook her head. "They usually reply within an hour."

So it had been almost twenty-four hours since Mira had heard from Rowan? Iris didn't like the sound of that. Not at all. Maybe she was overreacting, but she'd read about people being shipped off to conversion camps or getting locked up by their families. Unease jabbed at her insistently.

"I don't know what you're about to ask, but can we pick Rowan up? It sounds like they might not be safe. We can figure out the details afterward."

Mira stood. "I was hoping you'd say that. We have the little room ready here. I don't have a lot of cash right now, but I'll do an extra spell to cover their rent, or—"

"Nonsense," Henry Dale cut in. "We'll all chip in. Since I'm getting a discount for puttering, I can easily afford to contribute."

"As can I," Sally said. "Really, we're all getting a bargain, especially since the house is so much prettier these days."

"I can pay," Eli said, sounding slightly disgruntled. "I can send a year's rent for Rowan right now."

Iris waved her hands, demanding attention from everyone. "Hey! I'm the homeowner. I wouldn't charge Rowan *anything* under the circumstances."

"If you don't stop it right now, I'm going to cry," Mira announced, already putting on her coat.

"Let's go now," Sally urged. "If I'm right, Rowan's family is probably at Sunday night church, so we can do a stealth rescue. Ooh, should I put on my black coat and hat?"

"If you want," said Iris.

"If it's okay, I'll just take Iris and Sally," Mira said.

"Fine with me," Eli said. "Henry Dale and I will put sheets on the bed and dust Rowan's room."

"They'll be so happy," Mira said with another tremulous smile. "Should I send a text to let them know we're on the way? They're not answering, so—"

"Wait," Iris cut in, as something occurred to her. "When I got in trouble at home, my mom would usually take my phone away. If you send a message to Rowan and they don't have access, couldn't their family read the message first?"

"Oh damn," said Sally.

Mira slowly lowered her phone. "Do you think their family would do that?"

Iris lifted a shoulder. "We won't know until we get there."

"I'll try to call instead. If I can't get a hold of them..." She trailed off as the phone rang and rang before defaulting to voice mail.

Since Mira knew where Rowan lived, she drove and Sally

called shotgun. Iris gazed out over the cornfields as they left town. Somehow it was worse knowing that Rowan lived out in the country. It would be so easy for their family to isolate them, cut them off from friends who cared, and *ugh*. This line of thought reminded her of Lily, who was so glad not to be related, and of Rose and Delphine, who'd essentially ghosted her while claiming to put the ball in Iris's court.

Twenty minutes later, they arrived at a dilapidated farmhouse set well back from the road. It would take an hour to walk into town from here. Mira had grown more agitated from the silence, and by the time they got there, she raced to the front door, pounding on it with both hands. No answer.

"They're home," she whispered. "I *know* they are. The light's on in their room."

"We have maybe forty minutes," Sally said, checking the time on her phone. "And that's if their family socializes for a bit after services. We should put some pep in our step."

Iris had a bad feeling as she circled the house, trying to decide if they should just look for a way inside. Maybe she was overreacting, but—*oh. There's someone in the yard.* She called out, but the person didn't seem to hear her, and when she tapped their shoulder, they jumped so hard they nearly fell off the wooden swing.

"Mira, I think I found Rowan!" she called.

The person in question was young and slight, clad in dark jeans and a blue hoodie. They also held an old iPod with headphones askew on their ears. *They probably didn't hear us earlier.* Iris took a step back, not wanting to freak them out further.

"I think we ran into each other briefly at Fix-It Witches. You were getting your iPod repaired? Oh, and Mira was worried about you," Iris added. "That's why we're here."

Some of the tension drained out of Rowan's posture. *Yeah, I'd be wary too if someone startled me in the dark, and I lived in the middle of nowhere.*

"Oh! Yeah, I remember you. Turns out I needed the iPod," Rowan said in a cautious tone.

Soon, Sally rounded the house, followed closely by Mira.

The younger woman rushed to Rowan's side. "I was so worried when you stopped responding to messages and didn't answer the phone. Are you hurt?"

"I'm sad. And *pissed*," Rowan replied. "My parents confiscated my phone. They tried to make me go to church tonight too, but I refused. Things are...tense, to say the least."

"I can't believe Peyton did that to you." Mira shook her head, clenching a fist.

"It sucks. I trusted her at first because she had her own doubts about the lifestyle, but then they brainwashed her or something. Now she thinks she's doing this for my own good, and..." Rowan trailed off, glancing at Iris and Sally. "Who are these two anyway?"

"My housemates," Mira said.

Rowan seemed to put the pieces together then. "I've heard a lot about you. You must be Iris...and Sally, of course. Love your cardigan! It's too cute."

"Maybe now's not the time for a lengthy chat," Sally said.

They nodded. "Yeah, I need to get out of here. Don't know where I'll go, but—"

"You're coming home with us," Mira cut in firmly.

Rowan didn't seem sure about that, but they didn't argue. Just as well because Sally was right. It would be safer to avoid a confrontation with Rowan's family. Maybe they wouldn't make a huge fuss, but Iris would rather not test the issue. She focused on the practical side of the situation.

"Do you know where your phone is?" Iris asked.

"My dad put it in the locked file cabinet in his home office."

"I can retrieve it while you pack," Sally said.

Everyone just sort of...stared at her after hearing that. Iris had to smile over such a kindly, innocent old lady confessing to thieving skills. "Care to explain?" Iris asked.

Sally waved a hand airily. "Now isn't the time. Rowan needs to get their stuff. We can talk about it later."

Ten minutes later, they were backing out of the long drive onto the county road when a truck with high beams on came toward them. Rowan glared. "That's them."

"You don't have to worry about them anymore," Sally said.

"I prefer found families anyway," Iris murmured. "So it was a bit hectic back there, but...welcome to ours."

While Eli understood why he hadn't been chosen to be part of the liberation team, he still paced the front room until he saw headlights in the driveway.

Tension streamed out of him, leaving him weak at the knees. Maybe it was silly to worry, but so many things could go wrong. Things could get physical during the extraction, or maybe somebody in Rowan's family had a shotgun. He wished his imagination wasn't so great right about now. He held on to the wall, letting out a relieved sigh.

"They've only been gone an hour. You've practically worn a new groove in the floor," Henry Dale said.

Though Eli didn't say anything, he knew the old man was concerned too. Which was exactly why he was still looking out the window and not holed up in his room rereading *The Princess Bride*. Four people headed toward the house, and Eli went to open the door for them. Iris and Sally came inside first, leaving Mira to converse for a few moments with the newcomer. *That must be Rowan.*

They had a small suitcase, a backpack, and a duffle bag with clothes sticking out the top. *Yeah, definitely a stealth extraction.* Rowan looked nervous—completely understandable since everything was happening so fast. Eli decided that Sally's solution— warm drinks for everyone—made a lot of sense in this situation. He conscripted Henry Dale to help him, and the older man appeared to understand his intentions. Even in the kitchen, Eli could hear the conversation, however.

Mira had gotten Rowan into the foyer, but they were objecting. "I can't just move in. I don't have a *job*. I don't have anything. I need to—"

"Everyone needs a hand sometimes," Iris said. "Before I inherited this house, I owed so much back rent that I couldn't sleep for fretting over it. The room Mira mentioned isn't big, but when we heard about your situation, we collectively decided it should be yours."

"Let's take your things upstairs," Sally suggested. "If you decide you'd rather stay somewhere else, *you* have all the power."

Iris's voice came across as very gentle. "Definitely. I won't ask you to sign a rental agreement. The room is yours for however long you need or want it."

"I...wow." Rowan paused briefly, and Eli wondered what was happening inside that silence.

Mira spoke in a reassuring tone. "I've been here for a couple of weeks. Everyone is nice. Henry Dale can be a bit of a grouch, but you'll get used to him. Sally is pure sunshine, Eli is the brother I never had, and Iris is the glue that holds us together."

"Really? Not only because I own the house?" Iris sounded surprised at being described that way.

No, she's right. You drew all of us in, one way or another.

"We won't force you to stay, of course," Iris went on, "if you don't like the house or you'd rather make other arrangements."

"No, I like it," Rowan said quickly. "What I've seen anyway."

Eli filled the kettle, still shamelessly eavesdropping. There was a brief pause, then Rowan added, "It's just that when something seems too good to be true..."

"It usually is," Mira finished.

In time, Eli heard the four go upstairs, and he set up the drinks in the front room along with a plate of Sally's homemade cookies. The others were upstairs less than ten minutes, then they returned en masse. Eli waited for Iris to perform the introductions.

"Everyone, this is Rowan. Rowan, you've met Sally, and you know Mira. This is Eli and Henry Dale. Before we chat, I guess we should go over the house rules. We don't enter each other's rooms uninvited. There's a basic chore schedule, so we'll add you to the roster. What else? Oh! Mira gets the bathroom at 7 a.m. since she has a day job." Iris glanced at Eli, then Henry Dale. "Can you think of anything else?"

Eli shook his head. "Not off the top of my head."

Henry Dale said, "Washer and dryer's in the basement. The washer can be a mite tetchy. Holler at me if the wheel drum gets out of balance."

"Should we swap numbers?" Sally asked.

Rowan seemed entirely bemused as they added contact numbers to their phone. "I don't understand what any of you are getting out of this. I mean, I know why Mira's helping me. But the rest of you..."

"Everyone should be safe," Henry Dale said. "You deserve a lot of other good things, but that's the bare minimum."

"I don't think they'd *hurt* me," Rowan said uncertainly.

But Iris was shaking her head. "Look, we just met, so you don't know my...family. I'd have to dump a lot on you tonight to explain, but suffice to say, there are *layers* of damage. Even if it's not physical harm, they're hurting you with their words and with the way they treat you. Emotional wounds can be even worse—to the point that their words can become the mocking voice in your head, the one that cuts you down."

"And it's not right," Henry Dale added.

"Absolutely not," Sally agreed.

"People want to believe the best about their families. 'They'll come around. I just need to give them time.' But you don't owe them patience *or* tolerance when their love is conditional," Eli said.

He recalled how Iris's sister Lily had been glad to have a "get out of jail free" card after stealing Iris's boyfriend and how her other sister was thinking about litigating so she could profit from Iris's heartbreak. *Why are people like this?*

"And that's a lot. Let's eat before I get all mopey," Iris said, picking up the tea Eli had fixed for her.

It felt like a secret known only to them—the fact that she could tell that he'd made it from the amount of milk in the cup. The others grabbed their drinks and settled on chairs and couches around the living room. Rowan took two cookies first, scarfed them quickly, then washed them down with warm tea.

"Sorry. I didn't eat dinner," they said.

Sally got to her feet immediately. "Do you like eggs? I can scramble you some in a jiffy. I'll fix a nice plate of toast to go with them. We have homemade jam! Hazel brought it over, made from fresh raspberries."

Rowan smiled for the first time since arriving. "Is this what I have to look forward to? It's like I suddenly acquired the nicest grandma ever."

Mira grinned, a teasing light in her eyes. "Be warned, she's not on duty full-time. Sally spends a lot of time with her close, *close* friend Ethel these days."

Rowan brightened visibly. "I have a gay foster grandma?"

"Not gay," Sally said over her shoulder on the way to the kitchen. "But absolutely bi-curious. I'm trying things out with Ethel, it's true. But we prefer not to put labels on our relationship. She's not the type to settle down, and *I* was monogamous for far too long. I need to kiss a *lot* of people to make up for lost time."

"This is heaven," Rowan declared with an awed look. "It must be, right?"

"That's how I feel," Iris said.

Eli gazed at her, just...drinking her in and marveling at her ability to attract happiness like she cast it as a spell. *If this is heaven, you're the angel.*

CHAPTER EIGHTEEN

FOR THE NEXT FEW DAYS, Iris mostly left Rowan to their own devices.

This was a big change, and they wouldn't get comfortable if everyone hovered. She hadn't mentioned the "label your food" rule because the rest of her housemates had come to a tacit understanding that they'd take care of Rowan. Yesterday, Sally made a huge pot of vegetable soup and froze individual portions, so there was always something to be defrosted and eaten. She might claim she was tired of looking after people, but the instinct hadn't gone away, it seemed.

Besides, for the first time, Iris's shop had so many orders that she had no time left to work on designs or make jewelry. Almost every piece she'd uploaded had been sold, and now she was busy with the fulfillment end of the business. She had gift boxes stacked around, several thank-you notes and coupons, and another pile of padded envelopes that toppled over while she was looking for her address stamp.

"I started off so organized," she muttered.

But her bedroom/studio looked like a cyclone had hit it, and she hadn't even gotten the jewelry in the boxes yet. She let out a frustrated breath and tried to decide where to start. This was where her brain often got uncooperative. The more she had to do, the less she could do anything at all.

Just then, someone knocked. What a glorious excuse to procrastinate. Iris called, "Come in!"

And Rowan stepped into her room for the first time. "Oh, wow. You...seem to have a lot going on. This isn't urgent. It can wait."

"It's fine. I'm still trying to get my bearings. I hate being a failure, but I wasn't ready for success either." Ruefully, she gestured at the mess surrounding her.

"Is there anything I can help with?" Rowan asked.

She started to say, "No, it's fine," as a knee-jerk reaction, but then she paused. "I don't want you to feel like you *have* to offer, just because you're staying here."

"Actually, that's why I came up," Rowan said.

"Oh?"

"Well, Mira told me she's getting a discount on rent for spells, and Henry Dale fixes stuff around the house, right? So I was just wondering if there was anything I could do. I'm an artist...well, *aspiring* anyway. I'm hoping to take commissions eventually. I just wrapped up a web comic, and I'm taking digital art classes online."

"You're already an artist," Iris corrected. "If you make art, you're an artist. What you're trying to do is make it financially viable."

Rowan smiled. "True. Right now, I have a few subscribers, just enough to pay my phone bill and that's about it."

"It's a start!" Iris paused, considering the offer. "Okay, so, were you serious about wanting to help? I could use someone on the fulfillment end. I can show you how."

Iris pulled up the first order, matched it with the product purchased, printed the label she'd prepared, and affixed it to the center of the padded envelope. Next, she stamped it and put the thank-you note and coupon inside. Final step, check that she was enclosing the right necklace in the box, slip it inside, and seal.

"That's it. I have forty-three more orders to process, almost my entire backlog of jewelry. Which is *amazing,* but if I don't get some new pieces made, the shop will lose momentum. I'm finally getting eyeballs, so I can't afford to—"

"This looks simple enough," Rowan cut in. "If you trust me, I'm happy to take over. Minimum wage is fine, but I'd appreciate it if you would reduce the rent by that amount each month, however much I work."

"I told you not to worry about the rent," Iris said. "It's—"

"'It's not a big room, and it doesn't cost much.' But I *love* that little room. I'm putting my own art on the walls a little at a time, and I don't want to feel like I'm mooching off everyone else, okay? I understand Mira, she feels protective, but—"

"Nobody thinks you're mooching. It's only been a few days."

"I want to pay my own way," Rowan insisted.

Fine. I get it.

"Okay, Rowan. You have a deal. But if you put in more hours than your rent costs, I'm paying you." It hit her all of a sudden. "Oh, lord. This means I have to figure out W-2s or...what are those forms called?"

They stared at Iris blankly, then shrugged. "No idea. I've never officially had a job, so I never filed. I read that I don't need to worry about it if I earn less than five grand a year."

"You might want to check into that, just in case."

Rowan sighed. "I'll add it to my list."

As Iris settled in at her desk to bring some of her sketches to life, Rowan got to work packaging up the orders. Iris didn't pay attention to how long it took, but a beep drew her gaze. "That's fifty-six minutes. Everything is ready to ship. Do you want me to keep a log?"

"There's probably an app," Iris joked. "And if there isn't, Eli can make one."

As she'd suspected, she found a free one supported by ads and recorded Rowan's time. "All set. Let me show you how to schedule the pickup."

It was simple on the postal service website, but Rowan bit their lip, looking worried. "Is it really okay for me to use your login?"

Iris grinned. "I trust you. Besides, what can you even do in there besides order a bunch of stamps?"

"True enough. I'll take these downstairs and leave them by the front door. They'll be picked up at 10 a.m. tomorrow."

"That's perfect. I'll add an hour to tomorrow's time sheet since you'll be waiting for the mail carrier."

"That doesn't really count as work, though."

She folded her arms, brooking no disagreement on this point. "It absolutely does! That's time you could be devoting to your art."

Rowan appeared to consider arguing anyway, but they ended up yielding. "Okay. When you put it that way… Anyhow, it makes me happy that I can pitch in. I want to be useful to the Iris Collective."

She burst out laughing. "Is that what Mira calls us? I prefer Violet Gables." She took a moment to explain the name.

"That's so cute. It makes me want to draw the house even

more. I'm looking for my next web comic idea, wonder if people would be interested in reading about us…" Looking pensive, Rowan loaded the packages in the hamper Iris used for transporting her creations and wandered downstairs.

"I'd read it," Iris said to nobody in particular.

Then she got back to work.

—————————

Eli's phone pinged, signaling a new message. There were also several emails waiting for his attention, including an invitation to a Zoom meeting—to further discuss the huge proposal that Liz had been enthusing over for the past few weeks. He still had mixed feelings. While he might not be rich the way some app developers were, he also enjoyed the freedom he currently had in deciding how a project would go.

If he signed on, agreeing to work for someone else, even as a contractor, they could control more than he felt comfortable with. Which was why he'd agreed to attend the video conference but had yet to sign anything despite the seductive figures being tossed around as enticement.

Liz: Why aren't you more excited about this? This is life-changing! But instead of getting on board, you're fiddling around in Illinois. How long are you planning to stay anyway?
Eli: That's a good question. I admire your perspicacity greatly, have I said that?
Liz: And that's not an answer.
Eli: No idea. I'm…figuring some things out.

Liz: I...see.

Eli: Why? You don't usually ask personal questions.

Liz: And you don't usually move in with a gaggle of strangers. You're not acting like yourself, and it worries me. You
might blow this whole deal.

Eli could have written *touché*, but instead, he snapped his
phone shut. A while back, he'd spent a small fortune on a cutting-
edge smart flip phone, and there really was something ineffably
satisfying about closing it. He didn't get that mental boost with
a regular smartphone, no matter how emphatically he tapped the
screen or closed an app.

It was a good thing nobody had noticed how pricey his tech
was, as it would give away the fact that he could afford to make
other housing arrangements.

Iris will be so *hurt.*

If he'd learned anything, it was that she prized honesty, and
she thought everyone in the house had laid all their cards on the
table. No secrets. No lies.

Which made Eli feel terrible. But he wouldn't focus on that.
Other matters required his attention. As the weather turned colder,
Henry Dale had run out of house projects that could be tackled by
two people with a can-do attitude. Which meant he was crankier
than usual, likely stemming from the fact that he felt useless. It made
him even crabbier when Mira spent all of fifteen minutes keeping
her promise to update the paint in the second-floor hallway. Now
Henry Dale probably thought his own existence was pointless, as it
would've taken him several days and been messy and costly besides.

Normally, Eli wouldn't care about any of this. They weren't his people, right? He was alone in the world, soaring above it all. Untouchable and—

Nah. Not anymore.

An hour after the text chat with Liz, he was conspiring with Mira and Rowan to find Henry Dale a project. They were both in his room, away from any chance of being overheard by Henry Dale. He filled them in on his suspicions regarding Henry Dale's bad attitude and then said, "Any ideas?"

"Is that why he's in a mood?" Mira asked. "He seemed okay with my magic in the beginning, but now…"

Rowan nodded thoughtfully. "It makes sense. I was feeling kind of meh—like a charity project—until Iris hired me for her shop."

With a pensive frown, Mira paced a bit. "Hmm. I see why you wanted us to collaborate because I can't come up with anything off the top of my head."

"It has to be something we actually need," Eli cautioned. "Or he'll *know*."

The silence stretched for a few moments, then Rowan cleared their throat. "Uh. I have a want. Maybe even a need. A regular desk won't work in my room, but I was thinking it would be cool if I had, like, a fold-down table to draw on, something I could fasten to the wall when I'm not using it."

Inspired, Eli got out his phone and searched until he found an example of what he thought Rowan meant. "Something like this. With hidden shelving, maybe?"

"Oh, the Murphy bed of desks," Mira said, leaning in to see the picture better.

Rowan scooted closer on his other side and nodded, excitement flickering in their dark eyes. "Exactly like that."

In seconds, Mira had her phone out too. "Look, they even have folding ergonomic desk chairs. Maybe Henry Dale could work this chair into the design, so it all folds into the same cabinet when you're not using it?"

"That would be amazing. I hate clutter, makes me anxious. But do you think Henry Dale will get mad if I ask him about this?" Rowan let out a little breath.

Eli beckoned. "One way to find out. Since this was my idea, I'll see if he's interested."

Mira followed them out of Eli's room. "This is perfect. My spells are no good for creating something out of nothing. I hope this reassures Henry Dale that we still need him around here."

Rowan said, "It's kinda not good that he feels like he has to be *useful* to be wanted, but y'know, one issue at a time?"

Eli headed down the hall. "Exactly. I think he's in his room reading. Let's go talk to him."

On the way, Mira branched off to her own room, probably best since Henry Dale sometimes bristled over her abilities. Not that he disliked her, Eli thought, more that he had a fear of obsolescence. *What good is an old man who putters when there's magic like this?* Henry Dale never said it outright, but that was the gist, Eli suspected.

While Rowan made coffee—Henry Dale's favorite—Eli knocked. "Hey, if you're not too busy, I need to talk to you."

"About what?" Henry Dale asked in a snappish tone.

"Come out, we made coffee."

"We?" Henry Dale popped out of his room and smiled when he saw Rowan. "That smells really good, thank you kindly."

The old man had taken a shine to their youngest roommate, so this probably wouldn't be a difficult ask. If Henry Dale was feeling cooped up, this would help. Eli raised a brow, silently verifying if Rowan wanted him to broach the subject. He got a terse nod in response.

Okay, my time to shine.

"Rowan's got the smallest room, so they have nowhere to focus on their art. So we were wondering, if you have time…" He explained the project and showed Henry Dale some of the sample photos they'd found. "I'm planning to order this chair—"

"Nonsense. I'll make the chair too. It'll look better if it's all one set. I have plenty of lumber left in the shed, and I bet Sally would sew some memory foam cushions once we're done. I can draw up some designs… Is that all right with you, Rowan?" The old man had a happy gleam in his eyes, actually rubbing his hands together in anticipation.

Rowan blinked. "But we haven't even talked about how to pay—"

"I want you to use that new desk and draw me a unicorn. Can you do that for me?" Henry Dale cut in.

"Totally," said Rowan.

Henry Dale nodded once. "Then it's settled. I'll get to work right away."

"I don't think I'll ever understand him," Rowan said, as Henry Dale sat down at the kitchen table with a yellow legal tablet and a cup of coffee.

Eli smiled, imagining that unicorn framed and hanging in a place of pride in the old man's room. "Me either. But it's more magical this way."

CHAPTER NINETEEN

AT THIS POINT, THINGS WERE going almost *too* well.

In the usual course of events, Iris could expect life to throw her a curveball right about now, some terrible catastrophe that she hadn't planned for. Because, frankly, she wasn't great at planning or paying attention to details that might catch her unaware. But there were no problems she could pinpoint, so maybe she was creating that sense of foreboding, some kind of self-fulfilling prophecy.

I expect to fail, so I fail.

Hopefully that was the issue, not some pertinent minutiae that Iris should deal with before it snowballed. With a groan, she stood and stretched, pleased with her progress now that she had Rowan pitching in. With them tending to shipments like clockwork, she could devote herself to design, production, and photography. She'd even managed to order a reasonably priced lightbox with different backgrounds to showcase her jewelry professionally, even using a black velvet neck form to make her shots look high-end.

I finally feel like I know what I'm doing.

She left her supplies on the worktable and headed down for a bite. Something smelled delicious, but she was surprised to find

Henry Dale in the kitchen alone. Judging by the empty packages on the counter, he was making spaghetti with canned sauce. Not that she objected. Any meal she didn't have to cook counted as delicious in her book. He was definitely fixing enough for everyone too.

The old man had already come a long way from his "leave me alone, don't talk to me" days. He didn't even claim he only needed someplace to lay his head at night either. She'd noticed that he fretted over Rowan, if they were getting enough sleep and enough to eat. And these days, Henry Dale spent most of his time working on some project in the shed. He'd been at it for the last week.

"Need any help?" Iris asked.

He waved his long spoon in the direction of the fridge. "I was planning to make a salad, but you can do it if you want. There's lettuce, carrots, and cucumber in the crisper."

"No tomatoes?" she joked.

"They're in the sauce."

"You're making a lot of food."

He nodded. "Sally is inviting Ethel over, and Eli is bringing someone too."

She paused in pulling vegetables out of the fridge, trying not to show too much interest. "Oh? Anyone I know?"

Henry Dale shrugged, swirling the pasta around in the frantically boiling water. "He didn't say."

"Maybe I should call Hazel," Iris joked.

"If you want. I've made enough food to feed ten people."

She opted not to, mostly because Hazel might feel like she'd been added at the last minute, and it was better not to do things impulsively that could hurt people's feelings. *I'll invite her next time.* Quickly, she washed the lettuce and chopped the veg, throwing together a salad in record time.

"Looks good," Henry Dale said. "We have any Italian dressing left?"

Iris grinned. "It's cute you think we can't eat salad and spaghetti without it."

"Oh, go away." But he seemed to be smiling too.

At least she'd gotten a heads-up; that gave her time to head upstairs and put on some better clothes. It would've been embarrassing to receive visitors in paint-stained yoga pants and an old hoodie from a college she didn't graduate from.

"I'm definitely not competing," she said, rummaging through her options.

Obviously, it was a total coincidence when she came downstairs in a super cute blue-and-black-plaid dress, a bit retro with a black Peter Pan collar and pockets. She'd thought about adding tights, but that seemed like overkill. Her stomach felt odd and tight and knotted at the prospect of meeting Eli's guest. It wasn't like they'd discussed deepening their relationship, after all, but she'd thought maybe—

Get a grip. Whatever happens tonight, be an adult.

Rowan came down soon after to help set the table, and Sally breezed in five minutes later with an older woman in tow. Ethel was a curvy woman with silver hair and a flair for dramatic style; she came in like she owned the place and offered hugs to everyone who wanted them. Then Mira got home from work, which just left Eli. For so many dinner guests, they'd put the leaf in the table and added folding chairs from the basement.

Everyone was at the table looking at the two empty chairs when the front door opened and closed. Iris clenched a fist against her knee, resolutely pinning on a smile. Eli came in with a gorgeous Black woman. The lady was put together from head to toe, dressed in a blue power suit, and Iris's heart plummeted to her shins.

"Everyone, this is Keshonda," Eli said.

A chorus of "a pleasure" and "nice to meet you" sounded around the table, as Henry Dale plated the pasta and spooned sauce over it. Iris actually preferred cooking her pasta al dente and then stirring it into the sauce and cooking for five minutes more. Then she'd let it sit for another ten minutes to let it absorb the flavor. More delicious, less messy.

"I offered to take you out to dinner to discuss the offers," Keshonda said. "But I won't say no to a home-cooked meal."

Ethel was already twirling spaghetti around her fork, using her spoon to brace it. "I love doing this. Best pasta I ever had was in Venice. Little place on the corner, run by two delightful old gentlemen who had no idea where St. Claire was." She ate her bite with relish, seeming surprised to see she still had everyone's attention. "More about Venice? Okay. Surprisingly, I also had the *worst* shrimp cocktail. Different place, they put mayonnaise on it for some reason. But they also had a tiny balcony out back where you could eat by the canal, and they served food through the windows."

"Now I want to go to Venice," Keshonda said.

"Me too," Rowan agreed.

"I'm saving up for a trip," Mira added. "My dream vacation,

but it's not Venice. For me, it's New Zealand. What about you, Henry Dale?"

"What about me?" he muttered.

"Do you have anywhere you'd like to go?" Rowan asked.

He sighed. "I can't afford to travel."

Iris couldn't focus on that when she was so busy wondering what offers Keshonda was talking about. *Maybe...*

"But you can dream," Ethel pointed out.

"I'd really like to know," Rowan coaxed.

The old man could never say no to them. "Fine. If you must know, I always wished I had joined the Navy. So I'd like to own a boat and just sail wherever the whim took me."

"Oh, that sounds amazing. Do you need a first mate?" Ethel asked.

"I'd invite Rowan, not you," said Henry Dale.

Rowan grinned. "I might be interested in that."

"What about you?" Mira asked Keshonda.

The woman didn't contemplate for long. "Mm, I'm all about tropical islands and getting oil rubbed on me. I'm thinking Tahiti."

"Eli?" Sally asked.

"My turn? This might be weird, but...Veracruz," he said softly.

"Interesting. Veracruz, Mexico, right? Any particular reason?" Ethel asked.

He nodded. "It's a long story."

Thankfully, Sally was ready to ease the awkwardness, changing the subject smoothly. "So how do you know Eli?" she asked Keshonda.

Keshonda smiled. "I'm his real estate agent, and we've got

three offers on his house. Well, his grandmother's house. This is the ideal situation, so I wanted to do a business dinner to discuss the pros and cons of each. But he invited me home instead."

Oh my God. He's flipping his grandmother's house, and this isn't what I thought at all.

After dinner, Eli found the kitchen to be the quietest spot once everyone else wandered off.

He'd end up doing the dishes after Keshonda left, but that was fine. He listened as she summarized the offers, nodding along. He was inclined to go with the first couple, even if it wasn't the highest dollar amount—not because he felt like he had to honor first come, first served—but newlyweds, first house? He'd feel like a villain if he blew them off in favor of filthy lucre. Then again, he had a responsibility to get Gamma the best deal he could, as this was her financial security for the future.

Keshonda laughed, looking at his expression. "I can see the wheels in your head turning. You're in a good position, no matter what you decide. The first couple definitely plans to live in the house, promise you that. I suspect the second will rent the place. The third buyer I can't get a read on because they're using a proxy. That usually means vacation home or investment property, though."

"What would you do?" he asked.

She tapped the third set of documents. "I'd take the highest offer. If I'm selling a house, I don't care what happens to it after I move on."

"Pragmatic."

"But I can tell you have some qualms, so why don't you call your grandmother?"

"Good idea. I feel like Gamma might want to put Ruben and Natalie in her house, but who knows? She might prefer the twenty-five grand."

"That's a dream vacation or two, like we were talking about at dinner." With that, Keshonda packed her briefcase and headed toward the door. "Call me when you know what you want to do."

Eli walked her out. "I will."

There were so many cars parked here that it looked like they were throwing a wild party. Susan, the cranky neighbor, was probably on standby waiting to make a noise complaint. But things stayed chill, and Ethel left quietly an hour later. It was cute when Sally kissed her goodbye. Not that Eli was spying on them. He just *happened* to be collecting coffee cups to wash right then, a complete coincidence.

Sally danced upstairs humming "It Had to Be You," and Eli went back to cleanup duty. He checked the time and realized it was early enough to call Gamma, who was two hours behind in Albuquerque. The phone rang twice, then she picked up.

"It's my favorite little man! How are you?"

"Excellent. Listen, I called to tell you about multiple offers on the house..." He tried to be succinct in explaining the pros and cons of each.

When he was done, Gamma said, "The first offer. It's not even a question. I don't need the money that much, they offered first, and I *adore* the thought of giving newlyweds their first home."

"I'll text Keshonda and let her know. Everything good with you?"

"Fantastic. It's early days yet, but I met someone special in my Bunko club. I'm cautiously optimistic, but she seems *lovely*."

"I can't wait to meet her," Eli said.

"Maybe you can come for Christmas?" Gamma asked in a hopeful tone.

"Maybe." Fact was, the house would likely be sold by then. He didn't want to think about leaving. "I'll let you know."

"Love you, talk soon!"

Sighing, Eli got back to work, tucking his phone in the pocket of his sweats. He was almost done, dishes stacked in the drainer, pots and pans upended on the mat, when Iris came into the kitchen. She seemed...determined in a way he hadn't seen before, and he'd thought he was an expert on all her expressions.

"Hungry?" he asked.

They'd eaten every last bite of the spaghetti and salad feast, which had visibly made the old man happy. Being needed seemed to be a key component of Henry Dale's psyche. And on that note, Eli couldn't wait to see how the desk-chair combo cabinet turned out.

"No." She chewed at her lip and paced around the space, touching stuff here and there. What looked like restless hands made her grab a dish towel and start drying, all without making eye contact.

Okay, this is weird.

"Something wrong?" he asked.

"Not wrong. I'm just...*really* nervous. And I don't know what to say or how to say it or if I should say this at all. I might ruin everything."

Eli strode over to her and put his hands on her shoulders. *Maybe it's family stuff?* "Whatever's happening, we can figure out a solution together."

For some reason, that relaxed her. Iris smiled and took a breath. "I should've known you'd say that. Okay, here it is. I got upset when I found out you'd invited someone home because I thought it was a date. Lately, I've had…feelings for you. Romantic ones. And I was wondering if you feel the same at all. Is it just me?"

She peered up at him with hopeful gray eyes, as if she hadn't just made all his dreams come true, just like he'd named her contact info when they first met. And if he just happened to be here, if everything was random chance, then maybe they could—*no, I have to tell her. We can't date under these circumstances.*

But instead of the truth, he said, "I like you too."

Just that. And she was so happy; she hugged him. He stood there frozen until his arms came up and he held her close, the way he'd thought he never would.

This is bad.

"You don't know how much courage it took for me to speak up. I'm not a jealous person, but it *hurt* thinking about you with someone else."

He had to say it because it was so unbelievable, something he never could've imagined. Dreams were dreams for a reason—they didn't come true. Not like this.

"Because you want to be with me."

"Exactly. I'm so relieved you feel the same. I can't believe this worked! Violet Gables is the happiest place on earth, not Disneyland."

"Careful, the Mouse will get you for that."

Iris laughed, giddy and breathless. "We should probably lay down some ground rules. I don't want our relationship to make the others uncomfortable."

"Right, limiting the PDA." He started to step back, but she held on.

"Just a few seconds more. Let me be greedy. I doubt anyone will come to the kitchen before the dishes are done. They'd feel obligated to help." Her hands moved on his back, sending pleasurable chills throughout his whole body.

She felt so right cuddled against him, the way nothing and no one ever had. Before, he had been a tree unable to put down roots, and he thought it was because of his dual nature. He was meant to live in the skies, not to forge connections on the ground.

That...no longer felt true.

For a few moments, Eli reveled in the hug, breathing her in. This much was fine. Soon, he'd figure out how to tell her the truth, before things got more complicated. And then she kissed him.

The world melted away.

CHAPTER TWENTY

SOME KISSES WERE FIREWORKS.

Some were spiky aliens with lizard tongues, and others were summer nights by the ocean with sand between the toes. This one? It was the chill of an autumn night warmed by the sweetness of hot cocoa. It was soft and shy with a slowly building heat that felt like a roaring fire by the time Iris pulled back, breathless, to peer up at Eli.

He was smiling slightly, gazing at her with such affection that she felt a bit silly for not having noticed how much he cared before. *Those are the eyes of a man who—*

Okay, maybe not that *L word. A man who likes me. A lot. How's that?*

"Limited PDA, huh?" Then he did pull away, resuming the kitchen work with a haste she found mildly unsettling.

Maybe he's worried about getting caught. If she was smart, she'd share that concern because the last thing she wanted to do was make anyone else uncomfortable. She'd never been in this situation before, so she couldn't say what the etiquette was. In other roommate situations, the rules had been "Partners should stay no more than two consecutive nights and no more than seven nights a month total" and "Don't wake anyone up with your nocturnal doings." Since they lived together, the first rule didn't apply, but the second made sense. If she got teased by Sally the morning after—

"Oh God," she mumbled.

"Wow, you're really pink," Eli noted.

Despite being flustered, Iris decided to continue drying dishes and keep him company. "Are you selling the house soon? Keshonda said it was your grandma's place."

"Sales often don't happen fast, even after the offer. The process takes time."

"What will you do when everything is settled?" she asked.

It had been a couple of months already, so he only had a month left on his three-month rental agreement. She'd never bought a house, just inherited this one, but she knew there were usually terms like thirty or sixty days to close. But since he was out of the house already, the buyers could move in right away. Once the papers were signed, he could go.

Damn. He might go.

"I'm not sure yet."

Yeah, that wasn't what she wanted to hear. But one kiss didn't make a relationship.

And she had no clue where to go from here, because if she said something noncommittal, he'd probably sense her disappointment. Yet Iris was fully aware that she had no cause to feel that way. No promises had been made.

Changing the subject seemed like the best idea rather than

put weighty expectations on him when he hadn't suggested they become official after she kissed him. "By the way, my store is doing a lot better. I've been using all the techniques and strategies you taught me. Views and orders are way up. Rowan's helping with the shipments."

"I knew you'd do amazing," he said.

And his tone bothered her; there was a finality and a sadness in it, as if he had some bad news to impart, but he hadn't figured out how yet. *Shit, he's not sick, is he?* That...would explain a lot. His reluctance to let people close, the way he chose not to make major decisions or long-term plans... She gazed at him, wide-eyed.

What would I do if that's true?

And then suddenly, it was crystal clear. It didn't matter. Not to her. If he had two months, a year, two? Then she'd want to be with him. Life didn't come with any guarantees, after all. She'd rather be with Eli than look for someone else. Her "mother" would say this was just more of her romantic nonsense, utterly divorced from reality, but that only made Iris more certain.

In that moment, all her doubts disappeared.

"It doesn't matter," she told him.

Eli blinked. "What doesn't? Never mind that for a sec. I have to tell you something."

Here it comes. Cancer? Bad heart? I'm ready. I can take it.

Just then, Rowan dashed in, waving their hands wildly. "Hey, come up and see. Henry Dale finished installing my desk."

Iris hadn't even heard the banging, which proved how distracted she had been. Eli sighed a bit over the interruption, not so loud that Rowan noticed. He dried his hands on the towel and followed them upstairs to see the custom build. Iris was too curious to pass up the invitation, so she went along with them. Sally and Mira were already there, peering into the small room from either side of the doorway.

"Isn't it cool?" Rowan asked three or four times, getting affirmations from a different housemate each time.

"I love the detail work," Mira said.

There were fanciful cuts and grooves on the back of the unit, making it look like an art piece, and Henry Dale had painted it in different colors, so it brightened up the plain walls. He demonstrated how to lower and fold up the desktop twice, then Rowan took over. The chair really did get tucked away in the cabinet, leaving no trace once the cabinet was closed.

"You do great work," Iris said.

Eli agreed. "You should start offering custom builds to those who need special furniture for small spaces."

"I wouldn't even know how to start with that," Henry Dale muttered.

But Iris could see a thoughtful look in the older man's eyes, so she encouraged him. "If I can run a business, you can."

"I already did that! I'm retired."

"You were a general contractor," Sally said. "This is carpentry. I'm willing to make the cushions for you, as long as you don't work me too hard. And I'll need a cut of the profits. Thirty percent seems fair."

"Thirty percent?! You're delusional, woman."

The older couple went off bickering. Iris suspected they'd argue over the venture, but at least it would keep them busy.

Rowan slowly sat down at their desk and wriggled a bit, getting comfortable. She took that as the clue to step back. Mira nodded as she closed the door.

"They'll be lost for hours. I was thinking..."

"What?" Eli asked.

"Rowan's birthday is coming up, the day before Thanksgiving, and I want to get them a digital drawing tablet. I found one on sale, and I'm planning to get it, no matter what. But I wondered if you're interested in chipping in?"

"Absolutely," Eli said at once. "Is a hundred enough?"

"Too much! I only need about half that if everyone kicks in."

"Then I'll pay for Iris and me right now." Before Iris could stop him, he had his wallet out, counting bills.

Mira shot Iris an interested look, as if she had many thoughts and feelings about Eli offering to do that on her behalf. Regardless, Mira accepted the cash. "I...see. Then I just need to talk to Henry Dale and Sally. Thanks for supporting Rowan. They're really talented."

"I know," Iris said.

With that, Mira headed off, leaving Iris to wonder why Eli was so willing to spend money. Was it because he wouldn't need it for much longer?

Dammit, what was he about to tell me anyway?

Eli should have immediately followed up after the disruption.

There would never be a "right" time to explain things, but the longer he waited, the more difficult it got to raise the subject.

It seemed like such a tiny harmless misunderstanding back then. Now, he could see that Iris was worried about whatever his revelation might be, and he shamelessly chose the coward's path. It probably wouldn't make a difference if he waited a week or two, right? If he dumped this on her immediately after they started...dating? *Is that the right word?* Then it might end before even getting started.

If he tried to build a deeper relationship first, she'd be more inclined to examine events from his point of view. Probably. Hell, he didn't know anymore. This much he did know—he wasn't ready for this to end. And the minute he confessed the full story, she might ask him to move out.

I'll tell her when my rental agreement is up. Another month.

Not nearly long enough to do everything he wanted with Iris, but maybe, if the situation went sideways, those memories would be enough to console him. *Hmm. It'll be almost Christmas.* Gamma had never believed in the religious implications, but she liked sparkly trees, penguins in sock hats, and red-cheeked St. Nick with a bulging bag of goodies.

Eli felt more or less the same way.

"You look pensive," Iris said, worrying her lower lip with her teeth.

"My grandmother invited me to spend Christmas at her place in Albuquerque," he answered, and it wasn't a lie, though it *was* an evasion.

"Are you going?"

Is it my imagination or does she look sad?

"Not sure yet. We don't always spend the holidays together.

When I was in college, she went on a holiday cruise two years in a row, and after that, I started visiting friends."

Or I stayed home by myself while assuring Gamma I had my own plans. But he didn't tell Iris that.

"What about Thanksgiving?" she asked.

"I'll be here. We should get everyone involved. I bet Sally knows how to cook a turkey. Even if she can't be here, she can teach us."

Iris smiled. "That sounds fun. I'll ask who's going to be around."

"Does Mira have family in the area?" he asked.

He knew Rowan did, but they weren't likely to head back for Thanksgiving. To his knowledge, they hadn't contacted their relatives since moving out. Their family was looking for them, and they'd sent a number of messages demanding that Rowan return home at once. Thankfully Rowan was safe here. Henry Dale had said he didn't have anyone, so he'd be around. Sally was the big question mark, as she was the most social of butterflies and would likely have invitations from friends *and* family.

Iris seemed to be considering. "Honestly, I don't think she ever told me. I know her ex-girlfriend is here."

"Anyway, let's ask them about it tomorrow."

"We can plan the menu together! And then on the big day, we'll eat until we're sleepy. Sports or movies?" she asked quickly.

"Movies." A beat later, he understood what she was asking. "But I think Henry Dale will want to watch sports, so we should take turns voting on the entertainment."

"Ooh, or we could play games."

"Cards, board, or video?" he asked.

"Let me think about it." She stood on tiptoe and kissed his cheek. "Night, Eli. See you tomorrow."

After she dashed up the stairs, Eli touched his cheek, not realizing that he was smiling until Rowan cleared their throat. "You two are adorable. I ship it."

"You overheard?"

"Uh, *you* decided to be cute right outside my room. The walls aren't soundproof."

"Then what do you think about Thanksgiving?"

Rowan gave Eli a speaking look. "It's a terrible holiday for reasons that I think I don't need to articulate."

"Absolutely true. But are you on board for lots of delicious food?"

"I love turkey. I love gravy. I love gravy on turkey. And don't get me started on the stuffing. Mounds of mashed potatoes? Green beans, yams. Pumpkin pie? It's all *so* good." Rowan seemed to retreat into their mind for a bit, savoring some private fantasy feast.

"This is the most excited I've ever seen you," Eli teased.

"Gravy," said Rowan.

"You should come with us to Bev's," he suggested.

"What's that?"

"Only Henry Dale's favorite eatery. Iris ordered the biscuits and gravy plate when we were there, and she gave me a bite. So good. If you like gravy, you have to try it."

Rowan briefly affected a lofty tone. "I *do* enjoy a fine béchamel sauce. Anyway, I'd like to go next time."

"Movies or sports?" Eli asked.

"What?"

"Oh, Iris was asking what we should do after the big meal."

"Ah! I don't want to be that person, but...both. Let's switch it up. And play games too." They paused. "Huh. This might be the first Thanksgiving I've ever looked forward to. I still kind of can't believe I'm *here*, you know? We're a family, people who care about each other, but it's low-key. Nobody's in my business all the time, and I love that."

"I feel the same way," he admitted.

"Anyway, good luck with Iris. Night, Eli."

He was headed to his own room when he remembered he hadn't switched the kitchen light off. Henry Dale would do it, but he'd also offer a lecture about running up the electric bill. As Eli reached the first floor, a knock sounded at the front door. He went to answer, thinking Sally might have left her keys.

But no, it was Susan from next door, and she wore a particularly nasty smile. "I need to speak with the homeowner, Iris Collins," she demanded.

He didn't like this woman, and her tone set off all his internal alarms. "She's in her room. What's this about? I can pass along the message."

"No, this news shouldn't come through an intermediary. And I want to see her face when she finds out." The malevolent anticipation this woman exuded truly was worrying.

Just then, Henry Dale came out of the kitchen, and he strode toward the front door like a man on a mission. He stood at Eli's shoulder, blocking Susan's route. "I do believe Eli has made it clear that you can leave a message. It's nearly ten in the evening, and

Iris might be asleep. I used to think Robert Frost had the wrong idea about fences making good neighbors, but *you're* proving his point."

"Fine! The rest of you jerks should know too. I've filed a complaint with the city. So many cars, so much noise. There's too damn many people living in this house, and *that's* a code violation." She waved some kind of handbook. "'No more than four unrelated persons may share a residential domicile, lest they be...' Well, I don't need to tell you how you'll be punished. It'll be more fun when you find out the hard way." With that, Susan spun on her heels and stomped over to her house without looking back.

Even Henry Dale seemed shaken. "Are we really breaking the law?"

"I'm sure it's not a big deal," Eli said, trying to reassure the older man.

In truth, it might be a problem, though he had no sense whether it was major, minor, or somewhere in between.

CHAPTER TWENTY-ONE

SURE ENOUGH, IRIS'S INSTINCTS HAD been dead-on.

The day started out well enough. She had a relaxing shower and a bagel with cream cheese for breakfast and she made a few necklaces. Then Eli knocked on the door. Normally, that would be an awesome excuse to chat and maybe kiss him again, but his expression gave away the fact that he wasn't looking forward to this convo at all.

A man who looked this sad shouldn't also be that handsome. It was distracting. His dark hair tumbled in gentle waves; it had gotten longer since he'd moved in. His jaw was darkly stubbled, and his light-brown eyes were somber. Even in navy sweats and a purple hoodie with his lips downturned, she still felt like biting him. Just a little.

But her initial happiness at seeing him faded when he said, "We need to talk."

Oh no. Four super scary words.

Now, she listened, horrified, as Eli summed up the complaint leveled against them by awful Susan from next door. She started searching right away and saw with alarm and bafflement that they did, indeed, exceed the "four unrelated persons" rule for a single-family dwelling, and when she dug deeper, it seemed like they didn't precisely qualify for a rooming house license, which was a building big enough to rent to more than five people.

That's us, right there in the cracks. Maybe they could still get a license despite not quite meeting the size requirement? Presuming the house would pass all the inspections. *I doubt it would now, but maybe…* Panic blanked her mind, and she tried to breathe. Eli took her hand, a quietly calming influence.

"I had no idea I was breaking any rules. I mean, it's my house! If there's space for everyone, why should anyone else care?" She gazed at him with shock slowly searing its way down into her bones.

"Susan just lives to be mad," Eli said. "We haven't hosted any parties, we're not playing loud music, and it's unfair of her to be annoyed about us improving the property. As for the number of vehicles, we only have three. Yours, mine, and Mira's. A regular family might have that many if they have a teen driver."

The rightness of his statements made things feel worse because it highlighted how unreasonable Susan was being. Calling her an asshole and demanding that she go away wouldn't resolve the dilemma this time. *But what can we do instead?*

"I agree with you, but…what are we supposed to do? Will the city send out an inspector? Do we have to let them in? Will I be fined? I can't afford—"

"Calm down. Breathe."

Iris tried to do as he said, but the anxiety didn't abate. Looming failure threatened to crush her, and this time, she'd dragged a bunch of super nice people into her latest fuckup. *I should have known I'd just make a mess of this too. Everything my mother ever said about me was true. Ah. Right. She's not my mother after all.*

"I have no idea what to do. Henry Dale can't afford to move. Neither can Rowan or Mira. And I don't *want* you or Sally to go." She inhaled shakily, trying to fight off tears. "Can we keep this between us while I...figure things out?"

Crying wouldn't do any good, but she was trying so hard not to freak out that it felt like her eyeballs might explode. Eli sat beside her on the bed and pulled her into a hug, his hands moving in gentle strokes down her back. That was the last straw; she burst into noisy, messy tears that proved how woefully unprepared she was to own a home or a be a landlord or even complete the most basic of adult tasks. She had notes on her calendar to do certain things like pay the bills, and then she set alarms to remind her to check her calendar, or she'd just make jewelry all day.

Eli said gently, "Henry Dale already knows. He was with me when I answered the door last night. And...I don't know if secrecy is the answer. Maybe if we put our heads together, we can come up with a solution."

She sighed. "You're right. I'm no good at hiding how I feel, so everyone will know something's up. Better to deal with it up front, I guess."

He kept petting her. "These things take time. I'm sure that the city has limited personnel, so one approach would be for two of us to make ourselves scarce while the inspector is here. I could take Henry Dale on a road trip or something."

Iris shook her head. "No, that doesn't address the problem

long-term, and I don't want to solve this with lies. Susan will keep complaining unless we find a legal remedy."

"That's true. If we knew what was *really* bothering her, we might be able to address the root issue and talk it out."

Shrugging, Iris said, "I figure she's allergic to other people's happiness. She liked it better when my poor auntie lived in the house alone."

Eli snapped his fingers. "Oh! I can talk to Liz. She looks over—" Suddenly, he stopped talking, paused a beat, then said, "My friend Liz is a lawyer. She doesn't live in St. Claire, but she can definitely look at the housing laws here and advise us."

"That would be amazing. You don't mind asking her? What about her consultation fee?" Iris asked, dreading the thought of how much an email would cost. She'd seen the hourly rates billed to her great-aunt's estate, and while she was doing better, she still had credit card debt to pay down along with old student loans.

Why is nothing *ever easy for me?* This whole situation felt tremendously unfair, as Susan's enmity made no logical sense. *We didn't even do anything.*

"Don't worry about that," Eli said.

She should protest, as she'd taken a lot of help already—from Eli especially, but from everyone else as well. Henry Dale had done reno while Sally filled the freezer with food she never asked anyone to pay for; Mira was casting spells to fix up the house while Rowan worked fulfillment on Iris's jewelry business. Iris had wanted to be independent, but instead, she'd assembled a team.

No idea what that says about me—probably nothing good. Maybe I'm biologically incapable of succeeding on my own.

But Eli didn't seem to think there was anything wrong with her. And she'd smeared her tears all over his hoodie and he was still here, still cuddling her like he had nothing else to do for the rest of the day. God, he smelled fantastic, all woodsy and crisp, so much that she wanted to roll around with him.

Then he kissed the top of her head, and the tingle ran straight down to her toes. That gave her the courage to...*try*.

"I guess we need to have another house meeting," she said softly.

After Eli sent an email to Liz explaining the situation, along with some pertinent links to local housing regulations, he ran some errands.

Dish soap. Laundry detergent. Toilet paper.

He never mentioned buying this stuff, mostly because he honestly enjoyed making everyone's lives easier. Nobody else seemed to notice when they were about to run out, and he liked being the detail person, the one who made it so Iris didn't have to worry.

I wish I could spend my life doing this for her. For everyone, really.

On the way home, he stopped by Pablo's and ordered a bunch of tacos for dinner. They had the good kind here—his favorite, tacos al pastor. Gamma had introduced him to them on a vacation in Florida; she'd tried her best to give him a little Mexican culture, but he'd still lost a lot when his mom had passed so young, losing touch with her side of the family. Several times a year, he thought about looking for them—it probably wouldn't be that tough—but he always hesitated over taking that last step.

Would they be glad to see him, or would he be an outsider there because he only spoke a little Spanish? He'd tried to keep it up because he'd spoken it with his mom as a child, but his dad hadn't been fluent, and neither was Gamma. Eli had always felt that he wasn't quite one thing or another—that he only fit when he was flying, far above the treetops, away from the pettiness and problems that came from other people. Though he wouldn't admit it, he'd also been lonely.

I'm not lonely anymore.

While he waited for the food, he checked email on his phone. There was an urgent one from Liz, and he read it with a frown.

What is up with you? This is the third message I've sent. AroTech is talking about going with another candidate on this project. They said you came across lukewarm in the videoconference, and I can't say I disagree. Are you really letting go of this much money?

Don't make me fly over there.

I'm doing my best to reassure them, but they're insisting on a face-to-face to hammer out the particulars. They want your signature and a handshake by the end of the week, or this isn't happening. Get your butt to Seattle! Don't disappoint me.

Before he could type a reply, the counter guy shouted, "Tacos al pastor!" and Eli went to grab the piquant-smelling bags. Currently, there was just too much going on for him to worry about a deal he wasn't even sure he wanted. Pushing the issue to the back of his brain, he drove home in a hurry, keen to check on Iris.

The others greeted him at the front door, Rowan eagerly pulling the bags of food from his hands. "What did you get? Oh my God, it smells fantastic."

He spoke in a bullet list. "Tacos al pastor. Refritos. Red rice. Grilled onions."

Everyone helped set out the food and gathered around the table. Sally and Henry Dale watched Eli top his first taco with minced onion, green sauce, lime juice, fresh cilantro, and bits of pineapple. He devoured it in two bites while Mira, Rowan, and Iris fixed their own plates.

"I've never seen a taco like that in my life," Sally declared. "No lettuce? No cheese? No tomatoes or salsa?"

"It's more traditional," Eli said. "Go easy on the green sauce; it's pretty hot."

Henry Dale didn't say anything, but it amused Eli to see how carefully the old man added everything to the corn tortilla, like he was playing Jenga and one wrong move would collapse his meal. He went light on the green sauce, heavy on the lime, and the first bite put a big smile on Henry Dale's face.

Rowan had their phone out. "It says here that tacos al pastor were invented by Lebanese immigrants in Puebla, Mexico, in the 1920s. Originally, they were called *tacos arabes* and they used lamb."

Eli grinned. He'd done the exact same thing when he tasted these, looked up the history of the dish. "Yup. The recipe was tweaked by local cooks—hence the spices and marinade—and they switched to pork because it's more popular in Mexico."

Rowan ate another taco. "Oh, interesting! This article says that in the early 2000s, a chicken version of pastor arrived in Lebanon, and it's called *Shawarma Mexici.*"

"And we come full circle," Iris intoned. "But while we enjoy the delicious grub, we have something important to talk about."

Henry Dale said, "I think I know what this is about already."

"Don't keep the rest of us in suspense," Sally urged.

Mira folded her hands and looked attentive while putting pineapple on her second taco. Eli let Iris take the lead since this was her house. While she hesitated here and there, she got the problem into the open eventually, leaving everyone silent in the shocked aftermath. People swapped looks, but he couldn't read what those measuring glances meant.

"Does this mean we have to move out?" Rowan asked, their face still and sad. "I was the last person in, so I should probably—"

"No," Eli cut in. "Definitely not. I'll go if it comes to that, which it won't. The whole point of this get-together wasn't the taco chat."

"Though that was fun," Sally said cheerfully.

"Why aren't you worried?" Henry Dale asked.

"Isn't it obvious? Because we'll figure something out. So many smart people in one room? There's no way we don't knock this problem on the head before dessert."

Mira laughed. "I so enjoy the way you put things. And I agree with you. It's not great news, but there has to be something we can do."

"Off the top of my head, the quickest solution is marriage," Sally suggested. "We get some legal families, and boom, we're set. I nominate Rowan and Mira and...Eli and Iris."

Rowan dropped their taco with a shocked splat. "What the heck! I'm only nineteen. Why don't *you* marry Henry Dale?"

Sally narrowed her eyes, pointing a forkful of refritos in retaliation. "My backside! I'd rather marry the raccoon who rummages through our trash."

"Me too!" Henry Dale snapped.

Iris sighed, rapping her knuckles on the table. "Nobody's getting married. Let's confine our discussion to reasonable, actionable ideas."

"No doubt," Rowan mumbled. "Are we coming up with a feasible plan, or are we doing a 'wrong ideas only' meme?"

"Hmm," said Sally. "Well, I could stay part-time at Ethel's place. I believe you need more than thirty consecutive days for residency."

Eli shook his head. "That still leaves us with one too many. And we're trying to avoid having anyone leave. I like things as they are."

"Me too," Rowan whispered.

Henry Dale didn't chime in, but Eli could tell he felt the same way. While they didn't qualify as a traditional family, they *were* one. Mira shot a poisonous look toward Susan's house, though it wasn't visible from the kitchen.

"If I end up joining Ethel's coven, I'm so hexing that wench."

Eli blinked. "Why can't you do it on your own?"

"The hex will be stronger if I add more witches to the spell," Mira said, as if that was the only answer that made sense.

And it kinda was.

Suddenly Iris snapped her fingers and stood up. "You're a genius, Mira!"

"I am?" The witch sounded none too sure.

"I have a plan. Well, part of a plan. The germ of an idea, really. Sally, Mira? You're with me. I need to talk to Ethel."

With that, the three women headed out, leaving Eli to wonder what exactly went on in Iris's head. It must be a magical place.

CHAPTER TWENTY-TWO

"WAIT!" ROWAN CALLED.

Iris was by the front door, putting her shoes on. Mira and Sally were already heading out to Iris's car, which was parked at the front of the driveway. "Yeah?"

"Ethel's a witch, right? I want in! I know Danica and Clem, but I need to meet the rest of the coven if possible. It will make our web comic even more awesome."

Though the situation wasn't amusing in the slightest, she admired Rowan's inclination to capitalize on opportunity as it knocked. "Then grab your jacket and put on your sneakers."

"I'm on it," Rowan said.

Soon, the four of them set off for Ethel's place, and Iris was sort of surprised that nobody had asked what she had in mind. Maybe it was obvious.

Ethel lived on a cul-de-sac about fifteen minutes away, a cute bungalow with what was probably a gorgeous garden, though autumn had done a number on her annuals. Plants that had to be replaced every spring always seemed kind of sad while Iris admired the hardiness of perennials, returning year after year with steely determination. There were enough evergreens in Ethel's yard to keep it from looking desolate, however.

"Do you intend to tell us what you're planning?" Mira asked as Iris parked.

"It makes more sense to explain in front of Ethel since the whole thing falls apart without her cooperation."

"I think I know what you have in mind," Sally said.

"You love being mysterious," Rowan complained. "You never did explain how you got into my dad's locked file cabinet!"

Sally laughed. "Are you still thinking about that? It's not that interesting. We used to have file cabinets just like that and the keys got lost pretty often, so I learned to pop the lock with a nail file." She raised her voice, talking to the streetlight. "It's not even proper lock picking, which I *definitely* do not know how to do, any NSA officers who might be surveilling us."

Both Mira and Rowan burst out laughing, then Rowan whispered, "You know, I kind of love that I can't tell if she's joking."

Iris let that go as she hopped out of the car and tried not to feel like the worst kind of parasite. She was about to request help from people she'd never met—on the most tenuous connections. Sally was dating Ethel, and Mira wanted to join Ethel's coven. And Iris just happened to live with both of them, not too impressive a foundation upon which to request aid, but she had no better alternatives.

Sally motioned for Iris to back off as she knocked. Ethel opened the door a moment later and smiled at seeing Sally. They greeted each other with a soft kiss, which made Rowan smile with such brightness that even Iris allowed herself to enjoy the moment. Then Ethel glanced at the others waiting on her porch.

"Huh. I wasn't expecting guests. I should have scried more thoroughly, but here we are. Come on in, then."

"Pretty baby," a brightly colored parrot shouted as soon as Rowan stepped in.

Rowan colored, their cheeks washed pink. "Uh, thanks?"

"Don't mind Percy," said Ethel. "He has a favorite whenever I have new visitors."

Iris waited for Mira, then closed the door. Inside the room was warm and cozy, eclectic décor with all manner of bright colors. Sally went right in Ethel's kitchen and started making coffee, attesting to how comfortable she felt here. The two of them were definitely cute together, but that wasn't why Iris had bolstered her nerve. Normally, pride didn't let her ask for favors, but...

This isn't for me. It's for us. To keep everyone together. To... Protect our family?

They made small talk until Sally delivered all the drinks and Iris wrapped her hands around the hot mug, drawing comfort from it. "I don't know where to start."

"It must be important or you wouldn't have showed up at this hour," Ethel noted.

"I'll just start at the beginning, I guess, since it's my house. I had no idea there were rules about how many people I'm allowed to let live with me. No more than four unrelated persons are supposed to share a single-family residence."

"Ah," Ethel said.

"The crankypants next door reported us!" Outrage showed in every line of Sally's body, from her clenched fists to her furrowed brow.

"Rotten luck!" Percy called.

Rowan nodded. "Tell me about it. I just started feeling at home, and I can't get a deal like this anywhere else."

Iris went on, "If I'd known, I would have looked into my options before, so that's on me, but what's done is done. Now, I have people to take care of, you know?"

Ethel sipped at her coffee. "I get it, but where do I come in?"

"I intend to try and get licensed as a rooming house, but I doubt the wiring is up to code, and I can't afford to have the whole house physically rewired. Mira is a tech witch, but a spell to update all the house wiring is more than she can manage alone.

"She's been looking to join your coven, so I wondered if the rest of you would be willing to help with the spell." She took a deep breath. "I can pay, just not up front. It would have to be in installments. But...it would mean a lot to us if it was possible. If Violet Gables gets approved by the city, there won't be any basis for Susan's complaint."

"If you need a deposit, I can take care of that," Sally said.

Mira finally spoke. "This is awkward because I haven't been voted in officially yet. We're still getting to know each other, so I understand if—"

Smiling faintly, Ethel held up a hand. "Whoa, slow down. I didn't say no. I didn't say yes either."

"Do it!" Percy shouted. "Do it! Do it!"

The curvy witch laughed. "Well, if Percy thinks so. But seriously, I need to talk to Clem and Danica first since this is their wheelhouse. They'd be doing most of the heavy lifting along with Mira. The rest of us would be lending our power to pull off a spell of that magnitude. I don't think any of us have tried to cover a whole house."

"Would it be easier in stages?" Iris asked. She didn't want to be one of *those* people, asking for the impossible because she didn't really understand how the magic worked.

Mira laced her hands together in her lap, and Rowan touched her shoulder lightly. "It...means a lot to me that you'd even consider it. I'm new here, after all."

"But you'll most likely be one of us," Ethel predicted.

The other witch glanced up with a tremulous smile, one that touched Iris deeply, as she understood so well how it felt to crave belonging to that extent. "You think so?"

Ethel answered, "I do. I'll text you with the particulars after I call for a coven meeting. We're not due to meet again until next month, but we need to talk it over."

"I appreciate being included," Mira said softly.

"But..." Ethel fixed an acute stare on Iris, eyes narrowed. "Why don't you ask *your* people for help?"

Honestly, Iris had no idea what the witch meant. "Excuse me?"

"That's odd. Gladys mentioned you to me, and I just confirmed it myself. Why don't you ask the fae? Is it because so few stay in the sunset lands?"

Iris's heart started pounding so hard, she felt it in her ears. "I have *no* idea what you're talking about."

Sally whispered, "I *told* you, she's been fighting with her family. Because of the mix-up at the hospital."

"Holy shit," Ethel breathed. "That changes everything. No pun intended."

Iris wished the world would start making sense again. "Uh, what?"

"I think I get it," Rowan said. "It explains everything. You're a changeling, Iris."

———————————

Eli put away the remnants from their meal, wishing there was more he could do.

There were certain big moves he could make, like having the place completely renovated from the inside out, but he couldn't bankroll that without revealing his true financial situation. If he dumped big money on the problem to make it go away, Iris would probably feel upset and betrayed.

"You worry about her a lot," Henry Dale observed.

For once, the older man hadn't retreated to his room after eating, a fair measure of how concerned he must be. Though Henry Dale wouldn't admit it, he wanted to hear what went down just as much as Eli did. At first, Eli nodded without comment, then he added, "Do you think relationships are worth it?"

"You're talking to the wrong person. But...for most, they seem to be. Why?"

"Never mind," Eli said, wiping the countertops.

Happily, they didn't wait long.

Soon, three of their housemates returned, but there was an odd energy between them. Rowan looked tentative and sympathetic while Mira kept stealing glances at Iris, as if something had changed in the time they'd been gone. Sally must have opted to stay over at Ethel's when everyone else left.

Henry Dale wasn't great at reading people, so he asked outright. "Well? What happened? Are you working with the witches, or...?"

"They need to discuss it," Mira said. "But I'm hopeful."

Rowan sighed. "I wish I had as much faith as you do."

"Hmph. Well, tell me if there's anything I can do. You know, other than move out. I was here first. *I'm* not going." Henry Dale headed to his room, evidently not noticing how Rowan flinched and hunched their shoulders.

Eli wanted to comfort them, but honestly, Iris looked so shell-shocked that she was his first priority. She always would be, even if she wanted nothing more to do with him after she found out why he was really here. The others seemed to sense that they needed privacy and went upstairs while Iris just stood in the middle of the kitchen, lost as a person could be in her own home.

"What happened?" he asked.

"I'm fae," she answered in a bewildered tone. "That's what Gladys meant at the community center, why she called me 'Lady' like it was a title. The older witch *knew,* apparently, just from the way my energy looks or something. How is that possible?"

Eli took a moment, stunned by what she was saying. Then he gathered himself and reviewed what he'd read about the fae. "Maybe changelings aren't just stories. There are legends about the fae doing that, though the accounts differ on the details."

Her expression cleared slightly, and she focused on him, appearing to take interest in what he knew. "Like how?"

"Well, I've read stories where it was done for revenge. One house steals another's child and banishes them to the human realm where the real fae parents can't find them. In other versions, fae children are sent to the mortal world to protect them from their enemies. Maybe you're a lost fae princess," Eli suggested with a faint smile.

Iris scoffed. "Wouldn't *that* be wild?"

But at least she didn't look so broken or stunned anymore, so he risked sharing something else, trusting she could handle it. "I should say, in hawk form, I *did* notice that your energy shines differently than anyone I'd ever seen."

"Why didn't you tell me before?" she demanded.

"Because other than that, I didn't have anything concrete to tell you. And I thought you were a psychic vampire until discovering otherwise." Best not to linger over how hurt she'd been by what Lily had said. "On the bright side, maybe this means your real family is desperately searching for you as we speak."

She inhaled softly, swiftly. "Do you...think so?"

Maybe he shouldn't get her hopes up. It was also possible that she'd been swapped because her fae bio-family didn't give a damn and they'd desperately wanted a human baby for some unknown and likely nefarious reason. Eli tried not to even hint at that train of thought. "Hmm. Could be."

She paced the kitchen, waving her hands wildly. "Doesn't matter. Unless they show up at my door, I have other aspects to consider."

"Like what?" he asked.

"Like, what should I be able to *do* if I'm fae?" She ticked the questions off on her fingers, one by one. "Do I have magic? Can I shape-shift? Spin straw into gold? Wait, was Rumpelstiltskin one of the fae? I think I'm mixing up my fairy tales."

"In some versions, he was a hobgoblin, which makes him fae." Eli wasn't sure why he remembered that. "In other renditions, he was a lesser demon."

"Interesting. I haven't tried to turn straw into gold, so let's put a pin in that." Iris drooped visibly, like a daisy about to drop its petals. "More likely, I'm a dud, and I won't be able to do what other fae folk can anyway."

"You're perfect," Eli said at once.

"Pfft. You're my boyfriend; you *have* to say that." As soon as she said that, she pressed both hands to her mouth, eyes wide.

Eli could barely breathe for the joy cascading through him. He had no right to be delighted over hearing that word since they hadn't even talked about it. And that must be why she was so horrified about declaring it unilaterally.

"I am," he agreed easily. "So yeah, you shouldn't be looking for unbiased assessments from me. Clearly I have an 'Iris' bias. *You* are my bias."

She relaxed and wandered into his arms, nestling close. "That's so cute. No matter how bad things are, you start talking, and I feel better. If I'm your bias, you're my panacea."

Guilt prodded at him, but this wasn't the time to dump another revelation on her for the sake of clearing his conscience. He'd read that certain confessions were actually acts of selfishness, asking someone else to bear pain, and he rather agreed with that currently. *Not now. I can't tell her now. I'll do it when everything's resolved.*

Instead, he kissed her forehead and offered a different truth. "Funny, that's how I feel about you. Since my parents died, I've felt...rootless. Gamma did her best, but I always felt like...an interruption in her life. As soon as I could, I moved out and tried to find my own place to belong so she could do the same, but I didn't fit anywhere. Not ever. I was even thinking I might be better off as a hawk because nobody would miss me."

"Oh my God, Eli..."

Before she could say more, he went on, "That's not true anymore. And it's because of you. Because of Violet Gables and everyone here."

She seemed to take strength in his declaration, gazing up at him with overbright eyes. "We'll protect it, right?"

"Absolutely," he promised.

CHAPTER TWENTY-THREE

THE ROOMING HOUSE LICENSE APPLICATION was seven pages long.

In a fit of ambition, Iris had printed it out upstairs, intending to jump right on this problem. Now she lined the papers up in order on the kitchen table, staring at everything with a growing sense of despair. There was so much information, most of which she didn't know or even how to access.

Breathe. She heard the word in Eli's comforting, gentle tone, a welcome change from Delphine hissing poison about how she was disappointing and worthless. But as if Olive sensed she needed cheering up today, her phone buzzed.

> Olive: Don't know if I told you, but this was my last year. I'll be back for Christmas.
>
> Iris: Oh my God. You have to come! I want you to meet everybody. Can you?
>
> Olive: Are you kidding? I'd much rather stay with you.
>
> Iris: ...Even if there's drama?
>
> Olive: Obviously. I might bring someone. If that's okay.

Iris: Awesome! And absolutely. You two can have my boyfriend's room. He might be sharing with me by then anyway.

Olive: Ooh. I can see we have a lot of catching up to do. Love ya.

Iris: Love you too. See you soon.

It might be unwise to be making plans like that so soon, but she was too excited about seeing Olive again to care. *How long has it been since her last visit anyway?*

Three years? Damn.

That quick chat bolstered her spirits for about five minutes, just long enough for her to remember what she'd been doing. "I have to talk to the fire chief about a fire plan," she said to no one in particular.

Henry Dale popped into the kitchen. "I know him. I can do that for you."

She felt like hugging the old man. "Seriously? That would so helpful."

"I'm not a witch, but I know people," he said gruffly.

Yeah, that was *still* bugging him. She stifled a smile over how consistent he was. The fact that Mira could use magic to replicate some of his skill set? He was still miffed that she'd done the second-floor hallway and now the paint looked new. In the beginning, he deeply appreciated getting his Walkman fixed and he acted like he was cool with tech magic, but the man wasn't good at pretending long-term.

"I wonder if the shabby exterior will hurt our chances," she said.

The old contractor took a seat at the table, skimming the pages. "Probably not the paint, but maybe the rotten gingerbread.

It could conceivably be cited as a safety concern. I'm dead certain they'll say you need a smoke detector on each floor and probably a few carbon monoxide detectors as well."

"That's good to know."

"If you buy those, I can call install 'em for you."

Ugh. How much will all of that cost? She chose not to search to find out, at least not right now. "You don't mind?"

"Not at all. Whatever I can do to help bring the place up to code, I'm willing to pitch in." Actually, his expression said he was freaking *delighted.* His eyes sparkled at the prospect of another project.

Maybe it's okay to ask.

"Since you offered, on this page, they need precise measurements of every single room in the place. Do you think—?"

"I'll ask Rowan to give me a hand when they have a minute. We'll take care of it."

Henry Dale's easy use of Rowan's preferred pronouns made Iris curious, though. "Can I ask you something?"

"Sure, I can postpone my important business meetings." Henry Dale pretended to get on his cell phone. "Mildred, cancel my two o'clock and push my three to four. Unfortunately I won't be able to buy MySpace today after all."

Iris burst out laughing. "Sally's rubbing off on you."

"Hardly. My sense of humor is much sharper. Anyway, what did you want to ask?"

"Some older people complain that they don't understand and refuse to honor nonbinary pronouns, so I was wondering—"

"Everything comes down to manners," said Henry Dale. "Maybe I *don't* understand, but here's an example—you meet somebody who says, 'My name's Bradley, but everybody calls me Buzz.' So you call 'em Buzz. You don't need to understand, do you? They don't have to share their life story and justify that name. It's just good manners, so for me, it's that simple."

That made a lot of sense, given what she knew about him. "Thanks for telling me."

"It wasn't a secret, that's just how I feel." Henry Dale had inspections on his mind, though. "Oh, you'll likely need a fire extinguisher too. Maybe check into how many the house needs to get licensed."

More dollar signs flashed before her eyes. Iris tried not to panic. *I have some room on my card, but I thought renting rooms would help me get out of debt.* The barter system had made good sense when she agreed to it; otherwise, the house wouldn't look nearly as nice as it did now, but there was still a lot of work to be done.

I can't believe we're jumping through all these hoops because of one grouchy neighbor.

Nobody else on the block seems to care.

To her surprise, Henry Dale reached over and patted her hand. "I know it seems like a lot, but try making a list. And write down easy tasks for motivation. I enjoy drawing a line through the ones I finish. Maybe it'll help you too."

"Couldn't hurt," Iris decided.

Doing that also let her procrastinate filling out the licensing application, so she obviously decided to make the checklist first:

- Price fire alarms
- Price carbon monoxide detectors

- Price fire extinguishers
- Buy all of the above
- Repair rotten gingerbread (somehow)
- Fill out forms
- Turn in forms
- Bribe someone who works for the city
- Spin straw into gold???

Henry Dale watched her write things down for a bit, then he tapped the "gingerbread" one. "I have plenty of wood, and I *think* I can replicate those pieces if you let me take one down to use as a sample. Do you want me to try?"

"If you don't mind. You've already done so much, and I feel like I'm taking advantage." She should probably decline, but she couldn't bring herself to do it.

Not when everyone was counting on her to make this work. Screw my pride.

"No, I'm looking forward to it. I found a saw in the shed that makes complicated cuts, and I've been wanting to try it."

"Huh. I wonder why auntie had so many tools."

"Maybe she lived with someone who used them?"

Iris blinked. While Gertie had never married, Iris had no clue whether she'd always lived alone. Hazel might know more? Although that wasn't her most pressing concern.

"Anyway," Henry Dale went on, "I imagine you're joking about the bribery thing, but it might help if we could get in touch with someone who works for the city."

"Leanne's on the city council," Mira said.

Iris jumped a little, as she hadn't even heard Mira come in. "Oh wow, you're home already? How long have I been staring at these forms? What day is it?"

Laughing quietly, Mira sat down at the table. "I'm a professional at forms. Let me fill some of it out. Ah, lots of repeated data blocks. Give me five minutes."

Henry Dale got up. "That's my cue. I'll roust Rowan and start those measurements."

It took all of Iris's composure not to burst into tears. She was so bad at...freaking everything, and here her housemates were, taking up the slack. *Why am I like this?*

"There." With a satisfied pat, Mira angled the pages so Iris could see the parts she'd filled in. "It's not as bad as it looks, I swear."

"The paperwork or my life?" Iris asked wryly.

Mira chuckled. "Would you believe me if I said both?"

Later, Iris put the application in the mailbox and retrieved her mail. She had two letters from a new collection agency, telling her one of her cards had been closed and charged off. Now the real fun would begin. She sucked in a breath and tried not to cry as she opened the statement for the one card she'd managed to keep active. Even the minimum payment was too much.

Right now, *everything* felt like it was too much.

When Eli spoke to Henry Dale the next day, he had misgivings about stepping in.

But the more he saw of Iris's worried face, the less he liked it.

They still hadn't heard from the city, but at least she'd submitted the application. So if the inspector came regarding the complaint, they'd started the approval process. Liz said that should muddy the waters a bit, and at worst, they should receive a fine and time to get their documentation in order.

But Iris would panic if she got fined. Money matters scared the crap out of her since she was already in debt. After wrestling with the issue, Eli decided he couldn't wait it out. Money could solve a lot of her problems, and he had that. It really was that simple.

First he put in an order for the alarms, detectors, and extinguishers, then he quietly texted Sally, asking her if she could arrange for him to meet with Mira and Ethel's coven. She sent him a map pin to Fix-It Witches. Belatedly, he recalled Iris chatting with some witches outside during that graffiti incident. Apparently, those two belonged to Ethel's coven, and since it was a business, he could show up without an appointment.

He didn't say anything as he headed out because there was no guarantee this would work. Outside, he found a tall man in his early seventies on the front porch, and his heart sank when he realized Awful Susan from next door stood behind him, a smug smile creasing her cheeks. The two had just been about to knock.

"Can I help you?" he asked in an icy tone.

"I'm from HAPI. Susan has made a troubling report. Is it true that you're housing multiple paranormals here in violation of all city housing regulations?"

Suddenly, he recognized the man. Dan Rutherford was a big mouth who'd built himself a reputation for targeting paranormal citizens. He was wealthy, and he'd drawn support from a certain type of human. This didn't bode well.

"I don't see why I should answer that," Eli said. "There's no law that says we have to report where we live or with—"

"That will change if I have anything to say about," Rutherford cut in. "I'm talking to my pal about it. You might know him. He's proposed some protective legislation."

Eli needed to get rid of these two assholes immediately. Before Iris discovered that the situation could potentially get worse.

She'll find out if you do this. But even that awareness couldn't dissuade him. Whatever the personal cost, he'd fix things for her.

"Neither one of you is welcome. Susan, you've been warned before. If I see you across the property line again, I'm filing for a restraining order." He flipped open his phone with a purposeful snick. "Do I need to report you two officially?"

Not that he'd actually call the cops. They might side with Susan and Rutherford, but fortunately, they didn't call his bluff.

"Look forward to my next move," Susan said.

Rutherford followed her across the yard, and that didn't sit right either. Hell knew what they'd be colluding while he frantically tried to fix things. Eli understood that he was contradicting himself because he'd registered how much Iris wanted to be independent and that she didn't want to rely on others. *But she said I'm her boyfriend. That gives me the right to look after her.*

At least, that was what he told himself as he jogged to his truck and drove toward the business district.

Downtown St. Claire was busy this time of day, lots of cars jockeying for limited parking spots. He circled once and opted to park on a side street and walk five blocks. No big deal, as it wasn't raining, though he sometimes wished shifting was more convenient. If he changed, he'd show up naked, and that *really* didn't work.

St. Claire was more charming than he remembered with shops painted in whimsical hues. Brick and wood buildings broke up the visual monotony, and he passed the little bakery Gamma had mentioned. *I should get cinnamon rolls on my way back.* But his goal was Fix-It Witches first.

The sign literally had two witches on it, so he marveled over the fact that this pair had kept their true nature a secret before the big announcement a few years back. Inside, it was meticulously clean with an array of vintage appliances and electronics displayed for purchase. The pretty woman behind the glass case glanced up and smiled as the bell jangled to announce his arrival.

"Welcome! How can I help you today?"

He thought he recognized her, but admittedly he'd been paying far more attention to Iris the day they'd stopped by the shop. "Are you Danica Waterhouse?"

"Uh-oh. You're not trying to serve me a subpoena, are you?"

Eli laughed, showing that he had nothing up his sleeve. "Not even slightly."

"Then yes, I'm Danica Waterhouse. I didn't change my name when I got married."

"Congratulations. That's a beautiful ring." He felt pretty sure it wasn't his imagination that she'd held her hand gesture a little too long.

Definitely inviting a compliment on the jewelry. Normally, he noticed such details and didn't play along, but today, he was trying to make a good impression.

"Thank you," she said.

"I came to talk to you because you're considering an offer to help with a big spell over at my girlfriend's house."

"Oh, you're Sally's housemate!" Danica brightened, her faint wariness evolving into a genuinely pleased expression.

"That's me, Eli Reese. I just wanted to tell you something that might impact your decision. I realize that this is literally your livelihood and you might not be inclined to accept work with a deferred payment schedule."

"It's not wholly the money," Danica said quickly. "Sure, that's a factor for Clem and me, but the whole coven has to agree. Typically, we'd only do joint spells for one of our own members, but Sally's dating Ethel, so…"

Eli nodded. "It's a gray area, understood."

"What did you want to tell me?" It was a gentle prompt but a nudge nonetheless.

"Cost doesn't matter. I can cover it. I can wire the full amount right now, and if you need to charge more than usual since the spell is so broad in scope, that's fine."

"That would be…seven times our usual fee. You're really fine with that?"

Since the money had hit his account yesterday from the sale of What's Cooking?, he could answer with assurance, "Yes, completely. Price is no object."

"Deep pockets," Danica murmured with a surprised twitch of her brow. "You don't look like you have that kind of money."

"Do you need to see proof of funds?" he asked.

She shook her head. "That won't be necessary."

"Does that change anything?"

The tech witch laughed. "I hate to say it, but probably. The others don't have any emotional investment, unlike Ethel. So Clem was a no, Kerry was a no. I was undecided until now, as were Margie, Leanne, and Vanessa. You had Ethel in your corner. And Priya, of course. She's such a sweetheart."

"Mira doesn't get a vote?" Eli asked.

Danica shook her head. "Right now, she's provisional. We're still in the getting-to-know-you stage, and she's directly impacted by the situation."

"That makes sense. I'll give you my contact info. When you reach a consensus and a workable estimate, let me know. I'll pay up front." He touched his phone to hers.

She checked to make sure his details registered properly and nodded. "Nobody in the coven will mind an unexpected windfall. Since that's the case, I'll be in touch."

There, it's done. No turning back.

Iris would likely be livid when she found out, and then...she would have questions, ones he'd answer at long last. Maybe part of him would even be glad to have it over, even if it meant *everything* was. His chest ached, and he rubbed it reflexively.

On the way back to the truck, he popped into Sugar Daddy's to get the cinnamon rolls Gamma had raved about. A cheerful woman waved as he stepped in.

"What looks good today?" she asked pertly.

"Maya! What did I tell you about trying suggestive slogans

on the clientele?" A burly, bearded dude scolded from the galley doorway.

"Sorry, just trying to put a little fun in my day. You didn't mind, sir?"

Eli shook his head. "It's fine. I'll have a dozen cinnamon rolls and four éclairs."

Just in case somebody doesn't like cinnamon rolls. This might be the equivalent of his last meal, after all.

CHAPTER TWENTY-FOUR

"COME WITH ME," ELI SAID.

Unexpectedly, he'd rung the doorbell instead of letting himself in. When Iris answered, he gave her the sweetest smile, making her heart flutter.

It was early evening, and she had a lot to do, but nothing more important than this moment. He stood on the front porch with an unfamiliar look, an expression somewhere between mischief and tenderness. She smiled and took his outstretched hand, content to let him surprise her.

But she didn't expect him to lead her out to his truck. "Where are we going?" she asked.

"It's a surprise."

She didn't push for details since that might spoil the mood, and she was so happy about being swept away that she let it happen with delight popping like corn kernels in a hot pan. Soon, Eli parked next to the river. At night, it was quiet and romantic with the yellow lamps glowing along the walkway, but the chilly temperature kept most everyone else indoors. He got out of the truck and opened her door for her, and she had no idea what to expect, so she was properly startled when he dropped the truck's tailgate. Inside, there were a couple of blankets and an insulated chest, probably to keep something warm.

"Starlight picnic," she guessed.

"It's nothing special. Just some fresh cinnamon rolls and a thermos full of coffee. I thought you could use a break." Eli vaulted into the back of the truck and pulled her up beside him. "Hope this is okay?"

"It's perfect. I don't want to think about anything right now."

"Cinnamon roll?"

She took the soft, gooey pastry and peeled it apart, nibbling until she had only the soft, sweet core left. Afterward, she licked her sticky fingers and washed the treat down with hot coffee. Eli watched her with a smile, like he could sate his hunger with her satisfaction. Iris leaned in for a kiss, and he moaned against her mouth. He cupped the nape of her neck, fingers dragging through her hair, and his touch sent shivers down her spine. Their kisses drew out, at first delicate like the tremulous notes of a flute, and then they surged into operatic territory, leaving Iris breathless when Eli drew back.

"I could easily lose myself in you," he whispered.

"Same. But I don't want our first time to be—"

"In the back of my truck?" He laughed. "Me either. Want to cuddle for a bit?"

"I'd love that."

Iris knee-walked until she could settle between Eli's legs, and he drew her against his chest, linking his arms to make her feel even warmer and more cherished. Between the blankets, the warm drink, and Eli, she couldn't feel any cozier. Despite the general messiness of her situation—complaints being filed and another card gone to collections—she still let out a happy sigh.

"Comfortable?" he asked, his voice deep with amusement.

"Extremely."

"I know you have other stuff on your mind, but…have you learned anything more about your fae heritage?"

"Not really. There's a lot of lore, but the fae are incredibly reclusive, so the stories are impossible for me to verify."

She lapsed into silence, and Eli didn't push—a fact she appreciated. Just snuggling with him and looking at the stars, Iris felt like the luckiest person in the world.

All too soon, he stirred and touched her cheek. "You're getting cold, even with the blanket. We should get home."

Home. Hearing him use that word for Violet Gables brightened her mood even more.

"I'm all fueled up. Whatever comes next, I can take it."

In quiet accord, they drove home in contemplative silence. Eli headed upstairs to take care of some business, and Iris decided to spoil him with a cup of hot tea. It was nothing compared to *his* surprise, but she'd gotten to stay toasty warm in his arms while he leaned against the cold metal of the truck. He could probably use some warming up.

She came upstairs quietly and was about to knock on his door when she hesitated. Because she couldn't believe what she was hearing. Or rather, she didn't *want* to. But she was standing outside Eli's room and he was definitely saying, "Are you sure twenty-five grand is enough? I'm happy to pay twice that if you can perform the spell right away."

He has...fifty grand?

Dazed and confused, she stumbled upstairs and set the tea cup on her work table with trembling hands, feeling shaky and queasy at the same time. Nothing made sense, and as she opened her laptop on automatic—because that was what she always did, checked on her shop—she found herself keying in the name *Eli Reese* and *popular apps*. To her astonishment, he popped up in a few feature articles, and he had a freaking Wiki page. Realization hit her like a fist in the gut.

He wasn't somebody who needed to rent a room from her. *Why the hell is he even here?* The sense of betrayal hit her so hard that she almost threw up, quivering in reaction. God, he must've laughed at her pathetic efforts, trying to get her life together. *How much money does he have anyway?*

Fuck.

FUCK.

No damn wonder he was always offering to pay for shit. She felt like screaming or punching him or both. Her face felt hot with humiliation, and she fought back tears—rage, sorrow—so many emotions. Nothing about him made any sense whatsoever. She read more, learning facts he should have shared himself.

Her rage ballooned.

She had to nix whatever backdoor deal he'd arranged with Ethel and Mira's coven. Like hell was she okay with Eli waltzing in like a big shot and just...taking over. With his bullshit secret rich guy entitlement. Hmm. Maybe that didn't entirely make sense, but when Iris was this angry, making her thoughts flow in a straight line was freaking tough.

She stormed downstairs, ready to let him have a piece of her mind. But Eli was on another call, and this time, he was arguing with someone. "I don't give a damn. I can't leave right now, and that's final." A pause. "My answer would be the same even if it was ten million, Liz. Just tell AroTech there's no deal. I'm needed here, understand?"

Those words eviscerated her. Iris took a breath, another.

Not only am I a failure, I'm dragging Eli down with me.

Her righteous indignation yielded to an emotion altogether more painful. She tiptoed back to her room and gave in to heartbreak.

Iris wept. For the future she'd imagined they were building together and for everything he'd hidden while pretending to be one of them. Eli didn't belong on her island of misfit toys, and he never had. Even if she could forgive him for hiding such crucial information, there was no way she could picture herself beside somebody like him. A relationship between them would be too much like charity or pity or, hell, she didn't *know* what. Them being together made no sense at all.

He had opportunities she could never imagine. For him, there was no worry about making ends meet, no cutting corners. Insta models were probably whispering in his DMs, promising him the time of his life. Probably he could eat filet mignon every night, get the expensive wine with dinner, and follow it up with a vacation in France.

His dream vacation is in Veracruz? Yeah, right.

He must've been trying to seem relatable. That bastard.

The tears flowed down her cheeks until her eyes hurt and her cheeks felt sticky with the drying salt. Still, she tried to stay quiet. The last thing she wanted to do was worry her housemates, most of whom were wonderful humans. Of course, she didn't have a bathroom up here or even a pack of wet wipes, so she'd have to sneak downstairs to try and hide the evidence of this crying jag.

But first, she called Fix-It Witches. The woman answered on the first ring. "Fix-It Witches, this is Clem. How can I help you?"

"Uh, yeah. This is Iris Collins. I'm not sure who's been talking to Eli Reese, but he didn't have my permission to go around me and pay for anything behind my back. At this point, I'm withdrawing my request for assistance from your coven, and I'd appreciate if you would pass the word along. I'm sorry for bothering you and wasting everyone's time."

"Wow. This is awkward. Eli did talk to my cousin, and we thought it was fine since he's your boyfriend and everything. I'll... let the others know."

"Thank you again," Iris said, fighting the urge to snort-laugh at the idea that Eli was her boyfriend.

Fresh fury roiled through her as she tapped to end the call. Mira's coven must think Iris was a bitch on wheels for flouncing away from their kindness, but she couldn't let Eli fix her problems, period. Even if she knew what was going on with him, she still wouldn't be okay with any of this.

A bit later, Sally was at the door, tapping gently. "Iris? I just heard something strange from Ethel. Can I come in?"

Wow, the witchy hotline is faster than the speed of light.

There was no point in delaying the inevitable. "Sure. Door's unlocked."

The older woman noticed her swollen eyes and stained cheeks at once, gazing at her with open concern. "You've been crying."

Before asking anything else, Sally opened her arms, and Iris practically tumbled into them. The tears started again, this time so hard she couldn't even breathe. Sally just held her and rubbed her back, making comforting noises. This crying jag left Iris feeling light-headed, like she might actually pass out.

"Can you tell me what's wrong? Ethel shared the gist of what you said to Clem. But I'm confused; why are you upset that Eli's willing to help?"

Iris couldn't get the words out right, but she tried, explaining her reaction in fits and starts. Then she showed Sally just how freaking successful Eli was, the apps he'd developed and sold, the profiles and the Wiki page, and suddenly, she saw comprehension dawn in Sally's expression.

"That's why," Iris mumbled.

"Oh. I see. He's out of your league then?"

"Freaking obviously. Why would he hide this? And why the hell is he living here? And how dare he just...buy me peace of mind? This is *my* house. I want to solve my own problems. I'm not looking for a Prince Charming or a white knight, dammit."

"No, I quite understand that part, dear. But I think you might be leaping to conclusions. I'm sure he didn't have bad reasons for keeping those things from you. Eli is a gentle soul, I'm sure of it."

"He's a *liar*," Iris snapped.

A bag thudded to the ground at the base of the stairs, toppling what sounded like boxes onto the floor. She didn't get up to investigate. Iris waited with her arms folded until Eli appeared in the doorway of her studio, standing there with an anguished look. And she didn't have it in her to speak because she'd used up most of her voice crying. Now there were just jagged edges of her dashed hopes, scraping up her insides.

"I'm sorry," he said. "I never meant to hurt you."

Shit. You asshole. That apology might be what wounded her most of all.

———————

It's over.

Eli saw that from the dead look in Iris's reddened eyes, echoed in the tear tracks down her face. The defensive posture spoke volumes as well, warning him not to get any closer. *I really fucked things up, didn't I?* Of course he'd known she would be upset, but not...not heartbroken. *I did this, extinguished the light in her eyes. What her shitty family couldn't accomplish, I did.*

Sally cleared her throat. "I'll leave you two to talk."

He didn't blame her for retreating because the time had finally come to clarify matters, but Iris didn't wait for him to speak. "Who the hell are you?"

"Eli Reese."

She clenched her jaw, speaking through her teeth. "You don't flip houses. You don't do websites. You're an apps entrepreneur. You have a financial advisor, own multiple properties, attorney on call—a friend, my ass—and a damn Wiki page."

He took a breath, trying to pretend he wasn't more rattled than he'd ever been. "Okay. You looked into me. That makes things easier. No, I didn't need to rent a room when we ran into each other at the coffee shop."

"You mean when we met," she corrected.

Eli shook his head. "No. That wasn't the first time. We knew each other a long time ago." Eli dug into his pocket and drew out the little bracelet; he carried it like a good luck charm and often touched it when he felt nervous. Like now. "Do you recognize this?"

"No. Why?" Then Iris took a closer look, stepping nearer in the process. "Wait, I think I had one like that a long time ago."

Despite the circumstances, he smiled. "It's not like yours. It *is* yours. When I was ten, you stepped in when I was being bullied. I was a lot smaller then and very timid."

How am I supposed to tell her the rest without her concluding I'm a stalker or a creep or both?

She hesitated, her scowl wavering. "I don't remember that at all. But...can I see the bracelet?" After examining it, she seemed more baffled than ever. "It's really mine. It has my initials on the inside."

"That's right. You dropped it when you were walking away, and I was too shy to return it."

"And you kept it all these years?"

He nodded. "I always hoped to thank you and give it back. Which might seem like overkill, but that moment meant a lot to me. Nobody had ever stood up for me before."

"How did you expect to do that?" she demanded.

"In time, I found you on social media," he admitted.

"You've been stalking me online? For years, it seems." She took a step back, hands out as if to ward off his weird, obsessive tendencies.

Eli moved away as well, not wanting her to feel pressed. "No! Haven't you randomly wondered about someone you used to know and searched their name?"

Iris sighed. "Okay, I admit it. But only with certain exes. Like, I do sometimes wallow in anger and regret and look at pictures Dylan and Lily have posted."

Finally, a small break. Not enough to give him hope.

He glanced past her, watching a few crows settle on the electrical lines beyond her window. Crows were clever as hell, and they always seemed to know when something terrible was about to happen. How fitting.

Eli made himself say, "Then you understand to some degree. I looked up to you in grade school, that's it. And at one point, I was curious how you were doing. I thought about contacting you, but I was afraid you'd think it was weird."

She nodded sharply. "It would've been, yeah. Actually, I think I do remember now. Big kid, name was… Nope, it's not coming to me."

If anything, Eli *wished* he could forget, but his memory was uncomfortably precise on certain details. "Roddy Frierson. He made elementary school a living hell for me until you intervened. You threatened to tell his grandma."

Iris snapped her fingers, seeming pleased over retrieving the recollection. "Yeah! He cried. I'd forgotten about that until now." Her sudden smile faded. "You fixate, huh? That wasn't a big deal to me back then. Shouldn't have been to you either."

"You don't get to decide that."

Her lip curled. "Whatever. So I was your childhood hero and you looked me up later on socials. That's how you recognized me in the café. Did you go there intending to meet me?" Her expression gave nothing away now, but her gaze was cold and wary, as if she was already braced for the worst.

"No!" Maybe if he spoke quickly enough, she'd believe him. "I was in town working on Gamma's house before you arrived. Meeting you was a total coincidence. I went over, just intending to introduce myself and thank you. That's it! If you recall, *you* assumed I wanted to rent a room, so I was extremely confused, and then..."

"And then?"

Yeah, she won't like this. But it's true.

"When I understood your financial situation, I wanted to help."

"Which is why you rented my most expensive room. Because you *pitied* me. When you didn't even need a place to stay. Well, fuck *you*, Eli. You could've left St. Claire weeks ago there's nothing to hold you here."

You're here, he wanted to say. But she wouldn't believe any declarations at this stage, so he didn't speak the words. Better to keep them than hear her call him a liar again. That fucking stung, even if she had it right.

"I just wanted to repay you," he said.

"Let's say that's true... It's still important to get someone's consent. I never authorized you to act as my agent with the coven. I'm not okay with being sugar babied. Maybe you felt sorry for me this whole time, but I'm not interested in that either."

He stepped toward her, and she moved back. *Message received. We're not people who touch anymore. Fuck, that hurts.* "You can't turn away their help because of me."

"I already have. This is my issue to solve. I'll accept the bracelet and your thanks, nothing more. Any debt between us is more than repaid. You gave me a lot of emotional support these past months, and that's all I wanted from you. Sally said you had your reasons, but I frankly don't care. Lies are lies."

"So we're done?" he asked, not wanting the answer but needing it.

Her gray eyes were like a heavy bank of storm clouds. "I'm sure you foresaw that. If you move out, we're one step closer to solving the issue."

"What can I do?" he whispered. "How can I make it up to you?"

Iris replied with brutal honesty. "You can't. I fell in love with someone else, the person you were *pretending* to be. There's only broken trust now. The real you? I don't know that guy, and I don't belong with him either."

You do. You know everything about me that matters. But the words couldn't fit past the tightness of his throat.

She went on, relentless, severing their ties with words that wounded him surgically, each syllable a fresh slice. "I hope you'll figure out a plausible excuse for everyone else. I don't want them hurt."

He swallowed hard, past the ache that made him want to dive into hawk form and scream to the skies. Because of his own fuckery, he was losing the only home he'd known since his parents died and he realized that Gamma had put her life on hold to raise him. "I'll take care of it," he rasped.

It took all his fortitude not to cry in front of her; there was no point since he'd done this to himself, and he understood that well enough.

Everything ends. Always.

CHAPTER TWENTY-FIVE

THE REST OF THE DAY, Iris didn't go downstairs except to use the bathroom.

Somebody, probably Sally, left food outside her door, and apparently, she told their other housemates that Iris had caught a bug. A devastating, heart-destroying bacteria, yep. And while she was wallowing, Eli vanished as quietly as he'd come.

Gone, just like she'd asked. Ordered? Yeah, more like ordered.

Now she had no clue how to pass this inspection, but she had to start somewhere. The next day, she stumbled out of her sad lady lair and found boxes of alarms, detectors, and fire extinguishers piled up at the foot of the attic steps. Eli must have bought them before taking off, before the breakup.

Is that even the right word?

She couldn't obsess, not now. Gathering her resolve as she gathered the packages, she hauled them to Henry Dale, who was sipping a cup of coffee at the kitchen table. "You said you could install these?"

"I'll take care of it." The old man scrutinized her from head to toe. "Did you know that Eli left? He said he had to see his grandmother—that it was urgent and he didn't know when he'd be back."

She tried to keep her expression neutral. "He told me yesterday. In other news, I can't afford the major cost associated with such a big spell. And I guess the coven isn't enthusiastic about a payment plan. We're back to square one."

The older man patted her shoulder with a deadpan expression. "If all else fails, I'll marry you. But we're *not* sharing a room or a bed."

Startled to her soul, Iris cracked up laughing. "You've made my day, seriously."

"I live to entertain," he said in that same droll tone.

Though she still hurt, at least she wasn't alone. Eli might be. She recalled what he'd said about wanting to live as a hawk—was any of that even true? Still, part of her hoped that Eli had, indeed, gone to seek comfort with his grandma. *No, I won't waste my mental energy on him. Who is he again?*

Iris tuned back in to find Henry Dale was in the middle of an update. "I'm working on the gingerbread issue, but I'll have to pause to install the alarms. Just so you know."

"I appreciate everything you do," she said.

"What about me?" Rowan asked.

"I appreciate you as well," Iris said.

"Me too," Henry Dale added.

Rowan had a sketch pad tucked under their arm, and they seemed a bit subdued, likely because of Eli's sudden departure. But they'd get used to the new dynamic soon enough; everyone would. And Iris would act like she was fine until her heart stopped feeling like somebody had yanked it from her chest and stepped on it.

To avoid further conversation, she smiled and left the kitchen, heading to the foyer. She stopped to grab a jacket, then stepped outside, shivering at the icy touch of the wind. *Eli helped fix this porch. He sanded these boards. Applied the weatherproofing and the stain.*

OMG, stop, you're doing it again.

Zipping her hoodie, she went down the steps, now firm and sturdy, thanks to Eli and Henry Dale. As for Violet Gables, the house was like an aging actress with her makeup smeared. Iris could picture what it would look like if it was glorious, riotously purple—no, *violet*, just gleaming with color—but she didn't have the magic to make it happen.

Yet that didn't stop her from focusing all her anger, all her despair on the house. Iris closed her eyes and locked onto the word *violet*. V I O L E T. The letters danced in her head, spinning into flowers. Oh, African violets, how pretty, with their dainty little petals, and she fell into a field of them.

House.

Field.

Violet.

Violet Gables.

There was a snap or a spark, and she *felt* the world as she never had before. There were connections everywhere, and it seemed impossible that she'd never sensed them. Power surged through her as if she'd grabbed on to an electrical line. She felt like a dolphin skimming along the waves, singing with every other dolphin in existence. And in that dazzling brightness, she heard whispers and the lightest touch.

Ah. Yes. There you are, precious blossom.

Not her thought—someone else's—but then they vanished in the swirling stream. The universe in her head receded, leaving her dazed and disconnected. When she opened her eyes, she stumbled backward and fell down, gaping at what she saw. The stately old matron, this Victorian oddity, was *festooned* in violets, a field of them growing sideways, impossibly, all over the house. No soil. No explanation, just...violets. They rioted with life and color— magical, beautiful, and incomprehensible.

She sat in the yard, staring up at the miracle that had appeared...like a sign, almost. When she'd nearly given in to despair, the world rose up to meet her, and it was as if the house crooned, "Yes, this is right. I'm beautiful again."

"I really am fae," Iris whispered.

Instinctively, she *knew*. She didn't need a spell or other casters. *Witches use magic. The fae* are *magic.* That wisdom felt very old, and it tasted true on her tongue, a thing where she didn't understand the knowing, but the fact remained. *This is my home, my land, and I have power here.* Another truth, indisputable. Her environment would bend to her will.

Mira pulled into the driveway as Iris gazed fondly at the miracle she'd wrought. The witch gaped at the house, glancing from it to Iris and back again. "Uh, something you'd like to tell me?"

"I don't need a spell," Iris said.

The woman eyed her warily. "I can see that. Your power's awakened then?"

"Seems so."

Another sidelong look from Mira. "What can you do?"

"Not sure. I can't feel the cars parked on the streets or other machines—like lawn mowers—at all, but things that were alive like the wood on the house? It's mine to shape."

"A little like vivimancers, then," Mira mused. "Maybe they came from the fae?"

"You're asking the wrong person. I only found out who I am a little while ago."

Rowan popped out of the house to see what was up, and they too stared in wonder at Violet Gables. "Is...is this real? I'm not hallucinating, right?"

"No, we have a garden growing up the front of the house." After pacing twenty steps to the right, Mira added, "Oh, it's all over. I can't wait for the press to get hold of this."

"That cranky lady next door will be so pissed," Rowan predicted.

Iris allowed herself a faint smile as the faint fragrance of violets wafted on the autumn breeze. "I hope so. Because I'm just getting started."

Eli didn't leave town.

He could have, easily. And probably, he should have.

But instead, he spent the night in an expressway hotel; then the next day, he rented a studio apartment on a vacation rental site. It was an adequate space over a garage, and he didn't inter-act with the people in the main house at all. Instead, he received a code allowing him to let himself in using a separate entrance. At this point, Eli didn't even understand *himself*, so of course Iris thought the worst of his motives.

In hindsight, he shouldn't have panicked and gone around her. He owed her so many apologies that he could deliver one daily for the next two months and it still wouldn't be enough. Maybe that was why he couldn't cut his losses and move on. Sighing, he set his suitcase in the small bedroom and wandered out to the equally efficient living space.

Ironically, he'd *just* unpacked his bags, finally feeling comfortable about his place at Violet Gables. Hell, he'd started feeling like he belonged. But before he could get cozy in the hole he'd dug, his phone rang.

Caller ID said it was Henry Dale, and that made him feel a bit better. At least the rest of his housemates—former housemates—didn't hate him. "What's up?"

"Where are you staying?" Henry Dale asked without preamble.

"What?"

The older man made a skeptical sound. "You didn't expect any of us to believe you suddenly flew to Albuquerque, right? We pretended to because otherwise it would've been awkward, but you were *heartbroken* when you left, son. Not worried. As you would've been, had your grandmother actually needed you to make an urgent trip."

"Oh. You truly are a student of human nature, aren't you?" It was humbling how happy Eli felt over Henry Dale checking in like this.

"I've learned to read people over the years. I don't always *care* how they're feeling, but I usually know. And sometimes I *act* like

I don't because I'd rather not pussyfoot around. But you didn't answer my question."

"Uh, I rented a place. You're right, I just couldn't…walk away. Not yet. Not if there's a chance she'll eventually forgive me."

"Well, put a pin in that because you wouldn't believe what's going on here."

"Iris is burning effigies of me in the backyard?" he guessed.

Henry Dale laughed. "Dial back the self-absorption. It's… Actually, why don't you come pick me up? I heard you're rich, so you can buy me lunch, and I won't need to explain as much if you witness this with your own eyes. I've seen some stuff over the years, but *nothing* like this."

Despite Eli's grim mood, he started feeling intrigued by whatever had Henry Dale so lost for words. "Fine, I'll be there in twenty minutes. Should we hit Bev's?"

The answer came in a cheerful tone. Well, as cheerful as Henry Dale ever got. "I was hoping you'd say that. I'm craving a burger with fries and the big pickle on the side."

Just as he was about to hang up, he realized something important. "This isn't just about what's happening at the house, is it?"

"Of course not. I miss you." Henry Dale said it quickly, as if he might be arrested for possessing human emotions.

"Me too. See you soon."

Oddly, that made Eli feel better. *I wasn't just an accessory to Iris. I made impressions on my own.* Even if things didn't work out with her, he'd made real friends, connections he intended to keep. Maybe…he'd sell the condo in Ohio and look for property in St. Claire.

After grabbing his wallet and keys, he headed out. He'd been instructed to park on the far right of the cement pad so there would be no issues getting in and out. It took only fifteen minutes to get to Violet Gables, and Henry Dale was already waiting at the end of the gravel drive. Surprisingly, Rowan was with him.

And then he *noticed*. Once he did, he couldn't believe he'd processed anything else. The house was covered in violets, like something out of a fantasy book. He even rubbed his eyes, but the house-garden didn't go away. Only the doors, roof, gingerbread, and windows weren't blanketed in tiny purple blossoms.

Rowan hopped in the truck first and slid into the back seat; then Henry climbed in front. He slammed the door and motioned for Eli to take off. "It's not that I think we're doing anything wrong, but Iris is unsettled enough right now."

"What happened?" Eli asked, fighting the urge to keep looking back at the gorgeous, unearthly spectacle that was Iris's home.

"That's what *we* want to know," Rowan said. "We suspect it has to do with her fae heritage, but..." They shrugged.

"Honest to God, I don't know how I'll replace that trim now. I've got hay fever!" Henry Dale was so aggrieved that it made Eli smile.

Rowan suggested, "Maybe you could wear a mask?"

"I'll figure something out. You remember the way to Bev's?" Henry Dale asked Eli.

"Why don't you remind me?" Eli could have put it in the map on his phone, but Henry Dale had a complex about being needed. This was an easy way to reinforce that the older man had useful knowledge and others could benefit from his wisdom and experience. When Eli had first met the older man, Eli had never imagined that Henry Dale would reach out first. But here they were, going to lunch on his invitation.

Henry Dale gave some directions; then Rowan filled the conversational lull. "I was promised gravy! We're finally going to Bev's."

"I try to keep my promises," Eli said.

Rowan added, "So I got the gist of what happened with Iris. Sucks, but I understand why she's so upset."

"Yeah." His tense answer probably made it clear this was tough for him to discuss.

"But I came along because I wanted you to know I'm not taking sides. I like both of you, and I hope you can patch things up. I miss you around the house." Rowan grinned, affecting a childish voice. "Don't fight, Mom and Dad, it's my birthday."

Since he and Iris were of an age to be Rowan's older siblings, that genuinely did make Eli laugh and lightened the mood considerably. "Thanks. I miss everyone too."

Henry Dale snorted. "Does that make Sally and me the grandparents?"

"I mean, not collectively, but...yeah." Rowan seemed in much better spirits, now that they'd been out of their family home for a while. "Forgot to tell you. I've been kinda doing a new web comic based on...well, us. And it's getting major views. People are tipping a lot, begging for updates. Fans will lose it when the magic house becomes a botanical garden."

Before Eli could say anything, Rowan added, "I changed our names and everything, don't worry. And I changed some of the physical traits too. I don't think anyone would know where my inspiration comes from."

"So I'm a comic book character on the internet?" Henry Dale didn't seem to know how he felt about that.

"Is that...okay?" Rowan asked.

"Better to ask forgiveness than permission?" Eli joked. "But seriously, you might want to learn from my mistakes and let everyone else know. *Before* it blows up on you."

"Noted," said Rowan.

The rest of the ride was quiet, and soon they reached Bev's and ordered their food. Once that was taken care of, Henry Dale sat forward with a purposeful gleam in his eyes. "Now then, *here's* why I wanted to talk to you..."

CHAPTER TWENTY-SIX

IRIS EXPECTED SOMEONE FROM THE city to arrive the same day because catastrophes tended to cluster.

She was wrong about that, and it felt sort of...anticlimactic to go about her business like things hadn't changed irrevocably. But she still had bills to pay, jewelry pictures to edit and upload, and laundry to wash. After ticking the first two items off her list, she hauled her hamper all the way down from attic to basement. By the time she got to the washer and dryer, she was exhausted physically, a nice match for her emotional wreckage.

It was impossible to forget how Eli had offered to haul dirty clothes for her. But now he was gone, just as she'd demanded. Iris had no idea why a fleeting moment in childhood meant so much to him. She'd thought they knew each other well, but he was an enigma now, the type of person she never would've even met in the normal course of things. Hell, Eli probably had a private plane.

Ugh, stop thinking about him.

Tiredly, she plopped her dirty clothes in the washer, added detergent, and started the cycle. This machine was delightfully simple; there weren't a lot of options, mostly just hot and cold on the dial. She turned to go back upstairs when something odd caught her eye. Since the basement was a bit creepy, she didn't spend a lot of time here.

But surely I would've noticed...

A door. There was *definitely* a door etched into the foundation wall on the far side, right next to the shelving full of homemade canned goods of indeterminate age. *That wasn't there before.* A door there made no sense; it must lead right into the ground. As Iris stared, unable to understand she was seeing, the seams on the sides filled with light.

And then the door opened.

Or more accurate to say it dissolved and became...more of a portal. Two beings stepped through, lithe and graceful and ageless. At first they seemed to be made of light and flowers, but eventually her eyes resolved, or perhaps their forms did, assuming a more comprehensible guise. The taller one had ink-dark hair, skin and eyes like a starry night, while the more feminine-looking one had hair golden as a koi in a Japanese pond with eyes like the violets on the side of the house.

They're fae.

That was the only answer that made sense. Awe and wonder pervaded her from head to toe; this must be how humans felt since the dawn of time when confronted with immortality. Yet Iris had no sense of how she was supposed to handle a couple of powerful, ancient entities suddenly porting into her basement laundry room. Behind her, the antiquated washing machine sloshed without decorum, rumbling through the beginning of the cycle.

For lack of any better ideas, she bowed. "Uh. Hello. Welcome."

To her utter astonishment, they rushed to her and embraced her on both sides. They spoke in a strange language, except... the more they said, the more it started to feel familiar. Sounds gained meaning, and then, suddenly, she *did* understand every word.

"We found you," the fair one said.

"Our precious blossom," the dark one added.

Iris had a hard time getting her breath, let alone finding words. The hold they had on her wasn't painful, but it had a strange effect. "I don't understand."

"Come with us." The taller one pointed to the shimmering doorway. "You don't belong here. We'll explain everything once we're home."

Somehow, she found the fortitude to withdraw, stepping away from the powerful grasp that made her skin feel too small. "I... No. This is my home. I'm willing to hear you out, but I'm not just...following you into the light. In case you didn't know, for humans, that's a euphemism for death."

"But you're *not* human," said the fair one.

How freaking weird—it was like they spoke with the voice of a wind chime, eerie, charming, and wholly disconcerting.

"I'm still coming to terms with that, okay? But I've been raised as a human for twenty-seven years, so cut me some slack."

The taller being seemed surprised, touching their partner's arm in apparent dismay. "Twenty-seven mortal years? Has it been that long? We were looking for a baby. We didn't recall how differently time moves between the realms."

"Can we speak in more agreeable environs?" the fair one

asked with a flicker of distaste for the exposed pipes and wires suspended above the cracked cement floor.

"Oh, sure. Let's go upstairs." Iris led the way and ran into Sally, who was making tea in the kitchen.

The older woman nearly dropped the porcelain pitcher when the other two came in. "Uh. Holy crap. We have...guests. Otherworldly guests." She lowered her voice to a whisper that the others could doubtless hear. "Help me out. Angels? Demons?"

"Fae," said the fair one.

"I think it might unsettle them less if we conform to our environment." After saying so, suddenly, two human-looking people stood there instead of the flickering, light-crowned beings: a dark-haired, dark-skinned person and a second with blond hair, fair skin, and dark-blue eyes. "Is this less unsettling?"

"Sure," Iris replied because everything was surreal at this point.

"I'll bring the tea. Why don't you chat in the living room?" Sally pressed her hand to her chest; too many surprises, Iris guessed.

I feel the same. These must be my...parents, right? But I'm sure they didn't have me the human way. How did I end up here?

Iris glanced around the front room, wondering what they made of the place. Taking a breath, she sat in the chair opposite her baffling visitors, who were clearly trying to seem less...alien. And not wholly pulling it off—mostly because they still sparkled, glimpses of iridescent magic that couldn't be contained by a human exterior. She gazed at them with amazement and fascination, trying to find connections.

"I'm sure you have questions. First, I'm...Rain. I think that's how it would translate." The fair-haired one offered a gentle smile, reiterating their name in the fae tongue, which indeed was more of a feeling, like a gentle rainfall on a spring morning.

"And I'm Fen." The other guest proffered the same experience in their native idiom, only it was quieter and more somber, a pensive ramble through a rolling marshland while birds called among the reeds.

Rain added, "You are our beloved child, I have no doubt."

"And you must be wondering how we lost you."

The way they did that was freaking incredible, a seamless switch as if they shared the same brain. Iris wondered how she could possibly be related to such magical beings.

But before Iris could speak, Rain made a soft, pained sound. "Ah. I see how they've hidden you from us. Be still—this might hurt."

That was the only warning she got before her world exploded in agony.

"I don't think that's a good idea at all," Eli said, once he heard Henry Dale out.

The old man had evidently been bingeing old romantic comedies because he seemed to think a good grovel and a boombox would resolve the issue. *Who knew he's secretly a romantic at heart? For other people, anyway.*

Rowan was already shaking their head, echoing Eli's doubts. "You know I love you, HD, but that's a terrible plan."

"Why?" Henry Dale demanded in an earnest tone. "I've watched seven of those movies now, and it *always* works. I even doubled-checked it at the library. I borrowed four different romance novels! Eli just has to do a…'grand gesture' I think is what they're called. He needs to express how sorry he is, that's all."

Okay, that's adorable. Eli smiled, imagining Henry Dale locked on to this research like it was one of his DIY projects. Since the man had never been interested in romantic relationships, he was now taking notes to try and support a friend.

"Hate to break it you," Eli said, "but that only works in a script."

"Are you sure?" Henry Dale asked.

"Well, I haven't tested it, but I'm pretty sure if I blow off Iris's wishes and try to force a reconciliation, she'll call the cops and file a restraining order."

Rowan nodded emphatically. "And she'd be right to do so."

"Oh." The old man was visibly crestfallen.

Guess he really thought he had it all figured out.

At least the burgers were delicious, as were the milkshakes. Rowan had the biscuits and gravy plate, and Eli smiled because he remembered inviting them to go to Bev's before. He'd just thought it would be with him and Iris, not him and Henry Dale. Regardless, he savored the meal in good company, quietly taking comfort in the fact that Henry Dale wanted Eli and Iris to get back together so much. Hell, Eli wanted it too, but not at the expense of what was best for her. She needed time, and he planned to give it to her.

"My plan…is to wait," he said eventually.

"That's it?" Rowan asked.

"At some point, she might be willing to talk. I'll stick around and hope that day dawns." He dipped the last fry in ketchup and ate it.

"That's not very romantic," Henry Dale said. "At least, not according to the movies I've watched, which accounts for most of my knowledge. I got the rest from novels, but one of them was set during WWII, so I don't think Eli going off to war is a viable strategy."

Eli laughed. "I'm *not* enlisting. Hard pass."

Rowan shook their head, still seeming fixed on the older man's first point. "It's sweet that Eli is willing to live on her time, you know? Not asking anything. Not expecting it either. But...hoping. You screwed up, you owned it. That's all you can do."

"You're really wise for nineteen," Eli noted.

"People say I'm an old soul. I was the only one in my family who didn't see the point of trick-or-treating," Rowan confessed.

It took a lot for Eli to confide this. "Frankly, I've blocked out a lot of my childhood. My mother died when I was young, I was bullied afterward..."

"Been there. It sucks." Rowan reached over, touching his hand briefly in sympathy. Their mouth twisted. "With the bullying, I mean, not losing my mom. For better or worse, she's out there praying for my soul as we speak."

He smiled at Rowan. It felt good to open up, and Henry Dale was listening with full attention too. They both seemed to expect him to continue. "I lost my dad a few years later. I have relatives on my mom's side, but...I've never sought them out."

"Why not?" Henry Dale asked.

For the first time, Eli admitted the truth out loud, what he'd barely acknowledged to himself. "If there's no connection, if they just see me as an outsider, it will hurt so much that I don't think I'll ever recover from it. So I'm afraid to try."

"Wow," Rowan whispered. "This feels like a hugging moment. Do you *want* a hug?"

"Sure," Eli said.

They leaned over to give him a careful side hug, easily achieved since Henry Dale had commandeered the whole other side of the booth. The man didn't like sharing space.

"Better?" Rowan asked.

"Yeah. Thanks." Eli *did* feel better.

Henry Dale cleared his throat. "If you want my opinion, you should go see them. You have family you've never met, and I'm sure they wonder about you."

"If they even know I exist."

"Then you'll be an amazing surprise," Rowan said.

"I'll think about it." He signaled for the check, and the other two let him pay without argument. At least one good thing had come from everyone finding out about his streak of success with various apps. "Hey, I don't think I said so before, but I'm happy that your comic is taking off."

Rowan visibly glowed over hearing that. "Between the discount for helping with Iris's business and what I'm earning online, I'm pretty close to self-sufficient now. And it's *such* a relief. My parents have been saying, 'You have no marketable skills, no education,' and they had me scared that I'd end up homeless if I tried to move out."

"That's bullshit," Henry Dale said fiercely. "You're smart and resourceful, and lots of people care about you."

"Aw. You're making me want to hug *you* too, HD." Rowan grinned, likely knowing that the older man would rise to the bait.

Sure enough, Henry Dale pretended to glare. "The cheek!"

Taking that as his cue, Eli stood up and headed out, still thinking about what they'd said about his mom's side of the family. Once they got in the truck, he said, "Maybe I don't have to start with anything as big as a visit. I could look for cousins on the socials and reach out that way, see if anyone…"

"Cares?" Rowan suggested.

Eli started the truck and checked his rearview mirror. "Another issue is the language barrier. I feel guilty that my Spanish isn't better, like I'm letting my mother down."

"Then that's what you work on," Henry Dale said.

As Eli backed out of the restaurant parking lot, he shot the older man an inquiring look. "What?"

"Take Spanish lessons. If she'd lived, she would've taught you, and she would've introduced you to her family unless there was some bad blood you don't know about. It's best to assume otherwise if you didn't hear anything."

Eli considered. "I never did, no. To the best of my knowledge, they lost touch because of the distance. I'm sure my mom intended to reconnect, but then she got sick. I *think* Gamma said that my maternal grandfather had remarried, and Mom didn't like her stepmother, so that's why she stayed in the US. She was here on a student visa and then married my dad. But I'm pretty sure she had an older brother…"

"Families are complicated," Rowan said with a sigh. "But if your granddad started a second family, you *might* have even more aunts and uncles and twice as many cousins."

"Glad to see you're taking my advice on this much," Henry Dale added.

Eli grinned. "Don't hold a grudge because I shot down your plan for me to reenact a scene from an old John Cusack movie."

"Iris would so call the cops," Rowan said. "And if she didn't, Susan would."

"That's true enough. I truly do not like or understand that woman." Henry Dale scowled as if the mere mention of her was enough to blight his good mood.

Rowan said, "Maybe she's lonely."

"Not everyone who's lonely is also petty and mean," Henry Dale pointed out.

While the other two chatted and bickered playfully, Eli thought about what he'd gained in St. Claire—friends who were like family, a chance to reconnect with people he'd written off, and possibly...love.

If he was brave enough to see it through.

CHAPTER TWENTY-SEVEN

THAT MOMENT OF AGONY LASTED a lifetime and no time at all.

Iris's head went blurry, and she arched as the agony unspooled, leaving her soul to bleed. She opened her eyes again with great difficulty, locking onto Rain's hand motions. As Iris struggled to grasp how she could feel pain in parts of her that had no nerve endings, Rain pulled what looked like a thin silver cord *out* of her body. The ephemeral chain writhed like a snake and then vanished in a puff of smoke. She blinked several times, wishing the world made sense, but it hadn't since she'd found a door to fairyland in her grimy basement. Now weird things just kept happening.

"That's how you were hidden from us," Fen said.

"And how you were bound to this form, your magical nature stunted," Rain added.

"We should start from the beginning, my love."

Rain agreed with a regal little nod as Sally tiptoed in with a tray of tea and cookies. Bless Sally for taking this development in stride, Iris thought, until Sally caught her eye and mouthed, *What the hell,* as she backed out of the room.

Right, I'm on my own.

Both the fae took cursory sniffs of the drinks and didn't touch them as Rain went on, "I'll try to make this concise, as it covers a fair amount of fae history. Fen and I, we come from opposing houses."

"Seelie and Unseelie?" Iris asked.

"Oh, you've read some legends! That's delightful. Not exactly *correct*, but human versions of fae history rarely are," Fen said.

Rain sighed with an expressive flutter of fingertips so graceful that they reminded Iris of leaves dancing on the wind. "So true. But then, they don't even document their own history accurately, so what can one expect?"

Surreal. She returned to that word as she listened to her parents—her real fae parents?—talk blithely about inaccuracies in human historical records. "You were saying..."

Rain nodded. "Indeed. We tend to be less...direct in our communication styles, as we're not under any time constraints, so we're finding this dialogue a bit challenging."

"You two had a Romeo and Juliet situation then? Your families disapproved of your relationship, I take it?" Iris had managed to glean that much.

Fen smiled—or tried to—a wholly strange and uncanny expression. "Precisely. So dear Willie made a go of the writing then? How fascinating."

"You knew...Shakespeare?"

"He visited a few times when he was writing about the fae queen. What was that play called?" Rain fluttered their fingers, trying to remember.

"*A Midsummer Night's Dream*," Iris supplied.

"That's the one. My family thought Fen and I would go our separate ways if they...well, if they removed you. From us."

"But the search only brought us closer," Fen said. "We created you out of love, and you were stolen from us, sent *here* wrapped in an enchantment that hid most of your true nature. I'm so sorry, precious blossom."

Rain added, "The humans granted you a good name, at least."

"True. Iris suits you." Fen inclined their head as if they were bestowing a boon.

Iris tried to keep calm, despite the excitement flickering through her. "Okay, let's start with the creation part. You...made me? That means you're my parents, right?"

The two exchanged one of their silent, brain-sharing looks, then Fen answered, "Procreation is different among our people. Ideas can take form. So can emotions. It's more of a magical genesis than a physical interaction, but you do absolutely share energy with both of us."

Okay, I can work with that. Rain and Fen are *my parents.*

"So I was kidnapped by your family," she said to Rain. "Hidden in the human world. Did your family raise the real Iris Collins?"

"They did. Her name is Thea... *All* this time, we had no idea."

"What happened to her?" Iris wasn't even sure if she wanted to know, especially since she knew the type of family that awaited Thea, should she return.

"At her coming of age, she married a minor noble and drank from the Wellspring, so she's no longer mortal, strictly speaking.

My family said she was a foundling, when in fact she was a change-ling, taken when they stole her and left you in her place."

She wondered if that meant Thea would never return to the mortal realm since she had bonds elsewhere. "This...is a lot. I have so many questions that I don't even know where to start. What did you do to me just now?"

"Unbound you," Rain said simply. "Fae aren't constrained by gender or even form. But you've been locked into this *shell* for far too long."

Iris blinked. "Wait, so you can change shapes?"

"Of course, precious flower. You saw us do it, didn't you? I lived as a seahorse for a while," Rain said in a nostalgic tone.

"What?" The surprises just kept piling up.

"You've confused her," Fen said swiftly. "Rain means a fae horse that lives in the sea. Not the marine creatures from this world."

"Right, because *that* would be weird," Iris said with decidedly ironic intent. "But getting back to the original point, can I change shapes as well?"

"I hope so," Fen said. "It would be excruciating to realize that our forbidden love blighted your potential. But you might find it difficult or unusual at first."

Rain predicted, "Your mind will probably be your greatest barrier. You've thought of yourself as human. When you accept yourself as fae fully, your potential should expand."

Ohhh.

"To be honest, I think I did that earlier. You might not realize since you haven't been outside yet, but the whole house is covered in violets."

Rain beamed at her. "We certainly knew something happened."

Fen put in, "That's how we found you. Whether you intended to do it or not, you've turned this place into a fairy mound."

"That's a portal connecting our world to the mortal realm. There used to be a lot more of them. As I recall, the last one vanished..." Rain gazed at Fen with a beseeching expression, inviting clarification.

"In Wales, wasn't it? I'm not too clear on when."

Iris held up a hand, locked onto a more salient point. "Wait, back up. I created a portal? A link to the fae lands."

With a fond smile that looked more natural all the time, Rain assured her, "Indeed you did, precious blossom. That's how and why we're here."

"Huh. Okay, next question. What's my last name?" Iris asked.

"Your what?" Rain asked blankly.

"Surname. There are so many humans that they need multiple names to track them. I think they have numbers these days too," Fen whispered.

"Oh! I'm Rain of House Summer. They are Fen of House Winter. Any of those words would do, I suppose."

"So my choices are House, Summer, or Winter?" she asked, greatly bemused.

Fen tried to be helpful. "You can put them together if you wish."

"Iris Summerhouse?" She laughed and shook her head. "Never mind, I'll figure it out."

Rain gazed at Iris, their expression tenderly troubled. "We didn't expect to find you already grown. No need for us at all."

"She's still a baby," Fen protested.

"By *our* standards. But she's developed as a human. You'll excuse us, we have some mental adjustments to make," Rain added.

"So do I," Iris mumbled. "The biggest issue is, what does all this mean?"

―――――――――

Eli dropped Rowan and Henry Dale off at Violet Gables.

The house stood out from the rest, an upright botanical marvel, as the wind ruffled lightly through the purple blossoms. *I wonder if anything else has changed.* As he pulled away, it struck him as heartbreaking that something so major happened after he left. The worst part of all this was, he couldn't check in with Iris to see if she needed anything, He'd lost that privilege when he lost sight of the fact that he was part of her life because she allowed him to be.

Those thoughts would break him, so he forced himself to drive away. *It's not about me. It's about her and what she needs.* Knowing that he was doing the right thing didn't make it less painful as he drove across town. At least he had an appointment this afternoon, signing the closing paperwork to make somebody else's dreams a reality.

Eli went straight to Keshonda's office, and even though he was early, the newlyweds who'd offered first were already on site, happy as two summer days, and nudging each other in excitement. Their joy put a smile on his face. Everyone settled at the table in the conference room as Keshonda passed around the perfectly organized packets.

"Thank you for agreeing to let us move in right away," Natalie Moreno said.

Her husband, Ruben, echoed the sentiment. "Yes, thank you! Keshonda told us you had other offers, so we were on pins and needles until you confirmed."

"It's what my grandmother wanted," he told them. "She likes the idea of another family finding happiness in the house."

"The yard will be perfect for a playset," Natalie said.

"Yep, I'll build one next summer."

"The baby won't even be old enough to play on it," his wife protested.

He hadn't known they were expecting. "Congratulations!"

Keshonda sat at the head of the table and interrupted their chitchat with instructions on how to proceed. Really, it didn't take long at all to sign the forms, finalize everything, and get the funds released from escrow. They went straight to Gamma's account, and it made Eli happy knowing she was set financially. And if she ran into trouble down the line, he could afford to help out.

He shook hands with the Morenos, then waited for them to head out because he had a question for Keshonda. "I have a condo in Cleveland. High-end with amenities like climate-controlled parking and on-site fitness center. It's two bedroom, two bath, hardwood floors, view of the river, walking distance to everything, and a private rooftop deck accessible from the loft."

"It sounds gorgeous," Keshonda said. "But why are you telling me this?"

"Because I'm looking to sell it, and I might be interested in property in or around St. Claire. I don't expect you to help me with the first thing, but—"

"Oh, I can find you a place here," she cut in.

He nodded. "I'll be in touch once I get the ball rolling."

As he turned to go, Keshonda said, "Actually, I do know somebody in Cleveland. I met her at an expo in Florida. Let me see if I can find her contact info."

"That would be great."

Soon, she shot him a text with a name and a link to the real estate agent's website. "You can find everything you need to know about Maribel on there."

"Thanks."

Keshonda nodded briskly. "When you get time, shoot me an email with your must-haves in writing and your price point. Also whether you're looking for single-family, condo, how much you're willing to pay for an HOA, whether a duplex or multiple-dwelling structure might work. Some people like to buy a building, live in one unit, and rent the others. Well, provided they can afford it, but I already know you can."

At this point, what he wanted was to move back into Violet Gables, but the next best thing was making plans to stay in St. Claire, proving to himself that he wouldn't run away just because things got tough. He'd come a long way from the person with no close ties, inches away from retreating from society entirely.

"Understood. You'll hear from me tomorrow, probably."

Once I get my thoughts in order.

Ironic that he hadn't liked St. Claire as a little kid, and he couldn't wait to leave once he graduated from high school, but the third time was the charm, as now he couldn't imagine himself anywhere else. It felt faintly ridiculous to be homesick for a house he'd only lived in for a couple of months, but he missed the people too. Sally had promised him a scarf for the winter, and everyone had agreed to cook together for Thanksgiving. Christmas too. He'd been looking forward to all that, dammit.

Silently, he let himself back into the rented apartment and called Gamma. "Everything's finalized. You should have the money from the sale."

"Yes! I've got the wire transfer, though all the funds won't be available for twenty-four hours. Thanks so much, little man." Gamma paused, and he could hear somebody talking to her in the background. "Just a minute, Jim. I'm talking to my grandson."

"Did I call at a bad time?"

"Not bad. *Breaking Bad.*"

Eli laughed without quite understanding what Gamma was getting at. "What?"

"We're going on a *Breaking Bad* RV tour! We're leaving in ten minutes. I'd love to chat more, but I don't want to be the last one on board. I'll get stuck sitting by Mary Jo."

"Uh, yeah, definitely try to avoid that. Have fun!"

Gamma sounded as excited as a little kid. "I'll send pictures. Supposedly, we're visiting a bunch of actual film sites. I can't wait."

He couldn't resist teasing her a bit. "Who needs Universal Studios, right?"

"Exactly! Love you. Talk to you soon, little man."

The conversation lightened his worries a bit. At least Gamma wasn't regretting her decision to upend everything and move to a retirement community. It sounded like there was always something going on, new friends and new adventures. She'd carpe'd the hell out of that diem, by any standards.

Time for him to do the same. He sent the initial email at once with a subject of *I'm interested in selling my condo*. Next he went into his bathroom to strip.

For most people, that would mean he was taking a shower, but Eli opened the small window within the stall and shifted; then he swooped out into the waning sunlight. It had been a while since he'd flown, and the winds carried him toward Violet Gables.

No surprise there—it was where his heart and wings always led him. But today, the view was even more breathtaking.

The whole house glowed different than before, akin to the kaleidoscopic, incandescent hues that burned around Iris like a living rainbow. He circled overhead, taking in the new corona. He didn't know what it meant, but the change likely heralded some massive shift. Feeling like a stalker, he perched on the roof, watching the street for a moment or two. Home might be where the heart was, but it didn't mean he could stay.

So Eli soared away, wheeling toward open skies.

CHAPTER TWENTY-EIGHT

"WE WANT YOU TO COME home," Fen said, as if that should be obvious.

"Home, as in...fairyland?" Iris felt silly calling it that, but she had no other word. In fact, up until finding out that she was fae herself, she'd never given much thought to the lore, too busy trying and failing all over the place.

"There have been many names over the years," said Rain. "Avalon, Mag Mell, Elfhame, Annwn. But Otherworld works well enough."

Fen nodded. "Even better in modern tongue, I should think."

"Look, I might be willing to visit at some point, after I get to know you better, but...I have a life here," Iris said.

"If you stay, especially if you remain in that form, you'll age," Rain said softly.

"And eventually...cease," Fen added in an anguished tone.

"Okay, I *really* don't want to talk about my mortality right now. I get it. If I choose to go with you, I'll be immortal and learn how to turn into a fairy horse that lives in the sea. And admittedly, that sounds cool as hell, but..."

"You're not ready to sever all ties to this place," Rain said.

"I was unhappy here sometimes," she admitted. "But I'm just starting to figure things out. I love this house."

Fen glanced around, a faint smile creasing their extraordinarily beautiful features. "That much is clear."

That said, she did want to get to know her...parents? Progenitors? Whatever. "Can we leave the anchor in place? And the door in the basement. That way, you can visit whenever you want. Once we get closer, I'd like to see the Otherworld too."

"Bliss!" Rain exclaimed.

Fen took her hand and kissed both of her palms. It felt like an oddly reverent gesture, and Iris wondered if the twenty-seven years she'd been missing had felt like five minutes to them. "We have so much to show you, so much beauty that's not to be believed."

"No Thomas the Rhymer nonsense, okay? I don't want to be gone for seven years."

"We'll do our best to keep track of mortal time," Rain promised.

Fen knelt before her, dark eyes twinkling like a starry night. "I know you're struggling, but may we embrace you?"

She couldn't recall the woman who'd raised her ever asking for a hug or offering one. Tears prickled in her eyes. *I'm not unwanted. I'm not a fuckup. My people were just...misplaced. For a time.* Iris included everyone who lived at Violet Gables in that assessment, but she was glad to add Rain and Fen to the list of people who cared.

"Absolutely."

The two fae drew her close, bracketing her between them. Maybe it was her imagination, but Rain truly smelled like fresh droplets of water gliding over the flower petals, while Fen reminded her of freshly turned farmland and the verdant smell of new life breaking the surface of the earth after a long winter. Each embodied springtime in a different way, and Iris came out of the hug feeling dazed and delighted.

"I came from the two of you. *Really?*"

"Are you happy about that?" Rain asked.

"Yeah. It doesn't feel quite real, but I'm ecstatic."

"As are we," Fen said.

Before she could respond, a knock sounded at the door. Sally called, "Keep talking with your visitors. I'll get it."

The older woman darted from the kitchen, through the front room, and into the foyer, where Iris heard her speaking to someone. She couldn't make out the words, but Sally's tone shifted from inquiring to annoyed.

Then she came to the archway and said, "Looks like they need a word with you. It's about the complaint Susan Grumpyguts filed."

"Grumpyguts?" Rain repeated. "What a curious surname."

"It's not her legal name," Iris said, like that was the salient point here.

She gestured to indicate she'd be right back (hopefully). No way to be sure if Rain and Fen understood, but she shouldn't keep the inspector waiting. It was a middle-aged man, balding, plaid shirt tucked into a pair of khakis. He was carrying a sheaf of paperwork, and he radiated impatience as he waited for an invitation to enter.

"Come in, what's this about?" As if Iris didn't know perfectly well.

"It says here that you're the homeowner, is that correct?"

"Yes, I own Violet Gables."

He snorted. "Violet Gables, is it? Hopefully I won't be here long. By the way, the city may cite you for the unregulated application of hydroponics on the exterior of your house. Here I thought I'd seen everything."

"It's not hydroponics," she said, but he wasn't listening, moving down his list of questions like he'd be fined if he slowed even for a second.

"Are you Iris Collins?"

"That's correct." She was already tired of his attitude, but she couldn't afford to snap or act rude. Not when she still didn't know how she was getting out of this situation. "Do you want to sit down?" she added.

"Who is this man?" Fen demanded.

Iris shrugged. "He hasn't seen fit to introduce himself."

"That seems rude," Rain noted. "Or have customs changed this much?"

Sally chimed in then. "They haven't. This guy is being exceptionally impolite."

The inspector sighed. "This isn't a social call, people. But fine, my name is Melvin Terry. I work for the city of St. Claire. All good now, can we continue?"

"Go ahead," Iris said, trying not to wince at how peeved he seemed.

"Thank you. Now where was I…? The nature of the complaint is that there are too many unrelated persons living here. This is a single-family dwelling—"

"Who are you to arbitrate such a thing?" Rain asked in a deceptively gentle tone.

Melvin spared a baffled glance for the person questioning him. Iris could tell that the man registered...something being off, but she guessed he'd never imagine in a thousand years that he was being asked to justify himself to a pair of ageless fae. "I just told you, I work for the city."

"But Violet Gables is an anchor point," Fen said.

He turned to Iris with a scowl. "What are they yapping about?"

Yet Iris couldn't help because she had no idea either. Sally gave up pretending she wasn't involved and came to perch next to Iris on the sofa. "This is better than daytime TV," she whispered.

"We are fae," Rain said simply. "I am from the Summer House. Fen represents the House of Winter. Iris is *our* child, and she has established an anchor here, the first fairy mound in these lands since we withdrew in ages past. That makes this place *our* sovereign ground. Here, your petty mortal rules hold no sway." Then Rain grew in size to dominate the space, voice booming like a clap of thunder. "Do you understand, child of earth?"

Melvin blinked so much that it looked like he had dust in both his eyes, stumbling back in instinctive self-protection. He practically had his back wedged against the front door. "I, what? No. Are you joking right now?"

Fen rose and dropped some of their human shape, allowing their true form to bleed through at the edges. Magic stirred around them like a dragon waking from a long slumber. "Not even slightly. Do you *want* to start a war with the Otherworld?"

"No," Melvin said uncertainly. "But—"

Frankly, Iris was impressed that the man hadn't already fled.

Fen went on, "Think of it this way. This place is our embassy. We're willing to remain on good terms with you mortals as long as Iris is content here. Should that change, should you trouble her in any fashion, you will face our wrath."

"Uh. Yeah. I...see. I think I need to pass this up the chain of command. This is way above my pay grade. Sorry to bother you, Ms. Collins." The man raced out of the house as if he might be turned into a newt.

And who knows, maybe they can do that. Maybe I can too.

"Holy shit," Sally said. "I think your problem is solved, dear."

Eli opened his door to find a familiar dark-skinned woman reclining in the chair on his small porch.

She had her hair in cute Bantu knots, a different style than her social media photos showed. "Surprise," said Liz.

Elizabeth Fielding had been his attorney for several years, and they'd always skirted the line between colleagues and friends. So Eli couldn't believe she was *here*, checking on him in person just because he hadn't answered her last few texts. They hadn't spoken since he blew off the AroTech deal, and they didn't have this kind of a relationship—or at least *he* hadn't thought so. Liz apparently believed otherwise.

"How did you even find me?" he asked.

She waved a hand like that was no big deal for someone of her impressive abilities. "I talked to an old man at your former address. He said you were staying here for the time being while you 'iron out' some complications between you and your lady friend. His words, not mine."

"You met Henry Dale. He's a character. Come on in then." He stepped back and waved at the small living space. "This is me."

Liz swept past him with a small suitcase, looking none too impressed by his choices. "You're here in a sad single boy apartment when you have that gorgeous condo? It's not even seven hours away. Why didn't you get in your truck and go?"

Because I love Iris.

He didn't tell Liz because it felt wrong to say it to someone else first. And maybe Iris would never get over the betrayal of trust, which would mean he had to figure out some way to move on too. But *not* before he gave this everything he had.

"Because it's time for me to put down roots," he said.

"You? Really?" She set a bag of groceries on the coffee table. "Don't worry, there's nothing perishable. I know how you are, so I brought instant noodles and the like."

"Hey, I can cook."

"But you generally don't bother for yourself."

That...was true enough. When had she gotten to know him so well? They'd been working together for years, and Liz was observant. Maybe that was the answer.

"How can you afford to just pick up and come check on me?"

"Most of my work is done remotely, and I can check contracts anywhere. Plus, I was worried about you. I know you're surprised to see me, but would it kill you say, 'Thanks, Liz. I appreciate you caring enough to stop me from vanishing into the night sky'?"

"Oh. Is that what this is about?" He had a fleeting memory

of telling her that he couldn't see the point of it all. Modern life seemed sort of futile, so maybe he'd just vanish into the horizon and live out the remainder of his days as a hawk.

"Yes, you jerk! It's cool that you can fly and all, but I'd miss you if you just...disappeared. We're friends, even if you're too dense to realize it."

"Thanks, Liz."

"For what?" she asked in a grouchy tone.

"Caring enough to check on me. For that, you get a home-cooked meal, courtesy of me. But I do have groceries, you know. And some of them are even fresh fruit and vegetables."

He made her a nice meal of steamed broccoli and rice with mushroom chicken, and then he filled her in on how everything had gone terribly wrong. Once he finished the saga, she sighed at him. "That's pitiful. I don't blame Iris for being mad at you. But it's so cute that Henry Dale and Rowan were trying to help you patch things up. Sidenote—I'm totally reading their web comic. You mentioned it last time you texted me, and it's awesome. They're so talented. But...have you seen *today's* episode?"

"What about it?" Eli read Rowan's web comic about Violet Gables now and then, but he hadn't looked at the most recent update.

"Apparently..." In a burst of excitement, Liz pulled up the site on her tablet and passed it over.

He skimmed with dawning disbelief. Iris's fae parents showed up and established Violet Gables as inviolable territory since Iris was their scion and ambassador. That meant normal city regulations didn't apply, and Iris could do as she damn well pleased with her property. Eli stared at Liz, who was bouncing a little in excitement.

"Is that, like, really real? Are you actually in love with a fairy princess?"

Yeah...that would take some getting used to.

"Rowan doesn't make stuff up," he finally said. "So if it's in the comic, then I guess it happened. She definitely didn't need me to buy her way out of trouble. Things got resolved for her... because she's Iris."

"Not trying to be extra, but I need to meet these people. After reading the web comic, they seem like celebrities to me. But don't worry, I won't be weird. I can be chill, I promise. Also, unrelated, is Mira as hot in real life as she is in—?"

"Are you sure you're a licensed attorney?" Eli demanded. "Because you sound like a fangirl at her favorite concert."

Liz waved that away. "You've seen my diploma. Never mind, you don't have to answer about Mira."

"Good, that would be awkward. She's like a sister to me."

"Then I'll scout that myself when you introduce me."

"You seem so sure that will happen."

"It has to. I have my hopes up and everything. Which means we need to start thinking about how to get you back together with Iris."

"Now we get to the truth. You weren't worried about me. You just want to meet Mira and Rowan and meddle in my love life."

Liz picked up the tiny container of ice cream she'd found in his freezer. He'd planned to eat that alone, but sharing was okay too.

"And Iris and Sally and Henry Dale. Oops, already met him.

But the others, yeah. I need their energy in my life. Maybe I'll move to St. Claire too!"

Eli sighed. "Why are you like this?"

She dug in, waving the spoon to punctuate her monologue. "Because you need someone to counter the level of morose energy you discharge into the world. We're like magnets with an opposite charge. It shouldn't work, yet we stick together and wow the world with our friendship."

"Let's say I agree with you. I do want Iris back, but I won't pressure her."

"Yeah, that's the issue. But you can't leave these things too long either, or she might think you were just playing with her, you know? Since that's not the case, you can't leave any doubts about your intentions."

"Please say you're not thinking of a grand gesture," he begged.

Liz narrowed her eyes. "None of that quitter talk. We give her two weeks, which is up when?"

He counted the days and told her. *Funny, it seems much longer.*

"Great. Past that point, we pull out all the stops. Operation 'get the girl' is a go!"

CHAPTER TWENTY-NINE

RAIN AND FEN STAYED FOR a week, marveling over the way the "mortal realm" had changed.

They used the main bedroom, which had been Eli's up until recently, so that was a bit weird for Iris, but it was good getting to know her parents. They didn't eat food, and they drank beverages only to be polite, so that was interesting as well. She still didn't understand how her own body worked, though come to think of it, she'd never been sick in her life, never had a normal childhood illness or been rushed to the hospital. Even her cuts healed cleanly and quickly.

But that made her wonder. "Uh. I used to donate plasma quite a bit. Do you think the patients who received my fluids are okay?" she asked Rain.

"The binding made you essentially human, dear one. I'm not sure what would happen if you tried to donate now, however. But if you need funds, we can—"

"I'm fine," she cut in quickly.

She didn't want them dumping heaps of jewels through the portal, as would doubtless happen if she said a word. The tax laws probably couldn't even handle sudden largesse from the

Otherworld, though maybe they'd just class them as a bequest. But she hadn't wanted a handout from Eli, and she didn't mean to mooch from Rain and Fen either.

Her housemates were all fascinated by the impossible door in the basement, and Fen kept offering to take Rowan to the "land under the hill."

"We've always been welcoming to artists," Rain added with a radiant smile.

Rowan looked a little dazed and more than a bit dazzled. "That would be—"

"When I decide to go, Rowan can come with me. They're not going off with you all of a sudden," Iris said for what felt like the hundredth time.

"I'm sure it would be okay," Rowan said with an enraptured smile.

Well, crap. I think Rowan might want to start a poly relationship with my immortal parents, so that's cool. Totally fine.

Henry Dale made a disapproving noise. "Don't be silly. We don't know enough about these beings yet."

"We know they love Iris," Sally said. "And they took care of her problems with the city on day one."

That was true. Yesterday, Iris had received official correspondence on the mayor's letterhead. Hopefully, it was the last time he'd be using that letterhead since Leanne Vanderpol-Montgomery was running against Mayor Anderson. The coven had gotten behind her in a big way, and Iris had shared a few posts as well. Hopefully, Ms. Vanderpol-Montgomery could push back against the assholes in HAPI who were stirring up trouble in town.

Today, a formal statement from the freaking governor arrived by special messenger, acknowledging her status as a new supernatural ambassador. State officials would be in touch, apparently, to define her role and see what could be gained through an alliance with the previously reclusive Otherworld.

Fen smiled at Sally, still a faintly alarming expression because their eyes didn't match the mouth movement. Not in a sinister way, just...alien. "Caution is understandable. We have nothing but time. Any of you are welcome, should you choose to visit with Iris."

"I'll bear that in mind," Mira said.

She didn't seem charmed in the same way Rowan was, but she was definitely curious. As a witch, she must be wondering how her magic would function in the Otherworld and what insights she could bring back to the coven. Rowan could hardly contain their excitement.

"Really? You might come with us?" they asked.

"I'm definitely thinking about it," Mira answered.

"If they're going, I am too!" Sally declared, never one to be left out of anything.

Out of curiosity, Iris glanced at Henry Dale, who scowled at the whole room as if they'd done him a great personal wrong. "Fine, we'll *all* go. And when we drink cursed fae wine and end up indentured for forty years, don't come crying to me."

"We wouldn't let that happen," Rain protested.

The old man snapped his fingers. "See? That's basically an admission that it *could* happen. I knew it! All of those cautionary tales had a basis in fact."

Fen didn't avoid the accusation. "We have...made mistakes in the past, but since our scion has been raised as a human, we'll do our best to forge a respectful path forward."

"Scion," Mira repeated.

Rowan nodded, eyes sparkling. "Oh, I *love* that word."

"I don't understand why the government is bending over backward to please a couple of random fae," Henry Dale muttered.

Everyone shot him quelling looks, but Sally was the one who answered. "The way I see it is this. Historically, our government has tried to step on 'different' elements within their own populace. So witches and shifters might have trouble with the authorities.

"The fae don't live in our territory, but they have *access* to it. Our government doesn't know how powerful they are or what they can do to us. So the way they're handling the fae, it's more like careful first contact with an alien race. The government can't afford to piss off the Otherworld when they have no clue what could happen."

Iris considered that explanation and nodded. "Honestly, that makes total sense."

Her parents did, sometimes, strike her as alien beings.

"What an interesting thought. But we should go," Rain said then. "We'll return soon."

"Probably. We'll do our best to keep track of time on your side of the veil." Fen stood and offered their hand to Rain.

It felt weird as hell to walk her parents to the basement, but when was anything about her life normal? The others stayed upstairs, allowing her a final moment with Rain and Fen. As the light gathered in the seams of the portal, she blurted, "You said it's possible for me to change forms. How...how would I do that? If I wanted to."

Fen paused, energy wreathing them in garlands of light. "It's difficult to explain. In the Otherworld, it would be as simple as a thought. It requires more focus and more energy here where everything is..."

"*Heavier*," Rain said. "I would say that the first step is believing that you can, however. Believe that you're not limited. Believe that you're not chained. Believe in your own potential. You truly *are* infinite, precious blossom."

Rain kissed one cheek while Fen kissed the other, and then they went, melting into the light. Iris would be lying if she claimed she wasn't curious, but it was also a relief to some degree. She had so much to process, and that wasn't even factoring for Eli.

Now that she'd had a chance to calm down, she could see that maybe she'd overreacted. A tad. Not that she had no reason to be upset at all, but maybe it wasn't an offense worthy of cutting all contact and going scorched earth.

I miss him.

I miss us.

I miss dance lessons, and I miss hugging him when I feel low.

"Okay, so I wasn't trying to spy on you, but I couldn't resist seeing that portal magic in action," Rowan said from the middle of the stairs.

Iris jumped so hard, she nearly fell over. "Oh my *God*!"

Rowan rushed to her side, steadying her with a hand on her arm. "Sorry! I thought you knew I was there. Sidenote, I can't *wait* to capture the magic of this moment. Thanks again for the digital tablet! I can't believe how great everyone has been to me. I've literally never been happier in my whole life."

That was supposed to be for Rowan's birthday, around Thanksgiving, but nobody had been able to resist delivering it early. "Mira organized everything. She should get extra ice cream for a week."

"You always do that," Rowan said.

"Do what?"

"Deflect praise and appreciation instead of just saying, 'You're welcome.'"

"Oh. Okay. You're welcome?"

Rowan grinned. "That's much better! But...did I hear you right? Were you asking about changing shapes?"

Crap.

"I was just curious," she said.

"Are you interested in becoming a hawk, by any chance?"

Oh my God, how do they know?

She mumbled something noncommittal and rushed upstairs, but Rowan didn't let her off the hook. "You're trying to get closer to him, huh? Does that mean you're ready to make up?"

Iris sighed, sinking into a kitchen chair with confusion dancing the mambo in circles around her. "*Maybe.* I do feel like we should talk. I don't feel great about the way I just...evicted him. Yeah, he messed up, but I'm not perfect either." She paused. "Do you... happen to know where he is?"

"I do," said Henry Dale and quickly recited the address.

Once she had the info, she didn't know what she intended to do until she got upstairs. The normal reaction would be to call him or get in her car. *Since when was I normal? My parents are Rain and Fen. I'm extraordinary. I'm fae.* Calmly Iris undressed in the main bedroom and folded her clothes; then she opened the window.

She imagined her body getting lighter and smaller, feathers instead of skin, hollow bones, and wings that would ride the wind. Her body was only a suggestion, not the lines that confined her. A chosen shape, not the only one, and then—

She was a hawk. Like Eli. Flying felt so natural that she let out a triumphant shriek and caught the updraft, circling the house.

Then she arrowed in the direction of her heart.

First there was a red-tailed hawk, circling overhead in graceful motions, and then there was a naked woman on Eli's porch. Not just any woman.

Iris.

He hurriedly dragged her inside without asking a single clarifying question. Her eyes rounded when she spotted Liz, currently sprawled on his couch in comfy clothes. Liz had been sleeping on the sofa, but this probably looked bad. *Oh shit. What the...? Why now?*

"Uh, hello there. There's probably an interesting explanation," Liz said, carefully keeping her gaze on Iris's face. "I look forward to hearing it after you get dressed."

He pulled Iris through to his room and quickly found her a T-shirt and jogging pants. Eli turned to close the door as she put the clothes on. "It's good to see you," he said.

"*All* of me?" The laughter in her voice said she wasn't upset.

"Okay, admittedly, this isn't how I would've chosen to get you naked the first time."

"You've thought about that, have you?"

"I'm not a saint," he muttered. "Those dance lessons..."

"You can turn around. So are you crashing on your friend's couch or what?"

He let out a breath, relieved that she didn't think he was the kind of person who could go from kissing her to being with someone else at the drop of a hat. "That's Liz, my lawyer friend. She got worried when I wasn't responding to her texts."

"Afraid of you going hawk forever on her?" Iris guessed.

Eli had to smile over how well she knew him. "Yeah, that's exactly right. And honestly, I've told her so much about all of you that she was hoping to meet everyone before she heads back. She's even talking about moving to St. Claire."

A soft smile started in Iris's pretty gray eyes, rounding the corners of her mouth like she was stealing a base. "That's how awesome you made us all sound, huh?"

"Just the truth, as I saw it."

"You must be wondering why I chose to come over this way," she said.

"I *am* curious about the whole turning into a hawk thing."

"I did that for you. To see if I could. I'd already found out that I'm fae before you left. Well, some fairly critical developments have occurred since then..."

Eli listened as she filled him in; some of this he'd gleaned from Henry Dale and Rowan's comic, but he wanted Iris's words too. All of her words, always, every day of his life. At some point, she curled up on the bed while she talked and he sat beside her. And then she closed the distance, ever so slightly, until he felt bold enough to put his arms around her. She let out a gusty, happy sigh, snuggling close as if she'd missed this.

Missed *him*.

"That's incredible," he said when she finished her account.

"It is. And now we should talk."

"About us?"

Emphatic nod from Iris. He breathed her in, unable to believe how lucky he felt. He hadn't needed the grand gesture after all. It felt good to realize he had been right—that he just needed to give her time and space to make up her mind.

"I'm sorry that I drove you away. I was hurt, and I overreacted. I didn't want you solving my problems with money. Honestly, I was stunned that you have so much of it."

"Everything I said and did, I meant it, love. You claimed you didn't know the real me, but you *do*. You understand everything about me, better than anyone."

"I get that, but…you can't lie to me again. That's not the kind of relationship I want. And if I'm ever to trust you again fully, I need a promise."

"That I'll always be honest? You have it. You'll be the first person I tell when I have news, good or bad. I won't hide anything from you anymore." Eli paused, taking a deep breath. "This is hard to talk about, but…I've always been really…self-contained. I have a hard time getting the words out, especially when I'm nervous. I have a history of running away from things. Honestly, I tried five or six times when we were in school…"

"To do what?" she asked.

"To talk to you. To give back your bracelet. But every damn time,

I chickened out and ran away. That's who I was, until moving into Violet Gables. I had money, yeah. And I know it upset you, finding out as you did. But success didn't make me happy. Living with you and everyone else? That was the first time that I felt at home."

"You probably don't understand how sick I felt...when I found out I'd cost you such a big deal. I just—"

"That doesn't matter," he cut in. "You're the most important person in the world to me. And I have plenty of money already. I just want to be with you. If you can forgive me. " Eli paused, gazing earnestly into her eyes. "I'm so sorry. I swear I'll never hide anything from you ever again."

She took a deep breath. "I believe you. And now I feel like I bring something to the table. Something you can't get from anyone else. I can hawk with you. I mean, I'll always let you go for a solo flight, but if you want someone in the sky with you, I'm there."

Eli really couldn't believe this was happening. "I'll never want to fly alone if I have the choice. I always want you with me. I'm so sorry that I disregarded your wishes and tried to solve your problems for you. But...I don't really understand why it's okay that Rain and Fen did."

Iris smiled. "This might not track for anyone else, but...their power is *my* power. I'm fae. So it doesn't feel like someone else solved it. This is my heritage, and Violet Gables is *my* home. Does that make sense?"

He nodded. "When you put it that way, yeah."

"We should get out there and explain everything to Liz," Iris said.

But he noticed she didn't sound too eager, and her gaze lingered on his mouth.

"Liz can wait. We should make up properly, now that everything has been cleared up and we agree that we belong together."

"We agree on that, do we?" she asked in a teasing tone.

"Don't we?"

This amazing, magical person wanted to be with him. Somehow he couldn't wrap his head around it—didn't make sense that he should be so lucky—that the first thing she did with her newly awoken fae powers was fly straight to his arms. As if sensing his thoughts, Iris snuggled closer, tracing a path down his left cheek with a delicate fingertip.

"Yes." She was breathless, smiling up at him.

"I love you, you know." He couldn't hold the words back any longer. The warmth and joy of being able to tell her, at long last, felt like a shooting star.

"I love you too. So much."

"Thank you for coming back to me," he added.

"And…I still think it's weird that you remembered me all those years, but it also makes me happy, you know? Something I did mattered. When I think about you carrying my bracelet around, I get all teary."

"Really?"

"I've cried over you more than once," she joked.

Her teasing melted under the heat of his kiss. "Do you want me?"

"More than anything."

After that, there was no more talking, just endless kisses and touches and the joy of two bodies becoming one.

CHAPTER THIRTY
THANKSGIVING, A WEEK LATER

IRIS STOOD AT THE WINDOW, staring with delicious schaden-freude at the argument taking place in Susan Calhoun's front yard. She was shouting at Dan Rutherford, and they were both waving their arms a lot. Finally, the man stomped off, got in his car, and drove away. Then Susan angrily staked a FOR SALE sign deep into her front yard.

I win.

The rest of her roomies were in the kitchen, and Iris hurried to join them, not wanting to miss a moment of this historic meal. Soon, everyone had a seat at the table. Though the oven was off, it was still toasty warm, and the food smelled incredible. For a while, the others focused on eating, but at the first chance, Rowan eyed Iris with great curiosity.

"What?" Iris prompted.

"Can you turn into a unicorn?" Rowan asked.

"I can't believe you asked that," Liz said.

Rowan served themselves more mashed potatoes while Henry Dale carved the turkey with the concentrated air of a man performing major surgery. "What, like I'm the only one who was thinking it."

Mira confessed, "I was curious too."

"You could make a fortune selling photos of yourself in various forms," Sally added.

"Hmm. I'll take it under advisement." Honestly, the shop was doing well these days.

Mira had cast a viral spell to boost Iris's business, and now the orders were coming faster than she could fill them. Iris had been teaching Rowan how to make some of the simpler pieces, and she was paying them accordingly—profit sharing, not just an hourly wage. Between the jewelry business, Henry Dale's new endeavor selling DIY installs for small spaces, and Rowan's web comic taking off in a big way, nobody needed to worry about financial problems anymore.

"This is the best Thanksgiving ever," Sally said.

The older woman had surprised everyone when she opted to eat here instead of at her daughter's house. As she put it, "Howard doesn't have anywhere else to go. I'm lucky because I do, and I'd rather be here. With my found family."

"That's what I've decided to call my next app," Eli announced.

Iris reached for his hand under the table, silently showing support. "Just wait until you hear this. I love it."

"Stop bragging that you get early access to his brain," Henry Dale said. "Just because you're 'in love.'"

Sally laughed. "Quit complaining and let Eli talk. It's like Iris stole your boyfriend or something."

"He talked to me more before they got together," Henry Dale grumbled. "Now it's like he never needs my advice."

"*I* need your advice," Rowan put in. "I have four ideas for my next web comic, but I'm not sure which one to pursue."

The old man smiled. "I'd be honored to be your sounding board."

Liz waved a fork, nearly dashing some cranberry sauce on Mira's plate. The two shared a look, and then Liz dropped her gaze, gently abashed. Iris didn't think she was imagining the sparks there. Then Liz pulled her rapt attention away from Mira's pretty eyes and said, "Seriously, I want to hear what Eli was about to say. The app!"

Sally and Mira and Rowan took up the chant. "App! App! App!"

What the hell. Iris joined in. "App!"

"You realize you're just delaying his news further," Henry Dale grumbled.

"Anyway," Eli cut in. "Since I had a tough time getting in touch with my mother's side of the family on socials, I thought, *What if I made an app for people who have lost contact with their families?* But then I went a step further. What about people who don't have family to begin with? And the idea was born."

"I could use some clarification," Sally said with a confused expression.

"Same," Mira admitted.

"Okay, so on one side of the service, people can input data on themselves, looking for people who are similar. When you move to a new city, it can be tough to find a new group that you click with. On the other side of the service, users can literally look for family members they've lost contact with. I'm calling it..."

Rowan did a drumroll on the tabletop. "Wait for it!"

"Found Family," Eli finished.

"It's perfect," Liz said. "Dual purpose."

"That's what I thought." Eli was definitely pleased with Liz's feedback, and Iris leaned over to kiss his cheek.

"I agree. I'd use it," Sally added. "I mean, honestly, I don't need it now that I found all of you. And Ethel. But…"

"He gets your intent," Rowan reassured her.

"It's not a bad idea," Henry Dale said, like the compliment pained him.

"Who wants pie?" Mira asked.

Iris groaned. She wanted some, but there was no room in her belly. "I think I need an hour or so. Let's stream something while we digest."

Eli gently took her hand, drawing her attention. "I thought you might like to fly?"

Oh. My. God.

"Cancel that," she said at once. "I'm going out with Eli."

"In the car or on the wing?" Rowan wanted to know.

"Wing," Eli called over his shoulder, already hustling Iris toward the stairs.

"We'll be back soon!"

The others continued to talk amongst themselves. As Iris raced up the stairs behind Eli, she *definitely* heard Liz flirting with Mira. "I ship those two so hard," she whispered as they went into Eli's room.

"Liz and Mira? When she first got here, she said Mira was gorgeous—in the web comic—but I had no idea she actually planned to go for it in real life."

"Right? I so admire her drive."

Eli grinned. "What can I say? Liz wants what she wants."

"It was nice of you to let her stay in your rental." These days, Eli was back in his old room, letting Liz make use of the apartment while she was here.

"That just made sense. I hope she moves like she's been talking about," he added.

Iris gave him a sultry smile. It felt like foreplay when they slowly stripped, but instead of tumbling to the bed, they swooped out the open window. She couldn't understand his hawkish cries in this form—maybe if she was a natural shifter and not fae, she could—but it didn't matter. The joy in his wild dips and swoops told the whole story. Eli was alive for the first time, sharing everything with her as she shared everything with him. He'd never been up here with anyone before, and he said it was the biggest gift she could've given him.

And for Iris, it was more than enough, knowing nobody else could make him happier, as that was all she wanted in the world. She still didn't talk to her old "family" apart from Olive and Dad; like Rowan, she was happier having purged them from her life.

Success wasn't about money, after all. It never had been. And she would continue to share her life with Eli because she chose to. And they'd solve problems together, with nobody taking all the weight alone.

I love you, she sang to Eli in shrill, hawkish tones.

With all her heart, she sent thanks to Rain and Fen for creating her and giving her a life that she cherished, even if the path to happiness had sometimes been rocky.

But all of that badness led me here, so I wouldn't change a thing.

Eventually, Eli could tell Iris was getting tired.

She wasn't as used to long flights, and it took real effort for her to maintain that form. Though she could shift, she considered her human shape the "real" one, so he worried about her losing focus and plummeting from the sky. Since he wouldn't survive losing her for good, he kept their flights relatively short.

In his room, she arched and stretched, giving him a scorching stare. While ordinarily he'd be all for taking her to bed, he heard soft footfalls; then a knock sounded. Rowan spoke. "Uh, not to interrupt, but Rain and Fen are here."

"We're getting dressed," Iris called.

"TMI!" Rowan shot back.

"Not because of—" Eli tried to say, but Rowan ran off in a fit of giggles.

"They're so childish and cute sometimes," Iris said fondly.

"They're nineteen," he pointed out.

"True, true. It's also adorable how protective Henry Dale is. I swear, if Rowan starts dating, Henry Dale will absolutely make the 'I have power tools and a shovel' speech."

"Uh, speaking of protective, how much do I have to worry about meeting your parents?" Eli asked as Iris dragged him downstairs.

"Not at all. I mean, they're weird, but good weird. To me at least. Actually, now that I think of it, I'm not sure how they'll react to you. I'm basically a baby in their eyes."

Eli gave a mock shiver. "Great, now I'm bathed in fear sweat."

"Relax, it'll be fine. Probably." With that less-than-resounding reassurance, Iris went downstairs to join everyone else in the front room.

The house felt much warmer than it had when he first moved in. A scientific explanation would be that the living floral carpet provided another layer of insulation, but he preferred the enchanting explanation. That it was Iris and her magic and all the light and laughter she'd brought to Violet Gables that made the difference.

Eli spotted the newcomers right away. They were both slim and lithe, and weirdly, he could identify them by scent. He shook hands with Rain and Fen, though they barely touched him, eyeing him with a careful, fearsome sort of interest. He glanced at Henry Dale, who for once had no advice to offer.

While Eli had thought the others were joking about the supposed infatuation, Rowan did seem to be crushing on one or both of Iris's folks. "So about that visit to the Otherworld..." they mumbled.

"Soon," Rain promised.

"I understand it's a holiday," Fen added. "We brought a gift. I don't know if it's appropriate for the occasion."

With evident delight, Iris took the delicate basket that appeared to be woven from living flowers. What she withdrew was the most delicate hair ornament Eli had ever seen, and it caught the light, liberally embellished with flecks of gemstone.

Iris held it up, beaming. "It's gorgeous. I love it!"

"Sally was telling us that you make personal adornments," Rain said then.

"I would love to see your work." Fen moved as if to head to Iris's studio, but Rain put out a hand to stop them.

"First, we should greet Iris's special someone. Did I put that correctly?" Rain asked Mira, who nodded.

Liz was eerily silent. Eerie because if you knew Liz, she just didn't sit on the sidelines. Yet she gazed at these two beings with admiration and astonishment that verged on the religious. She opened her mouth once, but no words came out.

Mira laughed softly. "I know, right? Just wait until we tell our supervisors that we need vacation time to visit the Otherworld."

Liz bounced back quickly, though. "I'm my own boss, so I can pack whenever. Just let me know."

When Fen turned their full attention to Eli, it felt like their gaze would flay the skin from his bones, as if his every dark thought and insecurity was exposed for their inspection. His knees trembled slightly, but he didn't retreat. Instead, he focused on his love for Iris, and the intensity of that scrutiny abated.

"He loves her," Fen said to Rain without asking a single question.

"Enough?" Rain asked.

"Enough," Fen confirmed.

Without warning, they embraced Eli on either side and pressed burning-hot kisses to each of his cheeks. Then Rain said, "That is our blessing. It will bring you great luck, prosperity beyond all mortal reckoning. But should you hurt our scion, should you cause our precious blossom even a moment's unease, that boon will turn to poison on your skin, and you will perish in an agony unknown to modern medicine."

Even Henry Dale looked impressed by that calmly spoken promise. "Now that's how a parent *should* behave," he said.

Iris sighed. "That's a bit over the top. You could've just asked him to be good to me."

Rain flicked a strand of silky hair over one shoulder. "But that's no incentive. You know that the fae cannot lie. I've said nothing untrue."

"So I'm really blessed. Or cursed?" Eli asked, fighting the urge to scratch his face.

"There is nothing to fear if your heart is pure," Fen said in a jovial tone. "Who wants to sample some fae wine?"

The party got a bit wild after that. Rain produced a strange flute and played a tune so haunting that squirrels and raccoons came up on the porch and scratched to get inside. That amused the shit out of Eli because he truly had fallen in love with a woman who was like a damn Disney princess. Susan must be so pissed after putting her perfect house up for sale and all. But her petty disfavor didn't matter, not when he had everything right here. Happiness to infinity and beyond.

During a quiet moment, Iris slipped away, towing Eli to the kitchen for a private word. "I'm so sorry about the weirdness and the cursed kisses. Rain and Fen can be so extra. I'll see what I can—"

"Don't worry about it. I'll take that double-edged sword because I'll never hurt you. I don't know what life has in store for us, but with you at the center of my world, I know it'll be beautiful. Magical, even. I wouldn't change a thing."

"Me either," she said in a tender tone. "You're *everything*. Thank you for finding me."

"Thank you for waiting. Somebody else might've swept you off your feet while I was getting my courage up."

She shook her head. "Never. We're meant to be, you and I."

"Along with everyone we met, the family we found here."

"Violet Gables is pretty great," she said, smiling.

Eli followed her back to the party because he'd meant it when he said she was the center of his life. While he might fly off in different directions, she was the heart of him, a glorious fae queen who ruled all she surveyed with a lovely, chaotic flair.

Iris, don't worry about your last name anymore. One day, you can have mine if you want it. Or anything else your heart desires.

Together, here or in the Otherworld, they'd make everyone's dreams come true.

EPILOGUE
CHRISTMAS

VIOLET GABLES WAS FULL TO the brim.

When Iris had set out to have a holiday party and invited everyone, she hadn't imagined that they would all come. But the old Victorian house was full of candles and pine boughs and visitors in every room. Ethel's whole coven was here along with the usual residents of the house, plus Liz, who had made the move to St. Claire just a week ago.

Hazel was here—without her cat—and Sally had agreed that Howard could come as Hazel's date. Really, Howard and Sally were learning how to be friends who had divorced instead of a former couple who disliked each other. Bruce and Mitch came because Sally was here, and Kim would be stopping by later with Megan. Iris made the rounds, chatting with small groups of people, unable to believe this was her life.

Eli kept a watchful eye on Iris from across the room, ever attentive in case she needed to be extricated from an awkward conversation. But he never pushed. And she loved that about him.

Eli's grandmother was drinking with Rain and Fen, and someone rapped on the door as Iris was about to make a toast.

When she answered, she found Olive on the front porch with a suitcase and a bag of presents. Iris's mortal dad waited in her shadow, none too sure of his welcome, but the fact that he'd shown up meant everything. Iris let out a little scream and hugged them both. It was dark, and a light snow had just started, bespangling the trees in winter white. The outside of her house was still covered in violets, and they didn't die, regardless of what the weather was like. In the distance, she heard carolers.

She urged Olive inside with one hand, grabbing Dad with the other. He went in uncertainly, and his eyes widened when he saw the crowd. "I didn't realize you already knew so many people. You're so happy, flower. It does my heart good seeing you like this. Have you...talked to your mother?"

"We email sometimes. We're both processing."

"That's good." He wandered off in search of snacks and drinks, leaving Iris with Olive.

"You said you might bring someone."

"It...didn't work out," Olive said in a careful tone. "Let's not talk about me. It seems like everything's come up Iris?"

"Finally feels that way, yeah. Let me introduce you to everyone!"

Since there were so many guests, it took quite a while for Iris to make the full circuit with her sister in tow. She ended her jaunt with Rain and Fen, who were chatting with Eli. "These are my fae folks. And this is my boyfriend, Eli Reese."

"I've heard of you," Olive said. "You're the app mogul, right?"

Iris groaned and covered her face with her hands. "Am I the only one who hadn't seen news about him online? I still feel like such a—"

Eli pressed a quick kiss to her mouth, likely to stop her from saying something derogatory about herself. It was cute when he did that. "Let's not think about that tonight."

"Fair enough," Olive said.

"Have you eaten?" Iris asked.

Olive shook her head, so Eli fixed her a plate, and Iris basked in the glorious sensation of having brought all these people together. Everyone seemed to be having an awesome time, so she opened more wine and continued playing hostess. She chatted with Leanne Vanderpol-Montgomery, who was running for mayor, and got some tips from Trev Montgomery on how to promote her site more effectively.

Glowing from that convo, she headed for the next group— Ethel, Sally, Hazel, and Vanessa. They seemed to be planning a glamorous vacation, which didn't need Iris's input, so she kept moving, offering food and beverages until the smile cut into her cheeks and she wanted to kick off her shoes.

After a couple of hours, she darted off to steal a few quiet moments in the kitchen. And of course, Eli found her. Because he was drawn to her like a lodestone.

"Can't function without me, huh?"

"Not really," he admitted.

"I love you," she said.

"I love you too."

She leaned in for a tender kiss.

"Ugh, if you two were any more adorable, they'd put you on a greeting card." Eli's grandmother stood in the kitchen doorway, smiling in delight. Her expression didn't match her teasing words.

"Everyone's looking for you, by the way. Rowan wants to do the gift exchange before Rain and Fen open the fae wine."

"Oh no," Iris breathed. Without another word, she raced into the other room. "I'm here! Let's open presents."

To avoid anyone feeling financially pressed, they'd agreed to a Secret Santa–type swap, where they handed out a single name to different guests. Iris watched in delight as Fen got a plushie and Rain a set of bath salts; the two fae stared at each other's presents and then silently traded them. All around the room, the people she loved were laughing and spilling joy into the universe, so warm and tangible that she could practically see it. Iris didn't even register her own lack of a gift until all eyes were on her.

Sally frowned. "Did you leave yourself off the list?"

Then Eli sliced through the crowd, bearing an exquisitely wrapped box. "This is from all of us. We left it until the end because we wanted to focus on your reaction."

It was too big to be jewelry, and she didn't think he'd propose this way anyhow. Iris made a show of hefting the package. "It's heavy." Bouncing a little, she untied the ribbon and tore the paper while Mira recorded the unboxing for posterity.

Carefully, she extricated the gift from the tissue package, and when she realized what she was holding, tears filled her eyes. Iris held up the wooden plaque for everyone to see. Then she found Rowan and Henry Dale in the crowd. "You two made this, right?"

"Beautiful," said Eli's grandmother.

It truly was a work of art. They'd crafted a beautiful piece using Henry Dale's woodworking skills and Rowan's artistic gift. Fanciful creatures gamboled about the edges, hiding in the floral border. Somehow, it was both charming and carefully wrought, done in shades of purple and green. And in the center, in bold letters: VIOLET GABLES.

"Thank you so much! I love it. I'm hanging this up right now," Iris declared.

And she meant every word, so the party went on hiatus while she used her newly discovered magic to bond the plaque with the house. Delicately, carefully, and soon, it looked as though it had always been there. Everyone rushed back inside, eager to warm up and continue the festivities.

"This is it," Eli whispered.

"What is?"

"All we were missing. Now every last piece is in place."

She agreed with a happy sigh, nestling into his side. Here in St. Claire, she'd found everything she needed. Not success, but happiness.

Forever.

Acknowledgments

Thanks to my agent, Lucienne Diver, for giving the best suggestions and always being in my corner.

Thanks to my amazing editor, Christa Desir, for believing in our beautiful books and polishing them to a diamond shine. She truly turns dross into gold. Thanks to Alyssa Garcia for making my books stand out from the crowd, and the rest of the wonderful team at Sourcebooks. I treasure our partnership and enjoy making art with everyone on the team.

Thanks to my friends. You know who you are, but I'll name a few names, even if this worries me in case I leave someone out. Shawntelle Madison, Piper J. Drake, Charlotte Stein, Sarah Zettel, and Lilith Saintcrow. Thank you all so much!

Thanks to my family. You brainstorm with me, give opinions on my cover art, and wrangle pets so I can work. Truly, you're the wind beneath my wings.

Finally, thanks to the readers who take my (virtual) hand and let me lead them to the worlds I have dreamt. Your trust through the years means more to me than I can say.

Read on, you beautiful souls.

About the Author

New York Times and *USA Today* bestselling author Ann Aguirre has been a clown, a clerk, a savior of stray kittens, and a voice actress, not necessarily in that order. She grew up in a yellow house across from a cornfield, but now she lives in Mexico with her family. She writes all kinds of genre fiction, but she has an eternal soft spot for a happily ever after.

Currently an investigative reporter for *Four Corners*, Sophie McNeill was formerly the ABC's foreign correspondent in the Middle East. She has worked across the region in countries such as Israel, Iraq, Syria, Yemen, Egypt and Turkey, as well as the Palestinian territories. Sophie has twice been awarded Australian Young TV Journalist of the Year and in 2010 won a Walkley Award for her investigation into the killing of five children in Afghanistan by Australian Special Forces soldiers. She was also nominated for a Walkley in 2015 for her coverage of the Syrian refugee crisis. In 2016 she won two more Walkleys for her coverage of Yemen and besieged towns in Syria. Previously she worked as a reporter for ABC's *Foreign Correspondent* and SBS's *Dateline* programs and she is a former host of triple j's news and current affairs program *Hack*. *We Can't Say We Didn't Know* is her first book.

SOPHIE McNEILL

WE CAN'T SAY WE DIDN'T KNOW

ABC
BOOKS

A percentage of royalties from sales of this book will be donated to Médecins Sans Frontières Australia. Médecins Sans Frontières/Doctors Without Borders is an international, independent medical humanitarian organisation delivering medical care to people affected by conflict, epidemics, disasters, or exclusion from healthcare. Médecins Sans Frontières provides assistance based on need and irrespective of race, religion, gender, political or economic influences.

The ABC 'Wave' device is a trademark of the Australian Broadcasting Corporation and is used under licence by HarperCollins*Publishers* Australia.

First published in Australia in 2020
by HarperCollins*Publishers* Australia Pty Limited
ABN 36 009 913 517
harpercollins.com.au

Copyright © Sophie McNeill 2020

The right of Sophie McNeill to be identified as the author of this work has been asserted by her under the *Copyright Amendment (Moral Rights) Act 2000*.

HarperCollins*Publishers*
Level 13, 201 Elizabeth Street, Sydney NSW 2000, Australia
Unit D1, 63 Apollo Drive, Rosedale, Auckland 0632, New Zealand
A 53, Sector 57, Noida, UP, India
1 London Bridge Street, London SE1 9GF, United Kingdom
Bay Adelaide Centre, East Tower, 22 Adelaide Street West, 41st floor, Toronto,
   Ontario M5H 4E3, Canada
195 Broadway, New York NY 10007, USA

A catalogue record for this book is available from the National Library of Australia.

ISBN 9780 7333 4015 4 (paperback)
ISBN 9781 4607 1147 7 (ebook)

Cover design by Amy Daoud, HarperCollins Design Studio
Cover image: In January 2014, when UNRWA was able to complete its first humanitarian distribution in Yarmouk, Damascus, after almost six months of siege, it was met by thousands of desperate refugees on the destroyed main street © 2014 UNRWA.
Back cover image: by Peter Beaumont.
Author photo, page i: Sophie McNeill
Map on page viii by Map Illustrations www.mapillustrations.com.au
Typeset in Sabon LT Std by Kirby Jones
Printed and bound in Australia by McPhersons Printing Group
The papers used by HarperCollins in the manufacture of this book are a natural, recyclable product made from wood grown in sustainable plantation forests. The fibre source and manufacturing processes meet recognised international environmental standards, and carry certification.

*For my three greatest loves, Reuben, Nat and Quinn,
and all the brave, beautiful people I have met along the way
who deserved so much better in this life*

Our Country is a Graveyard

Gentlemen, you have transformed
our country into a graveyard

You have planted bullets in our heads,
and organized massacres

Gentlemen, nothing passes like that
without account

All that you have done to our people is
registered in notebooks

Tawfiq Ziad (1929–94)

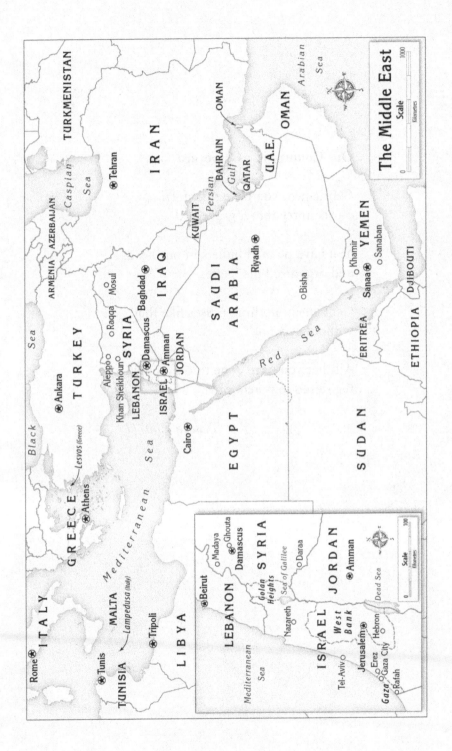

CONTENTS

Introduction

As I worked at my desk in Jerusalem, voice messages from Syria would pop up on my phone throughout the day and late into the night.

Some were from Dr Khaled Naanaa in his makeshift clinic in the opposition-held town of Madaya, near Damascus. 'Please, the international community must act fast to save the lives of the people,' he begged in one message. Khaled was only about 250 kilometres from where I sat, but his village was besieged, tightly surrounded on all sides by pro-regime forces loyal to Syria's brutal dictator, Bashar Al Assad. For the past five months, no food had been allowed in for Madaya's civilians and no one allowed out.

'People are starving here,' he said. He sent me images of a desperately ill, emaciated baby girl called Amal. Her mother had no milk and she was being fed just water and salt. Two babies in the besieged town had already died from malnutrition. Other small children stared into the doctor's camera, their cheeks hollow, their ribs jutting out of their malnourished frames.

I was the first to report the horrific pictures taken in this clinic. And, at first, people sat up and took notice. Children starving to death just 40 kilometres from Damascus? It was a shocking new low, even for Syria's depraved war.

Khaled's photos and videos featured on the front pages of newspapers and news channels around the world. The then US ambassador to the United Nations, Samantha Power, even referred to them at the UN General Assembly.

But nothing changed.

Over the next 15 months, medics documented the deaths of 73 more men, women and children in the besieged town. All had starved to death less than an hour's drive from UN warehouses packed full of food in Damascus.

For millions of people across the Middle East like Khaled, international law, the rules of war and the 'responsibility to protect'

seem like antiquated theories, discussed in New York at the UN, at legal conferences and in books, but not applicable in real life.[1] On the ground, it feels like the international rule book has not just been thrown out the window but shredded and set on fire. Because when it came to the crunch, most of the well-meaning international principles and systems proved meaningless as millions of the world's poorest and most oppressed people came under constant bombardment for years on end.

During my three years as the ABC's Middle East correspondent I filmed starving toddlers dying in front of me in Yemen, recorded doctors begging me over the phone for help as their hospitals were bombed in Aleppo, interviewed families who wept on the outskirts of Mosul as they described how ISIS used them as human shields during coalition bombardment, and met distraught children in Gaza whose parents had died after they were prevented from receiving cancer treatment outside the strip, because Israeli authorities wouldn't give them permission to cross the border.

The steady stream of human rights abuses, most perpetrated by state actors upon innocent civilians, was hard to comprehend.

What had our world become?

Ever since I can remember, I'd wanted to become a journalist and work overseas. Growing up in Perth, Western Australia, one of the most remote cities on earth, I dreamt of exploring beyond the confines of the small world in which I was raised.

I drew inspiration from reading and watching the works of trailblazing reporters like John Pilger and Max Stahl. When journalists were forbidden from entering East Timor under Indonesian rule, both men had sneaked in as tourists. There they bore witness to the horror of the Indonesian occupation before smuggling out evidence of massacres and torture, and their courageous reporting was critical to East Timor's path to independence.

I can still remember the night when I was 14 that I walked out of the Western Australia state library after watching John Pilger's documentary on East Timor, *Death of a Nation*.

I was in a daze, bowled over by what I'd learnt about the horrors of the Indonesian occupation since 1975, the struggle of the people of East Timor for their freedom, and my own country's complicity

in their oppression. I felt strongly that, now I knew what was happening to the people of East Timor, I had to act. I couldn't be aware of what they were enduring and just continue as normal. That felt criminal. I had to do something.

Then and there I signed up to volunteer to work with East Timorese groups, and spent the next few months helping organize rallies and public-awareness events around the upcoming independence referendum in August 1999.

More than 78 per cent of the population voted for East Timor's freedom. But we watched the news in horror as Indonesian militia attacked and killed civilians and set about burning East Timor to the ground.

Thanks to reporters like Marie Colvin and John Martinkus, who stayed behind to report what was happening on the ground, there was no denying the unfolding terror.[2] East Timorese were being taken at gunpoint by ship and truck to refugee camps in West Timor, and witnesses reported seeing civilians executed.

Thousands of Australians took action. Building unions laid down their tools, wharf workers refused to unload Indonesian ships, and protestors blockaded the counter of the Indonesian government-owned Garuda airlines at Sydney airport.[3] Meanwhile, tens of thousands of Australians attended snap rallies around the country, demanding the government send Australian troops to intervene and protect East Timor's civilians.

In an attempt to appease Jakarta, Canberra had spent months denying the need for an international peacekeeping force in East Timor for the controversial vote. But faced with growing public fury, the Howard government changed their tune, proposing that Australian troops be deployed immediately to lead a multinational peacekeeping force in East Timor.

After intense US and Australian pressure, Indonesia announced that it would accept a UN peacekeeping force. Within days, more than 5500 Australian troops arrived on the ground in Dili to lead the INTERFET peacekeeping force, to restore peace and security, and to facilitate desperately needed humanitarian assistance. A UN political mission, UNTAET, also temporarily governed East Timor and began to rebuild the new country, showing what the international community can do when it takes real action.

Hundreds of East Timorese families who had been sheltering in the UN compound in Dili had been airlifted to safety in Australia. Around 400 of them were staying at the Leeuwin Army Barracks in East Fremantle, just five minutes from my dad's house. Every day after school and on weekends I'd go there to help teach English to the kids.

A few months after the peacekeeping force arrived in East Timor, the families were sent back. My new friends would call me to talk about how the capital Dili was full of dengue fever and malaria and how much of the city had been destroyed.

During the school holidays, I sold chocolate frogs to fundraise an airfare, then borrowed my social studies teacher's brand-new video camera and headed off to East Timor. Once there, I made my first short documentary, about a clinic in Dili and the health crisis that was crippling the newly independent nation.

One film led to another and, at 18, I left my small town of Perth to join the SBS newsroom in Sydney. I was fortunate enough to spend most of the next decade on the road, reporting for SBS from Afghanistan, Gaza, Israel, Iraq, Pakistan, Syria and Egypt.

I also spent several years living and working in Beirut and Jerusalem, and fell in love with the Middle East and its passionate, kind-hearted, welcoming people. After returning home to Australia to have two sons, in 2015 I moved my young family to Jerusalem for my dream job: Middle East correspondent for ABC Australia.

I arrived to find the region ablaze.

In Syria, the civil war was about to take a deadly new turn as Russia intervened to help the Assad regime retake opposition-held towns and cities across the country.

Saudi Arabia had begun a massive aerial bombing campaign on its poverty-stricken southern neighbour, Yemen, as it tried to force Yemen's Houthi rebels, who had taken over the north, out of power.

Gaza was recovering from its third war with Israel in six years, with more than 1400 civilians killed in 2014, including 551 children.[4]

Islamic State militants had taken over large swathes of eastern Syria and northern Iraq, forcing millions of civilians to live under their brutal rule, as the coalition began a widespread campaign of airstrikes to try to defeat the jihadists.

My role was to work as a video journalist covering the whole of the Middle East. But in every story, civilians were enduring unspeakable fear and suffering. Civilian homes, markets and schools were being targeted. Food was being used as a weapon of war. Cluster bombs. Poison-gas attacks. Hospitals bombed. Doctors living in fear. Deliberate attacks on aid convoys. 'Double tap' strikes on rescue workers, where a bombsite is quickly hit a second time, with the aim of targeting the wounded and the medical personnel tending to them. The denial of medical care to civilians, including children, as a deliberate act to achieve a political objective.

Whether the aggressor was a jihadist group like ISIS, an oppressive dictatorship like the Syrian regime or a coalition of Western nations led by the US, civilians and civilian infrastructure were in the firing line. 'We know terrorist groups have little interest in international law. But too many governments now believe they have license to behave in rogue fashion as they lack consequence and incentive to change course,' argues David Miliband, the former UK foreign secretary and President of the International Rescue Committee, writing about Yemen. 'It is lame and inexcusable to claim that because terrorists do not live up to high standards neither should they. If the most powerful countries in the world do not set an example, then it is impossible to police the system.'[5]

We can't look back at what's happening now across this region and say we didn't know. The spread of information now is very different to the days of genocide in Rwanda, ethnic cleansing in the Balkans or the final stages of the Sri Lankan civil war. We have reached a point where the public can now know what is happening – how many are being killed, where and by whom. There was nothing we didn't tell you about Syria – that war is certainly the most reported conflict in world history. When journalists couldn't access sites, the evidence was clear from satellites and mobile phone footage filmed by the brave Syrians who chose to stay behind. In many cases war crimes were live-tweeted – you could watch them streamed live on YouTube. Sometimes they even went viral.

The endless suffering, violations of international law and litany of war crimes have been meticulously documented. Yet the world has chosen to look the other way. The precedents set during the last decade are staggering. The consequences will haunt us for years.

'Where there once was outrage and demands for action, complacency has set in,' says Philippe Bolopion, who spent years as Human Rights Watch's key advocate at the UN in New York.[6] 'How did it come to this?'

At first, I felt so privileged to be entrusted to tell the stories of incredibly brave Syrians like Dr Khaled. But after Madaya came Aleppo, then there was Ghouta and now Idlib; and the world watched time and time again as these desperate people were pummelled live on our timelines and televisions.

I strove to achieve what journalists before me did in East Timor. Make change. Influence policy. *Make things better.*

After a while, though, I became too ashamed to ask a Syrian trapped inside to give me any of their precious time or energy to help me report what was happening. What difference did it make? As one of my Syrian contacts said: 'Please, we are sick of filming it and taking pictures. You have seen it all. You know exactly what's happening to us. Just let us die in peace.'

Is this the price we pay for 24-hour news and social media? Are we all so overwhelmed by the horror, visible at our fingertips, of what's happening in the world that even the best of us with good intentions can't see where or how we can make a difference?

I now feel broken by what feels like a lack of cut-through.

I'm not alone. Many journalists, humanitarians and activists I speak to share similar feelings.

When I try to encapsulate how useless those of us whose job it is to tell the truth now feel, the notion of 'moral injury' comes to mind. Moral injury is the damage done to the soul of an individual. It's defined loosely as 'the injury done to a person's conscience or moral compass by perpetuating, witnessing or failing to prevent acts that transgress deeply held moral and ethical beliefs and expectations.'[7]

According to Professor Tom Frame from UNSW Canberra, moral injury is what happens when the moral norms that an individual uses to make sense of themselves and the world are destabilized. He describes the thought process of someone with moral injury. 'I thought there was a certain inherent moral logic in the way the world worked. The things I once believed, the things which once ordered my life – I'm not sure about them anymore.'[8]

American psychiatrist Grant H. Brenner has described the idea of 'collective moral injury' on a body politic as the result of ongoing, unrelenting moral transgression.[9] It feels, to those of us who put our trust in the idea that if the world knew what was happening it would be moved to stop it, that we are suffering from a collective moral injury.

Perhaps this collective trauma is now being experienced more widely, as the world witnesses attacks on democracy, the rise of authoritarian-leaning leaders and inaction in the face of what is now a climate emergency.

For those of us who trusted in the system, there is an overwhelming sense of betrayal as we witness a collapse in the order we had always believed in while feeling utterly powerless to stop it.

But we just cannot let this impunity continue.

This book documents the consequences for ordinary people when all the rules are broken and shows how this situation must be reversed if we have any hope of achieving a more peaceful planet in the future. In it you will meet amazing, brave, defiant people who bear the brunt of this lawlessness but refuse to kowtow to it and refuse to accept that they can't change the world for the better. They are people just like you and me. Many of them have lost everything in order to stand up for what they believe in.

I hope you draw the same inspiration from them as I have and that you too will no longer look the other way.

My book is just a small way of trying to honour these heroes.

These are their stories.

Sophie McNeill, January 2020

CHAPTER 1

A KNOCK AT THE DOOR

Noura

After seizing power in 1970, Hafez Al Assad ruled Syria with an iron-fist, brutally crushing any sign of dissent against his reign. Following a Muslim brotherhood uprising in the 1980s, the dictator sent regime forces to surround the town of Hama, where they besieged and then massacred the inhabitants inside. Amnesty International estimated that between 10,000 and 25,000 Syrians, mostly civilians, were killed in the crackdown, which for years stood as one of the most deadly atrocities committed in the modern Middle East by a government against its own citizens.[1] In the years after the Hama slaughter, anyone expressing political opposition to Assad's rule was hunted down and frequently jailed, a tradition continued by Hafez's son Bashar Al Assad once he assumed power in 2000 after his father's death. The story of Noura Ghazi describes just one of the hundreds of thousands of Syrian lives ripped apart by the unimaginable cruelty of a family desperate to hang on to power at any cost.

Syria, 1988

Seven-year-old Noura Ghazi watched out the car window as the border guards took away her mother for questioning. She and her six-year-old sister, Lama, were left alone in the car. It happened every time they crossed the border to Lebanon. Sometimes it lasted for hours. The security officers occasionally approached the young girls waiting patiently in the car, to see if any information could be gleaned from them. 'Where is your father?' they would demand. But Noura and Lama had been trained well. They never gave anything away.

It had all begun two years earlier with a knock at the door in the middle of the night. The security services had come looking for her father, but a friend had tipped him off. By the time the police arrived, Marwan Ghazi had already disappeared. In the weeks after her father vanished, Noura's mother and aunts would whisper in the kitchen, trying to smile reassuringly when she caught their gaze. 'Your dad is away working,' her mother told her, but Noura knew something wasn't right. He had been there one day and gone the next. One day, after her father had been gone for a lengthy period, Noura was shocked when a schoolfriend's dad came to do the school pickup. 'Your father lives with you?' she asked incredulously. She had thought all fathers were absent like hers.

After several months, her mother confided to Noura and Lama that their father was in Beirut and they were going to visit him. They mustn't dare mention his name at the border in front of the soldiers, she warned the young girls. The excitement of seeing him soon was overtaken by fear as Noura witnessed the Syrian intelligence officers interrogating her mother for the first time, but they were eventually allowed to cross.

It became a familiar pattern on school holidays: the three of them would pile into the car in Damascus and take the road west to Beirut, their mother steeling herself each time for the border guards' questioning. The visits were always too short. Memories of goodbyes, tears and tight embraces defined those years, not the time they spent together. Once, when Noura and her mother and sister were returning home, they carried chocolates and bananas with them, presents from their father which could be found much cheaper in Beirut than in Damascus. Syrian officials seized the items

from the car at the border, and Noura watched as they threw the precious gifts on the ground.

The trips to see her father in Lebanon went on for six years. Noura wasn't told exactly why her father was forced to live in exile, but as she got older what became clear in her mind was that he was a hero, one of a rare few who stood up to the Assad family and dared to ask for their freedom. 'We have to pay the price because the country is the most important thing in our lives,' she remembered him saying time and time again.

In 1992, when Noura was 11, her father was back inside Syria for a short visit, to meet with his fellow socialist-party activists and to pass on a gift for her mother's birthday. The gift never made it. He was arrested by the authorities and disappeared – the ninth time Marwan had been arrested for simply opposing the regime.[2]

After his arrest, Noura didn't see her father for months, and it wasn't long before his face began to fade in her mind. She had always thought he looked a lot like the famous Lebanese singer Azar Habib, so she listened to his songs and watched his performances; sometimes she would actually believe the singer was her dad – it was better than imagining what was happening to him in the custody of the feared security services.

Finally, Noura's father was brought to the military court for a hearing. The 12-year-old stood outside in the street alongside her mother, who was pregnant at the time with Noura's younger brother, watching as her handcuffed father was marched past by the guards. Noura ran up to give her father a hug, but before she could reach him, a military police officer stepped in front of her. The schoolgirl refused to be intimidated, pushing and trying to get past him, but the officer did not move, telling her it was forbidden to touch the prisoners. 'I shit on Hafez Al Assad!' the 12-year-old spat out in anger, repeating the curse she had heard her father and his friends utter at home.

The officer was shocked. Cursing the president was not something anyone would dare actually do in front of regime officials. 'Whose child is this? I will arrest her!' he snarled. Noura's mother apologised profusely and ushered her distraught daughter away.

That day, Noura vowed that she would become a lawyer, to defend prisoners just like her father.

The court declared Marwan Ghazi guilty of being a member of an opposition party – an illegal act in a one-party state – and a threat to the security of Syria. For the next two years, Noura and her mother and sister would visit her father once a fortnight at Adra Prison in Damascus, where he was held with other political prisoners. They were allowed to spend only two hours with him. Noura and Lama would spend the first hour talking with their dad, and then the second hour their mother would sit with him. There were two sets of bars separating the three of them from the man they loved, and this 40-centimetre gap meant months would go past without them so as much as holding his hand. When it was their mother's turn to talk, Lama would play with the children of other women visiting, but Noura would sit and discuss politics with her father's fellow prisoners, communists and labour activists also jailed simply for their opposition to the regime. It was a priceless education in social injustice.

When Noura was 14, her mother was washing dishes in the kitchen one night when there was a knock at the door. It was her father. Noura and her siblings smothered him in hugs and kisses, laughing and crying, unable to believe he was there for them to touch and hold. He was home.

Marwan didn't talk to his daughter about the torture he had suffered in custody, but when friends came to visit, she overheard them talking as they drank coffee in the living room. They would joke and laugh about what they endured in jail. Many times, Noura learnt, her father had come close to dying. Sometimes when Noura looked at her father, she could still see his face as it had looked in prison, peering out through the iron bars that had separated them for years on end. At those times, it felt like those bars could never be erased.

CHAPTER 2

YOU WANT FREEDOM?
Khaled, part I

In early 2011, a wave of pro-democracy uprisings swept across the Middle East and North Africa, as brave citizens went out on the streets and demanded the end of authoritarian regimes across the region. In March that year, the Syrian people rose up, holding widespread peaceful demonstrations calling for democratic reforms and the downfall of President Bashar Al Assad, whose family had ruled Syria for the past four decades. But the dictator responded with brutal force: unarmed protestors across the country were met with rounds of gunfire, and mass arrests saw thousands of innocent civilians rounded up and brutally tortured. Despite the threat of incarceration and death, citizens across the country risked all to join the uprising. This included doctors and nurses throughout Syria who joined the opposition movement to create a secret underground healthcare network, as a growing number of injured demonstrators could no longer safely seek shelter and treatment in public hospitals. Around this time, many Syrians felt like they had to make a choice: what side of history would they be on?

Damascus, Syria, 2011

It was close to midnight on Friday, 29 April 2011. A 25-year-old nurse, Khaled Naanaa, was doing his rounds inside Tishreen military hospital on the outskirts of Damascus when the ward phone rang. 'All nurses on duty, please report to Emergency immediately,' ordered the head of the nursing department.

The young nurse quickly finished what he was doing and rushed down the hall. *It must be a bad bus accident*, he thought as he headed towards the ER. Run by Syria's military, Tishreen hospital treats both soldiers and civilians. As Khaled entered Emergency, he noted that many off-duty, high-ranking staff were among those gathered, an unusual sight so late at night. None of the nurses knew why they had all been summoned. What was going on?

Within a few minutes, a large military truck rolled up outside the main entrance to the ER, followed by several buses. As the staff moved outside, Khaled could see dozens of dead bodies stacked up in the back of the truck. Syrian security forces started dragging wounded and bleeding men with obvious gunshot wounds out of the vehicles and dumping them on the bitumen near the young nurse's feet. Khaled stood shocked, frozen in horror and fear.

The uprising in Syria had started just a few weeks earlier. In the southern town of Daraa, 15 young boys had been arrested on 6 March 2011 for spray painting on a public building the slogan of the Arab Spring, 'The people want to topple the regime.' When the children were finally released two weeks later, they had been beaten and tortured, their fingernails pulled out by Assad's military police.

But this was the first time the young nurse had come face to face with the brutality of the government's crackdown on opposition supporters. Many of the medical staff at the hospital, particularly the department chiefs and head doctors, were known to be strongly loyal to the regime of Syrian president Bashar Al Assad, and came from the same sect he did, the Alawites.

Khaled, however, lived in a poor Sunni neighbourhood in Damascus, where many of the largest protests against the regime originated. In the last few weeks, he had been trying to keep a low profile at work, avoiding involvement in anything that would see him labelled an opposition sympathizer.

He bent down, but, before he could start treating the injured, some of his colleagues began kicking and beating the wounded men and yelling insults at them. Soldiers began using their rifle butts to deliver further, stunning blows and one of Khaled's male colleagues even urinated on the wounded men, laughing as they lay helplessly on the ground. A senior doctor remarked that the dead and wounded were 'terrorists' accused of planning an attack. But Khaled knew this was a lie.

The Syrian army had spent the previous few days besieging the southern city of Daraa in response to growing anti-government protests, and so civilians from surrounding towns had gathered that Friday to try to end the blockade.

'We held olive branches, and posters saying, "We want to bring food and water to Daraa." We had canisters with water and food parcels with us,' a witness later told Human Rights Watch. Another demonstrator spoke of the moment the unarmed protesters were shot. 'There was no warning, no firing in the air. It was simply an ambush. There was gunfire from all sides, from automatic guns. Security forces were positioned in the fields along the road, and on the roofs of the buildings. They were deliberately targeting people. Most injuries were in the head and chest.'

Witnesses reported that at least 62 people were shot dead by security forces, with dozens of others wounded.[1]

And now here some of them were – dead, cold and discarded like unwanted trash in the back of a truck. Those who had survived the shootings had been hunted down and dragged from their beds by the security forces. Here they were now, lying beaten to a pulp on the driveway, many of them still in their pyjamas and barefoot, bleeding and absolutely terrified. 'You want freedom? You want revolution?' the soldiers and staff taunted the wounded as they pounded them.

Khaled hung back, disgusted at what was going on but also terrified for his own fate. He knew that he could quickly join the ranks of those labelled 'terrorists' if he spoke out. While his sympathies lay with the crowds demonstrating for freedom and an end to the regime, he personally had not been involved in the street protests. The young nurse came from a large family of farmers from Idlib province in the north-west of Syria. Khaled was proud of his

university nursing degree and had spent the last few years working two jobs to try to pay off a small apartment he had purchased in the Damascus suburb of Darayya. He had also recently become engaged to Joumana, a sweet young art teacher he had met the previous year. Life was busy, and he was keen to settle down and start a family with his fiancée. His becoming involved in the revolution would risk losing everything he had worked so hard for.

Before their lack of participation was noticed, Khaled and a few other staff melted away. He drifted back to the hospital staff quarters and lay down on his bed, unable to get the horrific images he had just witnessed out of his head. He felt physically sick and terribly guilty. *Why did I just stand there?* he kept asking himself. *Why didn't I do anything?* He felt like a coward. Khaled knew he couldn't just continue as if nothing had happened.

Within a few days, Khaled formed a secret network inside the hospital, joining with his colleagues who had also chosen not to participate in that night's brutality. Together, they decided to formally document what they had seen and send it to a trusted contact working with Human Rights Watch.[2]

Over the next few months, Khaled and his colleagues at Tishreen military hospital became firsthand witnesses to the regime's systematic efforts to annihilate suspected opposition activists.[3]

Assad's security forces were abducting civilians off the streets and torturing them to death in military intelligence facilities. Their bodies would then be collected from regime cells and taken to Tishreen, where doctors were instructed by their superiors to write medical certificates stating that the detainees had died either from 'heart failure 'or 'respiratory failure'.

Amnesty International documented witness accounts from medical staff working at Tishreen in 2011:

They were sending us dead bodies from all of the prisons...
Medically I had to check them and see they were dead. I filled out a medical report – for example, this person, this ID number, died because of a sudden heart attack...The real cause of death is really hard to tell because the bodies were destroyed...At the beginning, they had wounds from electricity, burning, beating. They had broken legs and arms. Then we started to receive huge

numbers of deaths caused by diarrhoea and skin diseases. They were dying from scabies and tuberculosis.[4]

Each day, Khaled was terrified the authorities would discover that he and his colleagues were passing on word of what they were seeing. Government forces had carried out a wave of arrests against medical professionals in Damascus, and two of Khaled's Tishreen colleagues were among those arrested. [5]

Meanwhile, the regime's violent response to the protests only further fuelled demonstrations. The number of dead and wounded was quickly spiralling – but going to a hospital was no longer safe. Family members reported their loved ones missing after government-run medical facilities were increasingly being raided by Assad's secret police to snatch injured protesters and disappear them.[6]

In response, Khaled and his friends became part of a wider underground network of doctors and medical staff secretly treating activists. Under the cover of darkness, wounded opposition supporters would appear on the doorsteps of trusted medical staff across Damascus, where they could seek urgent medical care. Khaled's apartment was soon operating as one of these medical safe houses. He stole drugs and medical supplies from his hospital and smuggled them home to treat badly wounded activists in his kitchen in the early hours of the morning. The busiest night was Friday, where after a day of demonstrations that now regularly took place after lunchtime prayers, dozens of protesters might need lifesaving treatment.

The young nurse became increasingly committed to the opposition cause. He would work a full shift in the hospital during the day and then most of the night in his home, or in the homes of the wounded, treating everything from broken bones to head injuries and gunshot wounds. Like many of his colleagues, Khaled did this work in secret, unable to tell even his fiancée, Joumana, what he was doing, as disclosing it would expose her to great danger if she were ever detained or questioned by regime forces.

In September 2011, Khaled and Joumana married in a small, modest ceremony in Damascus, their joy of marriage overshadowed by the horror of the events surrounding them. Syria was now enveloped in violence and fear as Bashar Al Assad enforced a

full-scale crackdown on any sign of opposition. The uprising had begun to spiral into a civil war, with contingents of Syria's military defecting to form the Free Syrian Army, a self-declared armed opposition group. Many of Khaled's colleagues in the underground medical network had now moved to rebel-held areas of Syria where the need for doctors and nurses had increased dramatically. By December 2011, more than 4000 civilian protesters had reportedly been killed by government forces.[7]

Khaled was torn. He heard the horrific reports of wounded civilians coming in from rebel-held areas and felt deeply obliged to go and help. But Joumana was pregnant, and Khaled felt he couldn't leave until she had safely given birth. In July 2012, just sixteen days after Khaled held his newborn daughter, Ayaa, in his arms for the first time, he prepared to leave.

That night he tiptoed into his daughter's room and stood over her cot. 'Now I know you and your mother are okay, I must leave,' he whispered to his sleeping newborn, tears running down his cheeks as he bent over to kiss her goodbye. 'I must go and help my people.' Khaled then hugged Joumana tight and said goodbye. She knew he was going away for a few days, but he couldn't tell her exactly what he was up to, because it could place her and their new baby in danger.

Khaled walked downstairs and crossed the road, before pausing to look back at his home. *Please, God, protect my family*, he prayed. He quickly walked down the end of his street to catch a bus out of Damascus and towards Zabadani, a town near the Lebanese border. Before long, he alighted close to where regime territory ended and opposition control began. He set off on foot through the darkness. All he carried was a jacket, a fake ID and a small photo of his love Joumana and his newborn daughter, Ayaa, unsure of whether he would ever see them again.

THE BRIDE AND GROOM OF THE REVOLUTION

Noura and Bassel

In the weeks and months after the Syrian revolution erupted, anyone suspected of sympathising with the uprising was a target. Men, women and even children were snatched from checkpoints during the day, from their beds at night and while lying injured in hospitals. Some were never seen again, while others disappeared into the labyrinth of horror that was Assad's prison system. Haunted by his own experiences in jail, Noura's father was terrified of his daughter joining the opposition movement. But having learnt about her father's sacrifices in the struggle for freedom, nothing could have stopped her from taking to the streets. Noura had always dreamt of marrying someone as brave as her dad, and it was there during the early days of Syria's revolution that she met her match in Bassel.

Eastern Ghouta, Syria, April 2011

Noura Ghazi was trapped. Outside, the blood on the streets was still fresh. At least nine of her fellow protesters had just been shot dead by regime forces.[1]

Noura and her friends had gathered that day in Douma, a working-class neighbourhood in the north of Damascus, to join thousands of others marching to the central square after Friday prayers, calling for the downfall of Syrian president Bashar Al Assad's regime. They had been met with live bullets, unarmed protesters shot dead in the streets by regime forces. Now, Assad's thugs continued to roam the neighbourhood, arresting and beating suspected dissidents.[2] So Noura and a few of her fellow demonstrators sat besieged inside a friend's house, waiting until it was safe to go back onto the streets.

Noura had watched with bated breath as anti-regime demonstrations began sweeping across the country, with thousands filling the streets, bravely chanting, 'We are no longer afraid,' as they called for an end to the dictatorship that had controlled Syria for 40 years.[3]

At 30 years old, Noura had fulfilled the promise she had made to herself as the schoolgirl who witnessed her father marched off to jail simply for opposing the rule of President Hafez Al Assad. After graduating in law from Damascus University, she had dedicated much of her time to defending political prisoners. Noura now represented political prisoners jailed by President Bashar Al Assad, the son of the man who had jailed her father. Her legal work caught the attention of the regime, and they placed a travel ban on Noura to prevent her from leaving the country, a common punishment for anyone who dared challenge the system.

By early April 2011, as Noura sat trapped in her friend's house in Douma, tens of thousands of people across Syria were exhibiting the kind of bravery that had been instilled in her from a young age. Sheltering alongside Noura that afternoon was a fellow activist, Bassel Khartabil Safadi. Tall with short dark hair and a distinctive goatee, he spent the entire time on the phone, talking in rapid-fire English with a stream of different foreign news organizations, reporting to the world about the violence and death that had just taken place in Douma.

He was soon to become the love of Noura's life.

Bassel was born in Damascus in 1981, the son of a Palestinian writer and a Syrian piano teacher. A computer whiz at a young age, he developed a knack for coding. After completing a computer science degree at Damascus University and a master's in software engineering in Latvia, Bassel cofounded Aiki Lab in 2005, a collaborative research company and an accompanying tech space that became a hub for hackathons and teaching kids how to code. Passionate about internet freedom and information sharing, Bassel was an active member of Wikipedia and the Wikimedia Foundation as well as the project lead for Creative Commons in Syria, the global NGO that works to make creative content more freely available for others to build on and share. He wrote code for Mozilla to make the open-source web browser Firefox work in Arabic, and began a project constructing a virtual 3D version of Palmyra, the UNESCO world-heritage-listed ancient ruined city in Syria's Homs province. At a time when the Assad regime still blocked Facebook and Arabic Wikipedia in Syria, Bassel's advances and hacking projects were revolutionary, and he quickly became known in the global tech scene.

Jon Phillips, an American software developer, got to know Bassel online in 2004. 'I started all these open source projects and he came into a chat channel,' Phillips recalled. 'And he contributed some code as a gift and that's how I got to first connect with him. He was just like me.' After collaborating remotely for years, Jon first met the young Syrian at a Creative Commons conference Bassel had organised in Damascus in 2009. 'He was just this normal guy, jeans and everything...His favourite food was pizza...We just wrote code and drank beers.'

Through Bassel's innovations in social media, digital education and open-source software, he was credited with opening up the internet in Syria, an invaluable contribution in a society where the flow of information was tightly controlled in the hands of so few.[4] So, when the Syrian uprising began in March 2011, and that online expertise was called on, Bassel was perfectly placed to respond. News about demonstrations and protests was often issued through Facebook and other social media. Bassel's skills at bypassing government censorship became invaluable not just in

spreading information, but also in distributing videos and photos of the demonstrators and the brutal crackdowns that ensued.

At great personal risk, Bassel started to go back and forth to Beirut, smuggling smartphones, cameras, video cameras and computers into Syria for activists to document the unarmed protesters being repeatedly shot at in the streets, arrested and tortured. Bassel taught his fellow activists to set up proxies and virtual private networks so they could upload the evidence. With foreign reporters now banned from Syria, Bassel helped lead a network of pro-democracy campaigners operating in secret to bring what was happening to the attention of the world.

Three weeks after Bassel and Noura's initial meeting in the wake of the deadly protests in Douma, the two young activists met again when Bassel sought Noura's legal help following a friend's arrest by security forces. The revolution had become all-consuming for both of them, but the attraction was mutual, and they quickly became inseparable. 'It only took us a few days to fall in love,' Noura remembered happily. 'He had this kindness and smartness. I felt like my heart started beating so strong.' They began to work as a team, day and night, harnessing their skills for the revolution. Bassel would film demonstrations, sometimes streaming them live for overseas media outlets, while Noura worked assiduously to document the countless human rights abuses piling up and to advocate for the families of those arrested.

By now, regime forces with tanks and heavy weapons had begun mobilizing in Syrian streets across the country in an attempt to quell the pro-democracy uprising. In the six weeks since the uprising had begun, human rights groups estimated that more than 1000 protesters had been killed by Assad's forces, with more than 10,000 arrested.[5] All over Syria, innocent people were being snatched off the streets by security forces and disappeared.

No one was spared. Bassel heard about 13-year-old Hamza Ali Al Khateeb, a chubby-cheeked boy who had been arrested at a protest in late April in the southern city of Daraa and reportedly handed over to the notorious Air Force Intelligence Directorate. A month later, Hamza's mutilated body was returned to his family. The child had been tortured to death: his face was purple and battered, his skin covered in cuts, gashes, deep burns and bullet

wounds, his neck broken, his penis cut off.[6] Bassel verified the facts of Hamza's disappearance and sourced video of the child's body from his family. He then wrote, produced and edited a report about the murdered child that aired on Al Jazeera and quickly went viral around Syria and the wider Arab world, Hamza's story becoming a symbol of the Syrian revolution. In the Damascus suburb of Douma, protesters marched through the night holding signs declaring, 'We are all Hamza Al Khateeb,' while in Darayya, women and children held aloft signs that read, 'Did Hamza scare you that much?' as they shouted, 'The people want the overthrow of the regime!'

By June 2011, the Assad regime had begun using airpower to try to suppress the uprising, with Syrian army helicopter gunships firing machine-guns to disperse pro-democracy protests in the north-west of the country.[7] Meanwhile, 10,000 of the first Syrian refugees began spilling over the northern border into Turkey.[8] Defectors from the Syrian military announced the formation of the Free Syrian Army in late July, and the country began to slide into all-out civil war.

Bassel was on the run constantly during this time, staying in safe houses and changing location to avoid arrest. The Aiki Lab space closed after security forces confiscated all its equipment in a raid. The young activist could have fled Syria if he had chosen to. Over the years, he'd stayed in close contact with Jon Phillips, who, fearing for his friend's safety, had organised a job in Singapore for Bassel, with permission for him to bring along his whole family. Bassel chose to stay in Syria.

Every week, more of Bassel's and Noura's friends and fellow activists would vanish into the hands of the secret police, while others fled Syria with a price on their head. As the stakes got higher, Noura and Bassel feared one of them would be next. The intensity of their love was heightened by the death and destruction that continued to spiral around them. They soon became engaged, a short courtship by Syrian standards, as both felt time was of the essence. 'I knew there was a moment where I am going to lose him or myself,' Noura said, reflecting back on that time. 'Maybe that's why we got engaged very early.'

In a video taken by a friend around the time of their engagement, Noura sits on Bassel's lap as they joke and laugh about how they

fell in love.⁹ 'We love each other a lot and we are very compatible,' Noura says grinning into the camera before leaning back and planting a kiss on Bassel's cheek.

'When we met, we couldn't stand each other,' jokes Bassel, his chin resting on Noura's shoulder.

'I am the one who didn't like him!' Noura interrupts.

'Also, I didn't like you at the time!' Bassel teases, smiling.

The mood shifts as they talk about their fears for the future. 'I am always worried about him,' Noura says softly, glancing at Bassel, who has his arms wrapped around her waist. 'I worry a lot about him. A lot. I have fears.'

'Before we got together, I didn't have any fears, but now I fear for our relationship,' says Bassel, his brow furrowing. 'I didn't have any problem with getting arrested before we got engaged. But now I have a problem because I am worried about her.'

They both now had something to lose.

In September 2011, Bassel managed to travel out of Syria to attend a Creative Commons global summit in Warsaw, Poland. Jon Phillips was there too and tried again to convince his old friend it was too dangerous for him to go back to Syria. Late one night, over beers, they got into an argument. Jon recalled, 'I was screaming at him, "But you're going to die, man! You're going to die!" They were both in tears. Bassel ultimately shrugged apologetically, telling Jon that he was obliged to help his people. Bassel hugged Jon goodbye and flew back home to the death and despair waiting for him in Damascus.

In March 2012, nearly a year after they had met, Noura and Bassel were busy planning their upcoming wedding among their daily activism. One afternoon in Damascus, Bassel went out without Noura, which was unusual because they were always so inseparable, but he had a meeting and she was due to pick up her wedding dress with her mother. Later that night, they were going to visit the hotel where their wedding dinner would be held in three weeks' time.

'I felt something strange on that day,' Noura said, thinking back. 'I didn't want Bassel to go out, but he insisted.'

Bassel never returned from his outing.

Noura searched for him desperately, calling up everyone she knew in the movement to see if anyone had spotted him being abducted from a checkpoint or dragged into a police station. But

no one had seen a thing. Bassel had simply vanished. Eight sleepless nights later, the military police turned up at Noura's family home, where the couple had been living. And with them was Bassel – an exhausted-looking, dishevelled and pale Bassel.

He tried to smile reassuringly at Noura as the security forces swarmed the house, collecting all of his computers and his phone and notebooks, to use as evidence in a case against him. Noura's mother insisted on making coffee for the officers, buying her daughter a few precious minutes to hold her fiancé before he was torn from her arms.

When the military police gave the order that it was time to go, Bassel whispered in Noura's ear, 'Wait for me,' squeezing her as tight as he could. 'Please wait for me.' They quickly kissed goodbye before Bassel was bundled away in the military police van.

And then came complete silence. Their wedding date came and went, and Noura's white dress hung in her mother's cupboard collecting dust. Noura consumed herself with trying to find out Bassel's whereabouts and meticulously caring for Sissie, the white kitten Bassel had given her on Valentine's Day, just a month before he was snatched from the streets.

The young lawyer learnt a warrant had also been issued in her name, and she kept waiting for the security forces to come and arrest her too. Noura went into hiding, changing houses several times and ending her court work, but they never came. Later, Noura learnt from Bassel that he had made a deal with the intelligence officers: if he cooperated with them, they would cancel the arrest warrant against her. He would give them what they wanted in exchange for her freedom, essentially trading his own fate to ensure his love's safety.

Over months, news filtered out from previous detainees that Bassel was being held at the notorious military intelligence headquarters at Kafar Sousa. Jon Phillips and Bassel's other friends in the international tech scene went into overdrive. With the hashtag #FreeBassel, they launched an international campaign calling for Bassel's release, telling the world that the Syrian regime had arrested the 'Steve Jobs of Syria'. Awareness of Bassel's incarceration began to spread; he was named as one of the Top 100 Global thinkers of 2012 by the American magazine *Foreign Policy* for 'insisting against all odds on a peaceful Syrian revolution'.[10] More than a

thousand people from all over the world signed a letter addressed to the Syrian government calling for Bassel to be freed.

Noura had nightmares about what the security forces were doing to her fiancé. In July 2012, four months after Bassel disappeared, Human Rights Watch released a damning report, identifying 27 facilities across Syria where intelligence forces were torturing civilians.[11] The systemic pattern of the torture was so widespread, HRW concluded, that the regime was carrying out a 'state policy of torture and ill-treatment' which constituted 'a crime against humanity'. The report revealed that Syrian officers tortured their own people with prolonged beatings, electric shocks, acid burns, sexual assault, humiliation, pulling out fingernails and mock executions – and that women, children and the elderly were among those being tortured.[12] 'By publishing their locations, describing the torture methods, and identifying those in charge we are putting those responsible on notice that they will have to answer for these horrific crimes,' HRW said at the time. However, the Syrian government operated with impunity and the world proved it was indifferent to the lives of Syrians. Tens of thousands more Syrians would be tortured by the regime over the coming years.

In November 2012, eight months after Bassel's disappearance, a private number called Noura's mobile. She answered hesitantly; an unidentified call in Syria was usually something to fear. 'It's me,' Noura heard Bassel say. 'I'm in Adra Prison and you can visit me.'[13] It was the same prison Noura's father had been held in. Her life was once again about to become defined by iron bars separating her from the man she loved.

When Noura went to visit Bassel the next day, he was almost unrecognizable. He had lost a significant amount of weight and now looked emaciated and sickly. For the past eight months, Bassel had been beaten, tortured, abused and periodically starved, either held in solitary confinement or in a tiny room with 12 other detainees. 'I almost didn't know him because of the torture. He had become so unhealthy,' recalled Noura. 'It took me one minute to recognize him, and then I just hugged him, and I was just saying, "I love you, I love you, I love you," over and over again.'

The evidence of the suffering Bassel had endured was still there for Noura to see, including deep burn marks on his hands. 'It's

okay,' he told her with a sad smile. 'It is normal to be tortured. We live in Syria, baby.'

Bassel's release from the intelligence facility to Adra, a civilian prison with a mix of ordinary criminals as well as political prisoners, was seen as a win for the intense lobbying carried out by Noura, Jon Phillips and many other friends and campaigners. Despite the nine months he had already spent in military intelligence custody, there was no plan to free Bassel. He'd been charged with 'spying for an enemy state', but he was not given a trial or a lawyer. Bassel was going to be locked up in wing number seven of Adra Prison for the foreseeable future.

Noura quickly devoted her life to visiting her love. She would travel to Adra, on the north-east outskirts of Damascus, three times a week, smuggling in love poems, books and Snickers, Bassel's favourite chocolate bars. As she became accustomed to the jail and its routines, Noura would also sneak out letters Bassel had written to friends on the outside. 'Dear friends,' he handwrote to the team who had campaigned so intensely for him when he disappeared. 'I cannot find words to describe my feelings about everything you did for me. What you did saved me and changed my situation to better. Thank you all and big love!'

In early January 2013, Noura and Bassel married in a secret ceremony inside the prison. Their parents came along to witness the young couple's vows, which were exchanged in whispers through the bars, so the prison guards would not notice. Noura wore a blue dress, the couple's favourite colour. 'We have this rule that now, this moment, right now is the best,' Noura said firmly of their decision to get married in the jail. As Noura's father, Marwan, recited the wedding prayers, Bassel smiled at Noura and moved the wedding ring that had been on his right hand, to signify the engagement, over to his left. Noura did the same. They were now husband and wife.

As a lawyer, Noura was allowed special access to the jail that was not given to the wives of other detainees, and the guards wouldn't search her. Instead of just talking through the bars, she was allowed to sit with Bassel and hold his hand. She quickly became the conduit between dozens of jailed political prisoners and their families outside, passing urgent messages as well as cigarettes, medicines and sweets to men inside. During this time, when people asked

Noura what she did for work, she would always reply, 'I smuggle chocolate into Adra Prison!' Noura also used her time in the prison to work on the cases of other prisoners and pass messages to their families. Bassel would just sit there and watch his wife, his love for her the only thing keeping him strong and focused.

Not long after Bassel was moved to Adra, a young Syrian filmmaker called Wael Saad Al Deen arrived in Bassel's wing of the prison. The 29-year-old had been picked up by Syrian security forces while he was out on the streets filming protests. Like Bassel, Wael had initially been held in a military prison and tortured, spending three months in the notorious Palestine Branch 235. The young man had seen dozens of his fellow detainees die around him, from the beatings, sickness and a lack of food. Wael didn't think he would make it out alive. Adra Prison seemed like heaven in comparison to where he had been, and Bassel was soon to become his new best friend. The two discovered they had several mutual friends and quickly hit it off. 'Bassel knew how to navigate prison life, and he brought us food on the first day,' Wael remembers.

Adra Prison was becoming massively overcrowded. It was designed to hold only around 2500 people, but as the regime continued to carry out mass arrests of suspected political dissidents, the numbers swelled, with reports surfacing that the prison was holding as many as 7000 people.[14] In Adra's wing seven, where Bassel was in room ten and Wael in room three, each room held around 120 prisoners in spaces designed for 40 people.

Each morning, from 9 am to 12 pm, the doors between the prisoners' cells would swing open. Bassel and Wael would meet in the common area, where Bassel had arranged classes in Arabic, English and mathematics for his fellow inmates, while also tutoring Wael one-on-one in conservational English. The two would also spend hours walking up and down the hallway of the wing, deep in conversation about the revolution, philosophy and their dreams for Syria after the war. Bassel refused to let the prison walls impede his insatiable thirst for knowledge. When anyone asked what he needed in jail, he would tell them books. He devoured everything in the prison library and then began translating some of his favourite English reads into Arabic, including Lawrence Lessig's *Free Culture* and Karl Fogel's *Producing Open Source Software*.[15]

Wael would write poems in classical Arabic, and Bassel would illustrate them.

As Syria collapsed around them, Noura and Bassel's love was the only light in their lives. On the days Noura visited, Bassel would borrow T-shirts from his fellow prisoners, whatever was cleanest, in an effort to look his best for his bride. 'I would find them sitting like kids,' Wael remembered, grinning. 'She would play with his hair and they would hold hands. There was something beautiful about it.' Bassel could remember every little thing about his history and relationship with Noura, said Wael. 'He would write about their first protest together or when they first met. Every week, he would write about his love in a letter to Noura. And little did she know that I would proofread all those letters for him.'

The story of Bassel and Noura's incredible love grew, and the couple were soon dubbed 'the bride and the groom of the Syrian revolution' by their fellow activists. For the other inmates in wing seven, observing the thrice-weekly interactions of the two lovers provided a sense of faith and beauty amid the squalid depression of the prison and its walls. 'It was a story of love that gave everyone hope that perhaps tomorrow would be sweeter,' explained Wael. 'Noura was like a window to the outside. She was like the wind and the sun. She gave that sense of freedom to Bassel when she visited. And we all felt it too.'

Bassel continued to stay in touch with his dear friend Jon Phillips, who was trying to put together an art project to highlight his friend's incarceration and the plight of detainees in Syria. Bassel wanted to send some thoughts to inspire him. 'Cell no. 26 is the cell I spent 9 months in. It is 2-by-1 metre with no light at all,' Bassel wrote to Jon in a letter Noura smuggled out.

In my current jail I can see the blue sky for six hours each day, but I keep dreaming of the moment I can see sky with no walls and bars. Love is the main source of power to survive the darkness and hard times. Having Noura in my soul and my mind gave me hope when everything in my life collapsed in front of my eyes.

Bassel described to his friend how close he had come to ending it all, in the wake of the torture he endured at the military intelligence

facility. 'I decided to end my life in cell No. 26 after 8 months of no light and no hope. Then cancelled the idea when I thought of Noura's eyes and I got the feeling that I will see them again. That moment changed and saved my life and charged me with power.'

Bassel also started a Twitter account called @meinsyrianjail. He would scribble out thoughts to tweet on notes, which Noura would carry home in her pocket and email to Bassel's friend in Beirut, who would post them on Twitter. 'Jail is not walls, not the executioner and guards. It is the hidden fear in our hearts that makes us prisoners,' Bassel tweeted secretly from the account. Another tweet read, 'A world is the difference between life and death but most people don't know that.'

Every few weeks, the names of certain prisoners would be called out over the prison loudspeaker. Those men would be given a few minutes to collect their belongings before being taken away and never seen again. Rumours about mass executions of political detainees swirled around the prison and inside Bassel's head. 'Bassel [was] always anxious about this and talking about what would happen,' said Wael. 'He was terrified of this thought a lot.'

In March 2013, Bassel was given the *Index on Censorship's* Digital Freedom Award for using technology to promote an open and free internet.[16] His long-time friend Dana Trometer accepted the award on his behalf, telling the audience in London that Bassel was aware of the award and that he would like to pay respect to 'all the victims of the struggle for freedom of speech and especially for those non-violent youths who refused to carry arms'.

The brilliant young software developer was even asked to help with Adra Prison's aging computer system. 'He was so happy because he just wanted to touch computers,' said Noura. In a letter to his friends at the Electronic Frontier Foundation, who were campaigning for his release, Bassel joked about being forced to code with Microsoft in prison.

I'm living in a place where no one knows anything about tech, but sometimes the management of the jail faces problems on their win-8 computers, so they bring me to solve it. So I get a chance to spend few hours every month behind a screen disconnected. It was my first time with Microsoft, so it took me two hours to

learn their technology, four hours to write the code, and one minute to hate it. Don't tell anyone of that.[17]

He finished with a smiley face, jokingly signing off the letter as 'Bassel Safadi, Damascus Central Jail, powered by Microsoft'.

In another letter smuggled out, Bassel reflected on why the regime saw someone like him as such a threat.

I can tell how much authoritarian regimes feel the danger of technology on their continuity and they should be afraid of that. As code is much more than tools, it's education that opens youth minds and moves the nations forward. Who can stop that? No one...I'm in jail but still have thousands if not millions of my hands and minds outside writing code and hacking, and they will always keep doing that no matter what stupid action those regimes will take to stop the motion. As long as you people out [there keep] doing what you are doing my soul is free. Jail is only a temporary physical limitation.

In 2014, Noura wanted to give Bassel a special present for his birthday. What could she possibly give him apart from the standard books and chocolate she had already perfected the art of smuggling in? So she decided to tattoo his name in Arabic calligraphy on her back. On the next visit, Noura chose a special backless outfit to show it off. 'This is your birthday present,' she told him happily.

One night in September that year, Bassel was woken in his cell by explosions outside. The armed rebel group Jaysh Al Islam was fighting regime forces close to Adra Prison, with the stated aim of trying to reach the jail and free the prisoners. The inmates could hear the guards shouting and scrambling in the yard as the shelling got closer. Soon rockets were slamming into the roads surrounding the prison building, with several shells landing inside the prison itself. The battle continued for several days, and while the prison came close to being overrun, the opposition fighters were eventually pushed back by regime forces.

That year, a glimpse of the horror that haunted Bassel and his fellow prisoners was leaked to the world.[18] A military defector code-named 'Caesar' smuggled more than 50,000 photographs out of

Syria, showing the bodies of detainees who had died in the regime's detention centres. The collection was the stuff of nightmares. Verified by forensic experts and Human Rights Watch, the photographs contained the tortured, starved and beaten bodies of more than 6000 individuals.[19] Among the countless victims identified was a boy who was 14 at the time of his arrest and a female activist in her 20s. There could no longer be any doubt about the monstrously evil nature of Assad's rule. But nothing changed.

By 2015, Bassel had been detained by the regime for three years. Other activists who had been held that long without being killed had been released, prompting Noura to get excited that he too might be freed soon. 'All of us thought that, not only me,' explained Noura. On 30 September 2015, Noura turned 34, and the date coincided with a prison visit. As a gift, Bassel gave her a small set of scales – the international symbol of justice – he had fashioned out of materials in the prison workshop. He'd been working on the present for months and was immensely proud of his efforts.

Three days later, on a Saturday morning, Bassel and Wael were in their cells when Bassel's name was called out over the loudspeaker. Bassel quickly rushed to the payphone to call Noura. 'He told me they have come to take him. But he didn't exactly know where they were taking him or who was taking him,' Noura told me quietly. Wael watched helplessly as a military police unit arrived to suddenly remove his best friend. Bassel's face had gone a deathly pale, and he moved mechanically as he was ordered to grab his towel and change into his pyjamas. When he emerged from his cell, the officers pulled Bassel's T-shirt up from his back and over his head, completely covering his face in a makeshift hood. They roughly handcuffed his wrists together and Bassel was marched out of wing seven.

Noura was informed by the prison that military police had taken Bassel to the courthouse. Rumours circulated that the 34-year-old had been sentenced to death and executed. A lawyer Noura knew who had good relations with the government came to her house. 'I have to tell you Bassel has been killed,' he said.

Noura refused to acknowledge the exchange. To do so would be to accept the unthinkable. She had already lost and got him back once. How could they let him sit there for three years, allow her to visit him three times a week and hold his hand, and then just

rip him away from her like this? No, it didn't make any sense. She had promised she would wait for him, so she would continue to do so. Anything else felt like betrayal. 'I absolutely refused to hear anything about his fate. I just wanted to believe that he's still alive,' she said simply.

Wael held out hope that his best friend would return. They had spent much of every day together for the past two years and three months. But there was no sign of Bassel. After three days, Bassel's bed was given to someone else, and his name was removed from the prison register.

Noura and Bassel's friends mounted a relentless campaign to discover what had happened to him, refusing to accept that he had been taken from them. In December 2015, US Secretary of State John Kerry singled out Bassel as a 'prisoner of conscience' in his annual International Human Rights Day address.[20] The founder of Wikipedia, Jimmy Wales, recorded a video calling on the Syrian government to release Bassel, and in March 2016, on the fourth anniversary of Bassel's detention, protests were held in London, Paris and Berlin focused around the global hashtag #WhereIsBassel. But there was still no news.

Noura lay low, terrified the security forces would come for her too. Fleeing the country wasn't an option: she felt that would be betraying Bassel, and if she left it would be harder to obtain information about him. She spent most of her days talking to people all over Syria, secretly documenting human rights abuses for Amnesty International, focusing on executions.

Wael was released from Adra Prison in April 2016, having spent three years locked up there. In the end, he wasn't charged under the military court system as Bassel had been. His family managed to pay a big financial bribe to a judge, and soon after, Wael was deposited on the streets of Damascus. The bribe wasn't enough to take Wael's name off a wanted list, though, so to avoid being arrested again, he needed to be smuggled out of the country. It took 17 days of being swapped from car to car, walking across fields and sneaking across front lines, but eventually Wael made it to Turkey. One of the first things he did once he was free was go online and google his dear missing friend. 'As soon as I left prison, I found as many photos of Bassel as I could on the internet and I downloaded

them onto my laptop,' Wael told me sadly, trailing off. 'Photos of him before he was in prison, in the times I didn't know him. I have a huge folder of photos of him.'

By mid 2017, there was still no official news of Bassel's fate. In July of that year, fury overtook the sadness that had consumed Noura since Bassel had disappeared. 'I started to feel that I was being weak and a coward. And that I'm just hiding from knowing about Bassel,' Noura explained. The more she thought about it, the more certain she was that Bassel had given his life for hers. By giving the regime the evidence against him that they had demanded, he had successfully been able to protect her and have her arrest warrant withdrawn. The onus on her was to now honour Bassel's choice and tell the world his story. 'It's about justice in Syria, and if Bassel was executed, I know that I need to announce this and make a big noise about executions in Syria. And then maybe I will rescue other prisoners from this fate,' she explained.

Noura began to make inquiries with some of Bassel's friends who had connections with the authorities. Was there any chance Bassel was still alive? Was there any proof he had been executed in October 2015 as she feared? One day in late July 2017, a friend knocked at the door. He'd gone to the military court for Noura and had seen the official documents that authorised Bassel's execution. They confirmed that Bassel was killed just a few days after being taken from Adra Prison in 2015. Noura wrote the following post on Facebook.

Words are difficult to come by while I am about to announce, on behalf of Bassel's family and mine, the confirmation of the death sentence and execution of my husband Bassel Khartabil Safadi. He was executed just days after he was taken from Adra prison in October 2015. This is the end that suits a hero like him. Thank you for killing my lover. I was the bride of the revolution because of you. And because of you I became a widow. This is a loss for Syria. This is loss for Palestine. This is my loss.

Bassel's friends were stunned. 'I was trying to keep people's hopes up that he could come back out with us,' Jon Phillips explained quietly. One of the hardest parts about the confirmation of Bassel's death, said Jon, was the recognition that he didn't appear to have

been executed for any specific reason. He suspected his dear friend was just swept up as part of some clearing operation at the jail, where any individual suspected of opposing the regime is given a death sentence and quickly executed.

No details of how Bassel was executed or where his body ended up were provided. The bright spark that had brought so much happiness to Noura and everyone who knew him had been extinguished in a moment of sheer brutality and then discarded. One more body adding to the thousands and thousands of the Assad regime's own citizens that it had systemically murdered.

We know what might have happened to Bassel. Evidence collected by Amnesty International has found that civilians like him are often executed in mass hangings.[21] Once he was marched out of Adra Prison that day, handcuffed and with his T-shirt covering his head, Bassel was likely taken straight to a military field court and subjected to a short trial that lasted between one and three minutes. Condemned civilians are then placed in a basement cell. Many hours later, in the middle of the night, they are blindfolded and taken to the execution room. They are told that they have been sentenced to death only minutes before the executions are carried out; and they do not know how they will die until the nooses are placed around their necks. Between 20 and 50 people are often hanged to death at a time. After the executions, the victims' bodies are loaded into a truck, transferred to the regime's Tishreen military hospital for registration by Khaled Naanaa's former colleagues and buried in mass graves. It is a government-sanctioned system of extermination.

Noura was heavily medicated and didn't eat for 20 days after Bassel's death was confirmed. She wasn't sure she wanted to live in a world without Bassel. After a few weeks of lingering close to the edge, light began to overtake the darkness. Noura decided she would not stop fighting. Fighting was how she had met Bassel. It was why the regime had arrested and killed him. To stop fighting would be to let them win. He had made the ultimate choice, to protect her life over his. The least she could do was keep living. She posted an update. 'For the sake of my family and for Bassel's family, I have started eating today and have stopped the majority of medication,' she wrote. 'I will not kill myself. I will stay Noura. My journey is long and I will not go back or be broken.'

Noura threw herself into helping to create a new NGO, Families for Freedom, dedicated to raising awareness of the plight of the partners and relatives of Syrian detainees who have been disappeared by their own government. From Damascus, she travelled to London and Paris, standing on the steps of the British parliament and out the front of the Eiffel Tower, telling the world about her beloved husband and the thousands of other Syrians locked up in Assad's prisons. 'My aim now is to try to prevent any detainee in Syria having Bassel's fate,' she told reporters adamantly. 'I don't just sit and wish. I do.' Always, she spoke about her deep love for Bassel and how it kept her going. 'If I see him again, I might just pass out,' Noura responded to reporters. 'I just want to hug him and never let go. I want to tell him that my life isn't worth living without him. Our country is burning; Bassel and I are two small details amid the wreckage.'

Soon the threats arrived. Noura was one of the only people living in regime-controlled Syria who dared to speak out about such issues. She was clearly told that she would be arrested or killed if she didn't shut up. She didn't want to go. This is where the best days had been lived, where she felt closest to Bassel, and it felt disloyal to leave now. But she had promised herself that she would keep fighting, and she wouldn't be allowed to do that in Syria. Noura was left with no choice but to leave the only home she had ever known.

On 7 January 2018, the anniversary of her marriage to Bassel, Noura carefully packed up all of Bassel's books and the artwork he had created for her in prison. She squeezed the rest of her life into just a couple of suitcases and whatever could fit in the back of a taxi. She hugged her parents as tight as she could and jumped in the cab. In her lap was Sissie, the beloved white cat Bassel had given her, and Noura held her tight as they drove west out of Damascus towards the highway to the Lebanese border.

And there she was, 30 years later, forced to flee across the very same border as her father. Where she had sat tearful and terrified as the soldiers had interrogated her mother. Where she, as a stubborn, brave little girl, had defied them and refused to answer their questions, protecting her father. Where it had become engrained in her just what it meant to sacrifice everything for the Syria that she, her father and Bassel had dreamt of.

It is now Noura's turn to be visited in Beirut. Every few months,

her parents drive from Damascus to see her. Each time they return home, 66-year-old Marwan is questioned by security about Noura. He hides this from his daughter, just like he hid his torture in jail. But she knows from her brother that it happens.

Noura's father always wanted her to marry someone like him, someone who stood up to the system and fought for what was right for Syria. Everything Marwan went through – the fear the separation, the pain – was *for* Noura. To build a better Syria for his children. To give them the freedom and the choices he never had. The future was not supposed to be like this.

'Assad, or we burn the country,' the regime supporters had warned. And how they did. Noura and Bassel's love, hopes and dreams are among the millions now lost in the ashes.

*

In February 2016, investigators for the UN's High Commissioner for Human Rights announced that the Assad regime is killing so many detainees in Syria that it amounts to the crime against humanity of 'extermination'.[22] Investigators found that the crimes against humanity committed by the Assad regime in Syria far outnumber those of Islamic State (ISIS) militants and other jihadist groups. The UN said senior government figures clearly knew about and approved of the abuse.

An investigation released by Amnesty International in August 2016 found that nearly 18,000 people had died in Syrian government prisons since the beginning of the uprising in 2011.[23] Thousands of families began to learn of their loved ones' deaths inside Syria's torturous prison system in 2018, when the Syrian government began updating the civil registry.[24] After years of living in hope, mothers, fathers, daughters and sons across the country were given mass-produced death certificates, advising that their relatives had died in detention of a 'heart attack' or 'heatstroke', many learning about deaths that had occurred years before. The unprecedented release of thousands of names of allegedly dead detainees, and the thinly veiled attempts to account for the mass deaths, speaks to the absolute impunity of the Assad regime.

According to the Syrian Network for Human Rights, 130,000 Syrians have been detained or forcibly disappeared by the Syrian regime since the March 2011 uprising in support of democracy.[25]

CHAPTER 4

RUNNING FOR THEIR LIVES

Ahmad, part I

On 3 October 2013, a rickety 20-foot fishing trawler had drifted within sight of the Italian island of Lampedusa. The boat was packed with more than 500 asylum seekers and migrants, mostly from Eritrea, a small, impoverished totalitarian state in the Horn of Africa. After being adrift for two days on the Mediterranean Sea, the families and young men on board were desperate to be rescued. Someone set fire to a blanket to attract the attention of those onshore, but the flames were soon out of control. Terrified passengers flocked away from the fire, but as their weight shifted, the vessel flipped. Hundreds of men, women and children, many of whom could not swim, were flung into the sea. More than 360 people drowned just 600 metres from the shore, in what was one of the worst tragedies in recent memory in the Mediterranean.[1] The refugee exodus over the sea was also coming from the Middle East, as thousands risked the dangerous sea journey to Europe to try to escape war and oppression at home. Eight days after the Lampedusa disaster, nearly 30 refugees from Syria and Palestine also drowned

when their boat capsized between Malta and Lampedusa.[2] The mass drownings sparked national soul-searching in Italy. In response to the deaths, the Italian government announced it would begin a new effort to rescue migrants and refugees in the Mediterranean, called Operation Mare Nostrum. Despite coming from a land where we forcibly turn back boatloads of desperate asylum seekers, I was fortunate enough to be welcomed aboard the Italian navy operations to witness their 'open arms' approach to those most in need.

Puglia Coast, Italy, September 2014

Standing in the bridge of the 8200-tonne troop carrier *San Giusto*, captain Mario Matessi scanned the horizon as his ship steamed towards the Libyan coast. We didn't know how long we'd be gone for or which port we would pull back into – all we knew was that this ship wouldn't return to shore until it was full of asylum seekers. 'We're definitely heading towards the scene of action,' said Captain Matessi as he peered through his telescope. Our destination was 50 kilometres south of the Italian mainland, where Libya's sovereignty ends and international waters begin. This was where the boats were. The smugglers gave the boats only enough petrol to make it there, and the race was on to find them before the men, women and children on board ran out of water in the near 40-degree heat – if they were lucky enough to still be afloat.

The refugees knew the Italian navy were now here to help – they called the Italian emergency rescue number directly from satellite phones as soon as they were out of Libyan waters. 'We often get some very desperate phone calls,' Matessi explained. Inside the ship's crammed operations room, more than a dozen Italian sailors monitored satellite feeds and drones, scanning the sea for refugee boats in distress. Since Operation Mare Nostrum had begun nearly a year earlier, the Italian navy had rescued more than 100,000 migrants and asylum seekers, over an area of more than 40,000 square kilometres of the Mediterranean.

At the Italian navy headquarters on the outskirts of Rome, its commander-in-chief, Filippo Foffi, explained his government's new rescue policy. 'We have the duty in these cases, when we are at

sea, to intervene to save human life,' Vice Admiral Foffi said. My team from ABC's *Foreign Correspondent* program were the first international television reporters given permission to come on board to film the Italian operation. The vice admiral was acutely aware of Australia's reputation with refugees – and he was keen to highlight the difference between Italy's approach and the Australian 'turn back' policy. 'The phrase "turn back" is not applicable in these cases,' Foffi said intently, leaning forward. 'If we are not at sea then we can't see what happens, we can close our eyes, turn off the lights and in that way, there's no need to "turn back" the boats...Because they will die.'

Back on board the *San Giusto*, the crew of 350 sailors were poised for rescue action when the wind suddenly picked up and the swell started heaving. Not even a Libyan people smuggler would send a rubber dinghy off in these conditions. The ship would stand by for 24–36 hours while we waited for the seas to calm.

Downstairs, Marine Sergeant Major Francesco Cuonzo was making last-minute preparations for where the refugees would take shelter once they came on board. The *San Giusto* is an amphibious assault carrier designed to transport military vehicles and armoury – not hundreds of refugees – but Francesco and his men had turned the ship's massive under-deck hold into a makeshift refugee camp. The space was about 130 metres long and 30 metres wide, with portable toilets and special areas for families marked out with plastic flags. A medical triage zone, complete with an isolation tent, was set up in one corner. 'We really have two or three days in which we have close personal contact with the refugees, and you really understand their need to escape. Especially the children,' Francesco told me, as he and his fellow marines passed medical supplies from the storeroom into the large holding area.

Francesco had served as a peacekeeper in Albania, Kosovo, Lebanon, Iraq and Afghanistan, but he said this was his most important mission. 'In their eyes, you see the joy that they have arrived in a peaceful place. They don't hear the sounds of gunfire, bombs or airplanes above their head,' he said. He acknowledged, though, that the navy's rescue operation, which was costing the government more than A$13 million a month, was not popular with many Italians. 'Not everybody is in favour of this,' he said, sighing.

'My friends and family ask me, "What are you all doing with the mission? Why are these people coming to Italy?" I remind them that our ancestors also escaped when there was war. They went looking for their fortunes in America, in Australia, in Switzerland, in other places. When there is not war, it gives you hope of a better future.'

Up on the deck, the wind was easing. The sea would calm tonight. I looked out in the direction of the Libyan coast. In the next few hours, men, women and children would be setting off from those beaches in the dark of night. Mothers and fathers carrying crying children; young men with nothing but the clothes on their backs. Terrified, unable to swim and packed in like sardines to boats that were barely seaworthy. All praying that once day broke, the Italians would find them.

Early the next afternoon, a high-pitched emergency notice system started echoing throughout the ship. 'Loading dock to the bridge. Request permission to lower the dock!' Suddenly, it was on. An inflatable dinghy had been spotted nearby with about 100 people on board. The sailors started preparing their rescue boats to go and save them. Due to the recent Ebola outbreak in Western Africa, the navy had ordered that all crew wear full plastic body suits and face masks when interacting with the refugees. My cameraman Dave and I quickly suited up with the sailors and jumped on board one of the two small speedboats launched from the back of the *San Giusto*.

We started speeding towards a small boat a couple of hundred metres away. As we got closer, we could see dozens of young men packed onto the tiny vessel. Once they saw us, some of them started standing up, a dangerous precursor to the weight shifting in the boat, which could lead to it flipping over. We pulled up alongside the rubber dinghy. 'Everybody sit down!' the Italians yelled through a megaphone. 'There are life vests for everybody; we will give it to those in the middle to pass to the stern and the bow! Do you have kids?'

'No!'

'Do you have women?'

'No!'

'Is anybody sick?'

'Yes!'

'All right, and how many are you?'

'103!'

While some of the young men on board still looked frightened, a few were breaking out in smiles. More than 2000 people had died earlier that year trying to cross the Mediterranean. For these young men, from a mix of war-torn and poverty-stricken African countries, the risk of taking a journey that so many hadn't survived had paid off.

I called out to a young man grinning widely at me as he hurriedly put on his orange life jacket. 'How are you feeling?'

'Better!' he said, putting his hands together in prayer. 'Hope, hope! Thanking God.'

The transfer from one boat to another had to be done very carefully – before anyone panicked, because experience told the Italians that many of these guys wouldn't be able to swim. Slowly, one by one, all 103 men were brought on board. The majority were teenagers, many shoeless, without bags. They quietly took a place sitting on the now-crowded rescue boat deck. Some had tears running down their cheeks as they looked up to the sky and prayed.

Lamin from Gambia, aged 22, couldn't believe he had made it. 'So many dreams, I cannot tell you,' he said, shaking his head in disbelief.

'And you think you're going to find your dreams in Europe?'

'For sure,' he said, grinning. 'Yeah!'

Once all were on board, we headed back to the *San Giusto*. As the refugees disembarked from the rescue speedboat, medical staff checked their temperature, ready to isolate anyone showing signs of fever. Francesco the Marine was there in the landing area, coordinating where everyone would go. 'Fabrizio, it's Scorpio,' he said, giving orders into his radio under his code name. 'As soon as you finish at that station, send me the guests you've already processed.' Note the use of 'guests', not 'unauthorized arrivals', as they call them in Australia, or even 'migrants'. It took several hours for each refugee to be processed, checked by the medical team and given their first hot meal (of course, it was a steaming plate of pasta).

Another alert came through. A merchant ship several kilometres away had spotted a refugee boat in trouble and rescued all 230 passengers. The *San Giusto* crew set off to bring them on board too.

This transfer would be much riskier than that afternoon's mission, as by now it was night, and as we sped out towards the other vessel, the swell had picked up significantly.

After several miles in the pitch dark, we eventually spotted the lights of the massive Norwegian supply ship the *Bourbon Orca*. A friendly blond head popped out of a tiny manhole and waved to us. Several other members of the Norwegian vessel opened the hatch on the side of their ship and started trying to throw rope to help us dock. The Norwegian sailor in charge leant out of the hatch door and called out, 'They all come from Syria and they are escaping from the war there! When we told them they were not going back to Libya, everybody was very happy!'

In the swell, our small boat was bobbing up and down furiously, and it took several attempts before we were tied up securely alongside and could climb on board. As the Norwegian walked the Italian rescue team down a small passageway towards the back deck, he said, 'We heard of another vessel where 40 people drowned today. So we are happy here that everybody got saved. That nobody got injured. We've been giving everybody water and talking to everybody, so they feel safe. And especially trying to give attention to all the children, because the children have to live with this the rest of their lives, so it's important they have a good experience.'

He said that when they came across the boat, it was adrift quite far out in international waters. Its passengers 'had problems controlling it. There was nobody educated to be at sea, so they didn't know how to navigate, and they weren't on course anywhere!'

A metal hatch door swung open and we stepped out onto the deck. Waiting in the dark were hundreds of exhausted Syrian refugees – men, women and children. Several people smiled nervously at us and said hello, while others just stood there, still in shock after their rescue, not willing yet to relax and feel safe. The Marines started trying to sort out how best to transfer these 230 people to their two small rescue boats. They asked the women and children come forward first, but some of the small kids started to panic, thinking they were being separated from their fathers. 'Baba!' a little girl screamed hysterically, reaching for her dad. *Bad idea*, the Marines realised, changing the plan to families first, then the single men.

An old woman in a wheelchair was the first to be slowly passed down from the supply ship hatch to the speedboat as it rocked back and forth below. Two hulky Marines lowered her slowly to their colleagues. 'Okay, hold her under her arms,' one called out testily. 'Slowly, slowly! Tell her to stay calm.' Soon, a steady stream of mothers, fathers and children were being slowly passed down the Marine chain from one boat to the next. A small boy with a bandaged leg being held by his dad. A mum carrying a newborn, tears streaming down her face in relief. A little girl dressed in her best dress and white frilly socks. A toddler with wide eyes wearing a pink blow-up floatie, a seemingly desperate attempt from her parents to try to make the journey safer when no life jackets were available.

I was busy shooting video of the kids, when a young man who had just come aboard the rescue boat approached me. 'Thank you, thank you,' he said to me, grinning widely. His name was Ahmad, 22 years old and from the Syrian city of Aleppo. Ahmad spoke great English and had been translating for the Norwegian sailors.

I asked him how he was feeling in that very moment.

'The feeling is like reborn again, I was so close to death...' he said tearfully, pausing. 'God is the first one to thank, and you the second. Thank you for everything. From the morning till the evening.'

It took over an hour, but eventually all 230 refugees were safely transferred to the Italian boats. As we untied from the supply ship, a round of applause erupted from the Syrian families towards their Norwegian rescuers. The sailors hung out the hatch door waving goodbye as we sped off into the night towards the *San Giusto*.

The full extent of their journey seemed to hit the group as they disembarked the rescue boats and passed through the quick medical check. After first fleeing war in Syria, then facing more unrest in Libya and dealing with a people smuggler, to the very dangerous boat trip – finally, they'd reached safety. *San Giusto*'s newest guests lay down on the cardboard floor of the hold and quickly fell fast asleep.

The next morning, Ahmad from Aleppo was working alongside the Marines, helping to translate and hand out food. The 22-year-old had spent the last month in Libya preparing for the journey,

googling things like 'how to sail a boat'. He had studiously investigated other asylum seekers' trips that had ended in tragedy to try to understand what he could do to ensure his family avoided the same fate. 'Through my research, the main thing I found was that people need to stay calm on the boat. That's the advice I had for everyone. No pushing, just staying still,' he told me firmly, sitting on the floor of the hull with his family, who were enjoying their first hot meal in two days. 'The smugglers don't care if we arrive or not, their main concern is to get the money...When we boarded, I had with me the telephone number of the Italian navy. When we travelled well into the sea, I called them several times, and each time I gave them the location in which we were, until they were able to help us,' Ahmad said, smiling. 'Thank God!'

Ahmad explained that for him, the war in Syria left only three choices in life. 'The first option is to kill. Killing people is easy in Syria. When you have this option, everyone will help you to kill people,' he told me bitterly. 'Or being killed. It's even easier than option one. Because in every street in Syria, there are snipers and bombings. And option three, which we are taking, is to leave the country, and it's a most hurtful choice.' He shrugged sadly and smiled.

Ahmad had been about to start university in Aleppo when the war broke out. Slowly his friends started to either join the opposition armed movement or were forced into conscription in Assad's army. But Ahmad didn't want to fight. As the shelling and airstrikes intensified, and friends and neighbours started to be pulled from the rubble, Ahmad's family sold their apartment and flew to Libya where they waited for more than six weeks to organise their seat on a people smuggler's boat.

It was the first time in his life Ahmad had left Syria. Absolutely nothing remained of his previous life – his city, friends, school, relatives. Everything he once knew was either gone or so vastly changed, it was unrecognizable. And now he was floating in the middle of the Mediterranean, ecstatic to be alive but with nothing except for the clothes on his back, and no idea what would happen next. 'I want to tell people in general that they shouldn't lose hope regardless of what happens,' he said to me firmly. 'I was at a point when I saw death in front of me, and even I accepted it and stopped fighting for life, but, thank God, I and my family stayed alive. People

have to maintain hope in life, because at any moment your life will be changed forever. Keep hope,' he said, smiling.

It was now getting very crowded in the hold. In the past 40 hours, over 800 people had been taken aboard, and the jam-packed space resembled a refugee camp. Syrian families with children wandering around in nappies sat next to young African teenagers who had travelled alone. Clothes had been hung up around the walls and over ropes. It was so cramped, people took turns to lie down and rest on the cardboard-covered deck.

Francesco, the Marine sergeant major, stood surveying the scene. 'One day in the future, it would be lovely to meet someone who passed through one of our Italian navy ships on their way to firm ground in Europe,' he said pensively, 'and see that they have realised their dream. And that they have reached the hope they had the night they crossed the sea, with perhaps also the fear that they would never make it.'

For each life here before us that the Italians had saved, a new beginning in Europe now awaited. With Italy still in the grips of recession with high unemployment, most people on this boat were not planning on remaining there – nearly everyone I spoke to planned to sneak over the Italian border to a more prosperous European country, such as Germany or the Netherlands. And after bearing the full cost of rescue operations for a year without any help from the rest of Europe, Italy was pretty happy to see them go.

As we steamed towards the Italian coast, we heard news of a vessel sinking not too far from where we were, just near the coast of Malta. As many as 500 people drowned after a boat carrying Syrians, Palestinians, Egyptians and Sudanese was deliberately sunk by smugglers. Only 11 people survived after spending days in the water watching helplessly as family members and friends perished around them.[3] The BBC reported that the passengers, who included women and children, had been told to move to a smaller, less safe boat.[4] When they refused, the traffickers reportedly sank the larger vessel. Up to 100 children were believed to be among those who drowned.[5]

This latest tragedy meant that more than 2900 people had already drowned in the Mediterranean in 2014, compared with 700 the previous year. By October 2014, the number of people reaching

Europe had climbed to 165,000 – from just 60,000 the year before – with 150,000 of those rescued by the Italians during Operation Mare Nostrum.[6] But Italian navy commander-in-chief Filippo Foffi rejected the idea that his operation had encouraged more people to make the risky journey, pointing to the ongoing number of people displaced in Syria and northern Africa as the reason for the jump in migrants. 'There is a need to intervene at the origins of the problem; that is, before this horrible journey begins,' Vice Admiral Foffi told me. 'If in the world today there are those that suffer, they suffer because there are injustices and violence. If this violence is not managed and reduced, and if the hopes of these people for the future are not in some way met by countries who have the means to help, the complex disorder of a world so integrated and connected will continue to rise.'

Foffi said Operation Mare Nostrum would remain a source of pride for him and his men for years to come. 'What remains true for us is that that this very big effort and this commitment, both economic and human, has made us richer and has given great satisfaction and great motivation,' he said, smiling. 'I think that it has given every man and woman who has participated in this mission memories that they will never forget.'

After more than a week at sea, the *San Giusto* pulled into the port of Calabria in southern Italy, where hundreds of Italian volunteers waited on the dock to welcome the new arrivals. Ahmad and his family were beaming with excitement as they walked down the ship bridge and onto the wharf. They planned to buy new clothes and then spend the remainder of their savings on train tickets to Germany. It was a risky plan – they could be forcibly returned – but they hoped a set of Italian outfits would help them escape the border guards' attention. 'I'm so, so happy to be on land again,' Ahmad said on the dock, laughing. 'I never want to go on the sea again!' The Italians allowed the new migrants to have freedom of movement as soon as they passed the health checks on land, so we hugged Ahmad and his family, saying goodbye and good luck as they headed off to the train station.

A few days later I got a Facebook message: they had made it to Germany.

＊

After increased pressure from the EU countries receiving the majority of migrants, the Italian government declared the end of Operation Mare Nostrum just six weeks after our time on the San Giusto. A new EU-coordinated effort called Operation Triton began, but it had a different mandate from the Italian search-and-rescue efforts, focusing more on 'border protection'.[7] Operation Triton's budget was less than a third of what the Italians had spent on Mare Nostrum.[8] By April 2015, at least 1500 migrants had drowned en route to Europe, 30 times more drownings than at the same time the year before.[9] Human rights and aid groups attributed this increase to the end of the Italian operation. In response to the high rates of death, Médecins Sans Frontières and several other NGOs began carrying out their own rescues. MSF rescued or assisted more than 80,000 people in the Mediterranean Sea until December 2018, when the election of a new right-wing government in Italy saw the country's ports now closed to migrant rescue ships. MSF was forced to suspend its operations at Italian ports, rendering its search-and-rescue effort impossible.[10] The EU increased its support to the Libyan coastguard, which intercepted more than 14,000 people at sea and forcibly returned them to Libya, a clear violation of international law. In January 2019, a UN report found six migrants had died crossing the Mediterranean every day the previous year.[11] MSF was finally able to resume its life-saving search and rescue operations in the Mediterranean in July 2019.[12]

THE SYRIAN EXODUS
Nazieh, part 1

In the summer of 2015, the number of refugees fleeing the Middle East to Europe suddenly skyrocketed. The majority of them were Syrians, who after spending years being bombed and slaughtered by their own government, gave up waiting for the rest of the world to help them. In Jordan, Lebanon, Turkey and Iraq, nearly five million Syrian refugees had spent years living in decrepit refugee camps. Many of their children had not attended school since they were forced from their homeland years earlier, with refugee kids blocked from accessing free local schooling in most host countries for the fifth year running. With little access to legal work or affordable healthcare, and with no end to the war in sight, Syrian parents had no way of providing any future for their children. But Syrians are a determined, resourceful and brave people, and that summer, many took matters into their own hands. Over the next year, more than 650,000 Syrians fled, to begin new lives in Europe, aided by a Turkish government who, sick of bearing the load of hosting 3 million Syrian refugees, opened the floodgates and allowed hundreds of thousands to leave their shores.[1] Afghans, Iraqis and Palestinians joined the mass movement to escape war and persecution at home and

follow their dreams of life in Europe. I travelled to the shores of the Greek Islands to witness this history-making mass exodus that would have long-lasting effects on Europe.

Lesvos Island, Greece, September 2015

Faint orange dots appeared on the horizon, creeping over from Turkish waters towards this northern bay on the Greek island of Lesvos. As they got closer, the cheap inflatable speedboats slowly began to take shape. The boats sat low in the water, heavy with their precious cargo, heading straight for the beach I was standing on. The four small vessels each looked dangerously overloaded with people.

Thirty thousand people had landed on these shores in the previous fortnight. The Greek coastguard was so overwhelmed that people smugglers no longer sought the cover of darkness. On a calm day, it only took an hour or two to make the crossing. But if the wind quickly changed and the swell rose, these inflatable plastic vessels would be tossed around like bath toys – and many of these refugees couldn't swim. In the past few weeks, hundreds had drowned. Among them was a tiny three-year-old Syrian boy called Alan Kurdi. Dressed in his best clothes, he was photographed lying on the beach, face down with his shoes on, as if peacefully sleeping. The photo spread fast and wide around the world, yet nothing changed. None of the parents who had placed their child in a boat that morning knew if their baby might be the next Alan. When the alternative is daily bombings and airstrikes, a short boat ride is seen as a risk worth taking.

So those in front of me now were the lucky ones. They had made it. There was a cheer and a clap as the first boat ground up onto the sand. A group of young men were the first to jump off, amused to see a camera greet them as they stepped onto European soil. They gave each other high fives and hugs before tearing off the cheap fluoro life jackets that the smugglers had sold them as part of the travel deal. 'I'm from Syria,' declared a teenage boy as he jumped off a boat, wiping tears from his eyes. 'Thank you, thank you!' A man aged about 60 was so desperate to make it to Europe, he tripped as he tried to swing his leg over the edge of the boat and landed facedown in the water. Several people rushed to pick him up and help him to shore, where he collapsed on his back on the

sand and wept. 'Syria, Syria,' he said between sobs, unable to get anything else out. 'Syria!'

The families took longer to alight. Mums and dads stepped cautiously onto the sand holding babies, toddlers and small tote bags stuffed with belongings. A middle-aged mum in a headscarf, with two young sons, stood weeping on the beach. 'I'm planning on going to Germany,' she told me. A father carefully helped his son, who looked about eight, jump onto the sand. The dad shrugged sadly when I asked about the rest of the family. It had cost him US$1200 each to get on the boat, so he could only afford to pay for the two of them to escape Syria. His wife and younger children had to stay behind. 'On the way over, I told my son, I'm doing this for his future,' he said quietly, with his arm around his son, who stood, overawed and silent, next to his father. 'He is nine years old and has never been to school. You know what it is like in Syria.'

Everyone on board had spent the last few days under the control of a Turkish people smuggler. Crammed into small shoddy hotels, trying to avoid the attention of Turkish authorities, they were then packed into open-air trucks and driven at night to small coves, where they spent three nights in the bushes, cold, out of food and terrified of being arrested. Eventually the smugglers gave them the all-clear to make a run for the small motorboats that would take them on the short journey over to the Greek islands and on to Europe. 'Our kids were so hungry,' one mother told me with tears running down her cheeks.

'What do we do now?' the families on the beach asked. I felt terrible explaining that where they had arrived was on the other side of the island from the harbour where ferries to Athens left. The Greek authorities weren't yet stopping the boats, but they weren't exactly laying out the welcome mat, and the NGOs helping asylum seekers hadn't yet been given permission to operate by the local council. Those arriving from Turkey to seek asylum therefore had to walk 50 kilometres into Mytilini, the capital of Lesvos. It was still incredibly hot at that time of year, and the walk could take nearly two days.

The young single men were not discouraged by the idea of the trek, so they linked arms and started singing joyfully, heading up the path to start the next stage of the journey. The mums and dads took in the news with the quiet and steely acceptance of people used

to shielding their children from bad news. Clearly it was not the welcome to Europe they had dreamt of. (Not long after we arrived, Médecins Sans Frontières was finally allowed to set up a bus service to the main port, saving families days of walking.)

The few dozen families in front of me were just a tiny part of a modern exodus of biblical proportions. On this beach, the sheer size of this movement was obvious when you looked at the vast piles of discarded life jackets that lined the shore. Up and down this normally pristine coastline, tens of thousands of bright orange and yellow vests were now strewn across the beaches. We were witnessing one of the largest ever refugee waves to arrive in Europe. While Syrians made up the bulk of those fleeing, many Afghan and Iraqi families and young men were also among those arriving on these shores. In all, 1.3 million migrants applied for asylum across Europe in 2015, nearly double the previous record of around 700,000, set in 1992 after the fall of the Iron Curtain and the collapse of the Soviet Union.[2]

A few local Greek men waiting on the beach swooped like vultures on the plastic speedboats the refugees had arrived in, taking the spoils of this desperate trade. They used knives to hastily cut out the motors and throw them in the back of a waiting pickup truck. One man even appeared to be helping the refugees get out of their vessel, passing a baby to a parent waiting on the shore, before I realized he was just trying to secure the motor of this particular vessel for himself.

As the beach began to clear, I noticed one old man standing alone by himself, leaning on a cane and quietly crying. 'I've been separated from my wife and my children,' he said, wiping tears away with his hand. 'I don't know what to do now!'

I found out that Nazieh Abdul Rahman Husein, aged 61, had been born in Syria to Palestinian refugees and grew up in poor Palestinian refugee camp near the city of Latakia. When the Syrian war broke out in 2011, he tried to keep a low profile, but as time went on, life became progressively more unbearable and dangerous. Many of the young Sunni men in the Palestinian camp where Nazieh lived participated in demonstrations against President Assad and were known to strongly oppose the regime. In August 2011, Assad's forces surrounded the camp, firing at it from the sea with

gunboats, while ground troops shot at fleeing civilians.[3] Young men were rounded up and arrested, while thousands of camp inhabitants fled. Nazieh and his family stayed, as they had nowhere else to go. For the next few years the camp remained surrounded by the Syrian army, with men going in and out of the camp being continuously harassed at checkpoints and viewed with deep suspicion. Nazieh and his son lived in fear of arrest.[4] Opposition forces also constantly shelled Latakia, and many civilians were killed in the city as they tried to go about their daily lives.

Nazieh watched as each of his neighbours sold up their homes and possessions to try to make it to Europe. In August 2015, he decided it was time to risk the journey. Nazieh sold his house, said a painful goodbye to his eldest daughter and two grandchildren, and began the journey to Turkey with his 30-year-old daughter Mariam, his 25-year-old son Abdul Rahman and his wife, Basiyeh. All the family took with them were their identity documents and the family Quran, which had been wrapped in several plastic bags for protection. Each also carried the heaviest jacket they owned, having been warned of the freezing cold conditions they might encounter on the refugee path through Europe. Just escaping Syria was extremely dangerous and exhausting, as they had to pass through countless regime and opposition checkpoints, with each band of fighters demanding a sum for safe passage. After two days, they reached the Turkish border, where they were smuggled across before boarding an all-night bus to the seaside town of Izmir, the capital of people-smuggling operations for Syrian refugees en route to Europe.

In the summer of 2015 in Izmir, the smuggling business was doing a roaring trade. Turkish authorities turned a blind eye as hundreds of Syrian families sat each day in the Izmir main square, waiting for their smuggler to indicate it was time to leave. Parents sat clutching their few possessions, which were wrapped in black plastic for the boat journey. For many, the life jackets they had purchased with their precious savings provided no safety. Turkish traders made a mint selling fake jackets lined with foam, which does not float. Hundreds of Syrian men, women and children drowned that summer wearing these awful jackets.

Nazieh's family found a smuggler in Izmir who said he could get them to a Greek island for US$600 each. They handed over

their savings and waited for the smuggler to make contact. Late one night, they were summoned. A rendezvous spot was quickly arranged, and dozens of Syrian families piled into minivans driven by the smuggler's gang associates. The vehicles, designed to carry only eight people, were packed with around 20 people, squashed in so tight it was hard to breathe. The smugglers drove them north of Izmir to an area of desolate scrubland on the coast and ordered the families to hide in the bushes and keep quiet for several hours, as they made sure the area was clear of Turkish coastguards. They sat there anxiously in the dark as parents desperately tried to keep their children from crying.

After many hours, the smugglers reappeared and said that Turkish forces had been spotted in the area, so the dozens of families were ordered to quickly scatter. Panic ensued as parents tried to grab their small children and make a run for it. In the mayhem, Nazieh, who moves slowly with a cane, became separated from his wife and two children. 'We ran away because someone said the Turkish soldiers are coming!' he explained tearfully. 'My daughter and my son were helping their mum and went a different way. I was looking everywhere for them but couldn't find them.' Nazieh told me that he had wandered for hours by the side of the road, crying and lost in the dark.

Finally, he stumbled across some other Syrian refugees who were also preparing to depart in boats for the Greek islands. No one had seen his family. A smuggler took pity on the old man and found a spot on his vessel for Nazieh, saying it was likely his family had left and he would find them in Greece. He had arrived that afternoon, with no phone, no money and no contact numbers. All he had with him was his cane, his identity documents and the family Quran. He stood in front of me on the now-deserted beach and sobbed. 'I've been for two days with no food, nothing to drink,' Nazieh said sadly.

My editors had asked me to find a Syrian family and follow them as they tried to make it to the Greek mainland. But I couldn't just leave Nazieh here all alone. My producer, Fouad Abu Gosh, who had travelled with me from Jerusalem, agreed, as did the ABC's Middle East cameraman Aaron Hollett, who had been assigned to work with me on this trip. None of us wanted

to just carry on and pretend we had never met Nazieh and heard his desperate tale. We hugged Nazieh and told him not to worry, promising we would help him get to a safe place and put him in touch with groups who could begin the search for his loved ones. The authorities on Lesvos had implemented a law making it illegal to provide transport to asylum seekers, but our team agreed it was worth the risk to assist Nazieh.

Fouad put his arm around the old man and helped him walk along the beach and climb into our van. Ten minutes' drive down the road, we stopped at a small Greek café and the famished Nazieh devoured a cheese sandwich. It then took us nearly two hours to reach the island's main city, Mytilini. On the way, we passed hundreds of Syrian families making the hot, slow trek to the main port. That morning, following advice from our local driver Metin, we had filled our car boot with cases of water, dozens of packets of biscuits and also Band-Aids; many of those we had already met on this journey had had feet covered in blisters after walking many kilometres. Every time we passed families with children who looked like they were struggling, we stopped to pass much-needed supplies out the window.

As we drove, Nazieh quietly told us all the details of his missing relatives. 'My wife's full name is Basiyeh Musa Abdul Halek,' he said. 'She's wearing a long black dress. And my daughter Mariam is wearing a similar thing. My son Abdul Rahman is wearing glasses; he can't see without them.' He started crying again thinking of his family, telling us he had been married to Basiyeh for as long as he could remember.

In Mytilini, the main port resembled a refugee camp. With thousands of refugees arriving in the previous few days, every available space was filled with a family, resting after the long trek to the port before they continued their journey to Europe. The local park was packed with families sleeping out in the open, with most parents unable to provide their children with anything more than a dirty piece of cardboard to sleep on. The luckier ones had set up small tents in the main carpark of the ferry terminal. Dirty clothes had been washed in nearby public toilet blocks and carefully hung out to dry on tent roofs.

Mums sat outside the tents, which were boiling hot in the summer heat, holding babies and looking after small children who

ran in and around the rows of this tent city. Single men lined up at the one tap, taking turns showering in the open with their clothes on. One mother was perched nearby on a kerb with her children. She appeared to be travelling alone as she juggled several backpacks and a sleeping infant. Her daughter, who looked only about seven, struggled to hold the weight of a toddler who was passed out in her arms. The mother and little girl looked absolutely shattered. It was a look we saw on the face of nearly everyone here. The joy of leaving Syria had been replaced with the fear and uncertainty of what would happen next.

It was chaos down at the ferry ticket office. Many of the refugees didn't speak English, and the ticket sellers were struggling to communicate with these people, who were desperate to continue their journey towards mainland Europe before the cold weather hit in a few weeks' time. Many men waited in long queues, frowning as they carefully counted their family's savings, which would have a long way to stretch before they made it to their final destination. The ferry office had not been taking down the names of families who purchased tickets, and the local police were not registering names or keeping a list of missing relatives. We walked around the dock, Nazieh scouring the crowd for his relatives, with no luck. It was getting late, and all around us, exhausted families who hadn't scored tickets for the last ferry of the night started claiming space to lie down and rest until the ferries began departing in the early hours of the next morning.

Nazieh was also exhausted, having spent the last two nights sleeping rough in the scrub on the Turkish coast. We found him a hotel room so he didn't have to join the thousands of others sleeping on the streets. Nazieh's eyes filled with tears as he hugged us goodnight, telling us we were like his family now. He shuffled off to his room, clutching his Quran in its plastic bags and a change of clothes Fouad had given him.

The next morning we came to see Nazieh early. We found him outside, smoking a cigarette and staring off into space. He told us he was worried his family might already be searching for him on the Greek mainland, and he might never catch up with them. 'I just need to see them again,' he told us, tears running down his cheeks. 'This is my only wish in life.' I squeezed his hand and told him we'd

been advised that the International Committee of the Red Cross was operating a missing-persons tent in a camp 15 minutes out of town; it seemed like his best bet.

We drove over to the camp, the Red Cross caravan hard to find among the hundreds of people crowding the site. We finally located it and explained Nazieh's predicament. The volunteers wrote down the old man's details and took his photo to add to their family-tracing register. 'Your picture will be published on the Red Cross website and hopefully they will help you find your family,' a young Greek volunteer explained kindly to Nazieh via an interpreter. 'What was your family's target destination?'

'Almania,' Nazieh said sadly. Germany.

The Red Cross staff explained there were no services on Lesvos for someone like Nazieh. If he needed a safe place to sleep while he looked for his family, he would have to get to Athens, where he may be eligible for a room at a government-run camp. Near the Red Cross caravan, locals had set up a hot-food service, and dozens of refugees were lining up for a bowl of hot rice and vegetable stew. In the line, Nazieh spotted a family who had been on his boat coming over. They greeted him warmly and explained that they had purchased ferry tickets for Athens and would depart in a few hours.

Ehad, a Syrian from Damascus who speaks perfect English, offered to accompany Nazieh to Athens and help him find the Red Cross headquarters. Nazieh started crying with relief. We helped Ehad and his wife and family collect their belongings and gave them a lift with Nazieh down to the ferry terminal. As we waited, Nazieh looked around at the sea of Syrian families waiting in line at the ferry booth or sleeping with their kids on pieces of cardboard in the port parking lot. It was hard to believe it had come to this. 'What's happening in Syria is so unjust. It shouldn't be allowed,' he told us sadly.

Near us on the jetty was a young mother, visibly distraught, with her four young children sitting stony-faced next to her. Fouad discovered she had been separated from her sister on the journey. Their families had planned to travel together and she felt overwhelmed at the thought of continuing alone with her young children. We gave her some money to buy more phone credit, so she could hopefully track down her sister once she got to the Greek

mainland. Children playing on the dock ran past us with mobile numbers scribbled on their arms in permanent marker. Everyone was terrified of becoming separated from their loved ones on this arduous and long journey. Most of the refugee families would be travelling for the next week or two up through Greece, across Macedonia and Serbia, until they finally reached what they hoped would be safety in central European countries that had been taking in asylum seekers, such as Germany, Sweden or the Netherlands.

The boat pulled up, a mammoth vessel designed to ferry thousands of tourists between these luxurious Greek islands. Nazieh and Ehad and his family gathered up their few belongings. We had bought Nazieh a cheap mobile phone and some credit so we could stay in touch and let him know if the Red Cross had any news about the whereabouts of his wife and children. He hugged us tightly and we said a tearful goodbye before he limped up the long walkway leading onto the ship. He turned back and waved at us several times before disappearing inside.

That night we flew out of Lesvos. Our assignment was over, but I felt incredibly anxious. We had helped Nazieh as much as we could, but he still faced a dangerous and uncertain future. I looked out the window as we left this tiny island, feeling despondent about the desperation we had witnessed on its shores.

A few hours later, I was waiting at Athens international airport to board my flight back to Jerusalem when my phone rang. It was Ehad, the Syrian father who had promised to look after Nazieh and take him to the safety of the Red Cross headquarters in Athens. 'I heard they might close the Macedonian border,' he said worriedly. 'We have to leave Athens tonight and get there before dawn.' He told me they couldn't look after Nazieh anymore. He wanted to know what they should do with the old man.

My flight was boarding. It was nearly 2 am, and I was terrified that Nazieh might be dumped on the streets of Athens with no ability to communicate, no money and no proper jacket to keep him warm. It would take me a few hours to get out of the airport and into town, so Ehad said he would leave Nazieh with some Syrians who would deliver him to the Red Cross headquarters in Athens first thing the next morning. I promised to meet him there. I hung up and apologised to the Aegean Airlines representative at the gate,

saying I wouldn't be boarding the flight and needed to get my bag off the plane. I grabbed a taxi into Athens and found a cheap hotel close to the Red Cross headquarters, managing about two hours' sleep before getting up to meet Nazieh.

I arrived at the Red Cross just after 7 am and found no sign of Nazieh. After an hour, I started to get really concerned. Had he been left with people who knew he had nowhere to go? Had Ehad just dumped him somewhere in the city as they rushed to the border? Finally, at close to 9 am, I saw a figure slowly limping up the street with a cane. Nazieh! He saw me and started crying, and I rushed over to hug him and help him cross the road. He looked exhausted, and I felt terrible that we had told him Ehad would look after him but it hadn't gone to plan. He had had nothing to eat, so we found a small café, and he had a croissant and a much-needed cup of coffee. Nazieh's lack of English and my limited Arabic made conversation fairly short, but he was clearly relieved to see me. He kept beaming at me over his coffee cup, motioning to his heart and then pointing to me.

We headed into the Red Cross building and met the Syrian refugee case workers. They already had Nazieh's family-tracing report that we had registered on Lesvos, but they told us there was no news yet of his wife or children. They explained that the cash-strapped Greek government was overwhelmed by the massive asylum-seeker influx, with tens of thousands arriving each week, and hundreds of vulnerable cases needing help from the authorities. They didn't think they could help house Nazieh while he waited for news from the family-tracing team. I explained his inability to walk very far and his lack of money and language skills. They said they would double check and give me a call.

Nazieh and I headed out into the streets of Athens, downcast by our lack of progress. We had lunch, and I bought him some clothes and a small sports bag to put his belongings in. I emailed Greek refugee-support groups and sent messages on Facebook to asylum-seeker advocates in Athens. I couldn't leave Greece until I knew Nazieh would be cared for. We sat around for hours and drank coffee, waiting for news, and finally the Red Cross called. Amazingly, they had found a bed for Nazieh at the Eleonas refugee camp, in an industrial part of Athens just outside the city centre.

We jumped in a taxi and headed straight to the huge lot filled with lines of demountable trailers. Several hundred refugee families, mainly from Afghanistan, called it their temporary home. The staff were extremely welcoming to Nazieh, introducing him to the Arabic-language case worker and showing him to a little demountable hut with a small single bed and even air conditioning. A large mess tent served hot meals three times a day and a volunteer medical clinic operated several times a week. Refugees could come and go as they pleased, but most of the families didn't leave, as they needed the free services provided. Many people were waiting for other relatives, or had run out of money and needed to break their journeys in Greece before attempting to continue into Europe.

Nazieh and I sat together in the mess tent while he ate a meal of chicken and rice. A few other Syrian refugees were at the camp, and he said hello to them. Everyone who heard his tale promised to try to help him find his relatives. Before I said goodbye, Nazieh gave me the name of his eldest daughter who had stayed behind in Syria – Reem. He thought Reem used Facebook and that this could be a way of somehow getting in touch with Basiyeh, Mariam and Abdul Rahman. It was a promising lead. We hugged, and I promised I would call him the next day to make sure he was okay. He stood in the door of his demountable and waved sadly at me, motioning at his heart again and pointing to me. I waved back, sad to leave him, but happy I had found a temporary solution that would keep him safe.

It wouldn't be the last I saw of Nazieh.

CHAPTER 6

GERMANY OPENS ITS ARMS

Nazieh and Ahmad, part 2

By October 2015, tens of thousands of asylum seekers were arriving in mainland Europe each day. For the first time since World War Two, the United Nations High Commissioner for Refugees (UNHCR) had become fully operational in Europe, as officials tried to cope with the arrival of so many desperate people in need of food and shelter. German chancellor Angela Merkel took the lead, declaring that her country would welcome Syrian refugees and let them stay, no matter which country they had arrived in first. Day after day, the long processions of thousands of people continued, as asylum seekers trekked through the woods of Hungary to the highways of Austria, largely travelling on foot across Europe, with most aiming to reach Germany and start a new life.

Bayerisch Gmain, Germany, October 2015

In the days after our trip to Lesvos, my producer Fouad and I were consumed by trying to find Nazieh's missing relatives. We

scoured Facebook, trying different spellings and messaging as many accounts as we could find, in an attempt to track down Nazieh's eldest daughter, Reem, in Latakia, Syria. After several days of dead-ends, we finally got a message back from one of the women we had messaged. Yes! This Reem had a father called Nazieh and her family had been on their way to Europe.

We quickly gave her a call. 'Reem, my name is Fouad. I'm a journalist,' Fouad explained over a scratchy line to Syria. 'I met your dad when he crossed from Turkey to Greece. I met your father, Mr Nazieh, in Greece!' Reem was overjoyed to hear her father was safe. Her mother and two siblings had called her, distraught, a few days earlier after becoming separated from her father. She had advised them to keep trying to reach Germany, Reem told us, thinking it was best for them to get somewhere safe first. 'The last time I talked to them they were in Serbia, and they were trying to cross the border, and then their phone was off,' Reem told us despairingly. 'I don't where they are now!' She gave us the number for her brother, Abdul Rahman, and promised to let us know if she heard from them.

We tried Abdul Rahman's number countless times over the next few days, but the phone remained off.

Meanwhile, the Syrian refugee crisis was continuing to unfold, with hundreds of thousands of asylum seekers having already arrived in Germany. I received a message from Ahmad, the young Syrian man from Aleppo I had met on the Italian navy ship the year before. He and his family had been resettled in a small town in Bavaria state in southern Germany, right next to the Austrian border. Since the refugee crisis began, Ahmad had spent every day volunteering and translating for the new arrivals, and asked if I wanted to visit and film with him. It was a good chance to keep following the story, and if we heard from Nazieh's relatives it would be good to already be in Europe, so I booked a flight.

I flew into Salzburg, Austria; from there it was only a 25-minute drive over the border to the small village where Ahmad and his family were living. As I walked out of the arrivals gate, Ahmad was waiting, having caught the bus to the airport to surprise me. I almost didn't recognise him. He was dressed in a European-style cap, a cream jacket and a plaid scarf.

'You look so German!' I laughed, overjoyed to see him.

'I'm trying!' he says grinning and giving me a huge hug.

It was hard to believe how different these circumstances were to the last time we had seen each other: from a rescue boat in the middle of the Mediterranean to what felt like the set of *The Sound of Music*. As we took the short drive to his village, we were surrounded by jagged snow-covered mountains and rolling green hills. We passed traditional Bavarian beer gardens, and thatched-roof houses with chimneys and green shutters, window boxes overflowing with bright pink and red alpine geraniums.

Bayerisch Gmain, where Ahmad had been living, is a small town of 3000 people. It sits in one of Germany's most conservative regions; the population here is overwhelmingly white and Catholic. It was about as far from his hometown of Aleppo as you could get. We went into a cute little German café, where, over fresh apple strudel, Ahmad told me how difficult the past year had been. After the euphoria of making it to Europe alive had faded, he and his family faced the harsh reality of building a new life totally from scratch. 'During my first few months here, I felt optimistic. I had big hopes. But in reality, I was very surprised, it was different from my dreams,' he told me dejectedly. 'Before getting on the boat, I thought that this is the most difficult part of the journey to Europe. But when I stepped in Europe and I saw the situation, I realized that this is even more difficult than the boat journey.'

The family spent the first months in a camp, all six of them in one room, before they were moved to Bavaria. A rambling old motel in the centre of Bayerisch Gmain was now home. Several other Syrian families lived in the building, and we waved to a man sitting by himself, smoking a cigarette on the upstairs balcony. 'He has such a sad story,' Ahmad confided. There hadn't been enough money for the man to leave Syria with his wife and children. So the family had made the torturous decision for him to come Europe alone, and the others would follow as soon as they could. But it had now been more than a year, and the man was still waiting for his German residency to be approved, the first step before family reunification could take place. 'So this poor man will wake up every morning and sit on the balcony and wait for the postal car to arrive, hoping it will bring the good news of residency,' explained Ahmad. The man's wife and children were now trapped back in Syria in

the town of Zabadani, which was besieged by pro-regime forces and under constant bombardment. 'He will wait every day, even on holidays when there is no postal service, this man will wait, hoping for news of his residency,' Ahmad said sadly. 'Without residency you can't live, you can't study, you can't work, you can't do a thing!' After waiting more than ten months, Ahmad's family had recently had their residency approved, which meant they could apply for university and had the right to work. But it was bittersweet news as their friend upstairs continued to wait for his case to be approved.

We stepped inside the tiny two-bedroom apartment, in which all six members of Ahmad's family had been living, and Ahmad's mother and sisters gave me a big hug. They had been busy making kibbeh on a table in the crammed living room; I was about to be treated to a massive Syrian meal to welcome me here. Since gaining their residency, the family had been trying to move out of this temporary accommodation. They had put in hundreds of applications for rental properties in different towns all over southern Germany but had been rejected every time. One the hardest things, Ahmad said, was realizing that not everyone was pleased to have them here. 'Not many locals are willing to rent their homes to refugees,' he told me, shrugging sadly. 'I've witnessed some demonstrations in Munich by some people who were opposing the idea of having refugees in Germany. To me, this was very hard to be somewhere and feel unwanted.'

In recent months, there had been a wave of violence against refugees across Germany – with 200 attacks on asylum seekers' homes in just the first six months of the year, up on 175 for the whole of 2014.[1] Another incident saw a left-wing politician who stood up for refugees have their car firebombed, while in the Bavarian town of Bamberg, German police uncovered a plot by far-right extremists to attack refugee shelters using 'highly dangerous explosives'.[2]

Ahmad's mother and his two younger sisters didn't leave the apartment much. 'They're not used to seeing women with headscarfs here. So, when they go out, they always not be comfortable because all the eyes on them,' said Ahmad. They stayed inside, with news from Syria constantly blaring on the 24-hour Arabic satellite channel. His younger sister Hiba said she missed home deeply. 'The language, it's hard to communicate with people, it's hard to make friends,' she told me shyly over dinner. 'I find it hard here.'

Ahmad was desperately lonely, a feeling he had never experienced before. He's an easy-going extrovert, always ready with a joke and a smile. Growing up in a city like Aleppo means you are rarely by yourself. Life is lived in full view of your family and neighbours; everyone knows what everyone else is doing, and family and social networks are tight. So to suddenly live in a village where people don't even want to make eye contact, let alone say hello, is more than just isolating, it is a completely foreign way of living. 'Most refugees they come to the German suburbs, loneliness is a big issue,' Ahmad told me. 'To live alone is very hard.'

In order to try to make new friends, Ahmad had been going to the same coffee shop every day, hoping to strike up conversations with the other regulars. Ahmad noticed that one of his neighbours was in the garden most mornings. He decided to start waving and saying hello to the old man. For the first month, the old man consistently ignored Ahmad, but he persisted, waving and calling out hello whenever he passed. One day, the old man smiled back and started to return the greeting. 'I felt this was a victory to me,' Ahmad said, grinning broadly. 'I also would like to prove to the people who don't like to see us in Germany, that we are a good and positive people and not bad to this country.'

Once a month Ahmad had been meeting up with other members of a 'couch surfing' club, going to a nearby pub with young university students who like to host travellers and people from different countries (though no one had requested to surf Ahmad's couch yet, which was actually quite a relief, because his brother was sleeping on it). I headed along with him to the pub for one of the meet-ups. It turned out the others didn't even know he was a Syrian refugee. They were aware he was from the Middle East, but that was it. Ahmad sat on the edge of his seat, eager to engage in conversation and constantly smiling at people. Everyone else at the table was on the Bavarian beer, but Ahmad doesn't drink, so he downed a couple of Diet Cokes. When the two people on either side of him started chatting away to someone else in quick-fire German, Ahmad sat there nodding and smiling. The boy from war-torn Aleppo refused to be left out.

But beneath Ahmad's cheery persistence, the isolation had hit him hard. A few months ago, life in Germany was proving so difficult to adjust to that Ahmad considered returning home. 'As a result of

the stress, it even made me want to say, "Enough." To go home and choose the difficult life there, because here you feel so alone, and I miss my homeland,' he told me quietly, tears welling up in his eyes. As the news from Aleppo got worse, Ahmad felt increasingly guilty about leaving; life became filled with endless questions. Why did he deserve to live? Shouldn't he be at home like many others he knew, fighting against the regime that kept bombing his hometown? What help was he in Germany? He resolved to stay only after he realized that home as he knew it no longer exists. 'I will always belong to Syrian soil, but even if I went back, it's not the same,' Ahmad said, tears rolling down his cheeks. 'I lost so many really good friends there. It is so different now. I don't know if my street still even exists.'

It was the sudden arrival of hundreds of thousands more Syrian asylum seekers in Germany that transformed Ahmad's life. He suddenly had a reason for being here. Late one night, we took the short drive down to Freilassing train station, where Ahmad had been volunteering with German authorities. It is the first German station for trains arriving from just over the Austrian border in Salzburg. Germany, which pledged to take in around 800,000 Syrian refugees, was now dealing with the massive number of desperate people arriving on its doorstep. Local governments across Germany had been struggling to find adequate shelter for the massive number of asylum seekers, turning empty sport halls, campsites and schools into emergency accommodation.

Despite only being October, it was already bitingly cold, with temperatures just above zero. Local volunteers, rugged up in mittens and beanies, ran a hot-drinks station, making coffee and hot chocolate for the newly arrived refugees. Others sorted through second-hand clothes to get thick jackets and covered shoes ready for those who needed them. About a dozen German police were here too. The refugees wouldn't be processed here, but the adult males would have their photos and fingerprints taken as part of a quick security process run by the German Ministry of the Interior.

It was past midnight when the train from Austria slowly rolled in, carrying 430 new refugees. Little faces peered curiously out the window at us. A few kids waved. I climbed aboard the train with Ahmad and one of the local policemen. *'As-salaam alaykum!'* boomed Peitler, a six-foot-tall Bavarian police officer, smiling as

he walked through the crowded carriage. 'I'm with the German police. Peace be upon you!' Coming from Australia, where asylum seekers are labelled 'illegals' and politicians demonize refugees, I watched agape as the officer proudly welcomed the new arrivals to Germany with a friendly Islamic phrase. Little kids smiled up at Peitler and accepted his offer to shake their hand, with their parents shyly following. '*Alaykum salaam!*' said a little girl, grinning back.

Families with children were the first to file off the warm carriage and onto the freezing platform. 'Hello and welcome! Now, just small and simple procedures, fingerprints, nothing to worry about,' Ahmad told the refugees as they shuffled into lines. 'If anyone wants food or needs clothes, please ask, there are jackets. Come this way, this way, please!' The parents looked utterly exhausted. They stood in line, carrying sleeping toddlers while trying to keep their other children awake. Most of these families had been travelling for weeks, with many days on foot, carrying little ones and as many backpacks as they could manage, sleeping on the side of the road, giving children baths in public bathrooms, lining up for food at UNHCR- and charity-run facilities along the way. But they had finally made it. One father stood out in the line. He had his arms around his two young sons, aged around seven and nine. It was just the three of them. The dad looked dazed and overwhelmed. He kept bending over to kiss the tops of his boy's heads every few minutes.

Most people were not dressed for the bitterly cold night. A little girl had no coat or socks on. Young men wore only T-shirts. Ahmad and the volunteers busied themselves handing out warm clothes and snacks to those waiting in line. One older Syrian lady had cheap flip-flops on. She'd been wearing them since she left the refugee camp in Turkey several weeks ago, she told us. Ahmad found her a pair of socks and shoes in her size. She was so stiff and sore from travelling she couldn't bend over, so Ahmad sat her down and delicately put them on her feet, which had swollen and blistered from days of walking. 'Bless you,' she said tearfully to Ahmad. A mother with three children travelling alone collected jackets for her shivering kids. 'We have no money left, we paid it all to the smugglers in Syria and Turkey, they ripped us off, may God punish them,' she lamented.

Another father stopped Ahmad, worried about where his family was going to end up next. 'My concern is to live in a tent,' the man

confided. 'This my biggest fear. I just want to make sure the kids are looked after, not us.' Ahmad nodded, listening to the man and reassuring him that everything would be okay – eventually – but he knew better than anyone that it would take months and months before they would feel settled here.

It was not just Syrians arriving. Dozens of young Hazara men from Afghanistan, some who looked barely older than 13, stepped onto the platform. 'Is this really Germany?' one of them asked Ahmad apprehensively.

I was due to leave Germany in two days but we still hadn't made contact with Nazieh's family. The chances of them being on this train were ridiculously small, but that didn't stop me scouring the crowd on the platform to see if I could recognise them from the photos Reem had sent me. I saw no familiar faces.

The German security-processing system is speedy and efficient. All the security checks were completed within the hour and everyone was returned to the train. It rumbled off into the cold night, heading for Munich, where those aboard would have the choice of travelling to another part of Europe or staying in Germany.

Ahmad and I spent the next day driving around the foothills of the Alps and the gorgeous turquoise lakes of Bavaria, filming pretty pictures of the region to go with the other scenes I had shot at Ahmad's house and at the train station.

And then Fouad called. He had managed to get through to Nazieh's son, Abdul Rahman. We had found them. Nazieh's wife, Basiyeh, his daughter Mariam and his son, Abdul Rahman, had just arrived at a camp on the outskirts of Heidelberg. For the last two weeks, they'd been trying to make their way to Germany from Greece, sleeping rough on the side of the road and in UNHCR tents along the way. It had proved impossible to charge Abdul Rahman's phone. The camp they had been put in was more than five hours' drive north-west from here, towards the French border. 'Tell them I'll come see them tomorrow,' I told Fouad. Ahmad volunteered to come along for the ride and to translate for me.

The next morning, I crept out of my guesthouse at 5 am and picked up Ahmad in my hire car. We had to try to get on the autobahn, Germany's massive super-highway system, and past Munich before the morning rush-hour hit. We saw no evidence of

the hair-raising speeds on the German freeway that I'd read about. Instead, we crawled for hours in heavy traffic, as we traversed the bottom third of the country.

The camp where Nazieh's family was staying near Heidelberg is called Patrick Henry Village. It's a massive former US army base that once served as the Americans' headquarters in Europe after World War Two. The 100-hectare site that once housed 16,000 soldiers had become the centre of refugee processing in south-west Germany. As we approached the camp gates, hundreds of people were milling outside, waiting for the camp transfer bus into town. Asylum seekers were allowed to come and go as they pleased, but the security guards wouldn't let us inside. We perched on the footpath and called Abdul Rahman to let him know we were waiting outside.

Nazieh's relatives soon appeared. Basiyeh, his wife, walked out through the camp gate limping slightly, as her children supported her from each side. As I jumped up to say hello, deep sobs started racking her body as she wrapped her arms around me in a big embrace. 'We thought he was dead,' she cried, in between tears. 'I swear to God, I didn't sleep at nights, I was praying for him all the time. Last night, I was crying the whole night. I was crying and praying. Hoping to have him with us here.' Mariam and Abdul Rahman were also wiping back tears as they introduced themselves. 'Thank you so much for helping our father,' Abdul Rahman said shyly. Abdul Rahman was skinny and quiet with glasses and looked a lot like his father. Mariam greeted me warmly with a huge hug.

All five of us squeezed into my tiny hatchback and went into Heidelberg to find a quiet café where we could sit and chat. Over copious amounts of strong tea, the tale of how they became separated from Nazieh started spilling out. 'I thought Nazieh must be on the main road with the rest of the people,' explained Basiyeh, referring to the night they were separated on the Turkish coast. 'But we looked, and we couldn't find him anywhere. My husband wasn't there!' Basiyeh and Mariam stopped at a rest station, close to the last place they had seen Nazieh, while Abdul Rahman went on searching for his dad with other men. The other people they knew left for Greece, but Nazieh's family stayed put.

They put up posters with Nazieh's name and talked to as many Syrians as they came across. Had anyone seen their father? Had

anyone heard of an old Syrian man who had lost his family? 'We posted up our phone numbers just in case someone will find him, he can call us,' Basiyeh recalled tearfully. 'But no one called us. Then we waited another two days in Turkey, and we slept on the street waiting for him.' After two days with no leads they began to wonder if Nazieh had been put on a boat to Greece. So they decided that they should continue their search in Greece, praying they would find him along the way. 'When I got on the boat I was so upset to leave without my husband,' Basiyeh said. But the people smugglers sent Nazieh's family to the Greek island of Kos at exactly the same time as we were helping Nazieh search for them on nearby Lesvos. They spent the next ten days sleeping on the side of the road in their clothes, catching the occasional bus but largely travelling on foot, until they reached the German border.

They couldn't believe he was safely waiting for them in the camp in Athens. I played them the footage of when we found Nazieh alone on the beach, and his desperate attempts to find them. They watched, transfixed, tears streaming down all three of their faces. I told them how Nazieh had told me he didn't want to live without them, because he loved them so much. Basiyeh and Mariam started sobbing again, and I was crying too. We were all one big teary mess.

Ahmad, who had been a hero translating and providing us all with much-needed tissues, dialled up Nazieh on the phone. Fouad had given him the amazing news the day before, but I hadn't yet heard his voice. 'Hello?' Nazieh answered apprehensively.

'Hello, salaam!' cried Basiyeh jubilantly. 'How are you? How are doing? Thank God we are okay, and you? Thank God, listen, I'm with Sophie now…God sent you good people!' Basiyeh couldn't resist teasing Nazieh about his journey compared with theirs. 'We walked, we broke our backs from walking…In Hungary, I've walked for six hours…what are you complaining about…you got a ride in a car!'

We informed the Red Cross that Nazieh's family had been found in Germany. They told Nazieh to stay put in Greece and they would try to reunite the family as soon as they could. They warned us it could take several weeks. But now that he knew where his family was, nothing was going to stop him. Two days after speaking to Basiyeh on the phone, 61-year-old Nazieh, with his walking cane, caught buses and trains, sneaked over borders and walked in the cold and the rain

for hours to get to Germany. Five days later, he arrived at the gate of Patrick Henry Camp. I had flown back to the Middle East by then, but on hearing the news, I jumped on a plane to Frankfurt and drove down to the camp. This time the guards at the front let me in.

The family were staying in a small one-room apartment in a former Marine barracks. It's a rabbit warren of a place, but a friendly young Syrian guy helped me find the right building. Down a long hallway, I found the right number and knocked. The door swung open and suddenly I was being hugged by Nazieh, Basiyeh, Mariam and Abdul Rahman. There was laughing and crying, and none of us could quite believe it was happening.

Basiyeh had been sitting at the camp clinic two days ago when Nazieh had suddenly walked in. 'I hugged him and started crying and everyone at the clinic was looking at us!' Basiyeh cried, hugging Nazieh. 'They asked me, "Is this your husband?" I've told them yes! Everyone in the clinic was crying with us.' Nazieh looked like a different man, energetic and jubilant in the presence of his family. 'When we find each other again, we hugged, we cried, cried and cried,' he told me, grinning, sitting next to his wife and children. 'I felt so confused and I started crying, "What? Is this real?" I felt that I was dreaming and will wake up soon from this dream.'

An Iraqi woman from the camp in Athens had travelled with Nazieh all the way until Munich. He said he couldn't have made the journey across Europe without her. 'She was with me all the time, treating me like her own father,' he explained gratefully. 'I was very cold on the train. She was taking care of me, changing my wet socks. She promised she will stay with me until we get to Germany. We slept on the side of the roads under the trees.' Nazieh referred to the exhausting trek as 'the death journey. Little children were walking alone at night in the dark, kids were crying, mothers lost their kids. I had no idea where we were going at night and for how long we are walking. I had no idea where I was or in which country,' he recalled sadly. The Quran that Nazieh had been carrying in Lesvos also made it. Nazieh held it up proudly; it was the only thing he could carry all the way on his trip from Athens to Germany.

The family had no complaints about sharing a tiny one-bedroom apartment at the camp. They were together again at last. We perched on their foldup beds, drinking Arabic coffee and eating the

Palestinian sweets I'd brought with me from Jerusalem. Mariam joked that Nazieh would never be allowed out of their sight again. 'Like today, he went to pick up his medication, so I was with him all the time. He didn't expect me to wait for him, but I told him I'm not leaving you alone anymore!'

Basiyeh agreed. She was refusing to leave Nazieh's side for more than a few minutes. 'Yesterday he went to the doctor, Mariam had a German class, so I told him I'm waiting for you in the garden. I was waiting and waiting for him; I thought, "We've lost him again." I thought, "Sophie is coming tomorrow. What I'm going to tell her, that we've lost him again?"' Basiyeh said, giggling, glancing lovingly at Nazieh and waving her finger at him in mock anger.

There was one small shelf in their room. Carefully balanced on top of several piles of personal items were large photos of the three grandchildren who remained in Syria, Reem's children. It was a reminder of the bittersweet life the family now faced: safety and new opportunity in Germany, mixed with the overwhelming pain of leaving life as they knew it behind. 'Reem is telling me it's becoming very hard,' Basiyeh said tearfully. 'The Russian are now also bombing from the air. I can't get hold of her, so we just send voice messages. It's heartbreaking!'

Nazieh and Basiyeh came for a drive into downtown Heidelberg. We went for a slow walk along the river and gazed at the ancient cathedrals, red-roofed buildings and oak trees that lined the shore. A rowing club was training on the water and swans paddled around in the golden afternoon light. Nazieh shook his head in disbelief at how it had all worked out. 'I'm planning to stay here for good, for the rest of my life, I am happy here,' he told me firmly, looking out across the water. 'But I want to help my daughter Reem come to Germany too. I will beg on the streets. I will do anything to get my daughter, her children and my son-in-law here too.'

*

Nazieh and his family still live in Germany. Abdul Rahman works as a delivery driver while Mariam works in aged care. To Nazieh's utter heartbreak, despite numerous applications for them to resettle in Germany, his eldest daughter, Reem, and his three grandchildren remain in Syria.

THE SADDEST LITTLE HOSPITAL

Alaa, Salim and Farqar

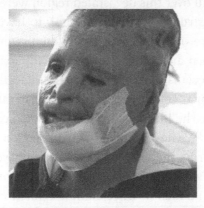

In 2015, innocent civilians across the Middle East were being maimed and slaughtered in horrifying numbers. After four years of government attacks and civil war, Syrian human rights groups put the estimated number of dead at 250,000 including 100,000 civilians, with indiscriminate air attacks by the Assad regime causing the vast majority of casualties.[1] A new Saudi-led aerial bombing campaign on Yemen had already seen hundreds killed and thousands wounded, while the people of Gaza were still recovering from the previous year's war with Israel, which had resulted in the deaths of 1462 Gazan civilians, including 551 children.[2] Meanwhile in Iraq, ISIS suicide bombers were exploding car bombs in the middle of busy markets in Baghdad, killing and wounding hundreds of people.[3] In all of these locations, staff from the medical charity Médecins Sans Frontières (MSF) were working tirelessly to treat those who often had no other source of the care they so desperately needed. Along my travels, I'd heard about an extraordinary new MSF surgical hospital in the Jordanian capital Amman, where

the most badly injured patients from across the region were receiving care.

Amman, Jordan, December 2015

It looked like just another dusty, rundown office block. But in a busy suburban neighbourhood on the outskirts of the Jordanian capital sat one of the world's most remarkable little hospitals. The worst war-wounded from all over this devastated region were being sent here, Al Mowasah reconstructive surgery hospital, to have their lives rebuilt. Its corridors were overflowing with children, women and men from Iraq, Syria, Yemen and Gaza – all horrifically maimed and awaiting life-changing specialist orthopaedic, maxillofacial or plastic surgery. 'We refer to them as cold cases,' explained hospital director Jean-Paul Tohme, who runs the 148-bed facility for the medical charity Médecins Sans Frontières. 'We have to take them again from scratch and repair them, to reconstruct them. Physically but also psychologically.'

The hospital's entrance was crowded with children on crutches, missing limbs, and men in wheelchairs. Yemeni victims of airstrikes waited, chatting with Syrian barrel-bomb victims next to Iraqi car-bomb survivors. The scene was a damning indictment of the lawlessness of today's wars – civilians unprotected and targeted across the Middle East, be it by ruthless dictators, the bombs of our allies and/or evil terrorist groups.

Downstairs in the operating theatre, surgeon Dr Rashid Fakhri was busy with two recently arrived Syrian patients, both suffering serious blast injuries. 'All our cases are challenging. It is not standard surgeries,' the surgeon explained as his latest patient was being prepped. 'It's war injuries with complications. We are not going into normal soft tissue or normal bones. The average time for our surgeries is five to six hours.'

The hospital was a new challenge for the medical charity that is better known for providing lifesaving trauma surgery and medical aid in warzones and emergency situations. It's a costly operation, one of the most expensive that MSF, which relies solely on donations, has ever run. There was intense debate within the charity as to whether they were ready to take on such a long-term complex operation. 'It is completely different from what we usually do. This is the first time

we do reconstructive surgery,' said director Jean-Paul Tohme. 'This kind of project is very costly and there were a lot of debate internally. Is MSF ready to run a hospital, such a big hospital? But there was one aspect that was not debated and that was the need.'

MSF's reconstructive-surgery program in Jordan began in 2006, specifically for Iraqi patients at a time when it was too dangerous for MSF to work in Iraq. When the bombs began to pound Syria, Yemen and Gaza, the demand for this kind of surgery skyrocketed. MSF went from renting one ward in the Red Cross hospital to securing a lease on this six-storey stand-alone building, with 600 surgeries performed in 2015. Using a network of MSF doctors working in Iraq, Yemen, Turkey and northern Jordan, potential patients are identified and brought to Al Mowasah, where they can spend months receiving state-of-the-art surgery, psychological support and physiotherapy free of charge. 'Many of the patients we see are infected,' explained Jean-Paul Tohme. 'They have been treated in their country, but they have been treated very quickly, and when they come here, we have to first treat the infection before we can operate.'

In the post-surgery ward, Alaa, a 32-year-old Syrian father of four was one of those who had spent years living in pain. The bones in his left arm were shattered when Syrian government warplanes bombed his hometown of Ghouta in 2012. He had never had the surgery needed to regain use of the limb.

Alaa, who has warm almond eyes and long eyelashes, smiled sadly as he talked about the day his house was hit. 'My brother and sister and I were injured, all three of us,' Alaa recalled. The former bus driver spent weeks lying in hospital next to his brother, whose injuries were far more severe than Alaa's and ultimately fatal. 'The hardest part was watching my brother dying,' Alaa said quietly.

Alaa's family escaped across the Syrian border to Jordan, where they had since been living in a refugee camp. He'd been unable to use his left arm for the previous three years. 'Until now I'm dealing with the pain,' he said. 'Lying in bed, going to the toilet, it's been really, really hard. I have to always call for my wife or my neighbour to help me. I have an eight-month-old baby that I can't even carry, because of my one arm.'

The previous day, MSF surgeons had reset Alaa's broken bones and put pins along his upper arm. It would take a few months, but

the surgeons were hopeful he would regain the use of his limb. 'My dream is to heal and to be able to work,' Alaa told me. 'So I can help my kids. Inshallah.'

On the fifth floor, I found 12-year-old Salim sitting on his bed next to his mum. Five months earlier, he had been watching television with his brother in rebel-held Eastern Aleppo, in Syria, when a bomb dropped by an Assad regime warplane slammed into their home. 'I remember I just heard this loud explosion,' his mother told me. 'The neighbour's house was hit and part of our house as well, two of the neighbours' children died, and Salim was injured.' Salim suffered horrific burns in the attack. The skin around his ears, nose and all over his little face and the side of his head melted in the heat. His features were hard to distinguish among the burnt tissue, and his disfigured mouth had made it difficult to eat. With no adequate medical care available in besieged Aleppo, Salim's parents had had no option but to lay their badly burnt son in a blanket and get a lift to the Turkish border, where they begged to be allowed to cross. There, in a camp, they met an MSF case worker who arranged for the 12-year-old to fly to Amman for state-of-the-art plastic surgery.

Salim had now been at the hospital for three months, receiving treatment for serious infections and undergoing surgery after surgery to try to improve his quality of life. Doctors were trying a special technique that stretched and expanded the skin on Salim's head to enable further skin grafts. Surgeons would then continue to reconstruct his face, trying to make it easier for him to breathe and eat. 'There was just no treatment at home; they didn't have any,' Salim's mother told me, as Salim sat next to her, quietly playing video games on her phone. 'We died 100 times and then came back to life 100 times. Thank God, he sent us to good people here. Hopefully, my son will recover, and we can return back to Syria; my husband and [other] kids are there. God help us.'

In the hallway Salim kicked a football back and forth with Talha, MSF's paediatric counsellor here. 'When he first came, he was very shy and always silent and socially withdrawn,' Talha explained to me later. Salim, like many of the other children Talha had cared for who were badly disfigured, played the 'bad guy' in games with other kids. 'That's what he thought he was,' said Talha sadly. 'He used to draw himself as a monster.'

Salim had made a new best friend on the ward, 12-year-old Farqar from Baghdad, who was injured in a car bombing six months earlier. 'It happened at the market,' Farqar's mother explained softly, with tears running down her cheeks. 'His father and little brother died. And Farqar was severely burnt.' Like Salim, Farqar had melted skin all over the side of his face and hands and was undergoing several rounds of specialist plastic surgery.

The two boys had become inseparable. They sat on Farqar's bed, cheekily discussing how much they both hated the hospital food, and how they planned to stay in touch over social media once they both got to finally go home. 'We go to activities together, physiotherapy together,' Farqar said happily, swinging his feet on the side of the hospital bed.

'Farqar's going to take me to his home in Iraq one day to play soccer,' Salim added, smiling.

The two jumped up and ran out of the room to hassle Talha the counsellor to play with them. 'These two are troublemakers,' Talha said, laughing as he threw a ball back and forth up the hall with the 12-year-olds.

After three months of sessions with the counsellors, and given his new friendship with Farqar, Salim was starting to feel less shy and embarrassed about his appearance.

'I keep telling him he is more beautiful than he sees himself,' said Talha. 'And he kept thinking of this for two or three days, and he kept asking me to repeat the same sentence for him. It made him delighted.' And Salim no longer drew himself as a monster. 'He now draws himself as a superman and says, 'It's me!' Talha said, smiling.

*

As of the end of 2019, MSF has performed more than 13,000 surgeries for nearly 6000 patients at the Al Mowasah reconstructive surgery hospital in Amman. In the past two years they have initiated a new 3D printed prosthetics program for amputees and increased mental health and psychosocial support for patients, including peer counselling and a school for kids who spend prolonged periods at the hospital. They have also developed a microbiology lab and an antibiotic stewardship team to help fight antibiotic-resistant infections in their patients.

'SURRENDER OR STARVE'

Khaled, part 2

Since that fateful night at Tishreen hospital in 2011, nurse Khaled Naanaa had devoted himself to treating Syrians living in opposition-controlled areas of the country. The Assad regime had now spent years pounding its own people daily from the sky, resulting in a rapidly spiralling civilian death toll. But the world's attention had turned away from the mass atrocities in Syria, focusing instead on ISIS militants who had taken over large swathes of eastern Iraq and north-west Syria and had begun staging deadly attacks in the West. Meanwhile, all across Syria, civilians living in opposition-controlled towns were being mercilessly targeted by the regime in devastatingly timed attacks: the bombardment of agricultural land with incendiary munitions just before crops were to be harvested, attacks on mosques during prayer times or schools during exams.[1] Confident of continued impunity, Assad's forces began to impose sieges through opposition-held areas across Syria, an illegal war crime that saw civilians like Khaled forced to choose between surrendering to the dictator or facing slow starvation.

Madaya, Syria, 2015

Madaya in Syria was once a holiday destination. It lies at 1300 metres and just one hour's drive north-west from Damascus; tourists from the capital would come for the day to enjoy the cooler temperatures in summer and the lush green views from the mountainous village.

But now regime snipers stalked the hills of Madaya. Civilians crept through their town in the shadows, staying close to the walls, the fear of the regime marksmen behind every step. And while they could try to avoid catching the sniper's eye, there was no escape from the tank and mortar rounds that slammed into Madaya's streets and homes at any time of the day or night. Just a quick whoosh and a deafening thud. And then blood, pain and tears.

Wounded men, women and children in Madaya were rarely given permission by the regime soldiers who controlled the checkpoint to be evacuated across the front line to Damascus. So they went to see 'Doctor' Khaled Naanaa. When the young nurse had originally arrived in the area in 2012, he spent the first few weeks working in the nearby town of Zabadani. But soon word emerged that help was more desperately needed in Madaya, a smaller town about five kilometres south.

By that time, fighters from Hezbollah, the Lebanese Shia militant group who fought alongside Assad's regime forces, controlled the hills that lay between Zabadani and Madaya. Khaled had had to sneak in the dead of night, with only the moon to guide him, from one opposition-held town to the other. He had stumbled over rocks and fields in the dark, crawling among sheep in the fields that were too close for comfort to regime checkpoints. Eventually, after many hours, Khaled made it to Madaya – and for the next three years he didn't leave.

As fighting spread across the suburbs of Damascus and wider Syria, many refugees sought shelter in the mountain town. The population swelled from 10,000 to around 30,000; the demand for medical care also skyrocketed. As in other parts of Syria that resisted the regime, Assad's forces harshly punished the civilian population of the town, with near daily sniper shootings, shelling and mortar attacks. Khaled became an invaluable addition to the town's only two doctors, who were struggling to deal with the overwhelming

and increasing load of casualties, plus the daily medical concerns of tens of thousands of people.

When Khaled first arrived, the clinic in the town had only two patient beds and very basic equipment. As the number of acute trauma cases grew, Khaled and his colleagues put out an urgent call for supplies. Drugs and medical equipment were soon smuggled into Madaya from across the Lebanese border, while the international medical charity Médecins Sans Frontières began to officially support the clinic, sending medicines and cash for Khaled and his colleagues to purchase much-needed prescriptions. A basic operating theatre was set up to perform emergency procedures for those unable to be evacuated out.

Khaled quickly earnt the respect of the town's residents. Just a few months after the 26-year-old nurse arrived, a barrage of shells hit the town, tearing into homes and people in the street. Five civilians were killed instantly and 30 injured, including many children. The survivors were rushed to the small clinic, bleeding, their limbs ripped open. Khaled calmly triaged the mass casualties, helped stabilize those critically wounded and quickly tended to the wounds of the others. His calm, gentle demeanour impressed the villagers, who were just getting to know this young volunteer from Damascus. After that day, everyone in the town referred to him as 'Doctor' Khaled.

Khaled threw himself into the clinic, working day and night to help as many people as he could. It was also the best means to distract himself from the aching loneliness in his chest whenever he thought of his wife, Joumana, and his young daughter, Ayaa, whom he had left behind in Damascus. Late at night, once all the patients were treated and the surgery cleaned for the next day's influx of patients, the young nurse would curl up next to the window in his small apartment and try to get a 3G signal good enough to call and send WhatsApp messages to Joumana and Ayaa. He hadn't seen his daughter since she was 18 days old. Sitting up, crawling, eating: Khaled watched all Ayaa's milestones on videos Joumana sent him.

Despite the fighting around Madaya, a segment of the population was still able to go back and forth across the front lines near the town, as long as their name was not on a regime blacklist of those suspected of actively working for the opposition. Several months

after Khaled arrived, Joumana was able to obtain the ID of a friend who looked like her and whose address was from an area not deemed sympathetic to the opposition movement. It would be a safe enough ID for Joumana and Ayaa to travel on through government checkpoints. Khaled waited nervously inside Madaya for them to arrive. The town was only 40 kilometres from Damascus, but the journey could take hours. Finally, they got through, and after four months of separation, Khaled was able to hold them in his arms. The joy was short-lived, as it was too dangerous for Joumana and the baby to stay more than a few days.

The news Joumana brought from home was sobering. Khaled's father had been rounded up by the regime in a raid on the Sunni neighbourhood where he lived. Overnight, he simply disappeared. Khaled knew the torture his 50-year-old father would be enduring inside the regime's cells. Three months after his sudden arrest, his father reappeared. He had been tortured, beaten and abused. The ordeal was so terrifying, Khaled's parents and some of his siblings soon fled Damascus to the north of Syria and then, as refugees, to Turkey.

About a year after Khaled arrived in Madaya, one of the doctors he had been assisting was badly injured when his ambulance was hit by a regime mortar round. Requiring urgent surgery, he had to be smuggled out of the town to Lebanon. Not long after, the only other doctor in Madaya received news that a large number of his family members had been killed in an attack in the south. He had to return to his hometown to help the surviving relatives and their children. Within a few months, both doctors had left, leaving Khaled all alone to run the busy clinic.

In the space of a year, the young nurse had gone from working on a hospital ward to being the only qualified medico caring for more than 30,000 residents. He had to quickly assemble a team to help him manage the load, seeking out the most qualified people in the town who could help. The options were limited, but a young dental student called Muhammad Darwish pledged to join the team, as did Muhammad Yousef, a middle-aged veterinarian.

The work for Khaled and his new team quickly grew as the regime began to attack Madaya by air with barrel bombs. Every week or so, a helicopter would hover in Madaya's skies, dropping one of

these crude, improvised weapons onto homes and streets below. The casualties would arrive, ten to 15 at a time, in Khaled's waiting room.

As it became increasingly harder for patients to be let through government checkpoints, Khaled was forced to perform lifesaving surgery in the makeshift operating theatre they had set up in the clinic; his operating skills were entirely self-taught online. 'I'd go on YouTube and follow the instructions step by step,' he later explained to me. 'The first operation was incredibly hard, but the second and third time it got easier.' He was soon performing stomach surgery and amputations, guided by YouTube and aided by his veterinary and dental assistants. Video from this time shows Khaled suited up in his green scrubs, a patient open in front of him as he delicately negotiates his way around stomach organs to try to stop the bleeding. He worked slowly and methodically, describing each step out loud to his colleagues. Another clip shows him sawing through the bone of a patient who urgently needed an amputation. This ward nurse was quickly becoming an experienced surgeon.

In April 2013, Khaled was in the middle of a long day treating patients when he received an urgent message from one of his brothers. 'Call me,' it read, 'something has happened to Ahmed.' Ahmed was the youngest of Khaled's siblings. He had only just started his compulsory military service when the revolution broke out in 2011. The 21-year-old had been sent to the south, to Daraa, the location of widespread anti-government protests. 'We were always begging him – me, my mum and brothers and my dad – not to participate in any military operation against civilians,' said Khaled. Ahmed had tried to keep a low profile and volunteer for mundane tasks in his unit, a near impossible task when Assad was ordering his forces to violently suppress any opposition to his regime. After being ordered to shoot at civilian protesters, the young soldier and some of his friends came up with a plan to defect to the opposition. But they were caught as they attempted to escape, with Ahmed shot in the legs by his superior. Khaled learnt that his young brother was then tortured by his unit captain as they tried to extract confessions. The next morning, Ahmed's body was found in a garbage dump, a bullet hole through his brain.

The brutal slaughter of his brave little brother hit Khaled hard. He kept imagining how terrifying Ahmed's last hours on this earth

must have been: his desperate attempt to flee, hours of torture. It made him even more determined to stay in Madaya and help. As the months went on, Khaled and his vet and dental student colleagues urged the rebels who controlled the town to try to avoid a confrontation with the Hezbollah troops besieging it. 'We told them this was like a refugee camp now in Madaya, there were so many civilians sheltering there,' Khaled explained.

Initially, the rebels in Madaya adhered to the medical team's requests. Periods of violence would be followed by brief negotiated ceasefires, each of which was soon broken by either Syrian government or opposition forces. As time went on and young men passing through the regime's checkpoints were increasingly kidnapped and forcibly conscripted, the rebels' desire to fight back against the daily shelling and sniping grew. Khaled's clinic was also attacked by government forces with airstrikes and constant artillery, a war crime that was being repeated against medical facilities across Syria. The medical team placed sandbags around the entrances and moved the surgery underground, into the basement of the apartment building.

Every few months Joumana and Ayaa would talk their way through the front line to Madaya, bringing a few days of joy and love into the darkness that surrounded Khaled. But soon it came too dangerous for them to try to cross the labyrinth of checkpoints to see their love.

In 2015, Hezbollah forces, with the support of Syrian-regime troops, edged closer to Madaya. Civilians faced increasing restrictions at checkpoints. Some left for day trips but were taken for interrogation by regime forces and never seen again. Only warlords working with both sides were able to get their goods in and out of the town. By July, Hezbollah had surrounded Madaya and planted landmines in the adjoining fields and mountains. Manned watchtowers and sniper outposts were set up, and all the checkpoints into the town were closed. Even the warlords could no longer get their goods in. Thirty thousand people were now trapped inside a 12-square-kilometre area. The citizens of Madaya were now boxed in with no escape, targeted from all sides. In August, a regime sniper killed a 70-year-old woman in the town's streets. Then, sharpshooters targeted mourners at her funeral.[2]

One night, not long after the siege had begun, a desperate knock came at Khaled's door. A friend stood there in tears. His wife had been in labour for more than 24 hours, but the baby hadn't come, and there was no way of leaving Madaya for a hospital. Could Khaled do an emergency caesarean? 'I've never done one before,' Khaled explained as they rushed to the clinic. 'I don't know how!' But no one else could help. The mother and baby risked both dying if the procedure wasn't done immediately, advised the local woman who had been acting as a midwife. Khaled quickly searched YouTube on his phone for 'how to perform a caesarean'. He studied the video several times. He had already performed delicate stomach surgery on victims after shelling, but this was a whole new league. Khaled said a prayer and cut into the woman's abdomen and uterus before reaching in and carefully pulling out the newborn, who let out a loud wail as Khaled handed the bub to her grateful father. Then he sewed up the mother, just as he had learnt on the YouTube video. It was a success.

As the weeks went on and the regime's blockade continued, food supplies inside Madaya started to dwindle. 'Not even a grain of wheat was allowed in,' Khaled explained. 'The prices were rising, basic supplies started to run out from the market. There was no baby milk, no food, no flour. People walked to the market and returned empty-handed. There was nothing to buy, nothing!'

Assad's policy was clear – surrender or starve.

Distraught mothers came begging at the clinic for Khaled's help. They were so malnourished, they were unable to produce enough breastmilk, but there was also no formula for them to buy in the market. Their newborns and young babies were constantly hungry. Desperate for help, Khaled contacted UN officials in Damascus.

After weeks of negotiations, on 18 October, a small food convoy was finally allowed into Madaya. The townspeople despaired when they discovered some of the food in the UN delivery had already gone bad – with 320 of the 650 crates of aid sent to Madaya and neighbouring Zabadani containing expired high-energy biscuits that were mouldy and rotten.[3] Many residents reported to Khaled's clinic with abdominal pain, vomiting and diarrhoea after eating the expired food.[4] The UN apologized for 'a human error' in the packing process. Pawel Krzysiek, a spokesperson for the International Committee for the Red Cross, had been part of

the October convoy. Months later, he revealed that at the time
distressed parents in Madaya had begged him for baby milk, which
the regime had forbidden from the aid delivery.[5] And while the UN
made general statements condemning sieges, it stayed silent on the
deadly conditions developing inside the town.

The UN supplies from the October delivery lasted only a few
weeks. Soon hunger set in again, and desperate parents scoured
garbage bins to feed their kids. 'But even the garbage had no food
in it,' Khaled said sadly. 'People started to look pale. Their cheeks
started to dissolve. No stomachs, the people started to look like
skeletons.' Like the rest of the town, Khaled was down to one meal
a day. He and his colleagues would mix one precious cup of rice
or lentils from a dwindling supply with salt and spices in a couple
of litres of water. 'We couldn't sleep at night,' he recalled. 'Imagine
a 30-year-old man crying because he is so hungry! I was crying. I
wanted to eat. We would just ask, "Why were they doing this to us?"'

Meanwhile, government authorities continued to forcibly
displace residents of Zabadani, the town next door, relocating
145 families from there to Madaya, putting additional stress on
Madaya's already overstretched resources.[6] 'You would think the
streets would be empty because people are exhausted and have
nowhere to go, but the town is full of skeleton-like people walking
around in a daze, looking for scraps of food from 6 am until sunset,'
Khaled described. 'People are in denial, every day they wake up and
think that they will miraculously find a store open.'

Khaled, too, was weak and dizzy from a lack of food, but his
workload was only increasing, as a growing number of townspeople
ventured into landmined fields, desperately looking for food. More
than 20 adults and children in Madaya lost their limbs in the
resulting explosions. 'We had so many amputation cases because
of the landmines surrounding the town and the many people who
tried to break the siege,' recalled Khaled. 'Some kids went too close
to the checkpoints as they tried to find food and had limbs blown
off by landmines.' Photos and videos taken of Khaled carrying
out amputation surgery show him deep in concentration in the
makeshift operating theatre. Dressed in green scrubs, the one-
time nurse had transformed into a surgical old hand, sewing up
the bloodied stumps of the town's residents as best as he could.

In the five months since the siege had begun, ten residents had been killed by landmines and five by snipers while trying to escape the town. In late December, a 26-year-old man was shot and killed by snipers while collecting grass for his family to eat.[7]

It had been months since Khaled had seen his wife and daughter. He would speak to Joumana and Ayaa late at night. He told his wife food was getting low but didn't disclose the severe hunger that he also was facing. By this stage he had lost at least 15 kilograms. His dreams were filled with food. 'I used to tell friends during the siege, my dream right now is to have a tomato, cucumbers, eggs and bread. If I had this food to eat,' Khaled said, smiling, 'I'll feel that I'm the richest man in the world.'

On top of everything, Khaled was then targeted from within. The rebel fighters in Madaya had initially pledged their allegiance to the Free Syrian Army, led by defecting officers from the Syrian national army. As the fighting continued, a steady flow of arms and money from Gulf Arab states and Turkey saw some of the fighters in Madaya join Ahrar al-Sham, a hard-line Islamist group. Around 20 of these Ahrar al-Sham fighters in Madaya soon broke off, pledging their loyalty to the ISIS jihadist terror group. Khaled disagreed with their radical ideology, which he thought harmed the opposition movement to Bashar Al Assad, and the ISIS fighters were aware of his disdain. 'I made it clear that I hate them,' Khaled said. 'I told them that ISIS is no less criminal than the Syrian regime. I still treated their families, but they knew I was against them.'

Several months into the siege, when Khaled was already weak with malnourishment, he was walking into his apartment after a long day at the clinic. It was already dark, but he could just make out two men on the back of a motorbike who drove past and shot at him. 'I recognized this man as one of the ISIS members. I yelled out, "Hey, why are you shooting me? I'm here to help. Only two days ago, I treated your mother!"' Khaled recalled angrily. Luckily, most of their shots missed Khaled, but one hit him in the calf, the bullet lodged deep in his bone. His colleagues quickly rushed the injured Khaled to the clinic and hoisted him up onto the surgery bed. The only problem was that Khaled performed all the operations in Madaya. He laughed when describing the options available: 'I had the choice of the dentist student or the vet!'

Khaled's colleagues gave him a local anaesthetic as he sat there, fully conscious, giving directions on his own surgery to remove the bullet and close the wound. Now, on top of his hunger, Khaled had to limp around town, in considerable pain as his wound was slow to heal.

Life was so dire that Khaled and his medical colleagues decided to sacrifice themselves to ensure the survival of Madaya's civilians.

'At one point, we offered to hand ourselves over to the regime in return for lifting the siege. We said, "Just break the siege on civilians and we will hand ourselves over, you can detain us." The regime simply said no,' said Khaled. 'You can't condemn 30,000 civilians to die for the actions of 100–200 rebel fighters!'

By December 2015, five months after the siege was imposed, there was almost no food left. Mothers desperately collected leaves and grass for their children to eat, but little was growing as winter set in. Most nights the temperature fell below zero, but there was no wood to burn and the electricity to the town had been cut off months ago. Families sat in the dark and the cold, praying for sleep that would bring temporary relief to the nightmare they were enduring. In desperation, some families started eating their pets, and the medical team had to pump a family's stomachs after they got food poisoning from eating cat meat.

The first to die from a lack of food was a three-month-old baby. 'I received a small baby at the beginning of December,' Khaled said quietly. 'When we asked why they didn't feed him, they said they had run out of baby milk two weeks earlier. The mother had tried so hard to give him milk or buy it, but at the end she fed the baby only salt and water.'

Khaled appealed to the UN and International Red Cross offices in Damascus, asking for aid to be urgently delivered to Madaya. 'We made so many calls to the UN offices. We explained, "People are starting to die, you must help to save lives." They never got back to us with honest promises or accurate answers,' he said. The UN told Khaled they couldn't deliver aid without the agreement of the Syrian government. After Khaled reported the baby's death, the UN then formally requested permission to send more food to Madaya, but, unsurprisingly, the Assad regime refused.

Kevin Kennedy, the UN Regional Humanitarian Coordinator for Syria, acknowledged that by early December, the UN were aware the situation in Madaya was extremely dire and food aid was desperately needed. 'We had requested a convoy and planned a convoy to go in on the 8th of December with a variety of food, non-food, medical and health items,' Kennedy said. 'Obviously... when we are going from a government-controlled area to a non-government-controlled area...it requires a green light from the government of Syria. That convoy was not allowed to go forward.'

What was happening to Madaya was a carefully executed war strategy by the Assad forces, with food as the weapon.

Soon, more patients started dying, primarily babies and the elderly. Mothers and fathers would bring their whole families to the clinic, begging Khaled to help their children. He was working 20-hour days, surrounded by a growing number of sick and starving children and adults, while he himself often felt like keeling over from exhaustion and hunger. 'It was so, so hard,' Khaled said. 'I felt responsible for these people. They are only suffering from hunger; they were coming to the medical centre, asking me, "Can you save our lives?"'

Khaled had a small supply of rehydration salts in the clinic. He would give the malnourished children a spoonful or two, to try to keep them going. Other children were given saline drips and cough syrup, more as a placebo than anything else. 'The children's skin was close to the bones, their muscles had started to deteriorate; it was clear by looking at their faces, too. There were no cheeks, no muscle, you can see almost their teeth. And they all had very bad breath, because of their empty stomachs and the hunger,' he described sadly. 'We were trying to tell the kids, their parents, they will live. We had to try and find something reassuring.' But his patients continued to die. 'I will never forget the looks on the children's faces,' he remembered. 'The way they were looking at us, in the hospital, they were hoping that we are the people who are going to help them. These children were denied their very basic rights. This was the biggest dream in Madaya: a piece of bread.'

Khaled was in regular phone contact with a UN staffer in Beirut, meticulously briefing her about the mounting deaths and suffering he was witnessing. Yet the UN office in Damascus, which sat only 40 kilometres from where civilians were being

deliberately denied food as a war tactic, still made no public comment about the situation. Warehouses full of food, paid for by international donors, sat in Damascus untouched, only a few minutes' drive away from the five-star hotel where many UN aid workers were based in Damascus. Meanwhile babies and children starved in the rebel-held town. Khaled's UN contact in Beirut, exasperated by her organization's silence, advised him that he should contact journalists instead. 'She told me, "Khaled, we failed to get any permission to allow aid in, you should approach the media,"' Khaled said. So the next day, when more starving, emaciated children came into his clinic, Khaled grabbed his phone and started filming.

By January 2016, I had started to hear rumours about the lack of food in Madaya and, from my ABC office in Jerusalem, had been trying to verify what was going on. Through the Syrian American Medical Society, a charity working in opposition-held areas in Syria, I'd been put onto Dr Ammar Ghanem, a critical-care specialist based in Oklahoma who had emigrated to the US from a town near Madaya in the 1980s. Dr Ghanem was in touch with Khaled via WhatsApp and gave me his number, so I sent him a message. Could he tell me what was going on? And did he have any video to prove the state of the people in Madaya?

The next day, a young boy was brought to the clinic by his mother, and Khaled filmed himself talking to the child on his mobile phone. 'It's January the 6th, 2016. I'm Doctor Khaled in Madaya,' he says, as he films the emaciated eight-year-old standing in front of him with his shirt off, the child's protruding ribs and skeletal frame clear to see.

'What's your name?' Khaled asks.

'Mohammad Eissa,' the boy answers, smiling shyly.

'How long has it been since you've eaten?' asks Khaled.

'Seven days,' replies Mohammad.

'Swear to God?' asks Khaled.

'I swear to God!'

In another clip, a seven-month-old baby girl lies on a blanket in the clinic. She has big dark eyes, and her tiny chest and arms are just skin and bones. There are no nappies left in Madaya, so the baby has a black plastic bag tied around her bottom.

'I'm Dr Khaled, from the Madaya field hospital. What's the name of this baby?'

'Amal Haddad,' replies the mother, out of shot.

'How long has she been without milk?' Khaled asks, filming the crying baby.

'Over one month!' exclaims Amal's mother.

'What do you give her to eat now?' he asks.

'Just water with salt,' says the mother.

A few hours after Khaled recorded the videos, they popped up on my phone in Jerusalem. I watched horrified. Here was the evidence – children, babies being deliberately starved as a tactic of war. Khaled sent me several voice messages along with the video. 'We want doctors to help. The UN should get involved to see how people are starving here,' he pleaded. I quickly got onto contacts I had within the charity Médecins Sans Frontières who were working on Syria, since Khaled had told me via voice message that MSF had been supporting them for several years. Could they confirm and verify these horrific images? A senior official quickly responded. Yes, they told me, we can vouch for Khaled and we believe the reports that civilians have died from a lack of food.

I posted the footage on Twitter and was quickly contacted by other journalists, with whom I shared the videos.[8] Within a few hours, it had gone viral. From Al Jazeera to CNN and the BBC, the video was playing on news channels around the world. The photos Khaled had sent were on the front page of newspapers in several capital cities. Khaled's wife, Joumana, was in Damascus at her parents' house when she heard her husband's voice on the television. 'I was in the kitchen, I heard Khaled's voice on the TV, it was during the news, I dropped everything from my hands and went to watch. This is Khaled's voice!' Joumana remembered.

In Madaya, Khaled couldn't believe how quickly the video had spread. 'The clip was all over the Arabic TV stations, on all the channels every hour. Joumana called me. She was surprised, asking, "Is it true? Are you guys starving?"' he explained. 'Twenty-four hours after I sent it, around 30 million people had watched this video clip. I told my colleague, "That's it, people worldwide saw us, now they will force the international community to allow aid to us!"' From Turkey, Khaled's parents called him. 'They said,

"Khaled is this true? Is this video clip genuine?" I told them, "Yes, this our life! This is reality!"' he said.

Khaled's images of the starving children prompted a global outcry. In New York, the US ambassador to the UN, Samantha Power, referred to Khaled's photos and videos in a speech to the UN General Assembly:

> Look at the haunting pictures of civilians, including children – even babies – in Madaya, Syria. These are just the pictures we see. There are hundreds of thousands of people being deliberately besieged, deliberately starved, right now. And these images, they remind us of World War Two; they shock the conscience. This is what this institution was designed to prevent.[9]

New Zealand, Spain and France called for an urgent UN Security Council meeting.

Despite the uproar, nothing had changed in Madaya. Khaled sent me more videos and photos, which I also put on Twitter. An emaciated little girl with sunken cheeks, holding up her jumper to show us her jutting-out ribs. An old man perched on the edge of Khaled's consulting bed, nothing but shrivelled-up skin and bone. The skeletal dead body of another man who had just succumbed to the hunger.

Meanwhile, senior British politicians were calling on the British Royal Air Force to airdrop food into Madaya. In a letter to Prime Minister David Cameron, MPs urged the government to 'strongly consider' the action, comparing the situation to when the RAF dropped aid to thousands of Yazidis fleeing genocide at the hands of ISIS in 2014. 'There are immediate steps we can take to stop more vulnerable people dying needlessly of hunger. We cannot sit by and watch this happen,' urged the former Liberal Democrat leader Lord Ashdown and the Labour MP Jo Cox.[10] David Blair, a columnist for UK's *The Telegraph*, noted that

> Madaya is only six miles from Syria's western border with Lebanon or about 40 seconds' flying time for a Hercules transport aircraft. If the RAF can't drop food to Madaya in Syria we shouldn't bother having an air force at all. Is it really

beyond the ability of the RAF to penetrate hostile airspace for a round trip of 80 seconds?[11]

Jonathan Jones, *The Guardian* UK's art critic, wrote that Khaled's photos were reminiscent of Don McCullin's images of the victims of the Biafra war in Nigeria in the 1960s:

> Photographs from this besieged city depict the stark reality of mass starvation. Children with barely covered ribs gaze at the camera. Emaciated corpses lie unburied…In Biafra in 1968, as in Madaya at this moment, people were starving not simply because of drought or crop failure but as a direct consequence of war.[12]

Supporters of President Bashar Al Assad spread wild accusations across social media, labelling Khaled's videos 'fakes' and the starving people as actors. They trolled western reporters, including me, accusing us of spreading 'lies'. The Syrian regime itself joined in the campaign of misinformation, labelling Khaled's videos 'fabrications'. Bashar Ja'afari, Syria's ambassador to the United Nations, denied anyone was starving in Madaya, blaming Arab television 'for fabricating these allegations and lies'.[13]

But thanks to Khaled, the evidence was overwhelming. Médecins Sans Frontières issued a press release, verifying Khaled's video and collating all the evidence he had been sending them.[14] 'Madaya is now effectively an open-air prison for an estimated 20,000 people, including infants, children and elderly. There is no way in or out, leaving the people to die,' MSF's director of operations announced, confirming that 23 patients in Madaya – six of them babies under one year old – had died of starvation in the previous four weeks. More than 250 people in the town had been identified as having severe acute malnutrition, including ten patients who were in immediate need of lifesaving hospital care. The charity highlighted the work of Khaled and his two assistants in trying to keep the town's residents alive: 'MSF has specific concerns also for the medical staff it is supporting. They are working under unbearable conditions, with already big medical needs now exacerbated by food insecurity and nutrition concerns, and there is an urgent need to resupply them with basic medical essentials.'

On 7 January, less than 36 hours after Khaled had recorded the videos, the Assad regime relented to the enormous international pressure, reluctantly granting permission for food aid to be delivered to Madaya. The United Nations, the World Food Programme and the International Red Cross began to negotiate specifics with the regime. They were allowed only to bring supplies approved by the Syrian government, which would grant access to Madaya only if aid was also delivered to Foua and Kefraya, two towns in the north of Syria besieged by rebels. (While there was no doubt these towns also desperately needed food, no one in Foua and Kefraya was starving to death; the regime made sure that towns supporting it were airdropped supplies.) As the negotiations dragged out over several days, five more people died in Madaya, a nine-year-old boy and four old men.

Khaled sent me urgent new voice messages. 'Every day passes by, it cost us lives of people,' he said desperately. 'Please, please, please the international community must act fast, please act fast to save the lives of the people here.'

On the morning of 11 January, three days after the permission had initially been granted, the UN aid convoy finally left Damascus and started to make its way to Madaya. The starving residents of the town began to gather in the streets from 11 am, with hundreds of families waiting in the cold until 9.30 pm, when the convoy rolled through the last regime checkpoint and into town. Children and parents wept in the streets with relief as they crowded around aid workers, begging for one of the few loaves of fresh bread that were being handed out. The adults hung back and let the kids devour the bread; they would have to wait until they got home with the flour and oil to break their own fasts. 'I felt like it was the happiest day in life. I don't think we will ever live happier days than that day, me and all the people of Madaya,' Khaled recalled, tears rolling down his cheeks.

He was determined the UN staff would tell the world that the situation in Madaya was as bad as he had claimed. Yacoub de Hillo, the top UN official in Syria, was part of the long-awaited convoy. 'The first thing I did was grab Yacoub El Hillo and without saying hello, I took him to the clinic,' Khaled said. 'We had been accused of lying and faking. So I told him, "I've got nothing to say to anyone from the UN. You can see for yourself."' Khaled led the UN and Red Cross workers into his basement clinic, where the worst cases

of malnourished Madaya residents lay on the floor in various stages of illness and distress. Video of that moment shows the Red Cross and UN staff standing on the stairwell in shock as they survey the morbid scene in front of them. Khaled walks from patient to patient, highlighting the most critical cases. Some of the mothers in the room start berating the aid workers and begging them for help. 'They all started to cry, all the delegation, when they saw kids, the women, the older people, even young men laying on the floor,' Khaled said quietly. 'Skinny people, skeletons, skin attached to the bones, nothing in between. Then the talk ended. No questions were asked.'

In the room was Pawel Krzysiek, the International Committee of the Red Cross spokesperson in Syria. He described entering Khaled's clinic as the 'most shocking' moment of the visit. 'It's really heartbreaking to see the situation of the people. I was just approached by a little girl and her first question was: "Did you bring food? Because we are really hungry." And I believe her. She looked hungry.'[15] One of the patients in Khaled's small clinic died soon after the aid officials entered. UNICEF's Syria representative Hanaa Singer told CNN later: 'There were two young men, I would say two skeletons really...it was shocking to witness the death of a young man in front of you, just like that.'[16]

Khaled took Yacoub El Hillo, the UN's Syria chief, aside, begging him to do more to stop Syrians starving to death in besieged areas throughout the country. 'My message to Yacoub El Hillo, when he was in my home, was that "I hope this village will be the last village going through this disaster." I said, "This is your real responsibility. Many towns are facing the same disaster as we did. I wish for you to take more responsibility." While Hezbollah forces did not allow reporters into the town, Yacoub El Hillo gave an impromptu press conference outside the main checkpoint, where several journalists had gathered, confirming that Khaled's reports of starvation were indeed true. 'I can confirm there are severely malnourished children in Madaya, that is a fact,' the UN aid chief in Syria told reporters unequivocally. 'It was at times difficult to determine whether what we were seeing was actually fabricated or exaggerated. It is not. It is not. I am sad to say it is not. These are true stories coming out of Madaya.'[17]

Aid officials worked through the night to unload the supplies they had brought from Damascus. Families stood waiting with their

bags packed, desperate to escape – but civilians were not allowed to evacuate with the convoy. After a mere few hours on the ground, the aid workers got back into their vehicles and returned to regime-controlled territory. The people of Madaya were once again alone.

After the convoy had confirmed the full scale of the horror in Madaya, anger quickly turned towards the UN. Why had they waited for an international media outcry before taking action? Despite the evidence humanitarian workers had seen in October, and Khaled's regular updates, Madaya was not even included on the UN's list of 'besieged' areas in Syria that it was monitoring. It emerged that the UN Office for the Coordination of Humanitarian Affairs (OCHA) had issued a secret 'flash update' on 6 January, the same day Khaled messaged me the photos and videos of the starving kids. The memo, classified as 'Internal, Not for Quotation', was leaked to *Foreign Policy* magazine.[18] Shockingly, it confirmed that as far back as October, community leaders in Madaya had reported 1000 cases of malnutrition in children under the age of one.

So why the silence? And why did the UN not condemn the Assad regime for their policy of starving their own people to death until they surrendered? In his comments to reporters in the days after his visit to Madaya, top UN official Yacoub El Hillo did not attribute any blame for the starvation of these children. He made no mention of the Hezbollah or Syrian government troops surrounding the town, blocking food from getting in and people from getting out.

I put these accusations to the Middle East spokesperson for the UN's OCHA, Iyad Nasr, who insisted: 'We have clearly and publicly expressed our demand and request to the Syrian government to access Madaya seven times in the past year. But we did not receive the green light. So even when people accuse the UN of not doing anything, no, we were not allowed to do what was required.'

Incredibly, it was also revealed that on 28 December 2015, once residents of Madaya had already begun to starve to death, aid officials operating on behalf of OCHA visited Madaya to evacuate injured fighters.[19] But they did not bring food aid, nor did they mention anything publicly about deaths from starvation.

The United Nations in Damascus stayed quiet. They didn't challenge the regime publicly. They didn't say a word until the world outcry at Khaled's images.

Instead, in December, the UN team had allowed the regime to amend the wording of its humanitarian plan in Syria, so it was more palatable to the government of Bashar Al Assad.[20] An earlier draft of the plan, leaked to *Foreign Policy* magazine, proved that the UN had removed ten references to 'sieged' or 'besieged' areas, such as Madaya, with the OCHA office in Damascus indicating that the alterations had been made at the behest of the Syrian government.[21] Iyad Nasr refused to comment to me on accusations that they had toned down reports to appease the regime. 'OCHA and all humanitarian actors have to keep a proximity to all parties to the conflict in order to have an effective engagement and effective negotiations to be granted access. It's not healthy if we are the enemy of any of the parties,' he said. A former Syrian diplomat who defected to the opposition told the *New York Times* that he wanted the UN to be pressing 'loudly and publicly for unconditional aid access'. Instead, he said, UN officials were privately telling opposition groups that they did not want Syrian officials 'to be upset and spoil the political process'.[22]

Madaya was not even classified by the UN OCHA office in Damascus as a 'besieged community' – which backed up accusations by several Syrian NGOs that the UN had been repeatedly under-reporting the number of people living under siege in Syria.[23] At the time of Madaya's starvation, UN figures said only 400,000 people were living under siege in Syria. The real figure, say the Syria Institute and the Syria Campaign, was closer to one million. While a senior official at Médecins Sans Frontières refused to comment on allegations that OCHA had under-reported the numbers, they did back up the Syrian NGOs' figure of one million people as accurate.

A report by Siege Watch, a joint initiative between the Dutch peacebuilding NGO PAX and Washington-based think-tank the Syria Institute, labelled international aid in the country a 'tool of war controlled by the most powerful party', with 'continued under-reporting of the siege crisis in Syria…creating a distorted and inaccurate view of the situation on the ground.' Siege Watch's most ominous finding was that the UN's practices 'may validate and inadvertently encourage the expansion of the Syrian government's "surrender or starve" strategy'.[24]

In the wake of the outcry over the starvation in Madaya, the

UN's Syria chief, Yacoub El Hillo, confirmed what many had long suspected – in 2015 only 10 per cent of all requests for UN aid convoys to hard-to-reach and besieged areas were approved by the regime.[25] Outraged at the UN's failure, more than 100 medical and humanitarian workers inside Syria published an open letter to the head of UN OCHA in Geneva, Stephen O'Brien, accusing the international body of kowtowing to Bashar Al Assad's regime. 'Mr O'Brien, your colleagues in Damascus are either too close to the regime or too scared of having their visas revoked by the same powers that are besieging us,' the letter read.[26]

> Those whose loved ones die from malnutrition-related illnesses or a lack of basic medical care will never forgive the UN staff who sit minutes away in luxury hotels, within earshot of the bombings...Meanwhile, the UN is delivering billions of dollars of aid to regime-controlled areas. By allowing the regime to veto aid to civilians in areas outside its control, you have allowed the UN to become a political tool of the war.

It was a damning indictment of how the UN was operating in Syria. I spoke to a senior UN official working in the country, who refused to be named but who confirmed that UN agencies in Syria were under 'enormous' pressure from the regime to downplay the humanitarian consequences of the war. 'We need to keep getting visas,' they said.

Khaled said he felt furious at the UN and what he saw as their complicity with the regime. 'I feel betrayed. They let us down.' Meanwhile, Khaled himself was soon paying the price for blowing the whistle on the Syrian regime's starvation tactics. Not long after the aid convoy arrived, Khaled began to receive death threats. 'I've received a phone call from a person who was from out of town, he was close to the Syrian regime and Hezbollah,' Khaled explained. 'He told me, "Your life is in danger, look after yourself. Hezbollah and the regime decided to kill you as revenge because of what you have done. They are recruiting people to do the job."'

Khaled was torn. After everything he had been through, he didn't want to abandon Madaya now. But he also didn't just want to throw his life away. The last three years of separation from

Joumana and Ayaa had been heartbreaking. He also wanted to make sure he survived so he could tell the world the full story of what had happened to Madaya.

On 14 January, three days after the initial convoy, the Syrian Red Crescent, UNICEF and the UN returned to Madaya, drawing up a list of the 400 patients Khaled had prioritised for immediate medical evacuation and treatment outside Madaya. Feeling reassured that his patients would now finally get the treatment they needed, Khaled decided it was worth trying to escape Madaya. The journey would be incredibly risky. He had to get past landmines and Hezbollah snipers and then sneak past regime checkpoints and over the Lebanese border. He didn't tell Joumana; he didn't want her to worry. If he was killed while escaping, his medical colleagues would be the ones to inform her.

On a snowy, freezing night in mid-January, with nothing but a small backpack and wearing the heaviest coat he owned, Khaled set out from Madaya. The first obstacle was the landmined fields. One wrong step could spell a disastrous end – he had treated countless patients whose limbs had been blown off by these horrific weapons. Also, his leg was still in terrible shape from the ISIS shooting, so it would be a slow journey. Khaled took a deep breath, trying not think of the wounds and the amputations he'd had to perform, and slowly began limping his way across the snowy terrain. It was just him, the moon and his prayers. After several kilometres, holding his breath and waiting for an explosion at any minute, he came to the end of the deadly no-man's land around Madaya. Khaled felt jubilant and reinvigorated. He could do this, he told himself, he could survive. 'I was so happy, I felt I've got more life to live,' Khaled said, smiling. 'I felt reborn.'

Khaled slowly walked west for the next few hours, making his way to a safe house in a village close to the Lebanese border, arriving just before the sun came up. His leg was aching and sore, and he was exhausted. He slept all day and got ready for the second part of his journey, sneaking over the Lebanese border. That night, he set out again, a slow limp towards what he dreamt would be freedom. Soon he saw the lights of the Beqaa Valley, and he began to sob, unable to believe he had made it. A friend of a friend was waiting for him in a car. Khaled had never been so happy to see anyone. He embraced

him, and they drove towards Beirut. Only then did he call Joumana. 'I told her, "I'm in Beirut." She said, "No, you're lying." I said, "Listen to the cars around me!"' Khaled recalled happily.

A photo of that night shows Khaled beaming as he tucks into a piece of cake at a friend's house in Beirut. His cheeks are hollowed and his face gaunt, testimony to the 15 kilograms he had lost over the previous few months. That night he ate his first proper meal in more than six months. 'I asked my friend for two fried eggs, cucumber and tomato, I told him how I've been dreaming of having this meal during the siege in Madaya,' Khaled said. While he devoured the food, what Khaled really craved was to see Joumana and Ayaa again. The siege meant it had been eight months since he had seen them. 'All what I wanted, is just to see them,' Khaled said firmly.

In Damascus, Joumana packed up a few suitcases. She knew she would probably not come back for a very long time, perhaps ever. She hugged her parents tightly, gathered up Ayaa, who was now four, and got the next shared taxi to the Lebanese border. To cross, she had to produce a fake document showing that she had an appointment at the French embassy in Beirut. She smiled sweetly at the guards, promising she would return. They were allowed in, and soon they were in Khaled's arms. 'When I saw them, Ayaa started crying, and I was crying,' Khaled says. He couldn't believe he had made it back to them in one piece.

Khaled and Joumana rented a small apartment on the outskirts of Beirut. Compared with Madaya, it was a dream. But Lebanon was no safe haven. They were all in the country illegally and risked deportation at any moment if picked up by the Lebanese police. Khaled was also wanted by Hezbollah, who have significant political clout in Lebanon and control large parts of the country. 'The fear continued with me here in Lebanon because of the Hezbollah presence,' Khaled explains. 'I was in fear all the time. I could have been identified by them, or by their supporters, or their members; this could be my end, they can kill me.'

Most of the time, Khaled, Joumana and Ayaa stayed inside, never straying far from their apartment. Khaled spent most of his days still living and breathing Madaya. He was in constant contact with his two colleagues, Muhammad Darwish and Muhammad Yousef, whom he had left behind. They would WhatsApp him photos of

wounds they didn't know how to treat and medical cases they didn't know how to deal with. Khaled would sit in Beirut, trying to give whatever advice he could to make it easier. Despite his joy at being reunited with his family, he was consumed by guilt at leaving.

Not long after they had moved into their new apartment, Khaled had to take a shared taxi to the other side of Beirut to see if the family could register as refugees with the UNHCR, the UN's refugee agency. The driver took a shortcut for another passenger and suddenly Khaled found himself in Dahieh, the suburb that is Hezbollah's headquarters in the city. He started panicking and sweating as the car approached a checkpoint manned by the Shiite militia. They were intermittently stopping cars and checking the IDs of passengers. 'I've been careful all this time with this issue, and suddenly randomly I'm in it!' Khaled explained. 'I felt this was my end. My heart was beating so fast!' Luckily, the soldiers waved Khaled's taxi through, but the incident shook him deeply. He hadn't survived all of this to suddenly disappear on a Beirut street. He had to try to get out of Lebanon.

He sent me a WhatsApp message. Did I know anything about applying for a visa to Australia? I knew that Khaled's life was in danger partly because of the photos and videos he had sent to me, and I felt deeply responsible for his fate. Australia had recently announced it would take 12,000 Syrian and Iraqi refugees as part of a one-off humanitarian intake. As I had covered this story, I had got to know a lovely Australian immigration officer working in the department's Dubai office, which had been tasked with overseeing this new intake of refugees. In March 2016, I sent an email outlining the details of Khaled's case and the ongoing persecution he faced in Syria and Lebanon.

A few days later, an official at the Australian embassy in Beirut called Khaled's mobile. Could he and his family come for an interview? Khaled, Joumana and Ayaa dressed in their best clothes and caught a minibus to the Australian embassy. 'I was very nervous, very tense. I was worried my case won't be approved,' remembered Khaled. 'Then I walked in to the interview room and the consular official greeted me, she was smiling. She told me, "Khaled relax, don't be nervous, we will listen to you, we have all day." This was at 9 am. They told me, "We have until 5 pm. Just be relaxed."' Khaled told them

everything – what he had witnessed at Tishreen military hospital in those early days of the revolution, the secret help he had given to the wounded protesters, the injuries he had treated in Madaya and the starvation he had witnessed, the incredible escape from Madaya and the threats he faced in Lebanon. The officials listened intently, taking notes and asking questions, over several hours. They thanked Khaled and promised he would hear soon if his application was successful.

While we were waiting to hear, a call came from Khaled's family, who had been living as refugees in Turkey. Khaled's mother had died from cancer. He hadn't seen her in five years. With no travel documents, he couldn't even go to her funeral. It was a crushing realisation of just how much he had lost over the past five years. He was devastated. The family bunkered down in their Beirut apartment in a kind of purgatory, unable to start a new life but not living this one either.

Three months later, on a Friday in July, the Australian embassy called Khaled. 'They said, "Congratulations, your visa has been approved! Do you have any problem travelling to Australia?"' Khaled recalled, smiling. 'I said, "This is my dream to go to Australia!"' Before they left, Khaled and Joumana had to attend special Australian cultural lessons run by the embassy. (They had to wear seatbelts in Australia, they were informed, and no, there were no crocodiles roaming the streets.) The best news was they were being sent to Perth, my hometown. I flew to Beirut to take the journey to Australia with them. It was an emotional moment to finally meet Khaled after so many months communicating by WhatsApp messages. In the days before their flight, I spent hours at their apartment, hearing Khaled's full life story and all of his and Joumana's hopes and dreams for their new beginning in Australia. 'My feelings now toward Australia is like a man who's left hell and is going to be rewarded with heaven,' Khaled told me. 'I never wished to leave Syria. But at the end this was not my choice, I was forced to leave, I was facing death.'

The night before we were due to fly out, I had dinner at their apartment in Mount Lebanon, a suburb near the airport. Not long after we finished eating, we heard the crack of a gun outside the window. Before long, a full-blown gunfight broke out in the street below between two warring neighbourhood factions. 'Thank God

we are leaving!' Khaled said as we sat on the floor of his bedroom, taking shelter as bullets whizzed past the window.

'It's not like this in Perth!' I promised.

The next day we could barely fit their suitcases into their taxi. After losing so much, and having nothing of the old existence with them, they wanted to bring everything they had in Beirut to Australia, even crockery, spices and their favourite ground coffee. Joumana had spent weeks carefully packing their whole life into several large bags, so big that the boot of the taxi had to be tied down because it wouldn't close.

At Beirut airport, Khaled was nervous. Despite his UN travel documents and Australian visa, he still needed to go through Lebanese security to leave the country. He was pulled aside at Customs, and the Lebanese security forces took him away to a small room. Joumana and I tried to keep our cool. Surely, we couldn't have got this far for it to all come apart here? He emerged, grinning, 15 minutes later. The Lebanese security services had made him sign a document stating that he was never allowed to return to Lebanon, but he was free to go. We boarded our flight excitedly. It was the first time any of them had flown. After take-off, Khaled turned to me and grinned. 'Now I can finally relax!' he said. Nearly 20 hours later we finally landed in Perth, Western Australia, about as far away from war-torn Syria as you can get. My younger sister Asha was waiting at the airport with a welcome sign and flowers. 'Welcome!' she said, hugging Khaled, Joumana and Ayaa.

Within a few days, the family had been settled into a small house and enrolled in English lessons. They couldn't believe how cheap meat is in Australia and how expensive vegetables are. They marvelled at the clean streets and 'how organised' everything looks. I visited them one afternoon and we went for a walk among the wildflowers in the hills of Kings Park, overlooking the Swan River below. The air was crisp and clean, and as we looked down, Perth sparkled in the afternoon light. 'To me, Australia is like heaven on earth,' Khaled said, looking out at the view. 'Not long ago I was under barrel bombings, snipers' shootings, amputating people's legs. I've gone from hell to heaven. It's an amazing feeling.'

Despite the overwhelming sense of relief from being safe in Australia, Madaya continued to haunt Khaled day and night. He

was still advising his colleagues inside. Each night, Khaled returned there, in a recurring nightmare where desperate injured people came to him for medical help that he just couldn't give. 'I still can't believe that I'm not in Madaya,' Khaled said quietly. 'When I eat and drink, I ask myself how the people in Madaya are living. "How are the patients? Is there someone who needs my help?" These questions are on my mind all the time.'

The hardest thing to live with, for Khaled, was that despite everything he had risked in proving to the world the deliberate starvation of people in Madaya, more than a year after that initial outcry, nothing had changed in the town. Evidence compiled by the Syrian American Medical Society and Physicians for Human Rights detailed how the Syrian government continued to block food delivery to Madaya.[27] The NGOs also revealed that when a UN aid delivery did make it to Madaya in February 2016, Syrian government officials removed numerous items from the convoy, including kits for treating malnourished children. In the two weeks after those supplies were not delivered, two children died of acute malnutrition. None of the aid that had been delivered to Madaya since the siege began in July 2015 contained fruit, vegetables, animal protein, eggs or dairy.[28] Children in Madaya began to present with extremely swollen bellies, characteristics of kwashiorkor, a form of life-threatening malnutrition caused by acute protein deficiency. Khaled's colleagues begged the UN to send food with protein, as well as fresh fruit and vegetables, as part of the next delivery. But when it arrived, the delivery contained virtually none of the requested items. The World Food Programme said that 'due to safety issues' and the 'long time it takes to deliver food to people in besieged areas', fresh goods could not be delivered to Madaya.

Patients who required urgent medical care were also not being evacuated out, and the medical team left in Madaya didn't have the expertise to help them. Two months after Khaled left, three young boys, two brothers – aged six and seven – and their seven-year-old friend, were going home from school on the outskirts of Madaya when a landmine exploded.[29] One of the boys was killed instantly, while the other two suffered severe injuries to the legs and stomach and shrapnel to the head requiring surgical intervention. Muhammad Darwish and Muhammad Yousef requested urgent

medical evacuation for the children so they could get the lifesaving care they needed, but it was refused. Both boys died within a day. All three were buried in the same grave.[30]

Despite the head of the UN in Syria being personally shown the evidence of starvation and lack of medical care, to Khaled's horror dozens more people starved to death in Madaya, even after the global outcry over his photos and videos. 'We lost our trust in the UN. I feel angry they let us down, and then just rushed in to save their faces into front of the international community. But now we are again seeing things beginning to repeat themselves,' he said bitterly in September 2016. 'We need to maintain our outrage, so the UN is forced to fix its own mechanisms to meet the needs of people, not only in Madaya, but in other areas in Syria. Starting from the UN Security Council and all the way down.'

Khaled hopes that one day the story of what had happened to Madaya would be used as evidence to charge the Syrian government with war crimes. 'No matter what I sacrificed it was worth it,' he says firmly. 'One day, when the Bashar Al Assad government falls, this documentation will be used to indict them in the courts of The Hague, God willing.'

*

The siege of Madaya continued until April 2017, when the regime retook the town. More than 3700 people, including Khaled's colleagues Muhammad Darwish and Muhammad Yousef, chose to be forcibly displaced to Idlib rather than submit to Assad's rule. In total, 81 people in Madya died due to a lack of food during the nearly two-year siege.[31]

The Syrian regime continued to impose surrender or starve tactics on other opposition-held towns throughout Syria, including Daraya, Al Waer, Eastern Aleppo and Eastern Ghouta. Hundreds of thousands of Syrian civilians were denied food and medical care as punishment for refusing to submit to Assad's rule.

Khaled and his family still live in Perth, Australia. After he has mastered English, he hopes to return to working as a nurse.

CHAPTER 9

THOSE LEFT BEHIND
Assia, Huda, Yazmin and Ibrahim

In 2015 and early 2016, nearly a million people arrived in Germany claiming asylum, the majority of them Syrians fleeing the civil war. But many families could not afford to send everyone to Europe, so they split up, with the hope that those left behind would follow soon after. However, with Germany overwhelmed by the sheer number of refugees, family reunification was not a priority. This left tens of thousands of Syrian families across the Middle East struggling to survive and suffering the heartbreak of being separated from their loved ones.

Amman, Jordan, March 2016

Seven-year-old Yazen stood next to his mother and looked out at the busy backstreets of the Jordanian capital, Amman. It was early, and hordes of schoolchildren headed off to their morning classes. Yazen's mother, Assia, looked pained as she watched the kids trot off for a day of learning – her little boy had never stepped inside a classroom. As they were Syrian refugees, the local school wouldn't let him attend, and they couldn't afford private education. 'I brought him some exercise books and I photocopy papers for him, so he

can learn how to write with me,' she told me sadly, looking down at Yazen, who was sitting in her lap. The curly-haired little boy flicked through the textbook his mother had bought him. He was wearing a Batman jumper and smiled at me cheekily through his long eyelashes.

Assia had been doing her best, trying to come up with lessons for him to work on at home. 'I teach him the letters, then after that I gave him grades, and I also encourage him with gifts and stars,' she explained proudly, showing us Yazen's workbook. 'I teach him math, in a way, so I ask him to draw triangles and squares, something like that.' Yazen's 15-year-old sister, Niveen, was quiet and withdrawn. She hadn't been to school since they fled to Jordan four years ago. 'Back in Syria she was a very good student, Assia said quietly, tears running down her cheeks. 'I talked to the principal, to the education administration; no one helped!'

Syrian refugees are not allowed to work in Jordan, but Assia's husband, Faris, had been doing some illegal labouring work to help the family get by. The previous year, Assia said, he had been picked up by the Jordanian authorities and threatened with deportation to Syria, a terrifying prospect for Faris, who had been arrested and tortured by Assad's security forces. So, nine months ago, Faris had packed a small bag and hugged Assia, Niveen and Yazen tightly. They sold their house in southern Syria and spent all their savings on a plane ticket to Istanbul for Faris. From there, he would take the bus to Izmir in Turkey and use the last cash they had to pay for one seat on board a smuggler's boat heading to Greece. 'I asked him to go to Europe, because the education is better for the kids there. Education is the most important thing for my kids. It was very hard for me when he left. It took me a while to accept the fact that he is away, now I'm carrying his responsibility here,' explained Assia. Each time Faris called, Yazen asked his father how much longer he would be gone for. 'Then my husband will start crying and he won't be able to stay on the line with him,' Assia told me quietly.

Assia had been trying to make money by cooking Syrian food and selling it to her neighbours, and Niveen would always help. It was the only kind of work Assia could do while also looking after the kids and teaching them what she knew; but she still was not making enough for them to survive.

'I live only for my kids. I need to take them to Europe, and after that, I don't care if I'll die, that's it. Doesn't matter to me anymore,' she said, crying.

I watched as the two spent hours stirring pots and carefully slicing up zucchinis and stuffing them with mince. They made huge platters of food to feed big families sharing a weekend meal. Assia beamed with pride as she handed over the food, profusely thanking her customers for the work. They ate the leftovers, just the three of them, on a mat on the floor of their flat, the noises of happy families in the apartment block next door drifting through the window.

This phenomenon of family separation was being repeated for thousands of the poorest Syrian refugee families spread across Lebanon and Turkey. 'You've had young men, fathers, the eldest male, or husbands leaving their families, not because they wanted to, but because they didn't want to put the rest of the family at risk,' Andrew Harper, the UNHCR's chief official in Jordan, told me. 'Many families also only had enough to pay the smuggler for one trip. So they left their families here in order to get to Europe, where they hoped to get asylum and then to be able to sponsor the rest of the family as soon as they could. We are doing what we can to support family reunification, but when you are speaking about hundreds of thousands of people, every refugee has a story. Every refugee has a nightmare.'

In a crumbling apartment block on the other side of town, 22-year-old Syrian refugee Huda sat despondent, her head in her hands. She had invited me over to hear her experience but broke down as soon as she started to talk. Huda has three small sons: a four-year-old, a two-year-old and an eight-month-old. Desperate to get ahead, and with no rights to work in Jordan, she and her husband decided that he should go to Germany and send for them once he had a job. But it hadn't worked out like that. Huda's husband was still stuck in a German refugee camp with no work rights, and they had no hope of being reunited anytime soon. Huda was now struggling to pay the rent and buy enough food to feed her boys. 'The kids get sick a lot, it's not easy,' she told me, wiping tears from her cheeks.

The small two-room apartment had no toys for these children, no balls, no books. There was barely any furniture – just a few

mattresses that served as couches during the day and beds at night. Huda's four-year-old son walked over and put his arm around his crying young mother. She tried to smile reassuringly at him through her tears, but he was not fooled. 'Mama? Mama?' he said, touching her wet cheeks.

'I've got no one to go to, because there is no one here for me,' Huda exclaimed despairingly. 'Now I can't take it anymore. I feel I'm gonna explode or die; it's been seven months and it's hard, can't take it anymore. I go to sleep crying, I get up crying, I don't know. This is how I feel!'

The extremely high demand for visa appointments on the German embassy website meant there were no vacant spots until October – eight months away. Yazmin, a 25-year-old Syrian mother of four, was so desperate to be reunited with her husband, she waited outside the German embassy to see if anyone could help her. Turned away at the gate, she said she was then approached by a man in the street who promised he could get her an appointment. 'This was four months ago!' she said desperately. 'He said, "Yes, I can set up appointment for you, there are many available." He took my money but then disappeared. And now he's not answering my calls.' My Jordanian translator, Sara, gently explained to Yazmin that it was probably a scam. Yazmin listened, ashen-faced, nodding. She had still been holding out a bit of hope it was real; tears started running down her cheeks as the devastation set in. 'After my husband travelled, I sold everything – stove, the oven, blankets – just to pay the rent, and now I can't. It's been two months without paying, and the landlord had said, "That's it. I can't wait. I'll ask you to get out,"' cried Yazmin.

The worst part, she told us, was that her husband was severely depressed in Germany, beside himself with guilt for leaving them and the thought of the reunion taking so long. 'He is telling me that he felt so bad that he had left us, whenever he hears the kids he will say, "What I've done? I've destroyed my own life with this immigration idea,"' she said. In many ways, this reality was worse than when she was trapped in Syria, explained Yazmin. 'Even in Syria during the war, we had him with us, he used to protect us, he will look after us. Now he is not with us,' she said, cuddling her toddler in her lap. 'There is no war here, but we miss him.'

Of all the Syrian refugee stories I had covered in the past year, these ones in Amman were by far the most heartbreaking. Every mother I spoke to was in a state of complete despair.

And then my translator and I met Yazmin's neighbour Ibrahim. 'His story is even worse than mine,' Yazmin said, leading us down her road to a small ground-floor apartment. We knocked at the door and Ibrahim, in his early 30s, opened it and invited us in. We were soon joined by Lama, his wife, holding their one-year-old girl, and the couple's two young sons, Bilal, aged four, and two-year-old Yakoub. But they actually have three sons. They began to tell us the story of Hamze, their eldest child, who was nine years old. Hamze hadn't been to school since they had fled Syria in 2012. So in August 2015, when Ibrahim's brother was heading to Turkey to try to make it to Europe, they decided to send Hamze with him. Ibrahim showed us a photo of the night he said goodbye to Hamze at Amman airport. Hamze has a green backpack on and is wearing his best clothes, a black and white checked shirt with a collar and new jeans. Ibrahim's top lip started trembling as he talked about how difficult it was to say goodbye to their young son. 'I was told, before my son travelled to Germany on August the 8th, last year, that after four or five months, you could join your kid in Germany legally,' explained Ibrahim sadly.

But it had now been eight months. To their horror, when Hamze reached Germany, the nine-year-old was separated from his uncle and placed with a foster family in a small town near Nuremberg. Ibrahim had no idea how to be reunited with his son. 'It's hard,' he said, choking up. He felt deeply guilty. Neither he nor his wife had thought the separation would last this long. 'Every time we sit down to eat, we remember Hamze, so we will start crying,' Lama, Hamze's mother, told us with tears in her eyes. 'I miss him very much, I'll never forget him. He is one of us, Hamze, now he is away, I miss talking to him, I want to go and see him, I miss him a lot...I love him.' Lama was now sobbing.

'Here there was no school for him. We've tried so hard to get him to go to school, but we couldn't!' Ibrahim said, leaning over and trying to comfort his distraught wife. Lama added anxiously, 'Life is much better for him over there. He has everything. His own room. Food, clothes. We are worried he will forget us. Over there he gets everything he wants.'

Twice a week, Hamze called on Skype with the help of his foster brother, and he was due to call soon. We stayed a while and drank the coffee Lama had made for us, playing with Hamze's two little brothers. When Lama's phone started ringing, she jumped straight up. 'Hamze! Hi, son! Are you okay? I miss you a lot, son!' Lama greeted her nine-year-old.

'Me too, Mama,' said Hamze in a small voice.

'Do you miss me a lot? Yeah? Hamze? Answer me, son. I miss you a lot. You are my darling...How is the foster mum?'

'She's okay, thank God,' replied Hamze.

'Oh, thank God, my darling,' says Lama. She put the phone in front of Yakoub.

'Hi, Hamze, how are you?' piped up little Yakoub.

'I'm missing you!' Hamze told him.

Lama passed the phone to her husband.

'How are you, Dad?' asked Hamze, sounding mature beyond his years.

Ibrahim could barely get a word out. 'We miss you, son,' he said, before his face crumpled up and he started to cry.

On the other end, Hamze began to bawl too.

The other three children sat quietly and watched their parents collapse in tears with their brother. It was a heartbreaking scene. Ibrahim and Lama said a tearful goodbye to their son and hung up. They profoundly regretted sending Hamze away and wished he could just come back to Amman. 'I don't wish this on anyone. I want to see Hamze, to reunite with him, we want to be with him, even if he is returned back to us,' Lama told me as we said goodbye. 'I didn't expect this delay, it's taking such a long time, nearly a year! If I knew it would be like that I wouldn't have sent him.'

My translator, Sara, had a contact at the German embassy in Amman. We called him the next morning and told him the awful stories of the families we had met. He replied that German authorities had been inundated with hundreds of thousands of requests to reunify desperate families like Hamze's. The official insisted he could do nothing from the Amman end, that all the immigration issues had to go through Berlin.

Ibrahim had been given the email for a lawyer in Germany that Hamze's foster family said had been assigned as his legal guardian.

He couldn't email or call himself, because of the language barrier, so we got in touch on his behalf, passing on the desperate messages from Hamze's parents, including the fact that they just would like him to be sent home if his case was going to take much longer. A few days later we heard back from the lawyer. He assured us that Hamze was doing very well with the foster family, but the nine-year-old's asylum application – a prerequisite for family reunification – could still take several months. The lawyer promised to use a translator and speak with Hamze's parents soon.

Ibrahim called us a few weeks later to let us know he had heard from the German lawyer. There was still no news on Hamze's asylum application, but he was going to school and learning German and Turkish from his foster family. Ibrahim thought they should wait a bit longer to see if the family could be reunited in Germany, before sending Hamze back to Jordan, where the schooling would end. He thanked us sadly and said he would update us when there was news.

Meanwhile, Ibrahim and Lama kept up their weekly Skype calls with their son, while promising they would all be together again very soon.

*

Hamze's parents waited 13 more months before they were finally reunited with their son in Germany. They had been separated for nearly two years. The whole family now lives together in Germany.

CHAPTER 10

A WAR ON CIVILIANS
The People of Yemen

It has been described as the 'hidden' or 'forgotten' war. Compared with Syria or the fight against ISIS in Iraq, Yemen has received a minuscule amount of attention from policymakers and the media – despite the UN labelling it as the worst humanitarian disaster on the planet.[1]

Yemen is a country of 29 million people, positioned on the tip of the southern Arabian peninsula. A neighbour of Saudi Arabia, it holds a strategically important position right next to the Gulf of Aden, gateway to one of the world's busiest shipping routes, and a crucial path for regional oil shipments.

The neglect of Yemen is partly due to how difficult the country has been for reporters to access, with large parts of it under aerial bombardment, countless active front lines and a real threat of kidnapping. In addition, as the list of war crimes committed by the Saudi-led coalition has grown, the Saudis have actively worked to block journalists and independent human rights observers from visiting the country, which it keeps under a tight air and sea blockade.[2]

Another reason this war has felt 'unseen' is that, unlike in Syria, where much of the population has a smartphone and can

upload videos of the latest atrocities to Twitter and Facebook, Yemen is the poorest country in the Middle East, and many citizens live without access to this technology. Despite these hurdles, Yemeni and international human rights observers have undertaken herculean efforts to meticulously document the cost of this war.

The war in Yemen can be traced back to the Arab Spring of 2011. That year, a popular uprising ousted Yemen's long-serving president, Ali Abdullah Saleh, who had ruled the country for more than 30 years. The political infighting continued, and in early 2015, the Iran-aligned armed Houthi rebels from Yemen's Zaidi Shia minority seized control of the Yemeni capital, Sanaa. Large sections of the Yemeni military, including the air force and the elite Republican Guard, switched their loyalty to the Houthis and forced Saleh's replacement, Abdrabbuh Mansour Hadi, into exile.[3]

In March 2015, Saudi Arabia, alarmed at the Houthis controlling large swathes of their southern neighbour, led a coalition – backed by the US and the UK – that began bombing Yemen, seeking to restore President Hadi's rule. The resulting war has led to the deaths of tens of thousands of civilians from airstrikes and starvation. Scared of losing access to the country to carry out lifesaving aid work, the UN has had to play a careful game with Saudi Arabia, which has essentially held the keys to Yemen, obstructing entry for humanitarian workers and aid deliveries whenever it pleases.[4]

In late January 2016, a leaked UN report painted a horrifying picture of what life was now like inside Yemen. Within the 51-page assessment, a panel of experts on the country accused the Saudi-led coalition of targeting civilians with airstrikes in a 'widespread and systematic' manner.[5] The detail was chilling. Civilians had been 'chased and shot at by helicopters'. Refugee camps, weddings, buses, schools, medical facilities, mosques, markets, factories and food-storage warehouses were reportedly among the civilian targets bombed by the Saudi-led coalition – actions that would constitute war crimes under international law.[6] And when they weren't being attacked, civilians were being 'deliberately starved' as a war tactic, the report found, with more than 80 per cent of the

population in dire need of food, water and other aid. 'Not a single humanitarian pause to alleviate the suffering of the Yemeni people has been fully observed by any Yemeni party or by the coalition,' the report read. By the start of 2016, more than 5800 Yemeni civilians had already been killed, with 60 per cent of those deaths attributed to 'air-launched explosive weapons' – bombs dropped from the sky by coalition planes.

Amnesty International's senior crisis response adviser, Donatella Rovera, explained in January 2016, 'We actually have said that war crimes have been committed. We didn't even put that in the conditional, because our investigation on the ground very clearly showed evidence of war crimes. Notably the indiscriminate bombardment of civilian neighbourhoods.' Rovera, who visited Yemen twice in 2015 to investigate what was happening on the ground, described the loss of civilian life and damage to civilian infrastructure in Yemen as 'absolutely staggering'. 'The kind of argument that we are hearing from the Saudi-led coalition, that they are only bombing places where there are combatants, is absolutely not true,' Rovera said. 'It is not true in the areas round the capital, where residential neighbourhoods are being bombed, day in, day out at all. It is not true in a place like Sa'dah, where the city itself, as well as its surroundings, have really been reduced to rubble for the most part.'

The coalition conducting the airstrikes on Yemen is an alliance of Sunni Arab countries, led primarily by Saudi Arabia and the United Arab Emirates, with Kuwait, Bahrain, Qatar, Sudan and Egypt also giving support. When the campaign first began in March 2015, Saudi Arabia deployed 100 fighter jets for the war effort, with the UAE dispatching 30 fighter jets to take part in the strikes.

It was the Nobel Peace Prize–winning US president Barack Obama who firmly backed Saudi Arabia when it announced the air campaign, authorizing US 'logistical and intelligence support' for the bombing 'in support of actions to defend against Houthi violence'. 'The United States coordinates closely with Saudi Arabia and our Gulf Cooperation Council partners on issues related to their security and our shared interests,'

Obama's National Security Council spokesperson Bernadette Meehan said in a statement on 25 March 2015.[7] There had been 'very little' debate over US involvement, reported the *New York Times*.[8] The US was keen to placate the Saudis in the wake of the Obama administration's signing of the nuclear deal with the Gulf kingdom's archenemy Iran.

The UK prime minister David Cameron and his government echoed the Obama administration, pledging the utmost support to the Saudis' operation and confirming that the Saudis were flying UK-manufactured aircraft over Yemen. 'We have a significant infrastructure supporting the Saudi air force generally and if we are requested to provide them with enhanced support – spare parts, maintenance, technical advice, resupply – we will seek to do so,' declared UK foreign secretary Philip Hammond one day after the coalition began its bombing campaign.[9] Britain would support the campaign, said Hammond, 'in every practical way short of engaging in combat'.[10]

To top it off, on 14 April 2015, the UN Security Council passed resolution 2216, which noted a request from the now-exiled president of Yemen, Abdrabbuh Mansour Hadi, calling for military intervention – this has since been used by the Saudis and their western allies as legal justification for the war. 'President Hadi has therefore requested and consented to Saudi assistance in Yemen in broad terms. As such, that consent provides a legal basis for the Saudi military intervention,' argued the UK Foreign and Commonwealth Office in 2016.[11] In the eyes of the west, this was a war that had the approval it needed – the *rules-based international* order' allowed for this one-sided, brutal air campaign on Yemen, which saw the poorest country in the Middle East essentially become a military training ground for the richest country in the region.

I

I finally had the chance to report from inside Yemen in July 2016. Our Yemenia flight from Amman, Jordan, to the Yemeni capital, Sanaa, should have only taken three hours. But Yemen does not control its own airspace. The only way our plane would be allowed

to land in Sanaa was if we first complied with a mandatory stopover at Saudi Arabia's Bisha airport. So, two hours into our journey, we began to descend, slowly coming in over the dry, barren Saudi desert until we landed at a small domestic terminal in what felt like the middle of nowhere.

Many of the travellers around me looked nervous. Most people on this flight were Yemenis – and for the past year, the Saudi Arabian–led coalition had been bombing their country on a near daily basis, killing thousands of civilians and decimating their infrastructure. Now they were about to come face to face with their oppressors. The plane door swung open and two tall Saudi intelligence officers climbed on board, each dressed in starched white robes with a red and white *shemagh* on their head. They started down the aisles, stopping at each passenger to slowly check all of their documents and make sure there were no unapproved passengers. Outside, more intelligence officers opened the cargo hold to search everything being brought into Yemen.

I was also nervous that this could be the end of my trip. It had taken months for us to get permission to visit Yemen, with just a few western journalists allowed on this flight recently. The intelligence officer examined my passport carefully and tossed it back quickly. He and his colleagues were much more interested in questioning several young Yemeni men who had been pulled aside. Eventually, they were allowed to return to their seats, and after several hours, the Saudis finally disembarked from our aircraft and allowed us to continue on our journey.

A year earlier, in April 2015, the pilot of an Iranian aircraft en route to Yemen had refused to land at Bisha to allow the Saudis to inspect his plane. To prevent him landing at Sanaa's only airport, the Saudis bombed both the take-off and landing runways.[12] The runways had since been repaired, but as our plane touched down, we were welcomed by the sight of the burnt-out shell of an aircraft that had been destroyed in that attack. It was an ominous forewarning of what the Saudis have done to this country.

We were warmly greeted by Hassan, our government minder. The Houthis, Iranian-aligned rebels from the Zaidi minority religious group who control Sanaa, had assigned him to follow us wherever we went – adhering to this strict supervision is the only

way reporters can access the areas the Houthis control. Outside the terminal, we piled our camera gear into our driver Mohamad's van. A jovial, heavy-set guy with a handlebar moustache, Mohamad reassuringly patted the AK-47 wedged in next to his seat and promised to 'look after us'. Seven months earlier, an employee of the International Committee of the Red Cross had been abducted by unidentified gunmen while on her way to work in Sanaa; and in the past, tribes in Yemen had abducted foreigners to use as 'leverage' in negotiations with the government, while militants linked to Al Qaeda forces had also claimed credit for kidnappings.[13]

We saw Houthi checkpoints all over the capital, manned overwhelmingly by bored teenage rebel fighters with AK-47s slung around their skinny shoulders and large wads of khat leaves, a mild stimulant, bulging in their cheeks. You have to be either extremely brave or perhaps ignorant of history to pick a fight with the people of Yemen. They have a long and proud warrior tradition – more people here carry guns, per capita, than in any other country except America. With their overwhelming airpower, the Saudis had been banking on an easy victory here – Saudi diplomats reportedly assured their US counterparts that the war would be over within six weeks.[14] But by the time of our visit, it had been raging for 16 months.

While the Saudi-led coalition and its Hadi government allies had been slowly taking more ground in the south and moving steadily north, Yemen's most populated areas in the north-west, including the key strongholds of Sanaa, Ibb and Taiz, were all still controlled by the Houthis. The coalition was enforcing a strict air and naval blockade on rebel-held areas, with very little getting in or out without the Saudis' approval. Flights were restricted and shipping movements slowed. The Saudis claimed the blockade was designed to stop weapons flowing to the Iranian-backed Houthis, but for a country that imports 90 per cent of its food, a humanitarian disaster was looming.

As we drove through Sanaa, we saw massive gaping holes where homes, public buildings and factories had once stood – all wiped out in the past year of airstrikes by the Saudi coalition. Even buildings in Sanaa's World Heritage–listed old city had been targeted. These towering, majestic rammed-earth structures dated back to the 11th century. Described by UNESCO as the 'world's oldest jewels of

Islamic urban landscape', they have distinctive, intricate white detail on their brown brick that gives them the appearance of a gingerbread house. But now several had been turned to dust, their occupants killed in their beds.[15]

'It's not the airstrike that we fear as much as the anticipation,' said political analyst Hisham Al Omeisy as he walked me around the destroyed Faj Attan neighbourhood near his home in Sanaa. The young father of two had become one of the best-known faces of the war to the outside world. Hisham had a popular Twitter account where he regularly posted videos of his family trying to live a normal life in a place where airstrikes suddenly rained down from the skies. It was a window into a world that was increasingly cut off, not just by fighting but also by Saudi restrictions that made it harder for people to travel into and out of Yemen. 'Usually before an airstrike, there are drones buzzing the sky, selecting targets on the ground,' Hisham explained. 'Sometimes the airstrike doesn't happen. But for an hour you've been sitting waiting for an airstrike, holding your breath. Imagine holding it for hours in anticipation of an airstrike that never came? It takes a toll, a huge mental toll. You don't sleep, you are very tense and nervous, you are anxious.'

The Saudi-led coalition stands accused of ignoring the risk to civilians when striking Houthi military targets in densely populated areas. Faj Attan is one of the worst-hit neighbourhoods in Sanaa, with nearly every block scarred by giant craters where houses used to stand. Hisham could clearly remember the day a huge Saudi-led coalition strike on a nearby Houthi weapons-storage facility killed dozens of civilians here. 'It actually happened in the morning. The kids were playing in the streets,' he recalled. 'I was having coffee right next to my window, and I suddenly saw this huge ball of fire. I was in total disbelief just standing there – and then the pressure wave came in, and it just knocked out the window right in my face and knocked me down.' The moment of the massive strike was captured on video, with a deafening boom and a mushroom cloud that shot high into the air, the blast blowing out the windows of homes for kilometres. More than 25 were killed and close to 400 injured in the attack.[16]

Despite the relentless airstrikes in the past year, Hisham said he believed Yemeni support for the Houthis had only increased in

the face of the Saudi attacks. 'They thought they could intimidate us. They could crush us. But they couldn't,' he said, smiling. 'They thought people would be driven by fear and surrender. What they ended up doing was really ticking off people – and now they are really mad and seeking vengeance.'

Hisham spoke frankly about what he described as a 'warrior' culture within Yemeni society. 'It's part of who we are,' he explained. 'When I was 12, my dad gave me a gun as a gift. When I was 16, he gave me a machine-gun. Ever since I was six, I've been carrying a *jambiya*,' he said, pulling out the small curved dagger that many Yemeni men carry tucked into the front of their trousers. 'It's very sharp! This is a very highly militarised society.'

Hisham took us back to his house where we met his sons, aged six and eight. We climbed up to the rooftop, and the three of them pointed out all the places they had seen bombs fall in recent months. The boys had trouble sleeping at night, constantly haunted by the fear of being hit by an airstrike. 'If I shut the door hard enough – they flinch now,' Hisham said sadly. 'I remember my wife was setting up the table for lunch, and she brought down the cup hard on the table, and my son just bolted out of the room...thinking it was a bomb.'

I met with Jamie McGoldrick, the chief UN aid official in Yemen, at the heavily guarded UN headquarters in Sanaa. The fast-talking, passionate Scot has a reputation for getting out from behind the blast-proof walls of his compound and travelling all around Yemen to document the cost this war is having on civilians.

McGoldrick told me UN data showed nearly 50 per cent of the casualties caused by fighting and airstrikes in Yemen to that point were civilians. 'When you visit the country here, the hospitals, the schools, public buildings have not been spared in this war, and that's been a tragedy. I think it's one of the hallmarks of this crisis, where there hasn't been enough care and attention given to protecting those and the people who use them,' he said.

McGoldrick described the Yemeni healthcare system as being on the verge of 'total collapse. The authorities here cannot provide the resources; they don't have the money to pay for medical services, to pay for health workers, to pay for resources to be imported to service these places, and that's where we are and that's why it's collapsing.'

The Saudi-led blockade was crippling Yemen's health system, because import restrictions had resulted in the supply of medicine being dramatically cut – with critical shortages of medications across the country. What little medicine was available had become so overpriced, the majority of the population couldn't afford it. A UN report leaked in August 2016 alleged that Houthi rebels had been diverting US$100 million a month from Yemen's Central Bank to support the war effort.[17] So while the money was going on guns and soldiers, the health ministry was unable to buy the drugs the hospitals required. Médecins Sans Frontières had stepped in and promised to airfreight critically needed drugs and equipment for the next six months – but even they couldn't guarantee a steady supply of fuel for hospital generators.

The lives of more than 4000 patients with kidney failure were also at risk after the Saudi blockade had prevented the importation of critical supplies for dialysis treatment. MSF had spent US$2 million over six months bringing in 240 tonnes of medical supplies for dialysis centres, without which thousands of patients would slowly die.[18] Meanwhile, in August 2016, the UN announced that more than 40,000 cancer patients in Yemen would no longer receive the medication they required because the Saudi banking restrictions on Houthi areas had dried up the funds to buy the drugs.[19] 'There are many people here dying silent deaths,' Jamie McGoldrick said bitterly. 'We're talking about the silent numbers who'll die because we didn't give them the drugs to prevent them dying of blood pressure problems, insulin problems, or cancer patients. They're dying deaths of preventable diseases that never should happen and that'll be on our conscience.'

In the packed hallways of Sanaa's Al Thawra hospital, ten-year-old Murad Sami waited with his father to get an X-ray. They had come from Saada, a northern city heavily bombed and shelled by Saudi forces. Murad had large sad brown eyes and a recently shaved head. Fresh wounds on his forehead marked where shrapnel had perforated his skull two weeks ago. 'I was playing football with my cousin and some other kids just next to our house,' Murad said softly, describing the moment he and his friends had found a shiny silver object in the grass. 'We didn't know what it was. It looked like a bottle. My cousin picked it up. And then it exploded.' The

object was a cluster bomb, and it blew up in the hands of his nine-year-old cousin Abdurazag, causing deep injuries to the little boy's stomach and thighs. 'We took him to the hospital; he was there for two days and then he died the third day,' Murad's father explained sadly, showing me a photo of Abdurazag. A skinny little thing, the nine-year-old stands solemnly in the picture, his small arms held straight by his sides as he stares into the camera.

Cluster bombs contain hundreds of little bomblets that scatter over a wide area. Their wide dispersal pattern and frequent failure to detonate on impact have been proven to disproportionately harm and kill civilians. In 2008, 102 countries, including the UK and Australia, signed a convention prohibiting the use of these deadly weapons – but Saudi Arabia didn't. The Saudis had repeatedly denied using cluster munitions in Yemen, but in May 2016, Amnesty International uncovered evidence that the Saudi-led coalition had dropped UK-manufactured cluster bombs in the north of the country.[20]

Amnesty researchers discovered scores of unexploded UK-manufactured BL-755 cluster bomblets 'strewn over a wide area' near a farm in Hajjah province, close to the Saudi Arabia border. The NGO documented the cases of 16 Yemeni civilians, including nine children, killed or maimed by cluster bombs in Yemen since the coalition bombardment had begun a year earlier – the incidents taking place days, weeks or sometimes months after the bombs were dropped by coalition forces in Yemen. Amnesty said the coalition members Saudi Arabia and the UAE both still held stockpiles of these now-illegal weapons, which the UK stopped manufacturing and exporting in 1989. The US, which also refused to sign the ban on cluster munitions, had continued to sell them to Saudi Arabia, with Riyadh reportedly buying millions of dollars' worth in recent years.

The cluster bomb that tore Murad's cousin to pieces was now also embedded in Murad's brain. 'There are two pieces of metal,' his father explained, pointing at two different spots on Murad's head. 'One is very deep and the second one is shallow. We hope the doctor can remove it. The surgery is very crucial for him to survive, because it has gone inside the skull very close to his brain. It has to be removed.' The ten-year-old had bad headaches, consistent nausea and trouble sleeping, but the brain surgery would cost the family

hundreds of dollars, which they didn't have. They had spent what little money they had on travelling to the capital to see if anyone could assist them.

'God willing, someone will help us,' Murad's father said, shrugging helplessly. They joined the long queue outside the MSF office and patiently sat down to wait their turn.

Down the hall in a crowded ward, I met eight-year-old Faris. He was laid out flat on his back in a bed by the window, with pins through his left upper thigh holding together a break in his bone. Deep burns scarred both his thighs, his little tummy and chest, and his right arm and left foot. All this meant Faris couldn't move, and the hospital had no television or books to distract him. The stiflingly hot room had no fans, let alone air conditioning. The eight-year-old stared up at the ceiling, a look of utter defeat in his eyes. His grandfather Salah sat next to the bed, cradling his grandson's small hand in his own.

The airstrike had happened when they were sleeping in their home in Al Jawf province, Salah explained. 'It was so difficult, so difficult,' he said, shaking his head at the memory. Faris had been the worst injured. His family had pulled him from the ruins of his home, but help hadn't arrived for hours. 'There were no cars. We tried to call the ambulance, but no one was able to come and rescue us straight away, because they were scared they might be hit again. They didn't rescue the injured till the morning at dawn,' explained Salah. 'The dead had to be picked up in pieces.' Salah leant in and whispered that Faris's mother had been killed in the attack, along with his five-year-old brother and three of his aunties. Salah had not yet told his grandson about these deaths. I asked if there were any Houthi military sites near their home. 'No,' Salah told me. 'There are mujahedeen in the markets where we go shopping, but they go one way and we go another.'

We sat with Salah and shared our cold water with him and Faris. Faris suddenly turned and told his grandfather in a small voice, 'I want to go out and play.'

Salah smiled reassuringly and patted the boy's hand, in a way that showed this was not the first time Faris had made this request. 'You know, we will take you home,' he told him. 'You will go and play, and go for a walk.'

Faris's next question to his grandfather took my breath away. 'Will I live?' asked the eight-year-old.

'Of course, you will live,' Salah answered, squeezing his grandson's hand. 'God will heal you. You will go home, play with other kids and study...' Salah trailed off, his voice overcome with emotion, before offering one more incentive for Faris to change the subject. 'I'll buy you a bike, huh? Okay? You will go with your friends and play.'

Two nurses came bustling into the ward with a metal cart full of fresh bandages and a large bottle of antiseptic. The dressings on Faris's wounds needed to be changed every second day to prevent infection – an incredibly painful procedure. 'Go away, please!' the eight-year-old begged as they started to peel away his old bandages. 'Please, doctor, don't!' Two nurses held his little arms while Faris writhed and cried when they applied Betadine to his wounds. 'Oh God, it burns! You're hurting me, you're hurting me! For God's sake, for God's sake!' he screamed, tears streaming down his cheeks.

Salah sat close to Faris, murmuring soothing words to console his grandson. But it had no effect against the searing pain as the eight-year-old's wounds were exposed to the burning disinfectant. The only worse thing than witnessing this was knowing that Faris would have to endure the same procedure every second day for countless weeks to come.

With Faris's painful screams echoing behind us, we quietly left the ward to check in with Murad and his father, who had just come from the MSF consulting rooms. Murad gave us a shy smile as his father explained that the charity had promised to fund the brain surgery needed to remove the cluster-bomb shrapnel from the ten-year-old's head. 'Thanks to God, we're hoping the surgery will be successful,' said his father joyfully, with his arm around Murad. 'It would have been hard, because we would have had to sell our belongings to pay. We are all a bit afraid for his life, because don't know if the surgery will go well or not...God willing it will!'

After revelations by both Amnesty and Human Rights Watch over the use of cluster bombs in Yemen, the Obama administration quietly blocked the sale of more cluster munitions to Saudi Arabia in May 2016.[21] But the hold on the sale of these deadly weapons was short-lived. In June, the US Congress voted to continue selling

cluster bombs to the Saudis, with Congress members concerned the ban would 'stigmatize' the munitions. 'The Department of Defense strongly opposes this amendment,' Republican congressman Rodney Frelinghuysen argued on the floor of the house. 'They advise us that it would stigmatize cluster munitions, which are legitimate weapons with clear military utility.'[22]

It took the British government seven months to admit that UK-manufactured cluster bombs had been dropped by their Saudi allies on Yemen. On 19 December 2016, in a speech to the House of Commons, UK defence secretary Sir Michael Fallon confirmed that a 'limited' number of cluster munitions exported from the UK in the 1980s had been dropped in Yemen, 'including by a coalition aircraft in the incident alleged by Amnesty International'.[23] Defending Britain's support for Saudi Arabia, the defence secretary insisted the Saudis hadn't breached international law because they had claimed the 'munitions were used against a legitimate military target'. No evidence was given to support this claim.

After the Saudis had denied use of the banned weapon several times, they finally admitted it, issuing a statement amusingly titled 'Coalition forces supporting legitimacy in Yemen confirm that all coalition countries aren't members to the Convention on Cluster Munitions'.[24]

Saudi Arabia was not just dusting off decades-old British cluster bombs to use in Yemen. In 2015, the Gulf kingdom became the world's third-largest military spender – after the US and China – spending US$87 billion on arms and aircraft.[25] So not only had the US and the UK given Saudi Arabia diplomatic cover for their bombing campaign on Yemen, they had also made billions out of it. Saudi Arabia was already one of the biggest buyers of UK defence equipment before the war began, but the supply of British weapons accelerated as the airstrikes got underway, with Saudi Arabia spending more than US$4.2 billion on UK arms in the first 12 months of the conflict in Yemen, from April 2015 to March 2016 – a 30-fold increase on the preceding 12-month period.[26] According to a report by a UK parliamentary committee, these arms sales included US$2.8 billion of fighter jets, US$1.1 billion of air-to-air missiles, US$79 million of bombs and US$669.9 million of military aircraft – by March 2016, Saudi Arabia reportedly had more British

fighter jets in its air force than the UK had in its own.[27] All the sales took place after the Saudi-led coalition began their airstrikes in Yemen in March 2015 and after serious human rights concerns were expressed and allegations of widespread war crimes made.[28]

But the largest supplier of weapons and aircraft to the Saudis, by far, is the United States. In 2010, US president Barack Obama signed what was then the biggest arms deal in American history, selling US$60 billion of advanced weapons and aircraft to the oppressive Gulf kingdom. Since the Saudis began their campaign against Yemen, the US government has authorized more than US$22.2 billion in weapons sales to them, including a US$1.29 billion sale of precision munitions announced in November 2015 'specifically meant to replenish stocks used in Yemen'.[29]

US arms sales to Saudi Arabia include everything from small arms and ammunition to tanks, attack helicopters, air-to-ground missiles, missile defence ships and warships – and the sales reached a historical high under Obama's presidency. A study by the US-based Center for International Policy found that since January 2009, Obama's administration had offered Saudi Arabia more than US$115 billion in weapons, other military equipment and training, the most of any US administration in the 71-year US–Saudi alliance.[30]

The receipts for these British and American weapons sales can be found among the rubble in Yemen. One of the deadliest strikes against civilians early in this war involved US-supplied weapons. On 15 March 2016, two Saudi-led coalition airstrikes hit a market in the Mastaba district of Hajjah province. According to the UN, more than 100 civilians, including 25 children, were killed.[31] Human Rights Watch investigators who visited the site discovered remnants of a US-supplied MK-84 2000-pound [900-kilogram] bomb fitted with a Joint Direct Attack Munition satellite guidance kit, also US-supplied.[32]

It's not just billions of dollars of American precision weapons that enable the Saudis to carry out this war – the Saudi coalition's bombing campaign relies on US air force fuel-tanker aircraft to refuel their warplanes. Democratic congressman Ted Lieu, who serves as a colonel in the US air force reserves, has been a vocal critic of this refuelling assistance. 'We are flying our tankers with US pilots, we are refuelling these jets of the Saudi Arabia-led military

coalition, and they are dropping bombs,' Lieu told the BBC.[33] 'But if you look at the laws of war and international law, you can be guilty of aiding and abetting war crimes.'

II

Our vehicle wound through green valleys and rocky mountain ranges as we made our way to the village of Sanaban in Dhamar province, about 150 kilometres south of the capital, Sanaa. The view out the window was pockmarked by evidence of powerful airstrikes, with destroyed homes, factories and government buildings lying in piles along each side of the highway.

It was a journey that needed to be taken with caution. Adding to the chaos and suffering in Yemen is the spectre of Al Qaeda and ISIS, with both groups exploiting the conflict and the resulting power vacuums to seize ground in the south and east of the country. Our driver told us that the frontier of Al Qaeda–held territory was about 20 kilometres from the roads we were travelling on, so we were keen to start our return journey before it got dark.

Travelling with me in our van was Osamah Alfakih, one of Yemen's leading human rights researchers at local NGO Mwatana. We were on our way to visit the scene of one of the worst alleged war crimes Osamah and his colleagues had investigated – where nine months earlier, Saudi coalition warplanes had transformed a wedding in Sanaban into a mass funeral.[34] 'Our research found that 40 civilians were killed in this airstrike, including 14 women and 13 children, and that 42 people were injured,' Osamah explained as we bumped along potholed roads on the way south. 'We found there was no purpose for targeting a wedding in that area. Only civilians were killed and injured. There are no military sites close to the targeted place. There are not even checkpoints!'

After nearly five hours of travelling, we reached the village. Sanaban is a sparsely populated town, with just a few hundred small stone houses scattered snugly along the highway. In the distance, craggy mountaintops pop sharply out of the green valley. On the edge of town, we followed a narrow muddy track up a small hill until it opened out to a clearing ahead of us, where once a home had stood. Only the charred skeleton of a building

now remained. Rubble and bricks were strewn in a 100-metre radius around the ruins, testament to the incredible force of the explosion that night.

Waiting to greet us as we stepped out of the car was 35-year-old Mohammad Jamal Al Sanabani. He shook our hands warmly, thanking us for coming. But the pleasantries were short; there was nothing at all pleasant about the purpose of our visit. 'Come, let's enter this way,' he said, and we followed him towards the remains of his family's home. The ground was still covered in remnants of the life that once existed here: a child's shoe poking out from broken bricks, a woman's scarf lying in the dirt next to broken glass, a baby's bottle half-buried in the dirt.

The celebration last October had been for the joint wedding of three of Mohammad's cousins, Moayed, Ayman and Abd Al Rahman.

Mohammad and the other guests could hear planes, he told us, as they had most nights since the war began. But Sanaban had never been hit before. In fact, some villagers had returned to the town from Sanaa in the belief that it was safer than the capital. There are dozens of videos of the celebrations that night before the plane struck. Mohammad's beaming relatives dance in a circle, holding hands as they step back and forth in time to the traditional Yemeni music. They laugh, sing and clap as the grooms waggle their hips and wave their ceremonial gold *jambiya* swords in the air. Colourful fake flowers are tacked up around the wedding tent, and large posters of the engaged brothers posing like movie stars adorn the walls. Glitter and rice are thrown. Everyone is dressed in their best clothes. I stare at each face in the clips, searching every grin and giggle and cheerful glance at the camera, as if looking for a clue of what is about to happen. But there is none – just unbridled happiness that is about to be torn apart.

The three young brides, Khetam, Hana and Jamila, were upstairs in the master bedroom. Aunts, nieces, sisters and mothers-in-law crowded the room to get a glimpse of the women in their bridal outfits. A faint buzz in the sky was heard by villagers, but in the room full of women there was no hint of what was about to happen. Hundreds of kilometres above, a pilot belonging to the Saudi-led coalition pressed a button in his aircraft. A missile weighing hundreds of kilograms began barrelling towards the house.

It was just after 9.30 pm when the missile from the coalition warplane slammed into Mohammad's father's home. The massive bomb immediately set on fire several vehicles that made up the bridal convoy, with gas cylinders causing secondary explosions around the property. Mohammad was thrown to the ground, temporarily losing consciousness from the enormous pressure of the explosions, as a massive fireball engulfed the yard. He soon came to and rushed to the main house, where he believed his five-year-old daughter, Jood, and his wife were. 'At that time the warplane was still hovering overheard,' Mohammad recalled. 'Everyone who was around was terrified they would drop another missile, so many people ran away.' Mohammad and others helped women on the ground floor break windows, so they could escape the engulfing flames. 'Inside was burning, and women were rushing to the door and were trapped. Some of them were jumping from the windows, and some jumped from the second-storey roof to escape,' he told me quietly. 'Women and children were burning in front of me while crying and screaming for help.'

Mohammad discovered his 65-year-old father dead on the ground 'swollen and split in half', while his mother was found in another part of the house, 'charred and burnt'. Eventually, he found his wife, who was not seriously hurt, but there was no trace of their daughter Jood, who had been playing in the yard with her cousins. The family searched frantically, going from house to house in the village, thinking she might have run away in fear. But no one had seen Jood. More than 24 hours after the strike, with the house still a smouldering wreck, members of Mohammad's tribe who had come to help with the rescue operation approached him and his wife. 'They said to me, "There are parts of a body, but the face cannot be recognized. Have you seen this hair clip before?"' Mohammad said sadly. 'Immediately we knew that it was our daughter Jood's hair clip, and then we knew she was dead. There was no face, no hands, only pieces of flesh.'

In all, out of the 40 people killed that night, 18 were Mohammad Jamal Al Sanabani's relatives – his daughter, his mother and father, his younger brother and nephew, plus many cousins and aunties and uncles among the dead. 'We didn't expect them to strike a wedding, because we are in a village, there are no military bases

here, no militants affiliating to any factions here,' Mohammad explained sadly as we stood in what was once a courtyard. 'I've lost all happiness in life,' he said soberly. 'We feel like we are living in a nightmare. I miss my dad and my mum, my daughter. We still can't believe the loss. Our life has become empty, without any hope.' Of the 42 people at the wedding who were wounded, many of them were children. Mohammad showed me photos of those who were rushed to hospital: children with horrific burns on their arms, legs and faces, with panicked and confused looks as they lie on hospital beds with soot covering their little bodies.

We walked through the yard, which was still filled with rubble and the burnt-out remains of cars. Mohammed pointed underneath one of the destroyed vehicles, where he said Jood's remains had been found. The doors to the house were still covered in debris, so we climbed inside a broken window to have a look at what remained. We climbed the half-destroyed stairs, bloodstains still smearing the walls where badly injured people had brushed them as they desperately rushed out. Upstairs, in the room where the brides and other female relatives had gathered, the jasmine wreaths still hung on a hook on the wall, dried and brown. 'Since the wedding day until today, we have kept it here,' Mohammad said, running his hand over the now-dead petals. 'The wedding turned into sadness, a funeral. The happiness is over.'

What makes this massive civilian toll in Yemen even more unconscionable is, apart from backing this war and providing the Saudis with much of the weaponry, British military advisers have been standing alongside the Saudis as the coalition picks its targets to bomb. Saudi foreign minister Adel Al Jubeir first revealed this in January 2016, telling reporters that British military advisers were present in the Saudi-led coalition's control rooms in the Saudi capital Riyadh as it carried out its intensive bombing raids across Yemen. The UK Ministry of Defence confirmed that British military officials, while not directly choosing targets or typing in codes for the Saudi 'smart bombs', were training their counterparts in doing so. 'We support Saudi forces through long-standing, pre-existing arrangements,' a UK Ministry of Defence spokesperson told *The Telegraph*.[35]

A UK parliamentary committee confirmed the detail of the British military adviser's assistance: 'UK liaison officers in the

air operations centre were not involved in targeting decisions, but instead conducted training on doctrine for using UK-supplied weapons systems and provided advice on targeting processes,' the UK's Minister for Defence Procurement, Philip Dunne, told a parliamentary committee.[36]

In March 2016, the *New York Times* revealed that a 45-person American military planning group with personnel in Bahrain, Saudi Arabia and the UAE was providing the Saudi operation in Yemen with 'advice and assistance'. 'We offer them coaching, but ultimately it's their operation,' Major General Carl Mundy, the deputy commander of Marines in the Middle East, told the newspaper.[37]

As time went on, the full extent of what this US military planning group was doing was leaked to reporters. The *New York Times* reported that at the flight operations room in Riyadh, Saudi commanders sat near American military officials who were providing intelligence and tactical advice. Describing a typical Saudi F-15 US-supplied warplane, the *New York Times* also wrote: 'American mechanics serviced the jet and carry out repairs on the ground. American technicians upgrade the targeting software and other classified technology, which Saudis are not allowed to touch. The pilot has likely been trained by the United States Air Force.'[38]

Just why his family had been bombed was something Mohammad Jamal Al Sanabani thought about a lot. Who had decided that his house should be targeted? Why? And what did they base it on? 'For the countries who are helping Saudi Arabia to strike Yemen, they share the same responsibility,' Mohammad said slowly. 'They are criminals as well. We won't forget them for this.' Later that night, after our long drive back to Sanaa, Mohammad emailed me photos of his daughter, Jood. Five-year-old girls who grow up in remote Yemeni villages are really no different from those in any other part of the world. In the pictures, Jood is laughing in a white party dress. Posing with her cousins in a pink floral gingham outfit with a cheeky smile. Wide-eyed, eating fairy floss with pigtails in her hair. And in the last photo, a proud-looking Mohammad holding Jood as a chubby-faced toddler.

In June 2016, the UN released its annual *Children and Armed Conflict* report, which identifies groups that 'engage in the

recruitment and use of children, sexual violence against children, the killing and maiming of children, attacks on schools and/or hospitals and attacks or threats of attacks against protected personnel, and the abduction of children'. The report documented that 60 per cent of the children killed in Yemen in the previous year were from Saudi coalition airstrikes, with 510 dead and 667 wounded.[39] It attributed 142 child deaths to the Houthis, while in some 324 incidents, the 'responsible party' for the deaths could not be identified. As a result, Saudi Arabia was placed on the UN's 2016 blacklist, alongside government forces in Afghanistan, the Democratic Republic of Congo, Somalia, Myanmar, South Sudan, Sudan and Syria.[40] Outraged, the Saudis swiftly threatened to revoke large financial contributions to UN programs throughout the Middle East if their name was not immediately deleted from the blacklist. The UN capitulated – with Secretary General Ban Ki Moon admitting to reporters that the intense pressure and threats from Riyadh had worked – and Saudi Arabia was removed from the list. 'This was one of the most painful and difficult decisions I have had to make,' Mr Ban told reporters. 'I also had to consider the very real prospect that millions of other children would suffer grievously if, as was suggested to me, countries would defund many UN programs.'[41]

Early on in the conflict, US military personnel reportedly identified why so many Yemeni civilians were being killed by Saudi warplanes – coalition jets were flying too high to accurately deliver the bombs to their targets, because inexperienced Saudi pilots were fearful of ground fire from the Houthi rebels. 'As a result, they flew at high altitudes to avoid the threat below. But flying high also reduced the accuracy of their bombing and increased civilian casualties, American officials said,' reported the *New York Times*. 'American advisers suggested how the pilots could safely fly lower, among other tactics. But the airstrikes still landed on markets, homes, hospitals, factories and ports.'[42]

Despite these concerns reportedly being raised within the first year of the war, the US continued its support of the Saudi war effort, providing crucial refuelling missions for Saudi jets and selling the Saudis massive quantities of weapons. When the Obama administration first discussed providing American support to the

Saudis, Samantha Power, the US ambassador to the UN and an expert on genocide and human rights, reportedly argued that American military support for the Yemen war might mean fewer civilian casualties.[43] It appears to have had the opposite effect.

I'd long admired Samantha Power. A former journalist turned academic, she'd written a Pulitzer Prize–winning book in 2002, *A Problem from Hell*, which examined America's failure and reluctance to prevent mass atrocities and war crimes. It had become a hugely influential text, laying out the moral imperative for the adoption of interventionist policies by governments to save lives around the world. Power had been appointed a foreign policy adviser to President Obama and then made US ambassador to the UN in 2013. It was perplexing to watch this brilliant mind, so passionate about the prevention of war crimes, becoming entangled in the Obama White House's failure to reduce violence in Syria and its appeasement of Saudi Arabia in Yemen.

I was fascinated by the fact that this human rights advocate stayed in the administration when so much of what it was doing (or was failing to do) appeared to be in sharp contrast to her own ideals. It got to the point where Power was just sending out helpless pleas on Twitter every time it became clear that Obama was incapable of acting or reluctant to: 'Strikes on hospital/school/infrastructure in #Yemen devastating for ppl already facing unbearable suffering & must end,' she tweeted in August 2016 from her official US ambassador to the UN account.[44]

Keen to hear more about her internal struggle, I emailed her in early 2019 to see if she would talk. I received a quick but blunt reply: 'Hi there. Yes I follow you on Twitter. Your tweets about me were often very harsh,' Power wrote back. Well at least she was reading them, and it was true that I hadn't failed to point out that the Obama White House's polices were in stark contrast to what she had advocated in her book. Power went on to say she was too busy finishing off her memoirs to talk.

'Dear Samantha,' I wrote back. 'Thanks for your reply. Yes, the stakes were extraordinarily high, weren't they? Aleppo, Yemen... And you had always been a bit of a hero of mine. I, like many others, had a lot of expectations riding on you – fairly or unfairly.'

She didn't reply.

III

It's not just the Saudis who have shown little regard for international law in this war – though being constantly trailed by our Houthi minder made it extremely difficult to document the war crimes they stand accused of. We were watched at all times and allowed to film only facilities approved by the Houthi Ministry of Information. One night, as we tried to sneak out and meet a human rights activist fiercely critical of the rebel group, we were stopped at the front entrance of our hotel by our friendly but firm Houthi intelligence officers, who demanded to know where we were going. No interviews would be performed without their approval.

According to the UN, there is evidence the Iranian-aligned rebel group is deliberately hiding weapons and military facilities in heavily populated areas, 'with the deliberate aim of avoiding attack. In doing so, the Houthis almost certainly deliberately endanger and expose the civilian population and civilian objects to the perils of conflict,' said a leaked UN report.[45] The rebels have also been indiscriminately shelling residential areas in the Yemeni city of Taiz and in southern Saudi Arabia, which has led to the death and injury of hundreds of civilians. Several human rights groups have also documented evidence that the Houthis have laid tens of thousands of landmines – internationally banned weapons – on front lines and around territory they hold throughout Yemen. In the southern portside town of Mokha, residents told a Reuters reporter than landmines laid by the Houthis had caused more casualties than fighting in the area. Saudi-aligned forces in the same region claim to have neutralized more than 40,000 landmines as they have advanced along the Red Sea coast.[46]

One of the Houthis' most egregious war crimes is the use of child soldiers. A panel of UN experts found that both the coalition-backed forces and the Houthi rebels have conscripted or enlisted children to participate actively in hostilities. 'In most cases, the children were between 11 and 17 years old, but there have been consistent reports of the recruitment or use of children as young as 8 years old,' said the panel.[47] The Houthis are allegedly the worst offenders, with UNICEF estimating that around 30 per cent of the fighters used by the armed group and its allies are minors.[48]

According to witnesses and sources, wrote the UN, in some areas, Houthi forces forcibly recruited children in schools, hospitals and door to door. All over Sanaa, we saw young boys – aged around 12 or 13 – standing aimlessly at Houthi checkpoints, with heavy AK-47s, half the length of their child-sized bodies, hanging over their scrawny arms.

One afternoon, as we were driving through the capital, we came across a funeral procession for a soldier killed fighting for the Houthis. Our minder was keen for us to film it. 'Show the world our martyrs who are sacrificing to defend their land!' he said proudly, as we swerved behind to join the convoy. The fleet of cars was headed by a pickup truck filled with young men pumping their fists in the air and chanting. Taped to the car bonnet, next to bouquets of pink and purple plastic flowers, was a large poster of the new martyr – a smiling young boy with curly hair and big green eyes. A child soldier.

A young mourner leant out his window to tell us that they were honouring Osama, a 16-year-old boy killed the day before by a sniper while he was fighting with the Houthi rebels on the front line, just a few hours' drive from Sanaa.

'God is great! Death to America and Israel! Victory to Islam! We don't be defeated! We won't be defeated!' the mourners chanted the Houthi slogan. *Crack-crack-crack crack-crack!* An AK-47 was fired into the air as the convoy of vehicles turned into a small street.

Osama's coffin was hoisted off the back of the truck by the crowd and carried inside his home, showered by grains of rice. We were invited inside to film. 'They want the world to witness their grief,' explained our translator.

My ABC cameraman Aaron Hollett was quickly pushed inside the house, where a room of wailing relatives sobbed and cried over the child's body. Osama's two younger brothers stood back, stony-faced, while the boy's father sobbed, leaning over the side of the casket to kiss his son's cold cheeks. A bandage was wrapped around the dead boy's head, with dried blood still caked on his face. Female relatives threw fresh jasmine leaves over Osama's body, weeping and holding each other up as many of the women collapsed in grief.

Soon it was time to take Osama to the cemetery for his burial. His brothers and father were among the men who hoisted the

wooden box containing Osama onto their shoulders and took him outside, where a large throng of people had now gathered. Osama's male relatives climbed into the pickup with the coffin, leading a procession through the streets. Mourners marched behind the truck, banging drums and letting off fireworks. When they arrived at a small blue mosque, Osama was carried inside and a sermon was given to honour his short life.

By this stage, my minder, who had been so keen for us to document the death of a Houthi soldier, had realised that this was a child fighter – definitely not something his superiors wanted the world to see. He looked panicked and started making a few calls. Aaron and I disappeared into the crowd before he could try and make us leave.

I spoke with some of Osama's fellow child soldiers, who stood guard around the building, holding their AKs. One of the boys, who looked around 14 and was wearing green and brown camouflage and several rounds of ammunition in a belt around his waist, shyly told me that, no, he never got scared. 'I'm just a fighter in the name of God,' he said firmly. 'Among many fighters who defend us against Saudi and American attacks on our country. The victory is with us who have God on our side!'

Once the sermon was over, the crowd spilt out over the front steps. But before Osama's body was taken for burial, a ceremonial dance was performed. A circle was created, and seven men lined up, slowly moving in unison with a drum beat as the rest of the crowd watched. Their AK-47s slung over their shoulders, they stepped back and forth to the beat as the drumming got faster and faster, waving their *jambiya* daggers in the air.

As the dancing continued, I was approached by Osama's father, a small wiry man with glasses, who introduced himself as Ahmad Mohamad Madhkour. He was keen to talk, angrily denouncing the foreign powers he saw as responsible for his country's suffering. Ahmad said he was willing to send his other two sons to fight for the Houthis too, explaining that, for him, the Houthis' battle against the Saudis was crucial to defeat what he saw as Sunni extremism.

'What if somebody invaded your country? Would you surrender?' Ahmad demanded angrily. 'Are you going to watch your country be destroyed and your kids and your families? All of the people of

Yemen are under siege. They have been killed by the sky and on the land. What have we done wrong to the world to be treated like this? Can anybody tell us what we've done wrong? Why is the whole world silent about Yemen?'

The grieving father turned to the crowd that had gathered around to hear him speak and raised his fist, leading them in the Houthi chant. 'God is great! Death to America and Israel! Victory to Islam! We don't be defeated! We won't be defeated!' A procession to the cemetery formed, with Ahmad leading the way for the hundreds of mourners. When we arrived, he and his other two sons carefully took Osama's white-shroud-wrapped body out of the coffin and slowly lowered it into the grave. Ahmad perched on the edge of his child's grave, wiping tears from his cheeks. He looked up to the heavens to say a prayer, as Osama's two younger brothers clutched each other tightly and sobbed. Mourners quietly filled the grave with dirt and the crowd melted away.

IV

All over Yemen, parents are burying their children. There are those like Jood and Osama, whose last moments on this earth have been filled with terror and fear. And then there are those who have quietly slipped away, as tens of thousands of Yemen's children are being starved to death. The tight Saudi-led blockade on the country has created a major humanitarian disaster – 14 million people in this country are now classified as 'food insecure', which basically means they are hungry and don't know where their next meal is coming from. As Saudi-led coalition forces surround Houthi-controlled northern Yemen, they are restricting supplies; since the blockade began, food prices have more than doubled. 'Since last year, the staple foods, such as wheat or rice, have gone up 60 per cent; cooking gas is 75 per cent more expensive than it was,' said the UN's Jamie McGoldrick.

Restricting flights and shipping to Yemen is not the only step the Saudis have taken. The coalition bombed Yemen's main seaport at Hodeidah on the Red Sea at the beginning of the war, rendering four of the port's giant cranes unusable. Unloading cargo now takes days, not hours – with items like corn funnelled by hand by workers

because the funnels and grain silos were also destroyed. Since Hodeidah port was bombed, food deliveries to Yemen have been cut by more than half, which is a death sentence for a country that used to import 70 per cent of its food through this Red Sea portal.[49] It is hard to see how this combination of actions is anything but a deliberate attempt to strangle Houthi-held areas into submission – food again used as a weapon of war.

The Yemeni Central Bank is not paying the salaries of thousands of civil servants, vastly diminishing the purchasing power of many families; for Yemenis without money to pay exorbitant black-market prices, there is precious little food or medicine. The economy in the capital, Sanaa, has largely collapsed, and its streets are filled with beggars. Children crowded around our car at traffic lights, asking for money. Women sat on the side of the road with their babies. Parents picked through rubbish in the streets for food. One day after we finished lunch at a Sanaa restaurant, two old men quietly entered as we exited, sitting at our table to eat the small amount of food scraps we had left.

The UN's Jamie McGoldrick said his figures showed that over a quarter of all local business has had to close. 'Seventy per cent of all small businesses have laid off large chunks of their workers. So that productive capacity that was there, that ability for people to earn money off their own bat, is gone. People who were coping a year ago are finding it harder to cope because of all the pressures on them, because of the price increases, because of the demands and the fact that they don't have an income,' he says. 'So, you can keep that going to a certain point, you live on your resources, you live on your savings, but that will then stop, and I think we're coming close to that point now.' In July 2016, the UN estimated 21 million Yemenis were now in now need of food assistance, but aid programs are desperately underfunded – there is just not enough to go around.[50] Astonishingly, it is estimated that some one-fifth of people in need around the world as a result of conflict, are in Yemen.[51]

At a food distribution point on the outskirts of Sanaa, a local Yemeni NGO was handing out large bags of flour and vegetable oil to around 60 needy families. But dozens more people had heard about the handout and gathered outside the gates of the compound,

desperate to see if their names were on the list to be allowed in. A guard tried to push people back as they crowded in. 'My name's on the list! My name's on the list!' a mother shouted desperately as she got caught in the throng. Another woman waved a piece of paper above her head, trying to get the guard's attention. 'I already gave my number to this guy! I need to take my share now!' One little boy who was too small to carry his family's bag of flour started crying in panic, seemingly concerned it might be taken off him. He stood over the sack, bawling but firmly staking his claim until his mother arrived to help him carry it. Those who received the food made a quick escape.

The dozens who missed out hung around the front gate, hoping there might be something left for them too. 'The lack of food is the most difficult part of life here,' a father outside the gate lamented. 'Wherever we can get food, we must just grab it.'

An old woman sat dejected on the edge of the road. There was no flour or oil today for her. 'I need my name to be listed! My husband's injured. I have nobody to help me but God,' she said mournfully.

Nearby, a mother gathered up discarded boxes, with the help of her three small children. She had missed out on the food distribution but was pleased with her new acquisitions. 'Once I get home, I will burn these, because there is no wood to cook,' she explained matter-of-factly, squashing up the boxes to carry under her arm. 'Our lives now are miserable and messy. We go around on the streets collecting garbage and taking things like this home with me, so in this case I can fill my kids' bellies.'

As difficult as life is here in the capital, outside Sanaa millions of Yemenis have been forced from their homes, fleeing coalition airstrikes and the continued fighting between Houthis and supporters of the exiled President Hadi. We drove several hours north to visit a camp for internally displaced families, near Khamir in Amran province. In a large clearing on the outskirts of town, hundreds of families had been sleeping in tents for the past six months to escape fighting and steady airstrikes near the Saudi border. With no trees, it was dusty and blisteringly hot. Little kids squatted in the shade of tents, while mums lined up to fill bottles with water at the communal taps. Food supplies were handed out once a week and

there were only two water tanks to share for the entire camp, which numbered more than 1000 people. Across Yemen, the UN estimates that there are currently 2.8 million displaced people living like this.

As we arrived, Médecins Sans Frontières was setting up a mobile clinic at the front of the campsite. They visited twice a week, bringing free medical care from doctors, nurses and nutrition experts. 'This is a catastrophe; this is a real humanitarian crisis,' MSF's project coordinator Francesco Segoni said, standing next to a long line of mothers and babies waiting to be seen. 'We see a lot of malnutrition among the kids. About 20 per cent of the children we see are diagnosed as malnourished. Half of them severely so. They don't have enough food, not nearly enough food!'

Inside the tent, 14-month-old Mazen was hanging in the doctor's scales. The baby had big brown eyes and extremely skinny arms and legs. A tape measure around Mazen's arm revealed he was as malnourished as he looked. 'You should give him milk. He is now 14 months. He needs toddler milk. Okay?' the doctor told Mazen's aunty. She spoke softly under her veil: they have no money for milk. Mazen's breastfeeding mother died two months ago from an illness. Since then, he had only been having bread and tea once a day, like the rest of the family. The doctor wrote a referral for Mazen, so he could go to the MSF-funded program at the local hospital for a week to receive milk. The aunty scooped up the baby and followed the nurse out to the charity's van, which would drive them straight there.

All over Yemen, MSF is conducting clinics like this, to try to identify the most malnourished children and offer them lifesaving treatment. But there is just not the staff or the facilities to help all those that need it. According to the UN, one in three kids under five in Yemen are severely malnourished – that's a staggering 1.3 million children.

The worst cases from the north of Yemen are sent to Al Sabeen hospital in Sanaa. In the corner of the children's ward there, I met little Eissa, who lay motionless on a small cot. His tiny body was so emaciated, it was difficult to tell how old he was – he looked no more than a few months old but was actually a year and a half. Eissa's skeletal chest laboured up and down slowly, each breath a struggle to get in and out. He had such severe malnutrition his little organs were beginning to shut down. There hadn't been enough food at home,

Eissa's father, Mohammad, explained sadly. 'He has been sick for ten months. Diarrhoea, bloated stomach and a mouth infection...We take care of him as best as we can. We don't sleep, day or night, worrying about him. What else can we do? My wife feels devastated and stays up all night crying. She's very exhausted looking after him.' Eissa's mum lay next to his tiny body, stroking her son. Even with her black abaya covering much of her face, you could see the tears in her eyes. Mohammad said the war had made it impossible to provide for his family. 'We don't get as much medicine and food since the blockade,' he said. 'People's situation has gotten worse. All we can do is pray to God and be patient. Some people cannot do anything but just see what's happening to their kids and be helpless.'

The emergency room doctors told me that Eissa needed to be in the intensive care unit, but to be moved there, you had to pay, and Eissa's family didn't have the money. I asked the ward paediatrician if they could make an exception for Eissa. 'No money, cannot do anything,' Dr Shariza, a young female doctor, said, shrugging apologetically. 'This is a big problem for doctors. If we do discount for all patients, this is big problem for us. Here in Al Sabeen hospital, there is no money from government!'

Lying in the next ward was Emtiaz. She was two but so acutely malnourished she weighed as much as some newborns. Her ribcage stuck out high and sharp, as did her collarbones. All that was left of this toddler was skin and bones. Emtiaz and her grandmother had travelled several hours from a small village in the north to be treated at Al Sabeen. All they had had at home recently to eat was tea and bread. 'It's hard, there's no money,' her grandma said quietly. Lying flat on her back, with her curly hair splayed out next to her gaunt face, Emtiaz looked like a delicate porcelain doll. A chest infection had left her gasping for breath. She was in desperate need of a ventilator, but they didn't have one in the emergency department, only in the ICU. Once again, it was the problem of not being able to pay.

The nurses were beginning to get embarrassed by our questions about who was and wasn't being allowed into the ICU. Two young male nurses came and stood next to Emtiaz's bed, whispering, before one called out to the main nurse's station. 'Hey, Mohamad! Talk to the doctor to get her to the ICU! They gave that order yesterday.'

'The grandmother doesn't have the money,' replied the head nurse, glancing over at me uncomfortably.

Emtiaz's grandmother explained that her husband had gone to look for money to pay for the hospital.

We offered to pay the US$20 needed for both Eissa and Emtiaz to be taken to the ICU. The ward manager declined our money, though he promised to grant exemptions for both children to receive the treatment they need. But the nurses reported that there was no room for either of them in the ICU, since there were no available functioning ventilators, the equipment Emtiaz desperately needed to help her breathe. A nurse showed me into a dusty storeroom containing six broken ventilators. The Saudi blockade had led to a shortage of vital spare parts for much of their equipment, she told me. Upstairs, within the pink walls of the malnutrition ward, a dozen tiny, skeletal children lay next to their mothers. All 12 beds here were full, and there was no money or more staff to add extra beds. Several weeks after I visited Al Sabeen, the Houthi-run government stopped paying 50,000 of the country's health workers – a move that would have seen many of the hardworking medical staff I met forced to leave and look for other sources of income.

'Seven hundred thousand children here need specialised support in terms of nutrition,' the UN's Jamie McGoldrick tells me. 'Of that 700,000 people, we've only got enough support for 70,000, so that's 10 per cent. We're only addressing the needs of 10 per cent. So who knows what's happened to the other 600-plus thousand people? We're not providing the nutritional support they deserve and need. What will happen is that in the future, the children will die unnecessarily, and on the death certificate it'll say 'pneumonia' or 'respiratory infection', but basically what it is…is the fact they've not enough nutrition, not enough health support, not enough access to drinking water.'

Just before I left Al Sabeen hospital that first day, Eissa was finally admitted to intensive care. His parents remained perched on the edge of his bed, stroking his back, holding out hope that the doctors would be able to save their son. But early the next morning, Eissa's bed was empty. The nurses informed me that he had died just hours after arriving in the ICU.

We drove to the outskirts of Sanaa, to the small brick home of Eissa's family. His father, Mohammad, invited us inside to where relatives had already gathered to mourn. Around 20 relatives sat around the living room, politely shaking my hand and inviting me to sit down with them. 'Eissa passed away just before the morning prayer,' Mohammad told me quietly. A plate of meat and rice sat in the middle of the room, a kindly donation from neighbours – the nutrition Eissa so desperately needed provided only to mark the occasion of his death. After drinking tea and paying our respects to the family, we followed Mohammad out the back of his house to a small dirt-filled field, where Eissa had been buried just a few hours ago. A small rock marked his grave; there wasn't enough money for a headstone.

Over my next few days in Sanaa, I went back to Al Sabeen hospital to visit two-year-old Emtiaz and her grandmother. Her condition had not changed. The doctors said she had been brain-damaged as a result of being so malnourished, and there was no prospect of her waking up from this coma. And then, one morning, Emtiaz was gone too. Her grandmother had taken her back to the village overnight. Death for the toddler was now a certainty.

Meanwhile, the Houthis discovered that we had filmed the funeral of Osama, the child soldier. They summoned us to meet with Ministry of Information officials who demanded we hand over the video. We gave them one of our camera cards, making a big show of appearing reluctant and disappointed to be forced into censorship like that. Thankfully, ABC cameraman Aaron Hollett had a backup copy already stashed on a hard drive that I had then hidden in the underwear section of my suitcase.

The Houthis made it clear our short time on the ground was up, we were not going to be allowed to stay any longer. At Sanaa airport, we waited all afternoon as stormy weather delayed our flight by more than five hours. After we finally took off, the aging Yemenia aeroplane we were on lurched violently up and down through the wet-season clouds that had clustered around the capital. The interior of the plane was like an emergency waiting room, with adults and children with bandaged limbs and IV drips filling the aisles. These injured and ill Yemenis were the ones lucky enough either to be able to afford the pricey airline ticket or to have been sponsored to receive medical care outside the country.

A few days after we left Yemen, peace talks between the Saudi-led coalition and the Houthis broke down, and the coalition began to pound the capital again on a daily basis with airstrikes. In just a few days, more than 80 targets were hit in Sanaa, including a site just one kilometre from where the emaciated babies lay inside the malnutrition ward at Al Sabeen hospital, the windows in their ward reportedly blown out by the force of the explosion.

Our flight out turned out to be one of the last commercial planes allowed to leave Sanaa. The Saudi-led coalition bombed Sanaa airport again, declaring that it was now closed and only UN humanitarian flights would be allowed in and out of Houthi-controlled territory.[52] It was a move that essentially trapped 20 million people, the majority of Yemen's 28 million–strong population, under direct siege, with no way in or out. And if getting food and supplies into north Yemen hadn't already been hard enough, the Saudis then also destroyed the main bridge on the road from the port city of Hodeidah to the capital Sanaa.[53]

Saudi Arabia became more audacious in its attacks on civilian targets. On 13 August 2016, ten children under 15 were killed, and 28 others injured, when the coalition bombed a school in the northern province of Saada.[54] Two days later, coalition planes attacked an MSF hospital in Hajjah province, killing 11 people and injuring 19 – the fourth attack against an MSF facility in less than 12 months.[55] 'The location of the hospital was well known, and the hospital's GPS coordinates were repeatedly shared with all parties to the conflict including the Saudi-led coalition,' MSF said in a statement. The very same day that the MSF hospital was hit, King Salman of Saudi Arabia announced that he was rewarding military personnel involved in his country's war on Yemen with an additional month's salary.[56]

These alleged bombings of schools and hospitals, all serious war crimes, passed with very little international condemnation or even attention. With no tangible consequence for such grave violations of the laws of war, what deterrent was there for the Saudis to avoid civilian deaths?

And so, on Saturday, 8 October 2016, when a Saudi coalition warplane was circling above a community hall in downtown Sanaa, where a funeral ceremony was packed with hundreds of civilians, the

pilot dropped his load. At 3.30 pm, a US-manufactured 500-pound [225-kilogram] bomb exploded through the roof – immediately burning dozens of civilians alive. Photos and video of the attack show charred and mutilated bodies strewn in and outside the hall, the once ornate building now a smoking wreck. 'When I got there, there were more than 50 burned bodies, many where you can still tell the features, but half of their body was gone, half of their head was gone, but the others, it was very, very hard to tell who they were,' a witness told Human Rights Watch.[57] Another witness, Abdulla Al Shami, spoke of the moment the bomb hit. 'I was inside sitting at the funeral when the airstrike happened...I couldn't see who was next to me, I was looking for an exit. There were dead bodies and body parts, some people under rubble...There were children inside before the strike, but I couldn't see anyone after the strike. It was dark. I just saw the light and ran toward it to escape,' he told HRW investigators.

As survivors and nearby civilians worked desperately to rescue those they could, a few minutes later a second bomb hit the site. It was a 'double tap' attack, designed to kill the survivors and the rescuers who had rushed to assist the wounded – an act clearly categorised as a war crime. 'The second air strike, which occurred three to eight minutes after the first air strike, almost certainly resulted in more casualties to the already wounded and the first responders,' UN monitors said in a leaked report seen by the Reuters news agency.[58]

A UN investigation found that at least 137 civilians were killed in the funeral hall attack, with 695 injured – the deadliest single bombing since the coalition bombardment had begun.[59]

The funeral gathering was to honour the death of the father of a senior official from the rebel Houthi group, and the evidence suggested that the Saudis had deliberately hit the funeral hall to target the collection of senior Houthi political and security figures who were in attendance, with no concern for the hundreds of civilians also present. The date and place of the funeral ceremony had been announced publicly on Facebook and on national TV, noted Human Rights Watch, while evidence provided to Nawal Al Maghafi, a BBC journalist, showed that informants were updating the Saudi coalition on who was in the funeral hall (they

had incorrectly claimed that Houthi ally and former president Ali Abdullah Saleh was inside).[60] The evidence also suggested the attack was planned. 'The afternoon hour of the attack would have been known to be the "peak time" when the funeral ceremony, open to the public, would have been very crowded. Coalition forces should have known that while a number of high-ranking commanders would be gathered, any attack on the hall would result in massive civilian casualties,' concluded Human Rights Watch.

Amid the rubble, Yemeni investigators discovered the tail fin of a US-made bomb used in the attack. The serial number showed that it was produced by the American weapons company Raytheon and fitted with a laser-guidance system, reported the *New Yorker*.[61] Such modifications in theory help to avoid civilian infrastructure by hitting military targets more accurately. But in Yemen the technology did little to help – if the Saudis were deliberately bombing civilian targets, it had the opposite effect.

By October 2016, the Obama administration was already on its way out. It had failed to rein in Saudi Arabia's conduct in any meaningful way, in a war that the US had fully backed diplomatically and with intensive refuelling efforts, intelligence and advisory support. With the White House now free of worry over any Saudi blowback, the day after the funeral hall attack, the US made an unusually blunt statement announcing it would 'immediately review its support for the Yemen war', saying that 'US security cooperation with Saudi Arabia is not a blank cheque'.[62] The UK government labelled the bombing as 'shocking' but did not follow the US lead and review British support for the Saudi-led coalition, saying it was 'comfortable' with the Saudi military investigating its own forces.[63]

After initially denying responsibility for the deadly strikes, the Saudis quickly changed their tune, calling the attack 'regrettable and painful' and pledging to investigate. The resulting inquiry by the Saudis' Joint Incidents Assessment Team concluded that coalition jets had 'wrongly' bombed the community hall. It blamed what it called 'incorrect information' received from Hadi-aligned Yemeni military figures, denying that the Saudi command centre in Riyadh had approved the attack. Yet evidence uncovered by BBC reporter Nawal Al Maghafi cast doubt on these claims. 'Does every

target need sign-off from the coalition?' Nawal Al Maghafi asked the chief of staff of the Yemeni army, Major General Al Magdashi. He replied, 'Sure, that's how we coordinate.'[64]

Two months after the funeral attack, the Obama administration announced that it would block the sale to Saudi Arabia of 16,000 guided munition kits from Raytheon, the alleged manufacturer of the bomb that the coalition had dropped on the hall. The technology is designed to turn so-called dumb bombs into smart bombs, so they can more accurately hit targets, similar to what was fitted on the 500-pound bomb that killed 137 civilians in the funeral hall. 'Administration officials said that upgrading the bombs would not help targeting if the Saudi-led coalition in Yemen did not choose its targets properly,' reported the *New York Times*.[65] But the move was small fry in weapons-sales terms – a loss of just US$350 million out of the $110 billion derived from Obama's new Saudi weapons deal.

Despite the hand-wringing over the massive death toll that October, the US did not seriously reduce its assistance to the Saudi war efforts, instead continuing with its critical refuelling of Saudi warplanes. In fact, according to evidence uncovered by the BBC, the US refuelled coalition jets the day after the funeral strike, and this operational support did not cease in the months and weeks after the massive civilian death toll.[66] The United States would refocus training with the Saudi air force in 'how to better choose bombing targets', reported the *New York Times*.[67]

Several months after my report on Saudi Arabia's alleged war crimes in Yemen aired in prime time on ABC's *Foreign Correspondent* program, and just weeks the funeral hall attack, Australian defence industry minister Christopher Pyne travelled to Saudi Arabia to try to get Australia a piece of the weapons sales action.[68] On 19 December 2016, he went to Riyadh to promote Australian military products and tweeted a photo of himself at a meeting with high-level Saudi military figures as well as a top Saudi prince.[69] 'The minister received a very positive reception, as did the business representatives who visited,' a spokeswoman for Pyne told the *Sydney Morning Herald*.[70] Three months after his trip, the *Herald* revealed that the Australian defence department had approved four military exports to the Saudi regime, but the Turnbull government had refused to release details of the approved

military sales, citing commercial-in-confidence rules. (Later, my ABC colleague Dylan Welch exposed how the coalition government spent $36 million in taxpayers funding to help Canberra-based defence company EOS systems develop remote weapons system units which were then exported to Saudi Arabia.[71])

As the war continued, food was becoming even harder for families to find. The charity Save the Children sounded the alarm in March 2017, calling on governments to put pressure on the Saudi-led coalition to immediately ensure urgent food aid could be delivered through Hodeidah.[72] The charity pointed the finger directly at the Saudis, accusing the coalition of preventing ships filled with urgently needed aid from docking at the port for 'security reasons'. 'We have had three shipments of life-saving medical aid delayed by the coalition so far this year, and our field teams tell us children have died as a result,' said Grant Pritchard, interim country director for Save the Children in Yemen. 'By bombing and blocking Yemen's main port – the country's lifeline for essential supplies – Saudi Arabia and its coalition allies are preventing the delivery of food and aid by sea. This crisis is not an act of nature. It is man-made. Food and aid are being used as weapons of war.'[73]

It was the same tactic that the American, British and Australian governments had condemned when Assad had used it against civilians in Syria. Yet when our Saudi 'friends' did the same in Yemen, and on a much larger scale, barely a word was said.

The high rates of malnutrition, lack of sanitation and clean water for millions of Yemenis laid the groundwork for a horrendous new medical emergency: cholera was now stalking the population. The waterborne disease caused by contaminated food or water started breaking out in small towns and cities all over the countryside. But there were few resources to help the thousands of children turning up at clinics and hospitals with the acute diarrhoeal infection. The World Health Organization reported that fewer than 45 per cent of health facilities in Yemen were fully functioning, and that the flow of 'essential medicines' had fallen by nearly 70 per cent. Saudi Arabia was blocking the supply of the lifesaving medications the people of Yemen desperately needed.[74]

Photos sent to me by UN contacts in Sanaa showed dozens of sick children and adults with cholera being treated in the halls of

the hospitals there – there were just not enough beds to go around. Aid organizations began setting up tents in hospital parking lots to host the hundreds of cases arriving every day.

I stayed in regular touch with my new friend and Yemeni analyst Hisham Al Omeisy. As the world's journalists were now blocked completely from flying into Sanaa to report on Houthi-held Yemen, Hisham became a vital voice advocating for Yemeni civilians and the horror they were continuing to suffer. We messaged regularly so that Hisham could update me on the worsening situation on the ground.

Hisham reminded the world that the people trapped inside Yemen were no different from any of us watching the horror from afar. 'Anything to make 'em forget war. #Yemen,' tweeted Hisham with photos of his two young sons rollerblading.[75] With the assistance of Hisham and Sanaa-based producer and cameraman Moohialdin Fuad, we produced a TV feature for ABC on the growing cholera epidemic that was regularly killing children within a few hours of them getting sick.[76]

'Last night at 10 pm he was fine,' said Abdo Ibrahim, a father in Sanaa who had rushed to hospital that morning with his eight-year-old son, Muhab, 'but in the morning he couldn't even stand up. I was on my way to the hospital. I thought, "He's dying." He was so weak. His eyes had rolled back into his head and I thought, "I've lost my child! He's dead, dead."' Mr Ibrahim's quick action in taking his son to hospital saved his life. But not all Yemeni parents could afford transportation or medical treatment. By June 2017, more than 800 Yemenis had died from cholera, a quarter of them children.

Part of the problem was that the UN had still not received the full funding it needed to carry out its operations in Yemen. 'The appeal for the humanitarian response plan is not fully funded. For 2017 we are at 39 per cent funded right now; we desperately need vaccines we don't have,' explained Hisham when my producer in Yemen filmed him for our second special report in August 2017.

Indeed at a UN pledging event to fund the response to the humanitarian crisis in Yemen in April 2017 in Geneva, only US$1.1 billion was raised, a figure that was US$1 billion short of the UN estimate of what would be needed 'to prevent a full-blown

humanitarian catastrophe in Yemen'.[77] An additional funding appeal at the event for $250 million specifically for combating cholera yielded only $47 million.

Yemen was by then officially classified by the UN as the world's worst humanitarian disaster.[78] Humanitarians warned time and time again of the impending public health catastrophe but were routinely ignored. Saving Yemeni lives was just not a priority for the international community. 'The health system is about to collapse,' UNICEF's Yemen spokesperson Meritxell Relano told me. 'With health workers who have not received a salary, with half of the facilities being closed and with very limited supplies coming into the country.'

V

One week after we interviewed Hisham for our report about cholera, his younger brother was driving his car through Saana's streets when he was suddenly surrounded by 15 armed men. The Houthis had decided they needed to arrest Hisham, as his independent voice and analysis on the war had come to be seen as a threat. Hisham's brother was forced call him and pretend he'd had an accident; he told Hisham to meet him at the hospital. When Hisham arrived, he was encircled by five armoured vehicles and countless masked men carrying guns. The thugs wanted to take Hisham and his brother initially, but the analyst convinced them to let his sibling go. The 38-year-old father of two was quickly blindfolded and shoved into a car. He then disappeared.

His family and friends outside launched a desperate campaign highlighting his kidnapping and disappearance, while reporters like me who had worked with Hisham produced a flurry of stories. 'Hisham Al Omeisy is a prisoner of conscience, whose only "crime" is peacefully exercising his right to freedom of expression, and he must be released immediately,' Amnesty International's Middle East campaign director Samah Hadid told me.[79] Human Rights Watch also called for Hisham's immediate release. 'Yemen more than ever needs activists like Hisham Al Omeisy to bring attention to the devastation that war, famine, and disease have wrought on the country and its people,' said Sarah Leah Whitson,

Middle East Director at Human Rights Watch. 'Houthi authorities should immediately release Al Omeisy and return him safely to his family.'[80]

But there was no official word on what had happened to Hisham. There were theories about where he might be being held and by whom, but no confirmation. The bombs continued falling on Sanaa, but now there was no Hisham to reassure his small sons as they lay terrified in their beds.

We learnt later that Hisham could hear the airstrikes from where he sat alone, in solitary confinement in a dirty cell measuring just 1.5 by 2 metres in an underground prison. At different times of the day, Hisham also heard his fellow prisoners being beaten, and screaming. He too was beaten, but not as badly as the others. Perhaps his media profile and the human rights groups' campaigns for his release helped spare him some of the worst abuse.

But the special treatment stopped there. For months, Hisham sat in his cell, occasionally let out only to be screamed at and beaten with a stick if he didn't clean the disgusting toilets as well as was demanded. The human rights defender now spent his days knee-deep in shit, unclogging drains. At other times, Hisham was blindfolded and taken upstairs for questioning. His jailers accused him of spying for the Americans, despite the fact that Hisham was one of the strongest critics of the US-supported Saudi bombing campaign on Yemen. Hisham insisted that he was simply an independent advocate, but his pleas were always ignored, and he would be marched back to his cell and left to sit alone for days and weeks on end, his only company a feral cat that roamed the jail, which Hisham had named 'Blacky.' Hisham would share his rations with the skinny animal and at night he'd hug Blacky, think of his boys and cry. Would he ever get out of this dungeon?

By December 2017, Hisham had spent five months in jail. By then, the World Health Organization was reporting that the number of suspected cholera cases in Yemen had surpassed one million, making it officially the worst epidemic of the illness in recorded history.[81] More than 2500 Yemenis – 58 per cent of them children – have died so far in the outbreak. What made these deaths so criminal was there is a vaccine for cholera – it is an entirely preventable disease. But when the WHO requested 3.4 million cholera vaccines for Yemen

in June 2017 it was too late – there were only two million vaccines globally in stock at the time.[82] While acknowledging the logistical challenges involved in distributing vaccines in Yemen, medical experts were critical of how the international humanitarian response to the cholera crisis was managed.[83] 'Whatever the reasons, OCVs (oral cholera vaccines) were not distributed until nearly 16 months into the cholera outbreak, by which time more than a million cases had accumulated...This should serve as a historic example of the failure to control the spread of cholera given the tools available,' wrote public health experts.[84]

In early November 2017, the Saudi-enforced blockade on Yemen tightened. After Houthi rebels fired a ballistic missile towards Riyadh airport, the Saudi coalition retaliated by totally closing Yemen's main port and stopping all UN humanitarian flights in and out of the country.[85] Yemen was now totally blockaded, with no way in or out for emergency aid or humanitarian workers, in a country where a quarter of the 28 million inhabitants were thought to be starving.[86]

In response to the total closure, the UN's global humanitarian chief in New York, Mark Lowcock, warned that Yemen would face 'the largest famine the world has seen for many decades, with millions of victims', unless the Saudi-led military coalition lifted its blockade.[87] The Red Cross announced that cities in Yemen had begun to run out of clean water because all imports of the fuel needed for pumping and sanitation had ceased.[88] The total closure of Yemen amounted to the 'illegal collective punishment of civilians', warned aid experts.[89]

'This is a man-made crisis. I mean it is not organic or natural. It is not something that just happened overnight. It was obviously planned,' the UN's Jamie McGoldrick told me in Amman, Jordan. He had been out of Yemen attending meetings when the Saudis announced the total closure. Like all other humanitarian workers he now had no way of getting back into the country. 'The humanitarian situation is only going to get more catastrophic and then [when] you put on shocks like a blockade that just basically tips things into a very difficult, more difficult situation, if it is possible.'

As the UN worked frantically to convince the Saudis to reopen the docks and airports to aid deliveries, I stumbled on a shocking

discovery – the Royal Australian Navy had been conducting training exercises with the Saudi navy in the Red Sea.[90] On the official 'Australian Defence Force in the Middle East' Facebook page, photos showed smiling armed Saudi sailors next to Aussie naval officers from HMAS *Newcastle*.[91] They had been participating in 'boarding party training', said the ADF – a questionable exercise given that the Saudis had been accused of enforcing an illegal naval blockade.

'I think it is disturbing to hear that the ADF is training a navy that is involved in this blockade,' Elaine Pearson, director of Human Rights Watch in Australia told me. 'We know that the Saudi-led coalition has been arbitrarily delaying and diverting ships carrying lifesaving goods to Yemen, and humanitarian assistance is clearly desperately needed right now.'

Oxfam, which is engaged in aid work on the ground in Yemen, said the news of the training was 'concerning in the context of the complete blockade of Yemen that is being maintained by the Saudi-led coalition'. Rebecca Barber, Oxfam's humanitarian policy adviser in Melbourne said, 'Oxfam will be asking the Australian government for more information. We are concerned by anything that could look like support to the implementation of the blockade...The blockade is directly contravening a series of UN Security Council resolutions and Security Council presidential statements calling for full and unimpeded, unhindered humanitarian access. [It] is in direct contravention of existing Security Council resolutions."

Even the executive director of the Australian Defence Association, Neil James, said he found the timing and location of the exercise puzzling. 'Particularly as the Saudis are a combatant engaged in a separate war zone,' he said. 'There's also the aspect of the perception that you give. Australia is not involved in the conflict between Saudi Arabia and the Gulf states in Yemen. And we should avoid any such connection.'

Questioned in parliament in the wake of our report, Australian defence minister Marise Payne defended the exercise, calling it 'opportunistic' and saying that such exercises take place from 'time to time' on an 'opportunity basis'. But as Human Rights Watch's Elaine Pearson told me, some opportunities 'just aren't worth taking up'. 'This is absolutely the wrong time for Australia to be sending the message to Saudi Arabia that it is just business as usual,'

Pearson said. 'We do absolutely have concerns if that training is about making the Saudi navy more efficient in how it carries out its business, because its business at the moment is about repeatedly violating international law.' The ADF did not reply to my questions about the specifics of the exercise and whether any future training exercises with the Saudi navy were being planned.

Meanwhile, a Reuters investigation revealed just how the Saudi navy had been blocking lifesaving aid from docking at Yemen's ports. Thirteen ships had been turned away or severely delayed from docking by the Saudis, even though the UN had cleared the cargo and there were no arms aboard. One of the vessels was carrying antibiotics, surgical equipment and medication for cholera and malaria for 300,000 people. 'The shipment was held up for three months, during which $20,000 worth of medicine was damaged or expired, according to UK-based aid group Save the Children.'[92]

The Saudi-led coalition also turned back four cranes the United States had given to the World Food Programme to replace those destroyed in coalition airstrikes in August 2015 and boost aid operations at Hodeida port. The ship then waited at sea for ten days before eventually sailing back to Dubai, reported Reuters. (The urgently needed equipment, which would have made an immediate difference by reducing the unloading time of aid and food from a week to three days, was blocked by the Saudis until January 2018.)[93]

After several weeks of intense lobbying by the UN, the Saudis finally allowed aid shipments to Yemen to resume in late November 2017. The International Rescue Committee (IRC) described the move as a 'half measure at best', warning that aid alone could not feed the country. 'We cannot celebrate this partial easing of access restrictions,' Paolo Cernuschi, Yemen's IRC director, said. 'Access by commercial shipments of food and fuel must be resumed immediately, otherwise this action will do little to turn Yemen back from the brink of famine and crisis.'

Meanwhile, Hisham remained behind bars, convinced this was how life was going to end for him. 'I really, really missed my kids and wanted to hear their voice. But they wouldn't let me. That was the worst torture. Not knowing what was going to happen next. Not knowing if I was going to see my kids again,' Hisham told me quietly. 'I had heard how people just went missing in these prisons. That once

you go there you don't leave. Or you leave dead. I knew it could be the end and I just wanted to hear my kids' voices one last time.'

Hisham paced back and forth in his cell during the day, trying to keep himself from going mad. Apart from his family, he yearned for the sky, the sound of birds chirping – anything to remind him that life existed beyond the four dark walls that surrounded his days and nights.

One day in January 2018, one of the guards arrived at Hisham's cell door and barked for him to get up. Hisham jumped to attention and began to prepare to be blindfolded – standard practice whenever he was taken out of his cell. But his jailer indicated that this time it wasn't necessary. He was whisked upstairs, where an adviser from the president's office suddenly walked in.

'You've been granted a presidential pardon,' the adviser told Hisham. He was stunned. Was he really going to see his family again? Hisham was put in the adviser's car and driven to a hall. He was going to have to give a press conference, he was instructed. And thank the president for the 'generous' pardon and his release. Hisham couldn't believe this was really happening. As he entered the building, TV and radio crews were gathered around a small table. And then suddenly two small figures nearly bowled him over. Hisham and his sons wrapped their arms around each other, the three of them crying tears of relief and joy as they hugged each other tighter than they had ever hugged before.

During the press conference, Hisham dutifully followed the strict instructions he had been given, acting grateful and thanking the president for the pardon. When he arrived home, his family couldn't stop hugging and holding him. Nobody could believe they had Hisham back. During this time, I tried to contact him, but there was no word from him except for one tweet in which he thanked everyone who had campaigned for his release.[94] Unbeknown to us, Hisham had been forbidden from speaking to reporters and instructed to remain at home under virtual house arrest. For weeks after his release, his boys refused to sleep in their beds: each night they would lie next to Hisham, refusing to let him go. Quietly and carefully, Hisham began to put together an escape plan. He'd never wanted to flee his homeland. Friends overseas had urged him to leave at the start of the war, but he had stood firm, even during the

worst airstrikes: he didn't want to abandon his people. But now he had no choice. He could be picked up and detained again at any moment. He'd come back from the dead once before, and he was determined to never again be separated from his loved ones.

Finally, in August 2018, the moment came. During the Eid holiday, when the checkpoints were manned lightly, Hisham and his wife and two boys wept as they said goodbye to his elderly parents and his siblings. Would they ever see them again? They crept out of their house in the dark and silently said goodbye to their home. They drove carefully along the back roads and less travelled routes, crossing several front lines of the war before leaving Houthi-controlled territory and finally arriving in Aden, the southern city controlled by the Hadi government and Saudi and Emirati forces. Given Hisham's loud criticism of the coalition war campaign, this was no safe haven. But air services were still operating there, so the family quickly boarded a flight to the Egyptian capital, Cairo. They were now refugees, cast out into a world indifferent to their suffering or their need for protection.

'We know Yemenis are not welcome anywhere,' Hisham said sadly. 'I was forced to leave. I don't know where I'm going to end up. I can't move back home. I can't move forward anywhere else. It's like you're in the middle of the sea and you don't know when you are going to reach safe shores.'

Hisham and his family still live in exile.

As of December 2019, the war in Yemen continues.

*

The UN estimates that by the end of 2019, 233,000 Yemenis had been killed as a result of fighting and disease. This includes 140,000 children under the age of five, many of whom starved to death.[95]

In the wake of the brutal murder of Jamal Khashoggi in the Saudi embassy in Istanbul in October 2018, the United States announced that it would halt the refuelling of aircraft from the Saudi-led coalition engaged in Yemen.[96]

In April 2019, the US Congress passed a bipartisan measure to end US military support for the Saudi-led war in Yemen. President Trump vetoed the motion.[97]

CHAPTER 11

WE CAN'T SAY WE DIDN'T KNOW

The Siege of Aleppo

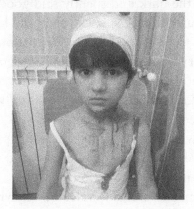

It was hard to imagine that the war in Syria could become any more brutal and deadly, but in September 2015 a ruthless new stage of the conflict began, with Russia intervening to help the weakened regime of President Bashar Al Assad win back territory from opposition rebels. President Vladimir Putin declared that his country was acting 'preventatively, to fight and destroy militants and terrorists'. Initially, Moscow claimed they would target only those areas of Syria controlled by ISIS jihadists, but within days Russian bombs were raining down on opposition-held towns and cities with no known ISIS presence.[1] The Russian warplanes became a deadly extension of Assad's propaganda campaign; anyone who didn't support the regime was a 'terrorist' and a target. The cost of Russia's intervention in Syria was soon clear: their airstrikes killed more than 2000 civilians in the first six months.[2] The Russian support swung the war in favour of Assad's forces, and the regime soon set their sights on retaking the eastern half of Aleppo city, which opposition forces had held since 2012.

I

The first airstrike hit at 9.37 pm on 27 April, slamming into a building just over the road from the Al Quds hospital. As medical staff scrambled to rescue the wounded, another missile hit the nearby hospital staff quarters. Then came a direct hit, pulverizing the entrance to the hospital's emergency room, killing and injuring staff who were ushering in patients wounded by the first bomb. Five minutes later, the last devastating attack blew apart the hospital's top two floors.[3]

Video of the aftermath shows desperate rescuers frantically shining torches on the mangled wreck of the hospital entrance as they searched for survivors.[4] 'Where did my father go? My family! Where is my family?' a hysterical young man howls in the street. Another clip shows a boy, no older than eight, stroking the dead body of his toddler brother.[5] 'I wish it was me, not you,' the child weeps.

Among the 55 people killed in the attack on 27 April 2016 were six medical staff, including the last paediatrician working in east Aleppo, 36-year-old Dr Mohammad Wassim Maaz.[6] 'He loved his country; he loved his city. He had to stay close to those babies. Who would treat those babies if everybody left?' his devastated colleague told the BBC.[7]

Since 2012, the Al Quds hospital had been supported by international medical charity Médecins Sans Frontières with training, drugs, medical equipment and cash funding. The charity had employed international staff to work at the facility until 2014, but once it became too dangerous for them to remain, MSF maintained regular contact with the Syrian hospital managers, doctors and nurses who refused to abandon their patients. In the wake of the strikes, Muskilda Zancada, MSF's head of mission for Syria, said, 'This devastating attack has destroyed a vital hospital in Aleppo and the main referral centre for paediatric care in the area. Where is the outrage among those with the power and obligation to stop this carnage?'[8]

The Assad regime were using a deadly tactic in Aleppo that they had employed with impunity in other parts of Syria: deliberately attacking medical facilities. Thirteen hospitals had been targeted by airstrikes in the Aleppo governorate since December 2015,

killing four medical workers and 45 civilians, reported the Syrian American Medical Society, an American-based NGO founded by expat Syrians.[9] 'Syrian and Russian forces have been deliberately attacking health facilities in flagrant violation of international humanitarian law,' Tirana Hassan, crisis response director at Amnesty International, told reporters. 'Wiping out hospitals appears to have become part of their military strategy.'

As early as September 2013, UN investigators had reported, 'Syrian government forces are systematically attacking hospitals and medical staff members and denying treatment to the sick and wounded from areas controlled or affiliated with the opposition.'[10] By killing a doctor, by destroying a hospital, the regime could efficiently multiply their death and devastation.

The Syrian regime were not the first to target hospitals, with previous conflicts in South Sudan, Sri Lanka and Yemen all experiencing this war crime. Yet in May 2016, the US-based advocacy group Physicians for Human Rights told *Foreign Affairs* that, in their 30 years of documenting such crimes, they found the frequency and brutality of the Syrian attacks to be unparalleled, with 240 medical facilities hit and 700 healthcare workers killed.[11]

'What we are witnessing is a sustained assault on, and massive disregard for, the provision of healthcare during times of conflict,' wrote Dr Joanne Liu, MSF's international president, in the wake of the Al Quds hospital attack. 'Under international humanitarian law and principles, health workers must be able to provide medical care to all sick and wounded regardless of political or other affiliation, whether they are a combatant or not. The doctor of your enemy is not your enemy.'[12]

Once Russian forces began supporting the regime's efforts, Assad had a UN Security Council permanent member stocking him with the weaponry and airpower needed to turn this illegal tactic on the people of east Aleppo. In the nine days surrounding the devastating attack on Al Quds hospital, the streets of Aleppo were steeped in blood and dust, as an overwhelming 193 civilians – including 40 children – were killed by airstrikes.[13]

More than 9000 kilometres away, 36-year-old Dr Samer Attar sat in his Chicago apartment, glued to the news from Aleppo. Known to his friends as Sam, the long-haired surgeon, who liked to surf in

his spare time, was an associate professor of orthopaedic surgery at Northwestern University. While Sam had been born and bred in the United States, his parents had emigrated from Syria in the early 1980s. Now he watched interviews with devastated medical staff talking about their dead colleagues at Al Quds hospital.

As the images of bloodied and broken children continued to stream out of Aleppo, Sam felt compelled to go over and help. The last time the surgeon had volunteered in Aleppo was in 2014. He would never forget treating a small boy whose school had been hit by an airstrike. Bone shards from the boy's school friends, blown up beside him, had been embedded in the boy's skin, and Sam had removed them without anaesthesia in a crowded ER. Sam had left Aleppo thinking the war couldn't get any worse. 'Syria can teach you that things can always get worse,' Sam said remorsefully. This time he wouldn't even tell his parents he was going.

From Chicago, Sam took the long flight to Istanbul and then Gaziantep in southern Turkey. Before the streets became too light, he was driven through the opposition-held countryside to the city's outskirts. This was the moment of truth: Castello Road into the rebel-held east Aleppo was then one of the world's most dangerous stretches of highway. You had to navigate a labyrinth of regime snipers, then say a prayer and drive at breakneck speed to avoid the airstrikes that could hit at any moment. Sam gripped the handle next to his head as his driver swerved around deep potholes left by previous bombings. They zoomed past blackened wrecks of cars and trucks, the smells of rotten human flesh and burnt metal hanging in the air. After several hair-raising minutes, their vehicle made it to the rebel-held east.

By mid 2016, Aleppo was a shell of its former self. Before the war, the northern city had been the most populous in Syria, home to more than 2.3 million people, and one of the oldest continuously inhabited cities in the world. Thousands of tourists had flocked to Aleppo each year, to explore the famous covered markets and visit the World Heritage–listed ruins of the ancient citadel overlooking the city. But Aleppo had since hosted some of the fiercest fighting in the Syrian civil war. In early 2014, after the regime began targeting Aleppo with a barrage of barrel bombs and airstrikes on the rebel-held east and opposition forces shelled the

west, hundreds of thousands of residents had fled north to live as refugees in Turkey. The UN estimated 200,000–300,000 civilians remained in the east, while over one million lived in government-held west Aleppo.

As Sam entered the opposition-held neighbourhoods, he saw an apocalyptic wasteland. Row after row of apartment blocks had been obliterated by the Syrian air force. Deeper inside the city, civilians scurried between the ruins, trying to retain some semblance of normal life, refusing to submit to the death that came in waves from the sky. Sam tried not to think about how difficult it was going to be to leave again.

By the time Sam arrived in mid 2016, the UN estimated that only 30 doctors were left in east Aleppo to treat a rising tide of complex, dramatic injuries. Sam volunteered in a hospital in the Sakhour neighbourhood, which, like all hospitals in Aleppo, used a codename to avoid the regime pinpointing its location for attack. Known as 'M10', Al Sakhour Hospital was supported by Médecins Sans Frontières and the Syrian American Medical Society. As the largest trauma unit and ICU centre hospital in east Aleppo, M10 saw the worst war injuries suffered by the city's residents, so it was exactly where a spare orthopaedic surgeon was needed.

The majority of patients who arrived at M10 were maimed civilians, but injured opposition fighters were also treated there. As with all hospitals in east Aleppo, M10 had no armed opposition presence inside or surrounding it. As a hospital in a war zone, it was supposed to be safe. Instead, M10 had been targeted by regime forces so many times it had been driven underground, concentrating its services in the basement. The staff were exhausted and under-resourced, the scalpels were blunt and the drugs were sparse.

One of the first to greet Sam when he arrived was Abu Rajab, M10's hospital administrator. A jolly, heavy-set 50-year-old with sparkling eyes and a salt-and-pepper beard, Abu Rajab was a permanent fixture in M10 hospital, rarely seen out of his blue scrubs. Before the war, the father of five had been a radiology technician at one of Aleppo's largest public hospitals. When the Free Syrian Army took over large parts of the city in 2012, Abu Rajab immediately volunteered to provide medical care for civilians living under opposition control. 'It's my duty, I will never leave it,'

Abu Rajab said simply. 'When the revolution started, we only had a Red Crescent clinic. And then we managed to turn that clinic into a hospital. Medical staff came from all over to help people in the liberated neighbourhoods.'

As the rolling emergencies continued in Aleppo and the number of medical staff dwindled, Abu Rajab inherited the role of hospital administrator on top of his radiology duties. It was a mammoth task, managing an exhausted staff and overwhelming patient load, sourcing hard-to-find medical supplies and food for the patients and doctors and nurses – all amid airstrikes targeting the hospital. Abu Rajab took it in his stride, always ready with a smile and a joke. The staff of M10 became his family and the hospital his home. 'All the staff, the doctors, the nurses, everyone, we all work with one heartbeat,' Abu Rajab explained happily. 'We work together, eat together, we share everything.'

When the madness hit and M10's ER was overwhelmed, Abu Rajab would be an extra pair of hands wherever needed, whether in the triage area, deciding which patient was going where, or in the operating theatre, helping the overworked surgeons. He could often be seen holding the hands of injured children who had arrived without their parents, comforting them until relatives arrived.

'My worst day, I remember it well,' Abu Rajab said quietly. 'There was a man, his wife and his three children, three daughters. The whole family had been injured in shelling and we took them in and welcomed them and treated them. And then the first daughter died. And the father carried her wrapped in a shroud to the street. But the second daughter died. And the third. And the father carried them both to the street.' The parents of the three dead sisters clutched each other and wailed. 'Don't cry,' Abu Rajab remembered the father repeating as he held his wife, 'our children have gone to heaven.'

As Aleppo became more and more dangerous, Abu Rajab's wife, five children and grandchildren fled over the border to Turkey in 2015, but he stayed. He would visit them regularly but always returned to east Aleppo – going against the flow of families fleeing the city as life inside became increasingly unbearable.

Despite the chaos of running an understaffed and under-resourced surgical hospital in the world's most dangerous city, Abu Rajab immediately helped Sam feel at home when he arrived. In the

basement there was no day or night, and it was always echoing with gunfire, motor shells, the screeching of jets and the whirling of helicopters. The rest of the staff were unfazed, going about their work as the hospital shook with the vibrations of war. 'Don't worry,' Abu Rajab assured Sam. 'If you don't see the rocket then you are safe.'

The Assad regime labelled everyone who chose to stay in the rebel-controlled east 'terrorists'. But each day, the patients that Sam saw being rushed into M10's ER were overwhelmingly civilians, pummelled from the skies by the regime and their Russian allies. A 40-year-old mother paralysed from the waist down. A child with shrapnel embedded in his spinal cord. A grandmother with half her face crushed and her arm bone sticking out. A boy with severe burns and his intestines protruding from his little belly.

Each family had a different reason for remaining, they told Sam. Many were terrified of crossing into regime-held territory after family members had been detained by Assad's security forces and never seen again. Some didn't have enough money to flee. Others felt that after everything they had been through, they would prefer to risk death than be forced from the only home they had ever known. 'They would rather be at home than on a boat trying to escape to Europe or living in a tent in Lebanon,' Sam explained.

One day, a market near the hospital was hit by an airstrike. Inside the ER, Sam felt a massive thud as the missile slammed into the ground. Soon the sirens started and patients started flooding in. There were not enough beds, so bloodied children were placed side by side on the same bed. When they ran out of space there, Sam triaged people on the floor. Soon blood pooled in the hallways, as the newly injured piled up around him.

With such limited resources, Sam constantly had to make life-or-death decisions. Should he continue with CPR on this child, who looked like he wouldn't make it, or stop and help the father lying next to him, who might have more chance of living? A photo taken in one of those moments shows Sam standing in a moment of stillness in the ER, his scrubs covered in blood. His face exhausted and fallen, he appears to be pondering where to turn his attention. 'There are children we literally saw bleed to death,' Sam told me. 'But there was just not enough blood to go around.'

Desperate resuscitation attempts were performed in the hallways alongside lifesaving amputations to stem bleeding. Anaesthesia was an unaffordable luxury in moments like this. And the hospital just didn't have the resources to save so many critically injured people at once. In photos taken by Sam, bodies of adults and children, wrapped in white shrouds, are piled up in the street outside the hospital. 'There was no room to store them inside the hospital,' Sam explained. 'They had to be placed in the street to make room for the freshly incoming wounded.'

Abu Rajab was deeply impressed by the young American surgeon. 'One day we did not have enough doctors. Dr Sam went into the surgical room and he did 13 operations in a row,' Abu Rajab remembered. 'He didn't stop to rest. I said to him several times, "Hey, you need to take a break," and he said, "I didn't come here to rest, I came to work and give." He lived with us as if he was one of us. He became absorbed in our reality.'

In the quiet moments between the shelling and airstrikes, as the emergency room sat waiting for the next wave of victims, Abu Rajab and the other doctors spoke to Sam about how they felt utterly abandoned by the world. 'One nurse said to me, he feels like they are getting crushed like bugs,' recalled Sam. They knew a siege was coming, but Abu Rajab and his colleagues did not even entertain the thought of leaving, telling Sam they would never abandon their patients. 'I had many chances to leave this work,' explained Abu Rajab. 'But I want to continue my duty towards my people until the very end.'

In the first two weeks Sam was in Aleppo, heavy aerial and artillery bombardment at times made Castello Road impassable, while the shelling was consistent and intense. Regime forces were advancing by the hour, and it was clear that soon there would be no way out of Aleppo. Sam wanted to stay but Abu Rajab urged him to leave. 'Go and tell the world what is happening to us,' he told Sam. They hugged each other and cried. Sam felt like he was abandoning his best friends, like Chicago no longer existed. Two weeks in M10 felt like a lifetime lived anywhere else. As the M10 staff lined up to hug Sam and say goodbye, he promised he wouldn't forget them or what he had seen in Aleppo. 'He saw everything that no reporters can show, but he saw it with his own eyes, he was an eyewitness.

He was there and being there means a lot,' said Abu Rajab. 'Dr Sam really means a lot to me.'

Sam set off in the pre-dawn darkness for the Turkish border, and his driver didn't dare turn on the headlights. It would all come down to a 500-metre section of the highway called the 'road of death'. Neither Sam nor the driver spoke, holding their breath as they sped along the exposed road, eyes on the dip ahead that signalled safety. They made it, but mere hours later the road was cut by regime forces.[14]

In the next 48 hours, the Syrian army and their allies completely encircled Aleppo. Fourteen civilians were killed while trying to flee via Castello Road over the next few days, reported Amnesty International. A witness told the NGO: 'The taxi driving a family in front of us was hit by an airstrike. The car burst into flames... we couldn't stop to check if anyone survived. On the way, I saw five human bodies rotting on the side of the road.'[15] There was now no way in or out of east Aleppo.

To Sam, escaping alive didn't feel worth celebrating. When I met him in Istanbul a few days later, he was so physically consumed with guilt that his face was grey and his shoulders slumped. We sat drinking tea in the garden courtyard of a hotel close to the famous Sultanahmet Square. It was a gorgeous summer day, but Sam was still cloaked in the darkness of Aleppo. 'How do you walk away from that?' he asked incredulously. 'I feel like I just lost a chunk of my soul.'

The UN issued warnings about the number of civilians trapped in east Aleppo, estimating there could be between 200,000 and 300,000, but officials were unsure of the exact count. 'We are extremely concerned because of the large number of people, it is a very high number,' Jakob Kern, the acting UN Humanitarian Coordinator for Syria, told me over a scratchy line from Damascus. UNICEF reported that a third of those trapped in east Aleppo were children.[16] As rebels tried to break the siege on the east of the city, they fired an indiscriminate barrage of rockets on government-held west Aleppo, killing at least 38 civilians, including more than a dozen children.[17] Both sides now seemed intent on fighting this battle to the end, with civilians trapped in the middle. But only the Assad regime and their Russian allies had

airpower – which was why the death toll inside the opposition-held east was skyrocketing.

As the siege set in, the cost of food and basic supplies inside east Aleppo greatly increased, while medical supplies ran dangerously low. One thing that did remain was satellite internet. After Sam left the city, he and his colleagues from the Syrian American Medical Society set up a WhatsApp group for reporters to contact Abu Rajab and the other medical professionals who remained inside. I started receiving a constant stream of video, photos and messages, informing me of airstrikes and falling bombs, of overcrowded emergency rooms, distraught parents and maimed children. Most images were deemed too graphic by my editors for the ABC to publish, so I'd describe them in detail for my radio broadcasts and post them on Twitter, because it felt criminal for these images to remain unseen. Tiny corpses wrapped in shrouds. Bodies lined up in the back of a truck. Babies missing limbs. Mums, dads, brothers and sisters clutching each other and weeping inconsolably over the death of a loved one.

I started to communicate nearly every day with Dr Farida, the last female obstetrician in east Aleppo, who worked out of the Omar Bin Abdul Aziz Hospital, codenamed 'M2'. Farida had a dry sense of humour, combining news of the siege and the challenges of treating her patients with scenes of daily life in the war-torn city. One night, an explosion in the street outside shattered the glass windows of her kitchen as Dr Farida was making dinner, with glass exploding around her. 'I am like cats, nine lives,' she said wryly. Dr Farida told me about doing emergency caesareans by mobile phone torchlight when the electricity cut out, and said that they were running out of basic supplies. 'In maternity section we finished all the umbilical cord clamps and we have to use the thread now,' she wrote, adding a sad-face emoji.

The obstetrics unit at Dr Farida's hospital, M2, was on the third floor, which left it more vulnerable to attack than the underground M10. Once, as she was performing a caesarean section, a missile struck the fourth floor of the facility, causing the ceiling to partially collapse. The rest of the surgical staff fled the room, but Dr Farida couldn't because she had to clean debris out of her patient's abdominal cavity. Extraordinarily, she was able to save her patient's life. On another occasion, a pregnant woman arrived with deep shrapnel injuries.

As a team of doctors worked to stabilise the mother, Dr Farida realised that her womb had been penetrated by the metal shards. She tried to do an emergency delivery of the five-month-old fetus but found it had been split in two from the waist down. They did, at least, manage to save the mother.

Dr Farida's eight-year-old daughter would often be in the hospital, waiting for her mother to finish work. With all the horror going on outside, they liked to stay close to each other. One day in July 2016, a regime attack near the hospital used a rocket containing chlorine gas. Dr Farida's daughter ran into the operating room, where her mother was performing surgery, crying and unable to breathe. The obstetrician left the patient and gave her daughter oxygen, holding her close.

On 23 July, the children's hospital in east Aleppo, where the babies Dr Farida delivered went if they needed more care, was hit by an airstrike, causing a power cut that led to the deaths of four newborns in incubators. According to UN investigators, the kids' hospital had been clearly marked with emblems on the roof as a place that deserved protection. After that day, the emblems were removed out of fear of being targeted.[18] It was an extraordinary reversal of the so-called 'rules' of war – rather than helping with protection in Syria, the Red Crescent insignia seemed to place medical facilities firmly in the crosshairs.

In the last week of July, Assad's forces launched airstrikes on six different hospitals in and around Aleppo, the worst week for attacks on medical facilities since the Syrian war had begun in 2011.[19]

Despite having shown little regard for the fate of civilians in rebel-held areas, the Russians announced that they would create safe routes out of east Aleppo for civilians, giving them food and medical care if they fled.[20] But how were those inside supposed to trust the allies of the man who had spent five years trying to wipe them out – particularly after the Russians had also bombed their neighbourhoods and hospitals? The proposal was feared to be just a fig leaf, allowing Assad and Moscow to claim civilians had been given an escape route before they unleashed their deadly arsenal on east Aleppo. The lack of trust was clear, as reportedly less than 200 civilians left the besieged east through the 'safe' corridors.[21]

As the operation to retake east Aleppo heated up, Abu Rajab

updated me most days on the trauma cases overwhelming his ER. 'Mona Masri, one year old. Was injured by a bullet in the picture and passed away during the operation,' he captioned a photo of a tiny baby girl covered in blood and bandages. 'A 16-year-old, name unknown with a head injury.' 'Mohammed Anas Jassem, 8, injured by a sniper.' 'This ambulance driver was targeted while helping the wounded.' 'Double tap airstrike. 24 civilians killed.' I verified the medics' photos and videos using several trusted sources inside and outside the city. It was the only way to report a war that reporters were blocked from accessing.

In mid August, the International Committee of the Red Cross backed up the reports of Abu Rajab and Dr Farida, announcing that hundreds of civilians had been killed in east Aleppo in just the past few weeks, with ICRC president Peter Maurer declaring:

> No one and nowhere is safe. Shellfire is constant, with houses, schools and hospitals all in the line of fire. People live in a state of fear. Children have been traumatized. The scale of the suffering is immense. This is beyond doubt one of the most devastating urban conflicts in modern times.[22]

Back in Chicago, Sam couldn't sleep or eat. He stayed holed up in his apartment, the screams and thuds of Aleppo haunting his every thought. All the surgeon wanted was to be back in M10 beside Abu Rajab, rolling up his sleeves and trying to save the next child and then the next. The urge to curl up and retreat was overwhelming, but he'd promised Abu Rajab and the other medical staff that he would ensure the world didn't forget them.

As Assad and the Russians tried to paint the city as full of 'terrorists' rather than civilians, Sam's eyewitness testimony from Aleppo was invaluable. He threw himself into a feverish campaign to try to persuade President Obama to do more to help the besieged civilians. Swapping his scrubs for a suit, the orthopaedic surgeon flew to New York to meet Samantha Power, the US ambassador to the UN. Sam showed Ambassador Power photos from his trip. Bloodied floors. Small bodies in shrouds. When he reached the images of maimed children, the US ambassador turned away, telling the surgeon she couldn't look.

Sam was given a slot as a guest speaker at an emergency side meeting of the UN Security Council, focused entirely on the situation in Aleppo. He scolded the diplomats for their lack of action. 'This body does have the power to make all of this stop. This body has the power to save lives and limbs on a scale that doctors cannot,' Sam told them firmly. 'It must pressure and threaten the Syrian government to do the same. It must enforce a no-fly zone, using coalition airpower already in place and in force against the Islamic State.'[23]

Sam wrote for the *New York Times*, campaigned outside the White House and did interview after interview with countless TV news networks. 'I plead with the Obama administration to act. It must boldly confront Russia to halt the bombardment of Aleppo and Castello Road,' Sam urged in the *Washington Post*.[24]

The American and British governments condemned the siege on Aleppo and the spiralling civilian death toll. But nothing changed.

On the ground in Aleppo, things only got worse. 'If the world isn't going to create a no-fly zone, we will do it ourselves,' activists in Aleppo declared, as they set fire to dozens of tyres, enveloping the city in acrid black smoke, a desperate attempt to provide rudimentary cover from the pro-government planes targeting and attacking their neighbourhoods.

As airstrikes continued to pound Aleppo, and an increasing number of people had to be pulled from the rubble of collapsed concrete apartment blocks, the rescue work of Syrian Civil Defence units known as the White Helmets gained notoriety among western news consumers. Since 2013, the group had been rescuing survivors of barrel bombs and blasts across Syria, receiving support, training and millions in funding from foundations and governments in the west, including the US, the UK and the Netherlands.[25] In 2016, after rescuing more than 60,000 Syrians, the group was nominated for the Nobel Peace Prize. In the wake of the White Helmets' growing fame, Syrian and Russian state media began a fierce misinformation campaign against the rescuers, falsely smearing them as allies of Al Qaeda and other jihadi groups.

The campaign to discredit the rescuers was cheered on by a legion of far-left media activists who classified the Syrian opposition as

part of a 'American imperialist' project. People who had admired my reporting from Lebanon, Gaza and the West Bank suddenly accused me of being a western agent because I used footage filmed by the White Helmets. Famous anti-war reporters like John Pilger, who had once done such groundbreaking work exposing atrocities in East Timor, joined the chorus of disinformation. 'We have the White Helmets, a complete propaganda construct, in Syria,' Pilger declared on RT, the international television network funded by the Russian government.[26] It was an astonishing and shameful parroting of Assad's and Putin's lines.

In 2017, an investigation by The Guardian newspaper uncovered that Russian interests had indeed funded the propaganda campaign that slandered the White Helmets.[27] But at the time, the disinformation led to a dangerous sense of confusion among many in the international community over what was happening in Syria, promoting the inaccurate idea that 'no good guys' were left there. The slurs translated into deadly results as the regime began to openly target the White Helmets, bombing their facilities and staging 'double tap' strikes that killed and injured the first responders as they arrived at the scene of attacks.[28]

‖

As the Syrian regime's bombing of Aleppo intensified, the distressing evidence of what was happening to the civilians trapped inside continued to be sent out. On 18 August 2016, one of Abu Rajab's colleagues from M10 sent my WhatsApp group a video of a young boy who had just been rescued from an airstrike by the White Helmets and brought to the ER. The clip, filmed by a cameraman working for the opposition-aligned Aleppo Media Centre, shows a dusty little boy sitting in the back of an ambulance, having just been pulled from the rubble of his home after an airstrike in the Al Qaterji neighbourhood. He sits on an orange seat that's too big for his tiny body, looking confused, his forehead and his shirt covered in blood. The child wipes his pudgy hand on his head, before looking down and realising it is now also covered in blood. But he doesn't cry. He just sits there resignedly,

seemingly accustomed to such horror. The doctors tell us that his name is Omran Daqneesh, and he is five years old.

Like most of the other photos and videos I had been receiving from medical staff in Aleppo, I posted the footage on my Twitter feed, as did other reporters in the WhatsApp group. 'Watch this video from Aleppo tonight. And watch it again. And remind yourself that with Syria #wecantsaywedidntknow,' I tweeted.[29]

Meanwhile, Abu Rajab was down in the M10 emergency room, triaging patients and treating those with less serious injuries. 'It was in the evening around 7 pm. We heard the siren of the ambulance. There had been a bombing in the Qaterji neighbourhood,' he explained. As Omran arrived in the ER with three other children, Abu Rajab and his nursing assistants immediately started treating the little boy, cleaning up and bandaging his head wound. 'My attention was caught when I saw this kid. He was different from the rest of the children. He was silent. The other kids were crying but he was not, despite the dust and the blood and the wound,' said Abu Rajab.

The little boy had very low blood pressure and remained silent. Concerned that Omran's deep shock was the result of a serious internal injury, Abu Rajab performed an X-ray on the little boy's chest and abdomen and an ultrasound on his stomach. But they didn't find any internal bleeding, so they stitched up the large cut on his head. 'He didn't say anything except to ask for his parents,' Abu Rajab said. 'They arrived shortly after, in a second wave of people. Only then, once Omran saw them, did he start crying.'

Meanwhile, the video and photos that I and other reporters had tweeted of Omran Daqneesh sitting stunned in the back of the ambulance went viral. Within hours, Omran's image was plastered across the front page of the *New York Times* with the headline 'An injured child, symbol of Syrian suffering'. He also made the cover of the *Financial Times*, *La Repubblica*, *El País*, the *South China Morning Post*, *The Times* of London and countless other newspapers around the world. By the next day, the video of Omran on the ABC News Facebook page had been viewed 13 million times, while the footage continued to make headlines around the world. 'We shed tears but there are no tears here. He doesn't cry once,'

a CNN anchor notes, crying live on air as the network repeatedly broadcast the image of Omran in the ambulance.[30]

Overnight, one child's suffering in Aleppo was suddenly front-page news. The charity CARE Australia contacted the ABC to say they'd had a surge in donations for Syria because of Omran's photo. My inbox filled up with dozens of emails from people all over the world, telling me they were distraught thinking of Omran and his family. 'I've asked my boss if I can work overtime, so I can send my overtime money to Omran. Can you help me and make sure it's given to him?' said one email. 'My heart is broken as soon as I saw his little face. My tears haven't stopped,' wrote Paul from London. 'How can I help?'

For weeks I had been frantically sharing other poignant and disturbing photos from Aleppo. The bloodstained white socks of a little girl wearing her best black patent-leather shoes. A baby's pram soaked in blood. What was it about little Omran that had cut through to people? Perhaps it was that, compared to the other pictures coming out of Aleppo, it wasn't *too* grisly. People could post it on their Facebook and Twitter feeds, feel engaged with the conflict and express their empathy without having to fully process the horror of the situation.

Activists inside Aleppo were outraged that many news organisations reporting on Omran's image attributed his injuries generally to the 'Syrian civil war', failing to point out that his house had been hit by an airstrike carried out by either Syrian regime or Russian forces.[31] 'Who has got warplanes in the sky of Aleppo, the people of Mars?' Abdulkafi Al Hamdo, an English teacher and opposition activist messaged angrily. 'We really don't want you to say we are being killed without saying who is killing us!'

Abu Rajab at M10 couldn't believe the reaction to Omran's picture. 'Dozens and dozens of journalists were suddenly asking about Omran. We didn't know this would cause all this noise, we looked after him the same as every other kid,' he told me. He hoped the attention given to Omran would spur on efforts to protect the people of east Aleppo from the regime's advance. 'This kid became like the face of the Syrian children's suffering. We thought maybe it will mean the international community will help us?' But Omran's story failed to translate into anything

more than temporary outrage and social media anguish. For one day, everyone talked about the horror in Syria – reporters who didn't normally cover the war wrote their think pieces and feature stories. And then they moved on.

Two days later, Omran's older brother, ten-year-old Ali, died from the injuries he sustained that night. But Ali's death didn't make the headlines, much like the more than 140 Syrian kids who had also been killed in the previous three weeks.[32] Just one week after Omran's video went viral, I was back reporting the same kind of evidence of horror inside Aleppo, but this time no one shared it:

> Eleven children, including an infant, were killed in a barrel bomb attack carried out by government forces on a rebel-held neighbourhood of eastern Aleppo. Video of the aftermath of the incident shows rescue workers pulling out the lifeless bodies of children from under the rubble. Two children were also killed in rebel shelling on government-held western Aleppo.[33]

Collectively the world heard, saw and felt the pain of Aleppo's people, but our global system had no functioning means of protecting these people. The UN had spent months trying unsuccessfully to pressure the Assad government into allowing them to monitor humanitarian corridors and get aid into Aleppo. Meanwhile, discussions between the United States and Russia over potential no-fly zones failed miserably. Russia's veto in the Security Council was used time and time again to block any resolution that would deter Assad from what he was doing to his own people.[34] Syria was put in the too-hard basket. Without firm action to deter Assad or Russia, the slaughter continued.

The photos and messages Abu Rajab sent me from M10 became more desperate as the hospital's ER overflowed with civilians. A seven-year-old boy whose skin was punctured all over by the hot shards of a barrel bomb. A crying three-year-old girl in pink shorts with a head injury from artillery shelling. A young man being frantically resuscitated by doctors on a blood-smeared floor, as his friends watched in horror. And to compound the dismay, a funeral was then targeted, killing 15 people, including several children.

In Chicago, Sam was finding the constant WhatsApp messages from Aleppo torturous yet addictive. Every image took him back

inside the ER. The smells, the sounds. 'I was anxious all the time, always checking my phone,' he said. 'Every morning you wake up, and it's just a race. A race to see if they're all alive, and if they're still around.'

At the height of the violence in Aleppo, on 5 September 2016, I interviewed Australia's foreign minister Julie Bishop when she visited Jerusalem, where I was based.[35] In the next few days, the US secretary of state John Kerry and Russian foreign minister Sergei Lavrov were holding crisis talks on Syria, and Kerry was reportedly planning to propose grounding all Syrian regime aircraft.[36] With Australian pilots flying over the country every day, as part of efforts to target ISIS militants in Syria's east, it was a relevant topic for Bishop to discuss. So the first question I asked her was: what did Australia think of Kerry's ambitious idea for Syria? She gave me a dose of her famous glare before excusing herself and racing over to admonish her aide. 'You didn't tell me they were going to ask about Syria,' she hissed. 'What's the latest?' It was a disappointing reality check on how little importance my government placed on the crisis.

But it wasn't as bad as the stumble made by US presidential candidate Gary Johnson. During a live interview on the US news network MSNBC, Mr Johnson was asked what he would do about the crisis in Aleppo if elected. 'And what is Aleppo?' Mr Johnson responded.

'You're kidding,' the stunned host replied.[37]

Shortly after, despite weeks of intense negotiations, the UN confirmed that it had still not received 'permission' from Assad's government to bring urgently needed food and medical supplies into Aleppo. And just like in other parts of Syria, they wouldn't try to deliver any aid without regime approval. Inside Aleppo, medical staff were devastated. Dr Farida wrote scathingly, 'We are trapped in Aleppo without food, medicine or fuel. Our children and patients are suffering because of the inefficiency and malaise of the UN. They are supposed to protect us and assure access to our patients. They are doing neither. They need a big shake-up. We lost trust with the UN long time ago.'

On 11 September 2016, John Kerry managed to secure a tentative ceasefire agreement, a seven-day pause in fighting across Syria to

begin at the start of the Muslim holiday of Eid Al Adha.[38] As part of the deal, the regime would suspend airstrikes, rebels would stop fighting around government areas, and a demilitarized zone would be established around the Castello Road leading into Aleppo so desperately needed aid could be delivered.

But the medical staff in Aleppo reacted warily to the good news. The ceasefire was not due to start until sundown on the next day, so Russian and Assad regime warplanes were pounding rebel-held areas while they still could. 'We fear ceasefires because of what happens first,' an activist inside told me. Indeed, in the same headlines announcing the agreement came the news that over 30 people had been killed that day across rebel-held east Aleppo.

The United States and Russia said that if the ceasefire held, they would share intelligence on areas in Syria where militants linked to ISIS and Al Qaeda were active, to coordinate airstrikes against both targets. It was a deeply ambitious plan, given that the Assad regime had labelled everyone in Aleppo's rebel-held territory 'terrorists' – including civilians and doctors. After such rhetoric from Assad, the cynics couldn't see how John Kerry would convince Moscow to end the widespread targeting of civilian infrastructure in opposition-held areas. The ceasefire seemed destined to fail.

But for a few days, with the skies quiet, the medical staff inside Aleppo managed to spend precious moments outside with their families to celebrate the Eid Al Adha holiday. Dr Farida took her young daughter to a small broken-down amusement park, where enterprising teenage boys had made a mini ferris wheel out of broken metal pipes retrieved from the sites of bombed-out buildings. The ride was turned by hand and in a fairly rickety state, but it didn't stop the kids from beaming with happiness; they hadn't been able to play out in the open like that for months. Inside M10, Abu Rajab organized a low-key party for injured children in the hospital ward, handing out small toys and clothes as the hospital enjoyed its quietest days in months.

The ceasefire, which had taken weeks of intensive diplomacy between John Kerry and Sergei Lavrov to secure, fell apart in just a week, with two deadly incidents destroying any hope of agreement between the United States and Russia on the fate of east Aleppo.

Five days into the temporary truce, in the afternoon of 17 September, warplanes with the US-led coalition against ISIS militants flew over what they believed was an ISIS training camp near the Deir Al Zour airport in Syria's far east. For days, coalition forces had been watching the camp with surveillance drones and reported seeing tents, tanks and armoured personnel carriers, as well as men wearing a mix of traditional, civilian and military-style clothing.[39] Deciding that the lack of uniform indicated these men were ISIS fighters, coalition commanders ordered a strike, which began at 3.55 pm Damascus time.

However, the men the coalition attacked were not ISIS, but pro-Assad forces who had been fighting the jihadists. Frantic to stop the attack, a Russian military officer called the US military headquarters in the Middle East, but the person he tried to contact was not at their desk. The Russians did not manage to speak to coalition military advisers until nearly an hour after the attack began. By then, 37 bombs and missiles, six dropped by Australian pilots, had already hit the site near Deir Al Zour. Eighty-three pro-regime militia were reportedly killed in the botched airstrikes.[40]

It was later revealed that while the US-led coalition had given the Russian military advance notice of the strike, they had provided the wrong location. Washington admitted their blunder within hours, apologising through the Russians for the 'unintentional loss of life of Syrian forces fighting the Islamic State'.[41] In all, the incident encapsulated the deadly omnishambles that had become the war in Syria.

Outraged, the Syrian regime accused the Americans of deliberately hitting their forces, claiming the airstrikes proved the US was supporting ISIS jihadists as part of efforts to oust Assad. How would Assad take revenge on the Americans?

Two days later, Damascus found the target for their retribution.

At 10.50 am on 19 September, a joint UN and Syrian Arab Red Crescent aid convoy rolled out of a warehouse in government-held west Aleppo. With bright blue UN flags fluttering on the side, the 31 trucks, packed full of food, medicine, clothes and other supplies, set off for the opposition-held town of Urum al-Kubra in the Aleppo countryside, 24 kilometres from the city. It was a delicate operation, with the convoy crossing from government-held territory

to opposition-held land, and the UN had spent weeks negotiating with the regime to secure permission for it to go ahead. The Syrian government had not allowed international UN staff to be on board, so the trucks were manned by local Red Crescent volunteers. The UN was required to inform the Assad regime of the exact route and coordinates of the convoy, with aid officials even tweeting about the mission. 'Inter-agency convoy is crossing the conflict line to Big Orem in #Aleppo #Syria to deliver aid,' tweeted officials from the UN humanitarian office, OCHA.[42]

At around 1.30 pm the convoy reached Urum al-Kubra, where aid workers started unloading the goods. As they unpacked, they noted aircraft in the skies but, assuming the aircraft were monitoring the ceasefire, continued working unperturbed. Russian drones were also seen in the sky for several hours following the convoy, with Moscow confirming they were tracking the aid delivery.[43]

At just after 7 pm, as the aid was still being unloaded, helicopters suddenly appeared overhead and dropped a barrage of barrel bombs on the UN-marked trucks and the civilian aid workers. As locals rushed to the scene to pull wounded aid workers from the wreckage of burning trucks, the helicopters returned, dropping a second round of barrel bombs.[44] The attack lasted about 30 minutes, with many of the aid workers burnt to death in the dark, some of them charred beyond recognition, their body parts scattered among piles of destroyed UN food parcels and boxes of medicine. In the ultimate horrific move, aircraft fired machine-guns at survivors as they tried to escape.[45] The attack killed 14 civilian aid workers and wounded 15.

The UN immediately suspended aid convoys throughout Syria.

All fingers pointed to the regime, and potentially their Russian allies, for the war crime of striking the UN-flagged aid convoy. A Pentagon spokesman told reporters:

There are only three parties that fly in Syria: the coalition, the Russians, and the Syrian regime. It was not the coalition. We don't fly over Aleppo. We have no reason to. We strike only ISIS, and ISIS is not there. We would leave it to the Russians and the Syrian regime to explain their actions.[46]

The UN secretary general, Ban Ki-Moon, slammed the attack as 'sickening, savage and apparently deliberate'. He said, 'Just when you think it cannot get any worse, the bar of depravity sinks lower.'

Both the Russian and Syrian governments denied being behind the attack, claiming that the trucks could have been destroyed in a fire, attacked by 'terrorists' or struck by an American drone – but the evidence lay there in the wreckage. The remains of barrel bombs and the tail fin of an OFAB, a Russian missile widely used by the regime, were strewn among destroyed goods.[47] Witnesses at the scenes also filmed footage and took photos that clearly showed the trucks had been hit by multiple attacks from warplanes, with the sounds of jets heard in the video.[48] A UN investigation into the attack on the convoy later found that it had been 'meticulously planned and ruthlessly carried out by the Syrian air force'.[49]

The brazen and ruthless bombing of the aid convoy signified the end of the ceasefire. Within a few days, Assad's push to retake east Aleppo was back on. Inside Aleppo, Abu Rajab and his colleagues despaired, feeling utterly abandoned. It seemed it would be only a matter of weeks before the regime forces were on their doorstep. And what then? Arrest and torture were the established pattern for dealing with opposition sympathizers.

On top of the fear that they were about to be cornered by the regime, no aid had reached the inside of the besieged sector during the ceasefire. Food was now scarce. 'The needs were becoming so dire,' explained Abu Rajab. 'I had so much responsibility. Just trying to provide meals and shelter for so many people.'

As Assad's forces and the Russians begin to pound east Aleppo with unprecedented force, Abu Rajab's ER was utterly overwhelmed. Children sat weeping and wailing as doctors checked for broken bones. Some had singed hair and burnt clothes from explosions, while other shook uncontrollably in fear and shock. Mothers clutched their dead babies, weeping up at the skies that had taken their children away.

Abu Rajab sent me through photo after photo of the horror. 'These are the children targeted by the Russian warplanes,' he wrote. 'They were pulled from the rubble.'

The daily death toll mounted.

49 dead.[50]
81 dead.[51]
104 dead.[52]

'Never has such horror been so well documented, so little done #wecantsaywedidntknow,' I tweeted.[53]

Parents rushed into M10 at all hours of the day and the night carrying their bloodied and limbless children. I was sent video of a traumatised toddler, covered in dust and blood from a head wound, flinging his arms around the neck of the nurse treating him. The nurse, trying to examine the child for serious injuries, gently tries to detach the little arms, but the boy won't let go. The bombardment was so fierce that pieces of children arrived at M10 – not bodies but pieces – the doctors unable to do anything but say a prayer and wrap them in shrouds for burial.

Abu Rajab sent a desperate voice message amid the carnage and the chaos. 'The matter is very serious,' he said, sounding panicked. 'This is a call for help to everybody who's listening. What's happening now we have not seen before!' With east Aleppo having been under complete siege for two months, his staff were running out of supplies to deal with the increasing number of patients with traumatic injuries. Meanwhile, fuel for the hospital's generators and ambulances was also beginning to run out. Dr Farida said it was the worst it had ever been. 'We need a miracle to save us from inevitable death,' she wrote after a day of bombardment. 'If we die, please have mercy on our souls.'

In the first week of bombing after the ceasefire expired, 96 children were killed and 223 injured in east Aleppo.[54] It was believed to be the deadliest three days in Aleppo since the war had begun. UN investigators confirmed that in a single day, on 23 September 2016, Russian aircraft conducted 42 air sorties over east Aleppo, making at least 28 confirmed airstrikes.[55] 'The children of Aleppo are trapped in a living nightmare,' declared UNICEF deputy executive director Justin Forsyth. 'There are no words left to describe the suffering they are experiencing.'

On 28 September, as the demand for the services of Abu Rajab and his colleagues was at its peak, they came under direct attack. At 4 am, a warplane fired a missile, slamming straight into one of

M10's walls. The impact was so fierce, rubble fell in on patients in the intensive care unit. 'The staff are in the shelter and no one can get out because of the intensity of the shelling,' messaged Abu Rajab as the attack was underway.

At almost the same time, M2, the second-largest hospital in east Aleppo after M10, was hit by artillery shelling, killing two patients and injuring three medical staff.[56] It was hard to see the bombing of the two hospitals as anything but a deliberate, coordinated attack.

'If the hospital falls on top of us, come pull us out from under the rubble but please do not take pictures,' messaged a nurse. 'We won't gain anything from it and our dignity is too precious.' One of Abu Rajab's colleagues, an anaesthesiologist, wrote to say that greatest thing he now wished for was a quick death. 'One that is more merciful than suffocating slowly under the rubble or the fire,' he wrote. 'We wish to be full bodies not scattered pieces if we die. We wish to have our own personal grave, not to be piled and buried on top of each other as we are doing now. A peaceful death is all but a dream now.'

After the missile attack, M10 limped along, largely out of service, with the intensive care unit no longer taking patients and all surgery cancelled. Civilians arriving with traumatic injuries were triaged and sent to the only two facilities still operating. Only six intensive care beds were reportedly left in the whole of east Aleppo, with anaesthetics supplies gone. Stoic as ever, Abu Rajab remained at the hospital site, trying to assess what needed to be done to make it operational again.

Three days later, at around noon on 1 October, an urgent SOS WhatsApp message from Abu Rajab popped up on my phone. A massive airstrike had just hit the already damaged hospital. 'Another direct target on M10 with cluster bombs. The hospital is being destroyed now!' he cried in the voice message. For several hours Abu Rajab and the other hospital staff and patients sought shelter in the basement as the attack continued.

The death knell for M10 came in the form of barrel bombs, cluster munitions and even a 'bunker buster', designed to penetrate underground targets, which left a large deep crater next to the site.[57] 'Women were crying, and children were screaming. It's as if death was falling upon us from the sky. We didn't know what they might

throw on us next. We almost suffocated from the smoke, the dirt, and the smell of gunpowder,' one of M10's doctors told Human Rights Watch.[58]

The massive barrage of airstrikes was the eighth attack on M10 in just two weeks. 'It was the most intense bombing,' said Abu Rajab. 'Death was chasing us at every direction. We had seven airstrikes hit us in just two hours. It was a tragic day.' Two patients in the street were killed and ten people injured. Among the wounded was one of the three orthopaedic surgeons left in Aleppo; with his hands burnt in the attack, he could no longer operate. The long driveway that led into the basement ER, where so many desperate families had run to receive urgent treatment and medical care, was now covered in rubble and twisted metal.

To Abu Rajab's despair, the hospital had sustained such severe structural damage it was unrecoverable; M10 would need to be abandoned. Abu Rajab led a local cameraman working for the BBC through the bombed-out facility that had been a home to him. 'This is one of the cluster munitions, it landed in front of the hospital,' he says in the footage, holding up the twisted metal cap of the weapons. He points out the destroyed wards and the collapsed walls of M10, taking the cameraman through the halls which were now empty of patients and covered in dust and debris. 'The laboratory was hit, as you can see, the electricity generators are not working,' he says, pointing through a blown-off doorway into what had been the hospital lab. 'May Allah punish those responsible.'[59]

With M10 inoperable, the UN humanitarian chief Stephen O'Brien issued an urgent statement, describing the healthcare system in east Aleppo as 'all but obliterated' and on the verge of 'total collapse'.[60] I interviewed Mr O'Brien's spokesperson Jens Laerke over the phone. The humanitarian situation in Aleppo was 'unparalleled', Jens told me. 'I don't remember any other point in time where we have collectively felt this agony about what we are seeing. We have not seen a humanitarian catastrophe almost played out in real time in front of our eyes. Frankly, it is agonising.'

But nothing changed.

Three days after M10 had to be closed, the regime hit it one last time for good measure, killing a technician who was trying to

recover any salvageable equipment. The power of the blast was so intense his body was thrown 100 metres from the site.

As international media attention focused on what was clearly a campaign to destroy east Aleppo's last hospitals, the Russian defence ministry hit back with disinformation, presenting their own satellite images that showed no sign of damage to M10. 'No changes to the facility can be observed on another image taken on October 11, or after the alleged airstrike. This fact proves that all accusations of indiscriminate strikes voiced by some alleged eyewitnesses turn out to be mere fakes,' claimed the Russian spokesperson.[61] But the fakes were all theirs: their satellite imagery was clearly from different dates, and the wealth of evidence unequivocally proving the strike included CCTV videos of the moment of impact, satellite pictures, and photos and videos of the scene.[62]

Bakeries were also being targeted by pro-regime forces to try to force the hungry population of east Aleppo to surrender. The same day M10 was obliterated, shortly before morning prayers, an airstrike carried out by either Syrian or Russian air forces demolished a bakery in the Al Maadi district that had fed almost 6000 families, killing eight civilians. Two days later, the Azizi bakery in the Al Haydaria neighbourhood was hit by an airstrike that killed more than 15 civilians.

Abu Rajab and the surgeons kept up their near daily chats with Sam in Chicago, confessing their fears that the worst days were near. 'They were telling me how bad it was and how they're operating without supplies, and how there's no food, they were just eating dry dates,' said Sam.

Pro-Assad forces continued to creep closer to east Aleppo. With so many Syrians having fled the country or moved to opposition areas to avoid being conscripted as cannon fodder for Assad's forces, by late 2016, the Syrian army was seriously depleted and reliant on a heavy network of national and foreign militia, including the Iran Revolutionary Guards Corps, Lebanon's Shiite Hezbollah, Afghan militias and the Iraqi Al Nujabaa and Al Fatimiyoon militias.[63] The presence of these notoriously violent and undisciplined groups, and the constant rhetoric from the regime that all those left inside Aleppo were 'terrorists', created a potential nightmare scenario for the weeks ahead.

In Geneva, the UN's Syria envoy Staffan de Mistura challenged the position of the Syrian government and Russia that all those under bombardment in east Aleppo were 'terrorists'.[64] De Mistura said that according to UN research, of the 8000 rebel fighters left inside east Aleppo, 900 were associated with the Al Qaeda-linked group Jabhat Al Nusra, which the Assad regime and Russia had declared were their main targets in taking east Aleppo. The civilian population was estimated to be around 275,000, said the UN official. 'So, are we talking about 900 people basically who are becoming the main reason for which there is 275,000 people actually being attacked? Is this going to be the alibi and reason for the destruction of the city?' he demanded. 'Are you rather ready to announce an immediate and total aerial bombing halt if al-Nusra leaves?'[65]

De Mistura said the departure of Al Nusra from east Aleppo would remove the justification for the ferocious bombardment. 'And if you did decide to leave in dignity and with your weapons to Idlib or anywhere you wanted to go, I personally am ready physically, to accompany you,' he offered. De Mistura invoked the 1990s atrocities of Rwanda and Yugoslavia's civil war, saying the UN were not willing to 'resign ourselves' to another genocide. 'Thousands of civilians, not terrorists, will be killed,' he stated firmly.

But just hours later, speaking to Danish television, Syrian president Bashar Al Assad made it clear he would ignore the UN's pleas. 'The moderate opposition in Syria is a myth,' Assad said. He said he put all opposition fighters in Syria in the same box as ISIS militants, and that it was his job to 'liberate' civilians in Aleppo, who he claimed were being used as human shields.[66]

Meanwhile, whole apartment blocks in east Aleppo were being obliterated as the waves of deadly airstrikes continued. At one scene in the Al Qaterji district, the White Helmets desperately picked through the rubble of a collapsed building that had buried several families inside. Twenty-five people had been killed, but extraordinarily, one teenage boy was spotted alive and dangling off the side of what had been his home.[67] The rescuers scrambled to reach him with their cherry picker, carefully extracting his legs from the rubble, slowly pulling the 16-year-old boy to safety. In the

Top: Democracy activists Bassel Khartabil and Noura Ghazi at their engagement party in Damascus in October 2011. *(Courtesy of Noura Ghazi)*

Above: Noura Ghazi holding a photo of her beloved Bassel with other members of 'Families for Freedom' at a demonstration in Geneva in February 2017. The advocacy group for Syrian detainees and their relatives campaigns on behalf of more than 98,000 Syrians who have disappeared during the Syrian war, the majority of those at the hands of the regime of Bashar Al Assad. *(Courtesy of the Syria Campaign)*

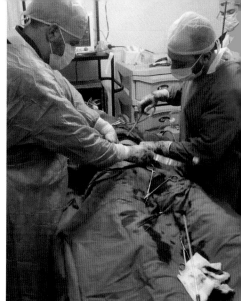
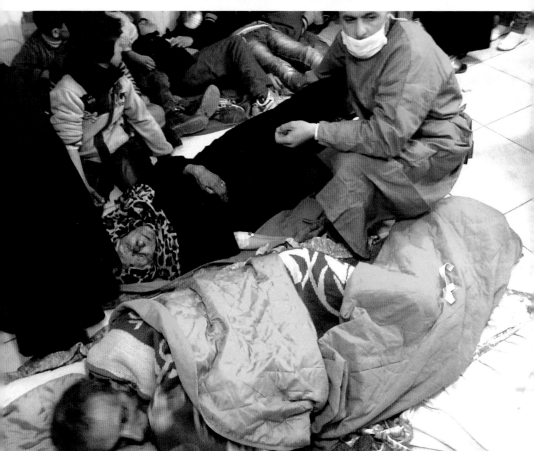

Top left: Khaled Naanaa with his medical colleague Muhammad Yousef in Madaya in 2016. Khaled was on crutches after being shot in the leg by ISIS sympathisers. *(Courtesy of Khaled Naanaa)*

Top right: Khaled operating in in Madaya. *(Courtesy of Khaled Naanaa)*

Above: Severely ill and starving civilians at Khaled's clinic in Madaya. *(Getty Images)*

Top: Khaled in Sydney in November 2016, accepting the Amnesty International Media Award for human rights reporting on radio, on behalf of Sophie McNeill and Fouad Abu Gosh *(Courtesy of Amnesty International).*

Above: Khaled's wife Joumana, Khaled, his daughter, Ayaa, and Sophie McNeill in Perth in September 2016 after the family was granted asylum by the Australian government. *(Sophie McNeill)*

Top: Syrian men react with relief after being rescued from the Mediterranean Sea and transferred to a rescue boat launched by the Italian navy ship *San Giusto* in September 2014. *(Sophie McNeill)*

Above: A jubilant Ahmad Sandeh aboard the *San Giusto*. The 22-year-old from Aleppo had just been rescued from the Mediterranean Sea. *(Sophie McNeill)*

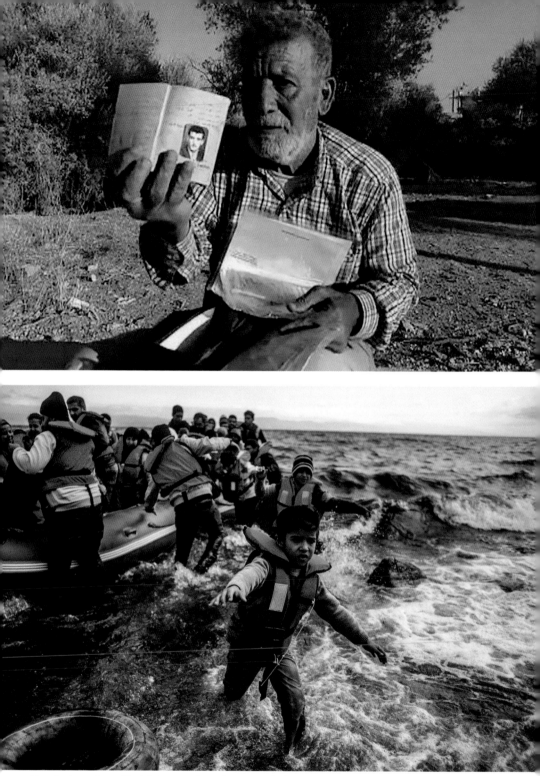

Top: Syrian refugee Nazieh Husein shows his ID card after arriving alone on the Greek island of Lesvos in September 2015. *(Aaron Hollett)*

Above: After years of being bombed by their own government and living in refugee camps, in 2015 650,000 Syrians fled their country for Europe, mainly by boat from Turkey. *(Getty Images)*

Top: Amhad Sandeh in his new hometown of Bayerisch Gmain in Bavaria, southern Germany, in October 2015. *(Sophie McNeill)*

Above: Sophie McNeill with Nazieh Husein after he was reunited with his wife, Basiyeh, daughter Mariam and son Abdul Rahman in Heidelberg, Germany, in November 2015. *(Sophie McNeill)*

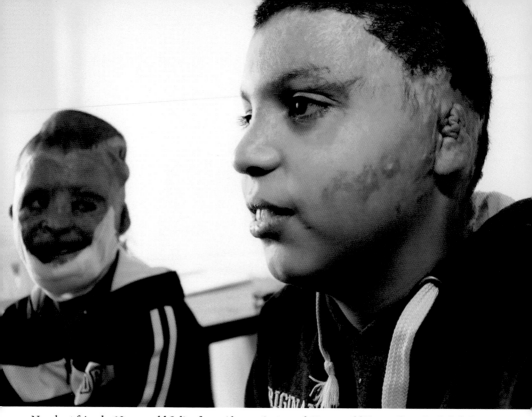

New best friends, 12-year-old Salim from Aleppo, Syria, and 12-year-old Farqar from Baghdad, Iraq, in December 2015. Both spent months receiving specialist surgery free of charge at the Médecins Sans Frontières reconstructive hospital in Amman, Jordan. *(Sophie McNeill)*

Above: As of October 2016, seven-year-old Syrian refugee Yazen had never been able to attend school. *(Sophie McNeill)*

Right: Similarly, Naveen, who wanted to become a lawyer, had been unable to attend school for four years, as of October 2016. *(Sophie McNeill)*

Top: On 7 October 2015, dozens of Yemeni families gathered at the small village of Sanaban, five hours' drive south of Sanaa, to celebrate the weddings of three brothers, Moayad, 25; Ayman, 23; and Abdurrahman, 21. *(Courtesy of Mohammad Jamal Al Sanabani)*

Above left: In the middle of the celebrations, a Saudi-led coalition plane dropped a bomb on one of the buildings hosting the wedding festivities, killing 40 people and injuring more than 40 more. *(Courtesy of Mohammad Jamal Al Sanabani)*

Above right: Five-year-old Jood was among the 14 children killed at the wedding by the airstrike. Jood's grandparents and uncle were also among the dead. *(Courtesy of Mohammad Jamal Al Sanabani)*

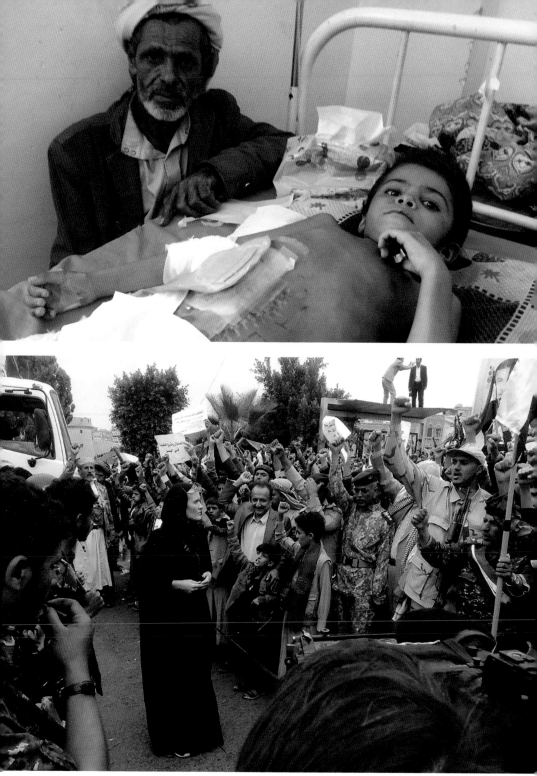

Top: Eight-year-old Faris was asleep in his home north of the Yemeni capital, Sanaa, when a missile from a Saudi-led coalition plane hit his house. His mother and brother were killed in the attack. *(Aaron Hollett)*

Above: Sophie McNeill at a Houthi rally in Sanaa in July 2016. *(Aaron Hollett)*

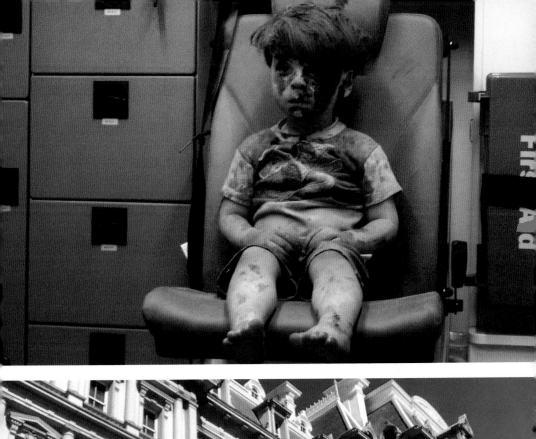

Top: Five-year-old Omran Daqneesh became a symbol of the suffering of Syrian children after he was photographed in an ambulance in besieged East Aleppo in August 2016. *(Getty Images)*

Above: American orthopaedic surgeon Dr Samer Attar (left) with Syrian medic Abu Rajab in Washington DC, March 2017. Abu Rajab had travelled to the United States to give witness testimony to the US Senate Committee on Foreign Relations. *(Courtesy of Dr Samer Attar)*

In December 2016, after years of airstrikes and months of siege, President Assad's forces took control of East Aleppo. To avoid living under regime rule and the risk of arrest and torture, tens of thousands of citizens chose to be evacuated from their hometown by bus. *(Getty Images)*

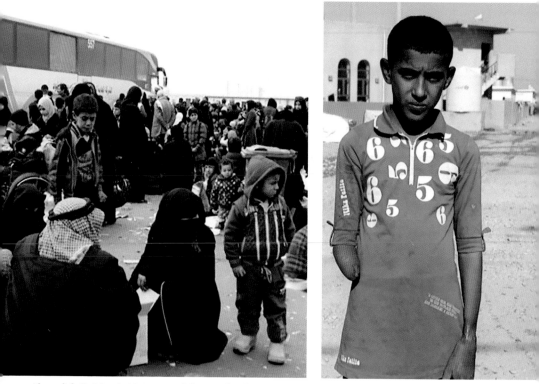

Above left: In March 2017, tens of thousands of starving, traumatised Iraqi families fled the war-torn city of Mosul, where they had been used as human shields by ISIS militants. *(Sophie McNeill)*

Above right: Thirteen-year-old Mohammad lived on the outskirts of Mosul under ISIS rule for three years and was severely injured during a gunfight near his home when the Islamic jihadists first arrived in the city. *(Sophie McNeill)*

Three-year-old leukaemia patient Retag underwent treatment alone in Bethlehem after the Israeli authorities refused her Gazan parents permission to go with her. *(Sophie McNeill)*

The Israeli authorities would not allow Gazan mother Feda to accompany her daughter Sara, aged three, when she had to travel to the West Bank for chemotherapy in 2016. *(Sophie McNeill)*

Hundreds of Palestinians cram into Bethlehem's Checkpoint 300 every morning from 4.30, waiting to be allowed into Israel to go to work, a process that can take hours every day. *(Sophie McNeill)*

Top: Over the last 30 years, as Dubai and Abu Dhabi have developed into major hubs of international business and tourism, Western governments have turned a blind eye to the United Arab Emirates' authoritarian government and repressive laws. *(Getty Images)*

Above: Human rights defender Ahmed Mansoor, a father of four, was sentenced to ten years in jail in May 2018 for speaking out against the UAE regime. Human rights groups believe he has been beaten and tortured in prison. *(Getty Images)*

First responders try to desperately wash off children exposed to sarin gas dropped by the Assad regime on the rebel held town of Khan Sheikhoun in April 2017. *(Courtesy of Syrian Civil Defence)*

According to the UN, at least 83 people, including 28 children and 23 women, were killed in the chemical attack on Khan Sheikhoun. *(Getty Images)*

Dr Mamoun Morad, who had spent years caring for war wounded, treated many of the people affected by the gas. He died of cancer in April 2019. *(Sophie McNeill)*

In 2017, aid officials spoke of a 'lost generation' of Syrian children, with half of those who have been displaced unable to attend school and many living with trauma and in poverty. A unique project by Australian artist Ben Quilty gave a heartbreaking insight into their world. *(Sophie McNeill)*

Above and right: Seven-year-old Wissam draws bleeding stick figures. She wants to be a doctor when she grows up. *(Sophie McNeill)*

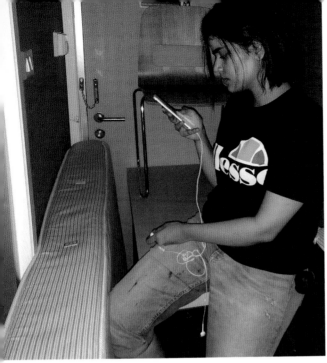

In January 2019, Sophie McNeill flew to Bangkok to support Saudi woman Rahaf Mohammed Alqunun, after Rahaf barricaded herself inside a hotel room at Bangkok airport to avoid being deported to Kuwait against her will. *(Sophie McNeill)*

In 2017, while attempting to flee to Australia, Saudi woman Dina Ali Lasloom was tied up at Manila airport and dragged back to Saudi by male relatives. *(Courtesy of Meagan Khan)*

Rahaf Mohammed speaks to reporters in Toronto in January 2019 after being granted asylum in Canada. *(Sophie McNeill)*

Sophie McNeill, Rahaf Mohammad and author Mona Eltahawy met in Canada after bonding on Twitter at the height of Rahaf's ordeal in Bangkok. *(Courtesy of Mona Eltahawy)*

footage of his rescue, we catch the English words emblazoned across his dusty, ripped T-shirt: 'Don't Shoot'.[68]

By now, a lack of medical supplies and general hospital resources was forcing doctors to amputate limbs which might have otherwise been saved.[69] Dr Farida sent through a photo of an airstrike that hit just outside her clinic, which she narrowly escaped but which killed 12 others. 'So many people are still under the rubble – even the man who I used to buy coffee from his market,' she said sadly.

The level of firepower used on the overwhelmingly civilian-inhabited besieged territory was astonishing. By comparing satellite images of east Aleppo taken on 18 October with those taken on 19 September, Human Rights Watch identified 950 distinct impact sites – an average of more than one blast an hour, day and night, for a month.[70]

In New York on 26 October, the UN's chief aid official, Stephen O'Brien, begged for action from the UN Security Council. 'Let me take you to east Aleppo this afternoon – in a deep basement, huddled with your children and elderly parents the stench of urine and the vomit caused by unrelieved fear never leaving your nostrils, waiting for the bunker-busting bomb you know may kill you,' the UN official said. 'Aleppo has essentially become a kill zone. If you don't take action, there will be no Syrian peoples or Syria to save.'[71]

O'Brien's blunt monologue was stunning as he tried to shame world leaders into acting:

> This is not inevitable; it is not an accident – it is the deliberate actions of one set of powerful human beings on another set of impotent, innocent human beings. There is no question today about whether you, Members of this Council, know what is going on – you clearly and tragically do. The question today is what you will do?

But Russia knew that, despite the diplomatic hand-wringing and lecturing, their brutal efforts to bolster Assad's dictatorship would meet no concrete resistance from the other Security Council members.

Inside Aleppo, Abu Rajab refused to kowtow to the impending doom. 'After M10 was targeted and destroyed, I started looking for another facility,' he said. He, the hospital's driver and another

colleague spent hours out scouring the streets, trying to find a building they could turn into a makeshift hospital. They were driving through east Aleppo's narrow, battle-scarred streets when a round of regime artillery exploded right next to them. It narrowly missed the hospital van, but hot metal perforated the doors, showering Abu Rajab with shrapnel.

The 50-year-old was rushed unconscious to M2, the largest trauma facility left in east Aleppo. Surgeons worked for hours to stabilize their friend, as Abu Rajab suffered extensive blood loss and internal bleeding. By the time Sam woke up in Chicago, Abu Rajab was stable. Sam couldn't believe his friend had made it through. It was a terrifying reality check on how bad things were about to become in Aleppo. 'They sent me photos from his hospital bed,' Sam said. 'He was awake and he was alive and that was all I needed to see.'

As the build-up for the final battle for east Aleppo intensified, armed opposition groups, fighting the regime's advance, fired barrages of mortars and rockets towards regime-held neighbourhoods in west Aleppo, killing more than 50 civilians, including 17 children. The rebels reportedly also used suicide car bombs and toxic gas in their attack.[72] On both sides of the divided city, parents were burying their children. 'Is this the revolution you wanted?' a distraught father in west Aleppo wailed as he cradled the body of his dead toddler killed by rebels' shelling. 'This is my son, I've only known him for two years!'

Amnesty International condemned the rebel fighters for their indiscriminate shelling of civilian neighbourhoods in the regime-held west.[73] 'We've reviewed video footage that shows that these armed groups are using mortars and Katyusha rockets. These are types of weapons that cannot be aimed at a precise target. So their use is unlawful,' Amnesty's Syria campaigner Diana Semaan told me. 'Breaking the siege must not be at the expense of civilians' lives.'

But the rebels' desperate shelling did not even break the siege, and, meanwhile, everyone I spoke to inside east Aleppo was running out of food. Residents were driven to burning plastic for fuel to cook and drinking large amounts of water to reduce the pains of hunger. One nurse sent a photo of a plate of rice, on which they had placed a scrap of paper with a drawing of a chicken drumstick

on it. 'Imagine eating it!' he wrote. It wasn't just the lack of food coming in that was the issue – some armed opposition groups had begun to confiscate and hide food to secure their own supplies.[74] The interests of civilians, who were estimated to make up 90 per cent of the population in besieged east Aleppo, had been abandoned by all sides to the conflict.[75]

Despite the lack of supplies and the reality that a final offensive to recapture the east was underway, many Aleppo residents rejected the idea of fleeing, convinced the regime would treat them as the enemy, even if they were clearly civilians, merely for staying in the east for so long. Abdul Naser Mashad, a 35-year-old father of four small children who worked as a driver for an international charity in east Aleppo, told me his family would stay, despite their deep fears of what lay ahead. 'We don't trust the regime, we don't trust Russia, we will not leave our homeland,' he said as we exchanged voice messages on WhatsApp.[76] His greater fear was for what Assad's security forces might do if he crossed into regime territory. 'The regime will torment us in the field. Or we all will be arrested or detained in their security facilities,' he told me firmly. 'We'd rather die here on our land.'

Such fears were well founded. By 2016, more than 65,000 people had vanished in Syria since the start of the war, the vast majority at the hands of Assad's forces, and more than 200,000 people were being detained by the Syrian regime.[77] Lama Fakih of Human Rights Watch's Middle East division told me, 'When the government took Homs city over, in those cases we did speak with individuals who discussed how their relatives were being detained and, in some cases, disappeared.'

On Friday, 4 November, the Syrian regime dropped leaflets on east Aleppo, warning civilians and armed rebels to leave the city's east by 7 pm, when heavy bombing would resume. 'If you do not leave these areas urgently, you will be annihilated,' the pamphlet read. 'You know that everyone has given up on you. They left you alone to face your doom and nobody will give you any help.'

But even for those who didn't fear regime arrest, by that stage there was no easy or safe way to leave east Aleppo. UN investigators later confirmed that militants from the extreme Jabhat Fatah Al Sham faction had threatened civilians who tried to flee certain

districts, arresting at least two people who attempted to negotiate the exit of fellow civilians, accusing them of 'inciting people' against the terrorist group.[78] A young woman told the UN that opposition fighters had killed her husband when he had attempted to flee.[79]

As the tension and threats built up, I was sent a surreal clip of a father who spotted a parachuted rocket in the sky near his house in the Aleppo countryside and started filming it on his phone, before realising it was going to drop near his house. He kept recording while screaming for his family to come inside. They quickly huddle together, bracing for the impact as the rocket explodes, and debris and dust fills the frame. The family's panicked screaming is the last thing you hear before it goes to black.[80] Amazingly, I learnt later from activists that no one in the family was killed.

It felt like D-day was coming for everyone inside east Aleppo, but they still managed to keep their sense of humour. In early November 2016, Abu Rajab and his colleagues followed the news that the United States had elected Donald Trump. 'At least Assad and his regime wasn't our choice,' one of them joked.

A new round of massive attacks began on 16 November. Modar, a young nurse at M2 hospital, sent through audio messages of bombs exploding around his apartment block. You can hear the steady roar of planes overhead and then BOOM, BOOM, BOOM. 'Warplane and helicopter in our sky hitting us,' said Modar.

The Aleppo children's hospital and the central blood bank in Al Shaar neighbourhood were attacked with a barrage of more than 20 barrel bombs.[81] CCTV footage of the moment shows nurses and staff calmly walking through the corridors of the only specialised paediatric hospital in Aleppo before dust and debris envelop them.[82] Nurses grabbed newborn babies from their incubators and rushed them downstairs, carefully laying them under blankets on the floor as rockets pounded the hospital. Three floors of the MSF-supported facility were destroyed, with two children and an ambulance driver among the ten civilians killed.[83]

Assad's forces and the Russians appeared to be conducting a final blitz on the healthcare system before pushing into the last stage of the offensive. But the bombing of such facilities in east Aleppo had become so horrifically routine that the day's attacks didn't generate the same headlines they had a few months earlier. 'Dear journalists,'

wrote a representative from the Syrian American Medical Society. 'The situation in Aleppo province in general today is again unprecedented. The world media doesn't seem to reflect that.'

The barrage continued. 'We are targeted now but I don't know with what,' messaged Wissam, an English teacher.

'Rocket launcher is hitting everywhere,' said his friend and colleague Abdulkafi, who was messaging from his apartment building, a ten-minute walk from Wissam's home.

'Many explosions!' said Wissam.

'More than 30 rockets,' replied Abdulkafi. 'I want to record but afraid to go close to window.'

'A strange mixture of warplanes attacks & artillery shelling,' Wissam said. 'Some news about troops of the regime approaching from Salhadeen neighbourhood which is next to my neighbourhood.'

It was one of the heaviest nights of bombardment yet.

In the morning, we checked to see if everyone was okay. 'Until now no one has died yet, from this group,' wrote back Dr Farida wryly. Within 24 hours of Dr Farida's message, her obstetrics facility, M2, was hit by a wave of artillery strikes, rendering it inoperable.[84] Thankfully, she wasn't there, but her colleagues and patients were trapped for several hours, some of them under rubble. 'The wounded are dying, a patient whose stomach is open in the operations room has to be abandoned, women are leaving delivery rooms still bleeding because the hospitals are getting attacked,' Dr Farida told *The Guardian*.[85] 'At this rate I cannot see us continuing for more than two weeks. They cannot take it from the ground, so they're trying to take it from the air. If it stays like this, people cannot wait it out. Nobody cares about us. We're just Arab Sunnis living in Aleppo.'

The World Health Organization (WHO) declared that all hospitals in the rebel-held east had officially suspended operations.[86] 'Although some health services are still available through small clinics, residents no longer have access to trauma care, major surgeries, and other consultations for serious health conditions,' the WHO said in a statement.[87]

The strategy was abundantly clear. By attempting to destroy all means for Aleppo's civilians to receive medical care, the regime hoped to break the will of the people inside and force a surrender.

Yet the doctors of Aleppo refused to submit. As the larger facilities were rendered inoperable, they opened pop-up medical clinics wherever they could to treat the massive number of patients flooding in every day.

The daily updates came in different waves. Some parents were weeping, hysterical, clutching the limp bodies of their children. Others were silent, slowly walking out of the ER holding the tiny shrouds of their children. In one video, a father wails next to his little girl. Her frilly blue dress is covered in blood, and she lies on a clinic bed deathly still as doctors desperately treat massive wounds on her tiny forehead.[88] 'Tank shells,' her dad says, struggling to breathe. 'Oh god, oh god!'

'Ahmad! Ahmad!' another father screams into the face of his dead teenage son, clutching at his bloodied body.[89] Someone out of shot tries to comfort the dad, telling him to leave Ahmad. 'I don't want to leave him!' the dad wails before a relative comes to comfort him. The medical workers put Ahmad in a body bag for burial. The father rushes over to it and peers again at his dead son's face, caressing the child's hair one last time. 'He is breathing, guys, I swear he is breathing!' he cries desperately, turning around and motioning for the medics, his hands covered in blood from stroking his boy. But Ahmad is not breathing.

Those inside said that, for the first time, Assad and Russian warplanes didn't leave their sky, day or night, with many of those I'd been speaking to trapped in their houses. 'The bombardment was so intense and from every direction. We didn't feel we would survive,' said Abu Rajab.

Children and babies were rushed into a clinic, struggling to breathe, after rockets filled with suspected chlorine gas were dropped on the Ard Al Hamra neighbourhood. A small boy coughs and splutters as a nurse helps him with an oxygen mask. 'Am I going to die?' he asks her, crying.[90] The lifeless bodies of four small siblings, two girls and two boys, are laid out carefully on the ground, with no obvious wounds, but blue lips and dark marks around their open eyes.[91] They were reportedly killed after some gas dropped from regime helicopters seeped into the basement where they were sheltering. The use of bombs containing toxic industrial chemicals, including chlorine, was later confirmed by UN investigators.[92]

As those inside east Aleppo were pummelled from the sky, the rebels hit back, sending an unprecedented barrage of mortars into civilian neighbourhoods in west Aleppo. A school was hit, with video and photos of the scene showing bloodied schoolbooks, upturned desks and distraught young children, eight of whom were killed.[93] On both sides of the city, the small bodies of dead children were piling up in increasing numbers.

As the bloody toll continued to rise, I tweeted a video of two young children who look like brother and sister. They clutch each other and cry hysterically in the street, in the aftermath of an airstrike on east Aleppo. The deluge of video and photos of dead bodies had been hard to bear, but it was the image of their terrified little faces that broke me. I sent the powerful footage to my foreign desk in Sydney straight away, but the news package I put together featuring the video of them was not played on the 7 pm Sydney news. There was nothing that new about today's developments, I was told, so it had been dropped for another story. To the annoyance of my ABC bosses, I tweeted my frustration with a link to the footage. 'What does it take to keep this horror in the news? Disappointingly my report (with this footage) didn't make the 7pm Sydney @abcnews #Aleppo.'[94] I was in trouble for airing my grievances publicly, but I didn't really care.

I knew it was repetitive. More pictures of dead people and distraught children. But to look away was criminal. If this was the world we had created, where war crimes were allowed to be carried out live, day after day with no consequence, then we were – at the very least – required to watch and recognise the full cost of our inaction. On 20 November, the White Helmets reported that 289 people had been killed in just five days of relentless attacks on Aleppo, with Médecins Sans Frontières reporting that 1500 were wounded in the ten days of mass bombardment between 15 and 24 November.[95]

The UN's most senior officials felt just as helpless as I did. 'Civilians are being isolated, starved, bombed and denied medical attention and humanitarian assistance in order to force them to submit or flee. I am more or less at my wit's end as a human being,' said the UN's chief aid official Stephen O'Brien to the Security Council. 'Horror is now usual – it is a level of violence

and destruction that the world appears to consider normal for Syria and normal for the Syrian people.'[96] But once again, no action was taken by the Security Council. 'Shame on us all for not acting to stop the annihilation of eastern #Aleppo and its people and much of the rest of #Syria too,' O'Brien tweeted after his impassioned speech had fallen on deaf ears.[97]

Kevin Kennedy, the chief UN humanitarian official for Syria, told reporters that after the massive uptick in violence, a growing number of families in the east wanted to flee. 'Forty per cent of the people surveyed wanted to leave,' Kennedy said. 'But they are concerned about getting out of East Aleppo and they are concerned about their arrival and welcome in West Aleppo.'[98] When dozens of families did try to flee east Aleppo at night, the Syrian Observatory for Human Rights reported that they were forced back by gunfire, though it was unclear whether rebel or regime troops had fired on them.[99]

As the airstrikes and shelling continued, a contact inside went out to try to film the latest injuries, but residents refused to let him take pictures. 'For five years we've been filmed and seen killed. What has changed? Now people here just want to die in peace,' they told him. I felt ashamed to admit they were right.

III

On Sunday, 27 November 2016, rebel-held east Aleppo began to fall. Pro-Assad forces took control of at least one-third of opposition-held territory in just 48 hours, recapturing key districts for the first time in years and effectively cutting east Aleppo in two. It was one of the most significant advances for the Syrian president in five years of civil war. As it became obvious the rebels could not hold back the regime's advance, thousands of desperate civilians suddenly fled east Aleppo. Carrying nothing but a few bags and suitcases, families clambered over rubble towards territory controlled by the government that had been bombing them. More than 16,000 people fled in just two days.[100]

No UN staff or international observers were there to monitor how the regime received these residents, but a few reporters living in government-held areas were allowed to film as the families

arrived. 'We lived a very terrible life. We were humiliated. We saw death. There is no bread, no food, no sugar, no anything,' one woman told a Reuters reporter as she boarded a Syrian government bus. While many had spent years resisting Assad's rule, now they were suddenly in his territory, some were quick to praise him. 'We thank the Syrian army and our President Bashar Al Assad!' one old man declared as he stood next to Syrian government soldiers and minders.

Inside the east, many were distraught. The day they'd long feared had come. 'For five years we were talking, but no one help us, except with hashtags,' Dr Farida wrote scathingly. They had watched the videos of those who'd fled now praising Assad. Wissam, the English teacher, told me he would do the same. 'If you find me on the Syrian TV, don't be surprised if I say, "Sophie put words in my mouth when I said bad things about the regime,"' he wrote. 'I'll say exactly what I'll be ordered to say.'

Tens of thousands of families also fled the other way, desperately moving further into rebel-controlled territory and towards the airstrikes.[101] With a few belongings piled into prams and trolleys, families trudge through the destroyed streets, pushing injured relatives in wheelchairs. To the Syrian government, all these people choosing to stay in rebel territory were 'terrorists'. But the vast majority of them were not part of the armed opposition and did not support the jihadi-sympathising militant groups. They were shop owners, traders, teachers, nurses, journalists – all people who chose to stay in the east because they vehemently opposed the brutal rule of Assad and were terrified of the regime's security forces.

For most of the activists and doctors I had been speaking to who had been publicly critical of Assad's rule, the idea of crossing over into the regime's control was unthinkable. Many had told me they would rather die than be put in Assad's hands, and now he was close they held true to their word, digging deeper into the small rebel territory that was left. I asked several of them if they could try to leave. Shave their beard. Throw out their ID. Wouldn't that be better than living under fear of death from the constant bombing and airstrikes? 'No, because we are all wanted,' insisted 26-year-old Yasser, who worked with Abu Rajab at the opposition-aligned Aleppo City Medical Council.[102]

Yasser firmly believed that if he crossed into west Aleppo he would disappear into Assad's prisons and die a slow death there. 'When you are a nurse [in east Aleppo] you are wanted, when you are a doctor, you are wanted,' he told me. 'Because we didn't join Assad's army we are wanted. We said no five years ago to Bashar, so we are wanted.' Yasser said he was not scared because he had chosen this fate, but he was very concerned for his pregnant wife who had insisted on staying with him. 'My wife is so, so scared. Her family is scared. Every woman, every child here is scared. It's the worst it's ever been,' he said.

Dr Farida, the obstetrician, had also decided that she couldn't go into regime-controlled territory. 'Death is better than this life,' she messaged me. But she was still terrified of what was about to happen.

Many I'd been speaking to for months went offline for long periods. 'I am so sorry, I couldn't communicate,' wrote Modar, a nurse, eventually. 'It's raining weapons. Heavy shells and rockets around us in Alsh'aar neighbourhood. Darkness and no charge for my mobile. Very dire situation.' He finished his message with a sad downcast-face emoji. 'The worse is coming,' Abdulkafi the teacher chimes in. It was hard to know what to write back. Others I had been in touch with simply dropped offline, their WhatsApp numbers no longer registered. I had been warned that if people had to cross over into regime areas, they would wipe their phones in order to try to avoid arrest.

Reports emerged of civilians from opposition areas being arrested by pro-Assad forces as they fled, with *The Guardian* reporting that as many as 500 men were missing after Iraqi militias and Hezbollah forces overran the Masakan Hanano neighbourhood in east Aleppo.[103] 'They took my nephew and my uncle,' a man told the newspaper. 'I don't know if I'll ever see them again.'

The next day brought tragic news. Modar Shekho, one of the nurses we had been talking to for months, had fled his home as the regime advanced. While he and his brother Mohammad searched for a new building to shelter their family, Mohammad was hit by an airstrike, killing him instantly. Then later that afternoon, as Modar and his father searched for somewhere to bury Mohammad, Modar's father was struck and killed by shelling. Unbelievably, this

was the second time that two members of Modar's family had been killed in the same day. In 2013, Modar's other brother, a doctor, and his sister, a nurse, had been killed together in a regime attack on a hospital. 'Modar is the kindest person you have ever met,' our contact Wissam said sadly. 'It's a great family. You can see, what happened to this family is what happened to Syria.'

Since I had begun covering Syria, I'd been in regular touch with Jan Egeland, a former Norwegian diplomat and now special adviser to the UN envoy for Syria. For months, Egeland had been working frantically behind the scenes to try to get aid into Aleppo and to secure safe zones for civilians. It was now clear that those efforts had been futile. The Syrian government had never intended to allow aid to enter; their forces had just been buying time. As we both watched the images of desperate families fleeing, Egeland didn't hold back. 'We have now 190 nations now watching the worst war of our generation and we have not been able to come to the protection or to the relief of the civilians in Syria. I find this indeed a very black chapter in the history of humankind,' he declared, clearly shattered. 'I mean, the security council was created to protect civilians. They have failed completely in the case of Syria.'[104]

Abu Rajab had never considered attempting to escape. He'd vowed never to leave his patients, and he had already decided that he would rather die than be arrested by the regime. 'The most frightening thing for us was to become a captive prisoner by the regime, by one of their forces,' the 50-year-old medic told me. 'Because we know they will torture us severely. It felt like we were being left with only two choices, both of them bitter. Either to be a captive or to be killed.'

Like Abu Rajab, Dr Farida chose to stay in rebel-controlled territory. But many of her friends and relatives fled to west Aleppo. 'They are neutral and just want to live and eat and drink,' she said bitterly. 'They don't care about the revolution and religion. Everyone sent me a message to tell me goodbye. I feel as if I lost a piece of me.'

Yasser, the young accountant for the medical council, made a gloomy declaration to our group: 'To whom it may concern, Aleppo has only two choices, death or Assad regime.'

'Don't be pessimistic,' scolded a doctor. 'The next few days will clarify our choices. May God be with us.'

'So, our choice is death?' asked Farida.

'Our choice is staying, the death is by Allah's hands,' Yasser responded.

The White Helmets announced they had stopped rescuing people in east Aleppo, having run out of fuel and lost much of their equipment in attacks. 'Thirty-five people are still stuck under the rubble because our team have not been able to reach them since yesterday,' they declared.[105]

More than 50,000 civilians were displaced by attacks in the four days after east Aleppo began to fall, according to the Syrian Observatory for Human Rights.[106] But even as they ran for their lives, civilians were targeted. As a group of families in Jub Al Quba neighbourhood desperately tried to flee the regime's advance, they were shelled by pro-Assad forces.[107] I tweeted the unbearable photos of the massacre.[108] A long line of bodies, torn apart by shells, strewn between nappies, backpacks and sports bags. Little kids in beanies and their thickest coats and boots, wearing gloves that their mother had jammed onto their hands that morning, lying on the ground cut in half. A father lying next to a carefully packed bag. A baby's bottle of milk. Twenty-six people, including seven children, had survived five years of airstrikes, months of siege, bombardment, hunger and fear, only to be massacred as they fled.

My contacts in east Aleppo had run out of hospitals, medicine and nearly all food, but they still managed to send messages online. So here we were, observing a horror movie in slow-motion, with no end in sight. It was a shamefully one-way flow of information. They provided us with evidence of what was happening inside, in the full knowledge that the world had deserted them and nothing they could say or do would change their fate. 'We are being targeted by heavy shelling,' described Wissam. 'But this time...[he pauses as an explosion sounds in the background]...it's worse than ever.' Keen to use one of the less graphic photos, one journalist doggedly asked our WhatsApp group for the photographer's name, presumably to caption it for his piece. 'It does not matter; we are about to die or arrest!' came the exasperated reply.

It was now freezing cold, with no power or gas for the people left in the east. Some had started chopping up furniture to burn to try to stay warm. Activists sent through a photo of a newborn baby they said had died overnight from the cold.

Another chlorine attack at this time saw Dr Farida's eight-year-old daughter among those struggling to breathe. Of all the things the doctor had witnessed, she said this was the worst moment. 'She was crying when she sniffed the chlorine gas, she was crying. She told me, "Mummy, I need oxygen, I need oxygen!" It was so bad,' Dr Farida said through tears. 'When she sniffed the chlorine gas, I cried because it was my fault, because I take the decision to stay in Aleppo.'

After that day, Dr Farida decided it would be less dangerous for her daughter to attempt to flee towards regime-held territory than to stay with her. 'I take the decision to send her to west Aleppo. So, if we died in Aleppo, she would live,' Dr Farida said quietly. The doctor's elderly aunt would accompany the eight-year-old. The moment of saying goodbye was the hardest thing Dr Farida had ever done. She was not sure if she would ever see her daughter again. 'It was a hard decision to take, but I want her to live, not to die in Aleppo. Because I couldn't imagine that I would get out of Aleppo alive.'

The people we had been communicating with for months were suddenly sending desperate SOS messages. 'There's a massacre 50 metres away from our house. People are injured! There's no one to help them. It's horrific!' said one panicked voice message from Abdulkafi, a young father of a six-month-old. In the background we could hear a barrage of heavy shelling. And then we were sent photos of blood-soaked streets.

In New York, Russia and China vetoed a UN Security Council resolution calling for a seven-day ceasefire.[109]

Regime forces were closing in. Someone wrote that face-to-face confrontations were happening near their home, while Dr Farida said she had heard that Assad's militia were approaching her neighbourhood. 'What should I do? Displace to an area away from the monster? Fight to death with all my family? Sprinkle some rice and smile to the monster?' she wrote.

Wissam, who was in a different neighbourhood from Dr Farida, offered this advice. 'Once you have to move, do it please. Keep moving until you get to the last free neighbourhood if things go on like this. Who knows what might happen then?'

'Dear international journalists,' another message read. 'How can you help?'

By 6 December it was clear that the rebels could not hold out for much longer, having lost two-thirds of their territory in the previous two weeks. They requested a five-day ceasefire to allow the evacuation of civilians.[110] But poised on the cusp of victory, the Assad regime announced it would not accept any truce in Aleppo.[111]

As reports of arrests and disappearances grew, there were urgent calls for the UN to oversee the immediate evacuation of civilians left in east Aleppo to other parts of Syria not controlled by the regime. Those inside east Aleppo kept asking the WhatsApp group if we had heard of any evacuation deals and if there was any chance of escape. 'In short answer we are dying, tens of injured, killed, children in front of me,' Yasser, the young accountant, wrote. He was starting to panic. After going to help out at a makeshift clinic, he heard reports that regime troops may have taken over his neighbourhood. He couldn't get through to his pregnant wife. 'I don't know anything about them, if they are alive or killed,' he said in a voice message, completely distraught.

Many people began to drop offline as they ran out of fuel for their generators.

'How are you guys today?' I asked.

'Alive,' replied a nurse.

There was not much else to say.

Someone in the group managed to venture outside. They found an old man pushing around the body of his dead wife in a wheelchair. He had been unable to find anyone to help him with her burial, but he couldn't bear to just leave her.[112]

Farida sent a photo of two small chickens covered in dust sitting among rubble and debris. 'My chicks are still alive, but the house and the plants have been destroyed,' she said with a sad-face emoji.

At the UN, Russia's foreign minister Sergei Lavrov announced that combat operations would be suspended to allow civilians to evacuate.[113] It was hard for those inside to trust Russia's

announcement. While the fighting eased, it didn't stop. Wissam sent a recording of mortars still being shot and of warplanes still firing rockets, as the dead kept piling up in east Aleppo's streets.

Then, a small piece of relief. Yasser heard from his wife. 'Today, my wife sent me a text message, they are ok,' he wrote with a happy-face emoji. 'She managed to flee to regime areas with family and is ok.' She would stay in the regime area with distant relatives while he had chosen to remain in east Aleppo, so he wasn't sure if he would ever see her again. 'I am really tired,' he wrote. 'There are hundreds of injured. Most of them are dying because the lack of hospitals and medical service.' Yasser was desperate to hear if the evacuation was going ahead. 'We just want safe passage to get out of here, we don't want to be arrested!' he messaged. 'They will force me to join the army.'

The White Helmets issued an urgent plea to the UN and the International Red Cross, begging for safe passage out of east Aleppo for them, their volunteers and other humanitarian workers in the city. 'If we are not evacuated, our volunteers face torture and execution in the regime's detention centres,' begged the rescue group in a statement:

> We have good reason to fear for our lives. The regime and its allies have falsely claimed many times that our unarmed and impartial rescue workers in the White Helmets are in fact affiliated with radical extremist groups. Our civil defence centres have been targeted and our rescue equipment destroyed. White Helmet volunteers have been purposefully killed in double-tap airstrikes. We believe we have less than 48 hours left.[114]

And then, evidence emerged to confirm what Yasser and Abu Rajab feared so deeply. The UN announced that they believed hundreds of men from east Aleppo had gone missing after leaving rebel-held areas.[115] Men were being separated from women and children, and families had not heard from them after that. 'Given the terrible record of arbitrary detention, torture and enforced disappearances, we are of course deeply concerned about the fate of these individuals,' a UN spokesman in Geneva told reporters. 'One has to ring some alarm bells. It could mean that some have been killed, it could mean

they have been arbitrarily detained and taken somewhere, we just don't know.'

We didn't need to look far for proof to back up the UN's claims. The Russian Anna News broadcast video of men taken by Syrian regime forces after they fled east Aleppo with their families.[116] The footage shows exhausted-looking young and middle-aged men sitting terrified in a field on the edge of Aleppo, surrounded by Syrian army soldiers. Some of the detained men look up at the camera desperately. It was clear they had no idea what their fate would be. 'Even the most determined terrorists are trying to find their way out,' declares the Russian TV reporter, explaining that these men are all suspected of 'terrorists association'. 'For now, we are holding them but later the Mahabharat [secret police] will pick them up,' says a burly Syrian army commander. The regime troops parade panicked young men in front of the camera, claiming they have confessed to being part of an extremist rebel faction. 'My name is Zuher and I served with Al Nusra,' a young wide-eyed man in a red jumper says hesitantly, looking straight down the camera barrel. We still don't know what happened to these men.

As Assad's forces retook the old city, the International Committee of the Red Cross discovered 150 wounded and disabled civilians sheltering in an old people's home.[117] The Red Cross said 11 civilians at the facility had died before they arrived, either being caught in crossfire or failing to receive the medical care they needed.

The situation had become so dire inside east Aleppo, those who'd sworn they would never leave were now praying for an evacuation deal. 'Please if anyone knows of any plan to evacuate medical staff please let everyone know, we don't want to left anyone behind,' a doctor pleaded in a voice message.

Abu Rajab couldn't believe how quickly Assad's forces had advanced. 'Every time we lost a neighbourhood it felt like losing a piece of my body. The city was falling piece by piece every day,' he said sadly. A nurse reported to the *New York Times* that opposition armed factions had stopped her parents and others from leaving the Bustan Al Qasr neighbourhood and threatened them for trying to leave.[118] Others managed to escape, with some reporting rebel fighters had shown civilians the way out.

The fear of civilian men being separated from their families when they arrived in west Aleppo was reinforced by terrifying images taken by a Reuters photographer on 11 December.[119] At a police centre in west Aleppo, around 80 men, young and old, have been rounded up in a courtyard. The men stand, cowed, as armed members of the regime's military police stand guard over them. They have all just arrived from east Aleppo and are being conscripted into military service to fight for Assad – exactly what so many activists in east Aleppo had warned of.

There were reports of the UN madly working behind the scenes to negotiate a safe passage for civilians, the White Helmets and medical staff out of what was left of rebel-held east Aleppo. Those fleeing only needed to cross four kilometres of regime-held territory to pass into opposition-held land on the outskirts of the city. But the potential exodus would require the agreement of the Assad regime and Russia. It was unclear how many people were left, with estimates ranging between 50,000 and 200,000.

In east Aleppo, armed opposition groups had withdrawn from a number of neighbourhoods and were believed to be controlling only around one square kilometre. My contacts left inside the tiny rebel-held corner firmly believed an evacuation deal was the only way they would get out alive. 'Are there any new discussions now about a deal to end the bombing/evacuate to rebel areas?' a reporter asked those inside. 'What message or request do you send to anyone we might talk to about the talks over a deal?'

'Doomsday, all of us are waiting, dying now in the last neighbourhoods,' Yasser, the 26-year-old hospital administrator, replied. 'Believe me, no one reject the safety evacuation.' He was in despair. 'Please all, stop asking us "what's happening". You only should ask if we're still alive or not. You all know what's happening,' he wrote.

'Families got together, waiting for death together. This is what's happening,' said Abdulkafi. 'We are not afraid of ourselves but of our wives and children.'

Yasser messaged me privately to see if I could ask any official organisations or UN body if they could send personnel into Aleppo as the regime advanced, to ensure protection for medical staff if the regime tried to take them away. 'Can someone be waiting to

take us to Idlib or to Kurdish areas?' he asked. 'Any young person who arrive to the first regime area, the Syrian army takes all his documents and even the mobile, so I can't contact you,' he said.

How could I tell him that none of the international conventions or 'rules of war' that are supposed to apply in such a situation were being followed? That Assad and his militia and Russian allies were carrying out wanton violence – as we watched live – ignoring every desperate plea from the UN and the International Committee of the Red Cross? It was such an embarrassing admission of the complete failure of our world system.

'I'm so sorry, I can't help organise for someone to help like that,' I told him.

As the regime forces inched forward, they captured the site of Abu Rajab's hospital, M10. A reporter for Syrian state TV recorded a report from the broken and damaged foyer of the bombed hospital, propagating false claims that those who had risked their lives to treat civilians were 'terrorists' paid by the United States. The reporter even pointed out a mammography machine manufactured by General Electric as 'proof' of an 'American' conspiracy to try to concoct regime change in Syria.[120]

The coordinators of the Syrian American Medical society were giving last-minute advice to their staff stuck inside. 'I urge everyone to do everything to protect yourselves and your families. Saving your lives should be a priority,' instructed Dr Zaher Sahloul, president of the Syrian American Medical society and creator of the WhatsApp group. 'In case that your hospital or neighbourhood was captured by the advancing forces and militias of SAA [the Syrian Arab Army], make all effort to leave to western Aleppo. I doubt very much that there will be any evacuation, but I hope that I am wrong.'

Abu Rajab was quoted on the front page of *The Guardian*, begging for humanitarian intervention.[121] 'This is a final distress call to the world,' he said. 'Save the lives of these children and women and old men. Save them. Nobody is left. You might not hear our voice after this. It is the last call.'

One of the doctors thought back to Hafez Al Assad's massacre of the Sunni population in the Syrian town of Hama in 1982. 'I was born in September 1982 when Hama massacre happened. I always asked the older people, "How come you guys stayed silent, how did

the world let such a monster rule his country for another 18 years, how did he meet presidents and kings and shake their hands, how come his minister gave speeches in the UN?"' Anas said. 'I was always told there was no media, there was no satellite or internet, and nobody knew what happened in Hama till few years later. Now, there is so much media but there is no ethics among the politicians now and then. Disgusting!'

Monther, one of just a few activists still communicating regularly, was scathing. 'This is not the '50s where no cameras or internet,' he said. 'That is happening in front of all the world's eyes. Our millions of videos will never be deleted, our pictures filled all this web.'

Dr Farida was suddenly removed from our doctors WhatsApp group. The hospital that she and her husband had worked at had fallen under government control. No one was sure if she was okay, but the group's administrators had decided to remove her as a precaution, in case her phone was examined by regime forces. It was a nerve-racking time as we imagined what might have happened to the obstetrician and her husband. After a while, one of the group reassured us that, while they did not know where Farida and her family were, they were understood to be okay.

Late on the night of 12 December, I heard from my dear friend Ahmad in Germany, whom I had met on the Italian rescue boat in the Mediterranean. He was beside himself with despair after reports from family and friends inside Aleppo. 'They entered my neighbourhood,' he said, referring to pro-Assad forces. 'Full families. At wall. Executed.' I had heard nothing of this scale in terms of deadly retribution against civilians. It sounded shocking and hard to verify. 'At Al Kallaseh and Bustan Al Qasr. I have friends, they saw it,' he insisted, distraught. Ahmad had been told it was pro-Assad militias, not the Syrian army, who had carried out the executions, and that women and children were among the dead. 'They collected families and put them at the wall of the cemetery and then shot them all,' Ahmad told me. He was inconsolable. 'After today...I just don't care about life...really don't care,' he said bitterly. I promised to follow up the reports with the UN and my contacts inside Aleppo the next day.

The following morning, before I'd had a chance to speak to my UN contacts, the office of the UN High Commissioner for

Human Rights announced that they had received credible reports of civilians caught and killed on the spot by advancing pro-Assad militia.[122] As I watched the press conference, I was stunned that many elements of Ahmad's claims to me were being echoed by the UN's human rights officials. 'We have also been informed that pro-government forces have been entering civilian homes and killing those individuals found inside, including women and children,' UN spokesperson Rupert Colville told reporters solemnly.

Colville said the UN had received reports from multiple sources alleging that tens of civilians had been executed by pro-Assad forces and their allies, including the Shiite militia group Iraqi Al Nujabaa. Colville said the incidents were reported to have happened in neighbourhoods including Al Kallaseh and Bustan Al Qasr – the same neighbourhoods Ahmad had told me about. 'In all, as of yesterday evening, we have received reports of pro-government forces killing at least 82 civilians, including 11 women and 13 children in four different neighbourhoods,' said Colville. 'We hope, profoundly, that these reports are wrong, or exaggerated, as the situation is extremely fluid, and it is very challenging to verify reports. However, they have been corroborated by multiple reliable sources,' finished Colville. 'We are filled with the deepest foreboding for those who remain in this last hellish corner of opposition-held eastern Aleppo.'

I called Colville's office straight after the press conference to see if they would release the names of the people killed. I wanted to check if any of them were Ahmad's relatives. They told me they couldn't release the names, but they believed the reports were credible. 'We received these reports from six different sources, one of whom we had been working with for a very long time,' I was told. The murder of Ahmad's relatives under the family name 'Sande' was later reported by the Violations Documentation Center in Syria and referred to in the Atlantic Council's *Breaking Aleppo* report.[123]

UN investigators also reported several other incidents of pro-government forces carrying out reprisal executions on civilians in east Aleppo, including Syrian soldiers killing their own relatives who were supporters of armed groups, and the wife and daughter of an opposition rebel commander being executed as they attempted to cross into west Aleppo.[124]

Back inside the last patch of rebel-held territory, the internet was going on and off, making it much harder to contact people. 'Is anyone there? Anyone online?' someone asked the group. A colleague noted that the silence in response was worse than everything that had gone before. A few hours later, Abdulkafi sent a photo of a building that had just been destroyed, a body visible amid the debris. 'Until now there are 12 people under the rubble. They died. No one could help them,' he said.

The Syrian Observatory of Human Rights announced that the battle for Aleppo had reached its end, with 'just a matter of a small period of time' before 'a total collapse' of rebel positions.[125] Firmly believing that advancing regime troops wouldn't spare them, many of the people I had been in touch with started sending goodbye messages and posting final videos on Twitter. Abdulkafi sent a video of him crouching in the rain, saying goodbye. 'The Assad militias are maybe 300 metres away. No place now to go. It's the last place,' he says, emotionally, pausing and taking a deep breath. 'We shared many moments inside Aleppo…really, I don't know what to say, but I hope you can do something for Aleppo people. For my daughter, for the other children…' Abdulkafi stops again, trying not to cry. 'I hope you can do something to stop the expected massacres.' The goodbye messages made headlines around the world.[126]

Abu Rajab was convinced Assad's forces could arrive any moment and would not spare him. 'Many times I felt this,' he said. 'I would farewell my family, farewell my wife, my kids, my siblings. I would say I may not be able to speak to you again and this is our last words.' Yasir, the young medical administrator, had been so brave all along. But now his simple words spoke volumes: 'I am afraid.'

In what might possibly have been the only concrete gain from months of desperate coverage of Aleppo, the distraught pleas and goodbyes broadcast around the world were too much for even Moscow to bear. Late on 13 December, the Russian ambassador to the UN announced that an evacuation deal had been reached. In exchange for a ceasefire, east Aleppo's fighters, activists and the remaining tens of thousands of civilians would be given the chance to evacuate to rebel-held territory in other parts of Syria.[127]

For 48 hours, the deal appeared to be on and then off, the shelling and bombing starting and stopping, with more people killed as the

powers that be fiddled with evacuation details in New York. But then, finally, came confirmation: all civilians, including medical staff, who wanted to leave the city would be allowed to do so. 'I will live!' Yasser wrote, overjoyed, adding a row of three smiley faces. 'I will see my wife!'

The last-minute deal was clearly the preferable option to what some had feared would be mass murder, but it meant the 36,000 Aleppo civilians left inside the rebel-held patch were being permanently exiled from the only home they had ever known.[128] 'A lot of people are crying now,' Abdulkafi messaged. 'They were crying yesterday because were afraid because they might die in any moment, but now they are crying because they are leaving their homeland.'

In the early hours of Thursday, 15 December 2016, hundreds of green Syrian government buses and Red Crescent ambulances slowly drove into devastated east Aleppo. Tens of thousands of civilians sat outside in the freezing cold, amid the ruins of their dusty, broken neighbourhoods, with only a few small bags per family. They were hungry and utterly exhausted. Some sat in wheelchairs or leant on crutches, while more than 400 seriously injured people were carried out on stretchers. All of them had been witness to unspeakable horror. 'Everyone was just dazed,' describes Abu Rajab.

Some residents burnt their belonging as they left, rather than leave them for Assad's forces to pilfer. Other residents graffitied their abandoned buildings with goodbye messages, reported *The Guardian*.[129] 'We will return, Aleppo. Our destroyed buildings are a witness of our resistance and your criminality,' read one. 'Under every destroyed building are families buried with their dreams by Assad and his allies,' said another.

The recapture of rebel-held east Aleppo and the evacuation of its remaining citizens was the most significant win for Assad's surrender-or-starve strategy. It also signified a momentous loss for the opposition – losing the city felt like losing the entire war. Assad, with his Iranian and Russian backing, had managed to claw back the majority of the towns and cities that opposition supporters had fought so hard to 'liberate'. Now, all the rebels really had left was the north-western province of Idlib.

For Abu Rajab, who had lived through so much death and destruction in the last few years, by far the worst day was the

one where he actually left Aleppo. 'It's an indescribable feeling,' he said sadly. 'All the sacrifices, all the people's lives. Everything we have been defending and have been holding so firmly to try and get freedom and dignity. We sacrificed so much, only to be forcibly displaced.'

The Assad regime had relented and allowed observers from the International Committee of the Red Cross to oversee the evacuation deal, but that didn't provide much comfort to those boarding the buses. They were still terrified of passing through the regime checkpoints. Like everyone else around him, Abu Rajab held deep fears over whether they were actually going to be allowed to depart safely on the buses or if Assad's forces would go through and drag out people like him, known to be opposition activists. Yasir said, 'We don't know who will be there. Red Crescent or Red Cross or UN or Russian generals!'

Yasir and Abu Rajab had been working non-stop to evacuate the badly wounded. Abu Rajab helped to escort out the only two ambulances provided by the Syrian American Medical Society that had not been destroyed. Amid the doom, it was a small victory that the vehicles were coming with him and the other medical staff. 'It felt like the hospital was leaving with me,' he said. 'I didn't want them to be left behind.' Abu Rajab stared out the ambulance window at his destroyed city as they were driven out. He hadn't been this close to the front line and seen the entire neighbourhoods flattened. *How had it come to this?* he asked himself, tears running down his face. All they had wanted was freedom and dignity. 'I can't fully describe this experience in words. It was so painful,' Abu Rajab said later.

IV

The evacuation of tens of thousands of people took nearly seven days. Despite having to cross only several kilometres of regime-held territory, evacuees were made to wait for 20 hours at dozens of regime checkpoints, in the freezing cold, with no food or water. 'We were so scared of what would happen to us,' said Abu Rajab. 'Some of the militias forced people to remove all their clothes and wait in the buses in nothing more than their underwear.' An observer from the International Committee of the Red Cross watching the

evacuation noted that they had 'never seen such levels of human suffering before'.[130]

Syrian Red Crescent volunteers on the buses warned those inside that they could be killed if they opened the bus doors and stepped outside. Children were forced to defecate on the floor of the packed buses. Abdulkafi spent 17 hours trapped on a bus with 41 children. His six-month-old baby girl, Lamar, was so parched he was concerned she would pass out. 'She was crying and crying,' he says. 'I told the Red Crescent official, "That's enough. I'm opening the bus door," but he wouldn't let me. It was torture.' Others reported Russian soldiers confiscating their laptops and phones.

At one point along the evacuation route where there was no Red Crescent presence, those in the green buses looked on, terrified, as four opposition fighters were dragged out of a bus. UN investigators later confirmed they had been executed by the side of the road by Assad's forces.[131] They also documented an incident where pro-government forces took away men and boys as young as 16 and forcibly conscripted them.[132]

After more than 20 hours of crawling along in the evacuation convoy, Abu Rajab's ambulance crossed into Idlib. He was finally safe.

In Chicago, Sam cried tears of relief when he heard his friend had made it. 'I was so very happy,' he said. 'But it's bittersweet, because all those people who have suffered and died, and some didn't make it.'

I finally heard again from Dr Farida. Five days earlier, regime troops had suddenly taken over the neighbourhood around M3 hospital, where she had gone to work after M2 was destroyed. Surrounded on all sides by pro-Assad forces and terrified they would be targeted for arrest, the obstetrician and her husband abandoned their medical IDs and scrubs and walked out of the hospital. They joined a crowd of thousands of civilians streaming towards government-held territory, trying to blend in with the crowd. 'Me and my husband and my friend and her father, we sneaked between these people,' explained Farida. 'There were Russian, Iranian, regime soldiers and everyone was just shouting in our faces, "You were with the terrorist!"' Amid the chaos, Dr Farida and her husband climbed aboard a government bus

going to west Aleppo. 'The good thing is they didn't ask us to take our IDs. They didn't realise we are doctors. They just told us to go to the buses,' she said.

After many hours, the obstetrician and her husband arrived at her father's house in west Aleppo, for an emotional reunion with her parents and daughter. Physically and mentally shattered, they were unable to believe they had made it out alive. But the strangest part, said Dr Farida, was seeing people in west Aleppo living mostly unaffected, when just a few kilometres away, they had been starved of food and sheltering from daily airstrikes and barrel bombs. 'When I saw the people just living their lives in a normal way, eating meat, it felt so bad,' she said.

To her amazement, some people in her father's neighbourhood were celebrating in the streets that night. 'They were partying in the streets because they had the victory against the "terrorists",' she said bitterly. 'That was us! They called everyone in [east] Aleppo as a terrorist. But the truth was that most of us were civilians. And the people fighting the regime, who were defending us, were just a few.'

Farida posted on Facebook to let friends inside know that she was okay, and at the same time expressed her disgust and anger at the regime and their supporters. She quickly received calls and messages from relatives and friends, warning her that she would be arrested and that she should delete her post. 'They were saying, "What are you doing? You are killing yourself! They will arrest you; they will take you!"' she said sadly. 'I told them, "I just want to die...I left all my life in Aleppo and I love it, but now I lost everything."'

The next day, Farida's father travelled back to her neighbourhood in the east, which was now controlled by regime forces, to check on her house and car. As the old man was outside her apartment block, a group of regime militia surrounded him. 'They told him, "Your daughter is a terrorist!" And they took him,' said Farida. The 60-year-old was beaten and held for several hours until the family paid US$2000 in cash to release him. Farida slept at a neighbour's house that night, firmly believing that the regime would soon come looking for her.

'So the next day I decided to get out of Aleppo, because I knew that they will take me too,' said Farida. Once again, Dr Farida, her

husband and their daughter had to flee. They said tearful goodbyes to her parents and got into a taxi. They'd spent nearly all their savings to release her father from the militia the day before, and with their last dollars, they paid a driver to take them out of the regime-held area. First, they drove to a Kurdish-held area in the north, before crossing over to territory in Idlib controlled by Syrian opposition forces. At last they felt safe. For now.

For Dr Farida and Abu Rajab, life in Idlib was bittersweet. There was proper food for the first time in months, and no helicopters over their heads for 24 hours a day. But the trauma and pain of what they had endured in Aleppo haunted their days.

Nearly three months to the day after they had been forced out of their hometown, Abu Rajab and Dr Farida each packed a small bag and crossed over the Turkish border, heading to a small airport in Hatay, Turkey. From there, they flew to Istanbul and on to Washington DC. The two medical professionals had been invited to the United States by the Syrian American Medical Society, the NGO that had helped fund the hospitals where they had worked in Aleppo. They were going to meet with senators in Washington and give witness testimony to the United States Senate Committee on Foreign Relations.

And Abu Rajab was going to see his dear friend Sam again. On a cold morning in DC, the medic from Aleppo and the surgeon from Chicago had an emotional reunion outside a French bakery near the Capitol. 'It was surreal,' said Sam. 'I'd only ever seen him in scrubs, but there he was wearing a suit, and I just ran up to him and I hugged him.'

Later that day, Sam was there to give emotional support as Abu Rajab and Dr Farida gave their evidence to the congressional committee.[133] Wearing a surgical mask, because she was fearful of publicly revealing her identity, Dr Farida gave her evidence first. 'I am here today not only as a doctor, but as a wife, a mother, and a Syrian. Throughout the past six years, I have witnessed unspeakable horrors,' she told the Senate Committee.[134] 'In the months leading up to our displacement, I can only describe the events as hell. Bodies parts scattered on the streets; blood everywhere; constant bombardment by air attacks; buildings reduced to rubble.'

The obstetrician explained why she and her husband had decided to stay in Syria, with their daughter, living in the rebel-held territory of Idlib and continuing to work in hospitals that remained targets for Russian and regime airstrikes. 'The reason is simple: it is our duty. As doctors, we have taken an oath to treat any and all patients, regardless of their affiliation. We have a moral obligation to try and save as many lives as possible, even if that means sacrificing our own lives,' Dr Farida said firmly.

When it was Abu Rajab's turn to address the senators, he spoke slowly and carefully in English, dressed in a crisp black suit with a red tie, to dozens of US senators. 'We moved from one hospital to another, as each was targeted and taken out of service. We struggled to eat, to sleep, and to protect our families. We were convinced that we were going to die. We lost many of our friends, colleagues, and family members,' he told the committee. 'I love Aleppo. It is my home. It is a part of me. I dream of one day returning to my home with my family and living in peace. But I need your help. I call on you to protect hospitals and health workers. This is a simple request. When you live in freedom, you must help others to be free.'[135]

Abu Rajab also had meetings in New York at the UN, with Médecins Sans Frontières and with President Trump's US ambassador to the UN, Nikki Haley. The ambassador held Abu Rajab's hand as he recounted the horrors of Aleppo and begged the US to do more to stop attacks on hospitals in Syria. After a long day of meetings, Sam and Abu Rajab got ice cream and wandered around New York's Times Square. Sam said, 'He was like a little kid, just like another tourist. And he wouldn't stop taking pictures, and he wouldn't stop taking videos, and he wouldn't stop taking selfies. After having lived under that sense of oppression and fear, and then being in New York, wandering the streets and having him see people from all over the world, wearing what they want, saying what they want, just being free. It was incredible.'

Abu Rajab was flown to Los Angeles to be the special guest at a gala dinner raising money for Syria. 'There were a lot of people who were speaking to me, I didn't know their faces. They were calling me "a hero from Aleppo". Everyone was running to me!' he said incredulously. 'I felt it was normal what I offered to my people. But they made it to be something big.'

While Abu Rajab was in the United States, many of the Syrian expats he met encouraged him to stay and seek asylum there, but he never gave it a second thought. 'I told them, "No way, there are people waiting for me back home. I need to go back and continue my work. And to provide help to who needs it in my country,"' Abu Rajab said firmly.

So, after a month travelling around the United States, the medic boarded his long flight back to Istanbul, flew down to the south and crossed over the border to Syria. He was working as a radiologist in a surgical hospital inside Idlib, the last rebel-held territory, but his wife, five children and grandchildren were now living in Turkey. He couldn't bear them going through the horror they experienced in Aleppo once again. But he would stay. 'My work is the most important thing in my life. It's my duty, I will never leave it,' he said.

Not long after Abu Rajab returned from the United States, the family of Omran Daqneesh, the little boy in the back of the ambulance whose photo went viral around the world, gave an interview to pro-regime journalists. The family were now living under government control in Aleppo. Omran's father Mohammed criticised the Syrian opposition and told Iranian and Syrian state TV that the international media had wanted to use Omran to 'attack' President Bashar Al Assad. Omran's dad made no mention of his other son, 10-year-old Ali, who had reportedly been killed in the strike. The family had been reluctant to speak after the incident, and it wasn't clear if they were now speaking freely or had been coerced to appear. 'Syrians appearing on state television or on channels associated with the Assad government are not able to speak freely,' noted the *New York Times*. 'The government exerts tight control over all information broadcast about the war, including interviews with civilians, who can be coerced and threatened with arrest if they criticize the government.' Abu Rajab commented, 'We were very surprised. All of us were surprised. I'm the one who treated him and went to their house. This was a very sad thing.[136]

Abu Rajab's happiest days, he said, were when he was working in M10 hospital. 'I lived a life of complete freedom and dignity,' he said, smiling as he remembered. 'I felt like I was a human giving to humanity. Despite the shelling and bombs and all that, I was free. The best moment in my life were spent at that hospital.'

Abu Rajab continues to do similar work in Idlib. It is the last province held by the rebels, and the regime and Russia are intent on retaking it too. The fear is that Idlib could become east Aleppo 2.0, except this time there will be three million civilians, rather than 200,000, stuck in the middle. The province is regularly bombarded, and so once again, Abu Rajab spends his days X-raying and doing MRIs on children brought into the hospital whose bones have been broken by airstrikes, and whose little bodies have been crushed by their collapsed homes.

Dr Farida is also there in Idlib, still delivering babies amid the airstrikes and dreaming of a free Syria. 'Every time I hear a new baby cry, I have hope,' she says, smiling. 'I haven't lost hope for a good future for Syria.'

*

At least 110,000 people are estimated to have lived through the horror that was the last six months of the battle for east Aleppo.[137] The Violations Documentation Center in Syria documented the death of 3497 civilians in east Aleppo between June and mid December 2016.[138]

Three months after east Aleppo fell, a UN special inquiry into the events in Aleppo, conducted by the Independent International Commission of Inquiry on the Syrian Arab Republic, found that both the pro-government and the rebel forces had committed war crimes.[139] The UN report found evidence to strongly suggest that the 'deliberate and systematic targeting of medical infrastructure' in east Aleppo by the Syrian and Russian air forces, with no military presence in the vicinity of those hospitals, was 'part of a strategy to compel surrender'.[140]

Physicians for Human Rights have documented the killings of 912 medical personnel in Syria since the popular democratic uprising began in March 2011. They suspect 54 per cent of these deaths were caused by shelling and bombing, and 21 per cent by small-arms fire from ground forces. They also suspect 13 per cent of victims were tortured before being killed and 7 per cent were formally executed. The Syrian government and its allies – Russia and the Iran-backed militias – are responsible for more than 90 per cent of the deaths of medical personnel documented by Physicians for Human Rights.[141]

In February 2018, the Syrian Army and their Iranian and Russian backers began a full-scale assault on Ghouta, the last rebel-held neighbourhood near Damascus. Nearly all of the tragedies of Aleppo were repeated: hospitals bombed; chemical weapons dropped by Syrian army helicopters; civilians massacred and blocked from fleeing by rebels; weeks of bombardment by the regime. The bombing was so fierce, there was average of 345 attacks each day on the enclave, or about 14 strikes per hour.[142] The death toll from airstrikes was so high that civilians were buried in mass graves. A litany of war crimes was committed by all sides, with rebels also firing a barrage of unguided mortars into Damascus. By the time government forces declared eastern Ghouta recaptured in mid April, some 140,000 individuals had fled their homes and up to 50,000 had been evacuated to Idlib and Aleppo governorates.[143]

As of September 2019, the Syrian Network for Human rights estimates that 224,948 civilians have been killed in Syria since March 2011 and that:

- 88.65 per cent (199,411) of that total were killed by Syrian regime forces and Iranian militants
- 2.9 per cent (6514) were killed by Russian forces.
- 2.43 per cent (5239) were killed by Islamist extremist groups like ISIS and Hayat Tahrir al sham.
- 2.33 per cent (5239) were killed by other parties.
- 1.83 per cent (4131) were killed by factions of the armed opposition.
- 1.35 per cent (3037) were killed by international coalition forces.
- 0.51 per cent (1157) were killed by Kurdish PYD forces and the Syrian Democratic Forces.[144]

CHAPTER 12

ESCAPE FROM ISIS
The People of Mosul and Raqqa

After taking over large swathes of eastern Syria and northern Iraq in 2014, the radical Salafi militant group Islamic State, or ISIS, forced millions of civilians to live under their brutal rule. To resist the violent jihadists or express any opposition to their sadistic ideology often resulted in execution. The UN found that the terrorist group committed systemic and widespread human rights abuses, including war crimes as well as genocide and the crime of extermination, with thousands of the Yazidi people of Iraq massacred, kidnapped and enslaved into sexual servitude. With the banning of the internet and mobile phones under ISIS rule, the true extent of the terror of the jihadists' reign was only revealed once towns and cities under their rule began to fall in 2016, after a major offensive by a US-led coalition of countries, including Australia.

Northern Iraq, October 2016

It was an impossible choice facing hundreds of thousands of Syrian and Iraqi parents forced to live under ISIS rule. Should they stay behind and face possible death in what was surely going to be a

fierce and deadly battle? Or should they risk their children's lives and flee, facing possible execution if caught by the militants?

As Iraqi and coalition forces ramped up their offensive to take back the towns and cities occupied by ISIS jihadists, the predictions from the UN and human rights groups were dire. They warned of a humanitarian disaster of historic proportions over the next few months, estimating that as many as 700,000 civilians would be in need of urgent assistance once Mosul, the largest city under ISIS control, fell. 'We don't know where they are going to come out, if they are going to come out and in what sort of numbers they will come out,' UNICEF's chief in Iraq Peter Hawkins told me. 'If they come out in large numbers, we will be overwhelmed.'[1]

By late October 2016, the first refugees to escape ISIS rule around their Mosul stronghold in Northern Iraq began trickling out. In a crowded refugee camp on the outskirts of Erbil, the region's Kurdish capital, I met some of the first families to flee the villages liberated in the new coalition offensive.

'I can finally show my face in public,' 18-year-old Shaima said, beaming, balancing her baby on her hip near the camp entrance. They had fled in the middle of the night. It had taken three days of walking to escape her village, but it was worth it, the young mother said – anything in order to escape the fear and punishment that had ruled their lives for the last two years. 'Everything was prohibited,' explained the young mother. 'Women weren't allowed to even show our fingers. Everything was banned. It was so strict and religious.' Shaima told me that she and her sisters dumped the long black niqabs that ISIS had forced them to wear as soon as they reached the safety of the Kurdish checkpoints. 'I will never wear it again,' she said happily.

As we talked, an older Iraqi woman perched on a pile of aid boxes next to us and inhaled a long drag of a cigarette. She caught my eye and smiled; cigarettes were among the long list of prohibited items under ISIS rule.

Despite their difficult journeys to escape, the families who had made it here were the lucky ones. ISIS wasn't digging into their villages and putting up much resistance. They were saving that for Mosul itself. Villagers from outlying areas around Mosul reported witnessing civilians being forcibly marched back towards the city,

with ISIS using women and children as human shields alongside retreating fighters as they withdrew into their stronghold.[2] Inside the city, reports emerged of civilians being shot dead by the militants after they were accused of leaking information to Iraqi forces. The bodies of more than 40 people were hung from electricity poles around the city to terrify and intimidate the civilian population.[3]

As I was filming in the camp, a little boy who looked about four years old wandered past. He was wearing a camouflage army jumper and holding a fake gun. I asked to take a photo. The little thing straightened his back, held up his plastic pistol and stared into my camera. His face was blank. He just cocked the toy weapon and confidently held it the way he must have seen many adults do in real life.

Of the more than one million people forced to live under ISIS rule in Iraq, it is estimated that more than half were children. They were forced to learn violent IS curriculum at school, attend public floggings and beheadings, and encouraged to spy on their own parents if they saw them breaking the militants' fundamentalist rules.

Thirteen-year-old Mohammad was one of the kids who gathered around as I filmed the camp streets. The teenager's right arm ended at his elbow. It was amputated after he'd been severely injured in a gunfight near his home when ISIS invaded his village. 'I was afraid of everything,' the young boy said softly, reflecting on the last two years. 'They used to bring people and slaughter them.'

In a corner of the camp, volunteers from UNICEF and the Norwegian Refugee Council had set up special play workshops for the youngest residents. Over a hundred kids squealed with delight as they danced, sang and threw balls with aid workers, clapping their hands in time to music being blasted over speakers. Parents watched on, a few with tears in their eyes, as they recounted how such activities had been banned under ISIS rule. 'Before they were locked up, scared, terrified from ISIS all day, every day,' a father said emotionally as he watched his kids play. 'Now here they are enjoying being looked after, enjoying this freedom.' The children threw balloons and giggled. There was even face painting. It was hard to imagine that just a few days ago some of these kids were living in a location where public beheadings were commonplace.

'My feeling as a mother watching my kids be happy again is a great feeling,' a grinning woman said. 'Thank God for this beautiful activity.'

In the other corner of the camp, volunteers from a European charity played volleyball with dozens of young men. About 50 boys aged between 12 and 17 were living in several large tents here. They had all arrived alone, many of them recently, as ISIS tried to recruit anyone they could for the upcoming battle for Mosul.

'I wanted to leave because they want me to join them and I didn't want to,' said 17-year-old Tariq, who fled his ISIS-held village in the middle of the night. 'If I didn't join, they would arrest me. I just didn't want to pledge myself to them.' The teenager felt terrible about leaving his parents and siblings behind. 'I didn't tell my family that I was escaping because this was very dangerous, and they wouldn't want me to go. Of course, this was a hard decision. This was my last chance,' he said quietly. 'If I got caught they will execute me.'

Inside the tents, the boys were mucking around, playing cards and styling each other's hair in front of a blue heart-shaped mirror. Twelve-year-old Abdullah sat quietly watching the older boys. He was a tiny little thing with curly hair and big eyes.

His left hand was missing the tops of four fingers, which he told me were blown off during his escape attempt. 'It was during the night; I dropped all my money,' the little boy explained shyly. 'I went to look for my money on the ground and the fuse of a grenade exploded.' Despite the injury, he was overjoyed to have escaped. 'My biggest fear was to get caught by ISIS. They killed my dad and my uncle,' he said. 'The only thing they know is how to kill.'

There used to be more boys staying here, but in the run-up to the Mosul operation, recruiters from the local Iraqi government militia group, Hashd Al Shaabi, came to the camp to enlist as many young men as they could to fight ISIS. The aid workers here told me that more than 200 unaccompanied boys were taken off in trucks to the front line. Seventeen-year-old Tarek had been thinking about joining too. 'If was offered to be recruited to go back and fight, I would do it,' he told me firmly. 'To liberate my people, I would sacrifice my life in order to free my village.'

Iraq and Syria, early 2017

One night, eight-year-old Hashim Abdul Fattah Al Ali was sitting with his family in their home in the town of Abu Kamal in Deir Ezzor province, Syria. That same evening a coalition warplane took off from a base somewhere in the Middle East and headed towards Hashim's village. Suddenly, they dropped their load, an airstrike slamming into a target not far from Hashim's house, causing a massive explosion. Little Hashim lost his life. But there was no blood; he reportedly died of a heart attack. The little boy was literally scared to death.[4]

By early 2017, there had been more than 17,000 coalition airstrikes on ISIS-held cities and towns across Syria and Iraq in an attempt to wipe out the jihadists.[5] But millions of innocent civilians were living in the same locations, trapped under the militants' rule – how many of them were also being killed in this massive bombing campaign?

At desks in the UK, Turkey, Jordan and Iraq, a fastidious team of researchers was trying to answer that question. They are part of Airwars, a non-profit NGO tracking coalition airstrikes on ISIS. Led by British investigative journalist Chris Woods, a team of eight researchers spent hours each day painstakingly sorting through whatever information they could glean: combing through mobile phone videos, Facebook posts, local media reports and official US military information to paint a picture of what was happening on the ground and just who was being killed.

'Everyone in Iraq and Syria has a cell phone. Everybody is taking videos, photographs, uploading stuff onto the internet. So we know a great deal about civilians – how they're dying, where they're dying, when they're dying,' Woods explained.

Their assessment of what was happening on the ground was grim – by February 2017, Airwars believed over 2500 civilians had been killed in coalition bombings since their air campaign on ISIS had begun in mid 2014. The team had compiled hundreds of cases of civilians allegedly killed in Syria and Iraq from coalition bombings, with the names, ages, locations and details of how those civilians were dying. They hoped their collation of data and the evidence of civilian deaths would force coalition nations to be more

careful in their targeting as they ramped up their airstrikes on Mosul. 'It's become much more difficult for militaries to ignore that information now,' Woods said.

One of the cases the Airwars team was investigating was an airstrike on 13 December 2016 that obliterated two neighbouring houses in Al Sukar neighbourhood in north-east Mosul. Footage of the site sent from family members trapped in Mosul and passed on to relatives in Canada shows desperate rescuers frantically trying to dig through the rubble and remains of the collapsed buildings. Eleven members of one family were killed, with five children among the dead.

Airwars ensured these civilians were not anonymous: 78-year-old grandfather Ahmed Nather Mahmood; his 68-year-old wife, Badreah; their son Shehab and his wife, Amear, and their children, Ahlam and Ali; and Ahmed's daughter Ekhlass and her children, Malak, Athear, Ali and Mohannad. Family photos show Ahmed as a proud man, posing in his crisp white Iraqi robe. Grandma Badreah has a warm smile and a white headscarf. One of the small boys wears a red polo shirt; his younger brother sits thoughtfully, hand on his chin, in a plaid red shirt and denim cap. A teenage son with a serious face flexes his muscles in a tight T-shirt.

It took 33 days for the surviving family members to dig out all the bodies and bury their loved ones. Who was responsible for their tragic deaths? Who decided to strike their house and why?

Only 60 per cent of coalition strikes on ISIS are carried out by the US military, with the other 40 per cent being conducted by other coalition partners; including Britain, France and Australia.[6] 'Now, we know the coalition bombed in Mosul that day. It may have been the US; it may have been Britain, Australia, Belgium, France, we don't know. We're reaching out to all four countries and saying, "Did you bomb here? Were you involved?"' explained Woods.

For many years, the US was criticised for the secrecy surrounding alleged incidents with civilian casualties, but there has since been a significant shift towards transparency. Airwars said the US Central Command (CENTCOM) now offered a level of cooperation with its investigations, providing dates, locations and GPS coordinates of alleged civilian casualty incidents. The NGO then cross-referenced that information with allegations of civilians being killed.

'The Americans come back, and they'll say, "Ah, no, we categorically weren't involved in this. We didn't bomb in this location," Woods said. 'They might come back and say, "Yeah, we've already got an assessment underway," or they'll say, "We're now going to trigger an assessment or an investigation because of your information."' By early 2017, the US were the only coalition member to admit that they had accidentally killed civilians, conceding they had unintentionally caused more than 220 civilian deaths, with many more still under investigation.

Airwars had a similar relationship of cooperation on a case-by-case basis with the UK, but Australia was refusing to cooperate with the NGO. 'The contrast with Australia couldn't be starker,' Woods said, frustrated. 'We're incapable of engaging with Australia because they won't tell us where they bomb, they won't tell us when they bomb, and they won't tell us what they bomb. And that's been going on for 30 months.' He considered Australia among the least transparent members of the coalition. 'In our view, there's just no real transparency from Australia here, and there's no real accountability, either.'

The Airwars team was shocked when a freedom of information request lodged with the Australian defence department revealed that the Australians were not even collecting data on alleged civilian casualty incidents. 'The department does not specifically collect authoritative, and therefore accurate, data on enemy and/or civilian casualties in either Iraq or Syria, and certainly does not track such statistics,' read the document released to Australian human rights lawyer Kellie Tranter.

It was a stunning admission. How could Australia investigate alleged civilian casualty incidents if it did not bother to track that information? 'Of the couple of militaries I've discussed this with informally, let's just say they've expressed surprise at the Australian position,' Woods said. 'Other nations are absolutely clear that it is their obligation to track and assess civilians they may have killed. Nobody else is going to do this for them. It's their job.'

This news also alarmed British QC Ben Emmerson, at that time the UN Special Rapporteur on Counter Terrorism and Human Rights, who reports annually to the UN General Assembly and the Human Rights Council on the impact of the military action against ISIS on civilians. 'I find it extremely surprising that there is

no central index kept of the number of combatants killed or civilian casualties,' Emmerson said. The expert suggested Australia may not be meeting its obligations under international law. 'A blanket refusal to release data on civilian casualties, regardless of the circumstances and regardless of any operational risk which there may or may not be, would not be consistent with any view of a state's responsibilities in international law.'

When I approached the Australian military for an interview about their policy, they refused. They told me that all Australian defence force personnel were required to 'immediately report suspected instances of civilian casualties' and 'all reports are investigated' – but they declined to say whether they were investigating any suspected civilian casualty incidents in Iraq or Syria. I was advised to take my questions regarding data on suspected civilian casualties to CENTCOM.

But when I asked the US military, they told me that each coalition country is responsible for tracking their own data in relation to suspected civilian casualties. 'We do not speak for our coalition partners and only talk publicly about US actions. Coalition nations speak for themselves.' It became clear the Australians were just trying to pass the buck. Why were they being so secretive and refusing to engage like the US and the UK?

Chris Woods believed that, given the number of airstrikes Australia had conducted in Syria and Iraq, it was 'impossible' that civilians would not have been killed. 'We're not saying these are war crimes or deliberate killings of civilians,' he explained. 'Even when your bombs are going to the right place, there's still human error, you still get civilians coming into the kill zone at the very last second, you can't avert the missile. If all we get is denial, how can we make things better? How can we improve on things?'

The stakes quickly escalated as the main battle to retake Mosul began. It was predicted to be the largest urban battle since World War Two, and with ISIS fighters deliberately hiding in densely populated areas, it presented a logistical and legal nightmare for coalition members. The risk of civilian casualties was incredibly high. By early 2017, experts and human rights groups had begun to urgently sound the alarm on a large uptick in the number of reported civilian deaths from coalition airstrikes.[7] For the first time since Russia's intervention to back up the Assad regime in

September 2015, civilian deaths assessed by monitors as likely caused by coalition strikes outweighed those attributed to Moscow's brutal air campaign in Syria.[8] 'You don't get to drop bombs on cities and towns and not kill civilians,' insisted Chris Woods.

Mosul, March–July 2017

By February and early March, a senior western diplomat told the Associated Press that civilian deaths had begun to dominate military planning meetings in Baghdad.[9] A few weeks later, I stood outside the main entrance of the Hammam Al Alil camp on the outskirts of Mosul, filming a steady stream of vehicles offloading the latest families who had managed to escape ISIS rule. Compared with when I had last been here, a few months earlier, the number of civilians fleeing was now massive.

The past week had seen the highest number of people flee Mosul since the battle to retake the city had begun five months earlier – 15,000 civilians had arrived at this camp alone in the past ten hours. It was standing room only in the large construction trucks, with dozens of people jam-packed into the back trays. Rows of heads peeked out, examining the desolate landscape where they were about to be unloaded. Iraqi soldiers formed a chain, helping mothers with babies climb out slowly first, passing smaller children down to colleagues, who placed them gently on the muddy ground.

Thousands of people were gathered outside the camp gate, but no one was being allowed in. This camp was now full. Parents stood around, clutching the hands of the children and a plastic bag of the few belongings they had been able to bring with them. It was raining and cold, and the four children standing next to me didn't have any shoes on. They held hands and shivered quietly next to their mother.

A young man spotted his relatives in the crowd and rushed towards them, sobbing and throwing his arms around their necks. 'We haven't seen each other in three years,' he cried. The three young men hugged, oblivious to the crowd around them, tears running down their cheeks. 'I escaped through the drains,' the young man told me, standing next to his cousins. 'The family is all together now. Thank God!'

Hundreds of families now sat around in the mud, exhausted from their journeys and unsure where they would be going next. Everyone looked shell-shocked and traumatised. For the previous few months, as the battle for Mosul had intensified, ISIS had held these men, women and children hostage as human shields – starving them as food and water supplies in the city dwindled, and then shooting at them when they finally managed to escape.

Mothers had resorted to drugging their babies, to ensure ISIS didn't catch them fleeing. 'I gave him some drops of medicine,' one mum told me quietly, holding her floppy infant tightly in her arms. 'I didn't want him to make a sound.'

Amid the confusion of fleeing Mosul, many were separated from their relatives. In the crowd, my Iraqi producer Adiba and I came across a boy in a blue jumper who looked about eight, clutching the hand of his wailing younger brother. 'We lost our mum,' the older boy managed to get out between sobs. 'We can't find her!' We stayed with the boys, trying to calm them down, until an aid worker from the NGO Save the Children arrived and took them to the place set aside for separated kids. Another aid worker walked past, carrying a crying toddler in his arms. 'Hey, families! Whose daughter is this?' he shouts out, walking through the crowds. 'Who has lost this girl?'

By the gate of the camp registration office, weeping mothers waited, desperate for news of missing loved ones. 'He was wearing blue trousers. He's sick. He can't walk properly,' sobbed Um Mohamad, who was searching for her 15-year-old son. He had been out searching for firewood a few days ago when bombing started in their neighbourhood. 'He's my only son,' she said desperately. 'I don't eat. I don't sleep. My heart is heavy for him.'

Many here were weak from a lack of food and water after being besieged in their houses for weeks and having run out of supplies. Hundreds waited in line for a plate of steaming rice and vegetable curry served up by volunteers. Meanwhile, a Kurdish aid group was swamped by a desperate crowd as they handed out bottles of water. Children clambered up the side of the truck, begging for a bottle. Iraqi soldiers pushed back the swelling number of people.

Inside the camp, the conditions were grim. Families tried to tread carefully around huge swathes of mud, but everyone was covered in

it anyway. The few toilet blocks were overflowing with sewage, the stench gag-inducing.

UNHCR had set up five huge tents for women with children who had not been allocated their own tent yet. We met Siham, a gentle 35-year-old mother of four, who had been sitting in the corner with her children for the past 24 hours. There were no blankets or mattresses or heating. Like everyone in here, she and her children were sleeping on the cold slabs of concrete, huddled up together to try to stay warm. 'My house was destroyed. And I don't have a place to go, and I don't have any money,' she explained despairingly. 'I will just stay here and wait for God.' The family had nothing but the clothes they had escaped in. Siham was worried about her two-year-old, who had diarrhoea. She had run out of nappies. For the past four weeks they had been trapped in a relative's house in west Mosul, where they had been drinking rainwater and running out of food.

'Can you believe it's been one month since we showered?' Siham asked sadly. 'I swear to God, one month without showering. You can't imagine how dirty my children are and covered in bacteria. We have learnt how to live on empty stomachs, but now my worry is they will get sick.' She paused and started quietly crying.

Siham's children sat and watched us chat, wide-eyed and silent. Their father had left their house one day several months ago and never returned. They didn't know if he was executed by ISIS or killed in an airstrike. 'All my life has been destroyed,' Siham said, tears running down her cheeks. 'Everything! We want the whole world to know what is happening to the people of Iraq.'

For months, the UN had been warning that the coalition's battle to retake Mosul had the potential to be one of the largest man-made disasters for many years. Despite their warnings and pleas for the international community to urgently increase its funding for the humanitarian response, the UN just didn't have the money to adequately look after the hundreds of thousands of people like Siham who desperately needed help. There were not even enough funds to house and feed the masses here, let alone provide the medical and social services they needed after being traumatised for so long.

On a quick visit to the camp, Bruno Geddo, the chief UNHCR official in Iraq, stood in front of reporters and begged for more

funds from international donors. 'There is a sense of urgency. At any time we could have a mass outflow. Because 400,000 people could still be trapped in the old city. The moment the corks pop, we could receive tens of thousands within the space of 48 hours. We have made an urgent appeal because we need to scale up,' Geddo insisted. The contribution of many countries to humanitarian efforts paled in comparison to what they were spending on the military campaign to unseat ISIS. By July 2017, only 42 per cent of what the UN required to provide a basic standard of care to people fleeing had been given – leaving a funding gap of US$570 million.[10] 'And the worst is yet to come,' Geddo told me gloomily.

As more truckloads of refugees arrived at the camp, it became clear that ISIS was not the only cause of fear, death and injury. Many civilians stopped us, wanting to talk about the massive number of civilian casualties they claimed were being caused by coalition airstrikes – the horrific cost this war was having on civilians was beginning to emerge. 'From one area to the next, there are just bodies everywhere,' a woman with an orange headscarf and three small children told me emphatically. 'Each neighbourhood you go, 100 houses are destroyed. Yesterday and today so many people were killed. As soon as you leave the house you see airstrikes! There are so many airstrikes on us. We were all stuck in our houses, we couldn't get out!' An old man who had just arrived on a bus claimed that dozens of people in his neighbourhood had been killed by coalition airstrikes. 'I lost three members of my family. Believe me. Believe me!' he yelled angrily.

On the edge of the camp parking lot, I met Khaled and his wife, Noura. Khaled was sitting in a wheelchair, while Noura perched in the mud, trying to breastfeed her newborn and not get dirt all over her and her children's clothes. Khaled had serious leg injuries after he was caught by a coalition airstrike on Mosul several months ago. 'I was parking my car and then the planes came and bombed. The planes bombed the parking lot,' explained Khaled.

Noura said civilians were increasingly being caught between ISIS on one side and airstrikes on the other. 'There is still shrapnel in his body from when the plane bombed, he can't feel his legs now,' she said, her face crumpling up in tears. 'We have no one to take care of me and my kids and my disabled husband!'

Next to the arrivals area, a crowd gathered around a small demountable caravan. Inside, an Iraqi medical charity was trying to perform a triage service for those arriving with injuries. On a chair in the corner, 35-year-old Khowlah was shivering and moaning in pain. She had spent the last 15 days with a broken leg after an airstrike hit her house. 'She was making bread, ISIS was in the neighbourhood and the plane bombed,' explained her brother, who said he had carried his sister out of Mosul on his back. 'So many families have been killed because of the airstrikes. They're being pulled from rubble.'

These accounts were not uncommon. A Human Rights Watch researcher in Iraq reported hearing a similar pattern of stories. 'Remarkably, when I interview families at camps who have just fled the fighting, the first thing they complain about is not the three horrific years they spent under ISIS, or the last months of no food or clean water, but the American airstrikes,' said Belkis Wille, the senior HRW researcher working on Mosul.[11] 'Many told me that they survived such hardship, and almost made it out with the families, only to lose all their loved ones in a strike before they had time to flee.'

We left the camp and headed towards a small town about 20 kilometres away, where some of the most badly injured were ending up. In a small field hospital, set back from the main road behind massive blast walls, more than 1000 Mosul civilians had received lifesaving surgery here in the past four months.

Fatima had been in her home in west Mosul three days earlier when an airstrike had hit. 'They bombed my house and it collapsed on me. My legs were broken, and my husband and daughter were also injured, and my neighbours were killed,' she told me from her hospital bed. The young mother spoke of families enduring unspeakable horror, trapped, cowering, in their homes as airstrikes pounded neighbourhoods all over the city. She questioned the level of force being used by the US-led coalition and the Iraqi army against ISIS. 'The missiles are so big they're destroying whole houses,' she insisted. 'It's a massacre. The planes need to take more care. That's why families are dying. Mosul is being destroyed!'

In the bed next to Fatima was a sleeping 18-month-old boy, a leg and an arm covered in plaster casts. Christine, an American

volunteer nurse, sat next to his bed stroking his hair. 'There was some type of blast and rubble fell down on top of him. And so he was trapped, from what I understand, in this rubble. It ended up breaking his right leg and arm,' Christine explained. She said the baby arrived several days ago in an ambulance, completely alone. 'Unfortunately, what we did find out with him, is that his entire family was killed. And now, we have the pleasure of caring for him, but unfortunately, he's a little orphan now,' said the nurse, tears welling in her eyes.

The evidence from this hospital and camps around Mosul backed up the urgent warnings from Airwars and other human rights groups that coalition airstrikes were having a devastating impact on civilians. 'I think what we're seeing in west Mosul is a shift. Instead of clearing a house, as they maybe would have done a few months ago, they're calling in an airstrike,' Chris Woods said. 'And it's transferring the risk from the military onto the civilians. That's a terrible choice that is having to be made.'

While I was on the ground in Mosul, reports began to emerge of a horrific incident in the Al Jadida neighbourhood in west Mosul several days earlier. Local officials claimed that as many as 200 people had been killed after a massive coalition airstrike. Some residents reported that the airstrike had hit an explosives-filled truck, detonating a blast that collapsed buildings packed with families.[12]

I met Ahmed, a 19-year-old from west Mosul, who had arrived in the camp several days ago. He showed me unanswered text messages he had sent to his 21-year-old sister, Ghofran, her two children and her husband. They had been sheltering in the Al Jadida neighbourhood, but he had not heard from her since the day of the airstrike. He was deeply worried they might be among those killed. 'We just want the authorities to tell us if they are dead or alive,' he told me worriedly. Ahmed said the jihadists had been deliberately hiding among civilians and the coalition needed to be more careful. 'In many of the neighbourhoods they are bombing, more families are being killed than fighters,' the young man said angrily.

Outrage grew as photos emerged from Al Jadida of dozens and dozens of bodies, including children, wrapped in blue tarpaulins, being buried in mass graves.[13] Locals reported that ISIS militants had positioned a sniper on the roof of the home that had sheltered

the largest number of people.[14] Majid Al Najim, a 65-year-old resident of Al Jadida who lost relatives in the airstrike, spoke to *The Guardian*: 'Is an ISIS sniper being on a roof enough of a reason to send a plane with a large bomb to destroy a house? They hit it many times. They wanted to destroy everything inside,' he said. 'The days after were horrible. There were children shouting under the rubble. Nobody came to help them.'[15]

The US military confirmed that coalition warplanes had struck in west Mosul on 17 March at 'the location corresponding to allegations of civilian casualties'. Claiming that their forces took reasonable precautions during the planning and execution of airstrikes to reduce the risk of harm to civilians, CENTCOM said in a statement, 'our goal has always been for zero civilian casualties, but the coalition will not abandon our commitment to our Iraqi partners'. The Mosul municipality chief supervising the retrieval of the bodies told the Reuters news agency that 240 bodies had been pulled from the location of the airstrike by 25 March.[16] The attack had one of the worst death tolls from a single airstrike in decades of modern warfare – reportedly one of the deadliest bombing raids for civilians since the US invasion of Iraq in 2003.[17] (The US military claimed later that the number of civilians killed was 105).

In Geneva, the UN's human rights chief, Zeid Raad Al Hussein, urged the US-led coalition and the Iraqi government to review their tactics in Mosul and take greater care for the lives of civilians being deliberately put at risk by ISIS. 'The conduct of airstrikes on ISIS locations in such an environment, particularly given the clear indications that ISIS is using large numbers of civilians as human shields at such locations, may potentially have a lethal and disproportionate impact on civilians,' he told reporters.[18]

Several days before the enormous death toll in the Al Jadida incident, the coalition had been behind two other deadly airstrikes that human rights groups said had also killed a disproportionately large number of civilians. On 16 March 2017, 38 Syrians, including five children, were killed when a US airstrike hit a mosque in northern Syria.[19] At the time, US officials insisted they had not hit a mosque but a separate building where they claimed Al Qaeda operatives were meeting. (They later conceded the destroyed building had indeed been a mosque, while a Human Rights Watch investigation found no

evidence to support the US allegation that members of Al Qaeda or any other armed group were meeting there.)[20]

On 20 March 2017, dozens of Syrian civilians were killed when another American airstrike in Raqqa province hit a school where refugees had been taking shelter.[21] (The US eventually admitted at least 40 civilians were 'unintentionally killed'.) 'We have until recently always credited the coalition for taking care to avoid civilian casualties, compared with the Russians,' said Chris Woods of Airwars. 'But since the last months of 2016, you have seen this steep climb in civilian casualties and public sentiment has turned very sharply against the US-led coalition.'[22]

In the wake of the Al Jadida massacre, Iraqi special forces told the *New York Times* that there had been a 'noticeable relaxing of the coalition's rules of engagement since President Trump took office'.[23] The officials claimed to the newspaper that under the Obama administration, many requests for airstrikes had been denied because of the risk that civilians would be hurt. Now, the officers claimed, 'it has become much easier to call in airstrikes'.

The US military denied anything had changed. 'There's been no loosening of the rules of engagement,' a Pentagon spokesman told the *New York Times* in the days after Al Jadida. But this contradicted previous statements made by the US military. The rules had actually begun to loosen even before Trump had become president. In December 2016, President Obama had given a new directive that allowed US and coalition advisers to call in airstrikes in Iraq without approval from the Baghdad operations centre, effectively reducing the number of steps required for some coalition units to authorize airstrikes. In February, the US-led coalition spokesperson, Colonel John Dorrian, confirmed that 'the rules of engagement in the fight against IS in Iraq were adjusted' two months earlier. Additional coalition ground commanders had been given the 'ability to call in airstrikes without going through a strike cell,' he said.[24]

Following on from Obama's December directive, President Trump, who famously had promised during his election campaign to 'bomb the shit out of' ISIS until there was 'nothing left' had ordered a review of the rules of engagement in the war against ISIS.[25] While the assessment had not been completed at the time of the Al Jadida massacre, there was concern that Trump's very public questioning

of Obama's battlefield strategy had led to a quiet acceptance within the US military of higher civilian casualty tolls.

Human Rights Watch linked the new US directive on airstrikes to the growing number of civilian dead. 'The high number of civilian deaths in recent fighting, as well as recent announcements about changed procedures for vetting airstrikes, raise concerns about the way the battle for west Mosul is being fought,' HRW said. It called out the US military's backflipping on whether their rules of engagement had indeed changed; saying it didn't matter how they chose to classify the new directive, the net effect 'appears to be that coalition aircraft are now able to conduct strikes in densely populated areas with less information and time to ascertain the number of civilians who may be injured or killed. This increases the likelihood of civilian casualties in an attack.'[26]

A former Obama administration official echoed HRW's concerns, telling Airwars, 'There is a tremendous disconnect between what we've heard from senior military officials who are saying there has been no change in the rules of engagement and clearly what we are seeing on the ground.'[27]

President Trump obviously hadn't read the memo denying a change in the rules of engagement. 'I totally changed rules of engagement. I totally changed our military, I totally changed the attitudes of the military and they have done a fantastic job,' Trump bragged several months later in an interview with CNN.[28]

Meanwhile, proof emerged from Mosul that ISIS jihadists were trying to lure the coalition into killing more civilians. The *New York Times* reported that American surveillance aircraft had filmed the militants herding Iraqi civilians into a building and then positioning their forces on the top, to bait the coalition into attacking with an airstrike.[29]

In May 2017, the US military announced the findings of their investigation into the Al Jadida massacre, finding that an American airstrike to target two ISIS snipers on a roof had inadvertently set off explosives laid by the militants (though it never explained why a 500-pound [225-kilogram] bomb had been thought necessary to kill two snipers). This had triggered a massive secondary explosion more powerful than the original airstrike, which had brought the buildings down on the civilians sheltering inside.[30] The US general

who led the investigation said tactics had been adjusted in the wake of the incident, to take into account such deliberate entrapment of civilians by ISIS.

That same month, after we featured several reports across the ABC focusing on civilian casualties in Mosul and the work of Airwars, human rights groups lobbied the Australian minister for defence, Marise Payne, demanding that Australia be more transparent with its operations in Iraq and Syria and over the issue of civilian casualties. Subsequently, the Australian military announced a significant change in policy. They would start publishing fortnightly reports on the airstrikes their personnel carried out in Syria and Iraq, including bombing targets and locations, allowing for the first time groups such as Airwars to compare claims of civilian casualties against the times and places of Australia's strikes.[31] It was a win for transparency and accountability, even if the Australians still insisted that not a single one of their airstrikes had killed any civilians.[32]

As the battle to take Mosul ground on, the final few weeks of the offensive created the absolute worst-case scenario the UN and humanitarian agencies had been warning of. More than 920,000 people had fled the city over the previous eight months of battle.[33] Fighting was now concentrated in the tiny backstreets of the old city, and those escaping had endured months and months of trying to stay alive under constant airstrikes and bombardment. It was now summer, and temperatures in Mosul were unbearably hot. Families limped out injured, exhausted and utterly traumatised. Small children arrived at the front line covered in wounds, carried out in sheets. Babies admitted to Médecins Sans Frontières hospitals were in a terrible state, suffering from acute malnutrition. 'Whenever we receive people from there, they look aghast. Like someone who has gone through an experience like hell,' Bruno Geddo, the UNHCR's chief official in Iraq told reporters. 'It is like coming back from the afterworld and so we are doing everything we can, but to be honest I don't think we have the tools to deal with this level of trauma. They have seen unspeakable violence.'[34]

On 20 July, nine months after those first refugees had fled to the camps, the battle for Mosul was over at last. In their final assessment of the battle, in a report called *At Any Cost*, Amnesty

International found that Iraqi and coalition forces had failed to take adequate measures to protect civilians, instead 'subjecting them to a terrifying barrage of fire from weapons that should never be used in densely populated civilian areas'.[35] Their investigation found that the efforts the coalition did make to warn some civilians simply provided them with a false sense of security. Families dutifully heeded the instructions given in leaflets dropped by the coalition, such as to hang children's clothes on their roofs to mark them as civilian homes. But Amnesty International interviewed people whose houses had still been bombed despite following these directives.

'The children's clothes were on the roof when the rocket landed on my house,' a father reported. Another resident was damning of the coalition's advice for how civilians could be safe. 'Leaflets were dropped continuously beforehand with warnings telling people to stay at home,' this young man said. 'But these were useless. Make sure you write that down. The. Warnings. Were. Useless.'

In December 2017, the Associated Press (AP) released an extensive investigation, reporting that between 9000 and 11,000 civilians had died in the Mosul assault, a civilian casualty rate nearly ten times higher than had been previously reported.[36] The report cross-referenced independent databases from NGOs such as Airwars with information compiled by Mosul's gravediggers, morgue workers and volunteers who retrieved bodies from the city's rubble. It found that while a third of the deaths of civilians in Mosul had occurred in a 'final frenzy of violence' by ISIS jihadists, at least 3200 civilian deaths were from airstrikes, artillery fire or mortar rounds on the city fired by Iraqi or coalition forces between October 2016 and July 2017. The AP could not determine who was responsible for the remaining deaths.

The AP's numbers were starkly different from how many civilians the US-led coalition had acknowledged were killed, which by the end of 2017 sat at 326. The US-led coalition told the AP they 'lacked the resources' to send their own investigators into Mosul in the aftermath of the battle.

Meanwhile, the news agency's reporter visited Mosul six times in six weeks, speaking to morgue officials and staffers dozens of times in person and over the phone. 'Most of those [civilian] victims are simply described as "crushed" in health ministry

reports,' the AP reported. 'As the fight punched into western Mosul, the morgue logs filled with civilians increasingly killed by being "blown to pieces".'

Raqqa, Syria, June–October 2017

There is no doubt that the enemy the US-led coalition faced in Mosul was horrifically cruel and morally corrupt. But no matter what barbarous tactics the jihadists employed, this did not relieve the coalition of their obligations to take all feasible precautions to minimize harm to civilians. Time after time, evidence built up that this was just not the case.

Despite the outcry over civilian casualties in Mosul, the US-led coalition showed no indication they had changed their operational behaviour by June, when they began the operation to liberate the Syrian city of Raqqa, the second-largest ISIS-held city.

When asked about the upcoming battle, US defence secretary James Mattis said that the US had 'accelerated' its tactics against ISIS from a policy of 'attrition' to one of 'annihilation'.[37] 'Civilian casualties are a fact of life in this sort of situation,' offered Mattis. 'We're not the perfect guys, but we are the good guys. And so we're doing what we can.'

Two weeks after these comments, UN war crimes investigators condemned what they said was a 'staggering' loss of civilian life as a result of the US-backed campaign to reclaim Raqqa.[38] 'The imperative to fight terrorism must not, however, be undertaken at the expense of civilians who unwillingly find themselves living in areas where [ISIS] is present,' Paulo Pinheiro, the chief of the UN Commission of Inquiry on Syria, told the UN Human Rights Council in Geneva. As the weeks went by, Airwars warned that the number of civilians reported killed in Raqqa was comparable to the worst periods of the Aleppo siege, when civilians there were under intense bombardment from Russian and Syrian forces.[39]

Up to 200,000 people were estimated to be trapped in Raqqa. With water and electricity cut off in the middle of summer in the desert city, reports began emerging of civilians dying due to a lack of safe water to drink. A citizen-journalist group known as Raqqa is Being Slaughtered Silently, with extensive contacts inside the city,

reported how desperate families trying to collect drinking water at the Euphrates River were being targeted by coalition aircraft. 'They are basically going with their cars to the river trying to get water, and then the coalition bombed their cars,' an activist told me.

The commander of the US-led coalition, Lieutenant General Stephen Townsend, attacked the UN over its criticism of the high numbers of civilian casualties. 'I would challenge anyone to find a more precise and careful campaign in the history of warfare on this planet,' he told the BBC.[40] 'I think we are being as careful as we need to be and as we can be, and I would challenge the individual from the UN who made this hyperbolic statement that civilian casualties are staggering. Show me some evidence of that.'

It was all there, if only the general cared to look. In the face of the coalition's lack of interest, it was left up to Amnesty International to uncover the evidence. In a devastating report, Amnesty found that the US-led coalition's campaign on Raqqa may have amounted to war crimes, saying that the coalition's claim that its 'precision air campaign' had allowed it to bomb ISIS out of Raqqa while causing very few civilian casualties did not stand up to scrutiny.[41]

The indiscriminate and disproportionate nature of the attacks on the city violated international humanitarian law, said Amnesty. 'When so many civilians are killed in attack after attack, something is clearly wrong,' said the report's author Donatella Rovera. 'On the ground in Raqqa we witnessed a level of destruction comparable to anything we've seen in decades of covering the impact of wars.' Just as they had in Mosul, the coalition repeatedly used heavy weapons and massive airstrikes in Raqqa, where civilians were trapped and held as human shields, with an incredible 30,000 rounds of artillery fired on the city. 'A senior US military official said that more artillery shells were launched into Raqqa than anywhere since the Vietnam War. Given that artillery shells have margins of error of over 100 metres, it is no surprise that the result was mass civilian casualties,' Rovera said.

Survivors of the Raqqa assault spoke of escaping only 'by walking over the blood of those who were blown up as they tried to flee ahead of us'. Rasha Badran, a young mother of one, had 39 relatives and ten neighbours killed over the course of several weeks in four separate coalition airstrikes, as they moved from place to

place inside the city, desperately trying to find somewhere safe to shelter. Her one-year-old daughter, Tulip, was among those killed.

'We thought the forces who came to evict [ISIS] would know their business and would target [ISIS] and leave the civilians alone. We were naïve. By the time we had realised how dangerous it had become everywhere, it was too late; we were trapped,' Rasha told Amnesty. 'I don't understand why they bombed us. Didn't the surveillance planes see that we were civilian families?'

Tulip had been born amid the horror of life in ISIS-ruled Raqqa. Her parents had debated the names of several flowers before settling on Tulip. 'She was an amazing baby, a joy,' her mother said. Photos of the one-year-old showed a pudgy little thing with a mop of dark black hair, long eyelashes and a pink headband, lying on her mat wearing a playsuit with pandas on it. But when the coalition came to liberate Raqqa, there was nowhere safe for Tulip and her young parents to hide. When they tried to escape, ISIS shot at them in the streets. Then, one night, the house they were sheltering in was bombed by a coalition airstrike. The family hid in the rubble until the morning, as planes continued to circle overhead. In the light of day they found Tulip's body. The house had been pulverised; nothing was left standing, there was only rubble.[42] Satellite pictures of the house Tulip was hiding in show it standing one day. The next, it has disappeared, wiped from existence, just like nearly everyone cowering inside.

In all the cases Amnesty investigated, coalition forces launched airstrikes on buildings full of civilians using what are known as 'wide-area effect munitions'. All the civilians killed and injured had spent long periods of time in the same location before the airstrikes, noted the investigators.[43] Why did the coalition not conduct rigorous surveillance before these devastating strikes? The coalition failed to provide Amnesty International with detailed information on the strikes they had investigated, including the one that killed baby Tulip.

Human Rights Watch conducted a similarly damning assessment of the coalition's tactics in Raqqa, examining airstrikes in small towns on the outskirts of the city.[44] I spoke with Ole Solvang, the deputy emergencies director at HRW, not long after he returned from conducting an on-the-ground investigation in northern Syria.

'We have serious concerns that the coalition did not take the necessary precautions before they launched attacks,' he told me. One of the incidents Solvang investigated was a massive airstrike near a bakery in the town of Tabqa. ISIS members had been reported in the vicinity, but there were also dozens of civilians lining up to buy bread when the airstrike hit. HRW collected the names of 44 civilians whom local residents and survivors said had been killed in the attack, including 14 children.[45]

'If the coalition did not know there were so many civilians there, then there is something wrong with their intelligence,' insisted Solvang. 'If the coalition knew that there were civilians, [then] there is the question [of] whether the attacks were proportionate. Under international law you can only launch attacks where the expected military gain exceeds the civilian harm.'

Amnesty International and Human Rights Watch staff had managed to safely visit Raqqa and surrounding towns to conduct investigations into coalition airstrikes, but the US military had apparently failed to carry out its own research. Yet Solvang claimed that American forces had been seen in the area, asking locals where foreign IS members lived. 'If they can do that, they can go and collect that kind of intelligence. They can [get on the ground and] investigate their own strikes. It's a matter of priority and how much they care about finding out the truth of those cases,' he told me. 'So what we are calling on the coalition to do is to conduct that full investigation, go to the sites, interview witnesses.'

When a UN team was finally able to enter Raqqa, its members 'were shocked by the level of destruction, which exceeded anything they had ever seen before'. The subsequent report from the UNHCR described how 'a cascade of rubble lies along the streets with hardly a single building intact', and estimated that more than 70 per cent of the city had been destroyed.[46]

When I contacted the US-led coalition body CENTCOM, requesting an interview to talk about the civilian casualty rates, they declined to discuss the issue. 'We are aware of the allegations and take all allegations of civilian casualties seriously,' they wrote. 'We can, however, say the coalition's goal is always for zero civilian casualties. The coalition has done, and continues to do, everything within its power to limit harm to non-combatants and civilian

infrastructure. We apply rigorous standards to our targeting process and take extraordinary efforts to protect non-combatants.'

So did the coalition really do everything within its power to limit harm to non-combatants and civilian infrastructure in the fight to defeat ISIS? 'Not at all,' former state department adviser Dr Larry Lewis told me recently. 'I mean so far from everything possible.'

A leading authority on civilian casualties during war, Lewis has spent over a decade working with the US military and has been behind every official US civilian casualty assessment since 2010. While working for the US military in Afghanistan, Lewis studied trends of civilian casualties and made recommendations that resulted in changes of tactics and a subsequent decrease in the civilian death toll. When he was given coalition data from airstrikes on ISIS in Iraq and Syria, he was shocked.

'I've done multiple assessments in Afghanistan, both for ISAF [International Security Assistance Force], and also for Special Forces. And then I was working for the US with the Saudis in Yemen. So, I can kinda look across these different operations, and go, "What do we do, what do we not do? Were we better, were we worse?" And Mosul and Raqqa were awful. It was damning, I mean it was just horrific.'

Lewis believes the comments by US Defence Secretary James Mattis about tactics of 'annihilation' in Raqqa influenced the US military's attitude towards the operation. 'It definitely had an impact. You had this idea of annihilation, and that shaped the whole operation in a bad way for civilians.'

In Afghanistan, according to Lewis, the US-led ISAF force developed a 'mindset of restraint' over time. 'There was an awareness of: "Is this strategically smart? We have the upper hand, so we're gonna use our superior capabilities, refine our ability to be precise, and to do it at a minimal cost to civilians." That was the overall evolution in Afghanistan.'

But those lessons were not taken aboard in Iraq and Syria, Lewis told me. He lays part of the blame on the desire to complete the operation quickly, but also on what he says was a lack of political pressure on the coalition regarding civilian casualties. Lewis believes the sectarian, Shiite-dominated nature of the Iraqi government meant that there was no strong lobbying on behalf of the mostly

Sunni families being killed by the airstrikes. 'There was very, very little pressure from the Iraqis. The only time they ever complained was [over] that one March 2017 incident [the Al Jadida airstrike].'

This contrasted greatly to the situation US forces faced in Afghanistan. 'I mean [tribal leaders] would go to the US commanders and say, "What do you not understand about not killing my people?" You had this external pressure that reinforced the strategic importance of reducing the civilian casualties. In Iraq there was no such pressure. So the sectarian factor, I believe was a factor to this. And there was this pressure to go faster, and of course, the US military doesn't need a whole lot of encouragement to go faster.'

While acknowledging the desire for civilians to be freed as quickly as possible from the jihadists who were using them as human shields, Dr Lewis believes that humanitarian concern for civilians was not the driving force behind the US approach. 'You can certainly make the argument about a sharp campaign, right? A sharp campaign is more humane, because it reduces the time that civilians are under this. And I think that is true to some extent, but then you go okay, well let's look at Mosul, and look at Raqqa, and they're destroyed, right? So, if the motivation was truly humanitarian, then it's hard to reconcile that to what actually is left.'

According to Lewis, the race for quick results limited 'tactical alternatives'. For example, if a sniper was spotted on a rooftop, it wasn't unusual for the Iraqi forces on the ground to quickly call in an airstrike to drop a 500-pound bomb. But, says Lewis, slower and more complex but potentially more accurate and less deadly alternatives could have been explored. 'Maybe I can bring in a sniper, maybe I can use a precision-guided hellfire [missile]. So ideally you would say "Okay, Iraqis, fall back, we're gonna move something in, and then in an hour we'll take care of it in a way that is not as destructive." But you didn't see that problem-solving process happen.'

Lewis believes the most significant influence on the rise in civilian casualties was another policy change implemented by President Barack Obama in late 2016. This increased what is known as the 'non-combatant casualty value' (NCV) – in other words, the maximum number of civilians that could acceptably be killed in any

operation within the normal approval chain. 'I'm not allowed to say the numbers,' Dr Lewis told me. 'Since I know it from classified sources, I'm not allowed to tell. But it was a significant change.'

Estimates of the change were, however, widely reported in the media at the time, with most indicating that the number jumped from zero civilian casualties to 10. The *Military Times*, for example, wrote: 'Military leaders planning operations against the Islamic State group in Iraq and Syria may authorize strikes where up to 10 civilians may be killed, if it is deemed necessary in order to get a critical military target. That is a change from the earlier policy that called for an assessment that zero would be killed. Officials said the change was made because of concerns that the military wasn't being aggressive enough in its targeting.'[47]

The change had a dramatic impact. 'I was shocked actually that [Obama] changed it,' Dr Lewis said, pausing and choosing his words carefully. 'I don't know if he really realized what effect that would have. When that number changed, basically it was carte blanche. "Hey, as long as you're below this number, which is much higher, it's okay."'

In April 2019, Members of the US Air Force 74th Fighter Squadron were celebrated with a special gallantry award for their work in the Raqqa offensive. 'I thought it was pretty awesome that we could go out there and affect the infrastructure as much as we did,' one of the pilots told the *Air Force Times*. 'Going back and looking at what we actually struck and the damage we did was pretty cool.'[48]

*

Between August 2014 and October 2019, the coalition conducted 34,706 airstrikes on Iraq and Syria. The US military says that at least 1347 civilians were unintentionally killed by coalition actions during that time.[49] Airwars believes that the number is closer to between 8,000 and 13,000 people.[50]

After initially denying they were responsible for any civilian casualties in the bombing campaign to defeat ISIS, the Australian Defence Force later admitted they had accidently killed civilians in several operations. In September 2017, the ADF detailed two incidents

of civilian casualties in west Mosul in March and June of that year involving Australian aircraft or personnel. Two children were feared to be among those killed in the separate bombing raids.[51] In March 2018, Australia admitted to killing two civilians and injuring two children in May 2017. That case had originally come to light during a field investigation by Amnesty International, when several family members reported attempting to evacuate a home they had been sheltering in when it was hit by an airstrike. The ADF said it had carried out two investigations into the attack and found that the civilians had been killed and injured by munitions dropped by an RAAF Super Hornet.[52]

In February 2019, ADF officials admitted that between six and 18 civilians had possibly been killed when two RAAF fighter jets were called in to bomb a house in Mosul in June 2017. The number of dead was based on estimates of population density, said the ADF. A local man told the ABC 35 people had been killed in the incident, including his brother and other family members.[53]

After being identified by Airwars in in December 2016 as one of the coalition's 'least transparent members', Australia has since been commended by the NGO for 'taking steps to improve the reporting of its actions.'[54]

NOT JUST A NUMBER
Adel Faraj

By mid 2016, US-led coalition forces had begun their efforts to take back large swathes of northern Iraq and eastern Syria that had been occupied by the ISIS terror group. Facing defeat, the ISIS jihadists turned to deadly guerrilla tactics, targeting civilians all over Iraq, but particularly in the capital Baghdad, with massive, deadly suicide bombings. Day after day, bomb after bomb went off in markets and outside mosques, and dozens and dozens of innocent men, women and children were killed as the summer went on. The civilian death toll in Iraq – approximately 940 civilians brutally murdered in that year alone – was much higher than the tally resulting from ISIS attacks in the west in the same period,[1] but we heard little about the lives of those Iraqi victims.

Baghdad, Iraq, July 2016

Late on a Saturday night during the holy month of Ramadan, Adel Faraj was shopping for clothes at Baghdad's Karrada market for the Islamic holiday of Eid. Despite it being close to midnight, the streets were packed as families and young couples celebrated the breaking

of the daily fast and enjoyed the cooler evening temperatures. At this midsummer time of year, many Iraqis would spend hours sheltering inside their houses as daytime temperatures soared into the high forties.

This evening, Adel had a spring in his step. Just days before, the handsome 23-year-old had graduated from Baghdad University with a law degree. He had also recently become engaged. But most importantly for Adel, he was now firmly on track to follow his dream – moving to the United States to try and make it as a professional dancer.

For Adel, dance had been a means of escaping the violence and fear that had engulfed his childhood in Iraq after the US-led invasion in 2003. He was largely self-taught, learning modern dance moves from watching hours of Michael Jackson DVDs and YouTube videos in his cramped family home in Baghdad. Pushing all the furniture in their living room to one side, Adel would spend hours in the world of dance, escaping the chaos that ruled the streets outside.

Despite Adel's obvious dance talent as he grew older, he often had to keep it under wraps. Dance, particularly by a male, was frowned upon by many in the conservative Iraqi society, which largely centred on religious identity and was deeply suspicious of western influence. Even some of Adel's own relatives were uncomfortable with his dancing, though his own parents and brothers were always very supportive.

As the years went by, Adel outgrew the confines of the family living room. Despite the risks, he would spend hours practising his moves in one of Baghdad's many parks. But the more power that religious forces gained in Iraq, the more dangerous this became. Once, when the young dancer was rehearsing in the park with a friend, strangers confronted Adel, accusing him of 'desecrating Islam' with his moves. Adel pretended he had been doing martial arts, quickly talking his way out of trouble. That didn't work on another occasion, and he ended up with a bloody nose after a police officer harassed and beat him, telling him 'dancing was not normal'.

As Adel's world became too small to contain his ambition, he scoured the internet, desperate to find a connection that could help him expand his horizons and follow his dancing dreams. In October 2014, he stumbled on news of an outreach program undertaken

by the prestigious New York dance company Battery Dance. Adel emailed the company's founder, Jonathan Hollander. Was there any way they could help him? He spoke of how desperate he was for some formal training in dance, given that he couldn't find a teacher in Baghdad willing to engage in the frowned-upon activity. 'He said he was a break dancer and hip-hop but that he really wanted to expand his repertoire,' Jonathan recalled. 'I said, "Let's see what we can do for you. Let's see what we can do remotely, long distance. Why don't you send me some videos of your practices?"'

Thrilled with the idea, Adel promised to send through some material soon. 'I thought I would see some handheld video of him doing tricks in a gym or something,' said Jonathan. Instead, Adel spent ten days working with a friend to film and edit a dramatized music video showcasing his skills. The New York producer was floored by Adel's talent. 'He had creativity coming out of every part of his body,' said Jonathan. 'His ability to reach across the world and capture me and engage me in this way was extraordinary.'

Battery Dance committed to helping Adel, scheduling weekly lessons on Skype from one of the company's leading modern-dance performers, Sean Scantlebury. Despite an often-dodgy internet connection, Adel threw himself into the practice, keenly following instructions from his American mentors. Video of their practices recorded for a *Wall Street Journal* report showed the persistence required to make the remote tutorship work, with the connection dropping out several times and an assistant holding the computer close to Sean for Adel to work out the exact moves.[2]

'I think he is extraordinarily talented, he has charisma,' Jonathan Hollander told the *Wall Street Journal* at the time. 'I have this feeling that if you give this person the opportunity, he will set fire to the world. He's phenomenal.'

One night Adel didn't show up on Skype at the appointed time, which was unusual for the normally punctual student. 'We found out about an hour later that he had been on the other side of a wall from an explosion,' said Jonathan. 'He said he survived simply because there was a wall between him and the bomb.'

When an opportunity arose for Battery Dance to perform at the Amman Contemporary Dance Festival in Jordan in April 2015, Jonathan and Adel moved mountains to raise the funds and arrange

the visa for him to join them from Baghdad. The young Iraqi arrived in Amman before the American team but returned to the airport to meet his mentors. In footage filmed by Adel's friend and published on his YouTube channel, the 22-year-old stands nervously in the arrivals area of the airport, wearing a suit jacket and slicked-back hair, clearly eager to impress his New York friends.[3] When the Battery Dance team come through the gate, they spot Adel's happy face in the crowd. He and Jonathan embrace tightly, like two long-lost friends. 'I lose my mind!' Adel says, grinning, before embracing Jonathan again.

'There he was,' Jonathan said, smiling. 'It was like a dream come true that we were actually able to meet in person and work together. It was like he was transported into another planet. It was completely different from Baghdad for him.' Videos posted by Adel on social media capture the young dancer's absolute joy. It was a week of milestones – his first trip outside Iraq, his first plane ride and, most significantly, the first time in his life Adel could dance freely without fear. The Iraqi trained for five hours a day in the lead-up to his solo performance.

His story attracted the attention of local reporters, and Adel told an Associated Press reporter about his fear of returning to Baghdad and his dreams of pursuing a dancing career abroad. 'If there were no problems in Iraq with dance and people liked dance, then I would have no problem being there,' he said. 'But that isn't so, and I can't imagine any other solution than to leave Iraq. There are people in religious groups who attack this kind of art.'

After days of intensive practice with the company, Adel's moment to shine finally came. On a dark stage, lit by just one spotlight, the young Iraqi moved gracefully in front of a packed house to a haunting soundtrack of Gary Jules's cover of 'Mad World'. As he confidently performed a combination of contemporary dance and hip-hop moves, he gave no hint this was actually his first time in front of an audience. At the end of the performance, the crowd erupted in applause. Beaming, Adel bowed multiple times, overflowing with excitement as he walked off the stage. 'I felt tremendous joy,' he told the AP reporter backstage. 'It is like a dream.'[4]

It was challenging for Adel to return to Baghdad after the workshop and performance had given him a glimpse of the life he

longed for. Fighting off the claustrophobic isolation of Baghdad, Adel continued his devotion to the long-distance tutorials with Battery Dance while also buckling down to finish his four-year law degree, hoping to then go to America and pursue his dream of dancing professionally.

Every now and then on his Facebook page, Adel alluded to the difficulty of life in the violence-ridden Iraqi capital. On 4 February 2016, he sounded distressed and fed up: 'This geographical location in which I live is a storm of destruction, killing, intolerance, lying, hypocrisy, dirty, Stupid!!!! Because of this thing I decided to make a private world for me to live away from these people and this storm.'

Life in Iraq was getting darker as the year went on, with Iraqi forces and the international coalition stepping up their battle to defeat ISIS forces in the north and west of the country. Weak on the battlefield, the militant group shifted their tactics, striking at 'soft' civilian targets. In April, 38 people were blown up as they walked to a Shia shrine. A string of attacks over six days in May left more than 200 civilians dead, as ISIS suicide bombers targeted checkpoints and crowded markets, while 31 people were massacred on a single day in June.[5]

But on that Saturday night in July, Adel Faraj was likely thinking of the future, not the past, as he wandered the Karrada market. Meanwhile, an ISIS suicide bomber carefully packed a refrigerator truck with explosives and set off through the streets of the Iraqi capital. A week earlier, Iraqi forces had driven the jihadists out of Fallujah, just an hour's drive west of Baghdad. The bomber's act of revenge was to pick the softest of targets – families out for dinner, crowds watching the Euro cup and shoppers like Adel. Just after midnight, on 4 July, the suicide bomber detonated his load, wiping out a massive section of the market. The overall number of dead was astounding – with 324 people killed, it was the single deadliest bombing in Iraq in more than a decade of war and insurgency.[6]

The scene was apocalyptic, with black empty shells where busy restaurants and shops had been. Video of the attack's aftermath shows stunned young men treading carefully through the ruins, carrying pieces of their friends and family members wrapped in blankets. A woman in a black abaya stands in the middle of the chaos, sobbing and beating herself in the chest over and over again.

'We could hear people trapped inside desperately calling their family and friends for help. In those minutes some could have been saved,' a rescue worker told the BBC.[7] Baghdad hospital officials told the *New York Times* 'they had never seen so many charred bodies, and that many of them could not be identified'.[8]

Adel's body was found intact, a small grace for his family. He was buried the next day in the Shiite city of Najaf.

The Karrada bombing was far deadlier than the November 2015 Paris attacks, the June 2016 Orlando shooting or the January 2017 Istanbul nightclub horror. But #PrayforBaghdad didn't trend on Twitter, and Facebook didn't give Iraqis the option to mark themselves as 'safe' in the wake of the blast. For the rest of the world, it was just another suicide blast in the Iraqi capital. When had it all become so horrifically routine?

Inside Iraq, people were outraged. How had such a massive bomb made it through the vast number of checkpoints that dot the city? Many wondered whether the fake bomb detectors sold to Iraqi police by British businessman James McCormick were to blame. In 2013 a London court had sentenced McCormick to ten years in jail for selling the fake detectors to war-torn countries, but many of the 6000 devices sold to Iraq were believed to still be in use.[9] In the wake of Iraqis' fury after the massive Karrada bombing, Prime Minister Haider Al Abadi demanded an immediate review and withdrawal of any suspected fake detectors across Baghdad.[10]

But the order came too late for Adel's family. 'I wish I had a time machine to go back and fix what happened,' Adel's grieving brother Bilal told the Associated Press.[11]

The news of Adel's death travelled quickly to his friends in New York. 'I was numb ... I was bereft,' Battery Dance founder Jonathan Hollander said, choking up. 'I had the privilege to meet this person and to become close to him; and to see through him how much talent and how much opportunity there would be for young people to develop and grow, just like they do here in New York City. But they don't have the space. They don't have the safety, security. They don't have the opportunity.'

In Adel's memory, Battery Dance established a fellowship program for Middle Eastern dancers from conflict zones to come and receive advanced dance training in New York.

'I really wanted his parents to know how much we loved Adel,' said Jonathan. 'I wanted them to have some kind of permanent memorialization of my feeling, of Battery Dance as an institution, what it meant to us to work with their son. I wanted to tell them that they are great parents and they did such an amazing job. Having a son who wanted to be a dancer in Iraq was so countercultural. How many families would embrace their son, and understand who he was, and embrace him?'

He paused before continuing. 'He's become a mythical creature to us. Someone so good and so talented with so much potential. And almost too good for this earth.'

PRISONERS IN THEIR OWN HOME

The People of Gaza

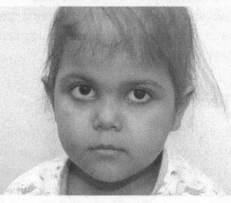

Around 1.9 million Palestinians live inside the Gaza Strip. It is a narrow band of land on the Mediterranean coast, only 45 kilometres long and between six and 12 kilometres wide, bordered by Israel in the north and the east and Egypt in the south. The strip feels like the world's largest open-air prison, with the vast majority of people locked inside this small territory and unable to access or visit the remainder of the occupied Palestinian territories or the outside world.[1] Huge, 6-metre-high concrete walls, watchtowers, electric fences and 'no-go' zones line the territory's borders; if you venture too close on the Israeli frontier, you risk being shot by the soldiers who are stationed all along the perimeter. Israeli warships prowl the coast and fishermen who drift more than 6 nautical miles off the shore may be arrested or shot and killed. Since 2006, when Gaza came under the control of the Islamic militant group Hamas, the territory has witnessed three wars between the militants and Israel. In the most recent conflict in 2014, 73 Israelis were killed and 2251 Palestinians, of whom 551 were children.[2] The UN accused both Israeli forces and Hamas of committing war crimes.[3] The population of Gaza is largely impoverished, with more than

70 per cent of Gazans receiving some form of international aid, the bulk of which is food assistance. Gazans cannot leave the strip without the permission of Israel or Egypt, even to receive desperately needed medical care not available within Gaza, and many are routinely refused exit permits. In 2017, I witnessed time and time again how the denial of healthcare was used by Israel and the Palestinian National Authority to punish civilians in Hamas-run Gaza. Israel and Egypt's 13-year blockade of Gaza by land, air and sea has been described by the UN as a 'denial of basic human rights in contravention of international law and amounts to collective punishment'.[4]

Gaza Strip, September 2016

Dozens of barefoot children chased each other through the unpaved, rubbish-filled backstreets of Shati Camp, one of the poorest neighbourhoods in Gaza City. It was summertime, and the heat and humidity combined to make conditions stiflingly hot. Families here receive just four hours' supply of electricity a day, if they're lucky, so once the sun starts to fade, many gather in the street to escape the sweltering temperatures inside.

I'd come here to explore a dark tragedy: child cancer patients being forced to endure painful treatments for weeks on end without their parents, reportedly because of Israeli security restrictions.

Up a steep, dark climb to the fourth floor of one of the dilapidated apartment buildings in Shati Camp, we found three-year-old Sara and her 32-year-old mother, Feda. The toddler had big sad brown eyes and wore a frilly blue dress and a floppy hat with purple flowers. She sat in her mother's lap, tightly clutching her hand. Feda took off her daughter's hat to show me her balding head, testament to the 22 days of intensive leukaemia treatment little Sara had just endured. 'She used to call us from the hospital, asking, "Mummy, Mummy, why did you leave me?"' Feda said quietly. 'She was crying all the time, "Mummy, Mummy!" Asking for me day and night.'

Leukaemia treatment for children is not available inside the besieged Gaza Strip, so Sara was forced to travel outside the strip for her three-week hospital stay. But Feda was not allowed to go with her. 'When she returned, it felt like I hadn't seen Sara in years. When she

walked into the house, I hugged her so hard,' Feda described tearfully. 'The doctors told us to be careful, she's in a delicate condition. But I had to hug her tight, hold her and not let her go!'

Almost ten years after Israel – and later Egypt – imposed a blockade on Gaza, medical facilities in the strip ruled by Hamas militants had significantly deteriorated. As a result, an increasing number of Palestinian patients were forced to travel to the occupied West Bank, or Jerusalem or elsewehere in Israel to receive treatment. Cancer patients made up a high number of these referrals, due to the lack of radiotherapy and specialised chemotherapies available in the impoverished strip.[5] But in order to exit Gaza for such treatment, residents needed the permission of the Israeli security authorities. 'I've been trying for 42 days to get a permit, and my daughter was in the hospital all this time...but no permit for me,' Feda said.

In the words of the World Health Organization, 'Israeli authorities have created an extensive bureaucratic apparatus to control the movement of Palestinians into and out of the Gaza Strip.'[6] All permit applicants are subject to evaluation by the Israeli security services, and there are no defined eligibility criteria, according to the WHO. In recent years, security procedures had become stricter, and processing times often extended weeks and even months past a patient's appointment dates. 'I called Doctor Mohammad from Beit Jala hospital and asked him to send another request on my behalf,' Feda explained miserably. 'He told me, "It's in the hands of the Israeli intelligence. We don't have any authority."'

The WHO has documented a clear decline in the number of exit approvals granted by Israeli security forces to Gaza patients' companions, who include the parents of young cancer patients. In 2012, 83 per cent of applications for companion permits were approved, but by August 2016 this fell to only 51.2 per cent.[7] The WHO explained that in previous years patient companions older than 35 had not required a security check, but Israeli authorities were now enforcing mandatory security clearances for anyone under 55 who wanted to leave Gaza.[8] Such 'security checks' took a significant period of time, with no priority given to parents of babies or toddlers who needed urgent cancer treatment.

The separation had clearly been traumatic for both Sara and her mother. As I talked to Feda, the toddler whimpered and cried in her

lap, clinging to her mother every time she tried to shift her weight. The three-year-old was due to return to Beit Jala hospital in the West Bank for another chemotherapy session in a few weeks' time, and her mother was desperately praying that this time the permit would be approved. 'I can't tell you how hard it was without her,' Feda said sorrowfully, patting the little girl in her lap. 'I really hope I can be with my daughter next time, because her next treatment will be much harder than the previous times. I pray day and night to be able to leave with my daughter.'

Sara's was not an isolated case. I discovered that dozens of desperately ill babies and toddlers throughout the Gaza Strip had been forced to endure traumatic medical care for weeks on end without their mothers or fathers by their sides. Inside the children's ward of Augusta Victoria hospital in East Jerusalem, the walls were painted deep blue with bright yellow smiling moon faces, but the cheerfulness ended there. In each room, sick children lay curled up next to their mothers, or in their arms, on narrow hospital beds. Except for 13-week-old Elias. His mother was not there; she did not get a permit.

Elias's 64-year-old grandmother Emtissa told us quietly, 'He got very sick. They could not help us in Gaza. We were referred urgently to this hospital.' Baby Elias was suspected of having a cancerous tumour, but because his mum was under 55 years old, she had needed an Israeli security clearance to leave Gaza – something she could not receive in the short timeframe before Elias needed to be transferred. 'We called the coordination office because it was a very urgent referral,' said Emtissa. 'They got back to us by the evening and told us only my request was approved, and this was because of my age. His mother's approval was not.' Emtissa rummaged in her overnight bag for the can of baby formula she had bought from a nearby supermarket. Tears slowly ran down her face as she prepared a bottle of milk for Elias, who was normally breastfed by his mum. She picked up the newborn and began to give him his bottle. 'How do you think a mother feels? She was staying up all night to breastfeed him,' the grandmother said, weeping. 'My daughter hasn't called me since yesterday. She's just sleeping, she's so depressed.'

At Beit Jala hospital in Bethlehem, three-year-old leukaemia patient Retag sat on her hospital bed, playing with a cheap plastic

doll as she waited for her next chemotherapy session. The chubby-faced toddler had a halo of curls and a bright red playsuit on, but no relatives in sight. Neither of her parents got permits. An elderly neighbour was the only one old enough to receive a quick security approval to make the journey. 'She's asking for her mum a lot. On the first day when I brought her here, she gave me a very hard time,' said the neighbour, who did not want to give me her name. 'She was asking for her mum all the time, and she was crying. Her eyes were full of tears. She refused to eat or drink because her mum wasn't here.' The worst moment, the neighbour said, was when they had to say goodbye at Erez, the border-crossing terminal between Israel and Gaza. 'Her mum held the girl's hand so tight she wouldn't let go. She was weeping and Retag was crying too,' she told me sadly. 'This is the situation. A daughter being separated from her mum. To be away from Mummy's lap. What kind of feeling is this!'

Retag's doctor, Dr Mohammad Najajreh, wandered into the room and started helping the toddler put clothes back on her doll. He was in charge of the children's chemotherapy program at Beit Jala, and every time a child arrived alone from Gaza without a parent, he tried to make sure they received extra attention. 'To accept the treatment is not easy for a child, with his neighbour or with somebody that he doesn't know,' the cancer specialist explained. 'It is very important to be with one of their parents. Most of them are not speaking properly, they are small, like Retag, so you need a translator! You need the mother.'

In the room next door to Retag was two-year-old Tarek, a sweet little thing with long eyelashes and cuddly blue pyjamas. His 29-year-old mother, Hanadi, sat dotingly by his hospital cot, holding his hand. 'Mamma?' said the toddler, looking up and catching his mother's eye. Looking at them, it's hard to believe they could ever be separated. But at the beginning of the year, when Tarek had first received treatment for his leukaemia, Hanadi did not get permission to come with him.

The memory of the three weeks they had spent apart clearly still traumatised her. As soon as she started talking about it, her eyes filled with tears. She quickly got up from her chair so Tarek couldn't see her cry, moving behind the hospital curtain, where sobs took over her body. 'When he saw me again, he hugged me so hard

and wouldn't let me leave,' she told me in between tears. 'He just stayed in my lap. He felt like he had lost me and then just found me again. Thank God it's over now and we're together.'

The second time, the Israeli authorities did grant the young mother permission to leave Gaza with Tarek. She was now so terrified of being separated from her ill son that they had not returned to Gaza in between Tarek's treatments, which had come at a heavy cost. Tarek also has a twin sister, Hanadi told us. They were born after ten years of trying to conceive and repeated IVF attempts. But Hanadi and Tarek had not seen Tarek's twin or his father for five months. 'Every day that passes is very hard. This situation is not easy, but this is my son, I have to suffer for him. My son needs me, so I left his twin sister behind and my husband,' she said tearfully, adding that Tarek had stopped asking for his father. 'It's very hard for him; it's hard for both of us. I feel like he is missing something.'

A spokesperson for the Israeli Ministry of Foreign Affairs refused to discuss with me why the parents of babies and toddlers with cancer were routinely being denied entry to Israel so they could travel to Palestinian treatment facilities in East Jerusalem and the West Bank. COGAT, the Israeli army's civil affairs unit responsible for issuing permits for Palestinians to leave Gaza, also declined my numerous requests for interviews. In a statement, COGAT told me that 'we should all remember that a hostile terrorist regime rules over Gaza. Erez crossing is constantly open for hundreds of people to receive medical treatment in Israel despite the fact that the Gaza Strip is controlled by the Hamas terrorist organization, which clearly and openly acts on the destruction of Israel. Our efforts to separate between terrorism and the population are of great importance.'

But there is little evidence that the Israelis are taking into account the horrific cost their blanket policies have had on these families. A few weeks after I first met Sara, the three-year-old with the floppy hat, we arranged to go and visit her in Beit Jala hospital in the West Bank, where she had just arrived from Gaza to receive her second dose of chemotherapy. Her mother had desperately been praying that this time the permit would come through. But when we walked into the hospital room, we found a downcast Sara. The approval had not come. Sara's grandmother said sadly, 'Her mum was crying. She escorted us all the way until the border crossing, then she returned

home, and I brought Sara to the hospital. Sara was crying all the way until we got to the hospital. She kept asking for her mum. Even until now, every time her mum calls, she will cry, she keeps asking for her mum.'

It's not just patient companions who are denied permission to leave the strip. Adult Gazan patients themselves must also apply to Israeli security services to access healthcare outside the territory. In June 2017, 50 per cent of such requests were either denied or delayed by Israeli security services. 'Some patients unfortunately die while they are on the waiting list to get the permit approval from the Israelis,' Dr Gerald Rockenschaub, head of the WHO in the occupied Palestinian territories, told me.

On the outskirts of Gaza City, down a long dirt road, I walked to a small house. Inside was a 22-year-old woman, Haneen Al Fayoumi. She sat quietly weeping on a sofa in the family living room. In the corner, next to the couch, was a large framed poster resting on a wooden easel, decorated with brightly coloured plastic flowers around its edges. In the middle of the poster was a photo of a smiling middle-aged woman sitting against a backdrop of white clouds in a blue sky and flanked by beautiful pink roses, as if she were looking down on us from heaven. It was the funeral poster for Haneen's late mother, Farha.

'My mum was in a bad condition. Her situation was very critical, she was struggling,' recounted Haneen.

A 53-year-old widow, Farha had been diagnosed with breast cancer. The mother of nine was desperate to receive the treatment she needed to beat the disease. But the ability of Gaza's hospitals to provide adequate diagnosis and treatment to cancer patients was severely limited due to chronic shortages of medicines and lack of medical facilities, as noted by the World Health Organization.[9] Nuclear-medicine scanning needed for determining the stage of a cancer, radiotherapy equipment, and some specialized surgeries are all unavailable.

So, in February 2017, Farha's doctors referred her to East Jerusalem for radiochemotherapy, a treatment not available within the Gaza Strip. Farha submitted three applications to Israeli security officials to obtain permission to leave Gaza, but each time the officials denied her permit application.

'What could my mum do?' said Haneen, sobbing. 'She was ill in bed, she spent all of her time in hospital or at home. How could she be a security threat? She suffered a lot. When she was in pain, she would say, "I want to run to Israel's hospital to get medical help, I want to beg them to treat me, not for me, just for my kids, nothing more."'

Farha died on 15 April, without receiving radiochemotherapy, the fourth Gazan to die during 2017 while waiting for Israel to approve their exit for medical care. There is no doubt about the impact Israel's security policies are having on the fate of women like Farha.

The World Health Organization says the five-year survival rate for breast cancer should exceed 80 per cent if early detection and essential treatment services are available and accessible. But in Gaza only 65 per cent of women with breast cancer survive five years after diagnosis.[10]

'She never got the full treatment that she needed to live, to survive,' Haneen said, tears running down her cheeks. 'I still need my mum, my mum was everything in my life, I wish the Israelis gave permits to mothers, so they can live for their kids, for their families!'

I asked the Israeli intelligence service, the Shin Bet, why they were blocking patients like Farha from leaving Gaza.

'This is an issue of entry of residents from a hostile territory,' a spokesperson for the Israeli security service replied in a statement. 'They are under the control of the terrorist organizations, led by Hamas, who have repeatedly exploited the humanitarian approach to promote terror attacks in Israel and to establish terror infrastructures. In recent years, tens of thousands of residents from the Gaza Strip have entered Israel, following security checks, most of them for medical treatment.'

The Israelis point to an incident in April 2017 when a 59-year-old Gazan woman was arrested as she travelled out of the strip with her ill sister. Israeli officials said they found explosive materials in her luggage.[11]

The UN's most senior official in the occupied Palestinian territories told me that incident was 'outrageous' but also unusual. 'It gives absolute ammunition to the security people in the Israeli system that say every sick person is potentially a fraudulent claim,' UN humanitarian coordinator Robert Piper said. 'Every sick person pays the price for that act and we condemn it absolutely, unambiguously.' (The smuggling incident also happened after Farha's death.)

The average yearly approval rate of only 54 per cent for Gazan patient permits by Israel in 2017 was the lowest on record since 2008, when the WHO first began actively monitoring Gaza patients passing through Erez crossing to access healthcare.[12] The organization says there has been a continuous decline in patient approval rates since 2012, when approximately 93 per cent of patient applications were successful.

After we reported Haneen's mother's tragic death, 50 more Gazans died that year while awaiting approval. The dead included a 17-year-old boy, a five-year-old boy, a five-year-old girl and another mother of nine.[13]

'We really are arguing and asking to de-politicize health. It cannot be that politics [should prevail over] vulnerable Gaza patients,' said the WHO's Gerald Rockenschaub.

For Gazans to leave for urgently needed medical treatment, they don't just need Israeli security approval – the Palestinian Authority (PA), the administrative body based in Ramallah in the West Bank, needs to confirm it will pay their treatment costs.

The PA is run by Fatah, a rival group of Hamas that was kicked out of Gaza in 2007 when the Hamas militants took over the strip. In mid 2017, Fatah began a campaign to squeeze Hamas. They started decreasing services to Gaza, first the supply of electricity and salaries for public officials and then, most alarmingly, funding for healthcare. Innocent Palestinian civilians found themselves caught between two bickering political parties – neither of which has their best interests at heart. Gaza is also not the kind of place where you can freely express your resentment and anger at what has now been more than ten years of oppressive rule by Hamas overlords. Opponents to the militant group live in fear, with those speaking out against them at risk of being jailed and beaten. Yet the PA was failing to distinguish between Hamas and the innocent civilians forced to endure its rule.

On 21 June 2017, Bara'a Ghaben was born, the first child of 22-year-old Hanan and her 25-year-old husband Mohammad. But soon it became clear that the tiny baby was not well.

'They told us he needed urgent heart surgery outside Gaza. He was classified as "top urgent" so it could happen straight away, within a few days,' Mohammad said, showing me a stack of his

son's medical papers. The medical referral could not have been clearer: 'Top Urgent' it read in big letters on the first page.

Yet Bara'a was not given any kind of priority at all. The surgery and care the newborn needed were available within a one-hour drive of his home, but just one week after being born, on 27 June 2017, while waiting for permission to leave Gaza – permission that never came – Bara'a died.

'They didn't tell us exactly why they denied it, but the request was ignored,' Mohammad told me. 'Nobody got back to us. My son's situation was getting worse by the minute. For every minute we waited his condition deteriorated.'

This time it was the PA that delayed the case by refusing to approve payment for Bara'a's treatment, not Israeli security restrictions. The authority had come to feel that it should not be paying for treatment that should have been covered by Hamas, and decided to block payments with the aim of making Hamas take responsibility for its territory – or return control of it to the PA. As a result, during the period from the end of May 2017 to June 2017, many such applications were rejected.

'My baby did not vote for Hamas,' Mohammad tells me sadly. 'He wasn't alive when Hamas took over. None of us are Hamas supporters. Not the baby, not his mother or father. It's not Bara'a's fault.'

Others suffered similar losses. North of Gaza City, in a poor rural area, I tracked down the family of toddler Yousef Al Aga. At the mention of his name, Yousef's mother Subheya broke down. 'I ask God to take revenge on everyone who was responsible for me losing my son,' she said, with tears streaming down her face.

She had spent 13 days desperately trying to get her critically ill son transferred out of Gaza. Yousef, who was nearly two, had been admitted to Gaza's Rantissi hospital on 30 May 2017 with a second episode of haemolytic uraemic syndrome, a rare blood condition where the blood vessels in the kidneys become damaged. Timely and appropriate treatment usually leads to a full recovery, but if proper care is not received the condition can lead to kidney failure.[14]

It could not be treated in Gaza.

'When I took my son to Rantissi hospital he had a low blood count and his kidneys were not functioning well,' Subheya said. 'He was very sick and his situation was deteriorating.'

Yousef's doctors told the ABC they had requested a transfer for the child right away, but it took nine days for the Ministry of Health in the West Bank to approve payment for his treatment outside Gaza. Subheya was then told Yousef could not be transferred until 13 June. The day before he was due to be moved, he suffered complete renal failure and fell into a coma. At that point, he was too ill to be transferred, and he died two weeks later.

Subheya sobbed as she took out photos of her boy. 'Yousef was the light of our family,' she told me while showing me pictures of the little curly-haired boy with big, dark eyes and a cheeky smile. 'If he had been born elsewhere, he would have had proper medical care. This is a political game, and our children are paying the price.'

The PA was clearly using Gaza's sickest and most vulnerable inhabitants to punish Hamas.

'The last few months we've seen this confrontation between the Palestinian Authority and Hamas. That's translated into some pretty tough measures that are being felt across the Gaza Strip,' UN Humanitarian coordinator Robert Piper told me later. Piper said the first sign of these measures was a sharp reduction in the amount of medicine the Ministry of Health sent to Gaza. 'There was an unambiguously substantial drop in the availability of essential drugs in Gaza. Some 35 to 40 per cent of essential drugs are now not available,' he explained. 'It's been almost three months since a bulk shipment of essential drugs has come from the West Bank to Gaza.'

The senior aid official acknowledged that the PA was withholding patient approvals. 'Someone appears to be taking some steps at least to slow down the approval process. That's very troubling indeed.'

The WHO agrees. 'There seems to be quite a backlog of patients who have applied for Ramallah financial approval, which they need [but] which has not been processed in time,' said Gerald Rockenschaub.

Despite the UN's comments and the mounting evidence I uncovered, the Palestinian Ministry of Health continued to deny any official change in policy regarding patient referrals. It did not respond to my requests for an interview or to our questions about delays for patients or the deaths of baby Bara'a or toddler Yousef.

But new data on patient referrals backed up my findings. The Palestinian Centre for Human Rights (PCHR) found that in March 2017, 2190 patients from Gaza received financial approval from the

Ministry of Health to be treated outside the strip. The tally for June was just 400 patients, a decline of more than 80 per cent.[15]

A source at a United Nations agency in Gaza told me the PCHR data was 'extremely alarming' and matched trends observed by UN staff in the strip. The UN's Robert Piper blamed all sides for playing politics with patients' lives. 'No one comes out of this looking good, whether you're Hamas, whether you're the Palestinian Authority, or indeed whether you're the Israeli government,' Piper told me firmly. 'Our message is the same to everyone, which is: there are some things that need to be protected. Access to urgent healthcare for a very sick person is one of those issues that we really all need to respect.'

*

The increasing number of delays and rejections from the Israeli authorities when processing applications for patient companions from Gaza continued into 2017 and throughout 2018. Despite consistent UN pleas for change, by October 2019 the approval rate was only 45 per cent, with more than half of all Gaza patient companion applications being denied or delayed by Israeli authorities.[16] The Israeli policy of separating sick Gazan children from their parents while they undergo medical treatment outside the strip received growing attention. A report by The Guardian in June 2019 highlighted the case of 56 Gazan babies who had been separated from their mothers and fathers, six of whom died while receiving medical care without a parent present, according to Makassed hospital in East Jerusalem.[17]

In 2019, the Palestinian Authority implemented a new policy aimed at reducing the number of Palestinian patient referrals to Israeli hospitals. According to the WHO, the reduction in referral destinations for Palestinian patients has initially increased strain on existing services and led to a backlog of patients waiting to receive care. Palestinian patient care has also been made more challenging in the wake of the Trump administration slashing US$25 million of funding to East Jerusalem hospitals.[18]

By November 2019, only 59 per cent of Gazan patients had their applications to leave the strip for medical care approved by Israeli authorities.[19]

CHAPTER 15

OCCUPIED LIVES
The People of the West Bank

The Six-Day War began on 5 June 1967 and ended with Israel's army capturing the West Bank and East Jerusalem. More than 50 years later, nearly 3 million Palestinians there continue to live under Israeli military control. Their lives are filled with checkpoints, walls, patrols, military posts and heavy restrictions on freedom of movement. Israel controls the people of the West Bank 'through repression, institutionalized discrimination, and systematic abuses of the Palestinian population's rights', according to Human Rights Watch.[1] Palestinians' ability to move unimpeded within their own country, to exit and return, to develop large parts of their territory, build on their own land, access natural resources or develop their economy is largely determined by the Israeli military.[2] Israeli authorities have seized thousands of hectares of Palestinian land in the West Bank for hundreds of illegal settlements where more than 500,000 Israelis now live, while it is nearly impossible for Palestinians to obtain building permits in East Jerusalem and in the 60 per cent of the West Bank under exclusive Israeli control.[3] Israeli authorities continue to expand settlements in the occupied West Bank and to discriminate systematically

against Palestinians in favour of Israeli settlers.[4] Only around 85,000 Palestinians out of the 2.5 million in the West Bank have a special permit granted by the Israeli authorities that allows them to work inside Israel.[5]

Bethlehem, West Bank, June 2017

It is only 4.30 am but already hundreds of men are lining up quietly in the dark outside Checkpoint 300, a massive Israeli army installation on the edge of Bethlehem. The checkpoint is one of the few entrances for Palestinians living in this part of the West Bank to enter Jerusalem. The men shuffle forward, slowly getting closer to the long, caged walkway they need to get through before the Israeli security inspection point. Standing in line is 25-year-old Ahmad from the West Bank village of Yatta. His alarm went off at 3 am, when the young labourer needs to get up in order to get through the checkpoint and avoid being late for his construction job, which starts in Jerusalem at 7 am. 'If you're just a little bit late the checkpoint can be a disaster,' he tells me.

Each morning, he creeps out of his house in the dark, leaving his wife and young son sleeping, and makes his way to Checkpoint 300 by shared taxi.

Thousands of these workers from around the southern West Bank converge at this spot at the crack of dawn each weekday morning to cross into Jerusalem. The line quickly gets jam-packed. There are younger guys in hoodies and concrete-splattered jeans, and older men in carefully pressed shirts and pants carrying briefcases; everyone looks exhausted and half asleep. Those desperate to get to the front of the line climb up the sides of the cages and carefully walk along a thin concrete edge, precariously holding onto the bars that line the walkway. Everyone is pressed up tightly against one another, and it's hard to breathe. There's a moment of panic as a surge of people pushes forward. It is hard to imagine that everyone here has to endure this every single morning, six days a week for their whole lives.

At the entrance, 47-year-old Alfred Khoury stands apart from the crowd, watching the spectacle around him with a look of

exhaustion. 'It's so depressing. We feel like animals. But these days not even animals get treated like this!' he says angrily, motioning at the cage the men are shuffling through. 'It's humiliating. Every day I'm here by 4.30 am to make sure I'm in my office by 8.30 am.'

At the very front of the queue, a teenage Israeli soldier buzzes people through the turnstile, one by one. Once they are finally through, most men hurriedly join groups stand waiting for minivans to take them to work. Others lie curled up on the footpath, trying to catch a few winks before their ride arrives. As some of the older men in suits rush to the vans, a few meet my eye and give me a sad smile. I feel ashamed as I take photos of people treated in such an undignified and humiliating way.

Two hours after I first spot Ahmad the young builder, he's finally made it to the other side. He probably won't return home until after 5 pm tonight. 'I don't have a choice but to do this,' Ahmad says, shrugging. 'The situation in Yatta is really bad. There are no jobs there!' I ask what living under Israeli occupation means to him. 'Please, let's not talk politics,' he says, laughing. 'Because tomorrow they might stop me and suspend my entry permit!'

By June 2017, Palestinians had endured 50 years of Israeli military occupation, with no end in sight. Generation after generation has been born into a life in which nearly every aspect is controlled by the Israeli army – where they can travel, which roads they can drive on, where they are allowed to build a house, if they can visit Jerusalem; the restrictions are endless. Which permit is or isn't granted by the Israeli military administration can determine where Palestinians can work or study, whether they can visit relatives, if they can afford to get married, and even who they marry.[6]

To try to understand the extraordinary impact this situation has on people's lives here, I spent a day observing life as a Palestinian. At 7.30 am, my producer Fouad and I head to the South Hebron hills, where 16-year-old Reem is wearing a crisp blue dress and a black headscarf. She smiles shyly, slightly embarrassed by having us follow her on her morning walk to school with her girlfriends. Home for Reem is a tiny village of 100 people called Tuba, while the school is in another small village on the other side of the valley.

The 2-kilometre route to class involves walking past the illegal Israeli settlement outpost of Havat Ma'on. After years of Palestinian

children reporting random attacks and harassment from settlers, since 2004 armed Israeli soldiers have escorted the schoolchildren on the journey each morning. Reem and her schoolmates pass the settlement, an armoured vehicle in front of them, and two soldiers carrying M16s bringing up the rear. Nathaniel is one of the Israeli troops protecting the children this morning. 'We have to escort the students when they come to school and when they finish,' the 22-year-old says. 'I heard there were a few problems with the settlers here in the past.' Often the soldiers run late. The schoolkids then wait by the side of the road until they arrive, afraid to venture on alone. 'The other way is 7 kilometres around that hill,' Reem says pointing to the left of the settlement. 'We are not allowed to walk through this shorter way without the escort of the soldiers. The settlers might attack us.'

Down the road from where Reem is receiving her armed escort to school, Ayman Abdullah is having a bad morning. It's now 9 am and the Israeli army has set up a 'flying' checkpoint at the entrance to his village of Beni Neiem – and he is running late for work. In the occupied West Bank there is a complex network of established checkpoints, but what's delaying Ayman this morning is the pop-up variety. There one day, gone the next. It makes life incredibly difficult to plan, says the 35-year-old father of five who works in a nearby stone quarry. 'What do I tell my kids?' he says. 'They always see the presence of soldiers. I try and tell them not to be scared. But this is not enough. They get scared because they expect the worst.' Israelis say such spot checks are needed for 'security reasons'. 'We are looking for guns,' the young soldier giving orders tells me. Palestinians and human rights groups label these sudden road closures and pop-up restrictions as collective punishment.

Ayman sits in his company car in the line of vehicles that are slowly moving forward, waiting for the soldier to motion that it's his turn to pass. A young Israeli recruit points his M16 at Ayman and jerks his head. Go! But whether it's the fact it's still early or only the third day of Ramadan and he hasn't had his morning coffee, instead of zigzagging through the traffic spikes the soldiers have laid out on the road, Ayman slowly drives a couple of metres forward. A depressing, slow hissing noise can be heard as his car rolls to a stop. He's burst the front two tyres. 'You didn't see the

spikes!' the soldier says. 'No, I didn't,' Ayman says quietly. 'I was looking at you.' The soldiers help him change the tyre, telling me to make sure I get photos of them assisting. Later that day, I speak to Ayman by phone. 'It cost me $150 for the new tyres. I only earn $700 a month!' he says bitterly. 'The checkpoint was there again on the way home, delaying me by half an hour. We have no freedom and we always live in fear. We can't live normally.'

Snaking across the hills of the occupied West Bank is a massive barrier to prevent Palestinians without permits from crossing into Israel. Around 70 kilometres of it consists of 8- to 9-metre-high concrete-slab segments that are connected to form a wall, while the rest consists of fences, ditches, razor wire, an electronic monitoring system, patrol roads and buffer zones.

The barrier cuts through towns and villages, separating Palestinian residents from their lands, crops, services, water and jobs.[7] The route of the barrier is about 708 kilometres long, more than twice the length of the 320-kilometre-long 1949 Armistice Line (Green Line) between the West Bank and Israel, which marks the pre-1967 border. Land required for the construction of the barrier is requisitioned from Palestinian owners by the Israeli Ministry of Defense.[7] Described by Israelis as a 'security wall' or 'separation fence', the barrier is often referred to by Palestinians as an 'apartheid wall'.

The Israeli human rights group B'Tselem describes the barrier as a 'major political instrument for furthering Israeli annexationist goals', as its route cuts into almost 10 per cent of the West Bank's territory.[8] In 2004, the International Court of Justice ruled that the barrier was illegal, saying that construction must stop immediately, and Israel should make reparations for any damage caused.[9] The Israeli government says the barrier and other restrictive measures in the occupied West Bank are needed for security reasons – there have been two violent 'intifadas' or uprisings in the past 50 years, with Palestinian suicide and car bombings common during the second intifada that ended in 2005. (The first intifada saw over 1400 Palestinians and 270 Israelis killed.[10] The second intifada claimed the lives of approximately 3200 Palestinians and 1000 Israelis over five years.[11]) A recent string of stabbings and car-rammings by Palestinians that began in late 2015 has so far killed 87 Israelis.[12]

These attacks included elderly people stabbed to death on a bus in a suburb of West Jerusalem and a 13-year-old girl killed after being knifed in her home inside a settlement as she slept.[13]

Palestinians say the violence is a result of the occupation and that they're fighting for their freedom and an independent Palestinian state. They say the arrival of 400,000-plus Israeli settlers in the West Bank in the past 50 years has resulted in the theft of their land, and they want the settlers out immediately. While settlements only make up 2–3 per cent of the West Bank, much of the land surrounding settlements is also blocked off to Palestinians for security reasons. And to protect the Israeli settlers living in the middle of 2.5 million Palestinians who do not want them there, Israeli soldiers maintain full control over more than 60 per cent of the West Bank.[14]

In a report to mark the 50th anniversary of Israeli military control of the West Bank, the United Nations attributed the violence to the Israeli occupation, saying it 'drives continued conflict'. 'The prolonged occupation, with no end in sight, cultivates a sense of hopelessness and frustration that drives continued conflict and impacts both Palestinians and Israelis,' said the report.[15]

Out the front of the Arroub camp, between Hebron and Bethlehem, 26-year-old Salah stands smoking a cigarette and waiting for the 11 am bus with a friend. His village is called a 'camp' because its residents fled here in 1948 when Israel was created. What used to be a collection of tents has now turned into a motley bunch of dilapidated houses and apartment buildings, but the name has stuck. An Israeli watchtower sits directly opposite the two main entrances to Arroub, one of which has been permanently closed by the Israeli military for the past 15 years. Large concrete slabs block the road; here people can only cross on foot.

'On a daily basis the Israelis enter our town,' Saleh tells me, keen to chat but refusing to let me take his photo. Two small boys stand next to him, silently looking up at the Israeli watchtower that looms over them. 'They detain. They arrest children,' Saleh tells me. He says he's spent five years going in and out of Israeli jails, for throwing rocks and Molotov cocktails at Israeli soldiers during demonstrations. 'My two younger brothers were also jailed,' he says with a gleam of pride. 'We were resisting the occupation. One of my brothers was arrested for the first time at 13. The other at 14.'

Saleh says he hasn't visited Jerusalem, just 15 kilometres up the road, since he was 12 years old. He can't get a permit he says, but he dreams of going. I asked Saleh if he's stopped going to violent demonstrations since his release from jail at the end of 2015. 'What do you think?' he says with a wink.

In downtown Hebron at 11 am, 16-year-old Ameer is trying to balance a box of tomatoes. Not an easy task at the best of times, but while going through a checkpoint turnstile it's especially trying. 'I feel like I live in a prison,' he says through gritted teeth. Ever since Ameer was born he has had to walk past armed soldiers and pass through checkpoints to leave his neighbourhood. He lives in what's called 'H2', one of the tensest and most heavily militarized parts of the West Bank. Protected by a large Israeli military presence, 800 Jewish settlers live in the midst of 30,000 Palestinians. Whole streets in H2 that used to be bustling Palestinian commercial areas are now closed by the Israeli army for 'security reasons'. Palestinians are only allowed to enter on foot, but Israeli settlers are allowed to drive their cars.

'Sometimes they close the checkpoint and we can't move. It's very hard,' says Ameer. My producer Fouad and I get buzzed in and we follow the teenager through the turnstile, showing our IDs to the Israeli soldiers and then going through a metal detector – all this just to enter the neighbourhood where Ameer lives. The long rows of barricaded shops and deserted streets make downtown Hebron feel like an eerie ghost town. 'I would like to move out of here,' Ameer tells us firmly. So where would he go? 'Anywhere,' says the teenager. 'Anywhere but here.'

Israeli settlements in the occupied West Bank, like the one near Ameer's home in Hebron, are considered illegal under international law and the Geneva Convention, but over the last ten years they have been steadily growing – on the land Palestinians want for their future state. In December 2016, the United Nations Security Council voted to adopt a resolution urging an end to Israeli settlement expansion, which it labelled a threat to the viability of the two-state solution.[16] The US decision to abstain from the vote was a rare step by Washington, which usually shields Israel from such action at the UN. The move was largely seen as a parting shot from the outgoing US president, Barack Obama, who had an acrimonious

relationship with Israeli prime minister Benjamin Netanyahu. (At the time, Australia was the only western government to publicly condemn the UN resolution, with Prime Minister Malcolm Turnbull calling it 'one-sided and deeply unsettling'.)[17]

As we leave Hebron and drive back towards Jerusalem, we encounter another 'pop-up' checkpoint, just next to the Israeli settlement block of Gush Etzion. It's 12 pm and two Israeli soldiers stand by the side of the road, checking the IDs of drivers as they go past – but not all drivers. In the West Bank, Israeli ID holders have yellow number plates. Palestinians have white and green. The yellow plates don't get stopped. 'That's just my orders,' said the young soldier when I asked, shrugging.

When I asked an Israeli spokesperson from the Ministry of Foreign Affairs about this incident, which is likely repeated hundreds of times a day across the West Bank, I was told the explanation for the difference in how Israelis and Palestinians are treated 'is very simple'. 'Israeli citizens don't spend their days trying to destroy the state of Israel,' said the spokesperson. 'So they don't need to undergo the same security checks and controls as Palestinians do.'

Fouad and I drive through Jerusalem to the other side of the occupied West Bank, close to Ramallah. It's a path not available to the majority of Palestinian residents of Hebron and Bethlehem. They have to go all the way around Jerusalem, a journey that takes an extra three hours, compared to our 40-minute drive. We arrive at Ofer military prison, where dozens of Palestinian families are standing around in the shade waiting for transport at the end of visiting hour.

Israeli authorities have incarcerated hundreds of thousands of Palestinians since the occupation began in 1967, the majority after trials in military courts, which have a near 100 per cent conviction rate.[18] Some are detained or imprisoned for engaging in non-violent activism.[19] Living under military occupation means Palestinians can also be held by Israeli authorities under 'administrative detention' without charge or trial; children are among those held under those conditions. According to Defence for Children International, an NGO, each year about 500–700 Palestinian children, some as young as 12 years old, are detained and prosecuted in the Israeli military court system. The most common charge is stone-throwing.[20]

When I meet Anan, he has just finished visiting his little sister in the prison. 'She's the first one in the family to go to jail,' he tells me through the fence, clearly a little embarrassed. 'She was arrested 40 days ago. She's only 24 and has three kids including a seven-month-old baby. She hasn't seen any of the kids since her arrest.' Anan and his family live in Hebron. He says his sister was going through a checkpoint when the Israeli soldiers found a knife in her handbag. So, does Anan think she was going to carry out an attack? He leaves the question unanswered. 'Life's hard there,' he says quietly. 'But it's harder in prison. She doesn't stop crying when we visit her.'

At 2 pm we visit Makassed hospital, in East Jerusalem. Like the West Bank, East Jerusalem was annexed by Israeli in 1967, and its continued occupation is deemed by the United Nations to be illegal under international law.[21] (In 2014, the then Australian attorney general, George Brandis, caused a stir when he said the Australian government should no longer refer to Palestinian East Jerusalem as 'occupied'.[22] When he was visiting Jerusalem in 2015, I asked him if he had gone to East Jerusalem on his trip and assessed whether it was occupied or not; he refused to answer.) Over the last 50 years, Israel has increasingly cut off East Jerusalem – once the focus of political, commercial, religious and cultural life for Palestinians – from the rest of the West Bank. Today, if you're a Palestinian from the West Bank and under 50 years of age (55 for men) you need a permit from the Israeli military to enter Jerusalem – even if you're the mother of a three-month-old breastfed baby who's just had brain surgery.

In the children's ward of Makassed hospital I meet Um Raed, a Palestinian grandmother from Jenin who is cradling her infant grandson Sajid. 'When he got sick again and it was an emergency, I was the only one who could come with him,' she says. Born with fluid on his brain, little Sajid, together with his mother Samera, spent a month at the hospital as he recovered from delicate surgery. Last Sunday, they went back home to Jenin camp in the northern West Bank. Just a day later it was clear that Sajid urgently needed to return to the hospital; a stitch had opened and fluid was leaking from the tiny baby's head wound. But his mother's permit had run out. 'At that moment when we needed to bring back the patient, she had no permit with her,' explains Sajid's neurosurgeon, Dr Hadi

Dababseh. 'Unfortunately, he had to bring his grandmother with him.' Um Raed tears up as she describes how her daughter-in-law can't be there to feed Sajid. 'He needs his mum to breastfeed him. He can't take milk from this bottle easily; it's hard for him. He was throwing up during the first few days; he's not used to this milk.'

Little Sajid now lies on the hospital bed, unmoving. He has a massive bandage wrapped around his head and tubes where fluid is slowly being drained. The grandmother says Sajid's mother Samera is distraught at the separation from her sick newborn. 'When I call her on the phone she can't talk, she cries all the time. She is going crazy without her baby,' says the grandmother. 'She is his mother. What do you expect?' (When I approached Israeli authorities about Sajid's case they told me they approved his mother's entry to Jerusalem two days after the baby returned to the hospital without his mum. They claimed the hold-up was the Palestinian Coordination Office's fault and that they gave entry permission on 'humanitarian grounds' once they became aware of the case.)

Medical staff at Makassed are not exempt from permit issues. Hospital director Dr Rafik Husseini tells me that almost 20 of his staff recently had issues with their permits. 'One of our senior nurses who's worked here for 15 years had her permit recently suspended,' he says. The director says a man with the same last name as the nurse had been charged with a security offence. It then took six weeks for the nurse's Jerusalem permit to be reissued by the Israeli military.

Not far from Makassed hospital is Shuafat camp. About 80,000 Palestinians live behind the huge 8-metre-high concrete wall that surrounds the impoverished Palestinian neighbourhood. It used to be part of East Jerusalem's suburbs, but since the wall was built after the deadly second intifada, Shuafat camp has been physically cut off. Now there are only two ways to exit, both through Israeli checkpoints, and only one that allows entry into Jerusalem. Residents spend much of their time lining up, waiting, getting their cars searched and their IDs checked. In and out, every day, trudging past the giant concrete structure that encircles their lives.

'I feel like a bird in a cage,' explains 26-year-old Yaseen. He doesn't stop to chat for long. He's late for work. Again. The line at the checkpoint this afternoon was long. 'We don't live like human

beings,' laments 26-year-old Firas who's on his way to his nursing shift at a Jerusalem hospital. The camp, which is one of the poorest neighbourhoods in the city, is also notoriously under-serviced and neglected by the Jerusalem authorities. 'Yesterday the power cut our five or six times, the running water cuts out. Ours is not a normal life!' says the young nurse. Thirty-year-old Suzan is unloading her shopping from her sister's car and is just about to venture through the checkpoint, carrying armfuls of groceries through the turnstiles and mazes of cages. She can remember what life was like before the wall was built. 'It was so much easier,' she tells me. 'Living like this is a disaster.'

Covering Israel and Palestine is one of the hardest jobs in journalism. Pro-Israel advocacy groups relentlessly target, bully and attempt to intimidate reporters in a way I have never experienced while covering any other story.

When my appointment as Middle East correspondent was first announced by the ABC, and before I had even started packing for Jerusalem, pro-Israel lobbyists were calling for my appointment to be overturned.[23] They mounted a steady campaign of intimidation, claiming I was unfit to fill the post because I had said that the blockade of Gaza amounted to collective punishment of a civilian population, had fundraised to help my fixer Raed rebuild his house after it was bulldozed and totally destroyed by Israeli forces during the 2009 war, and because I said 'one of the saddest things I've seen in my whole life is spending time filming in a children's cancer ward in Gaza'.[24]

The ABC's then managing director, Mark Scott, a fierce defender and supporter of his reporters, refused to kowtow. 'Before this reporter set foot in the Middle East, there was a campaign against her personally taking up that role. I am saying that she is a highly recognised and acclaimed reporter...she deserved that appointment and she needs to be judged on her work,' he told a Senate estimates committee.[25]

Having already lived in the region and covered it for years, I refused to be intimidated by the pro-Israeli lobby, despite their relentless attacks. For three years they wrote thousands of words criticising my work. Each report I did on Israel and Palestine was

meticulously dissected by armchair critics sitting in Melbourne or Sydney who never visited the prison that is Gaza under blockade or spent time with Palestinians living under occupation in Hebron.[26] Lobbyists used Twitter and Facebook to smear and attack me on a near daily basis, while conservative parliamentarians repeatedly used Senate estimates to question my work.

Dozens of people working at these organisations scoured every little piece of work I did in Israel and Palestine, desperate to have me trip up or make a small factual error they could use as proof that I was as terrible a journalist, as they had repeatedly accused me of being. (I was proud of the fact that throughout my three years of coverage of Israel/Palestine not a single complaint against me was upheld, because I made no factual errors, which is actually really easy and totally normal to do!)

One particular assault on my work blew up in the face of the attacker. In September 2017, Israeli authorities surrounded the home of 84-year-old Palestinian Ayoub Shamasneh and his 78-year-old wife Fahamiya in Palestinian East Jerusalem. For the past 53 years, the couple had lived in their home in the Sheik Jarrah neighbourhood as protected tenants, but an Israeli court had ruled that they had to get out. Under a decades-old Israeli law, if Jews can prove they lived in a property in East Jerusalem before 1948, they can demand the property be returned, and they receive the full ownership rights. The law allows Jews, but not Palestinians, to reclaim property or land they were forced to abandon in enemy territory during Israel's 1948 'War of Independence'.[27]

The Israel Land Fund, a right-wing pro-settler NGO, took the Shamasnehs to court on behalf of an heir who claimed that in the 1940s her Jewish relatives owned the land on which the Shamasneh family home now stood. After an eight-year court battle, an Israeli judge ruled that the land had to be returned and the Shamasnehs forcibly evicted. The case was significant because it was the first such eviction in the neighbourhood since 2009.

I had interviewed the elderly couple soon after the court ruling. Their house was small and dilapidated but well kept. It was full of doilies, tea sets and black-and-white photos on the walls of the life they had led in that house. Fahamiya relies on her son Mohammad to help look after her husband, who is very ill. He is confined to a

wheelchair and suffers heart problems. The elderly woman cannot believe that they might lose their home and is angry at what she sees as a racist application of law.

'If any refugee from the Palestinian villages wants to go back to his house, do you think they will let him return?' she asks me sadly. Human Rights Watch calls the Israeli laws 'discriminatory'. 'It's very clear from our analysis that Israel applies one set of rules for its Jewish citizens and one set of rules for Palestinians,' Omar Shakir from Human Rights Watch tells me.

On 5 September 2017, at 5.15 am, armed Israeli soldiers surrounded the Shamasneh home. I arrived at the scene as soldiers blocked off the street and tried to stop me filming as the family's personal effects were loaded onto a truck. Wheelchair-bound Ayoub had to be lifted out of the house. Fahamiya sat outside on a plastic chair weeping and looking at her old home. 'Honestly, I don't know what to do now,' she told me. ' I don't know. I need to look for a new home.'

Shortly after the elderly couple were evicted, Israeli soldiers escorted settlers into the Shamasnehs' house. 'We hope that all the houses in this neighbourhood will return to Jewish hands with the help of the Israel Land Fund and God almighty,' settler Yonatan Yosef told a local cameraman as he inspected his new house. The eviction took place while the latest appeal submitted by the family was pending before the District Court. According to the UN, at least 180 Palestinian households in East Jerusalem have similar eviction cases filed against them.

In the past decade, East Jerusalem has increasingly become a site for new Israeli settlements, with settler groups targeting densely populated Palestinian residential areas. Some 200,000 Israeli Jews now live in Palestinian East Jerusalem in settlement homes considered illegal under international law. (Under international law, the transfer and deportation of protected persons from occupied territory is illegal. As the occupying power in East Jerusalem, Israel is banned from changing the status and demographic composition of the occupied territory.)[28]

My TV story was a short two-minute piece that ran on the midday news.[29] I was so busy trying to finish writing a feature report about Iraq that I didn't even have time to file an accompanying online or

radio report. Three weeks later, a half-page advertisement in the *Australian Jewish News* appeared, attacking me over my reporting. The ad, featuring a photo of me in sunglasses and half smiling, had been stolen from my personal Facebook page. There was a photo of the western wall and what appeared to be blood dripping on my face. To my left was a photo of the elderly Palestinian who had been evicted, Mr Shamasneh, and to the right, members of the Salomon family who had been killed in a terrorist attack in July, stabbed to death during a Friday-night Shabbat family dinner in their settlement.

The ad had been placed by Australia's most renowned pro-Israel politician, Victorian Labor Member of Parliament Michael Danby. 'Why the double standards,' he wrote in a large headline over my photos. Drawing a line to the Palestinian family he wrote, 'Extensive ABC coverage', while over the Israeli family was the caption, 'No report'.

It was a blatant and disgusting lie designed to inflame opinion in Australia's Jewish community against me. The day the Salomon family were killed, I arrived back in Jerusalem late that afternoon with my small kids and was still technically on holiday leave. I was asked to work that night because three Palestinians had just been shot dead by Israeli soldiers in clashes around Jerusalem. I filed two short radio news pieces on the clashes, and just before I went to bed at about 11 pm, the news broke about the Salomon stabbing attack at the Halamish settlement. I filed new updated radio reports to include the attack and updated our online story.[30]

The next day I woke early to file a TV report for 7 pm ABC TV news bulletins across Australia, detailing the six deaths that had happened the day before, including those of the three members of the Salomon family. The following day I also did a live cross and another prime-time TV news story mentioning the stabbing attack on the family. 'Neighbours had rushed to help the 70-year-old father and his two children who were stabbed to death,' I reported.

Danby's accusation was demonstrably false and a lie. To make it worse, he had paid for the ads with $4574 of taxpayers' money.[31] It was a horrible moment. I was exhausted and burnt out from covering so many traumatic events, and here was an MP slandering and defaming me in such a public way. 'This is unfortunately part

of a campaign of attacks on me and other reporters who refuse to kowtow to intense and intimidating lobbying and dare report the reality of what is happening here on the ground,' I told *The Age* newspaper.[32] The ad soon became a political story in Australia. Danby's personal attack ad was roundly condemned. According to media reports, Labor Party leader Bill Shorten was 'deeply unimpressed' with Danby and reportedly had a heated phone conversation with the MP.[33]

In Jerusalem, I received a phone call of support from a Labor shadow minister. 'Don't pay attention to Danby,' the senior ALP figure reassured me. 'He's a fuckwit.' A few weeks later, when Bill Shorten visited Jerusalem for the centenary of the Battle of Beersheba, he gave a short press conference. When he finished, he and his colleagues, Warren Snowdon and Mark Dreyfus, came up to me and apologised for Danby's behaviour. (In the wake of the incident, Danby was encouraged to retire, which he did at the 2019 election.)

Since I left Jerusalem, the situation there has only become more tense. President Donald Trump's recognition of Jerusalem as Israel's capital in 2018 and the moving of the American embassy to the city has sparked more violence and despair among Palestinians. Every Friday since March 2018, thousands of young Palestinians in Gaza have protested at the border fence that locks them in. Known as the Great March of Return, this new protest movement calls for an end to the Israeli blockade and the right of return for refugees. While many in the protests are non-violent, the action is supported by the Hamas Islamic militants who run Gaza. Some members of the crowd throw stones at the Israeli soldiers on the other side of the fence and set tyres alight. Some demonstrators have also flown kites or balloons carrying burning rags towards Israel, which have ended up damaging Israeli property, including agricultural land.[34] Israeli soldiers have responded to these civilian demonstrations by using tear gas, rubber-coated bullets and live ammunition.[35] The number of Palestinians shot during these protests is extraordinary: between 30 March 2018 and 31 July 2019, 7500 Palestinians were injured by live ammunition from Israeli forces at the Gaza border,[36] and 206 Palestinians, including 44 children, were killed.[37]

With the world paying little attention to the Israeli–Palestinian conflict, Trump went one step further. In November 2019, his

government announced that the US had shifted its position on Israeli settlements in the occupied West Bank, no longer viewing them as illegal.[38] 'After carefully studying all sides of the legal debate the United States has concluded that the establishment of Israeli civilian settlements in the West Bank is not, per se, inconsistent with international law,' US Secretary of State Mike Pompeo told reporters. Israeli prime minister Benjamin Netanyahu said the policy shift 'rights a historical wrong' and called on other countries to do the same. Chief Palestinian negotiator Saeb Erekat told the BBC that the US decision was a risk to 'global stability, security, and peace' and said it threatened to replace international law with 'the law of the jungle'.[39]

To cap off 2019, in November, Omar Shakir, who investigates human rights abuses in Israel and the Palestinian territories for Human Rights Watch, was deported. The Israeli government had revoked his work visa. Human Rights Watch challenged the decision, but the Israeli Supreme Court upheld the government's deportation order. As Shakir was deported on 25 November, Israel joined the likes of Venezuela, Cuba, North Korea and Egypt as countries that have blocked access to Human Rights Watch staff. The NGO says this is the first time a country that calls itself a democracy has deported or blocked access to its staff members. 'Israel claims to be the region's only democracy, but, at the same time that I have been expelled from Israel, we have offices in Jordan, Lebanon, Tunisia where foreign colleagues work from,' said Omar Shakir.[40] 'I think this highlights not only the government's attack on human rights advocacy, but also its larger disdain for basic international norms.'

*

Between 2008 and the end of 2019, 248 Israelis were killed and 5578 injured in the conflict with the Palestinians. During the same period, 5559 Palestinians were killed and 112,001 injured as a result of the occupation and conflict with the Israelis.[41]

CHAPTER 16

BEHIND THE GLITTERING FAÇADE

Ahmed Mansoor

It took more than 25 years and millions of dollars, but when three-year-old gelding Cross Counter galloped across the finishing line to win the 2018 Melbourne Cup, Sheik Mohammed bin Rashid Al Maktoum was finally the winner of the prestigious race. It was only a matter of time before the billionaire ruler of Dubai achieved the victory, so accustomed is he to getting what he wants. The global horse-stable empire the sheik built up from scratch is one of the United Arab Emirates royal family's more famous exploits in the west. Since the 1990s, Sheik Maktoum has spent hundreds of millions of dollars on breeding and training potential winners across the globe. Victorian racing authorities praised the sheik for his persistence in entering the cup, with chairperson Amanda Elliott telling reporters, 'There is no one who has put more horses into this race and this is his wonderful first win.'

The English-based horse trainers of the winner dedicated the historic victory to their boss, saying it was 'all down to Sheik Mohammed, he's the one that's given us all the

encouragement'. This celebration of the sheik and his pursuits is quite an achievement for a ruling monarchy that has more in common with the Saudi royals than the UK's Windsors for behind the glitz and glamour of the skyscrapers and the beaches are the real emirates, home of a brutal regime, where dissent is not tolerated and those brave enough to speak out meet dreadful fates.

Dubai, UAE, 2017

It was nearly midnight on 20 March 2017 when uniformed security officers stormed the home of 47-year-old Ahmed Mansoor in Ajman, just a short drive from the Dubai international airport. The internationally acclaimed human rights campaigner had long been viewed as a potential threat by the regime that runs the UAE – facing years of repeated intimidation, harassment and death threats from the authorities and their supporters. And now, it appeared, they wanted to silence him for good. The security forces tore Ahmed's home apart, conducting an extensive and invasive search that included the children's bedrooms. Every single electronic device in the apartment was confiscated. In front of his four young sons and his wife, the mild-mannered engineer and poet was then dragged away into the night by officers and taken to Abu Dhabi's central prison, where he was placed in solitary confinement.

Ahmed's international human rights colleagues quickly sprang into action as news of his arrest spread. 'There just isn't another country where the government has jailed every single human rights defender,' one activist messaged me urgently that night. 'He was the last one left in all of the UAE!'

Since independence from the UK in 1971, the UAE have been ruled as a despotic monarchy, with an alliance of seven 'emirates' or sheikdoms run by six royal families worth billions of dollars thanks to massive oil revenues.

Over the last 30 years, as Dubai and Abu Dhabi have developed into major hubs of international business and tourism, as well as bases for foreign militaries, western governments have turned a blind eye to the emirates' authoritarian regime.

The regime's ruler-in-chief, President Khalifa bin Zayed Al Nahyan and his right-hand man, Sheik Mohammed bin Rashid Al Maktoum, ruler of Dubai and prime minister of the UAE, have established a complete dictatorship – all political parties are banned.

This hasn't prevented Australia developing extremely close ties with the Emirati regime. Since 2008, as many as 500 Australian military personnel have been permanently stationed at the Al Mihad airbase on the outskirts of Dubai. Operated by the UAE Air Force, the base has become Australia's regional military headquarters and the main transport and logistics hub for Australian operations in the Middle East.[1]

In 2010 when the UAE crown prince decided he wanted his tiny kingdom to develop its first ever elite fighting force, he turned to an Australian, Mike Hindmarsh, a former Australian Defence Force major general, ex–Special Operations Commander, and recent commander of Joint Task Force 633 in the Middle East Area of Operations. Hindmarsh had close dealings with the highest level of the UAE regime when Australia set up its new military headquarters in the kingdom. Clearly impressed, the crown prince offered him a massive tax-free salary reported to be around half a million dollars annually.

After months of secret negotiations, which reportedly involved the Australian Government approving the move, Hindmarsh became the commander of the regime's presidential guard. 'He reports directly to the crown prince, Mohammed bin Zayed of Abu Dhabi; he's obviously right at the top,' Rori Donaghy, founder of the Emirates Centre for Human Rights, who first reported on the Australian's appointment told me. 'Mike Hindmarsh has brought in a lot of his own men. There are dozens of Australians that are involved in command positions within the presidential guard.'

Apart from the actions of a brave few, there has been little internal dissent in the UAE. Many citizens have been placated with generous social services and high public-sector salaries compared with many other Middle Eastern countries, as the Emirati royals have shared a tiny percentage of their oil spoils with the relatively small UAE population.

But in the wake of the Arab Spring protests in 2011, some very brave, democratically minded Emiratis became increasingly vocal in

their opposition to the regime. Ahmed Mansoor was one of them. In April 2011, the then 42-year-old Ahmed was first arrested and charged with 'insulting officials', together with an economist and lecturer at the Abu Dhabi branch of the Sorbonne, Nasser bin Ghaith, 41, and online activists Fahad Salim Dalk, 39, Ahmed Abdul Khaleq, 34, and Hassan Ali Al Khamis, 39. Known as the UAE 5, the men were not accused of advocating for any violence or change of government – their 'crime' was to simply call for democratic and economic reforms and sign a petition in favour of an elected parliament.[2]

Ahmed was pulled into a car with blacked-out windows and taken to Abu Dhabi. He was held in the car from 3 pm until 1.30 am the next morning, and during those ten hours he was not allowed to go to the bathroom or move in any manner. After being questioned at the State Security prosecutions office, he was taken to Al Wathba Prison at 4 am, where he was placed in an isolation cell without water, a toilet or electricity.[3] He was only removed from isolation 11 days later, when he was transferred to a block holding prisoners convicted of various serious crimes.

Ahmed and his co-accused were denied bail. As a closed-door trial against the UAE 5 began, Amnesty International designated them 'prisoners of conscience' and called for their immediate and unconditional release. Seven months after their arrest, on 27 November, the State Security Court in Abu Dhabi announced that the five men had been convicted of insulting Dubai's rulers. The other four were sentenced to two years in jail while Ahmed Mansoor was given three – but in a surprise move, perhaps designed to avoid international outcry, the very next day all five men were given a presidential pardon and freed.[4]

Finally, Ahmed was allowed home to see his wife and four young boys. During his time in prison, he had lost more than 20 kilograms – leaving him so skinny his toddler didn't even recognize him. 'I went to hug my young kid, but he started to scream and cry because he seriously did not recognize me. It was really the most difficult moment,' Ahmed described in an interview.[5] His punishment didn't end there. He was fired from his engineering position in a telecommunications firm, a huge amount of money disappeared from his personal bank account, and he was banned from leaving the UAE, his passport confiscated. Ahmed was also denied a 'Certificate

of Good Conduct', ruling him out of any further employment in the UAE. As he was trying to complete his third year of law school, the father of four was physically attacked and forced to suspend his studies, while his car mysteriously disappeared.

The brutal crackdown in the UAE continued.[6] In 2012, one of Ahmed's UAE 5 co-accused, Ahmed Abdul Khaleq, was put on a plane to Thailand and warned never to return. A fresh wave of arrests saw dozens of men and women disappear overnight. Prominent human rights lawyer and professor Dr Mohammed Al Roken, who had represented Ahmed in court in 2011, was among those detained, as well as judges, teachers, student leaders, businessmen, bloggers and civil-society activists. Detainees were held incommunicado for months on end, with no explanation given to their loved ones – and inquiring after a family member was enough to see several people disappear themselves, swallowed up by the brutal secret-prison system, denied access to lawyers and contact with the outside world.

The UAE Attorney-General announced that the detainees had sought 'to turn public opinion against the government' and would stand trial before the State Security Chamber of the Federal Supreme Court. In March 2013, the 'UAE 94' trial opened. The accused were brought to the court blindfolded, some showing obvious signs of torture, malnutrition and mistreatment.[7] Some pleaded with their jailers to 'give them the tablets', wrote David Hearst in *The Guardian*, referring to the common practice of drugging political detainees. 'All were terrified to speak.' The son of one of the defendants was subsequently arrested after posting details of the trial on social media. In July of that year, the court convicted 69 of the accused, imposing prison sentences ranging from seven to 15 years. The sentences, wrote Amnesty International, meant that in one swift stroke the UAE authorities 'removed their most prominent critics and the country's leading advocates of reform from the public arena'.[8]

In a move that can only be described as astoundingly brave, Ahmed continued his human rights activism despite the growing numbers of arrests and ongoing death threats. He maintained regular contact with international human rights organizations, UN officials and foreign reporters to discuss the UAE's lack of political

freedom and harassment of activists like him. As he Skyped these international contacts, invariably one of his four young sons would come into the frame and ask him for help with something: 'Where is the football', 'When are we eating?' and so on. Those who know him well describe him as a loving dad, and very hands on. They also speak of his dry, cutting wit, and how he was never without his sense of humour, despite the massive risks he faced.

Meanwhile, the UAE government engaged the services of international public-relations consulting firms, paying millions for them to carefully craft an 'open and tolerant' image of the UAE to show the rest of the world, as brave dissidents continued to rot inside the emirates' jails. Levick, a US-headquartered PR firm, is one such company that has worked to provide a sheen of respectability to the Emirati regime. On its corporate website, the firm boasts about the 'seamless strategic service' they provide to governments worldwide, including the dubious provision of 'communication strategies during human rights issues'. Levick proudly advertise their relationship with the UAE – and their audacity is astounding as they openly brag about the work they have done to portray the UAE as anything but the oppressive dictatorship it really is: 'When Levick's Foreign Governments team partnered with Dubai, we effectively delivered the Emirate's [sic] messages about human rights and rule of law. Many NGOs were convinced. So was the State Department.'[9] Levick did not respond to a request to comment on their contracts with the UAE regime.

In 2015, Ahmed was chosen as the laureate for the prestigious Martin Ennals Award for Human Rights Defenders, but his travel ban prevented him from attending the ceremony in Geneva. In a short video made to commemorate the prize, Ahmed spoke of what his life had become.[10] 'I've been physically followed by the security authorities. I do check if cars are following me. I've got used to those kinds of things now,' he explains. 'They are trying to keep me under pressure and harass me. I was attacked twice within a week by unknown individuals at the university. The possibility is always there for me to be arrested for my activities.' In the film, Ahmed firmly pledges to continue his activism. 'There is no free will. People are afraid to talk. But we are not going to stop. We have to continue doing whatever we are doing. Even

removing one stone from this mountain is better than keeping this mountain as is.'

And so Ahmed kept chipping away at the mountain – giving interviews, tweeting in support of human rights and calling for the growing list of Emirati political prisoners to be released – until he was the last one left. And then they came for him again, late that night in March 2017. Arresting the last person brave enough to publicly discuss human rights in the country meant it was incredibly difficult to get any information about Ahmed's fate.

Internationally, there was very little outcry over his arrest, such was the power of the Emirate's PR machine over the years. In fact, the same day Ahmed was hauled off to solitary confinement, Australia's ambassador to the UAE, Arthur Spyrou, was in New York preparing to host a joint event with the UAE government. 'We are excited to co-host an event today with the UAE at the UN for the #InternationalDayOfHappiness' tweeted Ambassador Spyrou, complete with smiley-face emoji.[11]

Meanwhile, the UAE's official news agency reported that Ahmed Mansoor had been arrested on the orders of the public prosecutor for cybercrimes and accused of using social media websites to 'publish false information that harm national unity and damage the country's reputation'.[12] Ahmed was not given access to a lawyer – but the extent of the crackdown in the UAE means there are now no lawyers willing to risk their safety to represent someone like Ahmed; his last attorney, Dr Mohammed Al Roken, remains in prison himself. Both Human Rights Watch and Amnesty International issued urgent alerts calling for his immediate release and highlighting their real concerns that Ahmed was at risk of torture in detention.

A few weeks after Ahmed was dragged away in the middle of the night, his wife was phoned by the security authorities one morning and told to come to the State Security prosecutor's office in Abu Dhabi, where she was allowed to have just 15 minutes with her husband. Ahmed was brought to the meeting in chains, his head shaved. A few weeks later, during another short visit with his wife and one of his sons, Ahmed was just a shell of the man he had once been. He had lost a significant amount of weight, appearing gaunt and disorientated. He was incoherent and crying

all the time, begging to go home. His family thought he looked like he had been drugged.

By July, Ahmed had spent several months in solitary confinement, but reactions to his arrest from the outside world were still muted. Australia announced plans to position itself as a major arms exporter, highlighting the UAE as one of the key countries it wanted to increase defence exports to. 'So why wouldn't we want to cement our relationship with a country like the UAE, which shares many of our values in terms of the geopolitical issues that we face through things like defence exports?' Australian defence industry minister Christopher Pyne told reporters.[13]

A few months later, in November 2017, French president Emmanuel Macron was the guest of honour in Abu Dhabi as the regime opened an outlet of the famous Louvre Museum in the UAE capital, a project ten years in the making, which cost more than US$1 billion. The museum was 'a gift from the UAE to the world', the chairman of the Abu Dhabi tourism authority, Mohamed Khalifa Al Mubarak, said at the opening. 'When you're in this museum, we're all connected, we are all one. It's a centre of acceptance, it's a centre of tolerance,' he told reporters, without a hint of irony.

Meanwhile, there was no news on Ahmed's welfare. There were no more family visits. In early 2018, two Irish lawyers visited the UAE and asked to visit him in jail, but their request was refused, and they were quickly required to leave the country.

In May 2018, the UAE foreign minister, Sheik Abdullah bin Zayed bin Sultan Al Nahyan, visited Canberra, where he was enthusiastically welcomed by Australian government ministers. The Department of Foreign Affairs refused to comment when I asked if Foreign Minister Julie Bishop had raised the case of Ahmed Mansoor during the visit.

Just over two weeks later, on 29 May 2018, Ahmed was suddenly handed down a sentence, with the UAE government media reporting that he had been given a ten-year jail term and a fine of more than US$270,000 for the crime of 'defaming' the UAE on social media.

It is not just the silence of western governments that renders them complicit in the fate of Ahmed Mansoor and his fellow democracy activists. The brutal crackdown on Emirati human rights defenders would not be possible without the sale of advanced western security

equipment to the regime. Britain, Germany and Italy have made millions in recent years exporting cyber-surveillance software to the UAE that human rights groups believe is being used by the Emirati government to more efficiently control the use of communication technologies by dissidents.[14] The UK's BAE Systems were among the companies revealed to have made large-scale sales of mass surveillance technologies to the Emirati regime.[15]

In 2016, before Ahmed's second arrest, his phone was targeted by a previously unknown method of hacking, when he received a text message that invited him to click on a web link. Instead, he forwarded the message to researchers at the University of Toronto. The attack on Ahmed was the first known case of software that could remotely take over a fully up-to-date iPhone 6, reported Reuters.[16] 'Once infected, Mansoor's phone would have become a digital spy in his pocket, capable of employing his iPhone's camera and microphone to snoop on activity in the vicinity of the device, recording his WhatsApp and Viber calls, logging messages sent in mobile chat apps, and tracking his movements,' the University of Toronto researchers said. They attributed the attack software to a 'private seller of monitoring systems, NSO Group, an Israeli company that makes software for governments'.

While Ahmed's story has not received the attention it deserves, other high-profile human rights cases have emerged from the UAE. In March 2018, news broke of the disappearance of Princess Latifa, daughter of the Melbourne Cup winner and ruler of Dubai Sheik Mohammed bin Rashid Al Maktoum. A 39-minute video made by the princess was uploaded to YouTube on 11 March.[17] 'If you're watching this video, it's not such a good thing,' Latifa warns ominously to camera, explaining that she is about to attempt to escape Dubai and the control of the royal family. 'Either I'm dead or I'm in a very, very, very bad situation.' The 33-year-old Emirati royal speaks of a world without any freedoms, where she is regularly mistreated at the hands of her male family members. 'There's no justice here,' she says in the video. 'Especially if you're a female, your life is so disposable.' Latifa says her family has banned her from travelling and that she has not left the UAE for 18 years, claiming she is allowed out of the house only under the watchful eyes of the royal chauffeur. She describes an earlier failed escape

attempt that she claims saw her jailed, tortured and beaten for years. 'I hope I never use this video, that it just gets deleted and we are all okay,' Princess Latifa says in the YouTube clip.

But her worst fears were realized. A month before the clip was uploaded, Latifa and a Finnish friend, Tiina Jauhiainen, fled Dubai by land to Oman, before escaping the coast with jet skis and an inflatable boat. Once out at sea, they met up with a French sailor waiting with his yacht on international waters and set off for the Indian coast. It was straight from the pages of a spy novel, an audacious plan that was years in the making.

But just when Latifa thought she was free of her father's grip, the Indian coastguard and Emirati special forces raided the yacht just off the coast of Goa. Jauhiainen told the *New York Times* that armed men she identified as Indian and Emirati pushed her, the captain and the crewmen to the ground, tying them up and beating them. She said she witnessed Latifa also tied up on the deck, kicking and screaming that she wanted political asylum in India.[18] An Arabic-speaking man boarded the ship to retrieve the princess, Jauhiainen told the newspaper.

'Just shoot me here,' Latifa reportedly cried. 'Don't take me back.'

But she was whisked back to Dubai, with no word released on her fate for nine months.[19] In December 2018, the royal family released photos of Latifa, claiming she was 'fine' but 'troubled' and 'receiving support'. In the images, Latifa looks vacant, her eyes unfocused, her smile fixed, raising concerns she is being heavily medicated.

Another high-profile case hit the headlines when British scholar Matthew Hedges was arrested at Dubai airport in May 2018, after a two-week research trip in the country, and charged with spying after an Emirati local reported him to authorities for asking 'sensitive questions'.[20] The 31-year-old Brit spent six months in jail, mostly in solitary confinement, where he later claimed he was psychologically tortured, made to stand all day wearing ankle cuffs and force-fed a toxic cocktail of drugs by his jailers.[21] Hedges was given a life sentence in November, but after an international outcry, the student received a presidential pardon and was flown home to the UK. On his release, he told reporters that while he was jailed in

the UAE, he had been forced to 'confess falsely to being a British spy or face torture'.

Afterwards, Hedges used his detention to draw attention to the close relationship between western governments and the UAE regime, publicly questioning whether a desire to keep good relations with the UAE stopped Britain from acting faster to help him.[22] 'The question I would ask is: Are there any other vested interests here which may have slowed this process down or deliberately inhibited it?' he told Sky News UK. He called on the UK foreign office to conduct an internal review into its handling of his case. 'The idea of the UAE or wider Gulf influence in the UK decision making structure I think is very unhealthy,' Hedges said. 'We have a certain set of values and standards we like to try and live by and we should continue to do this without interruption.'

While Hedges's case and the fate of Princess Latifa have made the headlines, Ahmed Mansoor has continued to rot in jail.

In November 2018, the head of the Australian Federal Police, Andrew Colvin, travelled to Dubai, where he met the UAE president and signed a new memorandum of understanding between Australia and the emirates, allowing increased cooperation and 'information exchange' between Australian and UAE authorities.

A month later, the UAE state media announced that Ahmed Mansoor would have the chance to appeal his ten-year sentence on Christmas Eve, a clear sign they hoped everyone would be too busy to pay attention. On New Year's Eve, it was announced that his ten-year sentence had been upheld – Ahmed Mansoor would spend the next eight years in jail.

As Ahmed and his wife and four kids faced this massive blow, the UAE stepped up its PR efforts to project an image of itself as a progressive nation, declaring that 2019 would be celebrated as the 'Year of Tolerance' in the despotic monarchy. Under that banner of tolerance, the UAE regime managed to attract none other than Pope Francis to visit the country, in his first ever papal visit to the Arabian peninsula. In a video message released before his arrival, the head of the Catholic Church gave the brutal rulers of the UAE the sheen of respectability they crave, describing the country as one 'which strives to be a model for coexistence and human fraternity, a meeting point of different civilizations and cultures. A place where

people find a safe place to work, live freely and where differences are respected.'[23] While the Pope used his historic address in Abu Dhabi to highlight the suffering caused by wars in Syria, Yemen, Iraq and Libya, he made no mention of the brutal internal repression in the UAE.[24]

Jets spouting yellow and white smoke, the colours of the Vatican City flag, flew over the presidential palace in Abu Dhabi after Pope Francis met with the UAE's chief ruler, Sheik Mohammed bin Zayed Al Nahyan, and Latifa's father, Mohammed bin Rashid Al Maktoum. 'Mohammed bin Rashid & I were delighted to meet with Pope Francis,' tweeted the UAE dictator, 'in our homeland of tolerance.' [25]

A few months later a stunning abdication from the UAE royal family was further indication of the true nature of the Emirati regime. In July, news broke that Princess Haya Bint Al Hussein, the wife of Dubai's ruler Sheikh Mohammed bin Rashid Al Maktoum, had fled the United Arab Emirates with their young son and daughter and sought asylum in London.

The 45-year-old princess, who is Sheik Mohammad's sixth wife, was said to be living 'in fear for her life' and had gone into hiding, the BBC reported.[26] Sources close to the princess told the BBC she had 'recently discovered disturbing facts behind the mysterious return to Dubai last year of Princess Latifa, one of the ruler's daughters', and that she no longer felt safe in Dubai. The princess appeared in a London court for a hearing, as *Vanity Fair* reported that the 70-year-old billionaire dictator was suing her for the return of their two children, aged seven and 11, to Dubai.[27]

Meanwhile, Ahmed Mansoor languishes in jail. In October he turned 50 behind bars, and human rights groups reported that he had begun a second hunger strike, after receiving severe beatings in response to his complaints about his prison conditions and ongoing detention. 'Mansoor is reported to be held in prolonged solitary confinement, in a cell with no bed and no running water. His health is rapidly declining, and his life appears to be in jeopardy,' wrote the International Campaign for Freedom in the UAE. 'As his health declines and his life is put at risk, the international community has an obligation to take a stand and facilitate his unconditional release to ensure that he will spend his 51st birthday in freedom.'[28]

As Ahmed's unjust incarceration continued, the retiring Australian ambassador to the UAE, Arthur Spyrou, was busy praising Dubai's Attorney-General: 'Wonderful farewell call on Dubai Attorney-General, HE Issam Al Humaidan,' gushed Ambassador Spyrou, tweeting a photo of the two of them smiling broadly and shaking hands. 'Appreciate the close relationship and the kind cooperation over the last 4 years.'[29]

*

In January 2020, a Polish businessman who had spent months locked up just two cells down from Ahmed Mansoor spoke out about the jail conditions they endured in Abu Dhabi's notorious Al Sadr prison. Artur Ligeska spoke of the dank, insect-infested cell Ahmed was being held in, with just a hole in the ground for a toilet, and no lights. Ligeska told Human Rights Watch that the human rights defender had been told by prison guards that 'they had no control over his conditions and that all instructions came direct from the Presidential Palace'.[30]

CHAPTER 17

LITTLE BODIES LAID OUT IN A ROW

The Sarin Attack on Khan Sheikhoun

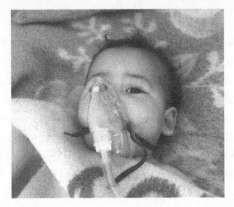

On 21 August 2013, two chemical weapons attacks on Ghouta, a Syrian opposition–held suburb of Damascus, killed between 800 and 1000 civilians.[1] Babies, toddlers, little boys and girls, men and women suffocated to death; many died with foam coming out of their mouths and blood out of their noses after they were asphyxiated by a gas that UN experts confirmed was the lethal nerve agent sarin.[2] Photos and videos of the aftermath of the attack show row after row of dead bodies, hundreds of civilians lined up on the ground. France, the United Kingdom, Germany, the United States and Human Rights Watch all attributed the attack to Syrian government armed forces. It clearly crossed the 'red line' US President Barack Obama had drawn, but no military action against the Syrian regime was taken. In the wake of the Ghouta massacre, the US and Russia brokered a deal requiring the Syrian regime to eradicate its chemical weapons stockpile. The Organisation for the Prohibition of Chemical Weapons was tasked with overseeing the destruction of all declared equipment and facilities related to Syria's chemical

weapons production. But the use of chemical weapons in Syria's conflict didn't end. Inspectors and diplomats suspect that while President Bashar Al Assad's regime appeared to cooperate with international inspectors, it secretly maintained chemical weapons capabilities.[3] A second sarin attack, on the town of Khan Sheikhoun in 2017, exposed the world's failure to protect the Syrian people from again being gassed to death by their own government.

Khan Sheikhoun, Syria, 4 April 2017

The first images showed nine small children lying next to each other, with their heads peeking out under the covers of a warm rug as if they were all cuddled up in a cosy double bed. But they weren't. They were cold little bodies lined up on the metal tray of a truck on a sunny morning in the opposition-held Syrian town of Khan Sheikhoun in the north-west province of Idlib. A little boy aged around three with a blue hooded jumper. Two small girls who looked like sisters, one in a purple top and the other in red polka dots, both with pierced ears and with long hair laid out wet behind them. Another girl, who looked around eight years old, with pink love hearts on her jumper. A toddler with wet locks stuck to his forehead, surely no older than two. Some looked at peace. Their eyes closed. Perhaps they had been asleep, I hoped, looking at them. Perhaps they never knew what was happening. But others had their eyes wide open. Staring up at the heavens. You didn't want to contemplate what their last few minutes on this earth had been like.

I'd received the first video of the aftermath of the suspected chemical attack just after 9.30 in the morning of Tuesday, 4 April 2017. 'We have 20 martyrs already and more than 150 injured after Khan Sheikhoun was targeted with gas in an air raid this morning,' a panicked message from a local activist read. Video kept coming through of the apocalyptic scene: a muddy parking lot, strewn with dead and dying civilians as rescuers from the White Helmets desperately worked to hose victims down, while others pumped frantically on the chests of unresponsive souls. Those still alive struggled to breathe, convulsing and shaking. A rosy-cheeked little boy with long eyelashes is filmed close up, his whole face filling

the frame. He grimaces in pain as you hear him desperately gasping for air. Nearby an old man lies motionless flat on his back, foam coming out of his mouth. A middle-aged man in a singlet wails in grief, clutching at a lifeless body next to him.

There was no doubt in my mind that this had all the indications of a chemical weapons attack. I started to tweet the horrific images.[4] Before long, a stern phone call came from one of my editors in Sydney. 'Do you need to put those horrible videos on Twitter?' they asked. 'And how do we know they're *real*?' I'd seen enough footage from Syria to know an authentic death scene when I saw one. I trusted the source who had sent it to me. I knew who controlled that town and what had been happening there in recent days. 'I'll resign if they're not,' was my short reply to my editor.

The images kept coming. More bodies of small children, as limp as rag dolls, being delicately placed in the back of a minivan. Tiny little feet intertwined, with no obvious trauma on their bodies except facial discoloration. They were all soaking wet and in their underwear; their clothes had been stripped off and their bodies blasted with water in a desperate attempt to get rid of the lethal fumes. But this substance was not something that could be washed off. It was sarin, one of the world's deadliest gases.

The chemical bomb had released a cloud that spread over the radius of between 300 and 600 metres from the impact point, UN investigators later determined.[5] The toxic substance had crept silently into homes in Khan Sheikhoun in the early hours of that morning, before children had left for school or parents for work. A Khan Sheikhoun resident who lived near the impact site described the gas as a 'winter fog – not quite yellow and not quite white' in an interview with the *New York Times*.[6] The head of a local ambulance service told the BBC that when medics first arrived at the scene, they found people, many of them children, choking in the streets.[7] A witness interviewed by the UN spoke of 'people dying in the street and children desperately crying for the help of their parents'.[8] Another resident described finding 'whole families dead in their homes'.[9]

In images filmed at a nearby medical clinic, doctors rushed from one bed to another, seemingly short of oxygen masks and unable to offer any real relief to those affected. 'I was asleep when the

warplane hit us,' a pale little boy says quietly when interviewed by opposition-aligned media activists. 'I went outside with Dad, but my head started hurting. I fell asleep and woke up to find myself here.' Doctors posted a video in which they shone a torch into a patient's eye, which maintained non-reactive pinpoint pupils, a tell-tale sign of nerve agent exposure. The local chief health official said the symptoms clearly indicated the presence of a poisonous gas. 'Suffocation, respiratory failure, foaming at the mouth, loss of consciousness, convulsions and paralysis,' described an official from the opposition-aligned Idlib Medical Council. A single mother returned home from farm work to find her four children dead, reported UN investigators, while the body of a woman and her six children were found in a basement, where they had desperately tried to take shelter from the gas.[10] At least 83 people, including 28 children and 23 women, were killed by the gas.[11]

What had happened in Khan Sheikhoun that morning was the deadliest chemical attack in Syria since Ghouta in 2013.

Idlib province was the last stronghold of the armed opposition groups fighting the Assad regime. By mid 2017, the region was controlled by factions of the nationalist Free Syrian Army, as well as powerful Islamist groups such as the former Al Qaeda–linked Nusra Front. Due to the high risk of being kidnapped by jihadists, plus frequent regime airstrikes, reporters from outside Syria rarely visited Idlib, but local Syrian reporters working for independent international media still operated in the region. Video and photos of the scene of the attack had therefore come from a multitude of independent sources, including the Agence France-Presse and Reuters news agencies, which had all sent journalists and photographers to report from Khan Sheikhoun that morning.[12]

All early evidence in Khan Sheikhoun pointed to the gas being dropped by a Syrian government warplane. At 6.26 on the morning of the attack, early warning observers reported that two Sukhoi 22 (Su-22) aircraft had taken off from Shayrat airbase in Homs, which was used by the Syrian air force throughout the conflict. At least one of the Su-22 planes (an aircraft used only by the Syrian government and not its Russian ally) was seen heading in the direction of Khan Sheikhoun. Witnesses recalled seeing an aircraft flying low over the town in a manner consistent with the airspeed

of the aircraft and the distance that needed to be covered, according to UN investigators. In a few minutes, the Su-22 made two passes over the town and dropped four bombs at about 6.45 am.[13]

Accounts from civilians, rescue workers and local media all reported shortly before the effects of the gas were felt that it was Syrian government warplanes that had bombed the village. As evidence mounted that the regime had carried out the attack, the Syrian military quickly rejected any involvement.[14] 'We deny completely the use of any chemical or toxic material in Khan Sheikhoun town today and the army has not used nor will use in any place or time neither in past or in future,' the Syrian army command said in a statement. But within hours, the United Nations Syria envoy, Staffan de Mistura, told reporters the 'horrific' chemical attack 'came from the air' – an indirect way of pointing the finger at the Syrian military. The opposition had no airpower and the Syrian regime was the predominant airborne force in that area – Assad had the motive to strike the rebel-held town, and it appeared he still had chemical weapons capability.

Later that afternoon, as medical staff continued to treat patients, Syrian government warplanes remained overhead, one striking a clinic as a journalist was addressing the camera – his cameraman capturing the moment as parts of the roof collapsed.[15] A reporter with the Agence France-Presse news agency reported seeing rubble coming down on top of doctors treating the injured.[6]

As world outrage grew, Assad's Russian backers and the pro-Syrian government media started spinning a different line, claiming the Syrian army had 'struck a jihadist gas factory' in Khan Sheikhoun that morning.[17] 'The Syrian aviation launched a strike on a large terrorist ammunition depot and a concentration of military hardware on the eastern outskirts of the town of Khan Sheikhoun,' Russian defence ministry spokesman Igor Konashenkov claimed in a prepared video statement. 'On the territory of this depot were workshops which produced chemical warfare munitions.' The Russians did not provide any evidence to support their claims of an 'ammunition depot'.

When Kareem Shaheen, a reporter for *The Guardian*, reached the town two days later, he found no evidence of any kind of rebel ammunition plant.[18] Just an empty warehouse and silos directly next

to where the missile had landed, covered in dust and with remnants of leftover grain and animal manure. What Shaheen did find in the town, which was now largely deserted, was a blackened crater where the bombs, laced with sarin, fell, and freshly dug graves in the cemetery for the dozens of dead who had been buried the day before.

As patients were evacuated from Khan Sheikhoun to northern Idlib and southern Turkey for urgent medical treatment, independent medical experts, including staff from the international medical charity Médecins Sans Frontières (MSF), backed up the claims of the opposition-run Idlib health directorate that people had been exposed to a toxic gas. 'An MSF medical team providing support to the emergency department of Bab Al Hawa hospital in Syria's Idlib province has confirmed that patients' symptoms are consistent with exposure to a neurotoxic agent such as sarin gas,' MSF said in a statement the next day.[19]

The photos from Khan Sheikhoun reached the White House. US President Donald Trump told reporters he had been deeply affected by the images of victims from the attack. 'I will tell you that attack on children yesterday had a big impact on me – big impact. My attitude toward Syria and Assad has changed very much. You're now talking about a whole different level,' President Trump said, laying the ground for possible retaliation.[20] But it wasn't just the horrific pictures of dead children motivating Trump. This was as much about ego for the narcissist in the White House. Trump wanted to be seen to be asserting the 'red line' that Obama had threatened but never acted on after the horrific Ghouta chemical weapons massacre in 2013.

Seventy-two hours after the gas attack, on 7 April, the United States launched 59 Tomahawk cruise missiles at Shayrat airbase in Syria, where the planes that dropped the sarin were. In all the years of the Syrian war and with all the atrocities that had been committed, this was the first time the White House had ordered military action against forces loyal to President Assad.[21] The targets included the runway, as well as aircraft, hangars and fuel facilities; between four and 16 Syrian soldiers were killed.[22]

'We are assessing the results of the strike,' a Pentagon spokesman told the *New York Times*. 'Initial indications are that this strike

has severely damaged or destroyed Syrian aircraft and support infrastructure and equipment at Shayrat airfield, reducing the Syrian government's ability to deliver chemical weapons.'[23] According to US Secretary of State Rex Tillerson, 'This clearly indicates the president is willing to take decisive action when called for. The more we fail to respond to the use of these weapons, the more we begin to normalize their use.' Tillerson's comments were a 'thinly veiled reference to President Barack Obama's decision to refrain from strikes in 2013,' noted the *New York Times*.[24]

Although several Syrian warplanes were reportedly destroyed, as well as a runway, it can be argued that the US attack on the airbase was mostly for show. The Pentagon confirmed that the Americans had given advance warning of the attack to the Russians, who in turn notified the Syrians, giving them enough time to remove many aircraft before the retaliation.[25] Just hours after the US strike on the airbase, Syrian warplanes defiantly took off again from Shayrat, carrying out air raids on rebel towns including Khan Sheikhoun, according to monitors speaking to the UK *Telegraph*.[26] The retaliatory strike did not make any real dent in Assad's war efforts; after all, he had 20 other airbases at his disposal. And Trump had his moment of being 'tougher than Obama', without inflicting any real damage or having to deal with serious consequences from Syria's Russian ally.

Three weeks after the chemical weapons attack, I flew to Istanbul. In a small café, I sat down with Dr Mamoun Morad, the first doctor present at the scene of the attack to get out of Syria so he could give his full account of what happened that devastating day.[27] 'Can you imagine how the end of the world will be like? Do you think anyone can guess what it will look like? It was a day from hell,' the surgeon says. 'No matter how much I'll tell you, or explain to you and what I say, I can't explain enough the scale of this.' The 65-year-old surgeon from Hama works with the Syrian American Medical Society and was one of the first medical responders to treat victims of the Khan Sheikhoun attack. 'I was among the people right here in the yard, in this yard. These were dead, they are all dead,' he recalls sadly. Dr Morad had to direct the medical staff amid utter chaos. 'We were treating them and crying. We were working and crying – the doctors, and all the medical staff

and the wounded too,' he says. He tells me that one little boy, who was filmed close up as he struggled to breathe and whose image was flashed around the world, didn't make it. 'We washed him, we gave him atropine, we gave him hydrocortisone, we also gave him oxygen and performed intubation. Then we referred him to the north, but he died on the road,' he said.

In the weeks after Khan Sheikhoun, Assad supporters and Russian state media swung into overdrive, attempting to cast doubt on the veracity of the photos and videos from Khan Sheikhoun, implying they were somehow 'faked' by opposition activists, or that they were taken during a 'false flag' attack aimed at baiting the US into retaliating against Assad and drawing America further into the Syrian conflict.[28] One of the leading voices spreading theories that it was opposition forces who had 'staged' the attack was a retired professor from the Massachusetts Institute of Technology, Theodore Postol.[29] His work was picked up and promoted by pro-Assad campaigners as well as leftist thinkers like Noam Chomsky and the Australian reporter John Pilger, whose work on East Timor I had once so admired, but who was now appearing on Kremlin-funded RT television.[30] (Tulsi Gabbard, a Democrat running for US president in 2020, is also among those who continue to spread Postol's discredited work.)[31]

The conspiracy theorists questioned why first responders at Khan Sheikhoun didn't appear affected by the gas.[32] But Dr Morad says this is untrue and that he and other medical staff and White Helmets responders were all contaminated by the sarin exposure, and he is among those still feeling the effects. 'I lost my voice. Now I'm in a much better situation, but in the past I couldn't talk even. I'm taking cortisone because my hands still hurt,' he says hoarsely, showing me his hands, which appear red and agitated. 'I didn't have time to wear my gloves even. It was happening so fast.' (UN investigators later found that first responders were unaware at the time of the possibility of the release of a chemical agent, so they did not carry respirators or other protective equipment. Several first responders fell ill upon arrival to the scene, and at least two died, the UN found.)[33]

Khan Sheikhoun was not the first time Dr Morad and his colleagues had been at risk of chemical attack since the Ghouta

massacre in 2013. In fact, it was now clear that international efforts to protect the Syrian people from being gassed again by their own government had failed – in full view of the world, the Syrian regime's use of chemical weapons in the lead-up to Khan Sheikhoun was widespread and systematic.[34]

In the wake of global outrage over the 2013 Ghouta massacre, and under an agreement negotiated between Russia and the United States, Syrian President Bashar Al Assad was forced to join the international Chemical Weapons Convention and surrender 1300 tonnes of stockpiled chemical weapons and industrial substances for destruction. But after its main toxic arsenal had been destroyed and once the world stopped paying close attention, Damascus turned to a widely available and hard to trace substance to make its rockets and barrel bombs more harmful – chlorine. The use of chlorine as a weapon is prohibited under the Chemical Weapons Convention; it irritates people's eyes and skin, burns the lungs and can be deadly when deployed in small confined spaces where the gas overwhelms and there is no oxygen to breathe.

In October 2016, a leaked confidential report to the UN Security Council concluded that Syrian government forces had used chlorine as a weapon at least three times in the past two years.[35] The report said that Syrian air force helicopters had dropped chlorine gas on rebel-held areas, once in April 2014 and twice in March 2015. In fact, a month before the Khan Sheikhoun attack, the US, the UK and France proposed a UN Security Council resolution to impose new sanctions on Syria over these chlorine attacks. If passed, the resolution would have banned the sale or supply of helicopters to the Assad regime and led to sanctions against 11 Syrian commanders.[36] But Russia and China vetoed the resolution in order to protect the Assad regime. The failure of the Security Council to pass the resolution would send a 'message of impunity', lamented French UN ambassador François Delattre. The attack on Khan Sheikhoun happened four weeks later.

And just nine days before the Khan Sheikhoun incident, there was a deadly chlorine chemical weapons attack that went largely unnoticed. On 25 March 2017, regime helicopters dropped bombs containing chlorine gas on an MSF-supported hospital in Hama province. Dr Morad's good friend, an orthopaedic surgeon and

father of five, Dr Ali Darwish, was killed. 'At around 6 pm on 25 March, Latamneh hospital in northern Hama governorate was targeted by a bomb dropped by a helicopter, which hit the entrance of the building. Information collected by the hospital medical staff suggests that chemical weapons were used,' MSF wrote on 2 April, just two days before the attack on Khan Sheikhoun. 'Two people died as a result of the attack, including Dr Darwish, the hospital's orthopaedic surgeon. Thirteen people were transferred for treatment to other facilities.'[37] The world paid little attention.

Dr Morad said he wants the world to be just as outraged by the Syrian government's continued bombing of hospitals as they were by the sarin gas attacks. 'I don't care about politics, I want the targeting of hospitals to stop,' he said. 'I don't care what the politicians are doing. According to international law, hospitals and holy places and schools should not be targeted. I'm a doctor. I have no relation with any organisation or faction or any terrorist. I'm a doctor and I'm treating patients who are less fortunate and who are under attack.' Dr Morad sometimes wonders how things might have been if Obama had enforced a 'red line' after the 2013 Ghouta attack, whether a campaign to take out Assad's air force and enforce a no-fly zone would have saved tens of thousands of his compatriots' lives. 'Now when people hear the planes they don't even bother hiding anymore,' he tells me sadly.

After several weeks' break and recovery in Turkey, Dr Morad returned to Syria to work. His wife, daughter and five grandchildren are living in America, while another son is a surgeon in Germany and has a new baby. He tells me he can't turn his back on his homeland and quickly shoots down my suggestion that he is a hero. 'I'm an ordinary person exposed to death just like any other person,' he tells me firmly. 'I don't feel I'm a hero and I believe I could die any time – we only live once.'

In the weeks after the attack, the US administration's outrage over what President Assad was doing to his own people subsided. And sure enough, the situation quickly went back to 'normal' after Khan Sheikhoun; Assad continued his bombing campaign with impunity. In the rest of April, about 400 civilians were killed in raids by Syrian and Russian warplanes and by regime helicopters, reported the Syrian Observatory for Human Rights.[38]

In August, a special Reuters investigation detailed how the Syrian government's efforts to voluntarily surrender and destroy their chemical weapons stockpile in 2013 was a 'ruse', and that while the regime appeared to cooperate with international inspectors, they secretly maintained or developed new chemical weapons capabilities.[39] 'The extent of Syria's reluctance to abandon chemical weapons has not previously been made public for fear of damaging international inspectors' relationship with Assad's administration and its backer, Russia,' wrote Reuters.

Then in September 2017, the UN released its investigation, confirming that evidence proved it was the Syrian regime that had dropped a sarin bomb on Khan Sheikhoun and declaring the attack a war crime. The UN Commission of Inquiry on Syria conducted 43 interviews with eyewitnesses, victims, first responders and medical workers, as well as collecting satellite imagery, photographs of bomb remnants and videos of the area allegedly affected by the air strikes.[40] 'Not having access did not prevent us from establishing facts or reasonable grounds to believe what happened during the attack and establishing who is responsible,' UN Commission chairman Paulo Pinheiro told a news conference.[41]

Addressing the Russian and Syrian claims that they had bombed a 'jihadist weapons depot', the commission said it was 'extremely unlikely' that an airstrike would release sarin potentially stored inside such a structure in amounts sufficient to explain the number of casualties recorded. The UN commission noted that if such a depot had really been destroyed by an airstrike, the explosion would have burnt off most of the agent inside the building or forced it into the rubble where it would have been absorbed, rather than releasing it in significant amounts into the atmosphere.

In October, the Organisation for the Prohibition of Chemical Weapons (OPCW) backed up the UN's findings, also concluding that the Syrian government was responsible for the Khan Sheikhoun sarin attack.[42] 'The sarin identified in the samples taken from Khan Sheikhoun was found to have most likely been made with a precursor...from the original stockpile of the Syrian Arab Republic,' said the OPCW report.[43] 'On the basis of the foregoing, the Leadership Panel is confident that the Syrian Arab Republic is responsible for the release of sarin at Khan Sheikhoun on 4 April 2017.'

*

For two years, a combined UN–OPCW Joint Investigative Mechanism (JIM) operated, investigating responsibility for chemical attacks in Syria. After the JIM confirmed that the Syrian regime was responsible for the April 2017 nerve agent attack in Khan Sheikhoun, Moscow used its veto at the UN Security Council to block several resolutions seeking to renew the JIM mandate. In November 2017, the JIM was abolished.[44]

On 7 April, nearly a year after the Khan Sheikhoun attack, 43 men, women and children were killed in the opposition-held town of Douma as a result of a chlorine-loaded bomb.[45] Syrian government helicopters are believed responsible for the attack.[46]

In February 2019, a study by the Berlin-based Global Public Policy Institute found that there have been at least 336 chemical weapons attacks over the course of the Syrian civil war. The report concluded that around 98 per cent of these attacks could be attributed to the Assad regime, with the Islamic State group responsible for the rest. About 90 per cent of all confirmed attacks occurred after Obama's infamous 'red line' statement of August 2013.[47]

On the first anniversary of the Khan Sheikhoun chemical attack, Dr Mamoun Morad was invited to New York, where he was recognized at a United Nations Security Council briefing for his role in saving lives that fateful day in Khan Sheikhoun. The 66-year-old had the chance to finally spend time with his US-based family, after spending years without seeing them while he worked tirelessly in Syria. While Dr Morad was in the United States, he fell ill and was diagnosed with terminal cancer. He passed away in April 2019, in his daughter's home, surrounded by his family.

THE FLOWERS ARE DEAD

Syria through the Eyes of Its Children

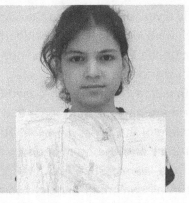

By 2017, 5.3 million Syrian refugees remained in temporary housing and refugee camps around the Middle East, years after they had fled their homes. The international community had failed to adequately fund the UN response: with only 53 per cent of the UN Syrian relief budget met, there was not enough money to fund healthcare or classrooms across the region. Aid officials spoke of a 'lost generation', with half of displaced Syrian children still unable to attend school while they lived with continuing trauma and in impoverished conditions.[1] An unique art project to hear firsthand from these kids provided a heartbreaking insight into their world.

Amman, Jordan, July 2017

'In my town, there are lots of wombats. Does anyone know what a wombat is?'

Thirty children stared blankly at Ben Quilty, one of Australia's best-known modern artists. It appeared the answer was no.

'It's like a small camel, but they have no hump. Very furry. Very short legs. And they dig huge big holes like a rabbit!' Ben explained enthusiastically, motioning his hands like two wombat paws tunnelling a burrow.

Some of the little girls glanced at me, giggling. Who was this guy?

Ben was laden with metres of drawing paper and dozens of watercolour pencils – everything he needed to run a summer-holiday art workshop for Syrian refugee children living on the outskirts of Jordan's biggest city, Amman. But first he needed to convince this tough audience why he thought their drawings were important. 'I hear lots of politicians and prime ministers and adults all round the world talking about what's happening in Syria,' he explained to the kids. 'All the world knows what all the adults think about what's happened to your country, but no one knows what you think. And I think it's really important. The one set of paintings that needs to be made is by you!'

Many of the children looked around, slightly chuffed. *Their* thoughts on Syria? Nobody had ever sought their advice before. Suddenly, the race for pencils was on. Dozens of tiny hands started grabbing the packets of colours and wads of paper.

Quilty's idea for the project came after visiting Syrian refugee camps in Lebanon's Beqaa Valley. Everywhere he went, he took along pencils and crayons for the kids in the families he was meeting. 'I just sat with the kids and drew,' he said. And each picture blew him away. 'So many of them instantly came up with these really intense drawings. It stayed in my mind, and I thought, *There needs to be some more documentation of this art.*' He secured funding for drawing and painting workshops, with the resulting art to be compiled in a book, its sale proceeds going to support work with Syrian refugee children.

The workshops were developed with assistance from UN-accredited child protection officers who had worked closely with Syrian refugees, explained project co-coordinator and Australian aid worker Conny Lenneberg. 'It is not a project where we say, "Tell us about the horrible things you have seen and experienced,"' she explained, as the kids started spreading out the art supplies on tables behind us. 'It's saying to children, "What do you want

the world to understand about your lives and your hopes and dreams? What do you want to draw about Syria?" We get some kids who draw the conflict in Syria and their story of loss and escape, but other children draw celebrations in the park with lots of food, playgrounds, fun and laughter. And everything in between. Children are remembering their homes, their farms. Some of them as they were and some of them are drawing them as they are now.'

Ben Quilty was walking table to table, introducing himself to all the kids. 'We tried to come up with questions that were healthy for them,' he told me. '"How do you remember Syria? Do you have memories of Syria? What do you hope for Syria?" In a way, empower the children to tell the story they feel is important that they want the world to know. They all answered the questions differently, but as kids do, they're all artists...We all start out as artists.'

A 13-year-old girl in a pink headscarf started to construct a vibrant garden image. Bright colourful flowers, green trees laden with fruit. And a house amid this joyful scene. 'I wanted to draw our home in Syria,' she said proudly. 'How life was and how we were so happy there.'

The workshops were held at different sites throughout Jordan and Lebanon, where hundreds of thousands of Syrian refugee children have spent years without access to proper schooling. Many of the kids in the room lived in informal accommodation, their parents working illegally as labourers or in the streets getting whatever work they could. They had been treated like second-class citizens in Lebanon and Jordan for years, with no rights to proper healthcare or education. Life was a hand-to-mouth existence.

I followed Quilty over to a table as he sat down next to a tiny little girl who was intently drawing four black stick people lying horizontally on the ground. Wissam, who was seven and wearing a frilly blue top, then grabbed a red pencil and started carefully colouring great spurts of blood coming out of the figures. A person with a hat on, wearing a spotted outfit, had been drawn in the corner, pointing a gun at the bleeding stick people. She looked up, grinning shyly at the attention. Wissam quickly moved onto the next picture. This time, a stick figure with a stethoscope, standing next to a baby. 'Here, I'm a doctor,' Wissam said proudly, pointing at the figure. 'I love drawing. I don't get bored when I draw.'

At the tables around us, beautiful homes in Syria were being drawn. But so were many tanks, helicopters, guns and dead people. A little boy around eight years old, Tarek, had drawn a building with people on the top holding rocket launchers. A big red helicopter dropped brown bombs. Stick figures underneath had sad faces, while the one figure holding a gun smiled. 'This is a helicopter bombing in Syria. These are people dying on the streets and people running away,' Tarek described, motioning at his drawing. 'Nothing explains my thoughts about Syria except for this.'

At the next table, a group of boys eagerly started using paintbrushes and jars of water to turn their drawings into watercolour paintings; eight-year-old Taim was excited to show us his drawing of 'fighters' with big muscles popping out of their arms. 'These are the strong men who will take Syria back,' he explained happily, pointing out every small detail in his work. The supermarket, the school – all surrounded by armed men. And why did Taim want to draw Syria like this? 'Because everyone in Syria is a fighter. They like fighting there. Syria is full of fighting!'

Taim's friend Zaid had not drawn any people or planes or helicopters. His page was full of big broad brushes of colour and nothing else. 'What is this, Zaid?' asked Ben. 'Tell me about your painting?' The ten-year-old shrugged. 'There is nothing in Syria anymore,' he explained in a small voice. 'But I remember the colours.'

Another little boy, Maha, pulled up a chair next to Ben and chatted him through his own intricate drawing. 'Here I am in school, this is the school. These are the police officers chasing the bad guys. This is my dad's car parked here, in front of them. This is how my dad got me just in time from school. And this is how we escaped to Jordan.'

Ten-year-old Ahmed was quieter than the others and didn't smile. He didn't need any encouragement, putting pencil to paper as soon as the supplies were handed out. 'This is my home in Syria,' he explained simply of his art. The rest didn't need any explanation. Lines of people were shooting at his house and bombs were falling on top of it. Even the sun in the corner of the page was crying. 'I've asked the staff here to give this boy special attention once we've gone,' Ben said quietly. 'Because he seems to just still be in complete shock. There is no smile in that little child's face.'

Ten-year-old Yasmin had been waiting patiently to show the acclaimed artist her work. She had drawn colourful panels: one green, one grey and one blue. She had drawn flowers all over the green, and little figurine people in the grey. But all was not what it seemed. 'These flowers are all dead,' Yasmin told Ben. 'And the people are stuck in the middle in the grey, they're stuck, they can't move anywhere. They can't move forward, and they can't move backwards, and they're dying in the grey.'

Ben Quilty saw these drawings as an important part of history that needed to be documented. 'When you see a child draw those things and you're sitting next to them, it's impossible not to be crushed, I guess. No kid should draw things like that,' he said. 'I don't know what is healthier, the children who are covering up the pain and drawing beautiful things, or little Wissam who is just going, "This is what my life is. This is what I want you to see, and the world needs to see it."'

As the afternoon wrapped up, all the children posed proudly with their art. They ate a hot lunch of chicken, rice and yoghurt and then played games outside.

'Through their drawings, it's impossible to ignore what has happened to those people. It has become so ugly and so harsh that we've forgotten the children, we've forgotten all of the refugees. Refugee has become a dirty word. When and how did that happen?' Quilty said despairingly. 'When you see a little person draw this thing, that's absolute truth. A six-year-old doesn't lie with a pencil; these children speak the truth. They are telling a story that is incredibly confronting, but, my goodness, we all need to hear this story.'

CHAPTER 19

ESCAPE FROM SAUDI
Rahaf Mohammed and Dina Ali

In 2019, a system still remains in Saudi Arabia that is akin to gender apartheid. Under the rule of the despotic Saudi royal family and an official male guardianship system sanctioned by the state, a woman's life in Saudi Arabia is controlled by a man from birth until death. Despite attempts by the new Saudi crown prince Mohammad Bin Salman to sell himself as a reformer, the country continues to force an archaic method of control upon female citizens – while those who try to advocate for reform are jailed and tortured. The significance of the story of Dina Ali, who was brutally forced back home after trying to flee the kingdom only became clear after another young girl called Rahaf turned up at Bangkok airport in January 2019. Her refusal to kowtow to efforts to silence her exposed to the world the Saudi regime's lies and cruel treatment of its female citizens.

Bangkok, Thailand, 5 January 2019

A few days into the new year, Bangkok's Suvarnabhumi international airport was heaving with holiday travellers. Amid the throngs of sunburnt tourists sinking beers and families rushing to their

305

gates, one young woman was on the run. Eighteen-year-old Saudi citizen Rahaf Mohammed Al Qunun filed nervously off her Kuwait Airways flight. The petite teenager clutched a small backpack, all she was taking to what she hoped would be a new life in Australia. On the plane, Rahaf had abandoned the black abaya she was forced to wear by her family and was now dressed in baggy jeans and a black sports T-shirt. Her dark hair sat in a jagged bob. She had cut it herself several months earlier in a defiant move against her family's wishes, an act that had seen her locked in her room for six months as punishment.

Growing up under Saudi Arabia's state-sanctioned gender apartheid, Rahaf, like every other Saudi woman, had to obtain permission from her male 'guardian' for the simplest of tasks – to study, travel, even attend medical appointments. Under the archaic system, the male guardian is normally a father or husband, but in some cases it can be a brother or even the teenage son of a professional middle-aged woman. A man controls a Saudi woman's entire life, and adult women are essentially treated as legal minors by the state.[1]

But as social media exploded around the globe, the despotic kingdom could not keep its younger citizens from learning how women were treated outside Saudi Arabia. Through Instagram, Snapchat and Twitter, Rahaf and her friends were acutely aware of the freedom women enjoyed in many other countries. Rahaf's iPhone gave constant reminders of the life forbidden to her just because she had been born a Saudi. She wanted out.

Rahaf connected online with other young Saudi women who had managed to escape. The most common method was to hack into their male guardian's phone and change the 'permission' settings for travel on the official Saudi state app Absher. The next step was to steal their passport and leave the country, praying they could make it somewhere safe before their family realized they were missing and notified authorities. The room for delay or mistakes was narrow, as the Saudi state would actively work with families to intercept such women – even outside the kingdom's borders.

The other method was to make a run for it while they were already out of Saudi Arabia with their family on vacation. This made it easier to catch a flight without being questioned about

travelling without a male companion. Rahaf had opted for the latter. Desperate to escape her controlling and abusive family, the teenager had seized the opportunity of a family holiday to the neighbouring country of Kuwait, where women are allowed to travel without a male guardian. A month earlier she had successfully applied online for a tourist visa to Australia – a popular destination for young Saudi women seeking asylum because they can be granted a tourist visa without physically visiting an embassy.

With a precious copy of the visa saved on her phone, Rahaf had woken at dawn that morning and packed a small backpack. While her family slept, Rahaf stole her passport, booked a flight to Bangkok with Kuwait Airways and took a taxi to the airport. She made it through customs and the seven-hour flight. It had all happened so quickly, she hadn't even booked her flight to Australia. This was the nerve-racking moment as she disembarked the flight. Her family would surely have noticed by now that she was missing. Had they raised the alarm?

Rahaf walked casually up the ramp with the other passengers into the terminal, trying not to betray how fast her heart was beating in her chest. Suddenly an Arab man in a suit appeared in front of her. 'Miss Rahaf Al Qunun?' he said. Rahaf was flooded with panic and fear, making it hard to breathe. She'd already decided that she would kill herself rather than be forced back to Saudi Arabia. 'Rahaf al-Qunun?' the man said again, reaching for her passport. The world started closing in. Who would help her now?

Sydney, Australia, 6 January 2019

I sat down at my desk on a Sunday morning in early January. For once, the house was quiet and still. The kids were away camping with their grandparents and my husband was at the Sydney Cricket Ground for the fourth day of the Test match. After a quick swim at the beach, I planned to get some writing done. But, as usual, the first thing I did when I opened my laptop was browse through Twitter.

One of the first tweets that popped up on my feed was by a young Saudi woman called Nourah. I follow a lot of feminist activists from Saudi Arabia, and that day they were all retweeting the short video

Nourah had posted.[2] The footage showed a young woman talking as she sat in what looked like an airport. It didn't show her face, just her jeans, and the legs and shoes of what appeared to be some officials. 'I'm a Saudi girl stuck in Thailand, please help me,' the voice on the video said. Nourah's caption on her tweet added, 'Help her please!! A Saudi girl stuck in Thailand.' It had been posted several hours earlier, at around midnight Bangkok time.

Intrigued, I started reading further. Another Saudi woman activist had tweeted, 'Please help us there is a Saudi girl tried to run from Saudi, but the Saudi embassy catch her at Thailand they arrested her they will kill her help us please.' Scrolling down, I found the Twitter account of the young girl the activists were talking about. 'I am the girl who escaped #Kuwait to #Thailand. My life is in real danger if I am forced to return to #Saudi Arabia,' tweeted someone with the handle @rahaf84427714:

> My name is Rahaf Mohamed. I will publish my full name publicly if my family and the #Saudi embassy and the #Kuwaiti embassy man don't stop chasing me…I should be able to live alone, freely, independent of anyone who does not respect my dignity and who doesn't respect me as a woman.

I sat back in my chair. This sounded just like the case of Dina Ali. On 10 April 2017, Saudi citizen Dina Ali Lasloom was in transit at Manila airport in the Philippines. The young English teacher was on the run. She had a ticket for a connecting flight to Sydney, where she planned to claim asylum, fleeing what she described as an abusive family. But her family had realised she was missing and contacted the Saudi authorities. Despite the fact she was 24 years old, the kingdom pledged to help force Dina back to her parents.

Once she touched down in Manila, Filipino airport officials, reportedly at the request of the Saudi embassy, confiscated Dina's passport and boarding pass and blocked her from boarding her flight to Australia. Dina posted a video on Twitter, begging for help, but none came. The young woman's male relatives flew to the Philippines, and witnesses interviewed by Human Rights Watch saw Dina Ali being carried screaming onto a Saudi Arabian Airlines flight, her hands and feet bound together with duct tape.[3]

Dina Ali Lasloom had not been heard from since.

I messaged one of the Saudi women activists on Twitter for more details of what was happening to this young woman 'Rahaf' at Bangkok airport. 'She was stopped by the Thai police,' Rosie, a Saudi asylum seeker in the UK, wrote to me. 'And they took her passport away.' They told the 18-year-old she was going to be deported to Saudi Arabia via Kuwait, because as a Saudi woman she didn't have the right to travel alone. Rahaf's passport was taken from her, and she was marched to the airport hotel where she was being held under surveillance. 'Taking her back is a death wish,' Rosie wrote next to a stream of crying emojis. 'She can't go back. Her family is very powerful.'

By then, it was about 10.30 am Sydney time. Rosie made it sound like Rahaf could be deported at any minute. *Shit*, I thought. *Rahaf could be another Dina Ali.* Dina Ali's story had always haunted me. At the time, I'd seen her tweets begging for help and had naïvely assumed someone would come to her aid. Reading of her forcible return, which had taken place in an airport full of people, I felt guilty. I, like others, had watched passively as someone live-tweeted their desperate situation, hoping someone would care enough to act.

But maybe this time, with enough attention, Rahaf might have a different fate.

I began emailing contacts at Human Rights Watch (HRW) and Amnesty International in Bangkok and Sydney, sending them Rahaf's tweets and reminding them of Dina Ali's case. Was there anything they could do to help? The world was still reeling from the horrific murder three months earlier of Saudi journalist and dissident Jamal Khashoggi. After his brutal dismemberment inside the Saudi consulate in Istanbul, which the CIA had concluded was at the request of Saudi crown prince Mohammad bin Salman, it was clear what the regime under his control was capable of.[4] I messaged my old friend Diana Sayed who worked at Amnesty International, but she was away travelling and told me they had no one currently in Bangkok. It was a bad time of year; everyone was still away on holidays. I tried calling the mobile number of HRW's Phil Robertson, who I knew lived in the Thai capital, but there was no answer.

Rahaf posted a video of being followed around by airport security if she tried to leave the airport hotel area. With no passport and a constant tail, there didn't seem to be any escape.

By that time, it was 11.30 am. How quickly would they deport her? I hesitated about what to do next. Should I message Rahaf directly? I couldn't promise her any help, but perhaps it was worth letting her know I was trying to get someone from an NGO directly in touch with her.

'Hi Rahaf,' I wrote to her via Twitter direct message. 'I'm an Australian journalist. I've asked Human Rights Watch and Amnesty to help you. Is there anyone in Australia who can help? Do you have anyone here you trust?'

Rahaf replied in a flash. 'No.'

'When did they say they are going to deport you?' I asked.

'Tomorrow,' said Rahaf. 'What time? Do you know the flight?'

'No. The Thai police have to help me. Otherwise I will be dead,' Rahaf wrote.

'Are the Kuwaiti and Saudi officials in your hotel watching you?'
'Yes.'

'Have the Kuwaitis and Saudis threatened you?'

'Yes. And they said don't dare to run away. And even if u could we will find u and kidnap u. They said that to me literally.'

'Honestly don't leave the room,' I advised her. 'Stay there. Amnesty International and Human Rights Watch have been given your details. I'm trying to find someone who can come and see you.'

'Yeah plz do that,' she wrote back. 'I really need someone who can be around me.'

I emailed the UN refugee agency (UNHCR) in Bangkok and the UN human rights office but received no response, and they weren't picking up calls. I also tried journalist colleagues in Bangkok with the ABC, Reuters, BBC and the *Financial Times*. 'Rahaf is at the Miracle Hotel in BKK airport Room 303,' I wrote. 'You would have to buy a plane ticket to get to her.' Again, no luck. It was a Sunday. People weren't answering.

It was now nearly 2 pm in Sydney, and 10 am in Bangkok. Rahaf had been detained for more than 12 hours and was starting to panic. Thai officials were continuing to refuse her request to talk to UN officials. She was trapped in the airport hotel, security

guards posted outside her room and men who she suspected were embassy officials sitting in the nearby lounge. There was no escape. Fortunately, the next Kuwait Airways flight didn't depart until Monday morning Bangkok time.

Meanwhile on Twitter, the renowned Egyptian feminist author Mona Eltahawy had been translating Rahaf's tweets into English for her more than 200,000 Twitter followers. 'I couldn't live with myself if this was a real person, and I didn't do what I could to help her,' said Mona. People around the world were captivated by the 18-year-old's plight. There were also many doubters who thought the whole story sounded fictitious, along with hundreds of pro-Saudi trolls flooding Rahaf's timeline to make fun of her claims. Mona was in constant touch with Rahaf, offering support and advice. 'I DMed her, and I said to her, "Rahaf, we need to see your face. People need to see you, so that they can believe that you exist,"' said Mona.

Rahaf decided she had nothing to lose. Disclosing her full name, she tweeted two photos: a selfie and a photocopy of her passport. 'My name is Rahaf Mohammed Mutlaq Alqunun, and this is my picture. This is a copy of my passport, Im sharing it with you now because I want you to know I'm real and exist.'⁵ Rahaf had now not only accused her family of mistreatment and abuse, she had publicly identified them.

Not long after, Rahaf also tweeted that she had decided to renounce Islam and was now an atheist. 'They will kill me because I fled and because I announced my atheism,' Rahaf said in an interview from her room. 'They wanted me to pray and to wear a veil, and I didn't want to.'⁶ The stakes had been raised significantly.

Thai immigration officials came to meet with the 18-year-old. They told her that her passport had been cancelled and she wouldn't be allowed into Thailand. Rahaf secretly filmed the meeting. The footage shows her telling the two officials that it is too dangerous for her to return to Saudi, with the officials insisting that she will need to leave. They state she will be boarding flight KU412 the next day at 11.15 am. The upside of this exchange was learning when exactly they were planning on deporting Rahaf.

'Lock yourself in the room until then,' I suggested. 'There is only one flight tomorrow with Kuwait Airways from Bangkok.'

'I will miss it. I will try to run and hide,' Rahaf wrote back.

By late afternoon, I managed to get through to Phil Robertson, Human Rights Watch's deputy Asia director who is based in Bangkok. A fluent Thai speaker, Phil is an incredibly efficacious operator who has close relations with the local UNHCR office and government officials – exactly the sort of person needed in this kind of situation.

'Okay. I'm on it,' he wrote reassuringly.

After getting a quick run-down on the case and its similarities to Dina Ali's, he started tweeting in support of Rahaf. 'Extremely worried that Saudi woman Rahaf Mohammed al-Qunun will face similar fate & abuse if she is forced back from #Thailand,' he said, linking to an earlier article about Dina Ali. 'She wants to seek asylum, currently being kept at #Bangkok airport hotel by representatives of #SaudiArabia embassy. #FreeRahaf'.[7] This was a significant move. Now it wasn't just Saudi activists and friends of Rahaf tweeting about her cause. If HRW was worried about Rahaf's fate and publicly willing to lobby for her, this would certainly help gain the attention of the UN and foreign embassies in Thailand.

But Phil couldn't go to the airport and be with Rahaf. He thought he needed to stay in the city and work the phones to lobby the UN. So, by 5 pm Sydney time, there was still no journalist or independent witness who had committed to visiting Rahaf at the airport hotel.

The thought of Rahaf being deported was absolutely gut-wrenching. In the wake of Dina Ali's forced repatriation, HRW had warned that 'Saudi women fleeing their family or the country can face so-called "honour" violence or other serious harm if returned against their will.'[8] Rahaf was in a very dangerous position. And despite all the tweets and online support, the 18-year-old asylum seeker was still alone, awaiting a forced deportation in a little over 22 hours to an unknown fate.

No reporter had been at the airport filming what they did to Dina Ali. No one had shouted questions at the officials and demanded to know why they were forcing an adult woman back to a dangerous and uncertain future against her will. I'd always thought if there had been, perhaps Dina Ali's uncles wouldn't have been able to tape up her hands and legs and drag her screaming onto the plane.

I began to do the calculations. If there was a flight leaving Sydney tonight, I could get there before the Kuwait Airways flight at 11.15

am. My husband arrived home to find me frantically searching for flights to Bangkok. Reuben, who is used to me running off on crazy adventures, barely blinked. 'How important is it?' he asked.

I gave him the quick recap. 'I don't know if me going will make a difference,' I explained. 'But if I don't do as much as I can, I will feel terribly guilty.'

'So go,' he said.

The cheapest flight I could find was with Emirates: $2300 to leave Sydney at 8.40 pm, arriving in Bangkok at 1.30 am local time. I looked at the clock. It was 5.20 pm. I had only a few minutes before the sales for that flight closed. My hands shook as I punched in my credit card details. Was it even going to work? What if Thai Immigration disappeared Rahaf hours before the flight? What if I flew all the way there for nothing? The website slowly processed my details. Waiting...waiting...confirmed!

Reuben helped me collect some socks and a jacket as I frantically shoved some undies and a few T-shirts into a small suitcase. We ran outside and jumped in the car. I had about 20 minutes to get to the airport before check-in closed. I messaged Rahaf.

'Hi, I'm coming to Bangkok. I land at 1 am on Emirates.'

Her reply was swift and blunt. 'Thankyou. I do appreciate it. I waiting for a saviour or death.'

I really didn't want Rahaf to get her hopes up. After all, there was no guarantee my presence would be of any help. 'I can't promise I can stop it,' I wrote as we raced to the airport. 'I just hope my presence helps. That the Thais are embarrassed and refuse to let it happen.'

I filled Reuben in on all the details as we drove. We arrived at Departures and I jumped out with my small suitcase. Reuben came around to hug me goodbye and I held him tight. I promised I'd be careful, before waving goodbye and racing over to the check-in counter. I didn't let on to Reuben how nervous I really was. A huge knot was forming in the pit of my stomach. It was a big gamble. I had no idea how the next 24 hours were going to play out.

The Emirates check-in lady took my passport and clicked her tongue disapprovingly. *Shit.* What was wrong? 'Your seat's pretty bad. Right in the middle of two others. Would you like an exit row?' she looked up and said, smiling.

'Thank you,' I said. This had to be a good omen. I headed through passport control and straight to my gate, where they were just beginning to board. Snapping a selfie at the gate, I sent it to Rahaf as I settled down in my seat. 'Just waiting to get on my plane! I arrive 1.30 am Monday morning. Flight on Kuwait airways is at 11.30 am.'

She called me on WhatsApp straight away. 'Someone knocked on my door. They say I have five minutes to get out. I think it was Thai police,' Rahaf said urgently.

Oh, fuck. 'Tell them that you have a UN lawyer coming. And that you need to wait for your lawyer,' I suggested. I hoped that Phil Robertson from HRW was having some luck with his calls.

'How long will you be?' Rahaf asked.

'This flight takes at least nine hours,' I told her. 'But I will come straight to your room when I land. Call Phil Robertson if they try again to make you leave. He was told by Thai contacts the plan is still to put you on the 11.15 am Kuwait Airways flight.'

I had to go. The plane was about to take off. 'I will call you as soon as I land,' I promised.

'Okay, thank you,' said Rahaf.

As the plane taxied from the gate, I tapped out one more quick message to Rahaf. 'Tell them that you will refuse. You will cry and scream. If you disappear, I will wait at the gate,' I wrote. 'If I can't find you, I will be there. Filming and yelling. Be calm. Try and sleep a little! You need to have strength tomorrow. Have some rest x.'

'I'm waiting for you,' she replied. 'Sophie plz help me. I might disappear in anytime.'

It would feel like the longest flight of my life. Drifting off to sleep a few times, I kept jolting awake, forgetting where I was and what was happening. The knot in my stomach grew the closer we got to Thailand.

Bangkok, Thailand, 7–11 January 2019

When the plane touched down on a warm Bangkok night, a message from Rahaf popped up straight away. Phew, she still had her phone.

'Sophie, where are you?' she wrote.

'Hey! I'm here! Are you there? Are you okay?'

'Yes. Okay. You can come right??' she replied.

'Yes. Just need to find the hotel. Coming.'

I hurried off the plane as fast as I could. Bangkok's airport was packed, hampering my progress. Through the heaving masses I spotted the transit sign, but I didn't have a connecting flight booked. Would they let me through? I smiled at the female security guard and casually tried to walk past her into the line.

'Where your ticket, miss?' *Fuck*.

'Oh, Emirates hasn't given it to me yet,' I bluffed.

'What about your e-ticket?' she demanded.

I got out my phone and tried to look as if I was searching for an onwards ticket. 'Oh, my 3G is not working in Thailand!' I exclaimed. 'What am I going to do?'

She gave me a strongly disapproving look.

'Please?' I begged, sounding as stressed and desperate as I felt. Sighing, she stepped aside and let me through.

I took a deep breath as I took out my laptop for scanning. *So far, so good*. After collecting my bags, I found a map and spotted the hotel. Concourse G. My plane had been a bit late to get in and it was now 3.30 am Bangkok time. 'Coming,' I messaged Rahaf as I hurried to the far end of the terminal.

I gathered myself before calmly walking into the Miracle Transit Hotel reception.

'Hello, miss, how can we help you?' asked the friendly receptionist behind the counter.

'I just need a room for the day,' I said.

'We only do it for six-hour sessions,' she replied. 'It's $200 US per six-hour block.'

'Okay, just one six-hour block, please,' I said.

'Your ticket, please?' she asked.

Not again. 'That's my problem,' I said, feigning exasperation. 'I'm waiting to try and get on this Emirates flight and they haven't given me the ticket yet!'

She narrowed her eyes.

I quickly produced my purse. 'So, $200 US you said? No problem,' I smiled hopefully, handing over my credit card.

She smiled and took it. *Thank God*.

I got my room key and walked down past the reception and breakfast buffet. There were only two levels in the small hotel, and

Rahaf was downstairs in room 303. I went down the escalator and wandered the corridor, rolling my little black suitcase and acting like a confused tourist as I checked out how Rahaf's room was being monitored. A hotel staffer was manning a desk just around the corner from her room while a Thai security officer sat watching at the top of the escalator.

Letting myself into my room, I was a bit worried. I'd hoped Rahaf could sneak from her room to mine without anyone noticing and then stay here until the 11.15 am flight left. But this wasn't going to be easy. The hotel was much smaller than I'd thought, and the guards would clearly be able to see her moving.

I gave Rahaf a call. 'Hey! I'm here. Upstairs! Room 606.'

'Hi! You're here!' said Rahaf, sounding pleased.

I told her about the security I had seen outside her room

'This is who is watching me,' she explained. 'They won't let me out of the hotel.'

I thought it over. 'Let's not blow my cover yet,' I said. 'If I come to your room now, they might make me leave straight away. So I will go sit in the breakfast area next to the reception and have a cup of tea. Come up so I can see what the guard does, but let's not show them yet that we know each other.'

'Okay. I will come up,' said Rahaf.

I came out of my room and wandered into the buffet. Making myself a cup of tea, I sat down by the window. A minute later, a petite teenage girl with a short dark bob, dressed in jeans and a sports T-shirt, walked down the hallway. Rahaf gave me a sneaky smile and I grinned back. The security guard who had been at the top of the stairs followed her up the hallway, hovering behind her as she took a seat near me at the buffet table.

She sat down and typed me a message. 'What should I do?'

It was 4.30 am. 'Did you have any sleep?' I asked.

'No, only one hour since three days.'

'I will sit in the lobby and watch so they can't get you. So go to sleep for a few hours,' I told her. 'If you don't have one or two hours of sleep then you won't have energy at the crucial moment. I'm sitting here watching. No one can take you now. Sleep just a little so you can think properly.'

Rahaf smiled at me. 'Yesss I can sleep now. Thanks,' she wrote back.

She got up and walked back down to her room, closely trailed by the security guard.

I made another cup of tea and settled into a low-backed chair by the window, looking out onto the busy terminal below. It was soon 5.30 am. My ABC colleague and Bangkok correspondent Liam Cochrane messaged me to say that he had arrived at the airport. The ABC News bosses' initial reluctance to allow Liam to buy a ticket and enter the transit area had changed as Rahaf's desperate Twitter messages began to get coverage from cable news channels around the world. The #SaveRahaf hashtag started by her friends was now trending in Australia and being retweeted thousands of times.[9]

About half an hour later, Liam entered the breakfast room and I gave him a big hug. It was a huge relief to have him there. Now there were at least two of us to witness Rahaf's fate. We nibbled on the croissants from the buffet and pretended to be two mates off on a holiday somewhere.

At this stage, while Rahaf's tweets had gone global, the UNHCR had still not reached out to Rahaf or confirmed to Phil Robertson from HRW that they would officially respond to Rahaf's tweets claiming she needed protection and asylum from Saudi Arabia.

I'd made contact with Drewery Drake, a London-based former Amnesty International researcher on human rights in the Middle East. He had spoken with UNHCR regional staff who had told him they were now very aware of Rahaf's case, but they'd refused to confirm if they would come to the airport. Drewery noted that while Rahaf had been asking for the UN and tweeting at them, she had not yet officially or publicly made a claim for asylum to the Thai authorities. He advised that Rahaf should do this as soon as possible, using a magic sequence of words that could help spur the UN into providing assistance. 'It is absolutely critical to say to a Thai official, face to face, her name and where she's from, and that she wants to seek asylum since she has a well-founded fear that her government will be unwilling or unable to protect her,' messaged Drewery. 'She should ask – clearly – to be given an opportunity to seek asylum with the relevant Thai authorities. Make sure she says the claim for asylum loudly and within the earshot of witnesses.'

If Rahaf did not do this soon, warned Drewery, the Thais could say she had never sought asylum. This would make it much easier to deport her, though since Thailand is not a signatory to the UN Refugee Convention, they were officially under no obligation to hear her claim. (The country has a history of returning refugees to the country they are fleeing, including China, Pakistan and Turkey.)

By that time, it was past 6 am. HRW's Phil Robertson had woken up and agreed with Drewery's advice for Rahaf to make an official asylum claim as soon as possible. Rahaf had barely slept. I could see from Twitter that she was awake, sending tweets and videos to ambassadors, pleading for them to help her seek asylum.

I gave her a call to let her know what Phil and Drewery had advised. 'Tell the ladies at the hotel desk that you need to see immigration officers about your case. And then Phil and Drewery say you need to ask like this, "I want to claim asylum with the UNHCR,"' I explained.

'Urgh, my English is bad. I hope I can talk with them,' said Rahaf.

A few minutes later she came back into the breakfast room, with the security guard trailing her. She gave me a little smile and walked up to the hotel reception desk. 'I want to see Immigration,' she said loudly to the staff and the guard. 'I want to seek asylum.'

The ladies at reception barely looked up from their desk. 'You supposed to stay in your room,' one lady said to Rahaf as she continued to stand there.

'I need to see Immigration,' Rahaf said slowly, louder this time.

The reception ladies turned to each other and chatted in Thai. 'Okay, we call,' one said.

Rahaf sat in a chair in the foyer. After half an hour, Immigration still had not arrived. Rahaf began to look more anxious. 'Do you think they deliberately delay?' she messaged.

'Maybe,' I replied.

I started tweeting about what I had witnessed. 'There are guards outside Rahaf's hotel room. It's 6.20 am in Thailand. She's been threatened to be put on the 11.15 am @KuwaitAirways flight. She's been denied access to a lawyer. She wants to speak to @UNHCRThailand and claim asylum #SaveRahaf'.[10]

As we waited to see if Thai Immigration would come, Rahaf sent me a screenshot of some of the advice she was getting on Twitter. A

former British diplomat, Craig Murray, with 60,000 followers, sent this advice for her to follow if they tried to force her onto the plane: 'Rahaf if you see this,' he wrote, 'go limp, be dead weight, then kick as hard as you can when they carry you and above all scream hard and do not stop screaming, especially on the plane. Resist being sat down with all your might. Try to buy time.'[11]

'I'm scared,' Rahaf wrote to me.

'We hope it won't get to that,' I replied.

By now, the media coverage of Rahaf's story was exploding. Phil Robertson was interviewed about Rahaf's case on the BBC News, and by 8 am, Rahaf's story was the leading item on the BBC News bulletin. Rahaf had done a phone interview with the AFP news agency, and by that morning the article was being republished by news websites around the world, with the headline 'Saudi woman held at Bangkok airport says fears death if repatriated'.[12] Importantly, the piece gave details of the Thai authorities' plans, with the country's immigration chief Surachate Hakparn confirming that Rahaf would be sent back to Saudi Arabia by Monday morning and that Thai authorities had contacted the 'Saudi Arabia embassy to coordinate'. BBC World tweeted a headline that said 'Saudi embassy says woman "still has her passport"'. Rahaf quickly retweeted the piece saying, 'They are liars!!!!!'[13]

Making Rahaf's situation all the more dangerous was that her father was an important public official in Saudi Arabia. He had been the governor of Al Sulaimi, a small governate in Ha'il region, since 2012. Her relationship to him was now public on Twitter and being discussed in the Saudi media. It was clear how high the stakes were. Not only had she renounced Islam publicly, which is punishable by death in Saudi Arabia, but her family had serious clout. There was no way she could be sent back safely.

A popular Saudi television program Ya Hala interviewed a Saudi official from the Bangkok embassy. He denied that Rahaf's passport had been taken (which was untrue) and confirmed that the Saudi embassy had called Thai authorities at the request of Rahaf's father after he noticed she had escaped.[14] He also claimed that Rahaf did not have a valid visa to Australia – another lie, as Rahaf had messaged me a photo of her visa before I'd flown out of Sydney.

The media arm of the Saudi Ministry of Foreign Affairs were also actively promoting disinformation about Rahaf's case, tweeting a media release headed 'The Fact About What Happened to the Girl Who Claims to Have Fled from Her Family to Thailand for Reasons of Family Violence'.[15] They claimed, 'The embassy does not have the authority to stop her at the airport or anywhere else.' But we had seen in Dina Ali's case how the Saudi embassy had pressured Filipino Immigration to detain her and confiscate her passport. Plus, this was a country that three months earlier had flown operatives to another country to murder and cut up a *Washington Post* columnist they didn't like, so who were the Saudis kidding?

'She was stopped by the airport authorities for violating the laws' was another claim, again incorrect. Rahaf had been detained as soon as she got off the Kuwait Airways flight. She was planning to enter Thailand on a tourist visa, which can be granted on arrival for Saudi citizens, stay there a few days and then continue to Australia, for which she had a valid tourist visa.

The most ominous 'fact' from the Saudi Ministry of Foreign Affairs was this: 'The embassy is in constant contact with her family. She will be deported to the State of Kuwait where her family live.'

Just after 8 am, more than an hour and a half after Rahaf had requested to speak with Immigration, a Thai immigration official in a crisp white suit arrived at the reception of the Miracle Transit Hotel. The official barely paused at the hotel door, just popping his head in to tell Rahaf she wasn't allowed out. Rahaf tried to talk but he did not allow her to make her plea for asylum; instead, he quickly and loudly spoke over the teenager.

'We will come and get you at 9 am, okay?' he said, before turning and marching off.

As he left, Rahaf turned and shot me a look of panic. This was the first confirmation of what time they would try to grab her. She legged it downstairs to her room.

'Sophieeeeee, people who know my father told me he planned to do a big problem to me,' she wrote once she got back inside. 'My father is rich and has power and everyone standing with him.'

'Okay, just relax,' I wrote back. I didn't want to be outside filming as they tried to make Rahaf get on the plane. They might

detain me before I could film the crucial moment. It would be better if I went down to her room and recorded what they tried to do from that side. I talked it over with my colleague Liam Cochrane. It made sense if he stayed here and kept watch, updating us on the movements of officials and security.

'I will come to your room?' I wrote.

'Okay,' Rahaf replied.

I wheeled my little black suitcase along the hall near the stairs down to Rahaf's level, doing my best to again look like a lost tourist. The security guard who had been keeping watch over Rahaf was sitting in his chair at the top of the escalator. His eyes were closed and his back hunched. It looked like he had dozed off.

I swiftly nipped down the stairs and knocked at room 303. Rahaf opened the door and ushered me inside, grinning widely.

'Lovely to properly meet you!' I exclaimed, as we gave each other a quick hug, laughing at the absurdity of it all.

Rahaf carefully locked the door behind me and put the chain lock across the entrance. She added a small chair in front of the door for good measure. It didn't look like she was going to go anywhere.

The room was a small twin-bed set-up, with a floor-to-ceiling window that looked directly onto the departure level. Behind a heavy curtain, tourists busily wheeled their suitcases just metres away from where Rahaf was making her pleas of freedom to the world. There was a TV on the wall but all it showed was the internal flights channel, so even though we had been told that Rahaf's story was now leading the BBC World News bulletin, we couldn't watch it. Rahaf set up a digital war room on her bed. She had two phones on charge and was constantly tweeting and checking her WhatsApp. By now it was nearly 9 am, the time at which the Thai officials had warned they would collect Rahaf to put her on the 11.15 am flight.

Suddenly, there was a knock on the door. 'Miss? Miss? Your flight, it's time to go?' a voice called from the hallway. It sounded like one of the ladies from reception. Perhaps it hadn't occurred to Immigration yet that Rahaf was going to put up a fight. Rahaf walked towards the door.

'No, I'm not going!' she called back.

The person outside hesitated for a bit before it sounded like they walked away. Rahaf sat down on the bed. It felt like it was all about

to kick off. Two minutes later the hotel room phone rang. We just looked at each other and didn't answer it.

'I'm scared,' she said quietly as I filmed on my phone. 'My father wants me back. People said, "They will kill you." My cousins.'

'What do you want?' I asked.

Rahaf paused for a second. 'To be free,' she said simply. 'To do what I want. That's it.'

Human Rights Watch's Phil Robertson was still in constant touch with us on WhatsApp. He advised that Rahaf should make a video of her asylum claim that the Thais has refused to let her make. If she posted it on Twitter, Thai immigration authorities couldn't deny that she had attempted to seek protection in Thailand – a claim they were legally obliged to hear under international law. Under the provisions of non-refoulment, no matter what convention any country has or hasn't signed, authorities are not allowed to expel an asylum seeker to their country of origin until they assess their refugee claim and find it to be not valid.

I sat on the bed holding up my phone, recording Rahaf as she looked straight into the camera, speaking slowly in English. 'I'm not leaving my room until I see UNHCR. I want asylum,' she said defiantly.

We sent the video to Phil.

'Stay strong,' he wrote back. 'Hold tight. Block the door with everything you've got. And hope the Thais will try to talk it out.'

I filmed as Rahaf dragged a small table to join the chair stacked in front of the door. She pushed the table right up against the frame and stacked the chair on top of it. She then pulled one of the twin bed mattresses off its base, stacking it behind the table and the chairs before deciding she might as well add the bed base too. She took a step back and proudly examined her barricade.

At just after 9 am, Phil posted the video we had just filmed on Twitter, saying: 'Video from @rahaf84427714 just sent from her hotel room at the #Bangkok airport. She has barricaded herself in the room & says she will not leave until she is able to see #UNHCR. Why is #Thailand not letting @Refugees see her for refugee status determination? @hrw #SaveRahaf'.[16]

Thousands of Twitter replies started pouring in.

'Rahaf, make sure you have the door jammed up good,' advised an American woman. 'Fill the tub up w/ water to be able to drink & flush the water in the toilet in case they turn water off. Keep phone/extra battery sources plugged in at all times. Keep the curtains drawn so no one can peek through. Hang tight!'

'Yell. Scream. Let everyone around you HEAR,' tweeted another. 'Fight Rahaf, kick and scream girl!'

A concerned German was trying to help. 'I have contacted the German embassy and Kuwait Airways, but no reaction. What else can I do?' asked Maik.

Some people were reaching out directly to offer help, but many were disingenuous. 'Look at this!' Rahaf showed me a message she'd just received on Twitter. Someone was offering to come to Bangkok airport and help her escape. 'He said if I give him 20,000 dollars cash, he will help me,' Rahaf read out.

'I wouldn't trust that. I'd ignore it,' I said.

Our internet was slow. While we could see that massive numbers of people around the world were engaging with Rahaf and calling on her to be given help by the UN, it was hard for us to stay on top of. Phil Robertson kept updating us to what was happening outside.

'Canadian ambassador on warpath. Banging on Thais,' he updated us.

Rahaf kept up the tweeting, appealing to ambassadors using the official UN language she had found online. 'Based on the 1951 Convention and the 1967 Protocol, I'm rahaf mohmed, formally seeking a refugee status to any country that would protect me from getting harmed or killed due to leaving my religion and torture from my family,' she tweeted. 'I seek protection in particular from the following country Canada/United States/Australia/United kingdom, I ask any if it Representatives to contact me.'[17]

It was now just before 10 am and no one had come back to the door. Rahaf and I sat on the bed and chatted. I asked why she wanted to go to Australia.

'Because I have a friend there and she said it's a good country. They have rights for women. I can work, I can study there,' she explained.

'What did you learn about women in Australia?' I asked.

'They have everything!' Rahaf said, her eyes shining. 'They can do everything. Everything we can't do.'

My ABC news colleague Liam Cochrane was still keeping watch upstairs in the lobby. 'Four Thai officials at lobby,' he messaged. 'Yellow polos, name tags. Immigration police.'

'They coming?' I asked. 'What's happening?'

'They're standing around the lobby,' he wrote. 'There are 10+ Thai officials.'

Liam had been joined upstairs in the hotel lobby by BBC and CNN reporters and camera operators. BBC correspondent Jonathan Head tweeted, 'Lots of immigration officials waiting at transit hotel preparing to force @rahaf84437714 onto a flight back to Kuwait. Not allowing any filming. They are forcing anyone caught filming to delete.'[18]

Rahaf had set up her Twitter account only the night before. In the space of 24 hours she had accumulated nearly 30,000 followers, with more than half a million tweets published carrying the #SaveRahaf hashtag.[19] Support on Twitter was pouring in, from normal citizens to high-profile celebrities and even the German ambassador to Thailand, Georg Schmidt, who tweeted: 'We share the grave concern for Rahaf Mohammed and are in contact with our Thai counterparts and the embassies of other countries she has approached for help #RahafMohamed'.[20]

Meanwhile, Egyptian author Mona Eltahawy's tweets were going viral as she urged people to get in touch with foreign embassies in Bangkok and demand action to protect Rahaf. 'The American Embassy, and all the other embassies were being inundated with phone calls!' Mona later said. 'This kind of small dedicated army also went into place, that was just to call embassies, so they'd be like, "I'm on the phone to all the embassies," and that's all they would do. It was incredible to just see how many people were invested in helping Rahaf. People were telling me, "I can't go to sleep. Is she okay?"'

As the Twitterverse went nuts, we received a new message from Phil Robertson. In the wake of Rahaf's plea to the UN and the media coverage, he'd been told that the UN were sending a team to the airport. However, it was unclear if the Thais would let them into see Rahaf or if they would try to deport her before the UN team arrived. Liam messaged to let me know that AP and Reuters news agencies had photographers and cameramen at the gate where

the Kuwait Airways flight would leave from. It felt like everyone was positioning themselves for a showdown.

At 10.12 am another knock came at the door. This time a male voice with an Arabic accent called out more forcefully. 'Rahaf?'

'Yes?' she replied, walking closer to the door. 'Who are you?'

'It's Ali from Kuwait Airways,' he replied.

Rahaf's eyes widened. Ali Alanazi was the Bangkok security supervisor for Kuwait Airways, who Rahaf told me had worked with the Saudi embassy the night before to confiscate Rahaf's passport. 'Kuwait Airways. It's him!' she whispered to me. (We didn't want the Thai officials to know I was in there, in case it gave them an extra reason to try breaking down the door.)

'What do you want?' Rahaf called out.

'Open the door. What's wrong with you?' Ali replied, clearly frustrated.

'I can't open the door,' Rahaf answered defiantly.

'Huh?' said Ali.

'I can't!' she called back loudly.

'Why?' demanded Ali.

'Just because,' replied Rahaf firmly.

'Can you open the door just a bit?' said Ali.

This time Rahaf ignored him.

Two minutes later, the voice of the Thai woman came back to the door. 'Miss, do you want breakfast? You must be hungry? You want breakfast?' It seemed they were going to try all sorts of ways to entice her out. But we knew from Liam that more than ten security officials were waiting in the reception. Their intentions were clear. Rahaf was not going to be allowed just to pop up and visit the breakfast buffet.

By now it was 10.15. The Kuwait Airways flight was in an hour. I tweeted an update. 'Official from @KuwaitAirways is at Rahaf's door but she's refusing to leave #SaveRahaf', with a photo of Rahaf perched on her barricade next to the door.[21]

Phil Robertson was in constant contact with the UN and the Canadian and German embassies, who were all trying to pressure the Thais to avoid deporting Rahaf. So far it wasn't clear if their lobbying was having any impact. 'Stay ready,' Phil advised in a message. 'She will have to fight if they try to take her.'

Another knock came on the door. This time, a different Thai female voice was at the door. 'Miss? Come out and talk to us, please? Just come and talk?' Rahaf stayed quiet and so did I. Soon it would be too late to try to get Rahaf on the flight. The knocking and calling out continued for a few more minutes. Would they try to open the door with force? We sat frozen with anticipation and fear.

Liam messaged from upstairs. 'AP is reporting that they've started boarding passengers at the gate.' He promised he would message as soon as he had news that the Kuwait flight had left. We sat on the floor watching the minutes crawl past. Surely the flight would be closing soon. Had she managed to avoid getting on it?

At 11.29 am came the message from Liam that we had been waiting for. The plane had departed without Rahaf.

'Rahaf, the Kuwait Airways flight has left!' I exclaimed.

'Seriously?' she said, smiling. 'Yes!' She lay back on the bed, exhausted. All her adrenalin had been leading up to that moment. She'd won the first battle by avoiding that flight, but it wasn't clear what her next move was.

'How long are you planning on staying in the room?' I asked.

'I don't know,' she answered uncertainly. 'As long as I can? I'm so happy I'm still here and safe. But I still need to go to another country.'

The video we had recorded two hours earlier, which Phil Robertson had posted on Twitter, had begun leading news bulletins across the world. From NBC in America to BBC in the UK, Al Jazeera and ABC Australia, Rahaf's plight had become the biggest news story in the world that day. 'The dramatic plea to the UN from 18-year-old Rahaf Mohammed Al Qunun of Saudi Arabia,' announced a newsreader on NBC, playing the video of Rahaf making her asylum request and the shots of the barricaded door. 'More than a day after her arrival, 18-year-old Rahaf Mohammed Al Qunun was still barring herself in her hotel room,' announced the BBC presenter at the top of the hour. Phil was doing back-to-back interviews. 'What country allows diplomats to wander around the closed section of the airport and seize the passports of the passengers?' he said to the AFP news agency.[22]

It was now past noon. Several flights were going to Kuwait that night on different airlines, but the story had become so big it was harder for airlines to be involved in the forced deportation; Kuwait

Airways was already receiving a huge amount of negative publicity. As the bad press against the Saudi government also grew, my fear was that the kingdom would send a private jet to Bangkok, forcing Rahaf onto the plane late at night when the world's attention had moved on to something else. We also stupidly hadn't brought any food into the room before barricading ourselves in. Would they just wait it out until we were so hungry Rahaf had to open the door?

Phil messaged to let us know that officials from the UNHCR had arrived at the airport – but Thai authorities were denying them access to Rahaf. I posted a photo of Rahaf still in the room, tweeting: 'So the 11.15 am @KuwaitAirways flight has left – Rahaf is safe and still at BKK. But the Thai government is reportedly blocking @UNHCRThailand from coming to speak with her? Why? #SaveRahaf.'[23]

News from Liam that several red-bereted Thai security officers had arrived in the hotel foyer in the past 30 minutes strengthened our concern that missing the Kuwait Airways flight had only been the first hurdle, and they were not going to give up trying to get Rahaf out. 'Security have a meeting nearby,' Liam messaged from his vantage point in the lobby. 'They're saying that Rahaf has a table against the door so they can't get in and they're angry about her social media posts. They're feeling the pressure,' he wrote. 'They have a red beret security guy (awake) at the top of the escalator.'

Rahaf sat on the bed, her head in her hands. She was utterly exhausted. It had been nearly three days since she had properly slept. She decided to try to have a nap while I kept watch on the door. We worried they would try to force her to leave later when she was even more exhausted and hungry. Within a few minutes of putting her head on the pillow, she was fast asleep.

As Rahaf slept, I used the time to back up all my videos of Rahaf and send them on WhatsApp to my husband Reuben and also to Sally Neighbour, the executive producer of ABC's *Four Corners*. I was worried that if Thai security forces arrested me, they might take my phone. Sally had my back as soon as I told her I was in the room; she knew this was a huge story that we were recording as it unfolded. But not all managers at ABC News were impressed to find out I was inside. 'I am concerned about the perception you'll be portrayed as an activist,' a manager in Sydney messaged me on

WhatsApp as I sat next to the sleeping Rahaf. 'We also need to be clear how we handle the reporting – it's difficult as you're not there as a dispassionate observer.' I thought of everything that had happened in the last 24 hours. Honestly, I didn't regret a thing. I knew how important it was to be there documenting Rahaf's story. I wasn't going to walk away now because a manager in Sydney was concerned it wasn't a good look for the ABC. Thankfully, I had the full support of my *Four Corners* boss, Sally Neighbour, who stayed constantly in touch, checking I was okay.

Some good news popped up from Phil Robertson. Nadthasiri Bergman, one of Bangkok's most renowned human rights lawyers, had filed an injunction in a Thai court to try to stop Rahaf's deportation. But other messages from Phil were concerning. 'Embassies are worried about an evening flight,' Phil messaged at 3 pm. 'Worry they will decide to break down door.'

By that time, the UNHCR officials had been at the airport for three hours but were still being denied access to Rahaf to officially hear her asylum claim. Clearly frustrated, they put out a statement:

UNHCR, the UN Refugee Agency, has been following developments closely and has been trying to seek access from the Thai authorities to meet with Rahaf Mohammed Alqunun, to assess her need for international protection. UNHCR consistently advocates that refugees and asylum seekers – having been confirmed or claimed to be in need of international protection – cannot be returned to their countries of origin according to the principle of non-refoulement, which prevents states from expelling or returning persons to a territory where their life or freedom would be threatened. This principle is recognized as customary international law and is also enshrined in Thailand's other treaty obligations.

The news coverage around the world kept growing. So did the support for Rahaf on Twitter, under the hashtag #SaveRahaf, with hundreds of thousands of people around the world sending their support.

I received a message that a senior Thai immigration official had told Reuters off the record that the strategy was to negotiate with Rahaf. 'They don't want the spectacle of dragging her through the

airport,' my contact wrote. It was heartening. Perhaps the media coverage and public pressure had made it too costly for the Thais to be involved in an ugly forced deportation. The number of reporters gathered upstairs in the hotel lobby was growing by the hour.

After several hours of quiet in the room, at just after 4 pm there was suddenly movement outside the door, several people talking and walkie-talkies beeping. Rahaf was still asleep. I was worried if she didn't answer, they might try to force their way in. I tried to wake her up. 'Someone's at the door!' I whispered.

'Madam? It's okay, we won't send you back to your country, so don't be worried!' called out a female Thai voice. 'Just tell me what you want! If you want to stay here for a long time you can. Just open the door!'

Rahaf opened her eyes and was listening intently. It sounded like the Thais were not going to make her go back. 'Madam, it's okay. Just open the door!'

The teenager got out of bed and went towards the barricade. 'I want to see the UN!' she called out to those behind the door.

'They coming here!' the Thai voice replied. 'Don't worry. You don't need to go back to your home, okay? If you want to stay here, you can.'

Another Thai female voice chimed in. 'Don't worry. If you don't want to marry, you don't have to. I'm a Muslim too and I don't want to get married and it's okay!' Rahaf gave me a weird look. This wasn't what we had expected to hear, but it was welcome.

'If you just open the door, we can talk!' the woman called out again.

But this was the Thai police rather than the UN, who were still not being allowed down. Rahaf sat on her bed wrapped in a blanket, unsure of what to do. If she could really trust them, then why were they still blocking the UN?

Phil Robertson messaged. 'Don't believe it,' he warned. 'Wait for the UN.'

When Rahaf didn't respond to the friendly women offering assurances, the people at the door tried a few times to turn the door handle, but of course the door was still locked.

'I want UN!' Rahaf called out, remaining steadfast.

I asked Rahaf what the plan was now.

'I will wait for the UN. It looks like now they will help me,' she said hopefully.

'And where do you want to go?' I asked.

'Still Australia. I want to go to Australia.'

But as Rahaf's news had gone global, it appeared that Australian immigration authorities had cancelled her tourist visa. When she logged into her online account, there was now a big red flag across the top that said, 'An error has occurred.'

'It wasn't doing this yesterday!' Rahaf said in despair. 'Is it really cancelled?'

It certainly looked that way. And it would make sense. The Australians, so notoriously strict about their borders, had seen that Rahaf was an asylum seeker who was planning on entering the country on a tourist visa. It was a stark contrast to the supportive tweets and messages from the Germans and the Canadians to realise the Australians had just quietly cancelled her visa. Rahaf sat there reloading the online visa page, but it kept coming up with the red error sign. She looked utterly dejected and devastated. That Australian visa was her ticket to freedom.

Then came amazing news: Thai immigration chief Surachate Hapkarn (known in Bangkok by his nickname 'Big Joke') had just given a press conference at the airport. He had told reporters that Rahaf would not be sent back, because the Thais believed her life was at risk if she returned, announcing that the UN would soon meet with Rahaf. 'Thailand is a land of smiles. We will not send someone back to die,' Hapkarn told reporters. 'We will take care of her as best as we can.'[24]

It was an incredible turnaround from the Thais. After realizing that Rahaf would not go quietly, they had gone from insisting the teenager board her flight to promising her safe access to the UNHCR. The news of the Thai backflip came together with a tweet from Melissa Fleming, the global head of media for the UN's refugee operations. 'Dear Rahaf, my @refugees colleagues are at the airport now and are seeking access to you!' she tweeted.[25]

But Rahaf was too shattered to be excited by what seemed like really good news. She stayed on the floor, wrapped in a blanket, her head in her hands. The hours of adrenalin-filled intensity combined with the lack of food had completely drained her of energy.

'Is UNHCR really coming?' I messaged Phil. 'She's gonna faint soon I reckon.'

He wrote back at 4.46 pm. 'UNHCR is coming. Told them to bring food.'

'Rahaf, the UN is coming! Phil's been promised they really will come,' I told Rahaf. She smiled weakly. I sat down on the floor next to her to wait. It was already 5.30 pm. What was the delay? Liam had seen the UN officials walk into the lobby more than 30 minutes ago.

Finally, at 5.57 pm a knock on the door. 'Rahaf, it's UNHCR,' a voice called out in Arabic. 'We work for the UN!'

Rahaf quickly got up and walked towards the door, but after everything she wasn't just going to open the door without proof. 'Show me your ID,' she called back.

A UN business card was slipped under the door. She picked it up and looked at me excitedly.

'Yep, it's them,' I said, examining it.

'Okay!' she called happily. Rahaf dismantled her barricade, slid back the chain lock and opened the door. The two UN staff, an Arab man and a younger Asian woman, walked into the room, stepping their way through the piled-up furniture.

Rahaf and I sat on the bed and hugged and cried. It was hard to believe they were finally here. The UN staffers sat down on the floor and explained they were protection officers, here to officially hear Rahaf's claim for asylum. It was UN protocol that only UN staff be present for the claim, so I had to leave the room.

'So Rahaf definitely won't be sent back to Saudi Arabia now? You promise that?' I asked. 'She will be safe?'

'Yes, she will be safe. She won't be sent back. We have been guaranteed this by the Thais,' the young woman told me firmly.

'Okay, I'll leave,' I said.

I immediately tweeted what the UN had told me, so they and the Thais knew they would be held to that guarantee. 'UN has arrived. They are interviewing Rahaf. They gave their word that she would remain in their custody & that she is now safe. This is what they promised,' I wrote.[26]

Rahaf and I embraced tightly, both of us crying.

'Good luck,' I said, tears running down my face.

'Thank you, Sophie,' she said, hugging me tight.

'You're amazing!' I told her. 'You're so brave. Look what you've done!'

We promised to stay in touch and vowed to meet up in Sydney one day. The UN staffers promised once more that they would not let Rahaf out of their sight until she was safe. 'Even if it takes a few days,' they reassured me.

After waving goodbye, I wheeled my little black suitcase to the door before opening it slowly and peering out. I'd never confirmed publicly on Twitter that I was in the room, not wanting to increase the Thais' annoyance with Rahaf. Were they going to question or detain me? It seemed unlikely now that they were being praised for refusing the Saudis' requests and working with the UN, but I wasn't sure.

Down one end of the hall was a bunch of Thai security forces in green uniform. They were busy chatting to each other and weren't looking in my direction. At the other end were several people who appeared to have UN lanyards around their necks. I quietly closed the door behind me and walked towards the UN staffers. I introduced myself and explained my predicament. Would one of them walk upstairs with me so it looked like I was with them and the Thais didn't question me? The head of the UNHCR in Thailand, Giuseppe De Vincentiis, offered to do so. The Thai security officials didn't give us a second glance. Coming into the hotel reception, I almost didn't recognize it. It was packed out with journalists, camera operators with their tripods and dozens of Thai police officers. Only Liam knew that I had actually been in the room. The other reporters gave me strange looks. Who was this tourist chatting to the head of the UNHCR?

I thanked Giuseppe and headed straight to the reception desk. I was supposed to have checked out six hours ago. I handed my key to the smiling reception lady and waited for the trouble I was about to be in.

'Madam! Where have you been?' she exclaimed once she realized how long I had been there.

'Oh, I'm so sorry, I fell asleep,' I said sheepishly.

'No, we checked! Where have you been?' she narrowed her eyes suspiciously. 'Were you in the room with that girl?!' she demanded.

'Here, look, so sorry. Put it all on my card,' I said apologetically, handing her my credit card, not wanting to draw the attention of the nearby police.

The receptionist continued to give me disapproving looks as she rang up my bill. I took the receipt and bolted from the scene. As elated as I felt to know that the UNHCR was hearing Rahaf's claim, there was still a lot of uncertainty around what would happen next. The AP news agency was reporting that Rahaf's father and brother were due into fly into Bangkok in the coming hours. There was fever-pitch speculation that the Thais might renege on their promise to keep her safe with the UN. As Rahaf was being walked out of the airport with the UNHCR, CNN was tweeting a headline that Thai immigration officials had advised them she was being returned to the Middle East.[27]

'She's now in a secure place,' a UNHCR spokesperson told the media, trying to clarify the misleading reports. 'She's now in a state of emotional distress after all she's gone through and she needs to be given a bit of breathing space, but in the coming days, we will keep on meeting with her to try to assess her protection needs.'

I took a cab into the city and booked a room at the Royal Princess Larn Luang Hotel, where the UNHCR had told me they would bring Rahaf. Early the next day I woke to an avalanche of tweets, messages and emails. While I hadn't publicly talked about being in the room, overnight Rahaf had blown my cover, tweeting a photo of the water bottle I had given her as a goodbye gift and thanking me for staying with her.[28] With Rahaf under UNHCR lockdown and no longer giving interviews, BBC World, NBC America, NPR and a bunch of international networks wanted to interview me. The demand was overwhelming. For the second day in a row, Rahaf was the number-one story around the world.

One determined and brave teenager had blown wide open the farce that was the Saudis' PR campaign around the kingdom's treatment of women. Since taking control in 2014, Mohammad bin Salman has portrayed himself as a reformer. Rahaf's story prompted new interest in Saudi Arabia's male guardianship laws, with the control men had over women's lives there suddenly front-page news. Nourah Alharbi, Rahaf's good friend in Sydney who helped start the Twitter campaign when Rahaf was detained, firmly attributed

the success of Rahaf's case – unlike Dina Ali's – to the attention it had received on social media, telling *The Guardian*: 'Yesterday, they [social media supporters] made the difference in Rahaf's life. You saved Rahaf's life yesterday: the people, the media.'[29]

But Rahaf wasn't completely safe yet. News came through that Rahaf's father and brother had arrived in Bangkok to try to force her home, prompting the UNHCR and the Thai police to increase security at the hotel. Even though Rahaf and I were just three doors down from each other on the same floor, I wasn't allowed to see her. UNHCR protection officers were in the rooms on either side of Rahaf's, and at least eight Thai police officers were keeping watch outside her room, guarding her against any kidnap attempt by the Saudis. There was serious concern that her life was in danger, and some fear that Thai officials might be persuaded to allow Rahaf's family to access her. Al Jazeera reporter Hoda Abdel-Hamid tweeted:

> If you want to know how much in danger is @rahaf84427714 just check the amount of Saudi tweets calling for her to be hanged. Her father & bro are now in Thailand. Whatever assurances they give, don't believe a word. It will all change if they take her back home.[30]

As Rahaf stayed in the hotel under close guard, the Saudi embassy met with Thai officials on behalf of her father and brother. The Thai immigration office released a video of the meeting, showing a Saudi official speaking in Arabic through a translator and telling Thai officials: 'When she first arrived in Thailand, she opened a new site [Twitter account] and the followers reached about 45,000 within one day. I wish you had taken her phone, it would have been better than [taking] her passport.'

As Rahaf's plight remained a huge story in Australia, I was flooded with WhatsApp, Facebook and Twitter messages from everyday Australians offering to help provide assistance to Rahaf. 'This is random as, but my husband and I live on the NSW north coast,' wrote Jessica. 'We heard your story of Rahaf. I don't know if you will have any influence but if she makes it to Australia and needs somewhere to live in safety we would love to help.' Patricia wrote, 'Hi Sophie I have been watching footage of the young lady

trying to come to Australia. I have a spare room which I would like to offer her if she ever gets to Australia.'

In the wake of such public outcry over her case, the Australian government would feel pressure to take Rahaf if the UNHCR assessed her as needing resettlement. In Canberra, federal health minister Greg Hunt told reporters, 'If she is found to be a refugee, then we will give very, very, very serious consideration to a humanitarian visa.'[31]

On Wednesday 9 January, less than 48 hours after assessing Rahaf's asylum claim, the UNHCR approved it under a fast-track system for those facing immediate threats to their life and referred her case to Australia.[32] The news broke in Australia after a government leak to local media. But Rahaf was still holed up in the hotel room, and the UNHCR had told her to stay off Twitter to protect her safety, so she wasn't aware of the news.

I messaged Rahaf. 'UN is saying you are a refugee! And they're asking Australia to take you!!'

'Yes!!' she wrote back with a dancing lady and a prayer-hands emoji. 'I'm so happy!'

Inside Saudi Arabia, Rahaf's story was still trending on social media, with a new hashtag being used by those Saudi women inspired by Rahaf that roughly translates to 'remove the guardianship system or we're all leaving'.[33]

Rahaf was taken to the Australian embassy in Bangkok to process her case. The Australian foreign minister, Marise Payne, was visiting the Thai capital but told reporters Rahaf would not be leaving the city with her, 'because there are steps which are required in the process which Australia, and any other country considering such a matter, would have to go through'.[34]

I flew back to Sydney, expecting Rahaf to arrive there soon. But by the morning of Friday, 11 January, Australian officials still had not confirmed to the UN that they would be taking the Saudi teen. With Rahaf's father and brother now in the Thai capital trying to gain access to her, UN officials told me they were still incredibly worried about Rahaf's personal safety and wanted her out of Bangkok as soon as possible. 'Why is Australia taking so long?' a UN official asked me, frustrated that Australia was not acting with the urgency they felt Rahaf's case needed. Australia's callous treatment of asylum seekers made the officials wary of trusting Canberra with such

a sensitive case. Their concern was reinforced by comments made by Australia's hard-line home affairs minister, Peter Dutton, that Rahaf's case would not be given special treatment.[35]

As the Australians continued to dither, the UNHCR decided to take Rahaf to the Canadian embassy. Canada had a strong recent record of standing up to the Saudis. Five months earlier, in the wake of a barbaric Saudi crackdown and jailing of women's rights activists, Canada's foreign ministry had condemned the move and urged the release of those arrested. In response, Saudi Arabia had expelled Canada's ambassador to the kingdom and withdrawn its own ambassador from Ottawa.[36] No country had publicly supported Canada's statement.

The Canadian embassy approved Rahaf's visa in a matter of hours. As Rahaf travelled to the airport for her flight to Toronto, I called advisers to both the Australian foreign minister and prime minister, but they were unaware of these developments. Canberra had badly handled the whole affair.

From Toronto, Canadian prime minister Justin Trudeau confirmed Canada's swift moves to approve Rahaf's visa. 'Canada is a country that understands how important it is to stand up for human rights, to stand up for women's rights around the world, and I can confirm that we have accepted the UN's request,' he told reporters.[37] In Australia, Channel 9 ran news headlines claiming Rahaf had 'snubbed asylum in Australia, opting to move to Canada instead'.[38] It was deliberately misleading and appeared designed to elicit ill-feeling towards the teenage refugee (I suspect the story came from those in the government who were embarrassed at how this had played out).

In the wake of Rahaf's case, we decided to make a *Four Corners* documentary about the treatment of Saudi women and what was driving them to escape. So, for the second time in less than six days, I raced to Sydney airport to catch an international flight for Rahaf, this time to Canada.

Ottawa and Toronto, Canada, 12–18 January 2019

As I waited for my bags in Ottawa, the only Canadian airport I had been able to fly to on such short notice, TV screens in the terminal played footage of Rahaf's arrival in Toronto a few hours

earlier, where she had been personally greeted by Canadian foreign minister Chrystia Freeland. It was snowing in Toronto, but since Rahaf had come from Thailand and thought until late on the previous day that she was headed for an Australian summer, she had only a dress to wear. Before she fronted the cameras, Canadian officials found her a big grey hoodie emblazoned with 'CANADA'. In front of dozens of cameras and hundreds of well-wishers, Rahaf smiled shyly as Foreign Minister Freeland put her arm around her and introduced her to the crowd. 'This is Rahaf Al Qunun, a very brave new Canadian,' Freeland declared.

I had a few hours' sleep in Ottawa before heading to Toronto to meet Rahaf. Fortunately, Egyptian author Mona Eltahawy, whose tweets had been essential in highlighting Rahaf's case, lived close by. She and her partner, Robert, picked me up from my hotel and we embarked on a five-hour road trip south to Toronto. It was a freezing minus-ten degrees, the snowy landscape zipping past out the window as we headed down the highway to the Canadian capital.

Mona talked about how she too had been inundated with messages from people around the world who had followed Rahaf's case and brought attention to it on social media. 'People write to me and say, "Oh, my God, I stayed up all night. Ah, this is the most intense thing I have ever been a part of." And people honestly feel a part of this!' Mona told me. 'So they'll write to me and they'll say, "Thank you so much for alerting us, and thank you for what you did, you gave me a chance to help her. I'm so glad we all came together. I'm so glad we all did our bit to help this young woman." So, I honestly feel it was like each person sitting there in their living room, bedroom, wherever they happened to be, thinking, "You know what? Fuck this world, but I'm going to try and save this girl, because at least I can do something."'

In Toronto, we met Rahaf at a low-key bistro in little Italy. There were lots of hugs and laughter as Rahaf and Mona met the first time, and we sat down and chatted, all of us in disbelief at how the week had panned out. After hot soup and pizza, we posted a photo of the three of us smiling together on Twitter. A few days later, a Saudi newspaper used that photo on its front page, decrying the western women who had 'corrupted' Rahaf. Hilariously, Mona, an award-winning author, was described as

a 'red-haired pornographer' while I was captioned as the foreign minister of Canada (quite a nice promotion).[39]

Rahaf told us how she had been approached by vocal lobbyists in Canada's anti-Islam movement to pose with them for their social media page and a newspaper column. She had initially thought they were pro-refugee advocates committed to helping Saudi women, but when she googled the individuals, she realized they would be using her story to advance their Islamophobic cause. 'I don't want to meet them,' she told us firmly.

Meanwhile, she was being hounded by reporters around the globe to do interviews. After consulting with her case workers at COSTI Immigrant Services, the NGO tasked with helping Rahaf settle into her new Canadian life, Rahaf decided to do just a few interviews, speaking to me for ABC TV, as well as the Canadian public broadcaster CBC and the *New York Times*. She would also read out a prepared statement at a press conference. She hoped that if she did that, the press would then leave her alone.

Exactly a week after we had been locked in that Bangkok airport hotel room, my ABC colleagues set up a camera and lights, and Rahaf and I sat down in an empty classroom in a refugee-education centre in Toronto for what would be her first proper TV interview. In just seven days she had gone from being in fear of her life to the most recognised refugee on the planet. 'I'm trying to absorb everything that has happened,' Rahaf said, shaking her head in disbelief.

That morning, Rahaf's family had released a statement, calling their daughter 'mentally unstable' and publicly declaring that they had disowned her: 'We are the family of Mohammed Al Qanun in Saudi Arabia. We disavow the so-called "Rahaf Al-Qanun" the mentally unstable daughter who has displayed insulting and disgraceful behaviour.'[40] The teenager was clearly upset by the statement. 'How can my family disown me?' she asked quietly. 'I just wanted to be an independent person and to escape their violence, so this has upset me.'

We talked about how lucky she was, with Rahaf expressing sympathy for the millions of refugees around the Middle East who had spent years waiting for UN resettlement. News had just broken that day that eight Syrian babies had frozen to death in the past month in a refugee camp on the Syrian–Jordanian border.[41]

Rahaf was clearly blown away by the attention her case had received and was feeling slightly guilty about it. 'I was so lucky that I was accepted so quickly,' she told me. 'They knew my life was in danger.'

Rahaf had followed very closely the case of Dina Ali, who was forcibly deported from the Philippines in 2017. 'Throughout this whole ordeal I was thinking about her case. I was very, very, very scared, like in a big way, that I would disappear like her,' Rahaf said firmly. 'That's why I wrote a goodbye letter,' she explained tearfully. 'I was expecting them to enter the room and kidnap me. I was intending to end my life before they could get to me and forcibly take me back to Saudi Arabia.'

Rahaf pledged to use her newfound freedom to campaign for women's rights in Saudi Arabia. 'I want to shine a light on life in Saudi Arabia. I think that the number of women fleeing from the Saudi administration and abuse will increase,' she told me. 'I hope my story encourages other women to be brave and free. I hope my story prompts a change to the laws, especially as it's been exposed to the world.' Ending the male guardianship system would be the best option, noted Rahaf. 'I'd rather the laws in Saudi Arabia change and rather they [women] not desperately need to escape and give up everything in their lives,' she explained passionately.

The world was desperate to hear what Rahaf had to say and our interview was quickly republished around the world. The next day Rahaf gave a press conference to satisfy the overwhelming media demand for her story. Nearly every single Canadian outlet plus the BBC, *New York Times* and CNN turned up. It was mayhem as the world's press crammed into the reception area of the refugee centre. Dressed in a new woollen dress and black boots, Rahaf nervously stepped up to the podium.

After her family had disowned her, Rahaf had decided to drop Al Qunun from her name and to be known as 'Rahaf Mohammed', so she spoke under this new name. 'Thank you to everyone for reaching out and making me feel welcome in my new home,' she said nervously, smiling at the multitude of cameras in front of her. 'I am one of the lucky ones. I know that there are unlucky women who disappeared after trying to escape or who could not do anything to change their reality. Any woman who thinks of escaping, or

escaped, will be at risk of persecution. Today and for years to come, I will work in support of freedom for women around the world.'

She then asked for some time out of the limelight to adjust to her new life, make friends and learn English. She smiled and stepped away from the podium. She wasn't going to take any questions. Rahaf disappeared into her new life, and the media largely respected her request for privacy.

While I was in Canada, I also wanted to meet with Meagan Khan, a young Canadian woman who had helped out Dina Ali while she was trapped in the Philippines. Meagan was the last person to see Dina before she disappeared. Meagan hadn't spoken publicly since the incident and had never shown her face in the media; I'd been told this was because she feared for her safety from the Saudi establishment, who resented the attention she had helped give to Dina Ali's case. Perhaps in the wake of Rahaf's story she would feel like talking. I had emailed Meagan just before I flew to Canada.

On the day of Rahaf's press conference, a message popped up on my phone. Meagan Khan! She had agreed to meet me, so I jumped in a cab and headed to a small vintage café not far from downtown Toronto. It was still minus 15 outside, with sleeting snow every few hours. I arrived early and ordered a big mug of steaming American filter coffee. Soon, Meagan walked through the door. She was a stunning woman in her late 20s, dressed in high pumps and a twinset suit with pearls. But the formalities ended there. 'Sophie!' she said, giving me a huge hug, 'So nice to meet you!'

It turned out Meagan had been following every development in Rahaf's case. After witnessing the horror that unfolded for Dina Ali, Meagan felt personally invested in Rahaf's fate and was overjoyed when she was granted safe haven in Canada. Having never publicly shared the full story of what had happened to Dina, Meagan decided now was the time. 'I saw Rahaf's story on Twitter when it first started and I thought, *It's happening again*. And I couldn't believe it,' Meagan told me, tears in her eyes. 'She reminded me so much of Dina. I'm so happy Rahaf made it.'

On the morning of Monday 10 April 2017, Meagan Khan had arrived at Manila airport in the Philippines for a long stopover on her way to a holiday in Bali. Exhausted by the 16-hour flight from

Toronto, Meagan, who was travelling alone, napped in the transfer waiting room. When she woke up, at around 10.30 am, Meagan noticed another young woman in the lounge. She was petite with short cropped hair and long dark eyelashes, wearing a stripy top and hipster reading glasses. It was 24-year-old Saudi citizen Dina Ali Lasloom.

After a while, Dina approached Meagan and asked to borrow her phone because her sim card was not working. 'She said, "Something's wrong with my flight." I said, "Okay. Sure." And I gave her my cell phone,' recalled Meagan. Dina told Meagan that her passport had been confiscated by a Saudi embassy official as she had disembarked her flight from Kuwait several hours earlier. Her next flight was leaving for Sydney at 11.15 am on Philippine Airlines and would start boarding soon, but airline staff were refusing to help Dina or tell her if she would get her passport back.

Meagan offered to help Dina try to get some answers from the Philippine Airlines staff. 'They said, "I'm sorry, but an important person called and told us to hold her documents and not allow her to leave." And they did not tell me who this important person was,' said Meagan.

Dina began crying and confided to Meagan what was going on. 'She was like, "Meagan, they're not trying to help me. They're not listening to me. They're just waiting for my family to come, who wants to kill me." And that's when she started sharing. "I'm Saudi and I'm not allowed to go anywhere on my own. I'm trying to get to Australia to seek asylum."' Dina told Meagan she had escaped from a violent family and a life with no freedom to make her own decisions, showing her the burka she had just dumped in the corner. 'I couldn't believe it, to be honest. I was in complete shock,' remembered Meagan quietly.

The two young women began desperately trying to contact anyone who could help. 'We tried to call a lot of human rights numbers that we were literally googling off online. We were calling everyone,' says Meagan. 'We were literally just in mission mode. Our mission was to find someone to come into the airport and help us.' They called local embassies, police stations and newspapers in Manila, leaving dozens of voice messages pleading for someone to help. But no one agreed to come to the airport.

A few hours before Meagan had arrived, Dina told Meagan, an official from the Saudi embassy had tried to grab Dina's arm and pull her out of the lounge. Dina had screamed, and an American man had stepped in to ask what was going on, stopping the Saudi official.

As the hours went by, Meagan learnt that Dina had just turned 24 and that she had been working as an English teacher in Kuwait, but that her family went back and forth between there and Saudi Arabia. She had kept her Australian visa application secret from her family and had picked Australia because it was easier to get a visa for there than any other country. She talked about the powerful connections her family had in the Saudi government, particularly her uncles, one of whom worked for the Saudi foreign ministry and another for a large phone company in Riyadh.

'She told me she wanted to escape that. She wanted freedom,' recalled Meagan. 'She said she wanted to live her life and that her brothers were abusive to her, but she did not go into detail of the abuse. Dina said she wanted to be away from them because she didn't feel like her family loved her.'

Dina told Meagan that she had sneaked out of the family home in Kuwait at 3 am to travel to the airport. She'd booked a week's stay at a Sydney hotel and had A$4000 on her, but Dina didn't have any further plans or know anyone there – she just wanted to start a new life. 'You have somebody here who just said, "No, I'm going to give up everything I have in my life and just completely start over." She didn't have a real game plan, but she really had taken the enormous risk and she just packed her bags and left,' said Meagan. 'She said she was from a family with some wealth, but she was willing to give everything up for that freedom.'

At around 2 pm, Dina asked Meagan to record a video of her explaining her case. Dina was scared to go public with her story, but she also wanted to make sure someone had recorded evidence of what was happening, in case things got any worse. Meagan held up her phone, recording Dina from the neck down because she was too scared to show her face. 'My name is Dina Ali and I'm a Saudi woman who fled Saudi Arabia to Australia to seek asylum. I start in Philippines for transit,' Dina Ali said solemnly and urgently to the camera. 'They block me for 13 hours just because I'm a Saudi woman, with the collaboration of the Saudi embassy. If my family

come, they will kill me. If I go back to Saudi Arabia, I will be dead. Please help me. I'm recording this video to help me and know that I'm real and here.'

Meagan and Dina were sitting in the lounge eating sandwiches together, taking a break from making calls, when Dina's worst fears were realized. 'And I remember, she was sitting, eating a sandwich and she was holding it, and then she just stopped. And I looked at her and I'm like, "What's wrong?" And she said, "Meagan, they're here." And I turned around and I saw these two, and she's like, "Those are my uncles,"' remembered Meagan.

Realizing that things were about to take a terrible turn, Dina told Meagan to quickly upload the video they had recorded. The two men came over to talk to Dina, who had begun crying. Meagan took a few more photos to show people that Dina's family had arrived. 'As the uncles tried to talk to Dina, she started getting upset, and saying, "I'm not going back with you." And I was sitting back down, trying to take pictures, and at this point, her uncle got up, and he's like, "What are you doing? Don't take pictures! Give me your phone. Delete those pictures!"' explained Meagan. But she refused to let them take her phone.

Dina went up to the Philippine Airlines desk and started pleading with airline staff for help. Video that Meagan took shows a clearly distraught Dina talking to officials. 'I beg for you, I beg. No one help me. No one help me,' she cried, sounding increasingly desperate. Airline staff and other tourists turned away from Dina in embarrassment. Nobody except Meagan wanted to get involved or inconvenience themselves to help her. 'You could tell she needed help,' Meagan said sadly. 'The confrontation with her uncles happened in this room in front of all these people. And she asked these people for help and they just did not help.'

Dina's uncles left the lounge, seeming uncomfortable with Dina's yelling. Meagan and Dina huddled together, unsure what to do next. They kept calling people and asked a Saudi activist in the US to retweet Dina's video so people could be made aware of her case.

After another hour or so, a Filipino man purporting to be a lawyer arrived, promising to help get back Dina's passport and ticket. 'For the last few hours she wasn't crying because we really thought that the Filipino lawyer was going to help,' Meagan said softly. 'She was

calm now because he said, "Just wait. I'm going to get you your plane ticket and your passport back so you can get to Australia."'

With both Dina and Meagan feeling hopeful it was going to be okay, Meagan decided to take her scheduled flight to Indonesia. The two women hugged each other tightly goodbye and promised to stay in touch.

But the lawyer was not who he purported to be – it appeared he had been working for Dina's uncles the whole time. 'I heard from Dina the next morning,' Meagan said, tears welling up in her eyes. 'She called me and she was crying. And she said, "Meagan, they tricked me. The lawyer wasn't real. My uncles tricked me and they are trying to get me onto a flight back to Saudi Arabia. And they have me locked up in a room right now. My uncles beat me overnight."' Down the line, Dina was crying hysterically. 'I think I was in shock,' Meagan said. 'I was like, *What am I doing? Why did I leave?* I felt really bad.'

Meagan started sobbing as she recalled the moment. 'I felt like I left her...I felt like I left her,' she said a few times, wiping her eyes. Meagan promised to call as many people as she could and let them know what was happening. Dina told Meagan she couldn't call her back because she was using the security guard's phone and hung up. It was the last Meagan heard from Dina before she was returned to Saudi Arabia against her will.

Interviews conducted by Human Rights Watch pieced together Dina Ali's last few hours of freedom. Not long after Meagan Khan left, Dina was forced into an airport hotel room by her uncles, where she was beaten. The next day at about 12.30 pm, a security guard – assigned by the airport to watch over Dina – talked to her in the lobby. The guard, who asked to not be named, told HRW researchers that Dina was in a panicked state and that he saw bruising on her body, which she told him was the result of her uncles assaulting her. 'He was really quite horrified by what he had seen,' Adam Coogle, HRW's lead researcher on Saudi Arabia, told me.

At just after 5.15 pm, nearly 24 hours after Meagan Khan had departed, the guard saw two airline security officials and three men of Middle Eastern appearance enter the hotel and go to Dina's room. He heard her screaming and begging for help from her room, after which he saw them carry her out with duct tape on her mouth,

feet and hands. He said she was still struggling to break free when he saw them put her in a wheelchair and take her out of the hotel.[42]

Bystander footage uploaded to YouTube shows a kerfuffle in the distance as Dina is dragged screaming towards the gate at Manila airport.[43] Tourists stand around looking mildly concerned. One woman is even heard saying, 'She has human rights!' while a Filipino-looking official mutters something about the embassy being involved. But nobody does anything. 'We did hear from other passengers who landed in Riyadh that a woman was dragged onto the plane screaming,' said HRW's Adam Coogle. HRW were sent evidence that Dina Ali Lasloom, along with her two uncles, were passengers on the kingdom's national carrier Saudia flight SV871, which departed Manila at 7.01 pm on 11 April.

Dina Ali Lasloom has not been heard from publicly since.

Meagan Khan was haunted by her decision to take her scheduled flight. 'It's not worth it to leave. It's better to stay. It's not an expensive flight to be there for. It's just a phone,' Meagan sobbed. 'You know, this person's life. Give them the phone. You know, there's things I learnt in that situation that I would do differently for her...I feel like I left her.'

Apart from the brutal behaviour of the Saudi foreign ministry officials, the complicity of Filipino authorities in Dina's forced return raises serious questions that the officials involved violated international law. As a signatory to the Refugee Convention and the Convention against Torture, the Philippines is legally obliged not to return anyone to a territory where they face persecution – but on the very same day that Dina was forcibly held in Manila airport, Philippines president Rodrigo Duterte began a three-day state visit to Saudi Arabia. 'Saudi Arabia is able to get away with this because they have a lot of money and they're able to exert influence on other countries,' HRW's Adam Coogle explained. 'Unfortunately, they're quite eager to cooperate and basically throw these women under the bus, so to speak.'

As Dina's plane made its way from Manila to the Saudi capital Riyadh, Saudi activists on Twitter were frantically spreading news of what had happened to her. A hashtag began circulating on Twitter urging people to 'receive Dina at the airport', a highly unusual and risky endeavour in Saudi Arabia, where any sign of

dissent can lead to arrest and possible jail time. Photos circulated on Twitter by activists showed what they said was an unusually high security presence around the arrivals area of Terminal 2 of the Riyadh international airport at around midnight, as Dina's flight was about to land. A Reuters journalist reported that around ten Saudi activists appeared to be waiting for Dina's flight.[44]

But after the Saudia flight landed, there was no sign of Dina Ali or her uncles in the arrivals area – she had clearly been whisked away from public view. Multiple disembarking passengers interviewed by the Reuters journalist said they had seen a woman being carried onto the plane screaming. A Filipino woman said, 'I heard a lady screaming from upstairs. Then I saw two or three men carrying her. They weren't Filipino. They looked Arab.' Reuters reported that one of the Saudi activists, a 23-year-old female medical student, was detained and sent to a police station in central Riyadh simply for approaching airport security about the case.

In response to questions from reporters about Dina Ali, the Saudi embassy in Manila issued a statement calling the case a 'family matter' and saying that Dina Ali had 'returned with her relatives to the homeland'.[45]

'Nobody has forgotten Dina Lasloom,' said Egyptian author Mona Eltahawy. 'Dina Ali now has become this awful traumatising worst-case scenario for Saudi women who try to escape and seek asylum. So we don't know: is Dina Ali alive, is Dina Ali free, is Dina Ali still in detention? We have no idea.'

HRW believes that Dina Ali had been taken to one of Saudi Arabia's notorious Dar Al Reaya, women's shelters that operate more like prisons. These state-run institutions, found in cities and towns throughout Saudi Arabia, are where women who disobey the male guardianship system or 'shame' their families – including victims of domestic violence – end up. HRW's Adam Coogle told me, 'What we understand, and we've heard from sources inside Saudi Arabia, is that Dina Ali was taken to a women's shelter in Riyadh and held there for a period of time. After that the trail more or less goes cold and there's not a lot of public information.'

Inside Saudi, 24-year-old Dina Ali would now be the one with a case to answer – for the 'crime' of running away – rather than her brothers for their alleged abuses or her uncles for the kidnap

of an adult woman. This reflects the reality for women inside the kingdom, where alleged abusers are protected by the Saudi state. 'Saudi women who attempt to approach police, for example, to report abuse by a male family member for example, sometimes they go to a police station or they call the police station and somebody there will tell them, "Well, you can't come here, you can't make a complaint unless your male guardian is with you." And in many cases that person would be the abuser,' explained Coogle.

Once women are taken inside a Dar Al Reaya, they are not free to leave or use mobile phones. 'Once they go in, they can't get out,' explained Coogle. Conditions inside are overcrowded, with reports of women being beaten, mistreated and prevented from continuing their education.

There are only two ways to escape the shelters. The first is to be signed out with the permission of your official male guardian, a laughable idea if you were put in the shelter for complaining of their domestic abuse. One case documented by HRW saw a young woman remain inside a Dal Al Reaya for three years because she did not have permission from a male relative to exit.[46]

The other form of escape from the shelter seems ripped from the pages of Margaret Atwood's novel *The Handmaid's Tale*: any man who comes to the Dal Al Reaya can pick a woman to marry, and if she agrees, he can sign her out and become her male guardian. 'In some cases, we've actually seen them encourage women to get married to strangers who will take them out and then become their new male guardians,' said Coogle. 'Some women actually do that. They just say, "You know, we'll roll the dice and hopefully we'll have a better chance with a new person." Right? So, so you know, once women go in their options are very limited, if they don't want to just stay in long term what feels like detention to them.' A Saudi expert told HRW that the government will find 'bad, random men...that just came out of prison, very dysfunctional men, who use [the women in the shelters] as concubines'.[47] In such cases a judge steps in to serve as the woman's guardian to authorize the marriage, and women are then permitted to exit the shelter under the 'guardianship' of their new husband.

A 2008 case documented by HRW saw a woman flee from her home to a shelter in Riyadh due to alleged abuse by her family

members. Her father and four uncles came to the shelter, arguing it was shameful for their daughter to remain there. The men signed papers promising not to harm her. But according to an account from an official at the Saudi Ministry of Labor and Social Development, the woman was later killed.[48]

Abused women are forced to make the unbearable choice between an arranged marriage, a life of imprisonment and a return to abuse.

There have been several reports of the suicide of women inside a Dal Al Reaya. In August 2015, the Saudi English daily *Arab News* reported that a woman committed suicide inside a shelter in Mecca, with a note purportedly written by the woman saying, 'I decided to die to escape hell.'[49] The paper reported that another woman at the facility spoke of 'days of oppression and darkness', adding, 'Dying is more merciful than living in the shelter. Food, which is supposed to be the easiest thing to get, does not come easily.' In July 2017, video emerged online of several women who had climbed out a window of the Dal Al Reaya in Mecca and were purportedly threatening to kill themselves.[50]

Author Mona Eltahawy compared the treatment of women in Saudi Arabia to apartheid in South Africa and was stunned by the world's acceptance of it. 'The entire world boycotted South Africa. The entire world wanted nothing to do with this pariah state. Saudi Arabia has been doing this to women for the longest time and no one gives a fuck. This is state-sanctioned patriarchy through guardianship laws,' Mona said angrily. 'So you can be the richest woman in the world in Saudi Arabia, but you're living under this form of gender apartheid, and when these women escape, like Rahaf, they're basically saying, "Fuck this golden cage. I want my freedom."'

Mona saw Rahaf Mohammed as a 'revolutionary', with her case bringing unprecedented global attention to the plight of Saudi women. 'When Rahaf escaped, and when Rahaf forced her issue on the global consciousness, thereby forcing onto the global consciousness the status of women in Saudi Arabia, I was like, "Thank you, Rahaf!' cried Mona jubilantly. 'I have never seen such global interest in Saudi women, and what the Saudi regime does to Saudi women, as I am seeing now because of Rahaf. It took the plight of an 18-year-old

young woman to finally make the world ask, "What the fuck is Saudi Arabia doing to women, that they are escaping?'"

Saudi Arabia, 2017–19

For years inside Saudi Arabia, incredibly brave women's rights activists have been challenging the male guardianship system and trying to end the kingdom's archaic treatment of women; among the projects they campaigned on was reforming and modernising women's shelters so they really provided a sanctuary for abused women. Many Saudis were hopeful women's rights would improve after 31-year-old Mohammad bin Salman (MBS) was anointed crown prince in June 2017, next in line to the throne held by his father, the aging King Salman. As MBS sought to consolidate his power, he sold himself as a Saudi visionary, pledging to carry out much-needed economic and social reform in the kingdom and return the country to 'moderate Islam'.[51] Manal Al Sharif, a Saudi women's rights campaigner living in exile in Australia, initially thought MBS would bring welcome change to Saudi Arabia. 'I was really hopeful, and I think it wasn't only me; it was a lot of Saudi youth,' she told me in an interview at her apartment in Sydney.

The turning point for Manal to fight against the male guardianship system, she explained, was when she became a mother. 'We were travelling to Dubai, and I had my son Abdallah in my arms (he was less than one year), and my mother-in-law, she was sitting at the front seat next to my ex-husband. While we're crossing the borders, they asked her – she's a 60-year-old woman – "Who's your guardian? You're not allowed to leave the country." And she pointed to her son and she said, "He's my guardian." And that minute shocked me. I looked at Abdallah, and I said, "One day this boy will be my guardian." This boy, who I breastfed and changed his diaper, and I'm like, "I'm gonna kick his butt, if he becomes one day my guardian!"'

In 2011, Manal, then 32, decided to publicly challenge the segregated treatment of women in her homeland. She filmed herself driving a car, an illegal act in Saudi for a woman, and posted it on YouTube.[52] The young mother was briefly jailed and then left Saudi after a campaign of harassment and death threats against her. In

September 2017, when Saudi Arabia announced that they would finally lift the ban on women driving, Manal began planning a trip home to celebrate the historic moment with her fellow activists. But her enthusiasm was curbed when, one day in Sydney, she received a threatening phone call from security officials in Saudi Arabia, warning her not to tweet or talk publicly about the decision. 'Why are they shutting up a woman who fought for this right?' asked Manal.

In March 2018, just before MBS embarked on a historic visit to the United States, the kingdom began a shocking new crackdown on Saudi women's rights activists, with 28-year-old Loujain Al Hathloul the first target. The outspoken Loujain had spent 73 days in jail in 2015 after she challenged the driving ban, but she showed she could not be easily silenced, bravely continuing to speak out despite further harassment and arrests by Saudi authorities. Egyptian author Mona Eltahawy said, 'She's become this really incredible young feminist who's out there and she's outspoken and she's willing to be arrested and she's willing to engage in civil disobedience.' But the new crown prince MBS could not tolerate such dissent, particularly the thought of Loujain giving interviews or commenting during his upcoming US trip, where he hoped to bask in the glory of his pitch as Saudi Arabia's reformer-in-chief.

Loujain was living just over the border from Saudi Arabia in the United Arab Emirates, studying for her master's degree in sociological research at the Sorbonne satellite campus in Abu Dhabi. She was also still working on projects at home, including setting up a new women-run domestic violence shelter called Aminah, which means 'safe' in English. On 15 March 2018, the 28-year-old was on her way to university when her car was suddenly surrounded by security force vehicles. Loujain was handcuffed, driven to the airport and thrown onto a private jet bound for Saudi Arabia.[53]

In Australia, Manal Al Sharif was horrified to hear what had happened to her close friend and fellow activist. 'Loujain was flown on a private jet to Riyadh where she was interrogated and placed under a travel ban,' she told me. Mona Eltahawy said the Saudi kingdom view feminists the same way they view terrorists, as a threat to the state and their autocratic rule. 'This is just, again, a reminder of the complicity of other regimes that help the Saudi authorities render back their women,' she said. 'As if an escaped slave was out

there, and you like send out this alert, "This enslaved person who belongs to me, bring them back." It's fucking horrendous.'

At the same time, Loujain's husband, the well-known Saudi actor and comedian Fahad Al Butairi, was in Jordan shooting a new project. Described as the 'Seinfeld of Saudi Arabia', he was one of the most popular YouTube stars in the country – but he too was seen as a threat by MBS, who had his henchmen hunt down Fahad and drag him back to Saudi. Manal Al Sharif explained, '[Loujain's] husband was kidnapped from Jordan. He was on a filming set, and he was flown, the only passenger on a commercial flight. The same way as Loujain, he was blindfolded and handcuffed.'

Three days later, on 18 March, MBS appeared on the American *60 Minutes*. It was appalling softball journalism, with MBS given free rein to espouse the lie that he was a 'social reformer'.[54] 'Are women equal to men?' reporter Norah O'Donnell asked him.

'Absolutely,' he replied, smiling. 'We are all human beings and there is no difference.'

As MBS appeared to lie to millions of Americans, Loujain sat in jail in Riyadh. After several days she was released to house arrest, placed under a travel ban and warned not to say a word publicly or use social media.

But in May 2018, just weeks before the new driving rules were to begin, MBS instead began an unprecedented and brutal new crusade against women's rights activists. Armed security officers stormed Loujain's family home, grabbing the young activist and disappearing her off to an unknown location.[55] 'They came in with so many people, there were so many cars waiting outside,' Lina Al Hathloul, Loujain's youngest sister, said, recounting to *The Guardian* what her family told her about that night. 'It was so spectacular that we thought it couldn't be real.'[56]

MBS then rounded up the rest of Saudi Arabia's best-known female activists who had campaigned for women's right to drive, among them Aziza Al Yousef, a 60-year-old professor, mother of five and grandmother, and Eman Al Nafjan, a university professor, popular blogger and the mother of four children, the youngest only a toddler.

In Sydney, Manal Al Sharif began receiving messages from Saud Al Qahtani, an adviser to MBS. He praised her opinion pieces on

the need for women's rights in Saudi and encouraged her to return and help out. Manal said, 'They were really keen. They asked me to go to the embassy here. They were really keen to grant my son a visa.' But Manal later realized what Al Qahtani had been trying to do. 'Apparently, they were just luring me to go back to Saudi Arabia to be put in jail. I barely escaped a very ill fate that is being served by my friends who fought for women's rights in my country,' she said sadly.

Loujain, Aziza and Eman had their reputations smeared by the Saudi state media and their pictures circulated on Saudi social media with the word 'traitor' emblazoned across their foreheads.[57] Official statements accused them and three other women of forming a 'cell' and of posing a threat to state security because of their 'contact with foreign entities'.[58] Loujain's sister Alia Al Hathloul wrote, 'A government-aligned newspaper quoted sources predicting the women would get sentences of up to 20 years – or even the death penalty.'[59]

Mona Eltahawy believed MBS arrested these women just before the driving ban was lifted because he didn't want them claiming credit for reforms. 'The Saudi crown prince wanted to send a very clear message, in which he said, "Don't think that activism works. You get what we want to give you, so rights are given, they're not taken,"' said Eltahawy. Adam Coogle from Human Rights Watch agreed. 'They did not want the image that women had campaigned, had generated international pressure, and that Saudi Arabia had capitulated to that pressure. They wanted it instead to look like MBS had decided to become a benevolent ruler and liberate his women,' he said.

MBS had the women taken to an undisclosed location. Their families had no idea where they were being held, and they were terrified of speaking publicly about what happened. Inside Saudi, the news circulated on Telegram and secret chat groups. Rahaf Mohammed was one of those who heard what had happened. 'They're secret heroes, because in Saudi Arabia we're afraid to be outspoken about these issues, so these conversations are secret,' she told me in Toronto.

Loujain is believed to have been held in solitary confinement between May and September 2018. As the months went on with

no sign of her release, the young activist's family started telling the world what was happening to their sister. Walid Al Hathloul, Loujain's older brother, who lives in Canada, told *The Guardian*, 'We were in a position where we had nothing to lose. We tried to be silent, we tried everything.'[60]

Loujain's sister Alia authored a shocking piece in the *New York Times* claiming the crown prince's most important advisers had overseen the torture and sexual assault of Loujain and other activists. She wrote:

> Even today, I am torn about writing about Loujain, scared that speaking about her ordeal might harm her. But these long months and absence of hope have only increased my desperation to see the travel bans on my parents, who are in Saudi Arabia, revoked and to see my brave sister freed.

When Loujain's parents were finally allowed to visit their daughter, Alia wrote, they found her:

> shaking uncontrollably, unable to hold her grip, to walk or sit normally. They asked her about the torture reports, and she collapsed in tears. She said she had been tortured between May and August, when she was not allowed any visitors. She said she had been held in solitary confinement, beaten, waterboarded, given electric shocks, sexually harassed and threatened with rape and murder.[61]

Loujain told her family she was taken blindfolded and in the trunk of a car to a secret place where she was tortured.[62] Her parents witnessed their daughter's thighs 'blackened by bruises'. Most shockingly, Loujain told her parents that MBS's top adviser, Saud Al Qahtani, had been present as she was being tortured. 'Sometimes Mr Qahtani laughed at her, sometimes he threatened to rape and kill her and throw her body into the sewage system. Along with six of his men, she said Mr Qahtani tortured her all night during Ramadan, the Muslim month of fasting,' wrote Loujain's sister Alia. She also wrote that a delegation from the Saudi Human Rights Commission had visited Loujain after reports of her torture were first published. Alia recounted, 'She told

the delegation everything she had endured. She asked them if they would protect her. "We can't," the delegates replied.'

Three of Loujain's siblings now live in exile, desperately campaigning for her release and for their parents' travel ban to be lifted. Her brother Walid spoke about the pressure placed on Loujain to break her spirit and try to persuade her to work for MBS. 'She said she was also offered the chance to work for them and go after Saudi women living in exile to bring them to Saudi Arabia. She, of course, rejected the offer, and because of that the treatment worsened,' Walid wrote for CNN. Manal Al Sharif was told Loujain's husband, Fahad Al Butairi, had been pressured by the Saudi regime into divorcing Loujain. Fahad's Twitter account, on which his bio had declared that he was Loujain's 'proud husband', has been deleted.[63]

Human Rights Watch reported that at least two other detained women's rights activists had reported being tortured. At least one of the eight women detained had attempted to commit suicide multiple times, sources told HRW.[64] 'Who are these people doing this? I've never heard of this in my country,' a distraught Manal Al Sharif said. 'And what disheartens me is the world's indifference about what's happening to these women there!'

In March 2019, ten months after their arrests, the Saudi public prosecutor's office announced that Loujain Al Hathloul, Aziza Al Yousef, Eman Al Nafjan and seven other women were accused of 'coordinated activity to undermine the security, stability and social peace of the kingdom'.[65] They were put on trial in the Riyadh criminal court, with the exact charges against them kept secret. The regime alleged the women had 'shared information' about women's rights in Saudi Arabia with journalists, diplomats and international human rights organizations, with such contact deemed by the kingdom to be a criminal offence. 'After nearly a year of accusations in Saudi government media that these brave champions of women's rights are "foreign agents", the actual charges against them appear to be simply a list of their efforts to promote women's rights,' Michael Page, deputy Middle East director for Human Rights Watch, said.[66]

In April 2019, three of the ten activists – including Aziza Al Yousef and Eman Al Nafjan – were released to what is believed to be house arrest, though the charges against them remain and the

trial continues. Loujain Al Hathloul remained in jail. That same month, she was named by *TIME* magazine as one of the 100 most influential people of 2019.[67]

In June, US president Donald Trump cosied up to MBS at the G20 forum in Osaka, Japan, posing with him, smiling, after they met for breakfast.[68] 'It's an honour to be with the crown prince of Saudi Arabia, a friend of mine, a man who has really done things in the last five years in terms of opening up Saudi Arabia.' Trump even singled out MBS's treatment of women for praise. 'I think especially what you've done for women. I'm seeing what's happening; it's like a revolution in a very positive way,' he said, standing next to a smug-looking MBS.

In August, Loujain's older brother Walid announced that the Saudi regime had offered to release her from jail if she agreed to say she was not tortured. 'They have asked her to sign on a document where she will appear on video to deny the torture and harassment. That was part of a deal to release her,' Walid tweeted.[69] But Loujain refused to be part of what she called a 'cover-up' for MBS's highest adviser, Saud Al Qahtani, who, she maintains, oversaw her torture. Walid described, 'When the state security asked her to sign the document for the video release, she immediately ripped the document. She told them, "By asking me to sign this document, you are involved in the cover-up and you're simply trying to defend Saud al-Qahtani who was overseeing the torture."'

As of December 2019, Loujain Al Hathloul remained behind bars.

Sydney, Australia, 2018

Three months before the world learnt the name Rahaf Mohammed, two young Saudi sisters arrived at Hong Kong airport in a desperate bid for freedom. Their story is further evidence of how the Saudi state is increasingly working to enforce male guardianship outside their borders – and how the policies of many countries, including Australia, have helped the kingdom prevent women from fleeing.

On 6 September 2018, Reem and Rawan, aged 20 and 18, stood in the Hong Kong international arrivals terminal, anxious and terrified.[70] The sisters had been dreaming of fleeing for years,

to escape the physical abuse and bullying they suffered at home, and a family holiday to Sri Lanka had provided the opportunity. After securing tourist visas to Australia online, they woke at 2 am and crept into their parents' room to steal their passports. Leaving behind their abayas, they jumped into a waiting taxi and raced to Colombo airport. There, they booked a flight to Melbourne, Australia, with a short layover in Hong Kong.

On landing in Hong Kong at just after 5 pm, the women were approached by two SriLankan Airlines officials. The men, smiling, told Reem and Rawan to follow them and took their passports. Under the impression they were being helped to transit to their Cathay Pacific flight to Melbourne, Reem and Rawan followed the men gratefully.

But unbeknown to them, the SriLankan Airlines station manager at Hong Kong airport was acting on behalf of the Saudi consulate. When Reem and Rawan made it through customs and into the ticketing area, they realised things were about to go horribly wrong: the Saudi consul general in Hong Kong was waiting for them. He took the sisters' passports, telling them their Melbourne flights had been cancelled and new flights booked to Dubai. One of the sisters said that when she tried to take their passports back, her hand was slapped away by one of the men accompanying the consul general. The sisters' lawyer, Michael Vidler, told CNN, 'We allege that they were the subject of an attempted kidnapping in an international airport in a restricted area.'[71]

Petrified they were about to meet the same fate as Dina Ali, Reem and Rawan began tweeting about their plight. 'Help me please, they will kill me. I'm stuck in Hong Kong i'm saudi girl with my sister,' one of the sisters wrote desperately.

Trying to escape the Saudi consul general, Reem and Rawan rushed to the Cathay Pacific desk, where they were told their tickets had been cancelled. Distraught, the quick-thinking pair made their way to the Qantas desk and booked seats on the next flight to Melbourne, due to leave at 7 pm. They were still being trailed by the Saudi consul general, who, they said, continued to threaten and intimidate them. The sisters then watched, horrified, as the Saudi consul general approached staff at the Qantas check-in desk. The sisters' lawyer claimed the diplomat told airline staff that the

women had stolen money, were planning on seeking asylum and should not be allowed to travel.

The commotion attracted the attention of an Australian Border Force (ABF) officer stationed at Hong Kong airport. After approaching the sisters, the ABF officer made a phone call, advising the Saudi women that he was speaking to someone in Canberra. He then told the sisters their visas had been suspended and they couldn't take the flight, reportedly because he correctly suspected they were going to claim asylum in Australia.

Devastated, the women tried tweeting again about what was happening, in the hope someone would help them. 'I book another flight and they tell the immigration guy that I'm going to take asylums and he didn't allow us to go! Please my family will kill me if I back to Saudi please help us,' one of the sisters tweeted.

Reem and Rawan decided to flee the airport and head into Hong Kong. They spent the night at the first hotel they could find. The next day, as they tried to visit the French consulate, they were convinced they were being followed along the street by a man of Middle Eastern appearance, and turned back. They changed hotels, but several officers from the Hong Kong police force then turned up in their hotel lobby. Police informed the young women that missing person's reports had been issued for them, and their father and uncle were in Hong Kong to track them down.

Despite their protests, the sisters were taken to the Hong Kong main police station and held there, while they refused repeated police requests to meet with their father and uncle. After six hours, the police relented and took the sisters back to their hotel. A refugee advocate in Australia who had noticed their tweets put them in touch with a local women's shelter and a lawyer.

Four days after the ABF officer prevented the women boarding their Qantas flight, Reem and Rawan received a letter from the Department of Home Affairs, confirming that their Australian tourist visas had been cancelled: 'On 6 September 2018 you attempted to board Qantas flight QF30 from Hong Kong to Melbourne. At that time, you were interviewed by an officer of the Australian Border Force (ABF) regarding the intentions of your travel to Australia.' Noting that the women had no checked luggage and demonstrated 'limited knowledge' of tourism activities in Australia, the Australian

immigration officer told the women their answers were 'not consistent with the responses of a genuine tourist in Australia. You and your sister stated to the ABF Officer that you intended to self-drive "the road around the ocean", likely to be the Great Ocean Road of Victoria,' said the letter. 'It was noted by the ABF Officer that despite your claimed intention to drive along the Australian coast that neither you nor your sister were able to produce a driver's licence of any sort to indicate a lawful capacity to undertake your stated activity.'

When I asked the Australian home affairs minister and the immigration minister about the sisters' case, and the failure of Australian immigration officials to help two distressed young women, both ministers declined to comment directly.

It would take three more months, but the two sisters would finally be given humanitarian visas by a western country (for the safety of the women, their country of final resettlement cannot be disclosed). 'The first thing I will do, I will dance in the airport, and like I will just express all my feelings there,' Rawan told CNN as they flew out of Hong Kong.[72] 'When I look into the future, it makes me happy and relieved because finally I have rights.'

As I investigated the treatment of Reem and Rawan and the experiences of other Saudi asylum seekers in Australia, a clear pattern emerged. As the number of Saudi women seeking asylum in Australia has rapidly grown, with more than 80 Saudi women believed to have applied for protection visas since 2015, ABF officers have been specifically targeting Saudi women travellers, suspecting they will apply for asylum. This has been happening not just in airports abroad, such as Hong Kong, but also by blocking them from entering the country when they arrive at Australian airports on tourist visas and deporting them to the country they just flew in from before they can submit a proper asylum claim. Some experts believe this return of prospective asylum seekers violates Australia's international legal obligations. 'If someone arrives at Sydney Kingsford Smith [Airport] and they raise a protection claim at any time, at or before immigration, the Australian Government is required, under internal and domestic law, to hear those claims,' says Regina Jeffries, an affiliate at the University of New South Wales's Kaldor Centre for International Refugee Law. 'There are clear arguments that this return, even just

to a transit country, where they might be indirectly returned, violates principles of international law.'

In the Sydney suburb of Parramatta, I visited an apartment being used as a safe house for Saudi women. Inside, I interviewed five young Saudi women, ranging in age from 18 to 28, who had all arrived in Sydney in recent years. Some were studying English, while others had found good jobs as receptionists and secretaries. All of them were terrified of being identified, concerned their families back in Saudi Arabia could track them down, so we filmed them in silhouette and have changed their names. We chatted for hours over tea and Arabic sweets.

They all had harrowing stories of escape – from abuse, arranged marriages and the lack of control over their own destinies. 'I took everything I need. One small bag. Nothing, nothing important. Just my life and my freedom. And I escaped. It wasn't easy, it's a long journey to be here in Australia. But it's worth it,' 20-year-old Nourah told me, smiling.

Another woman called Rawan, also aged 20, said she and her sister spent five years planning their escape. 'My dad basically has the same password to everything,' she explained matter-of-factly. 'So that's when we managed how to log in to his account, on the app that gives permission for women to travel. So we logged in and did our permission ourselves, we faked it, and then we deleted the messages, uh, on his phones, so he couldn't see it.' The sisters then raced to the airport before the family could discover they were missing.

Ranya, 28, arrived in Sydney two years earlier. She said she would never forget the first day she arrived in Australia. 'The first thing that I have done was running on the street,' she told me with a grin. Ranya had never before been allowed to run outside. 'I will never forget that moment. I wanted to try to understand the feeling of jogging in the open air.'

The women told me about the cases of two young women that are well known in their small tight-knit community of Saudi women in Australia – both arrived at Sydney airport in the past two years and were turned back when they made their asylum claims clear to Australian officials. In early 2017, Ranya waited at Sydney airport for a friend to emerge from arrivals, but she never came out. 'She was planning to apply for asylum here; she came from Saudi to

Indonesia and Indonesia to Sydney,' Ranya told me. 'And since that time, I never heard from her or what happened to her. We tried to reach her, but we haven't heard from her.' Ranya is convinced the woman made it to Sydney but was returned. She says she received a phone call from Australian officials asking her if she knew the woman. On the basis of that conversation, she believed it was clear they knew she was seeking protection in Australia but they were still going to put her on the return flight. Ranya showed me messages that backed up her story, and several other activists independently confirmed her version of events.

The women in the safe house told me of another case in November 2017, when a woman known as Amal reached Sydney airport. After questioning by ABF officers, she was rejected entry on a tourist visa. Amal then asked for asylum, reportedly telling the officials she couldn't return to Saudi Arabia, but she told her friends the Australian officers did not allow her to make an asylum claim. Amal messaged Dr Taleb Al Abdulmohsen, a Saudi refugee advocate based in Germany, and told him the Australians had put her in a detention centre and did not offer her a lawyer. Dr Al Abdulmohsen told me, 'After three days they forced her deportation. She was sent back to South Korea, where she had been in transit on her way to Sydney.' The activist heard briefly from Amal once she arrived in Seoul. She told him she was panicked about being stopped by Saudi officials and didn't know where she was going next. Dr Al Abdulmohsen said he then lost contact with Amal: 'We don't know what happened to her.'

With these stories becoming famous in the community of Saudi women attempting to seek asylum, fleeing women were preparing themselves for the questioning they would receive on arrival. But they were all shocked when one of the women who arrived in late 2018 at Sydney airport was asked by ABF officers where her male guardian was. 'They started to meticulously interrogate girls at the Australian airport at least since August 2017,' Dr Al Abdulmohsen told me. 'It is getting worse.' In another case, he said, 'They ask if her male guardian allowed her to travel. They ask for his phone number to call him. They also ask her to give them her mobile phone and read her SMS, WhatsApp and other chat messages and emails, searching for signs of asylum intent,

and they meticulously search the luggage to find any signs of asylum intent such as school certificates.'

When Nourah, a 20-year-old Saudi asylum seeker, arrived at Sydney airport in November 2018, Australian Border Force officials specifically asked her why she was travelling alone and where her male guardian was. She was astonished. Here she was. She'd managed to escape all the way to Australia, but the Saudi male guardianship system was still relevant to the authorities? Rahaf Mohammed had also heard about that particular line of questioning from the Australians. When I interviewed her in Canada, she was alarmed that Australian officials seemed to be helping to enforce the kingdom's archaic male guardianship system. 'Of course, I was surprised, why would they ask where my guardian is? They should let us enter because we'd be in grave danger staying in the airport or going back!' Rahaf said firmly.

The Australian immigration minister and home affairs department refused to respond to our specific inquiries regarding the targeting of Saudi asylum seekers.

Even when Saudi women do make it to Australia, many don't feel completely safe. Several Saudi women I interviewed in Australia showed me emails and messages they had received from Saudi men living in Australia – some just trying to get the women to meet them, others taking things a step further and trying to coerce them into returning home.

I looked up the name and email address of one of the men harassing Ranya – both his Facebook and his LinkedIn profiles said that he was employed by the Saudi Ministry of Interior. The women couldn't believe the Saudis would have the gall to harass them in a free country like Australia. 'I don't know how actually they got my email address,' Ranya told me concerned. 'He said, "Don't worry, we will meet and chat." Of course, I refused, and I said no way!'

Raneen, 20, had also received several harassing messages from Saudi men in Sydney trying to convince her to return to Saudi Arabia. 'They're saying that they wanna talk to you. "Can we meet, can we meet up in a coffee shop? We can get you what you want, what you like,"' she told me. 'They say, "Nothing is going to happen to you if you go back, don't worry, we'll try to talk with your male guardian there, it's okay, nothing's going to happen to you." They

lie to us so we can go back and not talk about what's happening inside Saudi Arabia for women, so they want to keep us silent.'

Many Saudi women asylum seekers who escape have extremely difficult hurdles to overcome. With the UN not classifying Saudi Arabia as a priority country for refugee resettlement, many women spend years waiting for their asylum claims to be processed. Starting life anew, after being cut off from all family, friends and financial support, is a lonely and testing task.

For two young Saudi sisters, seeking asylum in New York all became too much. Rotana, 23, and Tala, 16, had been living with their family in Fairfax, Virginia. In November 2017, they reportedly fled their home. After their family filed missing person's reports, the girls were found by police. When they alleged their family members had abused them, they were placed in a women's shelter. The two young sisters formally made applications for asylum in the United States. Eight months later, in August 2018, they sisters left the shelter and made their way to New York. Financial records obtained by police showed that in September and October the sisters stayed at a number of high-end hotels in the city. They would go out into New York during the day, shopping together, with CCTV showing them in good health. But by mid-October the money on the girls' credit card was running out.

On the morning of 24 October, a jogger in the Hudson River Park noticed two young women who appeared to be praying together while sitting in the playground. Later that morning, just a short distance away, the bodies of Rotana and Tala, taped to each other with duct tape, were found on the rocky bank of the Hudson River.[73] The New York police department's chief of detectives, Dermot Shea, told reporters there were no signs of trauma on their bodies. 'It is entirely credible that the girls entered the water alive,' he said, adding that the tape was 'not binding them tight together – more like keeping them together'. The detective announced they had uncovered 'statements made that they would rather inflict harm on themselves and commit suicide than return to Saudi Arabia'. The New York medical examiner determined that the girls had drowned, and the cause of both deaths was ruled to be suicide.[74]

The hopelessness and fear of the New York sisters is something all the Saudi women I speak to in Australia can relate to. The majority

of Saudi women asylum seekers in Australia are still on bridging visas, even though some of them have spent nearly three years in the country. They are terrified the Australian government might reject their asylum claims and send them back. 'I live with this fear every day because I know what's going to happen to me if I went back to Saudi Arabia,' Nourah told me, tears welling in her eyes. She paused and took a deep breath. 'It's really hard to say that but I'm not going back. I prefer to kill myself because, anyway, they will kill us but with torture.'

*

Since Rahaf successfully escaped, several other young women have also managed to flee Saudi, including two sisters who fled to Georgia and two to Turkey. All four have now been successfully resettled in third countries.[75]

Since Rahaf's story aired, Saudi women seeking asylum in Australia are reportedly no longer asked where their male guardians are when they arrive alone at Australian airports.

Despite the global outrage over Jamal Khashoggi's murder and the jailing and torture of Saudi feminists, in November 2020, the G20 Leaders' Summit will be held in the Saudi Arabian capital, Riyadh.[76]

CONCLUSION

As I write, a deadly new offensive by the Syrian regime has just begun in Idlib, in Syria's north-west. There are three million civilians trapped in the last rebel-held province, the vast majority of them women and children.[1] At least 300,000 people have fled their homes there in the past month as Assad's forces have advanced, and more than 1300 have been killed by airstrikes and shelling in 2019. The rebels in Idlib are now also dominated by Islamic extremists whose brutal, intolerant rule can often resemble life under Assad. Nine years later, this opposition bears no resemblance to the pro-democracy activists like Bassel, Noura and Khaled who started the revolution. But there is no escaping Idlib. Turkey has closed its border and is currently forcibly deporting Syrian refugees back to this hellhole, as is Lebanon. Meanwhile, Syria is rarely in the headlines anymore.

My greatest fear is that our collective indifference to the mass death, atrocities and war crimes in the Middle East over the past decade has sanctioned a broader unravelling of global order. World leaders, those democratically elected and authoritarian dictators, now know exactly what they can get away with. We have proved ambivalent to their slaughter. In the absence of any sufficient deterrence, they are now liberated from any pressure to rein in their murderous ways. As a result, we are now paying an unimaginable price – a world with seemingly no rules and no truth, where disinformation thrives.

It's increasingly clear that the rise of authoritarian rule and the climate emergency will be the greatest threats to peace on our planet and for our children in the years to come. But how can we win these monumental battles when our leaders have already squandered their moral standing? When facts and evidence are 'debatable' and easily dismissed, and 'truth' is subjective?

In 2019, I worked on one of the most heartbreaking stories I've ever investigated – the Communist Party of China's brutal treatment of its Muslim Uyghur people.[2] In Xinjiang province in China's north-west, more than one million Uyghurs and other Muslim minorities have been rounded up, detained and forcibly indoctrinated.

What makes it so horrifying is the ruthless, cruel and meticulous nature of this program: families systematically torn apart, the erasure of a people, a culture, a way of life, all conducted with the assistance of a surveillance system so dystopian it's like something from a science-fiction horror movie. What is happening in Xinjiang is likely to be the largest imprisonment of people based on religion since the Holocaust. Described by experts as an act of 'cultural genocide', it is arguably one of the worst human rights abuses of our time.

So it's astounding that, in this context, Beijing's unprecedented crackdown on the Uyghurs has never been formally or openly discussed by the United Nations Security Council. Clearly the council urgently needs major reform. Too often, Russia, China and the US use their veto power to block investigations into and action on alleged human rights abuses. (Russia and China recently used the same veto power to block the delivery of aid to war-ravaged areas of Syria.)[3] A French proposal to end paralysis of the council and suspend the use of veto power in cases of recognised mass atrocities needs to be urgently implemented if the UN is to have any relevance moving into the next decade.[4] Of course, veto power is not the only problem. By the time Aleppo was besieged in 2016, there had been 16 resolutions and 54 reports presented to the Security Council on Syria that called for an end to indiscriminate attacks, a halt to the violence, increased humanitarian access, the lifting of sieges and a cessation of hostilities, among other demands. But they were all consistently ignored and flouted by governments who knew there was nothing to fear by breaking them.[5]

Now, at a time when we need our leaders to lobby to uphold global rule of law, instead our prime minister is railing against what he calls 'negative globalism'.[6] In a major foreign policy speech in October 2019, Scott Morrison gave a Trump-like sermon, declaring that sovereign nations need to eschew 'unaccountable internationalist bureaucracy' – a clear swipe at the UN system. 'We should avoid any reflex towards a negative globalism that coercively seeks to impose a mandate from an often ill-defined borderless global community. And, worse still, an unaccountable internationalist bureaucracy...We can never answer to a higher authority than the people of Australia,' he declared.

The speech appeared designed to play down the significance of

the UN when Canberra is being criticised for its brutal treatment of refugees and its failure to take tough action on climate change. What message does this send to the growing list of authoritarian leaders in our region? And why should Beijing listen to Canberra when we urge them to operate within their international legal obligations in regard to the unfolding horror in Xinjiang? We can't just pick and choose when the 'rules' apply. Our hypocrisy erodes our moral high ground and impedes our ability to lead at a time when leadership in upholding international law is so desperately needed.

Back in 2002, the world set up the International Criminal Court (ICC), which was tasked with prosecuting those responsible for war crimes, genocide and crimes against humanity. Just 15 years later, the US administration threatened to arrest and sanction ICC judges and other officials if the court proceeded with an investigation into alleged war crimes committed by Americans in Afghanistan or by Israel or other US allies.[7] 'If the court comes after us, Israel, or other US allies, we will not sit quietly,' threatened John Bolton, Trump's then US national security adviser, in September 2018. 'We will let the ICC die on its own. After all, for all intents and purposes, the ICC is already dead.'

The US went one step further in May 2019, revoking the visa of the ICC's chief prosecutor because of her attempts to investigate allegations of war crimes in Afghanistan, an act described in the *New York Times* as 'unprecedented interference by the United States into the workings of the court'. 'In the past, we have always been on the side of prosecutorial and judicial independence, and against authoritarian regimes that demand that justice bend to political power,' Stephen Rapp, the former US Ambassador-at-Large for War Crimes Issues told the *New York Times*. By revoking the visa, he said, the US put itself 'on the same side as the world's thugs and dictators'.[8] Then the ICC itself controversially shut down the Afghanistan investigation commenced by its prosecutor, seeming to bow to US pressure (the decision is currently on appeal).[9]

As the US retreats from our global rules-based system, and Russia and China waste no time in taking advantage of this chaotic environment, it is crucial that middle powers such as Australia step up and work to help restore the international rule book. Australia is well placed to do so. The nation has enjoyed 27 years of

uninterrupted economic growth, the only country in the developed world to have done so.[10] It was a founding member of the United Nations in 1945 and, despite its recent failures, has a long history of supporting international law. Australia recently passed Switzerland as the richest country in the world as measured by household median wealth – meaning the typical Australian is richer than the typical person in any other country in the world.[11] Obviously not all Australians have shared this wealth, but many of us enjoy some of the highest standards of living in the world.

So if any country should be punching above its weight in advocating human rights, humanitarian assistance and the environment, it's Australia. Yet despite this record-breaking growth and wealth, Australia's foreign-aid spending is at an historic low.[12] The Coalition government has slashed the foreign-aid budget by $11.8 billion dollars in the past six years, with Australia now spending just 0.23 per cent of gross national income (GNI) on foreign aid, the lowest level ever.[13] In comparison, the Conservative government in the United Kingdom contributes 0.7 per cent of its GNI to international aid, a figure enshrined in legislation.

Real change in this fight takes self-sacrifice. Unless we're willing to sacrifice our time, energy and money to working together to make this world a more peaceful and liveable place, we must accept that not only will things not change, but they'll get worse. And while we work to encourage our governments to act, businesses and NGOs need to step up. We cannot afford to wait any longer. Citizens must demand it. Stop waiting for everyone else to act. Why not you?

I think of Saudi woman Rahaf Mohammad and how the bravery of one 18-year-old blew wide open the claims by the Saudi prince that he is modernizing and liberating women in his country, as the world learnt the details of his kingdom's archaic male guardianship laws. Saudi Arabia's recent historic announcement that it is easing travel restrictions on women is proof of the incredible 'Rahaf effect' that's been felt around the world.[14]

I draw inspiration from UK lawyers, brave Yemeni human rights activists and the work of the Campaign Against Arms Trade, Human Rights Watch and Amnesty International, who lodged a court case in London challenging the legality of Britain's weapons sales to the Saudi regime, which are worth billions of dollars.

And they won. In June 2019, the judge ruled that the UK government's process for licensing arms exports was unlawful. As a result, the government had to immediately suspend all future licences for arms sales to Saudi Arabia.[15] In its ruling, the Court of Appeal explicitly noted the discovery of a fragment of a UK-supplied bomb at the site of an attack on a Médecins Sans Frontières Hospital in Hajjah governorate in which 19 civilians were killed.[16] The UK government is appealing the verdict, but, in the meantime, they must review the legality of current sales and cannot grant any new arms export licences for use in Yemen. An incredible, almost unthinkable victory. The case is also a testament to the power of international law when it works. The global Arms Trade Treaty of 2014, which is binding on Britain, requires countries not to export arms to countries which would use them to violate international law.

I think of Greta Thunberg who, in August 2018, sat down, alone, to strike against the lack of action over the climate emergency. Just over a year later, we have millions marching in the streets.

I also draw inspiration from the incredible, brave people of Hong Kong I met while reporting there in August 2019. Right now, there's an extraordinary movement underway, as Hong Kongers from all walks of life unite to fight for freedom and democracy in the face of authoritarian rule from Beijing. Accountants, teachers, taxi drivers, stockbrokers, lawyers – all kinds of people are on the streets, risking years in jail, to demand their freedom and be on the right side of history.

As David Rennie, the Beijing bureau chief of *The Economist*, noted: 'The confounding part of watching the Hong Kong protests...is that based on everything known about the Chinese Communist Party the protestors must lose. This must end badly.'[17] And yet the people of Hong Kong keep coming out. They refuse to be intimidated. They refuse to follow the history we think has already been written for them.

I agree with China analyst Adam Ni, who observed that 'perhaps it takes such level of obstinacy, idealism and persistence to change the world we live in and forge a better future'.[18]

It is not hope that we need in these days. It is courage.

We can't say we didn't know.

The question now is, what are you going to do about it?

Endnotes

Introduction

1   In the wake of international inaction when confronted with ethnic cleansing in Bosnia and the Rwandan genocide, there was hope the world could develop a system to ensure that crimes against humanity would never happen again. A new global political commitment emerged under the notion of 'Responsibility to Protect' or 'R2P', which was adopted by all UN member states at the 2005 World Summit. The underlying philosophy of 'R2P' is that every sovereign state has a duty and responsibility to protect its populations from genocide, war crimes, crimes against humanity and ethnic cleansing. If a state manifestly fails to protect its people from mass atrocities, the international community has a responsibility to protect civilians with or without consent of the state in question and must be prepared to take appropriate collective action in a timely and decisive manner. 'About R2P', Global Centre for the Responsibility to Protect, http://www.globalr2p.org/about_r2p.

2   John Martinkus, 'E. Timor U.N. compound besieged', *Washington Post*, 10 September 1999, https://www.washingtonpost.com/wp-srv/inatl/daily/sept99/compound10.htm.

3   'What must be done in Timor', editorial, *Sydney Morning Herald*, 8 September 1999, https://www.unsw.adfa.edu.au/school-of-humanities-and-social-sciences/timor-companion/public-outrage.

4   'Key figures on the 2014 hostilities', OCHA Occupied Palestinian Territory, 23 June 2015, https://www.ochaopt.org/content/key-figures-2014-hostilities.

5   David Miliband, 'America is fuelling our age of impunity. Just look at Yemen', *The Guardian*, 5 April 2019, https://www.theguardian.com/commentisfree/2019/apr/05/america-impunity-yemen

6   Philippe Bolopion, 'Atrocities as the new normal', Human Rights Watch, 10 December 2018, https://www.hrw.org/news/2018/12/10/atrocities-new-normal.

7   'What is moral injury', Syracuse Project, http://moralinjuryproject.syr.edu/about-moral-injury.

8   Tom Frame, 'Moral injury and the inner wounds of our time', UNSW Alumni, 14 March 2018, https://alumni.unsw.edu.au/learn-lunch-professor-tom-frame-transcript.

9   Grant H. Brenner, 'Considering collective moral injury following the 2016 election', *Contemporary Psychoanalysis*, 2017, vol.53, no.4, pp.547–60, https://www.psychologytoday.com/sites/default/files/considering_collective_moral_injury_following_the_2016_election.pdf.

Chapter 1: A Knock at the Door

1   David Kenner, 'Massacre city', *Foreign Policy*, 5 August 2011, https://foreignpolicy.com/2011/08/05/massacre-city-2/.

2   Human Rights Watch, *Human Rights Watch World Report 1993*, Syria, 1 January 1993, www.refworld.org/docid/467fca761e.html.

Chapter 2: You Want Freedom?

1   Human Rights Watch, *'We've Never Seen Such Horror': Crimes against Humanity by Syrian Security Forces*, June 2011, p.24, https://www.hrw.org/sites/default/files/reports/syria0611webwcover.pdf.

2   Human Rights Watch, *'By All Means Necessary': Individual and Command Responsibility for Crimes against Humanity in Syria*, 15 December 2011, p.7, https://www.hrw.org/sites/default/files/reports/syria1211webwcover_0.pdf.

3   UN Human Rights Council, *Assault on Medical Care in Syria*, 13 September 2013, p.5, https://www.ohchr.org/EN/HRBodies/HRC/RegularSessions/Session24/Documents/A-HRC-24-CRP-2.doc.

4   Amnesty International, *Human Slaughterhouse – Mass Hangings and Extermination at Saydnaya Prison, Syria*, 7 February 2017, https://www.amnesty.org/download/Documents/MDE2454152017ENGLISH.PDF.

5   UN Human Rights Council, *Assault on Medical Care in Syria*, p.5.

6   Hugh Macleod and Annasofie Flamand, 'Syria's crackdown: why did Fawaz die?' *Al Jazeera*, 25 May 2011, https://www.aljazeera.com/indepth/features/2011/05/20115241653186869.html.

7   Human Rights Watch, *'By All Means Necessary'*, p.2.

Chapter 3: The Bride and Groom of the Revolution

1   'At least 9 killed as thousands defy Syria's Assad', *Sydney Morning Herald*, 2 April 2011, https://www.smh.com.au/world/at-least-9-killed-as-thousands-defy-syrias-assad-20110402-1cs35.html.

2   Neil Macfarquhar and Liam Stack, 'Syrian protesters clash with security forces', 1 April 2011, *New York Times*, https://www.nytimes.com/2011/04/02/world/middleeast/02syria.html?ref=world.

3   Hugh Macleod and a reporter in Syria, 'Syria: how it all began', *Public Radio International*, 23 April 2011, https://www.pri.org/stories/2011-04-23/syria-how-it-all-began.

4   European parliamentary question, 12 December 2013, http://www.europarl.europa.eu/sides/getDoc.do?pubRef=-//EP//TEXT+WQ+E-2013-014046+0+DOC+XML+V0//EN.

5   Nada Bakri, 'Syrian forces struck northern villages, activists say', 29 May 2011, *New York Times*, https://www.nytimes.com/2011/05/30/world/middleeast/30syria.html.

6   Liam Stack, 'Video of tortured boy's corpse deepens anger in Syria', 30 May 2011, *New York Times*, https://www.nytimes.com/2011/05/31/world/middleeast/31syria.html.

7   Khaled Yacoub Oweis, 'Helicopters open fire to disperse Syrian protesters', *Reuters*, 10 June 2011, https://www.reuters.com/article/us-syria/helicopters-open-fire-to-disperse-syrian-protesters-idUSLDE73N02P20110610.

8   Anthony Shadid, 'Violent clashes as thousands protest in cities across Syria', 17 June 2011, *New York Times*, https://www.nytimes.com/2011/06/18/world/middleeast/18syria.html?src=tptw.

9   'Bassel & Noura', YouTube video, August 2011, https://www.youtube.com/watch?v=VufA6ldkyG0.

10   Alicia P.Q. Wittmeyer, 'The FP Top 100 Global Thinkers 2012', *Foreign Policy*, 26 November 2012, https://foreignpolicy.com/2012/11/26/the-fp-top-100-global-thinkers-2/.

11   Human Rights Watch, *Torture Archipelago: Arbitrary Arrests, Torture, and Enforced Disappearances in Syria's Underground Prisons since March 2011*, 3 July 2012, https://www.hrw.org/report/2012/07/03/torture-archipelago/arbitrary-arrests-torture-and-enforced-disappearances-syrias.

12   Human Rights Watch, 'Syria: Torture centers revealed', 3 July 2012, https://www.hrw.org/news/2012/07/03/syria-torture-centers-revealed.

13   Eloise Anna, 'The bride and groom of the revolution', video, BBC News, 16 September 2018, https://www.bbc.com/news/av/world-middle-east-45521494/the-bride-and-groom-of-the-revolution.

14   'Damascus Madra prison massively overcrowded', *Daily Star* (Lebanon), 29 December 2014, http://www.dailystar.com.lb/News/Middle-East/2014/Dec-29/282494-damascus-adra-prison-massively-overcrowded.ashx.

15   Alice Su, 'How one Syrian fought to the death for a free internet', Wired, 27 September 2017, https://www.wired.com/story/how-one-syrian-fought-to-the-death-for-a-free-internet.

16   Sara Yasin, 'Winners – Index Awards 2013', Index, 21 March 2013, http://www.
      indexoncensorship.org/2013/03/winners-index-awards-2013/.

17   Electronic Frontier Foundation (@EFF), tweet, 3 August 2017, https://twitter.com/EFF/
      status/893176235781627904.

18   Ian Black, 'Syrian regime document trove shows evidence of "industrial scale"
      killing of detainees', The Guardian, 22 January 2014, https://www.theguardian.com/
      world/2014/jan/20/evidence-industrial-scale-killing-syria-war-crimes?view=desktop.

19   Human Rights Watch, If the Dead Could Speak, 16 December 2015, https://www.hrw.
      org/report/2015/12/16/if-dead-could-speak/mass-deaths-and-torture-syrias-detention-
      facilities.

20   John Kerry, press statement, 10 December 2015, https://2009-2017.state.gov/secretary/
      remarks/2015/12/250541.htm.

21   Amnesty International, Human Slaughterhouse – Mass Hangings and Extermination
      at Saydnaya Prison, Syria, 7 February 2017, https://www.amnesty.org/download/
      Documents/MDE2454152017ENGLISH.PDF.

22   'Syria "exterminating detainees" – UN report', BBC News, 8 February 2016, https://
      www.bbc.com/news/world-middle-east-35521801.

23   Amnesty International, 'It Breaks the Human': Torture, Disease and Death in Syria's
      Prisons, 16 August 2016, https://www.amnestyusa.org/reports/it-breaks-the-human-
      torture-disease-and-death-in-syrias-prisons/.

24   UN Independent International Commission of Inquiry on the Syrian Arab Republic,
      Death Notifications in the Syrian Arab Republic, 27 November 2018, https://reliefweb.
      int/sites/reliefweb.int/files/resources/DeathNotificationsSyrianArabRepublic_Nov2018.
      pdf.

25   Syrian Network for Human Rights, Documentation of 72 Torture Methods the Syrian
      Regime Continues to Practice in Its Detention Centers and Military Hospitals, SNHR,
      21 October 2019, p.1, http://sn4hr.org/wp-content/pdf/english/Documentation_of_72_
      Torture_Methods_the_Syrian_Regime_Continues_to_Practice_in_Its_Detention_
      Centers_and_Military_Hospitals_en.pdf.

Chapter 4: Running for Their Lives

1   'UN deeply concerned at rising deaths from boat accidents in the Mediterranean',
      UN News, 13 May 2014, https://news.un.org/en/story/2014/05/468152-un-deeply-
      concerned-rising-deaths-boat-accidents-mediterranean.

2   'UNHCR chief expresses shock at new Mediterranean boat tragedy', UNHCR,
      12 October 2013, http://www.unhcr.org/en-au/news/press/2013/10/52594c6a6/
      unhcr-chief-expresses-shock-new-mediterranean-boat-tragedy.html?query=Malta%20
      drowned.

3   'Mediterranean crossings more deadly a year after Lampedusa tragedy', UNHCR,
      2 October 2014, https://www.unhcr.org/en-au/news/latest/2014/10/542d12de9/
      mediterranean-crossings-deadly-year-lampedusa-tragedy.html.

4   'Malta boat sinking "leaves 500 dead" – IOM', BBC News, 15 September 2014,
      https://www.bbc.com/news/world-europe-29210989.

5   Peter Walker and John Hooper, '100 children among migrants "deliberately drowned"
      in Mediterranean', The Guardian, 17 September 2014, https://www.theguardian.com/
      world/2014/sep/16/migrants-children-drowned-boat-mediterranean.

6   'UNHCR concerned over ending of rescue operation in the Mediterranean', UNHCR,
      17 October 2014, https://www.unhcr.org/en-au/news/briefing/2014/10/5440ffa16/
      unhcr-concerned-ending-rescue-operation-mediterranean.html.

7   'Frontex Joint Operation "Triton" – concerted efforts to manage migration in the
      Central Mediterranean', European Commission, 7 October 2014, http://europa.eu/
      rapid/press-release_MEMO-14-566_en.htm.

8   Julian Borger, 'EU under pressure over migrant rescue operations in the
      Mediterranean', 16 April 2015, https://www.theguardian.com/world/2015/apr/15/eu-
      states-migrant-rescue-operations-mediterranean.

9   Patrick Kingsley, Alessandra Bonomolo and Stephanie Kirchgaessner, '700 migrants feared dead in Mediterranean shipwreck', 19 April 2015, https://www.theguardian.com/world/2015/apr/19/700-migrants-feared-dead-mediterranean-shipwreck-worst-yet.

10   'Aquarius forced to end operations as Europe condemns people to drown', Médecins Sans Frontières, 6 December 2018, https://www.msf.org/aquarius-forced-end-operations-europe-condemns-people-drown.

11   'SOS Méditerranée resumes Mediterranean migrant rescues', BBC News, 21 July 2019, https://www.bbc.com/news/world-europe-49065575.

12   'Mediterranean search and rescue', Médecins Sans Frontières, https://www.msf.org.uk/country/mediterranean-search-and-rescue.

Chapter 5: The Syrian Exodus

1   Phillip Connor, 'After record migration, 80% of Syrian asylum applicants approved to stay in Europe', Pew Research Center, 13 December 2017, https://reliefweb.int/report/world/after-record-migration-80-syrian-asylum-applicants-approved-stay-europe.

2   'Number of refugees to Europe surges to record 1.3 million in 2015', Pew Research Center, 2 August 2016, http://www.pewglobal.org/2016/08/02/number-of-refugees-to-europe-surges-to-record-1-3-million-in-2015/.

3   Press Association, 'Syria assault on Latakia drives 5,000 Palestinians from refugee camp', *The Guardian*, 16 August 2011, https://www.theguardian.com/world/2011/aug/15/syria-palestinians-latakia-assault.

4   Fabrice Balanche, 'Latakia is Assad's Achilles heel', Washington Institute, 23 September 2015, https://www.washingtoninstitute.org/policy-analysis/view/latakia-is-assads-achilles-heel.

Chapter 6: Germany Opens Its Arms

1   Kate Connolly, 'Germans greet influx of refugees with free food and firebombings', *The Guardian*, 31 July 2015, https://www.theguardian.com/world/2015/jul/30/germans-greet-influx-of-refugees-free-food-fire-bombings.

2   Justin Huggler, 'Police uncover far-right plot to attack refugee shelters in Germany', *The Telegraph*, 22 October 2015, https://www.telegraph.co.uk/news/worldnews/europe/germany/11948175/Far-Right-extremists-could-attack-refugees-with-acid-or-wooden-clubs-says-German-police.html.

Chapter 7: The Saddest Little Hospital

1   Human Rights Watch, *World Report 2016*, Syria, https://www.hrw.org/world-report/2016/country-chapters/syria.

2   'Crisis update', Médecins Sans Frontières, 10 November 2015, https://www.msf.org/yemen-crisis-update—-10-november-2015; 'Key figures on the 2014 hostilities', OCHA, 23 June 2015, https://www.ochaopt.org/content/key-figures-2014-hostilities.

3   Martin Chulov, 'Isis bombing leaves scores dead at market in Baghdad', *The Guardian*, 13 August 2015, https://www.theguardian.com/world/2015/aug/13/truck-bomb-leaves-scores-dead-at-market-in-iraq.

Chapter 8: 'Surrender or Starve'

1   Siege Watch, *Out of Sight, Out of Mind: the Aftermath of Syria's Sieges*, Pax, Utrecht, 2019, https://www.paxforpeace.nl/publications/all-publications/siege-watch-final-report.

2   Siege Watch, *Out of Sight, Out of Mind: the Aftermath of Syria's Sieges*, p.34.

3   Physicians for Human Rights and Syrian American Medical Society, *Madaya: Portrait of a Syrian Town Under Siege*, 1 July 2016, p.8, https://phr.org/wp-content/uploads/2018/09/madaya-portrait-of-a-syrian-town-under-siege.pdf.

4   Ghalia Muhkalalati and Samuel Kieke, 'Aid delivers food poisoning as residents' immunity "extremely weak"', *Syria Direct*, 26 October 2015, https://syriadirect.org/news/aid-delivers-food-poisoning-as-residents'-immunity-'extremely-weak'/.

5   'Syria conflict: civilians under siege', BBC News, 7 January 2016, https://www.bbc.
       com/news/world-middle-east-35250772.
6   Physicians for Human Rights and Syrian American Medical Society, *Madaya: Portrait
       of a Syrian Town Under Siege*, p.6.
7   Ibid., p.12.
8   Sophie McNeill (@sophiemcneill), tweet, 6 January 2016, https://twitter.com/
       Sophiemcneill/status/684724898305019904.
9   Samantha Power, 'Remarks by Ambassador Samantha Power at the commemoration
       of the 70th anniversary of the first meeting of the UN General Assembly', 11 January
       2016, https://www.belfercenter.org/publication/remarks-ambassador-samantha-power-
       commemoration-70th-anniversary-first-meeting-un.
10   Louisa Loveluck and Ben Farmer, 'Britain under pressure to send RAF to airdrop aid
       to starving Syrian town', *The Telegraph*, 8 January 2016, https://www.telegraph.co.uk/
       news/worldnews/middleeast/syria/12089872/British-MPs-call-for-RAF-airdrops-of-aid-
       to-starving-Syrian-residents-of-Madaya.html.
11   David Blair, 'If the RAF can't drop food to Madaya in Syria, we shouldn't bother
       having an air force at all', *The Telegraph*, 10 January 2016.
12   Jonathan Jones, 'Images of children starving in Madaya can still shock us into action',
       The Guardian, 14 January 2016, https://www.theguardian.com/commentisfree/2016/
       jan/14/images-children-madaya-shock-syria-compassion.
13   Kareem Shaheen and agencies, 'Madaya hospital must be evacuated, says UN', *The
       Guardian*, 12 January 2016, https://www.theguardian.com/world/2016/jan/12/sick-
       must-be-evacuated-from-besieged-syrian-village-of-madaya-says-un.
14   'Siege and starvation in Madaya: immediate medical evacuations and medical resupply
       essential to save lives', Médecins Sans Frontières, 7 January 2016, https://www.msf.
       org/syria-siege-and-starvation-madaya-immediate-medical-evacuations-and-medical-
       resupply-essential-save.
15   Kareem Shaheen, 'Aid supplies reach besieged Madaya: "The first impression is
       heartbreaking"', *The Guardian*, 12 January 2016, https://www.theguardian.com/
       world/2016/jan/11/aid-supplies-reach-besieged-madaya-syria-first-impression-
       heartbreaking.
16   'Mass starvation in Madaya, Syria', CBS News, 21 January 2016, https://www.
       youtube.com/watch?v=jvWa2l8Fsmo.
17   Sophie McNeill, 'United Nations confirm images of starving children in Madaya, Syria
       tell the real story', *PM*, ABC Radio, 12 January 2016, https://www.abc.net.au/pm/
       content/2015/s4387167.htm.
18   Roy Gutman, 'Exclusive: the UN knew for months that Madaya was starving', *Foreign
       Policy*, 15 January 2016, https://foreignpolicy.com/2016/01/15/u-n-knew-for-months-
       madaya-was-starving-syria-assad/.
19   Sophie McNeill, 'Madaya: United Nations humanitarian body rejects criticism it
       acted too late to aid starving Syrians due to close ties to Assad regime', ABC News,
       20 January 2016, https://www.abc.net.au/news/2016-01-20/un-knew-about-starving-
       madaya-children-for-months-critics-say/7099786.
20   Emma Beals, 'U.N. again allowing Assad regime to edit Syria aid document', Daily
       Beast, 23 December 2016, https://www.thedailybeast.com/un-again-allowing-assad-
       regime-to-edit-syria-aid-document?ref=scroll.
21   Roy Gutman, 'How the UN let Assad edit the truth of Syria's war', 27 January 2016,
       Foreign Policy, https://foreignpolicy.com/2016/01/27/syria-madaya-starvation-united-
       nations-humanitarian-response-plan-assad-edited/.
22   Anne Barnard, Hwaida Saad and Somini Sengupta, 'Starving Syrians in Madaya are denied
       aid amid political jockeying', *New York Times*, 10 January 2016, https://www.nytimes.
       com/2016/01/11/world/middleeast/syria-starvation-madaya-siege-united-nations.html.
23   Sophie McNeill, 'Accusations UN knew of Madaya starvation crisis for months', *PM*,
       ABC Radio, 20 January 2016, https://www.abc.net.au/radio/programs/pm/accusations-
       un-knew-of-madaya-starvation-crisis/7102742.

24 Siege Watch, *First Quarterly Report on Besieged Areas in Syria*, February 2016, p.10, https://siegewatch.org/wp-content/uploads/2015/10/PAX-RAPPORT-SIEGE-WATCH-FINAL-SINGLE-PAGES-DEF.pdf.

25 Yacoub El Hillo and Kevin Kennedy, 'Joint statement on hard-to-reach and besieged communities in Syria', OCHA, 7 January 2016, https://reliefweb.int/sites/reliefweb.int/files/resources/Joint%20Statement%20by%20Yacoub%20El%20Hillo%20and%20Kevin%20Kennedy_english%20FINAL.pdf.

26 'Besieged Syrians' letter to the UN: you are "complicit" in denying aid to starving civilians', The Syria Campaign, 15 January 2016, https://medium.com/@TheSyriaCampaign/besieged-syrians-letter-to-the-un-you-are-complicit-in-denying-aid-to-starving-civilians-58dfadde8be4.

27 Physicians for Human Rights and Syrian American Medical Society, *Madaya: Portrait of a Syrian Town Under Siege*, p.9.

28 Ibid., p.8.

29 Syrian American Medical Society, 'Three boys killed by a landmine in Madaya', 30 March 2016, https://www.sams-usa.net/press_release/press-release-three-boys-killed-by-a-landmine-in-madaya/.

30 Physicians for Human Rights and Syrian American Medical Society, *Madaya: Portrait of a Syrian Town Under Siege*, p.11.

31 Sophie McNeill, 'Syria: world "watched us die and did nothing", Madaya doctor says ahead of evacuation', ABC News, 12 April 2017, https://www.abc.net.au/news/2017-04-12/madaya-world-watched-us-die-and-they-did-nothing-doctor-says/8439854.

Chapter 10: A War on Civilians

1 'Humanitarian crisis in Yemen remains the worst in the world, warns UN', *UN News*, 14 February 2019, https://news.un.org/en/story/2019/02/1032811.

2 Ahmed Baider and Lizzie Porter, 'How the Saudis are making it almost impossible to report on their war in Yemen', *New Statesman*, 22 August 2017, https://www.newstatesman.com/world/middle-east/2017/08/how-saudis-are-making-it-almost-impossible-report-their-war-yemen.

3 David D. Kirkpatrick and Saeed Al Batati, 'Ex-Yemeni leader urges truce and successor's ouster', *New York Times*, 28 March 2015, https://www.nytimes.com/2015/03/29/world/middleeast/saudi-arabia-evacuates-diplomats-from-yemeni-city-as-houthi-advance-continues.html.

4 Sophie McNeill, 'Red Cross medicine and UN flights blocked after Saudi Arabia closes all of Yemen's borders', ABC News, 8 November 2017, https://www.abc.net.au/news/2017-11-08/yemen-crisis-grows-as-port-closure-blocks-aid/9128598.

5 'Yemen conflict: Saudi-led coalition targeting civilians, UN says', BBC News, 27 January 2016, https://www.bbc.com/news/world-middle-east-35423282.

6 Ewen MacAskill, 'UN report into Saudi-led strikes in Yemen raises questions over UK role', *The Guardian*, 27 January 2016, https://www.theguardian.com/world/2016/jan/27/un-report-into-saudi-led-strikes-in-yemen-raises-questions-over-uk-role.

7 'Statement by NSC spokesperson Bernadette Meehan on the situation in Yemen', White House Office of the Press Secretary, 25 March 2015, https://obamawhitehouse.archives.gov/the-press-office/2015/03/25/statement-nsc-spokesperson-bernadette-meehan-situation-yemen.

8 Mark Mazzetti and Eric Schmitt, 'Quiet support for Saudis entangles US in Yemen', *New York Times*, 13 March 2016, https://www.nytimes.com/2016/03/14/world/middleeast/yemen-saudi-us.html.

9 House of Commons Business, Innovation and Skills and International Development Committees, *The Use of UK-manufactured Arms in Yemen*, 15 September 2016, p.27, https://publications.parliament.uk/pa/cm201617/cmselect/cmbis/679/679.pdf.

10 Peter Foster, Louisa Loveluck and Almigdad Mojalli, 'UK "will support Saudi-led assault on Yemeni rebels – but not engaging in combat"', *The Telegraph*, 27 March

2015, https://www.telegraph.co.uk/news/worldnews/middleeast/yemen/11500518/UK-will-support-Saudi-led-assault-on-Yemeni-rebels-but-not-engaging-in-combat.html.

11   House of Commons Business, Innovation and Skills and International Development Committees, *The Use of UK-manufactured Arms in Yemen*, p.8.

12   Mohammed Ghobari and Mohammed Mukhashaf, 'Saudi-led planes bomb Sanaa airport to stop Iranian plane landing', Reuters, 29 April 2015, https://www.reuters.com/article/us-yemen-security-airport-idUSKBN0NJ24120150428.

13   International Committee of the Red Cross (ICRC) employee Nourane Houas was abducted while on her way to work in Sanaa, Yemen, on 1 December 2015 – see 'ICRC statement concerning abducted staff member in Yemen', 11 August 2016, https://www.icrc.org/en/document/icrc-statement-concerning-abducted-staff-member-yemen; see also 'Three westerners kidnapped in Yemen's capital, Sanaa', BBC News, 21 December 2012, https://www.bbc.com/news/world-middle-east-20817731.

14   Nicolas Niarchos, 'How the US is making the war in Yemen worse', *New Yorker*, 22 January 2018, https://www.newyorker.com/magazine/2018/01/22/how-the-us-is-making-the-war-in-yemen-worse.

15   Agence France-Presse, '"Air strike" kills five in historic district of Sana'a', *The Guardian*, 13 June 2015, https://www.theguardian.com/world/2015/jun/12/air-strike-kills-five-sanaa-old-city-yemen.

16   Mohammed Ghobari et al., 'Air strike on missile base in Yemen capital kills 25, wounds hundreds', Reuters, https://www.reuters.com/article/us-yemen-security/air-strike-on-missile-base-in-yemen-capital-kills-25-wounds-hundreds-idUSKBN0NB0R820150420.

17   Agence France-Presse, 'UN report says Saudi-led coalition and Houthis violate human rights in Yemen', *The Telegraph*, 5 August 2016, https://www.telegraph.co.uk/news/2016/08/05/un-report-says-saudi-led-coalition-and-houthis-violate-human-rig/.

18   'Yemen: crisis update – September 2016', Médecins Sans Frontières, 27 September 2016, https://www.msf.org/yemen-crisis-update-september-2016.

19   '"A political solution is the only solution," UN says, as rising violence deepens crisis in Yemen', *UN News*, 12 August 2016, https://news.un.org/en/story/2016/08/536562-political-solution-only-solution-un-says-rising-violence-deepens-crisis-yemen.

20   'Saudi Arabia-led coalition has used UK-manufactured cluster bombs in Yemen – new evidence', Amnesty International UK, 23 May 2016, https://www.amnesty.org.uk/press-releases/saudi-arabia-led-coalition-has-used-uk-manufactured-cluster-bombs-yemen-new-evidence.

21   John Hudson, 'Exclusive: White House blocks transfer of cluster bombs to Saudi Arabia', *Foreign Policy*, 27 May 2016, https://foreignpolicy.com/2016/05/27/exclusive-white-house-blocks-transfer-of-cluster-bombs-to-saudi-arabia/.

22   Alex Emmons, 'Worried about "stigmatizing" cluster bombs, House approves more sales to Saudi Arabia', *Intercept*, 17 June 2016, https://theintercept.com/2016/06/16/worried-about-stigmatizing-cluster-bombs-house-approves-more-sales-to-saudi-arabia/.

23   Sir Michael Fallon, Statement to the House of Commons, 19 December 2016, https://hansard.parliament.uk/commons/2016-12-19/debates/B8EBA03B-5FFC-44CF-8989-883F62F675D4/Yemen.

24   'Coalition forces supporting legitimacy in Yemen confirm that all coalition countries aren't members to the Convention on Cluster Munitions', Saudi Press Agency, 19 December 2016, https://www.spa.gov.sa/viewstory.php?lang=en&newsid=1571875.

25   Stockholm International Peace Research Institute, *Trends in World Military Expenditure, 2015*, April 2016, https://www.sipri.org/sites/default/files/EMBARGO%20FS1604%20Milex%202015.pdf.

26   House of Commons Business, Innovation and Skills and International Development Committees, *The Use of UK-manufactured Arms in Yemen*, p.28.

27   Ben Anderson, Samuel Oakford and Peter Salisbury, 'Dead civilians, uneasy alliances, and the fog of Yemen's war', *Vice*, 12 March 2016, https://www.vice.com/en_us/article/ev9myp/dead-civilians-uneasy-alliances-and-the-fog-of-yemens-war.

28 'Saudi coalition/US: curb civilian harm in Yemen', Human Rights Watch, 13 April 2015, https://www.hrw.org/news/2015/04/13/saudi-coalition/us-curb-civilian-harm-yemen.

29 Warren Strobel and Jonathan Landay, 'Exclusive: as Saudis bombed Yemen, US worried about legal blowback', Reuters, 10 October 2016, https://uk.reuters.com/article/uk-usa-saudi-yemen-exclusive-idUKKCN12A0BG.

30 Yara Bayoumy, 'Obama administration arms sales offers to Saudi top $115 billion: report, 8 September 2016, https://www.reuters.com/article/us-usa-saudi-security/obama-administration-arms-sales-offers-to-saudi-top-115-billion-report-idUSKCN11D2JQ.

31 UN Human Rights Council, *Findings of the Group of Eminent International and Regional Experts on Yemen*, 17 August 2018, p.6, http://www.securitycouncilreport.org/atf/cf/%7B65BFCF9B-6D27-4E9C-8CD3-CF6E4FF96FF9%7D/A_HRC_39_43_EN.pdf.

32 'Yemen: US bombs used in deadliest market strike', Human Rights Watch, 7 April 2016, https://www.hrw.org/news/2016/04/07/yemen-us-bombs-used-deadliest-market-strike.

33 Nawal Al-Maghafi, 'The funeral bombing' BBC World News, 14 December 2016, https://www.youtube.com/watch?v=-ZuIPXRrG0Q.

34 'From weddings into funerals', Mwatana Organization for Human Rights, 16 May 2016, http://mwatana.org/en/wedding-into-funerals.

35 Richard Spencer, 'UK military working alongside Saudi bomb targeters in Yemen war', *The Telegraph*, 15 January 2016, https://www.telegraph.co.uk/news/worldnews/middleeast/saudiarabia/12102089/UK-military-working-alongside-Saudi-bomb-targeters-in-Yemen-war.html.

36 House of Commons Business, Innovation and Skills and International Development Committees, *The Use of UK-manufactured Arms in Yemen*, p.30.

37 Mark Mazzetti and Eric Schmitt, 'Quiet support for Saudis'.

38 Declan Walsh and Eric Schmitt, 'Arms sales to Saudis leave American fingerprints on Yemen's carnage', *New York Times*, 25 December 2018, https://www.nytimes.com/2018/12/25/world/middleeast/yemen-us-saudi-civilian-war.html.

39 UN Secretary-General, *Children and Armed Conflict*, 20 April 2016, p.27, http://www.undocs.org/s/2016/360.

40 Michelle Nichols, 'UN adds Saudi coalition to blacklist for killing children in Yemen', Reuters, 3 June 2016, https://www.reuters.com/article/us-rights-un-saudi-yemen-idUSKCN0YO2RK.

41 Matt Brown, 'UN's Ban Ki-Moon says Saudi Arabia "pressured" him for blacklist removal', ABC News, 10 June 2016, https://www.abc.net.au/news/2016-06-10/saudis-pressured-ban-ki-moon-for-blacklist-removal-he-says/7498594.

42 Mark Mazzetti and Eric Schmitt, 'Quiet support for Saudis'.

43 Ibid.

44 Samantha Power (@AmbPower), tweet, 16 August 2016, https://twitter.com/AmbPower44/status/765682969520418817?s=20.

45 Agence France-Presse, 'UN report says Saudi-led coalition and Houthis violate human rights in Yemen', *The Telegraph*, 5 August 2016, https://www.telegraph.co.uk/news/2016/08/05/un-report-says-saudi-led-coalition-and-houthis-violate-human-rig/.

46 Aziz El Yaakoubi, 'Menace of Houthi-laid landmines adds to Yemeni misery', Reuters, 9 March 2018, https://www.reuters.com/article/us-yemen-security-landmines-idUSKCN1GK28Y.

47 UN Human Rights Council, *Findings of the Group of Eminent International and Regional Experts on Yemen*.

48 Agence France-Presse, 'Third of fighters in Yemen are children, says UNICEF', *The Guardian*, 9 April 2015, https://www.theguardian.com/world/2015/apr/09/third-of-fighters-yemen-children-unicef.

49 Reuters, 'Yemen's war-damaged Hodeidah port struggles to bring in vital supplies', VOA, 24 November 2016, https://www.voanews.com/a/yemen-s-war-damage-hodeidah-port-struggles-to-bring-in-vital-supplies/3610208.html.

50   'UN: more than 21 million people in Yemen need basic humanitarian aid', UN News, 24 November 2015, https://news.un.org/en/story/2015/11/516342-un-more-21-million-people-yemen-need-basic-humanitarian-aid.

51   House of Commons Business, Innovation and Skills and International Development Committees, *The Use of UK-manufactured Arms in Yemen*, p.2.

52   'Closure of Yemen's main airport puts millions of people at risk', Oxfam, 14 August 2016, https://www.oxfam.org/en/pressroom/pressreleases/2016-08-14/closure-yemens-main-airport-puts-millions-people-risk.

53   'Yemeni people's ability to access food threatened as main supply route to Sanaa targeted by airstrikes', Oxfam, 12 August 2016, https://www.oxfamamerica.org/press/yemeni-peoples-ability-to-access-food-threatened-as-main-supply-route-to-sanaa-targeted-by-airstrikes/.

54   Raf Sanchez, 'Saudi coalition kills 10 children in their classroom in Yemen air strike', *The Telegraph*, 13 August 2016, https://www.telegraph.co.uk/news/2016/08/13/10-children-killed-in-their-classroom-by-saudi-coalition-airstri/.

55   Noah Browning and Tom Brown, 'Air strike on MSF hospital in Yemen kills at least 11: aid group', Reuters, 16 August 2016, https://www.reuters.com/article/us-yemen-security/air-strike-on-msf-hospital-in-yemen-kills-at-least-11-aid-group-idUSKCN10Q1E0.

56   Mostafa Hashem, 'Saudi Arabia's king is giving military and security personnel an extra month's pay for fighting in Yemen', *Business Insider*, 15 August 2016, https://www.businessinsider.com/r-saudi-king-returns-home-gives-bonus-to-personnel-fighting-in-yemen-2016-8?IR=T.

57   'Yemen: Saudi-led funeral attack apparent war crime', Human Rights Watch, 13 October 2016, https://www.hrw.org/news/2016/10/13/yemen-saudi-led-funeral-attack-apparent-war-crime.

58   Michelle Nichols, 'Saudi coalition violated law with Yemen funeral strike: UN monitors', Reuters, 21 October 2016, https://www.reuters.com/article/us-yemen-security-saudi-un-idUSKCN12K2F1?il=0.

59   UN Human Rights Council, *Findings of the Group of Eminent International and Regional Experts on Yemen.*

60   Nawal Al-Maghafi, 'The funeral bombing'.

61   Nicolas Niarchos, 'How the US is making the war in Yemen worse'.

62   Patrick Wintour, 'US says support for Saudi Arabia not a "blank cheque" after Yemen air raid', *The Guardian*, 9 October 2016, https://www.theguardian.com/world/2016/oct/09/saudi-arabia-investigate-air-raid-on-funeral-in-yemen.

63   Raf Sanchez and Christopher Hope, 'Britain stands behind Saudi air campaign in Yemen even as strike on funeral prompts US to review its support', *The Telegraph*, 10 October 2016, https://www.telegraph.co.uk/news/2016/10/10/britain-stands-behind-saudi-air-campaign-in-yemen-even-as-strike/.

64   Nawal Al-Maghafi, 'The funeral bombing'.

65   Helene Cooper, 'US blocks arms sale to Saudi Arabia amid concerns over Yemen war', *New York Times*, 13 December 2016, https://www.nytimes.com/2016/12/13/us/politics/saudi-arabia-arms-sale-yemen-war.html.

66   Nawal Al-Maghafi, 'The funeral bombing'.

67   Helene Cooper, 'US blocks arms sale to Saudi Arabia'.

68   Patrick Begley, 'Senate pressure Defence for answers on Saudi Arabian military deals', *Sydney Morning Herald*, 30 March 2017, https://www.smh.com.au/politics/federal/senate-pressures-defence-for-answers-on-saudi-arabian-military-deals-20170329-gv996s.html.

69   Christopher Pyne (@cpyne), tweet, 18 December 2016, https://twitter.com/cpyne/status/810593290915430400?s=20.

70   Patrick Begley, 'Australia selling military equipment to Saudi Arabia during brutal Yemen conflict', *Sydney Morning Herald*, 24 March 2017, https://www.smh.com.au/politics/federal/australia-selling-military-equipment-to-saudi-arabia-during-brutal-yemen-conflict-20170324-gv5k7o.html.

71   Dylan Welch, Kyle Taylor and Rebecca Trigger, 'Australian Government under fire over export of weapons system to war-crime accused Saudi Arabia', ABC News, 20 February 2019, https://www.abc.net.au/news/2019-02-20/australian-firm-eos-weapons-systems-bound-for-saudi-arabia/10825660.

72   Sophie McNeill, 'Yemen: agencies call for aid as skeletal starving children on brink of death, ABC News, 17 March 2017, https://www.abc.net.au/news/2017-03-17/odds-are-stacked-against-us:-yemen-calls-for-aid-amid-famine/8362352.

73   Ibid.

74   Sophie McNeill, 'Cholera outbreak kills 34 people in Yemen as MSF calls for more aid', ABC News, 10 May 2017, https://www.abc.net.au/news/2017-05-10/yemen-faces-cholera-outbreak-msf-calls-for-humanitarian-aid/8512760.

75   Hisham Al-Omeisy (@omeisy), tweet, 8 July 2017, https://twitter.com/omeisy/status/883643437869936641?ref_src=twsrc%5Etfw%7Ctwcamp%5Etweetembed&ref_url=https%3A%2F%2Fwww.abc.net.au%2Fnews%2F2017-08-18%2Famnesty-calls-on-houthi-rebels-release-yemen-anti-war-activist%2F8822148.

76   Sophie McNeill, 'Yemen cholera outbreak reaches "devastating proportions" as deaths mount', ABC News, 12 June 2017, https://www.abc.net.au/news/2017-06-12/yemen-cholera-epidemic-at-devastating-proportions/8609246.

77   Frederik Federspiel and Mohammad Ali, 'The cholera outbreak in Yemen: lessons learnt and way forward', BMC Public Health, 2018, issue 18, p.1338, https://www.ncbi.nlm.nih.gov/pmc/articles/PMC6278080.

78   Sophie McNeill, 'Yemen cholera outbreak reaches "devastating proportions"'.

79   Sophie McNeill, 'Amnesty calls on Houthi rebels to immediately release Yemeni activist Hisham Al Omeisy', ABC News, 18 August 2017, https://www.abc.net.au/news/2017-08-18/amnesty-calls-on-houthi-rebels-release-yemen-anti-war-activist/8822148.

80   'Yemen: Houthis detain prominent activist', Human Rights Watch, 18 August 2017, https://www.hrw.org/news/2017/08/18/yemen-houthis-detain-prominent-activist.

81   'Suspected cholera cases surpass one million, reports UN health agency', UN News, 22 December 2017, https://news.un.org/en/story/2017/12/640331-suspected-cholera-cases-yemen-surpass-one-million-reports-un-health-agency.

82   Annie Slemrod, 'What's really stopping a cholera vaccination campaign in Yemen?', New Humanitarian, 17 October 2017, https://www.thenewhumanitarian.org/news/2017/10/17/what-s-really-stopping-cholera-vaccination-campaign-yemen.

83   Frederik Federspiel and Mohammad Ali, 'The cholera outbreak in Yemen'.

84   Ibid.

85   Sophie McNeill, 'Yemeni cities run out of clean water as Saudi-led blockade puts 1 million at risk of cholera', ABC News, 18 November 2017, https://www.abc.net.au/news/2017-11-18/yemen-cities-run-out-of-water-amid-saudi-blockade/9164458.

86   Reuters, 'Saudi-led coalition shuts off air, sea and land ports to Yemen in response to missile attack', ABC News, 7 November 2017, https://www.abc.net.au/news/2017-11-07/saudi-led-forces-close-air-sea-and-land-access-to-yemen/9124908.

87   'UN warns Yemen blockade may create largest famine in decades', ABC News, 9 November 2017, https://www.abc.net.au/news/2017-11-09/un-warns-yemen-blockade-may-create-largest-famine-in-decades/9134840.

88   Sophie McNeill, 'Yemeni cities run out of clean water'.

89   Stephanie Nebehay, 'Aid agencies say Yemen blockade remains, Egeland calls it "collective punishment"', Reuters, 24 November 2017, https://www.reuters.com/article/us-yemen-security-aid/aid-agencies-say-yemen-blockade-remains-egeland-calls-it-collective-punishment-idUSKBN1DN1NW?il=0.

90   Sophie McNeill, 'Joint exercise with Saudis during Yemen blockade "taints" Australian navy, say aid groups, ABC News, 15 November 2017, https://www.abc.net.au/news/2017-11-15/ran-exercise-with-saudis-criticised/9152438.

91   Australian Defence Force in the Middle East Facebook page, 9 November 2017, https://www.facebook.com/AustralianDefenceForceMiddleEastRegion/posts/1718313884870038.

92   Selam Gebrekidan and Jonathan Saul, 'Yemen's agony', Reuters, 11 October 2017, https://www.reuters.com/investigates/special-report/yemen-saudi-blockade.

93   Margaret Besheer, 'Urgently needed cranes reach Yemen port', VOA, 15 January 2018, https://www.voanews.com/middle-east/urgently-needed-cranes-reach-yemen-port.

94   Hisham Al-Omeisy (@omeisy), tweet, 19 January 2018, https://twitter.com/omeisy/status/954334368390172672?s=20.

95   Colum Lynch, 'Document of the week: UN study on the Yemen war's impact', *Foreign Policy*, 3 May 2019, https://foreignpolicy.com/2019/05/03/document-of-the-week-united-nations-yemen-war-impact-study.

96   Phil Stewart, 'US halting refuelling of Saudi-led coalition aircraft in Yemen's war', Reuters, 10 November 2018, https://www.reuters.com/article/us-usa-yemen-refueling/u-s-halting-refueling-of-saudi-led-coalition-aircraft-in-yemens-war-idUSKCN1NE2LJ.

97   Mark Landler and Peter Baker, 'Trump vetoes measure to force end to US involvement in Yemen war', *New York Times*, 16 April 2019, https://www.nytimes.com/2019/04/16/us/politics/trump-veto-yemen.html.

Chapter 11: We Can't Say We Didn't Know

1   'Russia joins war in Syria: five key points', BBC News, 1 October 2015, https://www.bbc.com/news/world-middle-east-34416519; Anne Barnard, 'Syrian rebels say Russia is targeting them rather than ISIS', *New York Times*, 30 September 2015, https://www.nytimes.com/2015/10/01/world/middleeast/syrian-rebels-say-russia-targets-them-rather-than-isis.html.

2   Emma Graham-Harrison, 'Russian airstrikes in Syria killed 2000 civilians in six months', *The Guardian*, 16 March 2016, https://www.theguardian.com/world/2016/mar/15/russian-airstrikes-in-syria-killed-2000-civilians-in-six-months.

3   Médecins Sans Frontières, *Review of Attack on al-Quds hospital in Aleppo City*, 30 September 2016, https://www.msf.org/syria-review-attack-al-quds-hospital-aleppo-city.

4   Anne Barnard, 'Divided Aleppo plunges back into war as Syrian hospital is hit', *New York Times*, 28 April 2016, https://www.nytimes.com/2016/04/29/world/middleeast/aleppo-syria-strikes.html.

5   Lizzie Dearden, 'Syria crisis: boy filmed weeping over brother's body after dozens of civilians killed in Aleppo', *Independent*, 29 April 2016, https://www.independent.co.uk/news/world/middle-east/i-wish-it-was-me-not-you-boy-filmed-weeping-over-brothers-body-after-dozens-of-civilians-killed-in-a7006231.html.

6   Rick Noack and Tiffany Harness, 'Aleppo lost one of its last paediatricians in latest hospital bombing', *Washington Post*, 29 April 2016, https://www.washingtonpost.com/news/worldviews/wp/2016/04/29/aleppo-lost-one-of-its-last-pediatricians-in-latest-hospital-bombing/?utm_term=.049a7b4625ed.

7   'Tributes for Syrian paediatrician Muhammad Waseem Moaz', BBC News, 29 April 2016, https://www.bbc.com/news/world-middle-east-36169170.

8   'Syria: airstrikes destroy Aleppo's al-Quds hospital, killing 14', Médecins Sans Frontières, 28 April 2016, https://www.doctorswithoutborders.org/what-we-do/news-stories/news/syria-airstrikes-destroy-aleppos-al-quds-hospital-killing-14.

9   'Syrian and Russian forces targeting hospitals as a strategy of war', Amnesty International, 3 March 2016, https://www.amnesty.org/en/latest/news/2016/03/syrian-and-russian-forces-targeting-hospitals-as-a-strategy-of-war/.

10   Nick Cumming-Bruce, 'UN reports Syria uses hospital attacks as a "weapon of war"', *New York Times*, 13 September 2013, https://www.nytimes.com/2013/09/14/world/middleeast/un-panel-accuses-syria-of-attacking-hospitals.html.

11   Betcy Jose, 'When hospitals are targets: how international law failed in Syria', *Foreign Affairs*, 10 May 2016, https://www.foreignaffairs.com/articles/syria/2016-05-10/when-hospitals-are-targets?utm_campaign=reg_conf_email&utm_medium=newsletters&utm_source=fa_registration; Physicians for Human Rights, 'Let Syria's Health Professionals Work', 1 February 2016, https://s3.amazonaws.com/PHR_other/let-syrias-health-professionals-work.pdf.

12   Dr Joanne Liu, 'The airstrike on an Aleppo hospital is a wake-up call for the UN. It must act now', 30 April 2016, https://www.msf.org.au/article/statements-opinion/airstrike-aleppo-hospital-wake-call-un-it-must-act-now.

13   Médecins Sans Frontières, *Review of attack on al-Quds hospital in Aleppo City*, p.15.

14   Sophie McNeill, 'Syrian army cuts off only road into rebel-held Aleppo, rebels say', ABC News, 7 July 2016, https://www.abc.net.au/news/2016-07-07/syrian-army-cuts-off-only-road-into-rebel-held-aleppo/7579172.

15   'Syria: safe passage for civilians will not avert humanitarian catastrophe in Aleppo city', Amnesty International, 28 July 2016, https://www.amnesty.org/en/latest/news/2016/07/syria-safe-passage-for-civilians-will-not-avert-humanitarian-catastrophe-in-aleppo-city/.

16   Sophie McNeill, 'Battle for Aleppo: six more hospitals struck by Syrian government airstrikes, relief agency says', ABC News, 4 August 2016, https://www.abc.net.au/news/2016-08-04/six-aleppo-hospitals-struck-by-syrian-government-air-strikes/7688504.

17   'At least 38 civilians killed in rebel fire on government-held part of Syria's Aleppo', Reuters, 9 July 2016, https://www.reuters.com/article/us-mideast-crisis-syria-aleppo/at-least-38-civilians-killed-in-rebel-fire-on-government-held-part-of-syrias-aleppo-idUSKCN0ZP0FP.

18   *Report of the Independent International Commission of Inquiry on the Syrian Arab Republic*, UN General Assembly, 2 February 2017, p.9, https://ap.ohchr.org/documents/dpage_e.aspx?si=A/HRC/34/64.

19   'Aleppo region suffers worst week of hospital attacks since Syrian conflict began', Physicians for Human Rights, 3 August 2016, https://phr.org/news/aleppo-region-suffers-worst-week-of-hospital-attacks-since-syrian-conflict-began/.

20   Ben Hubbard and Anne Barnard, 'Syria outlines plans for conquest of Aleppo, backed by Russian Power', *New York Times*, 28 July 2016, https://www.nytimes.com/2016/07/29/world/middleeast/syria-aleppo-exit-corridors.html?action=click&module=RelatedCoverage&pgtype=Article&region=Footer.

21   Emma Graham-Harrison, 'Starving families in Aleppo fear "safe passage" may be a trap', *The Guardian*, 30 July 2016, https://www.theguardian.com/world/2016/jul/30/aleppo-fear-safe-passage-trap.

22   'Syria: Aleppo "one of the most devastating urban conflicts in modern times"', International Committee of the Red Cross, 15 August 2016, https://www.icrc.org/en/document/syria-news-cities-aleppo-one-most-devastating-urban-conflicts.

23   Margaret Besheer, 'Doctors describe horrendous conditions in Syria's Aleppo', *Voice of America*, 9 August 2016, https://www.voanews.com/a/doctors-describe-horrendous-conditions-syria-aleppo/3456265.html.

24   Samer Attar, 'A doctor's plea to President Obama: please act to save civilians in Syria', *Washington Post*, 21 July 2017, https://www.washingtonpost.com/opinions/a-doctors-plea-to-president-obama-please-act-to-save-civilians/2016/07/21/092e081a-4f42-11e6-aa14-e0c1087f7583_story.html?utm_term=.7836d174867b.

25   'UK training for Syrian activists to save lives', UK government, Foreign and Commonwealth Office, 6 September 2013, https://www.gov.uk/government/news/uk-training-for-syrian-activists-to-save-lives.

26   Vanessa Beeley, 'John Pilger: "White Helmets are a complete propaganda construct in Syria"', YouTube, 26 May 2017, https://www.youtube.com/watch?time_continue=8&v=X27B0yuazGo.

27   Olivia Solon, 'How Syria's White Helmets became victims of an online propaganda machine', *The Guardian*, 18 December 2017, https://www.theguardian.com/world/2017/dec/18/syria-white-helmets-conspiracy-theories.

28   'Targeted air strikes kill five rescue workers near Syria's Aleppo', Reuters, 26 April 2016, https://uk.reuters.com/article/uk-mideast-crisis-syria-aleppo-idUKKCN0XN0LN.

29   Sophie McNeill (@Sophiemcneill), tweet, 18 August 2016, https://twitter.com/Sophiemcneill/status/766003327930949632.

30   'Story of little Syrian boy moves CNN anchor to tears', CNN, 18 August 2016, https://edition.cnn.com/videos/world/2016/08/18/syrian-boy-aleppo-omran-bolduan-breaks-down-ath.cnn.

31   Hady Al Khatib, 'Fact-checking Russia's claim that it didn't bomb a five-year-old in Syria', Bellingcat, 1 September 2016, https://www.bellingcat.com/news/mena/2016/09/01/fact-checking-russias-claim-didnt-bomb-5-year-old-syria/.

32   'Russian cruise missiles target Syria', Reuters, 20 August 2016, https://www.reuters.com/article/us-mideast-crisis-syria-aleppo-idUSKCN10U1EE.

33   Sophie McNeill, '13 Syrian children killed in Aleppo, one week after 5yo Omran's video shocked the world', ABC News, 26 August 2016, https://www.abc.net.au/news/2016-08-26/thirteen-syrian-children-killed-after-omrans-video-appears/7789404.

34   'Security Council fails to adopt resolution calling for ceasefire in Aleppo', UN News, 5 December 2016, https://news.un.org/en/story/2016/12/547002-security-council-fails-adopt-resolution-calling-ceasefire-aleppo.

35   Sophie McNeill, 'Julie Bishop starts visit to Israel and Palestinian territories', *AM*, ABC Radio, 5 September 2016, http://www.abc.net.au/am/content/2016/s4532609.htm.

36   Julian Borger, 'John Kerry lands in Geneva for Syria peace talks with Russia's Sergey Lavrov', *The Guardian*, 9 September 2016, https://www.theguardian.com/world/2016/sep/08/syria-peace-talks-geneva-john-kerry-sergey-lavrov.

37   Louis Nelson and Daniel Strauss, 'Libertarian candidate Gary Johnson: "What is Aleppo?"', *Politico*, 8 September 2016, https://www.politico.com/story/2016/09/gary-johnson-aleppo-227873.

38   Julian Borger, 'Russia and US reach tentative agreement for Syria ceasefire', *The Guardian*, 10 September 2016, https://www.theguardian.com/world/2016/sep/10/syria-ceasefire-deal-tentative-negotiate-kerry-lavrov-us-russia.

39   Brendan Nicholson, 'RAAF fighters bombed Syrian troops after vital clues missed', *The Australian*, 30 November 2016, https://www.theaustralian.com.au/nation/defence/raaf-fighters-bombed-syrian-troops-after-vital-clues-missed/news-story/7b0500e796f8e326086601f318585e72; Brigadier General Richard Coe, Memorandum for USAFCENT/CC, 2 November 2016, https://www.centcom.mil/Portals/6/media/REDACTED_FINAL_XSUM_Memorandum__29_Nov_16___CLEAR.pdf.

40   Andrew Greene, 'RAAF fighters dropped six bombs on government forces in botched air strikes in Syria' ABC News, 30 November 2016, https://www.abc.net.au/news/2016-11-30/syria-botched-air-strikes-australian-hornets/8077588.

41   Anne Barnard and Mark Mazzetti, 'US admits airstrike in Syria, meant to hit ISIS, killed Syrian troops', *New York Times*, 17 September 2016, https://www.nytimes.com/2016/09/18/world/middleeast/us-airstrike-syrian-troops-isis-russia.html?_r=0.

42   OCHA Syria (@OCHR_Syria), tweet, 19 September 2016, https://twitter.com/OCHA_Syria/status/777801927501447168?s=20.

43   Anne Barnard and Somini Sengupta, 'From paradise to hell: how an aid convoy in Syria was blown apart', *New York Times*, 24 September 2016, https://www.nytimes.com/2016/09/25/world/middleeast/from-paradise-to-hell-how-an-aid-convoy-in-syria-was-blown-apart.html.

44   *Report of the Independent International Commission of Inquiry on the Syrian Arab Republic*, p.17.

45   Ibid.

46   Julian Borger and Spencer Ackerman, 'Ban Ki-moon condemns "apparently deliberate" Syria aid convoy attack', 21 September 2016, https://www.theguardian.com/world/2016/sep/20/un-suspends-all-aid-convoy-movements-in-syria-after-airstrike.

47   Eliot Higgins, 'Confirmed: Russian bomb remains recovered from Syrian Red Crescent aid convoy attack', Bellingcat, 22 September 2016, https://www.bellingcat.com/news/mena/2016/09/22/russian-bomb-remains-recovered-syrian-red-crescent-aid-convoy-attack/.

48   Nick Waters, 'Analysis of Syrian Red Crescent aid convoy attack', Bellingcat, 21 September 2016, https://www.bellingcat.com/news/mena/2016/09/21/aleppo-un-aid-analysis/.

49   *Report of the Independent International Commission of Inquiry on the Syrian Arab Republic*, p.8.

50   Sophie McNeill (@Sophiemcneill), tweet, 22 September 2016, https://twitter.com/Sophiemcneill/status/778716456439586817?s=20.

51   Sophie McNeill (@Sophiemcneill), tweet, 24 September 2016, https://twitter.com/Sophiemcneill/status/779342051762589696?s=20.

52   Sophie McNeill (@Sophiemcneill), tweet, 25 September 2016, https://twitter.com/Sophiemcneill/status/779829672590782465?s=20.

53   Sophie McNeill (@Sophiemcneill), tweet, 23 September 2016, https://twitter.com/Sophiemcneill/status/779342051762589696?s=20.

54   'Children in Aleppo trapped in "living nightmare"', UNICEF, 28 September 2016, https://www.unicef.org/press-releases/children-aleppo-trapped-living-nightmare-unicef-deputy-executive-director-justin.

55   *Report of the Independent International Commission of Inquiry on the Syrian Arab Republic*, p.6

56   Kareem Shaheen and Julian Borger, 'Two Aleppo hospitals bombed out of service in "catastrophic" airstrikes', *The Guardian*, 28 September 2016, https://www.theguardian.com/world/2016/sep/28/aleppo-two-hospitals-bombed-out-of-service-syria-airstrikes.

57   *Report of the Independent International Commission of Inquiry on the Syrian Arab Republic*, p.9.

58   'Russia/Syria: war crimes in month of bombing Aleppo', Human Rights Watch, 1 December 2016, https://www.hrw.org/news/2016/12/01/russia/syria-war-crimes-month-bombing-aleppo.

59   'Syria news: Aleppo bombing shuts largest hospital', BBC News, 2 October 2016, https://www.bbc.com/news/world-middle-east-37528260.

60   OCHA, 'Under-secretary-general for humanitarian affairs and emergency relief coordinator Stephen O'Brien statement on Eastern Aleppo City, Syria', Relief Web, 2 October 2016, https://reliefweb.int/report/syrian-arab-republic/under-secretary-general-humanitarian-affairs-and-emergency-relief-50.

61   'Russia ready to deliver strikes on militants moving into Syria from Iraq', Russian News Agency, 26 October 2016, https://tass.com/defense/908612.

62   Eliot Higgins, 'Fact-checking Russia's claim that it didn't bomb another hospital in Syria', Bellingcat, 9 November 2016, https://www.bellingcat.com/news/mena/2016/11/09/fact-checking-russias-claim-didnt-bomb-another-hospital-syria/.

63   *Report of the Independent International Commission of Inquiry on the Syrian Arab Republic*, p.7.

64   Staffan de Mistura, press conference, United Nations, 6 October 2016, https://www.un.org/sg/en/content/sg/note-correspondents/2016-10-06/note-correspondents-transcript-press-conference-un-special.

65   The figure of 275,000 was an overestimate. Later assessments said at least 110,000; see OCHA, 'Syrian Arab Republic: Aleppo – situation report no. 13', Relief Web, 12 January 2017, https://reliefweb.int/sites/reliefweb.int/files/resources/aleppo_sitrep_13.pdf.

66   'Syria conflict: UN envoy offers to personally escort rebels out of Aleppo to end Russia, Syria air strikes', ABC News, 7 October 2016, https://www.abc.net.au/news/2016-10-07/un-envoy-offers-to-escort-rebels-out-of-aleppo/7911626.

67   'Aleppo bombing kills 14 members of one family', BBC News, 17 October 2016, https://www.bbc.com/news/world-middle-east-37675671.

68   'Syria crisis: footage shows boy dangling by legs from building after Aleppo airstrike', ABC News, 17 October 2016, https://www.abc.net.au/news/2016-10-17/young-boy-hangs-off-building-after-airstrike-in-aleppo/7937886.

69   *Report of the Independent International Commission of Inquiry on the Syrian Arab Republic*, p.8.

70   Digital Forensic Research Lab, *Breaking Aleppo*, Atlantic Council, February 2017, p.9, https://www.publications.atlanticcouncil.org/breakingaleppo/.

71   Stephen O'Brien, 'Statement to the Security Council on Syria', United Nations, 26 October 2016, https://www.unocha.org/sites/dms/Documents/ERC_USG%20 Stephen%20OBrien%20Statement%20on%20Syria%20to%20SecCo%20 26OCT2016%20CAD.pdf.

72   AP news agency, 'Syrian rebels' Aleppo offensive could amount to war crimes, UN envoy warns', *The Guardian*, 31 October 2016, https://www.theguardian.com/ world/2016/oct/31/syrian-rebels-aleppo-offensive-could-amount-to-war-crimes-un-envoy-warns?CMP=share_btn_tw.

73   Sophie McNeill, 'Aleppo siege: rebels accused over civilian deaths amid battle to end regime blockade', ABC News, 1 November 2016, https://www.abc.net.au/news/2016-11-01/rebels-accused-of-attacking-civilians-in-aleppo/7982414.

74   *Report of the Independent International Commission of Inquiry on the Syrian Arab Republic*, p.13.

75   Digital Forensic Research Lab, *Breaking Aleppo*, p.7.

76   Sophie McNeill, 'Aleppo: Fear and distrust in besieged Syrian city as army offers to let civilians flee', ABC News, 4 November 2016, https://www.abc.net.au/news/2016-11-04/syrian-army-urges-civilians-to-leave-alepp/7995068.

77   'The disappeared of Syria', Al Jazeera, 13 November 2016, https://www.aljazeera.com/ programmes/specialseries/2016/11/disappeared-syria-161110134005207.html.

78   *Report of the Independent International Commission of Inquiry on the Syrian Arab Republic*, p.14.

79   Ibid., p.14

80   Sophie McNeill (@Sophiemcneill), tweet, 6 November 2016, https://twitter.com/ Sophiemcneill/status/795220159296393216.

81   Kareem Shaheen and Emma Graham-Harrison, 'Children's hospital in Aleppo hit in airstrikes', *The Guardian*, 16 November 2016, https://www.theguardian.com/ world/2016/nov/16/horror-has-come-back-to-aleppo-airstrikes-continue-in-rebel-held-east.

82   'Moment of impact: children's hospital bombed in east Aleppo – video', *The Guardian*, 20 November 2016, https://www.theguardian.com/world/video/2016/ nov/20/moment-of-impact-childrens-hospital-bombed-in-east-aleppo-video.

83   'Multiple direct and indirect hits on hospitals in east Aleppo in the last 48 hours', Médecins Sans Frontières, 19 November 2016, https://www.msf.org/syria-multiple-direct-and-indirect-hits-hospitals-east-aleppo-last-48-hours.

84   Union of Medical Care and Relief Organizations, 'Omar Bin Abdul Aziz Hospital destroyed, eastern Aleppo without operating hospitals', Relief Web, 18 November 2016, https://reliefweb.int/report/syrian-arab-republic/omar-bin-abdul-aziz-hospital-destroyed-eastern-aleppo-without-operating.

85   Martin Chulov, Kareem Shaheen and Emma Graham-Harrison, 'East Aleppo's last hospital destroyed by airstrikes', *The Guardian*, 20 November 2016, https://www. theguardian.com/world/2016/nov/19/aleppo-hospitals-knocked-out-airstrikes.

86   'Syria war: all east Aleppo hospitals to suspend operations, health directorate announces', ABC News, 20 November 2016, https://www.abc.net.au/news/2016-11-19/all-east-aleppo-hospitals-suspend-operations-health-directorate/8039738.

87   'Eastern Aleppo without any hospitals for more than 250,000 residents', World Health Organization, 20 November 2016, https://www.who.int/news-room/detail/20-11-2016-eastern-aleppo-without-any-hospitals-for-more-than-250-000-residents.

88   Sophie McNeill (@Sophiemcneill), tweet, 18 November 2016, https://twitter.com/ Sophiemcneill/status/799592908907126784?s=20.

89   Aleppo Media Centre Facebook page, 19 November 2016, https://www.facebook.com/ AleppoAMC/videos/329369497440759/.

90   Ali Al Nasser Facebook page, 18 November 2016, https://www.facebook.com/story. php?story_fbid=193822801022445&id=100011841780925.

91   Sophie McNeill (@Sophiemcneill), tweet, 20 November 2016, https://twitter.com/ Sophiemcneill/status/800253107112267776.

92   *Report of the Independent International Commission of Inquiry on the Syrian Arab Republic.*

93   Sophie McNeill, 'Syria war: shelling kills eight children at Aleppo school; chlorine barrel bomb reportedly kills family', ABC News, 21 November 2016, https://www.abc.net.au/news/2016-11-21/syria-unrest-aleppos-children-slaughtered-on-both-sides/8041258.

94   Sophie McNeill (@Sophiemcneill), tweet, 20 November 2016, https://twitter.com/Sophiemcneill/status/800257158478708736.

95   Sophie McNeill (@Sophiemcneill), tweet, 20 November 2016, https://twitter.com/Sophiemcneill/status/800047610044280833?s=20; 'Crisis update: 28 November 2016', Médecins Sans Frontières, 29 November 2016, https://www.msf.org/syria-crisis-update-28-november-2016.

96   Sophie McNeill, 'US names Syrian generals accused of leading attacks on civilian targets', ABC News, 22 November 2016, https://www.abc.net.au/news/2016-11-22/us-names-syrian-generals-accused-of-leading-attacks/8044628.

97   Stephen O'Brien (@UNReliefChief), tweet, 22 November 2016, https://twitter.com/UNReliefChief/status/800718032163209216.

98   Sophie McNeill, 'East Aleppo: UN readies to send humanitarian help to Syria as rebels agree to aid delivery', ABC News, 25 November 2016, https://www.abc.net.au/news/2016-11-25/un-prepared-to-send-humanitarian-help-to-east-aleppo/8056808.

99   'Aleppo civilians try to flee as Syria army approaches', *Daily Star*, Agence France-Presse, 23 November 2016, https://www.dailystar.com.lb/ArticlePrint.aspx?id=382488&mode=print.

100 Hwaida Saad and Nick Cumming-Bruce, 'Thousands flee parts of Aleppo, Syria, as Assad's forces gain ground', *New York Times*, 29 November 2016, https://www.nytimes.com/2016/11/29/world/middleeast/thousands-flee-onslaught-in-aleppo-as-assads-forces-gain-ground.html.

101 Sophie McNeill, 'Aleppo: Syrian army seizes key district from rebels as thousands flee, observatory says', ABC News, 29 November 2016, https://www.abc.net.au/news/2016-11-28/syrian-army-seizes-key-aleppo-area-from-rebels:-observatory/8072852.

102 Ibid.

103 Martin Chulov, 'Aleppo families fear for 500 men seized by forces loyal to Assad', *The Guardian*, 30 November 2016, https://www.theguardian.com/world/2016/nov/29/residents-of-east-aleppo-fear-for-500-men-seized-by-forces-loyal-to-assad.

104 Sophie McNeill, 'Aleppo: Syrian army seizes key district from rebels as thousands flee, observatory says', ABC News, 29 November 2016.

105 'The statement of the civil defense in besieged Aleppo', YouTube, 28 November 2016, https://www.youtube.com/watch?v=vVHv7GwrwJw.

106 'Death toll rises in Aleppo – 50,000 flee in four days', Yahoo News, 1 December 2016, https://www.yahoo.com/news/death-toll-rises-aleppo-50-slideshow-wp-221648935/photo-p-search-rescue-team-members-photo-221648484.html.

107 Philip Issa and Sarah El Deeb, 'Syrians fleeing government advances in Aleppo shelled', AP news agency, 1 December 2016, https://apnews.com/7829d03698b04e07bdf86f903b0ae636.

108 Sophie McNeill (@Sophiemcneill), tweet, 1 December 2016, https://twitter.com/Sophiemcneill/status/804066136094490624?s=20.

109 'Aleppo battle: Russia and China veto UN truce resolution', BBC News, 5 December 2016, https://www.bbc.com/news/world-middle-east-38216969.

110 Ibid.

111 John Davison and Stephanie Nebehay, 'Syrian troops enter Aleppo's Old City, poised for war's biggest victory', Reuters, 7 December 2016, https://www.reuters.com/article/us-mideast-crisis-syria-wrap-idUSKBN13V26Y.

112 Sophie McNeill (@Sophiemcneill), tweet, 8 December 2016, https://twitter.com/Sophiemcneill/status/806597821830819840?s=20.

113 'Syria conflict: Army "suspends Aleppo fighting"', BBC News, 9 December 2016, https://www.bbc.com/news/world-middle-east-38257013?ns_mchannel=social&ns_campaign=bbc_breaking&ns_source=twitter&ns_linkname=news_central.

114 Patrick Wintour, 'White Helmets in east Aleppo plead for help after regime advances', *The Guardian*, 9 December 2016, https://www.theguardian.com/world/2016/dec/08/white-helmets-in-east-aleppo-plead-for-help-as-regime-advances.

115 Stephanie Nebehay, 'Hundreds of men from east Aleppo missing: UN rights office', Reuters, 9 December 2016, https://www.reuters.com/article/us-mideast-crisis-syria-aleppo-un-idUSKBN13Y14Y.

116 'Militants are leaving Aleppo disguised as civilians', Anna News, 10 December 2016, https://www.youtube.com/watch?v=bYrgR9FiT1s&feature=youtu.be&has_verified=1.

117 'SARC and ICRC evacuate 150 civilians from Aleppo front line', International Committee of the Red Cross, 8 December 2016, https://www.icrc.org/en/document/sarc-and-icrc-evacuate-150-civilians-aleppo-frontline.

118 Anne Barnard and Hwaida Saad, '"We are dead either way": agonizing choices for Syrians in Aleppo', *New York Times*, 10 December 2016, https://www.nytimes.com/2016/12/10/world/middleeast/we-are-dead-either-way-agonizing-choices-for-syrians-in-aleppo.html?action=click&contentCollection=Middle%20East&module=inline&region=EndOfArticle&pgtype=article.

119 'Members of government military police stand guard as men, who were evacuated from the eastern districts of Aleppo, are being prepared to begin their military service at a police centre in Aleppo', Reuters, 11 December 2016, http://news.trust.org/item/20161211134225-c8hau.

120 Mohamad Katoub, Facebook video, 6 December 2016, https://www.facebook.com/Katoub.Mohamad/videos/654656934694896/UzpfSTEwMDAwODE2NDUwNzM0NToxODEzNDAxNzQyMjc1Mjky/.

121 Kareem Shaheen, 'Aleppo: Assad forces within "moments" of retaking city amid reports of atrocities', *The Guardian*, 13 December 2016, https://www.theguardian.com/world/2016/dec/12/syria-assad-forces-close-to-capturing-east-aleppo.

122 Rupert Colville, 'Press briefing notes on Aleppo, Syria', Office of the UN High Commissioner for Human Rights, 12 December 2016, https://www.ohchr.org/EN/NewsEvents/Pages/DisplayNews.aspx?NewsID=21022.

123 'Sande family 1', Violations Documentation Center in Syria, http://www.vdc-sy.info/index.php/en/details/martyrs/182605#.XbXKLi--Jp4; Digital Forensic Research Lab, *Breaking Aleppo*, p.53.

124 *Report of the Independent International Commission of Inquiry on the Syrian Arab Republic*, p.19.

125 'Aleppo battle: UN says civilians shot on the spot', BBC News, 13 December 2016, https://www.bbc.com/news/world-middle-east-38301629.

126 'Aleppo: trapped Syrians say goodbye on social media', BBC News, 13 December 2016, https://www.bbc.com/news/av/world-middle-east-38309852/aleppo-trapped-syrians-say-goodbye-on-social-media.

127 Laila Bassam, Suleiman Al Khalidi and Tom Perry, 'Aleppo evacuation plan back on track to end years of fighting', Reuters, 13 December 2016, https://www.reuters.com/article/us-mideast-crisis-syria/aleppo-evacuation-plan-back-on-track-to-end-years-of-fighting-idUSKBN14300Y.

128 OCHA, 'Syrian Arab Republic: Aleppo – situation report no. 13'.

129 Kareem Shaheen, 'Hundreds leave besieged east Aleppo on first day of evacuation', *The Guardian*, 16 December 2016, https://www.theguardian.com/world/2016/dec/15/syria-ambulances-on-the-move-as-aleppo-evacuation-operation-begins.

130 Robert Mardini (@RMardiniICRC), tweet, 15 December 2016, https://twitter.com/RMardiniICRC/status/809362863068418049?s=20.

131 *Report of the Independent International Commission of Inquiry on the Syrian Arab Republic*, p.19.

132 Ibid.

133 'Six years of war in Syria: the human toll', United States Senate Committee on Foreign Relations, 15 March 2017, https://www.foreign.senate.gov/hearings/six-years-of-war-in-syria-the-human-toll-031517.

134 'Dr Farida opening statement', United States Senate Committee on Foreign Relations, 15 March 2017, https://www.foreign.senate.gov/imo/media/doc/031517_Farida_Testimony.pdf.

135 'Dr Abu Rajab opening statement', United States Senate Committee on Foreign Relations, 15 March 2017, https://www.foreign.senate.gov/imo/media/doc/031517_Rajab_Testimony.pdf.

136 'Omran Daqneesh, Aleppo's bloodied boy, shown in new images', BBC News, 6 June 2017, https://www.bbc.com/news/world-middle-east-40176781.

137 OCHA, 'Syrian Arab Republic: Aleppo – situation report no. 13'.

138 Violations Documentation Center in Syria, *Special Report on the Evacuation of Civilians from East Aleppo*, 6 January 2017, http://vdc-sy.net//wp-content/uploads/2017/01/Aleppo-report-En-.pdf.

139 *Report of the Independent International Commission of Inquiry on the Syrian Arab Republic.*

140 Ibid.

141 'Findings of attacks on healthcare in Syria', Physicians for Human Rights, September 2019, http://syriamap.phr.org/#/en/findings.

142 Atlantic Council, *Breaking Ghouta*, Washington DC, 2018, p.19, https://www.publications.atlanticcouncil.org/breakingghouta/wp-content/uploads/2018/09/20180924_breakingghouta_web.pdf.

143 'Siege of Syria's eastern Ghouta "barbaric and medieval", says UN Commission of Inquiry', *UN News*, 20 June 2018, https://news.un.org/en/story/2018/06/1012632.

144 'Civilian death toll', Syrian Network for Human Rights, 2019, http://sn4hr.org/blog/2018/09/24/civilian-death-toll/.

Chapter 12: Escape from ISIS

1 Sophie McNeill, 'Mosul: faces of the overflowing Debaga refugee camp as Iraqis flee IS stronghold', ABC News, 19 October 2016, https://www.abc.net.au/news/2016-10-19/mosul-iraq-faces-of-the-overflowing-erbil-refugee-camp/7945786.

2 Stephen Kalin and Ahmed Rasheed, 'Battle for Mosul: Shi'ite militias launch offensive to seal off western front', NBC News, 29 October 2016, https://www.nbcnews.com/storyline/isis-terror/shi-ite-militias-launch-offensive-seal-western-mosul-n674986.

3 'Mosul battle: IS hangs bodies of 40 civilians from poles in Iraqi city, UN says', BBC News, 11 November 2016, https://www.bbc.com/news/world-middle-east-37949714.

4 Alex Hopkins, 'Disturbing civilian death trends in Iraq–Syria war: a researcher's view', *New Humanitarian*, 20 June 2017, https://www.irinnews.org/opinion/2017/06/20/disturbing-civilian-death-trends-iraq-syria-air-war-researcher's-view.

5 Alex Hopkins, 'International airstrikes and civilian casualty claims in Iraq and Syria: January 2017', Airwars, February 2017, https://airwars.org/report/international-airstrikes-and-civilian-casualty-claims-in-iraq-and-syria-january-2017.

6 Ahron Meta, 'A10 forming 11 percent of anti-Isis sorties', *Defense News*, 19 January 2015, https://www.defensenews.com/home/2015/01/19/a-10-performing-11-percent-of-anti-isis-sorties.

7 Airwars (@airwars), tweet, 9 March 2017, https://twitter.com/airwars/status/839847129090834433.

8 Alex Hopkins, 'International airstrikes and civilian casualty claims'.

9 Susannah George, 'Mosul is a graveyard: final IS battle kills 9000 civilians', AP News, 21 December 2017, https://apnews.com/bbea7094fb954838a2fdc11278d65460/9,000-plus-died-in-battle-with-Islamic-State-group-for-Mosul.

10 UN OCHA, 'Iraq: humanitarians deeply concerned for remaining civilians in ISIL-held areas', 5 July 2017, https://www.unocha.org/story/iraq-humanitarians-deeply-concerned-remaining-civilians-isil-held-areas.

11   Samuel Oakford, 'Coalition civilian casualty claims double under Donald Trump',
     Airwars, 17 July 2017, https://airwars.org/news-and-investigations/trumps-air-war-
     kills-12-civilians-per-day/.

12   Patrick Markey, 'US confirms coalition strike in Mosul district where dozens reported
     killed', Reuters, 25 March 2017, https://www.reuters.com/article/us-mideast-crisis-
     iraq-mosul-idUSKBN16W0DZ.

13   Airwars (@airwars), tweet, 25 March 2017, https://twitter.com/airwars/
     status/845612680392134656.

14   Martin Chulov, 'Mosul's children were shouting beneath the rubble. Nobody came',
     The Guardian, 25 March 2017, https://www.theguardian.com/world/2017/mar/24/
     mosuls-children-were-shouting-under-the-rubble-nobody-came.

15   Ibid.

16   Patrick Markey, 'US confirms coalition strike in Mosul district where dozens reported
     killed'.

17   Tim Arango and Helene Cooper, 'US investigating Mosul strikes said to have
     killed up to 200 civilians', New York Times, 24 March 2017, https://www.nytimes.
     com/2017/03/24/world/middleeast/us-iraq-mosul-investigation-airstrike-civilian-
     deaths.html.

18   Stephanie Nebehay, 'Iraq, US must avoid civilian deaths in Mosul: UN', Reuters,
     28 March 2017, https://www.reuters.com/article/us-mideast-crisis-iraq-mosul-un-
     idUSKBN16Z12S?il=0.

19   Michael R. Gordon and Hwaida Saad, 'US military denies reports it bombed mosque
     in Syria', New York Times, 16 March 2017, https://www.nytimes.com/2017/03/16/
     world/middleeast/us-military-denies-reports-it-bombed-mosque-in-syria.html.

20   Human Rights Watch, Attack on the Omar Ibn al-Khatab Mosque: Authorities'
     Failure to Take Adequate Precautions, 18 April 2017, https://www.hrw.org/
     report/2017/04/18/attack-omar-ibn-al-khatab-mosque/us-authorities-failure-take-
     adequate-precautions.

21   Anne Barnard, 'US airstrike in Syria is said to kill dozens of civilians', New York
     Times, 22 March 2017, https://www.nytimes.com/2017/03/22/world/middleeast/syria-
     us-airstrike.html.

22   Martin Chulov and Emma Graham-Harrison, 'Iraq suspends Mosul offensive after
     coalition airstrike atrocity', The Guardian, 26 March 2017, https://www.theguardian.
     com/world/2017/mar/25/iraq-suspends-mosul-offensive-after-coalition-airstrike-atrocity.

23   Tim Arango and Helene Cooper, 'US investigating Mosul strikes said to have killed up
     to 200 civilians'.

24   Susannah George and Balint Szlanko, 'US changes rules of engagement
     for Mosul fight in Iraq', AP News, 24 February 2017, https://apnews.com/
     f084b4f094f440058e6b58318a67adce.

25   #MAGA, 'Donald Trump on ISIS – "I would bomb the SHIT out of 'em!"' YouTube,
     12 November 2015, https://www.youtube.com/watch?v=aWejiXvd-P8.

26   'Iraq: airstrike vetting changes raise concerns', Human Rights Watch, 28 March 2017,
     https://www.hrw.org/news/2017/03/28/iraq-airstrike-vetting-changes-raise-concerns.

27   Samuel Oakford, 'Coalition civilian casualty claims double under Donald Trump',
     Airwars, 17 July 2017, https://airwars.org/news-and-investigations/trumps-air-war-
     kills-12-civilians-per-day/.

28   Zachary Cohen and Dan Merica, 'Trump takes credit for ISIS "giving up"', CNN
     Politics, 17 October 2017, https://edition.cnn.com/2017/10/17/politics/trump-isis-
     raqqa/index.html.

29   Michael R. Gordon, 'New ISIS tactic: gather Mosul's civilians, then lure an airstrike',
     New York Times, 30 March 2017, https://www.nytimes.com/2017/03/30/world/
     middleeast/mosul-iraq-isis-military.html.

30   US Central Command, 'CJTF-OIR completes airstrike investigation', 25 May
     2018, https://www.centcom.mil/MEDIA/PRESS-RELEASES/Press-Release-View/
     Article/1193763/cjtf-oir-completes-airstrike-investigation/.

31   Caitlyn Gribbin, 'Australian Defence Force to begin releasing Syria, Iraq airstrike targets in fortnightly reports', 2 May 2017, https://www.abc.net.au/news/2017-05-02/adf-to-start-releasing-syria-iraq-airstrike-reports/8488470.

32   David Wroe, '"No civilian casualties" by ADF in airstrikes against IS, coalition reports', *Sydney Morning Herald*, 1 May 2017, https://www.smh.com.au/politics/federal/no-civilian-casualties-by-adf-in-airstrikes-against-is-coalition-reports-20170501-gvwq1k.html.

33   Michael R. Gordon, 'No escape from Mosul, and unlikely chance of surrender', 6 July 2017, https://www.nytimes.com/2017/07/06/world/middleeast/mosul-iraq-isis.html.

34   Megan Specia and Mona Boshnaq, 'Civilians emerge from Mosul's rubble starving, injured and traumatized', *New York Times*, 3 July 2017, https://www.nytimes.com/2017/07/03/world/middleeast/mosul-civilians-escape-isis.html.

35   Amnesty International, *At Any Cost: The Civilian Catastrophe in West Mosul, Iraq*, 11 July 2017, https://www.amnesty.org/download/Documents/MDE1466102017ENGLISH.PDF.

36   Susannah George, 'Mosul is a graveyard: final IS battle kills 9000 civilians', AP News, 21 December 2017, https://apnews.com/bbea7094fb954838a2fdc11278d65460.

37   Martin Pengelly, 'Defense secretary Mattis says US policy against Isis is now "annihilation"', *The Guardian*, 29 May 2017, https://www.theguardian.com/us-news/2017/may/28/james-mattis-defense-secretary-us-isis-annihilation.

38   Kareem Shaheen, '"Staggering" loss of civilian life from US-led airstrikes in Raqqa, says UN', *The Guardian*, 14 June 2017, https://www.theguardian.com/world/2017/jun/14/staggering-civilian-deaths-from-us-led-airstrikes-in-raqqa-says-un.

39   Sophie McNeill, 'Raqqa: monitoring groups sound alarm over civilian death toll as Islamic State fight heats up', *ABC News*, 28 June 2017, https://www.abc.net.au/news/2017-06-28/monitoring-groups-sound-alarm-over-civilian-deaths-in-raqqa/8658554.

40   Gabriel Gatehouse, 'Syria war: why the battle for Raqqa is far from won', BBC News, 30 June 2017, https://www.bbc.com/news/world-middle-east-40451093.

41   Amnesty International, *War of Annihilation: Devastating Toll on Civilians, Raqqa – Syria*, 5 June 2018, https://www.amnesty.org/en/documents/mde24/8367/2018/en/.

42   Ibid.

43   Ibid.

44   Human Rights Watch, *All Feasible Precautions? Civilian Casualties in Anti-ISIS Coalition Airstrikes in Syria*, 25 September 2017, https://www.hrw.org/report/2017/09/24/all-feasible-precautions/civilian-casualties-anti-isis-coalition-airstrikes-syria.

45   Sophie McNeill, 'Syria war: Human Rights Watch criticises deaths of civilians in airstrikes by US-led coalition', ABC News, 25 September 2017, https://www.abc.net.au/news/2017-09-25/deaths-of-civilians-in-syria-airstrikes-human-rights-watch/8980356.

46   Mysa Khalaf, 'First UN humanitarian mission to Raqqa City post-ISIS', UNHCR, 5 April 2018, https://www.unhcr.org/sy/11607-first-un-humanitarian-mission-raqqa-city-post-isis.html.

47   Lolita C. Baldor and the Associated Press, 'New war rules emphasize need to avoid civilian casualties', *Military Times*, 13 December 2016, https://www.militarytimes.com/news/your-military/2016/12/14/new-war-rules-emphasize-need-to-avoid-civilian-casualties.

48   Kyle Rempfer, 'Dropping sniper nests in four story buildings: A-10 Warthogs earn gallantry award in Syria', *Air Force Times*, 4 April 2019, https://www.airforcetimes.com/news/your-air-force/2019/04/04/dropping-sniper-nests-in-four-story-buildings-a-10-warthogs-earn-gallantry-award-in-syria.

49   'Combined Joint Task Force – Operation Inherent Resolve monthly civilian casualty report', Operation Inherent Resolve, 5 December 2019, https://www.inherentresolve.mil/Releases/News-Releases/Article/2032727/combined-joint-task-force-operation-inherent-resolve-monthly-civilian-casualty/.

50   Airwars, 'US-led coalition in Iraq and Syria', https://airwars.org/conflict/coalition-in-iraq-and-syria.

51   Andrew Greene and Ashlynne McGhee 'ADF's bombing raids could have killed two children in Iraq', ABC News, 30 September 2017, https://www.abc.net.au/news/2017-09-30/adf-bombing-raid-on-iraq-possibly-killed-children/9002852.

52   Samuel Oakford, 'Australia admits killing two civilians during battle for Mosul', Airwars, 29 March 2018, https://airwars.org/news-and-investigations/australia-admits-killing-two-civilians-during-battle-for-mosul.

53   Matthew Doran and Adam Harvey, 'Australian planes involved in Iraqi airstrike which killed civilians', ABC News, 1 February 2019, https://www.abc.net.au/news/2019-02-01/iraqi-civilians-killed-in-airstrike-australia-involved-in/10766770.

54   Samuel Oakford, 'Australia admits killing two civilians'.

Chapter 13: Not Just a Number

1   See 'Terrorist incidents in Iraq in 2016', Wikipedia, https://en.wikipedia.org/wiki/Terrorist_incidents_in_Iraq_in_2016.

2   Pia Catton, 'Skype connects US arts teachers with Iraqi students', Wall Street Journal, 26 December 2014, https://www.wsj.com/articles/skype-sessions-connect-u-s-arts-teachers-with-iraqi-students-1419616553.

3   Adel Euro, 'Reunion in Amman', YouTube video, 7 June 2015, https://www.youtube.com/watch?v=hIsHIYhV3WY.

4   Associated Press, 'Iraqi boy's dream of becoming dancer defied threats, borders', Daily Mail (Australia), 24 April 2015, https://www.dailymail.co.uk/wires/ap/article-3053518/Iraqi-boys-dream-dancer-defied-threats-borders.html.

5   Sarah Almukhtar and Derek Watkins, 'Major Islamic State attacks in Baghdad', New York Times, 30 May 2017, https://www.nytimes.com/interactive/2016/05/18/world/middleeast/baghdad-attacks-isis-map.html; Associated Press, 'Suicide bombings kill dozens in Baghdad area', New York Times, 9 June 2016, https://www.nytimes.com/2016/06/10/world/middleeast/baghdad-iraq-isis-suicide-bombings.html.

6   Ahmed Rasheed, 'Death toll in Baghdad bombing rises to 324: ministry', Reuters, 1 August 2016, https://www.reuters.com/article/us-mideast-crisis-iraq-toll-idUSKCN10B0VK?il=0.

7   Lyse Doucet, 'Iraq violence: did IS use new type of bomb for deadliest attack?', BBC News, 28 July 2016, https://www.bbc.com/news/world-middle-east-36910935.

8   Falih Hassan, Tim Arango and Omar Al Jawoshy, 'Bombing kills more than 140 in Baghdad', New York Times, 3 July 2016, https://www.nytimes.com/2016/07/04/world/middleeast/baghdad-bombings.html.

9   Kevin Rawlinson, 'Fake bomb detector conman's jail term extended over failure to pay back £1.8m', The Guardian, 26 April 2018, https://www.theguardian.com/uk-news/2018/apr/25/fake-bomb-detector-conmans-jail-term-extended-over-failure-to-pay-back-profits.

10   'Iraq PM Abadi orders police to stop using fake bomb detectors', Reuters, 4 July 2016, https://www.reuters.com/article/us-mideast-crisis-iraq-blast-detectors/iraq-pm-abadi-orders-police-to-stop-using-fake-bomb-detectors-idUSKCN0ZJ0WH.

11   Sam McNeil, 'Iraqi dancer who "just wanted to fly" among Baghdad's dead', Associated Press, 5 July 2016, https://www.apnews.com/464d74de8ee740148c3ad059c1295c26.

Chaprter 14: Prisoners in Their Own Home

1   OCHA, Gaza Strip: The Humanitarian Impact of the Blockade, https://www.ochaopt.org/sites/default/files/the_humanitarian_impact_of_the_blockade.pdf.

2   'Occupied Palestinian territory: key figures on the 2014 hostilities', OCHA, https://www.ochaopt.org/content/key-figures-2014-hostilities.

3   Sophie McNeill, 'UN accuses Israel and Hamas of war crimes during 2014 Gaza war', The World Today, ABC Radio, 23 June 2015, https://www.abc.net.au/worldtoday/content/2015/s4260226.htm.

4   'Humanitarian situation in the Gaza Strip: fast facts', United Nations, https://www.
     un.org/unispal/humanitarian-situation-in-the-gaza-strip-fast-facts-ocha-factsheet.

5   World Health Organization, *Right to Health: Crossing Barriers to Access Health
     in the Occupied Palestinian Territory 2016*, 2017, http://www.emro.who.int/images/
     stories/palestine/documents/WHO_-_Access_Report_2016_Book_Final-small.
     pdf?ua=1&ua=1.

6   Ibid.

7   Ibid.

8   Ibid.

9   'Gaza patients' painful journey to cancer treatment', World Health Organization,
     4 February 2019, http://www.emro.who.int/pse/palestine-news/gaza-patients-painful-
     journey-to-cancer-treatment.html.

10   Ibid.

11   Judah Ari Gross, 'Gazan sisters accused of smuggling explosives in cancer medicine',
     Times of Israel, 19 April 2017, https://www.timesofisrael.com/gazan-sisters-accused-of-
     smuggling-explosives-in-cancer-medicine.

12   World Health Organization, *Health Access for Referral Patients from the Gaza Strip*,
     7 February 2018, http://www.emro.who.int/images/stories/palestine/documents/WHO_
     monthly_Gaza_access_report_Dec_2017-final.pdf?ua=1.

13   Ibid.

14   See 'Hemolytic uremic syndrome', Mayo Clinic, https://www.mayoclinic.org/diseases-
     conditions/hemolytic-uremic-syndrome/symptoms-causes/syc-20352399.

15   'Minimizing medical referrals abroad jeopardizes patients' lives', Palestinian Centre
     for Human Rights, 10 July 2017, https://pchrgaza.org/en/?p=9231.

16   World Health Organization, *Barriers for Patients in the Occupied Palestinian Territory*,
     26 November 2019, http://www.emro.who.int/images/stories/palestine/documents/
     WHO_Oct_2017_Monthly_report_-FINAL.pdf?ua=1.

17   Oliver Holmes and Hazem Balousha, 'A Jerusalem hospital where Palestinian babies
     die alone', *The Guardian*, 20 June 2019, https://www.theguardian.com/world/2019/
     jun/20/a-jerusalem-hospital-where-palestinian-babies-die-alone.

18   http://www.emro.who.int/images/stories/palestine/documents/July2019-Monthly_
     report.pdf?ua=1.

19   http://www.emro.who.int/images/stories/palestine/documents/Nov_2019_Monthly.
     pdf?ua=1

Chapter 15: Occupied Lives

1   'Israel: 50 years of occupation abuses', Human Rights Watch, 4 June 2017, https://
     www.hrw.org/news/2017/06/04/israel-50-years-occupation-abuses.

2   OCHA Occupied Palestinian Territory, *Fragmented Lives: Humanitarian Overview
     2016*, May 2017, https://www.ochaopt.org/sites/default/files/fragmented_lives_2016_
     english.pdf.

3   'Israel: 50 years of occupation abuses'; Joseph Krauss and Mohammed Daraghmeh,
     'New data shows Israeli settlement surge in east Jerusalem', Associated Press,
     13 September 2019, https://apnews.com/98e4ad57e0784e05b9fdde2e0ffd7439.

4   Human Rights Watch, *World Report 2019: Israel and Palestine, Events of 2018*,
     https://www.hrw.org/world-report/2019/country-chapters/israel/palestine.

5   AFP, 'More Palestinians find Israeli work despite conflict', France 24, 16 September
     2019, https://www.france24.com/en/20190916-more-palestinians-find-israeli-work-
     despite-conflict.

6   Karin Laub and Mohammed Daraghmeh, 'For Palestinians, Israeli permits
     a complex tool of control', Associated Press, 30 April 2018, https://apnews.
     com/7cfac1e5441747da841e51fdf3851460/For-Palestinians,-Israeli-permits-a-
     complex-tool-of-control.

7   'Israel: West Bank barrier endangers basic rights', Human Rights Watch, 30 September 2003, https://www.hrw.org/news/2003/09/30/israel-west-bank-barrier-endangers-basic-rights.

8   OCHA Occupied Palestinian Territory, *Barrier Update*, July 2011, https://web.archive.org/web/20160912193655/http://www.ochaopt.org/documents/ocha_opt_barrier_update_july_2011_english.pdf.

9   'The separation barrier', B'Tselem, 11 November 2017, https://www.btselem.org/separation_barrier.

10   'International Court of Justice finds Israeli barrier in Palestinian territory is illegal', UN News, 9 July 2004, https://news.un.org/en/story/2004/07/108912-international-court-justice-finds-israeli-barrier-palestinian-territory-illegal.

11   'Fatalities in the first Intifada', B'Tselem, https://www.btselem.org/statistics/first_intifada_tables.

12   'Intifada toll 2000–2005', BBC News, 8 February 2005, http://news.bbc.co.uk/2/hi/middle_east/3694350.stm.

13   'Wave of terror 2015–2019', Israel Ministry of Foreign Affairs, 31 December 2019, https://mfa.gov.il/MFA/ForeignPolicy/Terrorism/Palestinian/Pages/Wave-of-terror-October-2015.aspx.

14   Sophie McNeill (@Sophiemcneill), tweet, 30 October 2015, https://twitter.com/Sophiemcneill/status/653841649353756672?s=20; Diaa Hadid and Myra Noveck, 'Palestinian, 19, stabs 13-year-old to death in West Bank settlement', *New York Times*, 30 June 2016, https://www.nytimes.com/2016/07/01/world/middleeast/west-bank-kiryat-arba.html.

15   Sophie McNeil, 'Australia too "one-sided" to help broker peace in West Bank, say Palestinian officials', ABC News, 22 February 2017, https://www.abc.net.au/news/2017-02-22/west-bank-settlements-a-right-says-israeli-austrlian/8291328.

16   OCHA Occupied Palestinian Territory, *Fragmented Lives: Humanitarian Overview 2016*.

17   'US rebukes Israel and allows UN condemnation of settlements', ABC News, 24 December 2016, https://www.abc.net.au/news/2016-12-24/us-rebukes-israel-and-allows-un-condemnation-of-settlements/8146442.

18   Andrew Greene, 'Australia distances itself from Obama administration's stance against Israeli settlements', ABC News, 30 December 2016, https://www.abc.net.au/news/2016-12-30/australia-rejects-obama-stance-against-israeli-settlements/8153504.

19   'Israel: 50 years of occupation abuses'.

20   Ibid.

21   'Number of Palestinian children (12–17) in Israeli military detention', Defense for Children International, Palestine, 23 November 2019, https://www.dci-palestine.org/children_in_israeli_detention.

22   'East Jerusalem', OCHA Occupied Palestinian Territory, https://www.ochaopt.org/location/east-jerusalem.

23   David Wroe, 'George Brandis' East Jerusalem stance labelled "radically pro-Israel"', *Sydney Morning Herald*, 6 June 2014, https://www.smh.com.au/politics/federal/george-brandis-east-jerusalem-stance-labelled-radically-proisrael-20140605-39lze.html.

24   Andrew Bolt, 'One case of ABC bias that even Malcolm Turnbull cannot ignore', *Herald Sun*, 16 March 2015, https://www.heraldsun.com.au/blogs/andrew-bolt/one-case-of-abc-bias-that-even-malcolm-turnbull-cannot-ignore/news-story/e1573f83e4d6c8877bad3205d3566455.

25   Amanda Meade, 'Pro-Israel advocates in Australia targeted three journalists, new book claims', *The Guardian*, 29 July 2017, https://www.theguardian.com/media/2017/jul/29/pro-israel-advocates-in-australia-targeted-three-journalists-new-book-claims.

26   Ibid.

27   Australia/Israel & Jewish Affairs Council, Sophie McNeill search results, https://aijac.org.au/?s=Sophie+McNeill+.

28 Nir Hasson, 'Israel evicts Palestinian family from East Jerusalem home to make way for pre-'48 Jewish owners', *Haaretz*, 5 September 2017, https://www.haaretz.com/israel-news/.premium-israel-evicts-palestinian-family-from-j-lem-arab-neighbourhood-1.5448364.

29 'Significant increase in risk of displacement in East Jerusalem', OCHA Occupied Palestinian Territory, 11 September 2017, https://www.ochaopt.org/content/significant-increase-risk-displacement-east-jerusalem.

30 Sophie McNeill (@Sophiemcneill), tweet, 5 September 2017, https://twitter.com/Sophiemcneill/status/905320985527803904?s=20.

31 'Clashes erupt in Jerusalem amid tension over metal detectors at holy site', 22 July 2017, ABC News, http://www.abc.net.au/news/2017–07–22/clashes-erupt-in-jerusalem-amid-holy-site-tensions/8733332.

32 Fergus Hunter, 'Michael Danby spent $4574 of taxpayer funds on ads attacking ABC journalist', *Sydney Morning Herald*, 6 January 2018, https://www.smh.com.au/politics/federal/michael-danby-spent-4574-of-taxpayer-funds-on-ads-attacking-abc-journalist-20180106-h0edli.html.

33 Michael Koziol, 'Jewish groups defend Labor MP Michael Danby over ad attacking ABC journalist', *The Age*, 6 October 2017, https://www.theage.com.au/politics/federal/jewish-groups-defend-labor-mp-michael-danby-over-ad-attacking-abc-journalist-20171006-gyw1jv.html.

34 Adam Gartrell and Broede Carmody, '"It's time": Labor MP Michael Danby under pressure after ABC attack backfires', *The Age*, 5 October 2017, https://www.theage.com.au/politics/federal/its-time-labor-mp-michael-danby-under-pressure-after-abc-attack-backfires-20171005-gyuvj7.html.

35 UN Relief and Works Agency for Palestine Refugees in the Near East, *Gaza – Great March of Return, One Year On*, https://www.unrwa.org/campaign/gaza-great-march-return.

36 Ibid.

37 'At least 1,200 people injured in Gaza demonstrations will require limb reconstruction', OCHA Occupied Palestinian Territory, 6 September 2019, https://www.ochaopt.org/content/least-1200-people-injured-gaza-demonstrations-will-require-limb-reconstruction.

38 Ibid.

39 'US says Israeli settlements are no longer illegal', BBC News, 18 November 2019, https://www.bbc.com/news/world-middle-east-50468025.

40 Ibid.

41 Scott Douglas Jacobsen, 'Ask HRW (Israel and Palestine) 3 – November–December: deportation from Tel Aviv, Israel for Human Rights Watch Israel and Palestine director', 25 December 2019, Canadian Atheist, https://www.canadianatheist.com/2019/12/ask-hrw-3-jacobsen/.

42 'Data on casualties', OCHA Occupied Palestinian Territory, https://www.ochaopt.org/data/casualties, accessed 22 January 2020.

Chapter 16: Behind the Glittering Façade

1 Michael Brissenden, 'Al Minhad Air Base: A closer look at Australia's base of operations in the Middle East', ABC News, 15 September 2014, https://www.abc.net.au/news/2014-09-15/al-minhad:-australias-base-of-operations-in-the-middle-east/5744620.

2 'UAE arrests democracy activists', BBC News, 11 April 2011, https://www.bbc.com/news/world-middle-east-13043270.

3 'UAE: expunge activists' convictions', Human Rights Watch, 28 November 2011, https://www.hrw.org/news/2011/11/30/uae-expunge-activists-convictions.

4 'Five jailed UAE activists "receive presidential pardon"', BBC News, 28 November 2011, https://www.bbc.com/news/world-middle-east-15922492.

5 Martin Ennals Award, 'Film portrait – Ahmed Mansoor – Martin Ennals Award laureate 2015', YouTube, 12 October 2015, https://www.youtube.com/watch?time_continue=324&v=eKfVe-xQSm0&feature=emb_logo.

6 Amnesty International, *'There Is No Freedom Here': Silencing Dissent in the United Arab Emirates (UAE)*, 18 November 2014, https://www.amnesty.org/download/Documents/MDE2500182014ENGLISH.PDF.

7 David Hearst, 'The UAE's bizarre, political trial of 94 activists', *The Guardian*, 6 March 2013, https://www.theguardian.com/commentisfree/2013/mar/06/uae-trial-94-activists.

8 Amnesty International, *'There Is No Freedom Here'*.

9 'Foreign governments', Levick, http://levick.com/experience/industry/foreign-governments#waypoint3.

10 Martin Ennals Award, 'Film portrait – Ahmed Mansoor – Martin Ennals Award laureate 2015', YouTube.

11 Arthur Spyrou (@AusAmbUAE), tweet, 19 March 2017, https://twitter.com/AusAmbUAE/status/843688553192329216.

12 Lisa Barrington and Stephanie Nebehay, 'UN says UAE activist Mansoor's prison conditions "may constitute torture"', Reuters, 8 May 2019, https://uk.reuters.com/article/uk-emirates-prisoners/u-n-says-uae-activist-mansoors-prison-conditions-may-constitute-torture-idUKKCN1SD1OE.

13 David Wroe, 'Defence Industry Minister Christopher Pyne wants Australia to become major arms exporter', *Sydney Morning Herald*, 15 July 2017, https://www.smh.com.au/politics/federal/defence-industry-minister-christopher-pyne-wants-australia-to-become-major-arms-exporter-20170715-gxbv4m.html.

14 'Motion for a resolution', European Parliament, 2 October 2018, http://www.europarl.europa.eu/sides/getDoc.do?type=MOTION&reference=B8-2018-0462&format=XML&language=EN.

15 'How BAE sold cyber-surveillance tools to Arab states', BBC News, 15 June 2017, https://www.bbc.com/news/world-middle-east-40276568.

16 Joseph Menn, 'Apple fixes security flaw after UAE dissident's iPhone targeted', Reuters, 26 August 2016, https://www.reuters.com/article/us-apple-iphone-cyber-idUSKCN1102B1.

17 'Sheikha (Princess) Latifa Al Maktoum – FULL UNEDITED VIDEO – #FreeLatifa', Free Latifa, YouTube, 11 March 2018, https://www.youtube.com/watch?v=UN7OEFyNUkQ.

18 Vivian Yee, 'A princess vanishes. a video offers alarming clues', *New York Times*, 10 February 2019, https://www.nytimes.com/2019/02/10/world/middleeast/princess-latifa-sheikha-dubai.html.

19 Emma Graham-Harrison, 'Missing Emirati princess "planned escape for seven years"', *The Guardian*, 4 December 2018, https://www.theguardian.com/world/2018/dec/04/missing-emirati-princess-latifa-al-maktoum-had-planned-escape-for-seven-years.

20 Nazia Parveen and Patrick Wintour, 'Matthew Hedges: British academic accused of spying jailed for life in UAE', *The Guardian*, 22 November 2018, https://www.theguardian.com/world/2018/nov/21/british-academic-matthew-hedges-accused-of-spying-jailed-for-life-in-uae.

21 Robert Mendick, 'Matthew Hedges force-fed cocktail of drugs during imprisonment on spying charges in the UAE', *The Telegraph*, 5 December 2018, https://www.telegraph.co.uk/news/2018/12/04/academic-jailed-spying-uae-now-suffering-severe-withdrawal-symptoms/; Matthew Weaver, 'Matthew Hedges: I'm determined to clear my name after UAE ordeal', *The Guardian*, 5 December 2018, https://www.theguardian.com/world/2018/dec/05/matthew-hedges-determined-clear-name-uae-spying-ordeal.

22 Deborah Haynes, 'Matthew Hedges: British academic freed from UAE concerned for detained UK football fan', Sky News, 11 February 2019, https://news.sky.com/story/

matthew-hedges-british-academic-freed-from-uae-concerned-for-detained-uk-football-fan-11634735.

23   Aya Batrawy, 'UAE's tolerance embraces faiths, runs up against politics', AP News, 2 February 2019, https://apnews.com/977d548fdf56424c8a9f027a3d816e20.

24   Al Jazeera, 'Pope in UAE: reject wars in Yemen, Syria, Iraq and Libya', 5 February 2019, https://www.aljazeera.com/news/2019/02/pope-uae-reject-wars-yemen-syria-iraq-libya-190204155801553.html.

25   Mohammed bin Zayed Al Nahyan (@MohamedBinZayed), tweet, 4 February 2019, https://twitter.com/MohamedBinZayed/status/1092358062575419398.

26   'Princess Haya: Dubai ruler's wife in UK "in fear of her life"', BBC News, 2 July 2019, https://www.bbc.com/news/world-middle-east-48843168.

27   Vanessa Grigoriadis, '"You're essentially a prisoner": why do Dubai's princesses keep trying to escape?', *Vanity Fair*, 11 November 2019, https://www.vanityfair.com/news/2019/11/why-do-dubais-princesses-keep-trying-to-escape.

28   'On his 50th birthday, ICFUAE calls for the immediate release of rights defender Ahmed Mansoor', ICFUAE, 22 October 2019, http://icfuae.org.uk/press-releases/his-50th-birthday-icfuae-calls-immediate-release-rights-defender-ahmed-msnsoor.

29   Arthur Spyrou, tweet, 30 October 2019, https://twitter.com/AusAmbUAE/status/1189465692078268416?s=20.

30   Human Rights Watch, 'Artur and Ahmed: prison mates in UAE hell', 8 January 2020, https://www.hrw.org/news/2020/01/08/artur-and-ahmed-prison-mates-uae-hell.

Chapter 17: Little Bodies Laid Out in a Row

1   Human Rights Watch, *Attacks on Ghouta: Analysis of Alleged Use of Chemical Weapons in Syria*, 10 September 2013, https://www.hrw.org/report/2013/09/10/attacks-ghouta/analysis-alleged-use-chemical-weapons-syria.

2   United Nations Mission to Investigate Allegations of the Use of Chemical Weapons in the Syrian Arab Republic, *Report on the Alleged Use of Chemical Weapons in the Ghouta Area of Damascus on 21 August 2013*, 16 September 2013, http://www.un.org/zh/focus/northafrica/cwinvestigation.pdf.

3   Anthony Deutsch, 'How Syria continued to gas its people as the world looked on', Reuters, 17 August 2017, https://www.reuters.com/investigates/special-report/mideast-crisis-syria-chemicalweapons; Patrick Wintour, 'Why does Syria still have chemical weapons?', *The Guardian*, 18 April 2018, https://www.theguardian.com/world/2018/apr/18/why-does-syria-still-have-chemical-weapons.

4   Sophie McNeill (@Sophiemcneill), tweet, 4 April 2017, https://twitter.com/sophiemcneill/status/849151622223736833?s=21.

5   United Nations Human Rights Council, *Report of the Independent International Commission of Inquiry on the Syrian Arab Republic*, 6 September 2017, p.24, https://www.ohchr.org/EN/HRBodies/HRC/IICISyria/Pages/Documentation.aspx.

6   Patrick Kingsley and Anne Barnard, 'Survivors of Syria gas attack recount "a cruel scene"', *New York Times*, 4 April 2017, https://www.nytimes.com/2017/04/04/world/middleeast/syria-hospital-airstrike-gas-attack.tml?action=click&module=RelatedCoverage&pgtype= Article&region=Footer.

7   'Syria chemical "attack": what we know,' BBC News, 26 April 2017, https://www.bbc.com/news/world-middle-east-39500947.

8   *Report of the Independent International Commission of Inquiry on the Syrian Arab Republic*, 6 September 2017, p.24.

9   Raf Sanchez, 'Syria "chemical attack": 11 children among at least 58 people reported killed in alleged regime strike on Idlib', *The Telegraph* (UK), 4 April 2017, https://www.telegraph.co.uk/news/2017/04/04/syria-gas-attack-nine-children-among-least-35-people-reported/.

10   *Report of the Independent International Commission of Inquiry on the Syrian Arab Republic*.

11   Ibid.

12 Ellen Francis, 'Scores reported killed in gas attack on Syrian rebel area', Reuters, 4 April 2017, https://www.reuters.com/article/us-mideast-crisis-syria-idlib-idUSKBN1760IB?utm_source=twitter&utm_medium=Social.

13 *Report of the Independent International Commission of Inquiry on the Syrian Arab Republic*, 6 September 2017, p.23.

14 Anne Barnard and Michael R. Gordon, 'Worst chemical attack in years in Syria: U.S. blames Assad', *New York Times*, 4 April 2017, https://www.nytimes.com/2017/04/04/world/middleeast/syria-gas-attack.html?module=inline.

15 Raf Sanchez, (@rafsanchez), tweet, 4 April 2017, https://twitter.com/rafsanchez/status/849269313026609156.

16 'Syria conflict: "chemical attack" in Idlib kills 58', BBC News, 4 April 2017, https://www.bbc.com/news/world-middle-east-39488539.

17 Leith Aboufadel, 'Syrian army strikes jihadist gas depot in southern Idlib: report', AMN, 4 April 2017, https://www.almasdarnews.com/article/syrian-army-strikes-jihadist-gas-depot-southern-idlib-report/.

18 Kareem Shaheen, '"The dead were wherever you looked": inside Syrian town after gas attack', *The Guardian*, 7 April 2017, https://www.theguardian.com/world/2017/apr/06/the-dead-were-wherever-you-looked-inside-syrian-town-after-chemical-attack.

19 'Khan Sheikhoun victims have symptoms consistent with exposure to chemical substances', Médecins Sans Frontières, 5 April 2017, https://www.msf.org/syria-khan-sheikhoun-victims-have-symptoms-consistent-exposure-chemical-substances.

20 Luke Harding, '"It had a big impact on me" – story behind Trump's whirlwind missile response', *The Guardian*, 8 April 2017, https://www.theguardian.com/world/2017/apr/07/how-pictures-of-syrias-dead-babies-made-trump-do-unthinkable.

21 Michael R. Gordon, Helene Cooper and Michael D. Shear, 'Dozens of U.S. missiles hit air base in Syria', *New York Times*, 6 April 2017, https://www.nytimes.com/2017/04/06/world/middleeast/us-said-to-weigh-military-responses-to-syrian-chemical-attack.html.

22 'Syrian monitor says at least four soldiers killed at airbase', Reuters, 7 April 2017, https://uk.reuters.com/article/uk-mideast-crisis-syria-observatory-idUKKBN1790IO?il=0; Raja Abdulrahim, 'Rebels hail U.S. strike, Syria says 16 killed', *Wall Street Journal*, 7 April 2017, https://www.wsj.com/articles/syrian-media-say-u-s-attack-caused-damage-to-air-base-multiple-casualties-1491535071.

23 Gordon, Cooper and Shear, 'Dozens of U.S. missiles hit air base in Syria'.

24 Ibid.

25 'Syria war: why was Shayrat airbase bombed?', BBC News, 7 April 2017, https://www.bbc.com/news/world-us-canada-39531045.

26 Josie Ensor, 'Syrian warplanes take off once again from air base bombed by US Tomahawks', *The Telegraph* (UK), 8 April 2017, https://www.telegraph.co.uk/news/2017/04/08/syrian-warplanes-take-air-base-bombed-us-tomahawks/.

27 Sophie McNeill, '"Day from hell": doctor reflects on deadly Syrian chemical attack', *Lateline*, ABC TV, 2 May 2017, https://www.abc.net.au/lateline/day-from-hell:-doctor-reflects-on-deadly-syrian/8491298.

28 George Monbiot, 'A lesson from Syria: it's crucial not to fuel far-right conspiracy theories', *The Guardian*, 15 November 2017, https://www.theguardian.com/commentisfree/2017/nov/15/lesson-from-syria-chemical-weapons-conspiracy-theories-alt-right; Kylar Loussikian, '"Trump is a vanity terrorist"', *Daily Telegraph*, 11 April 2017, https://www.dailytelegraph.com.au/news/nsw/sydney-university-academic-claims-us-is-the-mastermind-of-terrorism-denies-syrian-gas-attack/news-story/fd752c1d6df60b1515fd8e49a9fd650d.

29 Theodore A. Postol, *Addendum to A Quick Turnaround Assessment of the White House Intelligence Report Issued on April 11, 2017, about the Nerve Agent Attack in Khan Shaykhun, Syria*, 13 April 2017, https://phaven-prod.s3.amazonaws.com/files/document_part/asset/1862086/BCI9ExNk1DbCJB809IPlDfi8xqE/ADDENDUM_TO_-

-_AQuickTurnaroundAssessmentoftheWhiteHouseIntelligenceReport-Issued_on-April-11_2017_About-the_Nerve_Agent-Attack-in-Khan_Shaykhun__Syria__April13_2017__.pdf.

30   'Chomsky on Syria: we must help fleeing refugees & pursue diplomatic settlement', *Democracy Now*, 26 April 2017, https://www.democracynow.org/2017/4/26/chomsky_on_syria_we_must_help; Monbiot, 'A lesson from Syria'.

31   Tulsi Gabbard, 'Reports on chemical attacks in Syria', https://www.tulsi2020.com/issues/reports-chemical-attacks-syria.

32   Ian Wilkie, 'Now Mattis admits there was no evidence Assad used poison gas on his people: opinion', *Newsweek*, 8 February 2018, https://www.newsweek.com/now-mattis-admits-there-was-no-evidence-assad-using-poison-gas-his-people-801542.

33   *Report of the Independent International Commission of Inquiry on the Syrian Arab Republic*, p.24.

34   Human Rights Watch, *Death by Chemicals: The Syrian Government's Widespread and Systematic Use of Chemical Weapons*, 1 May 2017, https://www.hrw.org/report/2017/05/01/death-chemicals/syrian-governments-widespread-and-systematic-use-chemical-weapons/.

35   'Syria blamed for chemical weapons attack in 2015', BBC News, 22 October 2016, https://www.bbc.com/news/world-middle-east-37736184.

36   'Syria war: Russia and China veto sanctions', BBC News, 28 February 2017, https://www.bbc.com/news/world-middle-east-39116854.

37   'Syria: medical staff and patients killed', Médecins Sans Frontières, 2 April 2017, https://www.msf.org.au/article/project-news/syria-medical-staff-and-patients-killed.

38   Syrian Observatory for Human Rights, 'About 2800 persons including 938 children, citizen women and men were killed in April 2017', 1 May 2017, http://www.syriahr.com/en/?p=65659.

39   Deutsch, 'How Syria continued to gas its people as the world looked on'.

40   *Report of the Independent International Commission of Inquiry on the Syrian Arab Republic*.

41   Stephanie Nebehay, 'Syrian government forces used chemical weapons more than two dozen times: U.N.', Reuters, 6 September 2017, https://www.reuters.com/article/us-mideast-crisis-syria-warcrimes/syrian-government-forces-used-chemical-weapons-more-than-two-dozen-times-u-n-idUSKCN1BH18W.

42   Rodrigo Campos, 'Syrian government to blame for April sarin attack – U.N. report', Reuters, 27 October 2017, https://uk.reuters.com/article/uk-mideast-crisis-syria-un/syrian-government-to-blame-for-april-sarin-attack-u-n-report-idUKKBN1CV3GF.

43   United Nations Security Council, *Seventh Report of the Organisation for the Prohibition of Chemical Weapons-United Nations Joint Investigative Mechanism*, 26 October 2017, p.10, https://www.securitycouncilreport.org/atf/cf/%7B65BFCF9B-6D27-4E9C-8CD3-CF6E4FF96FF9%7D/s_2017_904.pdf.

44   Wintour, 'Why does Syria still have chemical weapons?'.

45   OPCW, *Report of the Fact-finding Mission Regarding the Incident of Alleged Use of Toxic Chemicals as a Weapon in Douma, Syrian Arab Republic, on 7 April 2018*, 1 March 2019, https://www.opcw.org/sites/default/files/documents/2019/03/s-1731–2019%28e%29.pdf.

46   Alan Yuhas, 'Evidence of chlorine found in Syrian town of Douma, investigators say', *New York Times*, 1 March 2019, https://www.nytimes.com/2019/03/01/world/middleeast/syria-chlorine-douma-report.html; 'Open source survey of alleged chemical attacks in Douma on 7th April 2018', Bellingcat, 11 April 2018, https://www.bellingcat.com/news/mena/2018/04/11/open-source-survey-alleged-chemical-attacks-douma-7th-april-2018/.

47   Global Pubic Policy Institute, *Nowhere to Hide: The Logic of Chemical Weapons Use in Syria*, February 2019, https://www.gppi.net/media/GPPi_Schneider_Luetkefend_2019_Nowhere_to_Hide_Web.pdf.

Chapter 18: The Flowers are Dead

1 'UN and partners launch plan to support five million Syrian refugees and countries hosting them', UNHCR, 12 December 2017, https://www.unhcr.org/en-au/news/briefing/2017/12/5a2ffd534/un-partners-launch-plan-support-five-million-syrian-refugees-countries.html.

Chapter 19: Escape from Saudi

1 Human Rights Watch, *Boxed In: Women and Saudi Arabia's Male Guardianship System*, 16 July 2016, https://www.hrw.org/report/2016/07/16/boxed/women-and-saudi-arabias-male-guardianship-system.

2 Nourah (@nourahfa313), tweet, 6 January 2019, https://twitter.com/nourahfa313/status/1081584253358333953?s=20.

3 Human Rights Watch, 'Fleeing woman returned to Saudi Arabia against her will', 14 April 2017, https://www.hrw.org/news/2017/04/14/fleeing-woman-returned-saudi-arabia-against-her-will.

4 Shane Harris, Greg Miller and Josh Dawsey, 'CIA concludes Saudi crown prince ordered Jamal Khashoggi's assassination', *Washington Post*, 17 November 2018, https://www.washingtonpost.com/world/national-security/cia-concludes-saudi-crown-prince-ordered-jamal-khashoggis-assassination/2018/11/16/98c89fe6-e9b2-11e8-a939-9469f1166f9d_story.html.

5 Rahaf Mohammed Al Qunun, tweet, 6 January 2019, https://twitter.com/rahaf84427714/status/1081785232280428544?s=20.

6 Richard C. Paddock, 'Fleeing Saudi woman, facing deportation, is allowed to remain in Thailand, *New York Times*, 7 January 2019, https://www.nytimes.com/2019/01/07/world/asia/saudi-thailand-asylum-rahaf-mohammed-alqunun.html?smtyp=cur&smid=tw-nytimes.

7 Phil Robertson (@Reaproy), tweet, 6 January 2019, https://twitter.com/Reaproy/status/1081811017007394823.

8 Human Rights Watch, 'Fleeing woman returned to Saudi Arabia against her will', 14 April 2017.

9 Trends Australia (@TrendsAustralia), tweet, 7 January 2019, https://twitter.com/TrendsAustralia/status/1081914398288109573.

10 Sophie McNeill (@Sophiemcneill), tweet, 7 January 2019, https://twitter.com/Sophiemcneill/status/1082054125976580096?s=20.

11 Craig Murray (@CraigMurrayOrg), tweet, 7 January 2019, https://twitter.com/CraigMurrayOrg/status/1082071593407430657.

12 'Saudi woman held at Bangkok airport says fears death if repatriated', AFP news agency, 7 January 2019, https://sg.news.yahoo.com/saudi-woman-held-bangkok-airport-says-fears-death-132515817.html.

13 Rahaf Mohammed (@rahaf84427714), tweet, 7 January 2019, https://twitter.com/rahaf84427714/status/1082080876823928832?s=20.

14 Nora Abdulkarim (@Ana3rabeya), tweet, 7 January 2019, https://twitter.com/Ana3rabeya/status/1082049188140060673.

15 Communication and Media Center, Saudi Ministry of Foreign Affairs (@CMCMOFA), tweet, 7 January 2019, https://twitter.com/CMCMOFA/status/1082073793869299714.

16 Phil Robertson (@Reaproy), tweet, 7 January 2019, https://twitter.com/Reaproy/status/1082096485079048192?s=20.

17 Rahaf Mohammed (@rahaf84427714), tweet, 7 January 2019, https://twitter.com/rahaf84427714/status/1082005121016320001.

18 Jonathan Head (@pakhead), tweet, 7 January 2019, https://twitter.com/pakhead/status/1082117175559614464?s=20.

19 Heather Chen and Mayuri Mei Lin, 'Rahaf al-Qunun: unpicking the tweets that may have saved her life', BBC News, 10 January 2019, https://www.bbc.com/news/world-asia-46819199.

20 Georg Schmidt (@GermanAmbTHA), tweet, 7 January 2019, https://twitter.com/
GermanAmbTHA/status/1082118497893736448.

21 Sophie McNeill (@Sophiemcneill), tweet, 7 January 2019, https://twitter.com/
sophiemcneill/status/1082114498708746241?lang=en.

22 'Saudi woman held at Bangkok airport says fears death if repatriated', 7 January
2019.

23 Sophie McNeill (@Sophiemcneill), tweet, 7 January 2019, https://twitter.com/
sophiemcneill/status/1082054125976580096?lang=en.

24 Richard C. Paddock, 'Fleeing Saudi woman, facing deportation, is allowed to remain
in Thailand, 7 January 2019.

25 Melissa Fleming (@MelissaFleming), tweet, 7 January 2019, https://twitter.com/
MelissaFleming/status/1082212629148565504?s=20.

26 Sophie McNeill (@Sophiemcneill), tweet, 7 January 2019, https://twitter.com/
Sophiemcneill/status/1082233244504928256?s=20.

27 CNN (@CNN), tweet, 8 January 2019, https://twitter.com/CNN/
status/1082267491328512001.

28 Rahaf Mohammed (@rahaf84427714), tweet, 8 January 2019, https://twitter.com/
rahaf84427714/status/1082297101239836672?s=20.

29 Jamie Fullerton and Helen Davidson, '"You saved Rahaf's life: online outcry
kept "terrified" Saudi woman safe', *The Guardian*, 9 January 2019, https://www.
theguardian.com/world/2019/jan/08/rahaf-al-qunun-saudi-woman-under-un-
protection-as-australia-urges-asylum-claim.

30 Hoda Abdel-Hamid (@HodaAH), tweet, 8 January 2019, https://twitter.com/HodaAH/
status/1082608715696529408?s=20.

31 Lisa Martin, 'Rahaf al-Qunun: Australia will "consider" granting Saudi woman a visa',
The Guardian, 8 January 2019, https://www.theguardian.com/australia-news/2019/
jan/08/rahaf-al-qunun-australia-asked-to-clarify-reports-it-has-cancelled-saudi-
womans-visa.

32 'Rahaf al-Qunun: UN "considers Saudi woman a refugee"', BBC News, 9 January
2019, https://www.bbc.com/news/world-australia-46806485.

33 Nora Abdulkarim (@Ana3rabeya), tweet, 8 January 2019, https://twitter.com/
Ana3rabeya/status/1082525869774647296?s=20.

34 Press conference, Bangkok, Minister for Foreign Affairs, 10 January 2019, https://
www.foreignminister.gov.au/minister/marise-payne/transcript-eoe/press-conference-
bangkok.

35 'Labor urges government to offer Saudi woman asylum in Australia', SBS News, 10
January 2019, https://www.sbs.com.au/news/labor-urges-government-to-offer-saudi-
woman-asylum-in-australia.

36 Ashifa Kassam, 'Saudi Arabia expels Canadian envoy for urging activists' release', *The
Guardian*, 6 August 2018, https://www.theguardian.com/world/2018/aug/06/saudi-
arabia-expels-canadian-ambassador-for-urging-release-of-activists.

37 'Saudi teen Rahaf Alqunun granted asylum in Canada, Justin Trudeau confirms', ABC
News, 13 January 2019, https://www.abc.net.au/news/2019-01-12/saudi-teen-rahaf-
alqunun-granted-asylum-in-canada/10710626.

38 *The Today Show* (@TheTodayShow), tweet, 12 January 2019, https://twitter.com/
TheTodayShow/status/1083818419844145152?s=20.

39 Sophie McNeill (@Sophiemcneill), tweet, 18 January 2019, https://twitter.com/
Sophiemcneill/status/1086089624169066502?s=20.

40 Sophie McNeill, 'Rahaf Al Qunun pledges to use her freedom to campaign for
others after being granted asylum in Canada', ABC News, 16 January 2019, https://
www.abc.net.au/news/2019-01-15/rahaf-alqunun-speaks-first-time-from-canada-
asylum/10716182.

41 Geert Cappelaere, UNICEF Regional Director for the Middle East and North Africa,
press release, 15 January 2019, https://www.unicef.org/mena/press-releases/lack-access-
medical-care-syria-putting-childrens-lives-risk.

42   Human Rights Watch, 'Fleeing woman returned to Saudi Arabia against her will', 14 April 2017.

43   steve bob, 'Saudi woman captured in airport', YouTube, 15 April 2017, https://youtu.be/qxrdLvX4cRM.

44   Katie Paul, 'Saudi woman seeking asylum in Australian returned to Saudi Arabia', Reuters, 13 April 2017, https://www.reuters.com/article/us-saudi-women-rights/saudi-woman-seeking-asylum-in-australia-returned-to-saudi-arabia-idUSKBN17E1WP.

45   Ibid.

46   Human Rights Watch, *Boxed In*, 16 July 2016, p.41.

47   Ibid., p.46.

48   Ibid., p.40.

49   'Woman ends life at Makkah shelter', *Arab News*, 26 August 2015, https://www.arabnews.com/saudi-arabia/news/797071.

50   ExMuslim TV, 'The Saudi prisons for women VICTIMS of abuse', 21 March 2018, https://www.youtube.com/watch?v=d8xF7E3Ve5E&feature=youtu.be.

51   Martin Chulov, '"I will return Saudi Arabia to moderate Islam, says crown prince', *The Guardian*, 25 October 2017, https://www.theguardian.com/world/2017/oct/24/i-will-return-saudi-arabia-moderate-islam-crown-prince.

52   Michael Buchanan, 'Freed Saudi woman driver vows to continue campaign', BBC News, 21 July 2011, https://www.bbc.com/news/world-middle-east-14240340.

53   Ben Hubbard, '"Our hands can reach you": Khashoggi case shakes Saudi dissidents abroad', *New York Times*, 8 October 2018, https://www.nytimes.com/2018/10/08/world/middleeast/saudi-jamal-khashoggi-dissent.html.

54   Norah O'Donnell, 'Saudi Arabia's heir to the throne talks to 60 Minutes', *60 Minutes*, 19 March 2018, https://www.cbsnews.com/news/saudi-crown-prince-talks-to-60-minutes/.

55   Ben Hubbard, '"Our hands can reach you"', 8 October 2018.

56   Lauren Aratani, 'Family of Loujain al-Hathloul fight to free imprisoned activist', *The Guardian*, 14 July 2019, https://www.theguardian.com/world/2019/jul/14/loujain-al-hathloul-family-imprisoned-saudi-activist.

57   Nora Abdulkarim (@Ana3rabeya), tweet, 19 May 2018, https://twitter.com/Ana3rabeya/status/997654098718744578?s=20.

58   Amnesty International, 'Saudi Arabia: chilling smear campaign against women's rights defenders', 19 May 2018, https://www.amnesty.org/en/latest/news/2018/05/saudi-arabia-chilling-smear-campaign-tries-to-discredit-loujain-al-hathloul-and-other-detained-womens-rights-defenders/.

59   Alia Al Hathloul, 'My sister is in a Saudi prison. Will Mike Pompeo stay silent?', *New York Times*, 13 January 2019, https://www.nytimes.com/2019/01/13/opinion/saudi-women-rights-activist-prison-pompeo.html?module=inline.

60   Lauren Aratani, 'Family of Loujain al-Hathloul fight to free imprisoned activist', 14 July 2019.

61   Alia Al Hathloul, 'My sister is in a Saudi prison', 13 January 2019.

62   Walid Al Hathoul, 'While my sister is in a Saudi jail, Mariah Carey could use her voice to help her', CNN, 31 January 2019, https://edition.cnn.com/2019/01/31/opinions/walid-alhathloul-opinion-intl/index.html.

63   Ben Hubbard, '"Our hands can reach you"', 8 October 2018.

64   Human Rights Watch, 'Saudi Arabia: detained women reported tortured', 20 November 2018, https://www.hrw.org/news/2018/11/20/saudi-arabia-detained-women-reported-tortured.

65   Vivian Nereim, 'Saudi Arabia puts group of women's rights activists on trial', Bloomberg, 13 March 2019, https://www.bloomberg.com/news/articles/2019-03-13/saudi-arabia-puts-prominent-women-s-rights-activists-on-trial.

66   Human Rights Watch, 'Saudi Arabia: Abusive charges against women activists', 21 March 2019, https://www.hrw.org/news/2019/03/21/saudi-arabia-abusive-charges-against-women-activists.

67 Sarah-Jean Whitson, 'Loujain al-Hathloul', *TIME* magazine, 16 April 2019, https://time.com/collection-post/5567677/loujain-al-hathloul/.

68 'Remarks by President Trump and Crown Prince Mohammad bin Salman of the Kingdom of Saudi Arabia before working breakfast', White House, 28 June 2019, https://www.whitehouse.gov/briefings-statements/remarks-president-trump-crown-prince-mohammad-bin-salman-kingdom-saudi-arabia-working-breakfast-osaka-japan/.

69 Walid Al Hathloul (@WalidAlhathloul), tweet, 14 August 2019, https://twitter.com/WalidAlhathloul/status/1161280885829844993?s=20.

70 Reem's and Rawan's names have been changed to protect their identities.

71 Hilary Whiteman, with Ivan Watson and Sandi Sidhu, 'Desperate and alone, Saudi sisters risk everything to flee oppression', CNN, 21 February 2019, https://edition.cnn.com/2019/02/20/asia/saudi-arabia-sisters-flee-hong-kong-intl/index.html.

72 Hilary Whiteman, Sandi Sidhu and Ivan Watson, 'Saudi sisters free but questions remain over 6-month stay in Hong Kong', CNN, 25 March 2019, https://edition.cnn.com/2019/03/25/asia/saudi-sisters-hong-kong-intl/index.html.

73 CBS New York, 'NYPD update on deaths of Saudi girls', YouTube, 2 November 2018, https://www.youtube.com/watch?v=_Fp7nNyZgaI.

74 'Deaths of Saudi sisters found bound together in New York river', *The Guardian*, 22 January 2019, https://www.theguardian.com/us-news/2019/jan/22/saudi-sisters-deaths-new-york-river-ruled-suicide.

75 Umberto Bacchi, 'Runaway sisters leave Georgia to start new life', Reuters, 7 May 2019, https://www.reuters.com/article/us-georgia-saudi-sisters/runaway-saudi-sisters-leave-georgia-to-start-new-life-idUSKCN1SD15J, and Lindsey Hilsum, Saudie sisters on run from authorities – and father they say abused them', Channel 4 News, 8 July 2019, https://www.channel4.com/news/exclusive-saudi-sisters-on-run-from-authorities-and-father-they-say-abused-them.

76 Dominic Dudley, 'Civil society groups pledge to boycott Saudi Arabia's G20 presidency', Forbes, 13 January 2020, https://www.forbes.com/sites/dominicdudley/2020/01/13/civil-society-boycott-saudi-g20/#4ac12a4734ba.

Conclusion

1 'Syrians face "daily nightmare" in Idlib, says top UN official', UN News, 7 January 2020, https://news.un.org/en/story/2020/01/1054871.

2 'Tell the world', *Four Corners*, ABC TV, 15 July 2019, https://www.abc.net.au/4corners/xinjiang-tell-the-world/11350450.

3 Michelle Nichols, 'Russia, backed by China, casts 14th UN veto on Syria to block cross-border aid', Reuters, 21 December 2019, https://www.reuters.com/article/us-syria-security-un/russia-backed-by-china-casts-14th-u-n-veto-on-syria-to-block-cross-border-aid-idUSKBN1YO23V.

4 'The UN reform', Permanent Mission of France to the United Nations in New York, November 2019, https://onu.delegfrance.org/The-UN-Reform.

5 Syrian American Medical Society, *Fuelling the Fire: How the UN Security Council's Permanent Members Are Undermining Their Own Commitments on Syria*, March 2016, https://www.sams-usa.net/wp-content/uploads/2016/08/Fueling-the-Fire.pdf.

6 Eliza Laschon, 'Scott Morrison uses Lowy Lecture to take veiled swipe at UN while urging against "negative globalism"', ABC News, 4 October 2019, https://www.abc.net.au/news/2019-10-04/scott-morrison-takes-jab-at-united-nations-during-lowy-lecture/11572804.

7 Owen Bowcott, Oliver Holmes and Erin Durkin, 'John Bolton threatens war crimes court with sanctions in virulent attack', *The Guardian*, 11 September 2018, https://www.theguardian.com/us-news/2018/sep/10/john-bolton-castigate-icc-washington-speech.

8 Stephen Rapp in Marlise Simons and Megan Specia, 'US revokes visa of ICC prosecutor pursuing Afghan war crimes', *New York Times*, 5 April 2019, https://www.nytimes.com/2019/04/05/world/europe/us-icc-prosecutor-afghanistan.html.

9   Courtney McBride, 'ICC won't launch formal investigation in Afghanistan', *Wall Street Journal*, 12 April 2019, https://www.wsj.com/articles/icc-wont-launch-formal-investigation-in-afghanistan-11555081875.

10   'Australia holds world record for longest period of growth among developed economies', Australian Trade and Investment Commission, 28 November 2018, https://www.austrade.gov.au/international/invest/investor-updates/2018/australia-holds-world-record-for-longest-period-of-growth-among-developed-economies.

11   Christen Tilley, 'Chart of the day: Australia nudges Switzerland off top of global median wealth list', ABC News, 23 November 2018, https://www.abc.net.au/news/2018-11-23/australia-tops-median-wealth-per-adult-list/10518082.

12   Dr Tania Miletic, 'Australian foreign aid is at an all-time low and should be dramatically increased', Election Watch, University of Melbourne, 2 May 2019, https://electionwatch.unimelb.edu.au/articles/australian-foreign-aid-is-at-an-all-time-low-and-should-be-dramatically-increased.

13   Latika Bourke, 'Labor MPs call for Scott Morrison to back bipartisan aid spend', *Sydney Morning Herald*, 16 October 2019, https://www.smh.com.au/politics/federal/labor-mps-call-for-scott-morrison-to-back-bipartisan-aid-spend-20191014-p530o0.html.

14   'Saudi Arabia: travel restrictions on Saudi women lifted', Human Rights Watch, 22 August 2019, https://www.hrw.org/news/2019/08/22/saudi-arabia-travel-restrictions-saudi-women-lifted.

15   'UK arms sales to Saudi Arabia unlawful, court rules', BBC News, 20 June 2019, https://www.bbc.com/news/uk-48704596.

16   'UK arms licences to Saudi-led coalition up by almost half despite arms trade treaty', Oxfam Great Britain, 24 December 2019, https://oxfamapps.org/media/press_release/uk-arms-licences-to-saudi-led-coalition-up-by-almost-half-despite-arms-trade-treaty/.

17   David Rennie, (@DSORennie), tweet, 12 September 2019, https://twitter.com/DSORennie/status/1171797398760259590?s=20.

18   Adam Ni, (@adam_ni), tweet, 12 September 2019, https://twitter.com/adam_ni/status/1171866005582340096?s=20.

Acknowledgements

To all the brave, dignified people I met across the Middle East, thank you for teaching me life.

To Noura Ghazi, Wael Saad Al Deen and Jon Phillips, thank you so much for your patience and trust. To my brother Khaled Naanaa, you are my hero. I am so grateful to have you, Joumana, Ayaa and Julie in my life. To Ahmad Sandeh, you are such a beautiful soul. Thank you for everything. To Nazieh, Mariam, Abdul Rahman and Basiyeh, thank you for sharing so much. Hisham Al-Omeisy, you are a champion and an amazing father. Thank you for your bravery. Osamah Alfakih, thank you for your incredible work, you're an inspiration. To Abu Rajab and Dr Farida, I am in awe of you both. The world needs more people like you. May you return home one day. Thank you so much to Dr Sam Attar, Dr Zaher Sahloul, Mohamad Katoub, Dr Amjad, Adham Sahloul, Dr John Kahler and everyone at the Syrian American Medical Society. You are all angels. Jonathan Hollander at Battery Dance, thanks for being so special. Adiba Qasim, you are amazing, thank you. To the late Dr Mamoun Morad, may you rest in peace knowing you did all you could. Connie Lenneberg and Ben Quilty, thanks for being such gorgeous humans. To Rahaf Mohammed, thank you for teaching me what true courage looks like. May you have a wonderful life – you deserve so much love. To Dina Ali, wherever you are, we will never forget you. Meagan Khan, thank you for your trust and patience, you are such a special soul. Nourah, may your life be filled with joy and happiness. You deserve the best. To Sarah Ruby, you are a saint. Phil Robertson, what an honour to work with you. Thanks for all you do. To Mona Eltahawy and Robert Rutledge, thank you for being there along the journey, every step.

Thank you, a million times, to my incredible husband Reuben, for all the days and the nights you held the fort alone. I adore you.

Thank you for always reminding me of the beauty in the world. Nat and Quinn, thank you for sharing your mum with so many people. All those hours I was away, I always had you boys there in my heart. All this is for you. Thank you to my amazing parents, Gerard and Elise. I'm so sorry I caused you such worry over the years. Thanks a million times for everything you taught me and for making me who I am. To my amazing sisters, Courtney, Asha and Ella. What would I do without your advice! Clinton and Leonie, thanks so much for all your amazing support and love over the years. I am so lucky to have you three. To Jane, Mark, Sandy, Amelia, Holly, Aimee, Greta, Dede and Pop, thank you for your love and support.

Diaa Hadid and Molly Hunter, thank you for always being there, my besties. Thanks for always letting me edit radio, no matter what bar we were in. Thank you to my favourite sub editor Joe Dyke, I'm nothing without you. Kate Macdonald, Olivia Rousset, Sarah Parker, Amos Roberts, Martin Butler, Liz Jackson, Mark Davis, Liz Lacey, Lucy Lyon, Roslyn Boatman, Robert, James, Amanda and Oren Yiftachel, thank you for all your friendship and support. It has been invaluable.

To dear Fouad Abu Gosh, for always being such a dear friend, gun researcher, amazing producer, so patient and kind with everyone and most importantly always putting 110 per cent into the story. Thank you to Raed Al-Athamneh and Samy Zyara, for your incredible spirit, despite the hardest circumstances. Thank you to Zahed Cachalia for all your support, encouragement and always being there. I couldn't have done any of this without you. Aaron Hollett, thanks for working so hard and having such a big heart. To everyone at ABC International, the foreign desk, the overnight radio desk, radio current affairs, *7.30*, *Lateline*, the Brisbane online team, *Foreign Correspondent*, thanks a million for all your hard work and support. Amy Donaldson and Jeanavive McGregor, you are my dream team! Marianne Leitch and Mark Corcoran, thank you for making Yemen happen! Thank you, Michael Carey, Gaven Morris, Alan Sunderland, Craig McMurtrie, Mark Maley, Jo Puccini, John Lyons and Sarah Ferguson, for your incredible support. Thank you so much to Sally Neighbour at *Four Corners* for always having my back and for trusting me. To Morag Ramsey, Sharon Davis, Mary Fallon and Michael Nettleship, thank you for

working so hard to make that story happen. Thank you, Sally Sara and Stephanie March, for subbing my scripts and being my best ladies. Mike Carey and Steve Taylor, thank you for giving me my big breaks.

Thank you so much to all the amazing staff at Médecins Sans Frontières. Thank you to all the brilliant people at Human Rights Watch, particularly Elaine Pearson and Adam Coogle. Thank you to all the fantastic, dedicated people at The Syria Campaign, Amnesty International, the Norwegian Refugee Council, Save the Children, Oxfam, World Vision, B'Tselem, the Red Cross, WHO, OCHA, UNRWA and UNHCR. Thank you to the incredible Chris Woods and everyone at Airwars for your extraordinary work.

Rifaie Tammas, this couldn't have happened without you. Ben Saul, thank you for always being so helpful and generous with your time. Thank you to Rina Rossi, Paul Duff, Chris Hill, Paul Roberts and Vicky Mason for being such amazing teachers. Thanks to the Bay Bakehouse and all our dear Maroubra friends.

Huge thank you to Jude McGee and Scott Forbes at HarperCollins for making this book happen.

Picture credits

Introduction: Sophie McNeill working as a video journalist in Gaza *(Sophie McNeill)*

Chapter 1: Noura Ghazi and her father, Marwan *(courtesy of Noura Ghazi)*

Chapter 2: Khaled Naanaa working as a nurse in Damascus *(courtesy of Khaled Naanaa)*

Chapter 3: Noura Ghazi and Bassel Khartabil *(courtesy of Noura Ghazi)*

Chapter 4: An Italian navy officer motions to a boat of migrants and refugees in the Mediterranean *(Sophie McNeill)*

Chapter 5: Nazieh Husein and Sophie McNeill on Lesvos Island *(Aaron Hollett)*

Chapter 6: Nazieh Husein and his wife, Basiyeh, in Germany *(Sophie McNeill)*

Chapter 7: Twelve-year-old Salim at the MSF hospital in Amman, Jordan *(Sophie McNeill)*

Chapter 8: Khaled Naanaa in besieged Madaya *(courtesy of Khaled Naanaa)*

Chapter 9: Little Hamzeh says goodbye to his parents at Amman airport *(courtesy of Hamzeh's family)*

Chapter 10: Children in the Yemeni capital Sanaa *(Aaron Hollett)*

Chapter 11: An injured little girl in Aleppo *(courtesy of Syrian American Medical Society)*

Chapter 12: A mother who has just escaped Mosul with her children *(Sophie McNeill)*

Chapter 13: Adel Faraj in Baghdad *(courtesy of Battery Dance)*

Chapter 14: Three-year-old Sara in a Bethlehem hospital without her mother *(Sophie McNeill)*

Chapter 15: Israeli soldiers in the Palestinian city of Hebron in the occupied West Bank *(Sophie McNeill)*

Chapter 16: Ahmed Mansoor *(Getty Images)*

Chapter 17: A child struggles to breathe in Khan Sheikhoun *(Getty Images)*

Chapter 18: Ten-year-old Yasmin holds the drawing she created in an art workshop with Ben Quilty *(Sophie McNeill)*

Chapter 19: Rahaf Mohammed in her hotel room in Bangkok *(Sophie McNeill)*

Conclusion: Sophie McNeill in Fallujah, Iraq *(Shaun Filer)*